KU-786-441

JACQUELINE CAREY

NAAMAH'S CURSE

Copyright © Jacqueline Carey 2010
All rights reserved

The right of Jacqueline Carey to be identified as the author
of this work has been asserted by her in accordance with the
Copyright, Designs and Patents Act 1988.

First published in Great Britain in 2010 by
Gollancz
An imprint of the Orion Publishing Group
Orion House, 5 Upper St Martin's Lane,
London WC2H 9EA
An Hachette UK Company

This edition published in Great Britain in 2011 by Gollancz

1 3 5 7 9 10 8 6 4 2

A CIP catalogue record for this book
is available from the British Library

ISBN 978 0 575 09362 1

Printed and bound in Great Britain by
CPI Mackays, Chatham ME5 8TD

The Orion Publishing Group's policy is to use papers
that are natural, renewable and recyclable products and
made from wood grown in sustainable forests. The logging
and manufacturing processes are expected to conform to
the environmental regulations of the country of origin.

www.jacquelinecarey.com
www.orionbooks.co.uk

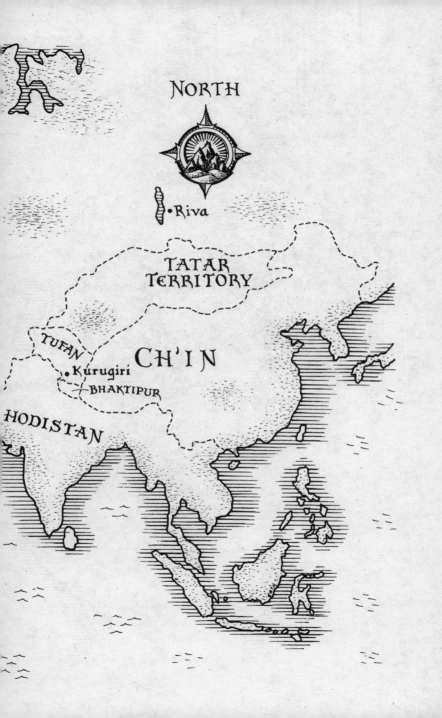

ONE

As the city of Shuntian dwindled in the distance behind me, a mixture of dread and exhilaration filled me.

I was all alone in the vast empire of Ch'in.

It was by choice, my choice. If I had wished it, the Emperor's daughter would have spoken a word in her father's ear, and his Celestial Majesty would have provided me with a mighty escort. Indeed, the princess had begged me to let her do so, and I suspected there would be times that I wished I had consented. I was a young woman, a foreigner, travelling alone in a country halfway around the world from my home.

Home.

It was a bittersweet word. I no longer knew what it meant to me. Once, home had been a snug cave in the Alban wilderness where I was Moirin, daughter of Fainche, child of the Maghuin Dhonn.

That was still true; in a sense it would always be true. The folk of the Maghuin Dhonn carry our *diadh-anams* inside us, the divine spark of the Great Bear Herself that gives us life and guides us. It is the part of our soul that connects us to Her. To lose it would be like dying, worse than dying.

I knew, because I had lost half of mine.

Not lost, exactly. In fairness, I had given it away, although I hadn't known what I was doing at the time.

My mind shied away from the memory. The noble chestnut

gelding I rode flattened his ears and tossed his head, sensing my unease. I stroked his neck, soothing him with my thoughts. "Peace, brave heart," I murmured.

He settled. On the lead-line, the pack-horse plodded patiently behind us.

They were gifts from Emperor Zhu, both of them. I carried a good many gifts. My rich silk robes were embroidered with bronze and amber chrysanthemums. Jade bangles rattled on my wrists and around my neck, hung on a silk chord, was a jade medallion carved with the Emperor's chop on one side and the Imperial dragon on the other. It would grant me safe passage anywhere in the empire of Ch'in.

Your jade-eyed witch soothes the dragon.

Memories.

The chestnut sidled and pranced beneath me. I soothed him once more, and forced myself to cycle through the Five Styles of Breathing.

The Breath of Earth's Pulse, drawn into the pit of the belly and the depths of the groin, inhaled and exhaled through the mouth.

The Breath of Ocean's Rolling Waves, drawn in through the nostrils to the middle belly, out through the mouth.

The Breath of Trees Growing, circulating energy to the limbs, trading nourishment with the world.

The Breath of Embers Glowing, in and out through parted lips, quickening the heart and warming the blood.

The Breath of Wind's Sigh, pulled and expelled through the nostrils into the space between my eyes, making my head light.

I breathed the entire cycle as I rode, and while the discipline calmed and centered me, with every breath I drew, a memory assailed me. Stone and sea! There were so *many* of them.

Master Lo Feng.

He had taught me the Five Styles, taught me all that I knew of the Ch'in manner of meditation and harmony he called the Way. It had served me well in the conflict I was leaving behind me. It had let me find the strength and courage to serve as a companion to Princess Snow Tiger and the dragon whose indomitable celestial spirit was housed within her mortal flesh. Were it not for Master Lo's teaching, I would never have been able to help free the princess and the dragon from the curse that bound them together in the midst of a bloody civil war.

Nor could I have endured the aftermath, in which I put my small gift of magic in the service of Emperor Zhu, breathing in and swallowing the memories of hundreds upon hundreds of men who had conceived, built, and wielded the terrible weapons known as the Divine Thunder. I carried the ghosts of those memories within me yet, tasting of brass and sulfur, blood and smoke and horror.

I returned to the Breath of Wind's Sigh, willing it to carry away the lingering acrid tang.

My *diadh-anam* burned steadily within my breast, calling to its separated half somewhere to the northwest. Since there was no escaping the memory, I let myself think about Bao, the stubborn Ch'in peasant-boy who had walked away with half my soul inside him.

Bao hadn't liked me much at first, nor had I cared for him. He was Master Lo's apprentice, guide, and companion—his magpie, Master Lo called him. I remembered my first sight of him, a lean-muscled young man with dark eyes glinting with disdain under a shock of unkempt black hair, carrying a steaming pot of bone-marrow soup over his shoulder on a bamboo staff.

That had been in Terre d'Ange, the land of my father's birth, the land toward which I first set out in pursuit of my destiny. A quest laid upon me by the Maghuin Dhonn Herself.

In my youth and folly, I thought I had found it straightaway in the form of Raphael de Mereliot, the healer with the charmed touch—Raphael, who was able to merge his gift with mine, to channel my magic to heal others. Raphael, the Queen's favorite courtier and lover.

We had wrought miracles together.

And it had nearly killed me.

If it hadn't been for the Queen herself, it very well might have killed me. Jehanne de la Courcel. There, at least, was a memory that made me smile. Gods, I'd gotten myself involved in an almighty tangle when I came between Jehanne and Raphael. And yet in the end, it was Jehanne who had rescued me from Raphael's ambition, and Jehanne whom I had come to love. My father was a priest of Naamah, the D'Angeline goddess of desire, and his line was ancient in her service. Naamah's gifts ran strongly in my blood. I had found pleasure and pride in serving as Jehanne's companion.

It had hurt to leave her. It had been too soon. When my infernal destiny summoned me to accompany Master Lo Feng, Jehanne was carrying the King's child, and she was frightened. I wished I could have stayed until the child was born.

I couldn't regret leaving, though. Not after the purpose I had served in Ch'in. I had seen the dragon, once restored, launch himself in glory from White Jade Mountain, his undulating silver coils gleaming against the blue sky. I had ridden in his claw; I'd seen him summon the rain and drown the terrible weapons of the Divine Thunder, ending the war. I'd seen my impossibly valiant princess Snow Tiger restored to honor.

And yet...

Bao.

My *diadh-anam* flared as my thoughts circled back to him. When had I even begun to harbor a fondness for him? I couldn't say. Somewhere in the long hours we spent together in Terre d'Ange while Master Lo Feng taught us the Five Styles. Mayhap it was the first time I'd won an almost-smile from him.

It was on the long journey on the greatship to Ch'in that matters had changed between us. Thrust into constant companionship, Bao and I had become friends, then lovers. I'd caught a glimpse of the complicated knot of pride, stubbornness, and romantic yearning that lay behind his insouciant exterior. And Bao...

I don't know what Bao felt for me, not really. Out of bed, we were always a little bit guarded with one another, neither of us certain how much our relationship owed to convenience, proximity, and Master Lo's unsubtle encouragement.

If things had fallen out otherwise, it might have been different.

But once we reached Shuntian, the imprisoned dragon's jealousy had come between us, forcing us to be circumspect in our behavior. Later, we had said to one another; later. Over and over, in stolen moments throughout our long quest, we said this to one another. When this is all over, if we live through it, we will talk. Later.

A lump rose to my throat, forcing me to swallow hard.

My hands trembled on the reins.

There had been no later, because Bao had died. It was a moment etched in my memory. The captured sorcerer Black Sleeve turning in a graceful, unrepentant arc, the deadly sleeve of his robe flaring wide. A spray of poisoned darts.

The dragon's helpless roar.

Bao whirling, his broken staff in two pieces in his hands, intercepting the barrage.

Bao, dying.

One dart, a single dart, had gotten past him, had pierced his throat beneath the chiseled angle of his jaw. It had been enough.

I breathed the Breath of Ocean's Rolling Waves, the most calming of all the Five Styles. I let the memories wash over me.

I should have known; of course, I should have known. Master Lo had as good as told me. *Today, I realize I have lived too long,* he said. Emperor Zhu had known what he meant. For the first and only time, Master Lo had asked me to share my gift with him, his dark eyes grave and anguished. *Are you willing to give a part of yourself that my magpie might live?*

I remembered my frantic reply.

Anything!

I should have known, but I didn't. When Master Lo Feng placed his hands on Bao's unmoving chest, I laid my hands over his and poured my energy into him, until I felt myself begin to fade and go away, until I saw the stone doorway that represents the portal into the afterlife for the folk of the Maghuin Dhonn. For a moment, I thought I would pass through it, and the thought was not unwelcome.

Then my *diadh-anam* blazed and doubled...

...waking inside Bao.

Bao came to life with a startled shout, thrust out of the realms of death. Master Lo passed from it peacefully, his chin sinking to his chest, his eyes closing forever.

What would I have done if I had known, if I had grasped what should have been obvious? I cannot say. And in truth, it does not matter.

What was done, is done.

On that day, my stubborn peasant-boy went away from me. He told me he did not blame me for our mentor's death. He told me that if he had been given the opportunity to choose, he would have chosen to spend his life with me.

But he died without being given that chance, and what Master Lo did in restoring his life, dividing the divine spark of my *diadh-anam* between us, bound us together in a way that only a second death could undo.

And Bao needed to find a way to choose this, to make it his own. To reconcile the hard choices and uncertainties that had yoked my destiny to his, to believe that I had chosen him out of genuine desire and love, that it wasn't merely Master Lo's art at work.

So I let him go.

And I waited for him to come back to me. All the while I travelled Ch'in and served as the Emperor's swallower-of-memories, I waited for Bao. The Imperial entourage returned in triumph to Shuntian, where I waited for Bao. In the gardens of the Celestial City, I listened to poetry with the princess and waited for Bao.

He didn't come.

Instead, I sensed him moving farther away from me, carrying the twinned flame of my *diadh-anam* inside him. Moving away from me, toward the outskirts of the empire, toward the Great Wall that kept the Tatar horde at bay.

It was the princess—Snow Tiger, my brave, lovely princess—who reminded me that I, too, had a choice. She had given me the greatest gift of all, the fragile gift of trust. In the beginning, I had been nothing but an unwelcome burden to her; her necessary inconvenience, she had called me. Much had changed between us by the end, and I carried private, tender memories of her that warmed my heart.

But nothing, *nothing* could replace what I had lost. And yes, I had a choice. So I had set out to find my stubborn peasant-boy.

If Bao would not come to me, I would go to him.

At least, I hoped so.

TWO

I took a room at a travellers' inn that first night. There was a time when I would have eschewed man-made walls for the freedom of the outdoors, but I had grown more civilized since leaving my home in Alba. After a long day's ride, the notion of a hot meal and a roof over my head appealed to me.

The ostler at the stable gaped at the sight of me, revealing a few missing teeth. On the road, I'd managed not to attract overmuch attention merely by dint of keeping my head lowered and my eyes averted. To be sure, a seemingly well-off young woman travelling alone drew curious glances, but at a quick, stealthy glance, with my coloring I could almost pass for Ch'in. My straight, black hair, I'd inherited from my mother. My skin was a warm golden hue, fairer than my mother's, but not nearly so fair as my D'Angeline father's milk-white skin.

I had his eyes, though. Green as grass, green as the rushes grow. And I had a measure of the fearful, keen-edged symmetry of D'Angeline beauty, coupled with the untamed spark of the Maghuin Dhonn. No one looking me full in the face could mistake me for aught but what I was: the Emperor's jade-eyed witch.

The ostler barked at a young stable-lad in an unfamiliar dialect. The boy went pelting toward the inn proper. I settled my battered canvas satchel over my shoulder and followed him. I hadn't gone ten steps before a solidly built middle-aged woman, clearly the proprietress of the establishment, came bustling down the path toward me. Her shrewd gaze raked me over, taking in my fine robes, my jade bangles, and the Emperor's medallion.

I bowed in the Ch'in manner, hand over fist, and spoke in the Shuntian scholar's tongue, the only one I knew. "Greetings, Honored Aunt. I seek lodging for the night."

A smile broke over her face. "You are the foreign witch, are you not? The one who freed the dragon?"

"Aye," I agreed. "I am."

She clutched my arm in a companionable manner, tugging me toward the inn. "Come, come! We are honored to give you hospitality. No charge, no charge at all. You must call me Auntie Li."

"You're very kind," I said politely. "But I can pay."

The proprietress snorted, squeezed my arm, and gave me a conspiratorial wink. "I'm nothing of the sort, child. I'm a greedy old widow who knows that folk will pay to hear tales of the Emperor's witch's stay here. Indulge me."

I smiled. "All right, Auntie Li."

She was right, of course. A silence fell over the common room of the inn when she ushered me inside. Men paused, teacups halfway to their mouths, staring.

But I was used to it.

I'd been stared at a great deal in my short life. In Alba, I had been my mother's well-kept secret—not due to any sense of shame, but simply my mother's own taciturn nature. Folk there had found it startling that a woman of the Maghuin Dhonn, a descendant of Alais the Wise, had borne a half-D'Angeline child.

In Terre d'Ange, folk had found it just as startling that a full-blooded D'Angeline man—a Priest of Naamah, no less—had chosen to couple with one of the infamous bear-witches of the Maghuin Dhonn, fathering a child on her.

And in Ch'in...

Vast as it was, the mighty empire of Ch'in was insular, circumscribed by its Great Wall and its outer shores. No one in that inn knew or cared aught about my heritage. I was the foreign witch who had helped free the dragon. It was enough.

"Sit." Auntie Li showed me to a low table, pressed on my shoulder.

I sat.

She clapped her hands together. Food came—hot, steamed dumplings with spiced pork and a dipping sauce. Noodle soup with green onions floating atop the broth and chicken feet stewed until they were gelatinous and tender. Auntie Li hovered over me, pouring hot water into my teacup whenever it grew low, nodding approvingly as I shoveled noodles into my mouth and sucked chicken flesh from the bone, tilting the bowl to slurp the dregs of the broth.

"You eat like a proper Ch'in woman," she observed.

I lowered the bowl. "I've had practice."

"Huh." Her shrewd gaze measured me. "Is it true you seek the twice-born one?"

I paused. "Twice-born?"

Auntie Li beckoned to one of her servers. He bowed and brought a small porcelain jar with two cups. She made an impatient gesture. "Drink your tea, drink it down. Indulge me, child. I will read the leaves for you while we enjoy this wine."

I downed my tea, leaving the leaves strewn and stranded on the bottom and the sides of the thin porcelain cup. Auntie Li studied them, tilting the cup this way and that. She set it aside and poured a measure of rice-wine for both of us, motioning for me to drink.

"So?" I obeyed. "What did you mean by the twice-born one, Auntie?"

"Born once into life, twice out of death, or so they are saying." Her brow furrowed. She drank her own rice-wine, then picked up the teacup again and bent her head over it, a straight white line delineating the part in her hair. "Hints of your fate are written here. Do you see? Here and here?"

I peered at the tea leaves. Despite Snow Tiger's best efforts, I was fairly illiterate when it came to reading Ch'in characters. During that last week I had lingered in Shuntian, she had teased me about it, wielding her long, braided hair like a ticklish brush and drawing characters on my bare skin.

Surely you recognize that *one, Moirin.*

The memory made me smile. I saw the shape of that character echoed in the pattern of the tea leaves. "Desire?"

"Desire, yes." Auntie Li nodded. Her forefinger moved, pointing. "But you see here, it lies in conflict with judgment. Does that mean anything to you?"

I thought about it before shaking my head. "No. I don't know. Whose judgment, Auntie? Mine?"

She shrugged. "I can only tell you what the leaves say. I cannot tell you what it means. Desire in conflict with judgment lies ahead of you."

"To be sure, it lies behind me." Raphael de Mereliot's face surfaced in my thoughts, his grey eyes stormy with anger. Even though there were untold oceans between us, it made me shiver. I had been very young and very foolish. I'd let Raphael use me to summon fallen spirits. If it hadn't been for Bao and Master Lo, a terrible force would have been loosed into the world. "But that is not a mistake I will make again."

Auntie Li smiled wryly, refilling our cups with rice-wine. "There are no end of mistakes to be made, dear."

"Am I making one now?" I asked her.

Her face softened. "Ah, child! I cannot tell you that, either. Do you love the boy? Is that why you seek him?"

A hundred memories of Bao cascaded through my mind: Bao staring insolently at me as I sought to master the Five Styles of Breathing, Bao shouting at me as he drove the demon spirit back, Bao helping Master Lo tenderly to his feet, Bao sporting his battle-grin as he sparred with Snow Tiger.

It should have been simple, only it wasn't.

I *did* love him. I remembered the moment I had realized it. When I had first fled Shuntian with the dragon-possessed princess and a handful of loyal ruffians, Bao and Master Lo had gone ahead to lay a false trail. They had been late in returning, and I'd begun to fear they weren't coming.

I would not let that happen, Moirin.

Those were the words Bao had spoken when they did arrive and I confessed my fear to him, the closest he'd ever come to a declaration of love. My heart had leapt.

And yet...

It wasn't why I was following him. I was following him because he had half of my *diadh-anam* and I couldn't do otherwise.

"I don't know, Auntie," I said truthfully at last. "It's a question I'm hoping to answer, and I cannot do it alone."

"Poor child." Auntie Li patted my hand. The look of kindness in her shrewd eyes nearly undid me. "Don't pay too much heed to an old lady's rambling. If the boy's got a lick of sense, he won't run far."

I smiled despite the sting of tears. "I'm not sure he does."

She sipped her rice-wine. "That probably makes two of you."

I laughed. "You're probably right."

THREE

So began the pattern of my days.

For the most part, it was a lonely time. I thought I was accustomed to solitude. I'd grown up in the Alban wilderness with only my mother's companionship. But she had been a constant in my life; and later, there had been Cillian, my lost first love, killed in a foolish cattle-raid.

Here, I had no one.

Oh, there were folk I met along the way, though none who took so lively an interest in me as Auntie Li. But with each new day that dawned, I was forced to leave them behind and set out on my lonely road.

I was grateful for the company of my horses. I named the chestnut saddle-horse Ember, and the grey pack-horse I called Coal. As a child of the Maghuin Dhonn, I was able to sense their thoughts and moods in a way most folk couldn't. Betimes I would let my thoughts drift, touching theirs, enjoying the simplicity of their reactions to the world around them.

Betimes I immersed my own thoughts in the world around me, breathing the Breath of Trees Growing and listening to nature.

Winter was coming, sooner than I would have hoped. I heard it in the sleepy murmurings of the trees, the sap growing sluggish in their veins. I heard it in the anxious whispers of the winter wheat in the fields, straining to outrace the coming frost. I saw it in the worried faces of farmers along the way.

The days began to grow shorter.

I wasn't worried, not yet. So long as I was in the empire of Ch'in, I was safe. I could always find a place to lodge, supplies to purchase. It grew harder to communicate as I rode, for the farther away from Shuntian I went, the fewer folk spoke the scholar's tongue. Still, I managed with friendly gestures and a few words of dialect picked up along the way; and the Emperor's seal spoke for itself.

But I was fairly certain Bao was no longer in Ch'in.

I couldn't be sure beyond doubt. It was a vast country. Still, when Snow Tiger had bade me consult my *diadh-anam* in conjunction with a map, it had been clear that Bao was headed for Tatar territory.

And I had a suspicion of the reason why.

Master Lo's tranquil voice echoed in my memory. *Through no fault of his own, Bao is a child of violence.*

Violence.

Rape, he meant—the crime D'Angelines called heresy. Folk who know no better reckon D'Angelines are a licentious lot. They are not entirely wrong—in Terre d'Ange, all manner of love and desire is freely celebrated—but it is far from the whole truth. Blessed Elua, the earth-begotten son of Yeshua ben Yosef and Mary the Magdalene, the deity who Naamah and the other Companions chose to follow, turning their backs on the One God's Heaven, gave his people one simple precept: *Love as thou wilt.*

So they do, but it is within the bounds of the sacred tenet of consensuality. To violate it is to commit heresy.

Bao's mother had been raped during a Tatar raid, that much I knew. When it became evident that he was the result of that violence, and not the legitimate offspring of his parents' marriage, they had sold him into servitude to a travelling circus. He had been trained and raised as an acrobat, but fighting was in his blood. At the age of thirteen, he had begged the troupe's best stick-fighter to teach him. And Bao had been willing to pay any price to learn.

He say, you be my peach-bottom boy, I teach you.

Thinking on it, I shuddered.

In some ways, I think it troubled me more than it did Bao. I hadn't been raised to think of myself as a D'Angeline—indeed, I was ten years old before it occurred to me to wonder who my father was—but I had always felt Naamah's presence in my life. The bright lady, I had called her. When the Maghuin Dhonn Herself at once accepted me as Her child and sent me forth to seek my destiny, I had no idea where to begin. So I set out to solve the only mystery I knew, and crossed the Straits to seek my father in Terre d'Ange.

I had found him, too; and as it transpired, he was one of the loveliest, gentlest souls I had ever encountered. When I was in a mood to resent my infernal destiny, one of the things I resented the most was that it had taken me away from my father so soon, when I'd scarce had a chance to know him.

The other, of course, was leaving Jehanne.

Well and so, it was done, and even on my darkest days, I could not deny there was a purpose in it. And I could not help but think that Bao travelled a similar path. He had *died*. His soul had travelled to the Ch'in spirit world. Because he had died a hero's death, the merciful Maiden of Gentle Aspect had intervened to spare him the judgment of the Yama Kings. And then he found himself reborn into his body, with his soul inextricably yoked to mine and his mentor Master Lo Feng dead.

None of that was reason to seek out his marauding rapist of a father, of course. Not at all. On the surface of things, it made no sense. But I thought he would do the same thing I had done when confronted with an unwanted destiny, and set out to solve the only mystery he knew. With Master Lo dead, Bao had nowhere else to go.

Besides, I could sense him somewhere beyond me, moving farther and farther away.

If I could have followed him as the crow flies, I could have closed the distance between us more swiftly, but I was constrained by the terrain to follow the roads. Still, Bao would have faced the same constraints. In village after village I asked after him as best I could, usually with mixed results.

I didn't have the luxury of keeping a low profile in face-to-face encounters. Bao did. A young Ch'in man travelling on his own, carrying little more than a satchel and a battered bamboo staff across his back, was not a remarkable sight. And I didn't even know for a surety under what name he went. I knew him as Bao, but I had learned that that wasn't a proper name, but the baby-name his mother had called him. Treasure, it meant; at least when spoken with the right intonation.

It was a name Bao had reclaimed when he cast his lot in with Master Lo Feng, abandoning the stick-fighters and thugs in Shuntian he had once led, leaving everything behind to become Master Lo's magpie, a journey that had taken him all the way to Terre d'Ange. For a long time, I'd wondered why he'd made such a choice.

It wasn't a pretty tale.

Bao had told me on the greatship. A young boy had come to him and begged him to teach him to fight. Bao had agreed . . . for the same price that the man who taught him had charged.

I don't know how I would have responded to Bao's tale had he gone through with the bargain. I might not have been raised with Blessed Elua's precept and the sacred tenet of consensuality, but I was Naamah's child as surely as the Maghuin Dhonn Herself's, and I had taken those beliefs deep to heart.

But he hadn't gone through with it. Confronted with the naked, shivering, stripling boy, Bao had walked away from his bargain, walked away from his life. He had taken Master Lo's offer, an offer he had jeered at only days before, and reinvented himself.

Everything I have done in my life, good and bad, I have chosen. But this, I did not choose.

That was what Bao said the day he left me.

"Stupid boy," I muttered to myself as I rode, not really meaning it. I tried not to dwell on it, tried not to wonder if he would be angry at me for following him. He had to know I was on his trail. He could feel my presence as surely as I could sense his.

And I tried not to worry about the distance that yet lay between us, the shortening days, the trees growing increasingly barren of leaves, the chill in the air.

Here and there, I found folk who remembered Bao's passage. He might not have stood out as unmistakably as I did, but he was memorable in his own way. Even from the beginning, there had been an air of coiled intensity to him, a feral glitter to his dark eyes that put me in mind of my own people. It was not unthinkable; although the Maghuin Dhonn have dwelled in Alba for time out of mind, there are tales among us of an older time, when the world was covered in ice and we followed the Great Bear Herself out of a frozen wasteland to warmer climes.

That was when there were still great magicians among us, shape-changers capable of taking the form of the Maghuin Dhonn Herself. We lost that gift generations ago when the magician Berlik broke an oath he swore by stone and sea and all that they encompass, on his very *diadh-anam*. Now, only small gifts remain to us; or so I had thought. My mother taught me to summon the twilight when I was but a child, a gift meant for hiding and concealment.

But as I'd grown to adulthood, I'd found it has other uses. To summon the twilight is to take half a step into the spirit world. It could also serve to make a gateway that allows the energy of the spirit world to spill into ours.

I discovered first that I had a knack for coaxing plants to grow. It seemed a simple and benign gift, mayhap a legacy of my father. Although he is a child of Naamah through and through, the lineage of Anael, the Good Steward, also runs in his veins.

It was Raphael de Mereliot who discovered that my gift could be used for other purposes. In a twisted way, I supposed I owed him a debt of gratitude. Had he not done so, had he not used my magic to work miracles of healing, my lovely father would have died of an infection of the lungs. Had Raphael not persuaded me to help him summon fallen spirits, I would not possess the gift one of them gave me on a whim, a charm to reveal hidden things. Were it not for that charm, Snow Tiger would have drowned in the lake below White Jade Mountain with the pearl that lodged the dragon's soul hidden in her mortal flesh.

Gods, the links that bind one person's ambition and desire to another's fate are complicated things! One could go mad thinking on it. But I knew for a surety that if Raphael had not used my gift thusly, Bao would still be dead. Master Lo Feng would never have known to use my gift to exchange his life for Bao's.

Being touched by death had changed Bao. Its touch clung to him, lent him a faint aura of shimmering darkness. Bao had died, and yet lived. He alone in the world was twice-born. So it did not surprise me to find folk who remembered him along the way.

And having guessed at his purpose, it should not have surprised me to come across the village of his birth as I followed in his tracks.

Yet somehow, it did.

FOUR

━━━◆━━━

T he village was called Tonghe. There was nothing to distinguish it
from the dozens of others through which I had passed along the
way, and I would not have chosen to stay there if my inquiries in the
market had not proved fruitful. When I described Bao using a combination of dialect and gestures, an elderly woman selling squashes
nodded vigorously and pointed across the square toward a handful of
men huddled over a set of dominoes.

Even though my *diadh-anam* assured me that Bao was many,
many leagues away, my heart soared, and I had to look twice to assure
myself he wasn't among them. The squash seller tugged my arm and
spoke volubly.

"I'm sorry, Grandmother." I shook my head. "I don't understand."

She scowled at me, then gave a penetrating shout. A boy of some
ten years came at a pelting run, listening and nodding as she spoke
to him.

"Greetings, Noble Barbarian Lady!" Despite his rough-spun attire,
he addressed me in the scholar's tongue, speaking with careful precision. He bowed three times in rapid succession and then straightened, his wide eyes taking in my horses, my robes, and the Emperor's
medallion around my neck. "I am Hui. Grandmother Fang says I am
to translate for you. You seek the stick-fighter from Shuntian?"

"I do." I smiled at him. "Was he here?"

"Oh, yes!" Hui pointed at the men playing dominoes. "That is his father." His grandmother cuffed him and muttered. He lowered his voice. "Or at least, that is the husband of his mother."

I tried to guess which of the men he was indicating. None of them looked like Bao—but then, none of them would. "I see."

Grandmother Fang offered helpful commentary. The boy listened, then translated. "Once he was a farmer. Now he does nothing but drink rice-wine and gamble at dominoes all day. Do you want to meet him?"

"I do," I said. "Is the stick-fighter's mother here, too?"

Hui nodded and relayed the question to his grandmother. "Yes, but she works in a sewing shop, she and her daughter. They must make a living since Ang Shen has become a drunk."

"I would like to meet all of them." I clasped my hand over my fist and bowed from the saddle. "My thanks to you and your honored grandmother. Is there an inn where I might lodge?"

He shook his head, then turned to his grandmother. After another exchange, he said, "Grandmother Fang says you must stay with us as an honored guest. Your horses can stay in the pen with the goat."

I inclined my head, touching the purse that hung from my belt. "Of course, she will allow me a small gesture of thanks."

That at least needed no translation. Grandmother Fang grinned and gave an effusive nod.

I let Hui lead me to the home he shared with his mother, father, two younger sisters, and his grandmother on the outskirts of town, collecting my thoughts while he chattered excitedly, telling me that he was the prodigy of the family and he meant to sit for the scholar's examination that would allow him to become a civil servant when he came of age. In the doorway of their humble house, his mother greeted us with gracious amazement, a round-faced toddler peering out from behind her skirts.

"Come around back!" Hui reached up to tug on Ember's reins. "I will show you the goat pen."

In the rear of the house, there was a sizable garden with well-tended crops of squash and soybean—and indeed, a small pen with a wise-eyed goat. With Hui's assistance, I unsaddled Ember and unloaded Coal's packs, stowing the gear beneath a weathered lean-to. He fetched a fresh bucket of water and watched with avid curiosity as I checked both horses' hooves for cracks or stones.

"Why do you not have servants, Noble Barbarian Lady?" Hui asked.

I worked at prying a pebble loose from the frog of Ember's right front hoof. The chestnut bent his neck and lipped my hair with idle affection. "Because I do not think the man I am following would like it if I came after him with an army of servants. And you may call me by my name, which is Moirin."

"Moirin." He pronounced it with the awkward Ch'in lilt I found charming. "Is it true what he said, then? The stick-fighter from Shuntian?"

"I don't know." I released Ember's foreleg and stroked his neck. "What did he say?"

Hui glanced around. "It is rumored that he claimed to be one of those who guarded Princess Snow Tiger on her quest to free the dragon and end the war."

"Aye," I said. "It's true."

"You were there?"

I nodded. "I was there."

Hui's dark gaze travelled from the medallion around my neck to my face. "You're *her*. The Emperor's jade-eyed witch."

I smiled. "Some say so. I say I am my own, and no one else's. But aye, the tales are true, and I was there. So was Bao."

"Oh." The boy whispered the word, then swallowed visibly. "Ang Shen did not believe the stories. He told the stick-fighter to go away."

My heart ached for Bao. "Mayhap Ang Shen will believe it when I tell him."

Hui looked dubious. "Mayhap he will."

He didn't.

In the early hours of the afternoon, I returned to the village square to meet with Bao's father—or at least, the husband of his mother.

Hui came with me to translate, his pride in the task offset by a certain degree of anxiety. There were four men yet huddled over the dominoes, sharing a jar of rice-wine.

"Ang Shen?" I bowed politely to the man Hui pointed out to me, a Ch'in fellow with a prematurely lined face, his black hair peppered with silver, clad in well-mended clothes. Since he did not rise, I knelt to offer him the respect due an elder in Ch'in society, sitting on my heels in the D'Angeline courtesan's manner that Jehanne had shown me. "I would speak to you of your son, Bao."

Hui translated.

The other three domino players left off their game and stared at me with open fascination. Villagers drifted near to eavesdrop. Ang Shen grunted, fingered the tiles, and refused to meet my eyes. "I have no son," he said in a rough variant of the scholar's tongue.

"Your wife's son, then," I said.

His shoulders tensed. "My wife bore no sons."

"Aye," I said softly. "She did. And it seems he sought you out. 'Tis no business of mine to tell you how to respond to such circumstances. But one thing I will tell you. Whatever Bao told you was true, and I doubt he told you the half of it. He is a hero. I know, for I was there. He saved the princess' life and mine at the cost of his own. He died, and was born again."

Ang Shen shuddered and lifted his head, his expression fierce. *"Would I have sold such a son away?"* he demanded of me. Startled, I rocked back on my heels. *"No!"* His eyes blazed. "No, no, no! I would not have done such a thing, so this man claiming to be such a person must lie. Else, what am I? What monster, what waste of flesh? It cannot be true!"

"It is!" I insisted.

Both of us surged to our feet.

I hadn't expected violence. If I had, I would have kept my distance from him. I would have brought my bow and quiver, the sturdy yew-wood bow my uncle Mabon had made for me. My fingers twitched, longing for the string as Ang Shen breathed hard in my face, leaning forward, his breath smelling of stale rice-wine, his expression adamant and anguished. *"I have no son."*

I bowed. "My mistake, sir. If you did, and if he had come seeking your acceptance, you would have been proud of him."

I left.

Hui trotted after me. "That didn't go so well, huh?"

"No." I spied the slender figure of a girl hiking her robes to her knees and beating a hasty retreat across the square, the soles of her straw sandals slapping against her heels. Her fleet, agile grace struck a familiar chord. "It is obvious that Ang Shen is a proud man who feels grief and guilt. Hui, would that be his daughter?"

He glanced at her. "Uh-huh. That's Ang Song."

"Let's follow her."

Hui beamed. "Yes, Moirin!"

We followed Song to a modest sewing shop, arriving in time to see her being scolded by the proprietress, who had the girl's earlobe pinched in a firm grip as she harangued her. Song protested and squirmed, more with dismay than discomfort.

"Excuse me, madame," I said politely. "I would like to speak to this girl."

Hui translated.

The proprietress turned on me with irritation, then gaped with comical surprise. She let go of Song's earlobe and stroked the girl's braided hair with an absentminded affection that belied her scolding, then questioned Hui in the local dialect. He grinned and replied. The proprietress bowed and spoke rapidly, gesturing at the door.

"Auntie Ai says you are most welcome here, Moirin," Hui said helpfully. "Of course, you may come in and speak to Song and her mother. If you would like to purchase some very fine embroidery work, that would also be good."

I smiled. "My thanks."

Auntie Ai led us through the crowded front room with squares of embroidered fabric stacked in piles. Although most of the material was plain cotton, the quality of the embroidery was indeed quite fine.

The girl Song stole glances at me, her face alight with eager curiosity. She was a pretty girl, and I saw traces of Bao in the shape of her ears, the angle of her jaw, and her full lips. She couldn't have been more than twelve or thirteen, hovering on the brink of womanhood.

"You're her?" she asked me shyly, speaking the scholar's tongue with more skill than her father.

"I'm her," I agreed.

She clapped her hands together with unbridled delight. Auntie Ai shook her head, but she smiled, too.

I knew Bao's mother at a glance. She rose to her feet in amazement as we entered the sewing chamber, a tangle of fabric and silk thread spilling from her lap. One hand touched her lips, her eyes brightening with tears. "It's true?"

"Aye, my lady," I said gently.

A joyful laugh spilled from her. "I knew he would not lie! Oh, tell me! Tell me everything!"

So I did, once Auntie Ai had bustled around and served cups of hot, fragrant tea and sweet bean-cakes. I told the whole long story of how I had met Bao and Master Lo Feng in Terre d'Ange, how Master Lo had taken me on as a student. How I had accompanied them across many seas in a greatship when the Emperor's men came to fetch Master Lo to tend to the afflicted princess.

"Is it true that Princess Snow Tiger *killed* her husband on their wedding night?" Song asked in a hushed whisper.

"Oh, yes." I nodded. "It was a very awful thing. Everyone thought it was a demon that possessed her. But it was the dragon, waking in terror and panicking at finding himself trapped in her flesh."

It was worse than they knew. The dragon had awoken while Snow Tiger and her bridegroom were engaged in the act of love. In his panic, the celestial creature had struck out in blind terror, and with dragon-infused strength, the princess had torn her bridegroom from limb to limb. I knew, I had seen her memories. After she had come to trust me, I had held her in the small hours of darkness when the nightmares came.

"But *you* saw the dragon inside her!" Song said triumphantly.

"Aye." I smiled. "I did. And with the magic that is the gift of my mother's people, I was able to let the princess see the dragon in the mirror."

Bao's mother, whose name was Yingtai, shook her head in wonder.

I told the rest of the story, from our escape from Shuntian and our journey in disguise across Ch'in to our victory at White Jade Mountain. Hui translated in a low tone for Auntie Ai. They knew it, of course. Everyone in Ch'in knew it. Bao had told it to them himself. But it was the sort of story that bore hearing over and over, the sort of story for retelling during long winter nights around the fire.

When I had finished, Yingtai sighed with profound pleasure. "I knew he was not lying," she said in a soft, wistful voice.

"Your husband did not believe him," I said.

"No." Her brow furrowed. "Ang Shen is a good man at heart. After the Tatar raid, after it was clear that Bao was not his son...the shame of it broke him." She glanced at her daughter. "Then, for many years, I did not get pregnant again. He...perhaps we did not try often enough. In ten years of trying, Song is our only child. When my Bao returned claiming a hero's status, it broke him all over again."

Song fidgeted. "Father is disappointed that I am a girl."

"Perhaps he might think on the pride that Emperor Zhu takes in his daughter," I suggested. "A pride the entire Empire shares."

That made her smile. "Is Princess Snow Tiger as beautiful and brave as they say?"

"Every bit and more," I assured her. "Now, tell me about Bao. How long did he stay? How long has he been gone? Did he say where he was bound?"

"He was troubled." Bao's mother's gaze rested on me, careworn and concerned. "I did not understand...he *died*? And you brought him back to life?"

I had skipped that part of the tale, reckoning it was not something a mother wanted to hear. "He died, yes, struck by one of Black

Sleeve's poisoned darts. It was Master Lo Feng who used my magic to trade his life for Bao's."

Yingtai looked away. "I could see that there was a shadow over him. He was at odds with himself. He asked me...he asked me about the Tatar who fathered him. If there was aught I could tell him."

The sewing room was very quiet.

"Was there?" I asked at length.

"Yes." She looked back at me. "He had a scar, here." She drew a line from brow to cheek over her right eye. "I have not forgotten."

"I'm sorry," I murmured.

Yingtai gave a stoic shrug. "Men can be cruel. I begged Bao not to seek him out. Even if he succeeds, I can see no reason for it." She folded her hands in her lap, studying me. "Although he did not declare his feelings, his face changes when he speaks of you," she said softly. "At last, I asked him. Why, when his feelings for you were written so clearly on his face, was he going in the opposite direction? He could not explain it to me."

"I don't think he knows," I said. "Not really."

She nodded. "He is searching for an answer for which no question exists."

I smiled ruefully. "That sounds about right." Feeling the weight of strong emotion in the cloistered room, I changed the subject. "How did you learn the scholar's tongue? You speak it well."

"From my grandfather." Yingtai stroked her daughter's hair. "A long time ago. I taught Song as much as I remember."

Song cast a sharp glance toward Hui, who was surreptitiously stuffing the second to last of the sweet bean-cakes into his mouth. "If I were a boy, I would sit for the examination one day!"

He sputtered a defiant, unintelligible reply. Auntie Ai cuffed his head absently and snatched the plate away, offering it insistently to me. I took the last sweet out of politeness, the jade bangles around my wrist tinkling as I reached for it.

"Oh!" Song touched one of the bangles. "So beautiful! May I see?"

"Of course." I extended both arms. Her slender fingers danced over the polished stone bracelets. "That one is the exact color of the reflecting pool beneath White Jade Mountain, where the dragon gazes at himself," I said when she paused over my favorite, a vivid translucent green bangle. "The very place where we freed him. Princess Snow Tiger chose it herself."

"And this?" She pointed at the bangle next to it, a deeper, more intense shade of green.

"That's called Imperial jade." I touched another, a pale milky-white bangle with cloudy patches. "This is leopard jade. And this, this red one is said to bring luck. Which is your favorite?"

Song contemplated the six bangles I wore with great seriousness. "This one," she said at length, touching a clear, pale green piece with honey-colored highlights. "It looks like a river in sunlight with fish swimming in it."

I worked it free. "Then it is my gift to you."

Auntie Ai's eyes bulged, and she hissed in urgent dialect.

"No, no!" Bao's mother said in protest. "It is too much!"

I ignored her. "Pick one for your mother," I whispered conspiratorially to Song. "Which one do you think she would like?"

"Moirin." Hui tugged at my sleeve, glancing over his shoulder. "Ah...Auntie Ai does not think you know how much those are worth."

I ignored him, too. "Which one?"

One by one, Song walked her fingers over the remaining five bangles that hung from my wrists, slow and deliberative. "I think Mother would like this one that looks like the dragon's pool," she said somberly. "But it would be wrong to take it from you. So I choose this one." She touched the bangle of Imperial green jade, glancing up at me. "The one that is the color of your eyes."

I smiled and began to work it loose. "A very good choice."

"*No!*"

I pressed the jade bangle into Yingtai's resistant hands. "Bao came to you penniless, didn't he? If he had stayed, if he had not fled, the

Emperor would have rewarded him generously for his service. Please."
I folded her hands over the bracelet. "Accept this small token."

Bao's mother shook her head. "Ang Shen will insist—"

Song flinched.

"I will speak to him," I said. "I will tell him that if he sells these bracelets to drink and gamble, it will bring such a curse down upon him that he will reckon his life has been paradise before now."

Hui stared at me, his eyes stretched wide. "Can you do such a thing?"

"Of course," I lied. "I am the Emperor's witch, am I not?"

Tears filled Yingtai's eyes. "You cannot understand what this means." She turned the bangle in her hands. "A jade piece of such quality, a gift from his Celestial Majesty's own hands...Moirin, it is enough to provide Song with a dowry to marry well, better than I ever dared to hope for her."

I smiled at her. "Then I have done a better thing than I reckoned," I said.

We spoke for a while longer. They told me about Bao's visit, and that he had departed several weeks ago, bound to cross the Great Wall through the gateway a dozen *li* to the north and enter Tatar territory.

"You mean to follow him?" Yingtai asked me. "Even *there*?"

I nodded. "I do. What Master Lo did to restore Bao to life...it bound us together. I have waited long enough. If he will not come to me, I will go to him."

She shuddered. "I will pray for you every day."

"Will you come back?" Song asked.

"I don't know," I said honestly. "I cannot promise it. No matter what happens with Bao, I have a home of my own, or at least family of my own, far, far away. I miss them. Especially my mother. I would like to see her again very much. But I do promise that I will never, ever forget you."

Song smiled at me with shy pleasure, toying with the bangle around her slim wrist. "I understand. I will pray for you, too, Lady Moirin."

With their assistance, I chose two embroidered squares to purchase from Auntie Ai—one of Song's worked with a pattern of flowering bamboo, and one with a stark black-and-white pattern of magpies that Yingtai had just completed.

"I thought of my Bao as I sewed this piece," his mother murmured. "He told me that the Venerable Master Lo Feng called him his magpie."

"Aye, he did." A wave of sorrow came over me. "I hope it will remind Bao of many glad memories."

"I hope so, too," she said.

Outside the sewing shop, we said our farewells. A small crowd had gathered to watch, trying without the slightest bit of success to appear nonchalant. At Auntie Ai's urging, Hui made a point of displaying the fabric squares I had purchased ostentatiously over his arm. I didn't begrudge her, for it was obvious she had shown much kindness to Bao's mother and sister. Let the tale spread that the Emperor's witch had found her wares worthy.

Yingtai bowed formally to me, her eyes bright with fresh tears. "I bless the gods for sending you to us, Lady Moirin. I pray they guard your path."

I returned her bow. "And yours, my lady."

In a public display of emotion uncustomary to the Ch'in, Song flung her arms around my neck and hugged me hard. "Thank you, thank you, thank you!" she said fervently aloud, then whispered in my ear, "I hope my brother chooses to be with you. He would be very, very stupid not to, I think."

I laughed and kissed the top of her head. "I think so, too. Be well, little sister."

Hui and I retraced our steps to the village square, our indiscreet entourage of onlookers trailing behind us.

Ang Shen and his companions were still there, squatting beside a jar of rice-wine and lingering over their dominoes in the slanting, late-afternoon sunlight. His head tilted at our approach, although he didn't deign to look up.

"Ang Shen?" I called. "I have given your wife and your daughter gifts of jade today. I am told it is sufficient to provide Song with a good dowry. And I am telling *you* that these gifts carry a blessing and a curse. Do you leave them be, it will be a blessing on your household." Thinking of my mother and how imposing she could be, I made my voice stern. "But do you think to take and sell them, my curse will be upon you, and I swear to you by stone and sea and all that it encompasses, you shall wish you had never been born."

Lest my words be mistaken, Hui translated them in a high, clear voice.

The village onlookers murmured.

Without looking at me, Bao's mother's husband gave a subtle nod of acknowledgment. I nodded in an unseen reply and turned to go.

"*Moirin.*"

I turned back.

Ang Shen had risen. He wavered a bit on his feet, but his gaze was steady. "That is your name, is it not?" I nodded. He executed a precise bow. "Moirin, I thank you for this gift you have given my family."

Unexpectedly, my heart ached for him.

"Here." I worked loose the last bangle on my right wrist, the red jade bangle, and held it out to him. "Take this. If it does not bring you the luck it promises, you may sell it and do what you will with the profit. It is yours, and yours alone."

For a moment, I thought he would refuse my gift; but then he took it, clutching it in gnarled, work-worn fingers, a world of wariness in his dark eyes. "Do you seek to force hope upon me?"

"I do," I said.

He bowed a second time. "I accept it."

FIVE

—✦—

On the morrow, I departed Tonghe.

   I left in the early morning. As much as it had delighted me
to meet Bao's mother and sister, the increasing chill in the autumn air
made me eager to be on my way. My young companion Hui's father,
a gentle, sensible fellow, advised me to make haste.

"Winter's coming sooner rather than later, Lady Moirin," he said
with concern, his son translating for him. "You don't want to be
caught out on the steppes without shelter."

"I grew up in the wilderness," I said with an assurance I didn't
entirely feel. "I can take care of myself."

He shook his head. "You will not have experienced a cold such as
this one. Perhaps it would be better to turn back. You could winter
in Shuntian."

I had suggested that very thing to Snow Tiger. Gently but firmly,
she had sent me on my way, telling me it was time to go.

My *diadh-anam* agreed. And I was too close to crossing a thresh-
old to turn back now.

So I set out, armed with Hui's father's advice regarding items to
purchase at the Blue Sky Gate market. Hui followed me, shouting and
waving, until I lost him in the distance.

It took no more than an hour to reach the Great Wall, the Blue
Sky Gate, and the market that sprawled within the shadow of the
wall. For those who have not seen it, the wall that the Ch'in built

to keep the Tatars at bay is an awe-inspiring sight. It is high and unthinkably vast, sprawling for countless leagues in both directions. It is constantly being built and repaired, and an untold number of laborers have died in the process.

This northern section was one of the oldest in its original incarnation, which had been little more than fortified earthworks that had crumbled over the centuries, allowing the Tatar raids that had begotten Bao. Since that time, it had been replaced with new construction, solid and imposing, with an outpost of Imperial soldiers manning the gate towers and a market sprung up to serve them.

I wandered the marketplace astride Ember, my pack-horse, Coal, trailing behind us, listening to the shouts of the hawkers falter as they paused to stare at me, a buzz circulating in my wake. It wasn't long before one of the Imperial soldiers hurried over to approach me on foot, a handsome young fellow with a merry face beneath his conical helmet.

"Greetings, Noble Lady," he said with a bow, speaking a dialect close enough to the scholar's tongue that I understood him. "I am Chen Peng. And I think you must be—"

I smiled. "The Emperor's jade-eyed witch, aye."

He laughed. "Swallower-of-memories, I was going to say. Is it true that you seek the twice-born one?"

"It is." It occurred to me that for a country as vast as Ch'in, it had a powerful and extensive rumor network.

Chen Peng read my expression. "I fought at White Jade Mountain," he said in a more somber tone. "When the dragon descended onto the battlefield, I was there. So please tell me, how may I assist you?"

I stroked Ember's neck. "I'm in the market for attire fit to endure a Tatar winter. And such supplies as I will need to survive, at least until I find my stubborn peasant-boy."

He bowed. "I will see to it."

He was as good as his word, marshalling other soldiers to the task. Within an hour's time, I had acquired a variety of supplies, including a long coat of padded cotton, worn sashed over thick trousers tucked into leather boots lined with layers of felt.

A fur-trimmed hat of felted wool that smelled of lanolin topped the ensemble. I wrinkled my nose at it. "Is this necessary?"

"Where you are bound, yes." Peng adjusted it over my ears, tugging it in place. His fingertips brushed the skin of my temples, and he flushed at the unintended intimacy, taking a quick step backward. "It is a dangerous journey. Are you quite certain you must go?" He cleared his throat. "And quite certain that you must go without an escort?"

Desire.

I saw it in his flush, in the sudden heat of his eyes. There was a part of me that responded to it, my blood quickening. He was handsome and pleasant, and I was lonely. I did not know how many days or weeks or months it would take before I found Bao. When all was said and done, I was Naamah's child, and I responded to desire. It was the path I trod and the element in which I swam.

My *diadh-anam* flared in rebellion.

"Aye," I murmured. "I am."

Chen Peng bowed. "Will you permit me one indulgence? I would beg you to ascend the wall and behold the scope of your task."

I nodded. "All right."

He escorted me to the right-hand gate tower. We climbed a winding stair and emerged atop the wall. The sky overhead was impossibly vast, a fathomless vault of vivid blue. I stood silent beneath it, gazing out at the endless expanse of grassy plain that stretched into the horizon as far as the eye could see. There were no farms, no villages. Nothing but grass and sky, and a few dots in the distance that might have been animals grazing.

"There is not even a road, you see," Peng said quietly, watching me. "In the summer during peace-times, the Tatars drive their livestock here to trade."

I felt Bao's presence far away, the twinned spark of his *diadh-anam* calling to mine over the leagues. "I do not require a road."

"They are a war-like folk." The soldier nodded at the Emperor's medallion. "And that will mean nothing to them."

"I know," I said. "But Ch'in is at peace with them now, is it not?"

He shrugged. "Peace is never certain with the Tatars. I beg you one last time, Noble Lady. Allow me to assemble an escort."

The wind was cold on my cheeks. Standing atop the wall, I consulted my own *diadh-anam* one last time, trying to tune out the insistent call of Bao's to discern the will of the Maghuin Dhonn Herself.

The open space of the gate yawned beneath the stone ramparts of the Great Wall. A powerful memory came to me unbidden. I had passed through another stone doorway long ago in Alba. It was a rite of passage among my people. Alone, I went through the stone doorway in the valley beyond the hollow hills into a world of dazzling night and shadowy day, a world of piercing beauty deeper and more profound than my soft, familiar twilight, a world where darkness and light were one and the same.

There, I had waited and waited, until the Great Bear Herself came to me, the Brown Bear of the Maghuin Dhonn.

At first, She came as a presence so immense She blotted out the stars. The earth had trembled beneath Her tread. With each slow, mighty pace, She had dwindled and shaped Herself to a mortal scale.

Her eyes had been so kind, so wise, so filled with compassion and sorrow.

She had breathed upon me, claiming me as Her own; and I had rejoiced, happy to bask in Her presence. And then She had shown me a vision of sparkling oceans filling the stone doorway behind me, and I had understood that I had a destiny to fulfill.

I still did.

And I would not find it until I found Bao, and somehow managed to reunite my divided *diadh-anam*.

I sighed.

Dangerous or no, foolish or no, this was my quest; and I was bound to undertake it alone. That was the meaning of my memory's vision, confirming the truth of my reluctant heart. I breathed the Breath of Wind's Sigh, feeling the space behind my eyes expand to encompass the enormous ocean of grass I beheld.

My kind soldier Peng waited patiently, hopeful.

Standing atop the wall, I turned back to face the Empire of Ch'in itself, breathing the Breath of Earth's Pulse to ground myself. The land that had once seemed strange to me had become a familiar place, filled with folk I could easily love.

Somewhere behind me, Auntie Li was reading tea leaves and regaling customers with tales of the Emperor's jade-eyed witch, who had seen fit to patronize her inn. Closer, Auntie Ai was fondly scolding Bao's mother and sister, bent over their embroidery, jade bangles on their wrists, exchanging glances and smiling.

No doubt young Hui was already boasting of our acquaintance to anyone who would listen.

Snow Tiger... what was my valiant princess doing? Sparring, mayhap, her slender sword darting and flashing steel-bright in her hands. Taking counsel with her father, the Emperor. Shooting at targets, reading the poetry she loved in the gardens of the Celestial City. Mayhap she was listening to music. Whatever she was doing, her faithful, hopelessly enamored guardsman Ten Tigers Dai would be hovering in the background, his bamboo staff at the ready. I hoped that when she thought of her erstwhile necessary inconvenience, she thought of me with the same poignant affection I held for her. I thought she did. My princess had sent me away with a smile as tender as a kiss.

The dragon...

The dragon would be drowsing atop the peaks of White Jade Mountain—sleeping or near to it. His opalescent eyes would be half-lidded, gazing at his reflection in the translucent waters of the pond below him, his coils and possessive claws sunk into stone and indistinguishable from the mountain, guarding the secret treasure that might grow upon its inaccessible slopes, the Camaeline snowdrops I had planted there at the dragon's bidding.

Master Lo Feng.

I bowed and breathed the Breath of Trees Growing, drawing strength from it. "Forgive me, Master," I whispered, turning away from my past. "I will do my best to be worthy of the sacrifice you made."

Beneath the vast blue sky, the distant horizon beckoned me.

"You are going alone," Chen Peng said with regret.

"Aye." I had nearly forgotten his presence. "I am."

SIX

G rass.

    Grass, and grass, and grass.

Once the Great Wall was no longer visible behind me, that was all I saw. Grass and sky. Grazing animals here and there, mostly sheep and cattle. Those, I avoided, knowing it meant there were herders nearby. Betimes, herds of wild gazelles.

It was lonely and peaceful.

I gave a wide berth to the Tatar encampments I saw, the distinctive domes of white felt dotting the plain. If Bao was living among the Tatars, sooner or later I would have to come into contact with them and discover if they were as fearsome as their reputation, but I was content to let it be later. There was no need to go begging for trouble, and I had no need to ask if anyone had seen Bao. Always, always, I could sense him ahead of me.

Hoping to catch up with him before the temperature dropped further, I travelled as fast as I dared; but even in the vast, empty plains, there were constraints. Travelling alone as I was, I couldn't carry much fodder for my mounts. Chen Peng had assured me that the horses would find sufficient grazing to sustain them, but that meant a good portion of each day was devoted to allowing them to graze.

Then there was the matter of water. Again, I had waterskins that allowed me to carry enough for myself to live on for days, but not enough for the horses, too. I didn't dare go more than a day or two without being in sight of water. When I found rivers winding in Bao's general direction, I followed them.

Bit by bit, I made progress.

The nights were the hardest. During the day, I had the sun to warm me and lift my spirits.

At night it was different. It was cold—gods, so cold! It frightened me to think how much colder it could get. I slept in my clothing beneath a fur blanket in the small tent of felted wool that was the bulk of the burden my pack-horse, Coal, carried. Inside the tent, the warmth my body generated was enough to sustain me for now, but every night seemed a little colder than the night before.

The Tatars may have lived behind felt walls, but their walls were thicker and they had one gift I lacked: fire.

It wasn't for lack of skill. I carried a good flint striking kit. And I'd helped my mother tend our hearth since I was four or five years old... but, of course, I'd grown up in a forest.

There were no trees on the empty plain.

From time to time, I passed through an abandoned pasture where I could collect dried dung. Not often, for the Tatars scoured the plains and left little behind when they moved to new pastures. On those occasions when I was able to collect enough to build a campfire, it seemed like a profound luxury. I would fill the little iron pot I carried with water, dried noodles, and bean curd and nestle it amid the burning dung-coals. The resulting soup was chewy and flavorless, but it was wonderfully warm in my belly.

Alone save for the horses, I would huddle over my tiny, smoldering fire, watching the immense sky change colors as the sun sank below the horizon.

Most days, I made do with tough strips of dried yak-meat, gnawing as I rode, chewing and softening it until my jaws ached.

Most nights, I crawled into my narrow tent without the comfort of a fire, tying the flaps tight against the bitter cold and burrowing under my blanket.

It was harder than I had reckoned. Anywhere else in the world, I would have been well equipped to survive. I'd grown up in the wilderness. If there had been edible plants to forage, I would have found them.

There weren't.

I was skilled with a bow. If there had been game to shoot, I could have shot it. But mostly, there wasn't. Such birds as I saw were poor eating—buzzards and raptors. The small game mammals of the plains were already hibernating.

There were the occasional wild gazelles, growing shaggy with the increasing cold. If I'd had fodder for a proper fire, it might have been worthwhile.

But I didn't.

It is a thing we take much for granted, fire. When all is said and done, it is the first, most primordial thing that separates humans from animals. Being children of the Great Bear Herself, the folk of the Maghuin Dhonn are closer than most to the animal realm; and yet, deprived of fire, I craved its reassurance.

I found myself scheming ways to attain it. I eyed the fresh, steaming turds of dung Ember and Coal deposited on the plains, wondering if there were some significance to the fire-names I had given them, wondering if I might rig some manner of woven rack that would allow their dung to dry as it was transported.

Of course, if I had had the materials to build such a rack, I would have had materials to build a fire.

I didn't.

So I gnawed on my strips of dried yak-meat while we plodded westward, ever westward. I did my best to meditate on the lessons Master Lo had taught me. I cycled through the Five Styles of Breathing. I measured the dwindling distance between my *diadh-anam* and the spark of Bao's.

I let my thoughts wander as far away as Terre d'Ange...

Jehanne.

It was at night that I thought of her most, when the immense canopy of stars flung itself across the night sky. As fair as she was, with silver-gilt hair and skin so pale it was nearly translucent, blue-grey eyes that held an impossibly charming sparkle, I'd always thought of Jehanne in terms of starlight and moonlight.

She would have been appalled to find me here.

But she would have understood it.

I pictured her, her fair brows frowning. *This peasant-boy, do you love him?*

I think so.

Jehanne would have shrugged, her slender shoulders rising and falling. *Well, then, mayhap you do.* She would have smiled and beckoned to me anyway, her eyes sparkling. *But you are still mine for now, my lovely savage.*

And I would have gone to her. Once, on the greatship, I had asked Bao why he was jealous of Raphael but not of Jehanne. *Might as well be jealous of the moon for shining as that one,* he had said in a philosophical tone. There was no one in the world Jehanne couldn't charm when she chose.

Thoughts of opulent Terre d'Ange were an incongruous thing on the Tatar plain, riding with dung beneath my fingernails, but they helped sustain me. It was good to remember that there had been a time when my world had consisted of more than endless grass plains, frigid, shivering nights, and dried yak-meat. There had been feasts with all manner of delicacies, bottomless pitchers of wine. There had been balls with music and dancing, splendid garments, a thousand shimmering lanterns. I'd had my own quarters at the Palace, the enchanted bower that Jehanne had caused to be made for me, warmed with braziers and filled with every kind of green, growing plant imaginable. Fragrant orange and lemon trees, dwarf firs in pots, tall fronds of ferns casting green shadows over my bed.

Here, there was grass, grass, and more grass.

I missed trees.

One day, I came across an unfamiliar structure. From a distance, it looked like a mound of sticks tied about with blue rags. Wary of human presence, I hesitated to approach it, but I sensed no one, and the prospect of wood drew me.

At closer range, I saw it was true. It was a conical cairn built of weathered branches—wood, firewood, enough for half a dozen merry campfires. I dismounted in haste, already calculating how best to bundle and load it, and how much additional weight Coal could carry, my cold fingers reaching eagerly to dismantle the structure.

And then my *diadh-anam* stirred in warning, and I hesitated.

Scarves of vibrant blue silk hung from the branches. There were little bowls nestled around the base of the cairn, tucked into niches. Some held a dried residue that might have been milk. Others held what looked to be the petrified remains of some kind of dumpling, pale and smooth as river-stones.

I sighed.

"This is a sacred place, isn't it?" I said aloud, gazing at the immense blue vault of the sky. A breeze sprang up as if in answer, setting the blue scarves fluttering.

So be it.

I didn't have milk or dumplings to offer, but I worked a strip of dried yak-meat free from the pouch that hung from my sash. Although I was worried about my stores growing low, I had learned in my travels that it was always wise to offer respect to foreign gods. I bowed and placed the meat in a bowl, hoping that it would not offend the original donor, hoping that whatever gods the Tatars worshipped would not think me stingy.

And then I heaved myself back astride Ember, and we continued on our plodding way across the endless plains, Coal trailing behind us.

It was two or three days afterward that I saw the herders. I saw the cattle first, scores of them ambling from the northwest on a course to intersect mine. I heard the shouts of the boys before I saw them. It was another cold, clear day, and their young voices carried across the plain.

I glanced around, but there was nowhere to hide on the flat, empty expanse of grassland. For the first time in longer than I could recall, I summoned the twilight.

Despite my lack of practice, it came easier than I had reckoned. I had seen dusk fall over the plain many, many times since I had passed through the gate, and the discipline that Master Lo taught me had focused my gift. I breathed the living memory of Tatar dusk deep into my lungs, feeling my *diadh-anam* flicker and glow. I breathed out the twilight, letting it settle over the horses and me.

The sunlit world turned shadowy and dim, the grass silvered, and the sky filled with deep purple and indigo hues.

With a silent thought, I asked the horses to remain still and quiet. They obeyed willingly, pricking their ears and watching with curiosity as the stream of cattle and the two young Tatar herdsmen passed before us. The boys looked to be thirteen or fourteen, and they rode in the saddle as though born to it, prodding the cattle with long poles, chattering back and forth to one another with cheerful urgency, all unwitting of our presence. A keen-eyed dog trotted alongside one of them.

I smiled quietly.

When they were no more than specks on the horizon, I released the twilight. The bright daylit world returned in a rush of color. Green grass was green once more; the arching sky overhead was blue. Ember tossed his head a few times and blew through his nostrils as though to comment on the phenomenon.

"Come, brave heart." I patted his withers. "We've a league or two to go before we make camp for the night."

Had I been wiser in the ways of winter in Tatar territory, I might have thought to wonder where the young herdsmen were bound, and why they went about their task with a certain sense of urgency.

I found out soon enough.

Within an hour's time, the temperature began to drop precipitously. The wind sharpened. It cut through my thick coat of padded cotton, it found its way up my sleeves, it froze my cheeks until my entire face felt stiff. The air began to smell like snow. Toward the west, the sky took on a dark, ominous hue, a tall stack of clouds growing on the horizon.

There was a storm coming.

A very, very big storm.

And ah, gods! It was so *sudden*. I don't know what early warning signs I missed, what signs the Tatars were able to read. It was unfamiliar terrain, an unfamiliar climate, unlike any I had known.

I broke to make camp as soon as I saw the clouds massing. It was my custom to tend to the horses first, unsaddling Ember, unloading all of Coal's packs, checking their hooves, and turning them loose to graze. This time, my heart beating hard in my chest, I begged their forgiveness and set about erecting my sheltering tent, fearful for my vulnerable human flesh.

I couldn't do it.

It was a task that had grown more difficult every day. Bit by bit, the farther I rode, the colder it got, the more the turf had hardened.

Today, it had hardened further. My wooden mallet skidded futilely off the frayed heads of the wooden tent-stakes. The points of the stakes splintered against the frozen ground, unable to penetrate the sod. I swung and pounded until my arm ached, my chest heaving and my breath rising in frosty puffs, all to no avail.

My eyes stung with frustrated tears. I dragged my padded sleeve over them. "Gods bedamned, Bao! Stupid, stubborn boy! Could you not stay put for one minute? Did you *have* to put me through this?"

The only thing to answer was the storm.

It descended on us with an unearthly howl, fierce as a dragon's fury, the wind filled with pellets of ice. It snatched the dense felt of my tent away from me, plucking the fabric and lines and stakes from my helpless fingers, sending it careening across the grassy plains under a glowering sky.

Flee.

The word resounded in my head. I did not know who or what spoke it—whether it was the Maghuin Dhonn Herself, the D'Angeline gods Naamah or Anael, the unknown gods of the Tatars, or merely my own panic speaking.

It didn't matter.

I fled. I ran toward Ember, hurling myself across his saddle. It struck me hard in the chest. I hauled myself astride, flinging my leg over him. I found the reins, and gave him his head.

"Go!" I shouted. "Go, go, go!"

My valiant chestnut arched his neck and thundered southward; poor Coal, half-unladen, laboring in his wake. All around us, the storm howled, pursuing us.

Flee.

Snow and bits of ice pelted us. I could not tell if it was day or night. All the world was chaos. We rode and rode and rode, trying to outpace the storm. I was a frozen creature, clinging to another frozen creature. The whipping wind howled. Frost gathered on my eyelashes. Ember lost his footing and staggered hard beneath me, pitching me onto his neck. He caught himself from falling, but came up lame, lurching every time he put weight on his left foreleg.

I slipped from the saddle and leant my face against his ice-crusted neck in despair. With an effort, I pushed myself away and set about trying to unbuckle the straps that lashed Coal's load to his back.

It was impossible. The straps were stiff and frozen, and my fingers were so numb I couldn't get any purchase.

So I did the only thing I could think to do. I took up Ember's reins and began trudging on foot, the horses trailing behind me.

How long I walked, I could not say. It felt like an eternity. The storm was like a mighty hand shoving me from behind. I concentrated on putting one foot in front of the other, convinced that if I stopped moving, I would die.

I don't doubt that it was true. Allowing my gift to be used in an unwise manner, I'd come close to dying before, but I never felt anything that sapped my will to live the way that bitter, cold wind did. Would that I could say it was hope that kept me going, but no such thing existed in that raging darkness. It was the irrational spark of anger I harbored toward Bao, the sense that this was all his fault, that gave me the will to keep taking one step, then another, long after my legs had begun to feel leaden.

Head down, I trudged blindly—trudged, and trudged, and trudged. Until I bumped into something large.

I went still.

The large thing bumped me back—*several* large things. A choked sound of fear died in my throat. There were large figures looming in the darkness, and yet I sensed a benign intent. I rubbed the frost from my eyelashes and squinted.

Cattle.

I was surrounded by cattle—big, shaggy cattle with short, curved horns and lambent eyes rimed with frost. They bumped, jostled, and nudged me and my horses, herding us forward, a dim sense of concern in their thoughts. And then, ah, gods!

There was a wall, a stone wall that blocked the worst of the blizzard's knifing wind. I'd never been so glad to see a man-made wall in my life.

If there was a wall, doubtless there were humans nearby, but I couldn't make out any of the Tatars' felt domiciles in the storm; and the cattle were insistent, nudging me into the lee of the wall. I let go of Ember's reins and slid down the wall in relief, resting my back against the rough stone and huddling into my coat.

With low groans, two of the cattle sank down on either side of me, pressing flanks and haunches against me. Their concerned thoughts gave way to complacent, bovine ones. Within minutes, I could feel the warmth of their shaggy hides penetrating my clothing.

I laughed, and wept tears that froze on my cheeks. "Thank you," I whispered—to the cattle, to the Maghuin Dhonn Herself, to the D'Angeline pantheon, to the Tatar gods, and to stone and sea and sky and all that they encompassed. "Thank you."

SEVEN

Impossible as it may seem, I fell asleep amid the cattle.

I was tired beyond exhaustion, as tired in spirit as though I'd been drained almost to death, and as tired in body as though I'd climbed White Jade Mountain all over again. The presence of the cattle was warm and soothing, and the stone wall blocked the worst of the storm. There was nothing I could do for my horses until the storm passed.

And so I closed my weary eyes, thinking only to rest them a moment, and fell into a black pit of unconsciousness.

I awoke to a startled shout.

I opened my eyes to find calm morning light, and one of the young Tatar herdsmen staring at me. He loosed another shout when I opened my eyes, gripping his herder's staff with both hands. The dog beside him planted its haunches on the frozen ground and wagged its tail, bright-eyed, its tongue lolling.

I shouted too, scrambling to my feet. The cattle on either side of me heaved themselves upright in their ungainly, rear-end-first way.

The boy yelled questions at me, his voice high and fierce. More cattle milled between us. I shook my head and spread my hands help-lessly, eyeing Ember amid the herd and wondering if I could get to the bow and quiver strapped to the saddle.

The boy hesitated, then turned and raced toward the felt dwellings now visible some thirty yards away, shouting all the while.

I hesitated, too.

I was alive, and so were my mounts. It looked as though most of the supplies loaded on Coal were intact.

But I had no tent, and it was ungodly cold. Snow dusted the frozen sod, not as much as I would have expected, but I supposed the fierce wind prevented it from accumulating. I sidled through the cattle and reached Ember's side, unlashing my bow. My fingers had thawed just enough that I was able to string it.

More folk spilled out of the felt huts—men, women, and children of all ages. I held the bow loosely in my left hand and plucked one arrow from the quiver without nocking it, trying to look calm. I didn't want to present myself as an enemy, but I didn't intend to appear an easy victim, either.

The Tatars fanned out as they approached, pointing and exclaiming to one another. I stood my ground uncertainly. A man of middle years whose coat and hat bore finer embroidery than the others beckoned to a young girl and spoke to her. She dashed back to the nearest hut, returning with a thick woolen blanket.

The man took it from her and began to push his way through the cattle toward me, holding out the blanket, uttering a sound such as one might make to soothe a fractious horse. "Ha, ha, ha!"

I eyed him, bow in hand, unable to determine whether he meant to offer the blanket to me or capture me in it.

He clucked his tongue, shaking the blanket at me in a way that could have been inviting or menacing. "Ha, ha!"

"I'm sorry!" I said aloud in the scholar's tongue. "I don't understand what you're trying to do."

One of the women said somewhat in a sharp tone. The adult Tatars argued amongst themselves. Wide-eyed children with round faces stared at me. I tried smiling at one, and he burst into tears.

Another woman emerged from the felt huts, walking slowly and carefully—in part because her pregnant belly strained against her long coat, and in part because she carried a small bowl of steaming liquid. She paused to dip her fingers in it, scattering droplets on the frozen earth.

All the Tatars murmured in approval.

The pregnant woman and the man with the blanket exchanged glances. He shrugged and stepped backward to let her pass him. She came toward me with those delicate little steps, smiling at me with weary sweetness. This time, the cattle moved out of the way of their own accord.

A few paces away from me, she raised the bowl to her lips and mimed drinking from it, then held it out to me. I paused, then slung my bow over my shoulder and returned the arrow I had drawn from my quiver. The pregnant woman nodded encouragingly. She cradled the bowl in one hand, pointed at it, then pointed at the ground, raising her eyebrows in question.

I felt foolish.

"Thank you," I murmured, cupping my hands together in a gesture of gratitude. "I recognize an offer of hospitality. You do not need to treat me like a wild creature."

She beamed, holding out the bowl with both hands.

I bowed in the Ch'in manner and came forward to accept it, taking it in both hands and lifting it to drink.

It was tea, hot and salty, rich with milk-fat. Another time and place, I might have found the taste repugnant. Here, it tasted like heaven. I meant to sip it politely. Instead, I downed the entire bowl.

The Tatars I had been so assiduously avoiding all made sounds of welcome and approval. Still beaming, the pregnant woman turned to her husband—as I later learned he was—and extended her hand for the woolen blanket. He gave it to her with an affectionate, rueful smile. She raised her brows at me once more, offering the blanket to me.

"Thank you," I said a second time, accepting it with another bow and wrapping it around my shoulders.

She touched my sleeve, then touched my face, her fingertips gentle and inquisitive. I held still and let her. Her dark, angular eyes searched mine. At length, satisfied, she nodded, turned and said somewhat to the others. Her husband nodded and said somewhat more, making a firm gesture of dismissal.

With obvious reluctance, the others began to disperse, returning to their felt huts or setting about various chores.

The couple turned their attention back to me. The woman asked me a question, speaking as slowly and carefully as though to a very young child. I shook my head helplessly. After another exchange with her husband, she pointed toward the felt huts. She mimed eating and sleeping, first raising an imaginary spoon to her lips, then pressing her cheek against folded hands.

Given my fears, I was embarrassed by their kindness. "Thank you," I said for the third time. "But I must tend to my mounts first." I pointed to myself and then at Ember and Coal, still saddled and loaded amid the meandering cattle, then mimed awkwardly to indicate what I needed to do.

The man's face cleared with understanding. He nodded in approval and called over the boy who had first discovered me. The boy went to work straightaway at unloading Coal's packs, blowing on the frozen buckles to thaw them. With an elaborate series of gestures, the man indicated that the boy would unload the horses and carry my gear and supplies to the hut, then turn the horses loose to graze on the frozen plain. He finished by echoing his wife's gesture with the imaginary spoon.

His wife didn't wait for my reply. Grasping the fur-trimmed cuff of my sleeve, she tugged me firmly toward the encampment. Wrapped in a warm blanket and their generosity, I went willingly.

There were some two dozen of the felt huts, which I later learned to call *gers*, in the camp. At close range, they were much larger and more substantial than I had reckoned, and infinitely more sophisticated than the simple tent that the storm had snatched away from me, thick felt layered on dome-shaped lattices. All the *gers* faced south, with brightly painted wooden doors. Smoke drifted from a hole at the top of each dome.

My hostess led me to the *ger* with the most elaborately painted doorway, ushering me inside.

Warmth struck me—warmth, and the smell of the rich, salty tea she had brought me. There were thick woolen carpets woven with intricate designs covering the floor of the *ger*, keeping the cold of the frozen ground at bay. Overhead, the poles of the lattice framework radiated like the spokes of a great wagon-wheel. Beneath the smoke-hole, two pots simmered atop an iron stove. I inhaled deeply, letting the blanket slide from my shoulders. My hostess smiled and took the empty bowl from my hand, then said somewhat in a formal tone.

I bowed in response. Even if she couldn't understand my words, it seemed important to speak them aloud. "May all the gods bless you for your hospitality and generosity, my lady."

"Eh?" On the far side of the *ger*, a seated figure lifted a wizened face, cupping one ear. Her bright eyes squinted in a parchment map of wrinkled skin. With an effort, the oldest woman I'd ever seen in my life, older than Old Nemed of the Maghuin Dhonn, dragged herself to her feet and hobbled across the carpets.

My hostess offered her what sounded like a bemused explanation.

The old woman nodded absently, peering at me. She had to crane her neck since a hump atop her spine wouldn't allow her to stand entirely straight. Licking her weathered lips, she essayed a question, starting and stopping several times, pausing to search her memory. At last she got it out, each syllable rusted and creaky. "Did I hear you speak the scholar's tongue of Shuntian?"

I blinked in surprise. "Yes, Grandmother."

"Thought so." She poked me in the breast-bone with one gnarled finger, her eyes sharp and inquisitive. "Who are you? *What* are you? And why in the world are you *here*?"

My hostess glanced back and forth between us, perplexity on her kind face. A boy toddler wobbled over to clutch at her coat; another child, a young girl, sidled up behind her, peeking out at me.

"I am Moirin," I said politely. "Moirin mac Fainche of the Maghuin Dhonn. And as to what that means and why I am here, I fear it is a very long story."

"Oh, good." The old woman doubled over and coughed deep in her chest, then straightened to the best of her abilities, dark eyes glinting at me in her wrinkled face. She yawned widely, covering her mouth to hide it. "And after I've finished my morning nap, you can tell it to me." She turned to hobble away, offering one last comment over her shoulder. "And take your time about it, because it's going to be a long winter."

EIGHT

So it came to pass that I wintered amongst a Tatar tribe.

It wasn't my intention to stay with them, but from the beginning, it was obvious that the weather gave me little choice. Once winter arrived in earnest, even the hardy, nomadic Tatars with all their knowledge of surviving on the plains settled in for the duration.

On that first morning, I sat cross-legged on the carpeted floor of the *ger*, feeling awkward at my unintentional imposition, trying to stay out of the way while I waited for the old woman to finish her nap. My pregnant hostess brought me a bowl of hot, stewed meat to eat. I accepted it gratefully. When I had finished, the little girl—her daughter, I guessed—approached me shyly at her mother's urging. With gestures, she showed me I was meant to wipe the bowl clean with my fingers, gathering the last of the juices. She bobbed her head in cautious approval when I obeyed.

The boy tending to my horses entered the *ger* along with a blast of cold air, staggering under the weight of my packs and gear. He darted back out before I could even thank him.

My hostess bustled around, scouring dishes and stirring pots. When I offered with gestures to assist her, she smiled and shook her head. She pointed across the *ger* to the pallet where the old woman was now snoring deeply, made a circling gesture with one finger that indicated time passing, then mimed two mouths talking with both hands.

"I understand," I said. "We will speak when she awakes. I only wanted to help in the meantime."

She pointed firmly at the carpeted floor and said something in a stern tone. Although she couldn't have been more than ten or twelve years older than me, it sounded for all the world like a mother's reprimand.

I sat, chastened.

My hostess smiled and went about her business.

Lulled by the warmth of the *ger* and the hot stew in my belly, I felt the weight of my exhaustion settle over me. Although I'd no intention of falling asleep amongst these strangers, hospitable though they seemed, my head grew heavy, my chin sinking to my chest. I fell into a light doze.

I awoke to find the family gathering around a low table for a mid-day meal of more stewed meat.

The old woman glanced over and gave a creaking laugh. "Aha! The slumbering forest spirit is awake." She beckoned to me. "Come, come, eat," she said, adding something in the Tatar tongue.

My hostess rose with ungainly grace to fill another bowl for me.

"Thank you." I accepted it with a bow, then took a seat at the table at her insistent gesture. "You're very kind. Grandmother, will you thank her for me?"

"She knows." The old woman's mouth worked as she chewed. "You've been bobbing up and down like a courtier since you came through the door. So! Begin your story, will you?"

I paused, the spoon halfway to my mouth.

My hostess spoke gently to the old woman, who sighed. "Oh, fine! My granddaughter says eat first, talk later."

They waited patiently for me to finish. There were six of them present: my hostess and her husband; the young herdsman, who I guessed to be around thirteen and their eldest son. The little girl's age I put at six or seven, and the toddler at two or three; and of course, there was the old woman, whose age I couldn't begin to guess. All of them gazed at me with polite curiosity while I ate.

After I had finished and wiped my bowl with my fingers in the prescribed manner, my host addressed me in a formal tone.

"My grandson Batu welcomes you into his dwelling," the old woman translated. "He hopes you find it a place of peace."

"Batu." I echoed his name. "Yes, thank you."

"Good." The old woman took a noisy slurp of tea, fixing me with her sharp gaze. "Now tell me who in the name of the ancestors you might be, and what in the name of all the gods and the great blue sky you're doing here."

I did my best.

It wasn't easy. There was far, far too much to explain, and I didn't know how much of my tale might give offense. The Tatars and the Ch'in existed in an uneasy truce in the best of times, and I did not care to reveal myself as an Imperial favorite. So I simply told her that I had come from faraway Terre d'Ange, travelling to Ch'in to continue studying with my mentor, the venerable sage Master Lo Feng. That I had fallen in love with a fellow student, who had fled after our mentor's death, venturing into Tatar territory to seek his father; and that I had set out in pursuit of him, driven by love.

She listened, drinking salty tea and pausing from time to time to translate for the benefit of the others.

Batu interjected a comment.

The old woman's wispy brows rose. "Huh! Was this young man carrying a powerful medicine?"

"No...wait. Aye, mayhap." I remembered the Camaeline snow-drop bulbs that Master Lo had transported all the way from Terre d'Ange. Only three of them had survived, and I had planted them atop White Jade Mountain, where the dragon had promised to guard and cherish them. The rest had been sacrificed, left to dry in the lodgings we had rented in Shuntian. When I had gone there to ask after Bao, the new tenants told me he had returned to retrieve the bulbs, which were capable of being rendered into a powerful aphrodisiac. "What manner of medicine, Grandmother?"

The old woman cackled. "The kind of tonic to stiffen a man's spear!"

I flushed. "Ah...yes. That would likely be Bao. Although he might have been calling himself Shangun. I do not know."

She eyed me. "Lightning Stick?"

I shrugged. "It is a name he took for himself when he was young and foolish."

The old woman conversed with Batu. Aided by her daughter, my hostess began to clear and scour our dishes. I waited.

"Yes," the old woman said at length. "My grandson has heard of your young man Bao. With his strong tonic, he bribed his way into General Arslan's favor before the winter winds blew. It seems that General Arslan has claimed him as a son. Come spring, you ought to be able to find him."

I stood, so quickly it dizzied me. "Spring! I can't wait that long."

My hostess hurried over to me, urging me to sit with gentle hands. She and her husband exchanged worried words.

"Strange girl, you are not going anywhere for a very long time!" the old woman announced in an acerbic tone. "No one travels in winter. You barely survived a single storm. You would only die."

My *diadh-anam* flared within me. "I *need* to go!"

The old woman sighed. "Oh, child! It only feels that way. Such is the nature of young love. It will pass."

"You don't understand," I whispered.

Her wrinkled mouth pursed. "So they all say. I was young once, too. Young and beautiful. It fades, child. All beauty and passion does. Stay the winter here, and in the spring, the tribes will gather in the northwest. You will be reunited with your young man, and see how well his passion has endured. Perhaps you will be fortunate. If so, I say well done. If not, it is not worth dying for now."

I hesitated.

Small hands tugged at the sash around my waist. I glanced down to see Batu's daughter yanking at me. Her eyes were wary, but her face was set and determined. She said something fierce in the Tatar tongue.

Her mother echoed it, and her father nodded.

"They do not want your blood on their hands," the old woman translated. "They beg you to stay."

I knew myself defeated. I sank to the floor, bowing my head. The little girl climbed into my lap and nestled against me, no longer fearful. Absentmindedly, I stroked her black hair. "I do not wish to be a burden."

"Then work for your keep," the old woman said forcefully. "My soft-hearted granddaughter-in-law Checheg will show you how. Live, endure, and learn."

I glanced at my hostess. "Checheg? Is that your name?"

She nodded, hands pressed against her swollen belly.

I touched my breast. "Moirin."

"Moirin." It was Batu who said my name in a strong voice, rising to his feet. He placed his hands on my shoulders as though to claim me, but there was only kindness in his grip. He smiled down at me, gave me a little shake, then turned me loose, ruffling his daughter's hair. "Moirin."

I was grateful for his kindness. "Your people are not what I was led to expect, Grandmother."

She snorted. "Do I *look* like a Tatar, child?"

"Ah..." I peered at her. With her shriveled-apple face, I couldn't tell. The little girl on my lap plucked at the silk cord around my neck. "Are you from Shuntian, Grandmother? Is that how you come to speak the scholar's tongue?"

"I am an Imperial princess descended from his Celestial Majesty Zhu Daoyu," the old woman said with steely dignity. "I was given in marriage to the tribal khan Oyugun as part of a peace treaty."

I blinked. "You were?"

She gave a dismissive wave. "Oh, it was a very long time ago. No one remembers. But you may call me Grandmother Yue, and yes, that is why I speak the scholar's tongue." She pointed at my chest, her eyes keen. "It is also how I know that is an Imperial seal you wear around your neck, which leads me to suspect part of your tale is either missing or a lie."

I glanced down in alarm to see that Batu and Checheg's daughter had pulled the Imperial jade medallion from beneath my coat and was toying with it, tracing the carved curves of the dragon's coils with her small fingers. I felt the blood drain from my face.

"So?" Grandmother Yue asked in a sharp voice. "Which is it, child? An omission or a lie?"

I swallowed hard. "Missing, Grandmother. Perhaps you heard, there was a civil war in Ch'in. I played a role in it and won the Emperor's favor."

"Ah!" Her lips worked. "Now, that's more like it. Yes, yes, we have heard rumors and gossip. A warrior princess possessed by a demon, great sorcerers doing battle in the south with dreadful weapons." She nodded. "That's a tale fit for a long winter. You'll tell it in full, of course, with no details omitted."

I looked around the *ger*. It was a scene of domestic tranquillity, filled with folk who had shown me nothing but generosity. "They will not take it amiss?"

Grandmother Yue took a noisy sip of tea. "The world is a complicated place, child. I have lived most of my life among the Tatars, and they are no better or worse than any other folk. Today, they are content to be peaceable. If the Emperor had lost the Mandate of Heaven and Ch'in lay in chaos, perhaps the khans would be plotting an invasion. They have conquered and ruled Ch'in before, you know."

"Oh." I hadn't known.

She shrugged. "It would not matter anyway. Hospitality is sacred to them, and my grandson Batu has offered you the protection of his roof. No tale you tell will cause him to violate that trust." She sipped her tea. "So tell your tale from the beginning. The *very* beginning."

"As you will, Grandmother." I took a deep breath and began. "I was born to the Maghuin Dhonn. We are the folk of the Brown Bear, and the oldest magic in Alba runs in our veins—"

The old woman smiled, her bright eyes disappearing in a nest of wrinkles. "Yes, that's definitely more like it!"

NINE

———◆———

Over the long winter months, I spun out my story—my true story, the one I had told to Bao's mother and sister, with a wealth of detail added to it. And Grandmother Yue was right, no one took it amiss. There was little else to do, and Batu's family was glad of the distraction.

I was glad, too. It gave me a sense of purpose during those early days when I was more hindrance than help in the camp. Bit by bit, as Checheg showed me how to prepare salty tea and cook in the Tatar manner, I felt myself become more useful. During Grandmother Yue's prodigious naps, we communicated with gestures and the few words of Tatar I began to acquire. As Checheg's belly grew ever larger, I sensed she was increasingly grateful for my aid.

After meals, I told my story, eking it out slowly while Grandmother Yue translated.

Unlike most folk I had encountered, the Tatars did not find it strange that the Maghuin Dhonn worship the Great Bear Herself. They simply nodded, accepting it as a matter of course; and I found myself grateful for that simple acceptance.

Like folk everywhere, they marveled at the opulence and licentiousness of the D'Angeline lifestyle. Although I couched the details in discreet terms for the benefit of the children, Batu and Checheg were shocked to learn that the King of Terre d'Ange not only wed a courtesan, but allowed her to take lovers.

"Heh!" Grandmother Yue cackled with delight. "I say good for her!"

Some details, I chose to withhold. Reckoning they would find it too unlike their customs to understand, I didn't tell them that Jehanne had seduced me quite thoroughly, only that she had rescued me from Raphael's deadly ambition.

Everyone agreed that Raphael was a right scoundrel, but they reveled in the tales of the fallen spirits we summoned and how they tricked Raphael and his companions. Checheg and Batu's daughter, Sarangerel, especially loved to hear about the spirit Caim, who had eyes like an owl and antlers with a bird's nest caught in them. According to lore, Caim could bestow the gift of communicating with all living creatures. He tricked Raphael and the others by teaching them the language of ants, which was composed wholly of scent. They gave up before the spirit Caim moved on to crickets.

It was a time of peace, but it was also a time of prolonged yearning, that endless Tatar winter. The warmth and kindness everyone extended to me made me miss my home. Gods, I missed *having* a home. I missed my taciturn, oh-so-familiar mother in Alba, and the lovely, gracious father I had discovered in Terre d'Ange. I missed my sparkling lady Jehanne, with whom I would always be a little bit in love. I missed Snow Tiger, whom I had come to cherish in a very different way.

I missed the dragon, my splendid friend.

And always, always, always, I ached for Bao's presence. I could sense his *diadh-anam* burning like a beacon, near enough that I could have ridden there in ten days were it not for the deadly cold. I ached to be reunited with the missing half of my *diadh-anam*. That was a constant. And it frustrated me, not only because I could not go to him, but because I could not sort out in my confused heart what was real and what was the result of the binding Master Lo Feng had laid upon us.

I knew where my feelings began and ended. They began with a sneaking fondness for Master Lo's magpie, the proud, stubborn peasant-boy with whom I had bickered and quarreled for so long, before we fell into bed with one another and began a thorny love affair. They ended with Bao walking away from me, leaving me alone and bereft, the spark of my sundered *diadh-anam* burning steadily inside him.

It was the missing parts in between that confused me.

There were good days and bad days. On good days, I thought mayhap it was for the best that I had this time to reflect. As harsh as they were, the frozen Tatar grasslands had a sweeping majesty to them. Although I felt guilty whenever I wasn't aiding Checheg in the *ger*, I liked being outdoors, liked the impossibly vast blue sky arching above me.

I liked doing simple tasks like fetching water from the nearby river, or even gathering cow-dung to dry. I liked to practice the Five Styles of Breathing in the achingly cold air. While I still missed trees, I liked the elemental rhythm of Tatar life.

On the bad days...

On the bad days, I questioned myself. If I had not tarried in the Celestial City in Shuntian an extra week, dallying with the princess, mayhap I would have beaten the weather and gained Bao's side before winter's onset, so we might use these long nights to resolve matters between us.

That had been my doing, all my doing.

Snow Tiger had asked me to invoke Naamah's blessing on her behalf, and I had done it gladly. She had not asked me to tarry. *I* was the one who had badgered her to let me stay, at least for a week's time. She had agreed to it without much persuasion needed. And I did not want to regret it, for it had been a time of profound grace.

I would have stayed longer had she let me. I would have spent the winter in Shuntian with her.

The Emperor's daughter's face swam in my memory, her dark eyes grave. *It is too easy to accept the comfort you offer, Moirin. I have duties that lie elsewhere. You have a destiny to follow.*

She was right, of course. But it didn't stop me from resenting my everlasting destiny on the bad days. It seemed unfair that it constantly drove me away from people for whom I cared deeply, and doubly unfair that the one person to whom my destiny *was* inextricably linked was bound and determined to evade me.

I wondered what Bao was feeling.

Bit by bit, I learned more about his circumstances. I learned that General Arslan was high in the Great Khan's favor. Batu confirmed that he would have been the one to lead a raid on Tonghe village twenty-some years ago.

"Very good warrior," he said slowly to me. "Strong man."

"Why?" I asked. "Why fight and kill?"

Batu frowned and shook his head, deciding it was too complicated a matter to explain to me with my limited Tatar language. He beckoned Grandmother Yue over and spoke to her at length.

"Ah, child!" she said when he finished. "It's the way of the world, that's all. The Ch'in raided Tatar camps, too. When the men were away, they kidnapped women and children and enslaved them, put them to work building the wall."

I took a sharp breath. "Put them to work building the very wall meant to keep them out? That's a piece of bitter irony."

She nodded. "I told you, it's the way of the world. Arslan lost his young wife. He was only taking vengeance."

"By raping an innocent woman?" I asked in outrage.

"I did not say I agreed with it," Grandmother Yue said in a gentle tone. "I said it was the way of the world, Moirin. It is in the nature of mankind."

I thought about her words when I breathed the Five Styles and meditated, doing my best to be mindful of Master Lo's teaching and let one thought give rise to another. It was hard, and I thought mayhap there were things in the world I didn't *want* to understand. In my travels, I had learned that the followers of the Path of Dharma believed that to live was to suffer. I was not willing to accept their wisdom as truth, but I could understand why many did.

Master Lo had allowed the possibility that mayhap I had my own path of enlightenment to follow, the Path of Desire.

These days, it seemed a very distant possibility.

Oh, I could have taken a lover if I had wished it. After the initial shock of my appearance, almost everyone at Batu's camp treated me with genuine warmth. I had a way with animals, and that endeared me to their keepers. The Tatars lived closer to nature than any folk I'd encountered save my own. I continued to be surprised and pleased by their acceptance. Although I understood there was some lingering debate as to whether or not I was a forest spirit from the distant mountains, it was generally agreed that it was a *good* thing if it were true. From time to time, I caught sidelong glances from some of the bolder young men in the camp, suggesting a tryst would be welcome.

But my *diadh-anam* disapproved, and the bright lady was silent. It seemed Naamah's gift had gone dormant for the winter.

Life held other pleasures. Living in the *ger*, I came to value Batu's quiet strength, his obvious love for his wife and children. I treasured Checheg's steady kindness and guidance. Their eldest son, Temur, spent a good deal of time blushing in my presence, but that was to be expected at his age, and he was a good-hearted lad.

Their daughter, Sarangerel, was a delight, bright and lively. Having adopted me on that first day, my small friend staked a relentless claim on me. Under her mother's indulgent gaze, Sarangerel followed me around the *ger*, tugging at the hem of my coat, her little brother, Mongke, toddling in her wake, babbling nonsense words. Among other things, she insisted on teaching me a complicated Tatar game in which both players made a fist with their right hands, then shot out several fingers and uttered competing rhymes based on the total number showing.

"Nine!" she would say in triumph, waiting for me to respond.

"Mine?" I would hazard.

Sarangerel would shake her head in mock disappointment, and rattle off a string of better rhymes. I never won a single game, but it improved my skills with the Tatar language considerably. And she was unstinting with her affection, always eager to climb into my lap and rub her cheek against mine, while her little brother pulled jealously on my sleeve until I made room for both of them.

It soothed that part of me that yearned for human contact in a way I had never known before, filled with tender innocence. Growing up in isolation, I'd had precious little contact with children.

I liked it.

I liked the simplicity and purity of it. In a strange way, it was a relief to develop a complex set of relationships in which carnal desire played no part. It occurred to me that this had happened seldom in my life since I came of age, and there was probably a lesson to be learned there.

And then a month into my stay, Checheg went into labor.

I had been expecting it; we all had. Day by day, we had waited and wondered. How could we not, her belly as swollen as it was? Still, it came as a shock.

For one thing, the men abandoned us.

For another, I was left in charge.

"What?" I said in dismay. "Batu, I do not know what to do!"

Batu jiggled young Mongke in his arms, not meeting my eyes. His eldest son, Temur, lurked behind him, peering at me. "You are a woman, are you not? This is women's business. Grandmother will help you. After all, she has done it many times before; and so has Checheg, three times. Men do not belong here." He gave me a furtive glance. "We will return after the child is born," he said firmly, exiting the *ger* and closing the brightly painted door behind him.

"Eh?" The old woman rose from her pallet and tottered in my direction, cupping one ear. "Ready to pop, is she?"

"Aye." I blew out my breath, trying to remember what Raphael had taught me. I had assisted him with a difficult birth once, although I'd come in at the end of the process. "Sarangerel, you will bring a bucket of water, please?"

"Yes, Moirin!" She dashed away.

One thing about the Tatars, they were not much for bathing, at least not in the dead of winter. I had not seen anything resembling soap in the *ger*; but I had a dwindling ball of soap in my battered canvas satchel. As soon as the water was warming on the stove, I scrubbed my hands and arms thoroughly, raising a goodly amount of lather. "Good," I said. "We need blankets and cloth. Clean."

"You needn't fuss so," Grandmother Yue said irritably, taking Checheg's arm and helping her walk around the *ger*. "Nature will take its course."

Checheg grunted in assent, rubbing the small of her back.

"I am trying to do a good thing!" I said in frustration. "Clean is better. Not to make sick."

They exchanged a glance and shrugged.

It was a long process.

When the contractions began to come hard and steady, Checheg lay down, propped against pillows, her knees spread apart. She did not protest when I eased the cleanest of the felt blankets beneath her. Gently, I removed her thick, felt-lined boots and woolen trousers. Half undressed, she seemed much smaller to me.

Ah, gods! Mortal flesh is a fragile and vulnerable thing. I knelt between her wide-spread thighs and placed my hand on her immense belly, feeling it harden and tighten, then ease, over and over. Checheg groaned with pain, eyes squeezed tight.

"Breathe," I murmured to her. "Push, yes, but not hard."

Eyes closed, she nodded.

I bowed my head and centered myself, breathing the Breath of Earth's Pulse. I breathed the Breath of Ocean's Rolling Waves, slow and deep. It eased Checheg, and she breathed with me—until the pace of her breathing quickened again, one breath coming hard and fast after another.

Delicate flesh tore and parted.

"Gods!" I whispered in awe, seeing the infant's head crown. I put my hand beneath it to support it as it emerged, first the head, then the narrow shoulders following. "Stone and sea!"

Checheg hissed between her teeth.

All in a rush, the infant slithered loose from her body, tethered by a pulsing cord. I caught it in my hands, gasping with wonder.

"You've got to turn it upside down so it can breathe," Grandmother Yue counseled, hovering over my shoulder.

Carefully, so carefully, I tilted the tiny, slippery creature so its head was lower than its miniscule feet. It drew a choked, soggy breath, and made a bubbling sound. Mucus and fluids sputtered and drooled from its mouth and nostrils. It drew another breath, and squalled. It was a healthy sound.

I laughed out loud.

Checheg opened her eyes and smiled wearily. With cloth boiled in the water Sarangerel had brought, I wiped the babe clean of blood and birth fluids, then wrapped it in the cleanest dry woolens I'd been able to find.

"Boy or girl?" Checheg whispered, reaching out feebly with both arms.

"Girl." Gauging the length of the birthing cord, I set the swaddled babe on her belly.

"I'm glad," Sarangerel announced, seeming not in the least unnerved by the entire process. "I wanted a sister."

"Well, that's done, all but the messy afterward bit." Grandmother Yue gave a mighty yawn. "I'm off for a nap. Keep them warm. Wait for the rest to come out before you tie and cut the cord, you hear?"

I nodded. "Yes, Grandmother. Thank you."

While I waited for the messy afterward bit, I draped more warm blankets over Checheg, checking beneath them when she grimaced in the throes of a secondary contraction. For the most part, she reclined against the pillows looking tired and peaceful, her thick coat unbuttoned beneath the blankets as she coaxed the babe to nurse. Sarangerel cuddled against her mother's side, peering at her new baby sister with fascination.

I gazed at them, filled with complex emotions.

"Why do you look sad, Moirin?" Checheg asked me, her voice soft with concern and exhaustion. "You did well. I have never known a birth so easy."

"Oh…" I smiled, knowing there was a shadow of sorrow in it I could not hide. "Yes, today is a day for joy," I said, choosing my words with care. "Only I am thinking of my Queen very far away. She was with child. She was afraid of this day when her time came. She did not want me to leave. I wanted to be there for her."

Checheg understood. "And instead you are here for me." She cradled the back of her babe's head with one hand, summoning a sweet, tired smile. "But now you see there was nothing to fear. I am sure it was so for your Queen."

"I hope so." Although I had underestimated her before, I could not imagine Jehanne facing the ordeal of childbirth with the same calm, steady courage.

"You will see." Checheg closed her eyes. "*I* will be sorry when you leave. All of us will." Her voice took on a dreamy tone. "But you will find your legendary peasant-boy, and together you will return to faraway Terre d'Ange with its white walls and great palaces, and forests growing beneath glass pavilions, and there you will find that all is well with this Queen of whom you are so very fond."

I had not spoken of my role as Jehanne's companion, since it was foreign to Tatar customs. Now I flushed, suspecting I was not as good at concealing my feelings as I thought.

"By then her baby will be as big as my little brother Mongke," Sarangerel added. "Already making trouble!"

It was a charming thought.

I wondered if Jehanne's child, boy or girl, had inherited its mother's mercurial temper or its father's sense of grave resolve. Secretly, I hoped it was the former. And I gazed at the babe in Checheg's arms, hoping she inherited a measure of her mother's innate kindness; hoping she would come of age in a time of peace, and need not believe that to live was to suffer.

Like as not, I would never know. But I could pray for it.

The babe stirred in its mother's arms.

I reached out to stroke her tender cheek with one finger. "Welcome to the world, little one."

TEN

They named the baby girl Bayar, which meant joy.

"It was your idea, Moirin," Checheg said to me, eyes dancing. "Remember? When she was born, you said it was a day for joy."

"I remember," I said, touched.

Grandmother Yue chewed her lips. "Too bad it wasn't a boy."

Batu smiled, the corners of his eyes crinkling. "I do not mind. I like daughters, too."

Life settled into a new rhythm in the *ger*. Having been trained by Checheg during my first month among the Tatars, I took on her duties, letting her rest, recover her strength, and nurse the babe while I saw to the daily preparation of tea and food, ladling it out at meal-times in the correct order of precedence.

Days passed, one by one.

Betimes, I grew restless and stifled, the felt walls and dried-dung smoke of the *ger* closing in on me until it was hard to breathe. When it happened, Checheg was sensitive to it. She would rise from her pallet, Bayar cradled in one arm, and tilt her head toward the door in an implicit command.

I went.

Outdoors, I could breathe. I sucked the achingly cold air deep into my lungs, breathing out plumes of frost.

I took part in surreptitious horse-races arranged by the young men of the tribe, marveling at how their sure-footed shaggy ponies were able to outpace my proud gelding Ember, an Emperor's gift. Since the strained foreleg Ember had sustained on our journey had healed entirely, I had no excuse. The Tatars were incredible horsemen.

I helped herd the cattle, who listened to me; and the sheep, who did not.

I took part in archery challenges, shooting at tiny, distant targets. There, I more than held my own, to which the young men responded with a surprised and begrudging respect.

"No one shoots as well as us," Temur said to me, his cheeks ruddy with the cold and his habitual embarrassment. "Maybe you are part Tatar, Moirin."

"Mayhap," I agreed. "My people remember coming from very far away long ago when the world was covered with ice. But we followed the Great Bear Herself, and there are no bears here."

The young men conferred.

"Not here, no," Temur said. "But there are bears elsewhere in Tatar lands." He nodded to himself. "It must be so. Otherwise, you would not be so skilled with a bow."

I lost track of the days, each much like the next. When I had been some months among the Tatars, there was a ceremony to celebrate the New Year. With unwonted shyness, Checheg presented me with a vibrant blue silk scarf.

"I have seen these." I remembered seeing similar scarves fluttering from the wooden cairn. "It is special?"

She nodded. "It is the symbol of the sky. Today, it means you are kin."

"I am honored," I said sincerely. "But I have no gift to give in turn."

Checheg shook her head. "It is not required."

"Wait." Remembering the dwindling store of Imperial generosity I carried, I rummaged in my packs and found a beautiful sash of celadon silk embroidered with birds and vivid pink peonies. "Maybe it is not tradition, but I would like you to have it."

She hesitated. "It is too nice."

"No, no." I pressed it into her hands. "Please, take it."

For three days, we celebrated the New Year with feasting and well-wishes. On the night of the third day, a great bonfire was built outdoors and a table set forth with incense and ritual offering bowls of food and water.

Bundled in layers of felt and wool, I watched the fire burn, sending sparks into the night sky. Overhead, the stars shone brightly.

Somewhere in the not-too-distant west, the other half of my *diadh-anam* shone, too. I wondered if Bao stood beneath these same stars, watching a similar bonfire. I wondered, as I often did, what in the name of all that was sacred was going through his mind.

The festival marked the first new moon after the point of midwinter, and I felt my blood begin to quicken as the days grew longer.

I struggled for patience, which had never been my strong suit. Oh, in some ways I had the knack of it. I could be patient with animals and children. I could be patient in enduring the foibles of people for whom I cared. It had served me well with Jehanne's temper and Snow Tiger's proud reserve, and it had served me badly with Raphael's ambition.

But in matters of desire, I had always been impulsive; and with the slow, inevitable coming of spring, desire was rising in me.

It made me more restless than usual, until Checheg began dismissing me from the *ger* more often than not.

"You are like a wild thing caged," she scolded me. "Go, go!"

When there were no chores with which I could assist outdoors, I would saddle Ember or Coal and ride as far as I dared, always ranging westward, always feeling the incessant pull of my *diadh-anam*.

Alone, I would summon the twilight. It was one of the only things that soothed me. In the dusky, shimmering half-light, time's slow passage did not seem so onerous, and distance did not seem to matter so much.

I thought of the dragon, content to regard his own silvery coils reflected endlessly in a mirror, in a river, in my own dark pupils.

The dragon had counseled patience.

You are very young, he had said to me. *Live. Learn. Love.*

I was trying.

To be sure, I was grateful for what I learned of love, kindness, and hospitality amidst Batu's family. They were lessons I took to heart. Were I to start a family of my own one day, I would remember them. I regretted nothing of my own upbringing, but I did not have my mother's taste for solitude. I yearned for connection.

Day by day, I endured.

At last, spring came. It came slowly and tentatively, but it came. The frozen ground began to thaw. Murmuring grass shook itself awake, sending out tender new shoots. Cattle, sheep, and horses grazed gratefully, nibbling it to the sod's quick.

One day, I awoke to the knowledge that Bao was on the move. I could sense his presence moving away from me.

"Batu!" I said in distress. "General Arslan...his camp, I think they must be moving. Is it not time we went, too?"

"Soon." Batu gripped my elbows, hard. His gentle eyes gazed into mine with unwonted intensity. "They go to their spring pastures. Here, it is not time yet. Soon. Wait. Do not wish ill upon my herds with your haste. The gathering of the tribes will come."

I bowed my head. "I wish your herds to prosper."

He smiled. "Thank you."

I waited and waited—and gods! Waited. At last, it was time to move the camp to our spring pastures, a week's ride away. The felt *gers*, which had come to seem such substantial man-made structures to me, were dismantled and taken down easily, packed for transport in a matter of hours.

We moved.

Save for the fact that the grasslands were not overgrazed, there was little to distinguish the new campsite from the old. We followed the twisting, shallow river that was our source of water.

We established a new camp.

It went up as swiftly as it had been taken down. But my impatience continued unabated, for Bao had moved, too, and I was no closer to him than I had been before.

I very nearly struck out on my own. Only Sarangerel's tears persuaded me to wait for the gathering of the tribes.

For as much as I thought I might strangle on my own ever-growing impatience, I survived. And when the day came that Batu and a handful of others made ready to set out for the gathering, I found myself in tears, too. Checheg, Grandmother Yue, Sarangerel, little Mongke, and the baby Bayar—all would be staying behind. Blushing Temur, too—left in charge as the eldest male. I embraced them all, suddenly reluctant to say farewell to them.

I gave away two of my last three jade bangles, keeping only the translucent green bracelet the hue of the dragon's pool. The pale, spotted bangle of leopard jade, I gave to Sarangerel, knowing it was her favorite. I gave a bangle of lavender jade to Checheg in keeping for Bayar, whom I had helped deliver.

"Moirin, you *cannot* keep giving valuable things away!" Checheg protested. "You are a long way from home, and you may need them."

I touched the blue silk scarf draped around my neck. "You have given me more valuable gifts, Checheg."

"We did but honor the laws of hospitality," she said stubbornly.

I smiled through my tears. "No. You offered me kinship. That is a great deal more."

She sighed and gave me a hard, fierce hug. "You are a very strange girl."

I laughed. "You are not the first person to tell me this."

When there were no more good-byes to be said, Batu gave the command to mount and ride.

Once again, I was leaving behind people I had come to care for. As grateful as I was to answer the relentless call of my *diadh-anam*, it hurt, too. Mayhap Checheg was right and I would come to regret it, but for now, I was glad I had given away such gifts as I had. They left behind a trail of mementos among the lives that had touched mine. Whether they knew it or not, Bao's sister Song's story was linked to my young friend Sarangerel's.

It pleased me to think on it. And I had kept the tokens that were the most important to me.

I had my dragon-pool bangle—and another gift from Snow Tiger, a dagger with an ivory hilt carved in the shape of a dragon. I had the Imperial jade medallion. I had the squares of cloth that Bao's mother and sister had embroidered.

I had the blue silk scarf Checheg had given me.

Somewhere in the depths of my battered canvas satchel, I had a crystal bottle of perfume that had been Jehanne's parting gift.

I had a signet ring my mother had given me so very long ago, etched with twin crests—the boar of the Cullach Gorrym in Alba and the swan of House Courcel in Terre d'Ange, signifying my dual inheritance.

And I had the yew-wood bow my uncle Mabon had made for me, still resilient and sturdy.

It was enough.

ELEVEN

———◆———

Twenty-one of us rode to the gathering of the tribes—twenty Tatars, plus me. Among the Tatars, there were sixteen men and four women.

It seemed I fell somewhere in between.

I had not come to know any of the women outside Batu's *ger* well, and nothing changed on our journey. When we made camp at night, the women demurred politely, refusing my assistance. We travelled lightly, subsisting on dried meat and chunks of hardened cheese aged to the point that it took forever to soften in the mouth—at least when there was nothing better.

During the day, the younger men invited me to hunt with them as we rode, shooting at the thick-furred groundhogs that had emerged from hibernation. These were cooked by virtue of slitting their bellies, removing their entrails and inserting heated stones inside the carcasses.

It was not very tasty.

I didn't care.

We rode beneath the blue sky, and slept beneath the stars. And with every league that passed, my *diadh-anam* sang inside me.

I didn't even care when I sensed Bao on the move once more. Wherever he was, he was travelling slowly and in the same direction.

"Yes," Batu agreed when I remarked on it. "If he is with General Arslan, he is going to the gathering of tribes."

"What happens there?" I asked, curious.

He stroked his chin. "There will be feasting and games. There will be delegates from other nations. Strategy is discussed. The Great Khan will make his wishes known to us."

I raised my brows. "Oh?"

Batu's shoulders moved in a faint shrug. "Do not be concerned. I do not expect there to be talk of war, Moirin. The Emperor of Ch'in's hand has been strengthened in this last year, in part thanks to you. Of that, I will not speak at the gathering. But we have agreements with others regarding securing the overland trade routes. Vralians, perhaps even northern Bhodistani. Some will be present."

"Oh," I said a second time, frowning. I knew the names. Bhodistan—that was the birthplace of Sakyamuni, the Enlightened One, whose followers travelled the Path of Dharma.

Vralia...

I knew that name, too.

Berlik had fled there—Berlik the Oath-Breaker, the last great magician of the Maghuin Dhonn.

The last shape-changer.

He had met his death in the northern wilds of Vralia, hunted down by the relentless D'Angeline prince he had betrayed. In the end, Berlik had sought out his death, seeking to make atonement. He had knelt in the falling snow and bowed his head to the sword. Prince Imriel had slain him and wept at the deed. When I was ten years of age, my mother had taken me to visit the green mound in Clunderry where Berlik's severed head was buried, a reminder of my people's folly.

I shivered.

"Do not be afraid, Moirin," Batu said, mistaking my unease. He leaned over in the saddle and patted my shoulder awkwardly. "I promise you, no one speaks of war this year, only treaties and strategy."

"I am glad," I said sincerely.

He lowered his voice. "So am I."

Eight days into our journey, Bao stopped moving and stayed in one place.

Bao knew I was coming; he *had* to know. The spark that burned in me, burned in him. And at least he was not fleeing it.

That was something.

Much of the entry into the campsite is a blur in my memory. There were *gers* and tents erected, that I remember. There were Tatars, more than I could count—and other folk, too. Vralians in thick, woolen clothing trimmed with a great deal of fur. After so long among the Ch'in and Tatars, it came as a shock to me to see Western features, and fair skin and light eyes and hair on many of them. There were others I thought must be Bhodistani, with warm brown skin, clad in many layers of bright attire.

Bao.

I felt his presence like a drumbeat in my heart—in my heart, and on my skin. So close; ah, gods! I barely took stock of the camp, wandering like a blind woman, driven by my *diadh-anam's* insistent pulse.

Batu understood. "Go," he said gently to me. "Go, and find him."

I went, following the call of my soul.

There were folk milling everywhere—folk, cattle, horses, and dogs. Astride Ember, I picked my way through them. Even here, people paused to stare. The Vralians in particular whispered and murmured amongst themselves. I wasn't sure why, since it didn't seem green eyes would be unusual for their kind. I supposed it was because I was dressed as a Tatar, despite my green eyes and half-D'Angeline features.

It seemed the games had already begun. Outside the perimeter of the vast campsite, I caught glimpses of boys racing on horseback. Within the camp, I passed men wrestling, stripped to the waist and grappling with one another.

I heard the sound of staves clattering.

My *diadh-anam* flared inside me.

Even at a distance, I picked Bao out of the fighters. Although his back was turned to me, there was no mistaking his acrobat's agility, his quickness and grace, coupled with the sense of unbridled glee with which he fought, toying with his opponents. The air felt thick and dense around me, and I struggled to draw breath. Forcing myself to breathe the Breath of Wind's Sigh, I approached slowly. Some yards from the makeshift fighting ring, I drew rein to watch.

Bao froze, his head tilted.

He knew I was there. Although he did not turn around, he knew it. I saw it in the tension of his strong, lean shoulders, the taut cords at the back of his neck.

The two husky Tatars he was fighting shouted and converged on him, staves whistling through the air.

In the blink of an eye, Bao went from utter stillness into blurred motion, spinning and vaulting. No longer toying, he dispatched his opponents with ruthless efficiency. One went down with a hard blow to the back of his skull, sprawling to measure his length on the trampled grass. The other, Bao tripped and laid flat in a move too quick for the eye to see. Seeing the butt of a staff poised to crush his throat, the man called out an urgent surrender.

Bao took a step backward, whipping his bamboo staff upright. He planted it in the dirt, standing with his head bowed.

I swallowed hard and dismounted, my heart thundering in my breast.

With his head lowered, his unruly black hair hung over his brow, obscuring his eyes. Absurdly, I thought how much it had grown since I had seen him last. I'd shaved it myself when Bao and Master Lo Feng and the others had taken on the guise of travelling monks sworn to the Path of Dharma.

He was clad in felted trousers and thick Tatar boots, bare-chested save for a woolen vest with ornate embroidery. His chest rose and fell swiftly, and sweat glistened on his sleek brown skin.

His knuckles were pale where they gripped his bamboo staff. I knew that staff well, bound with metal, carved with characters. It had been broken in two during the battle for White Jade Mountain.

I had made it whole.

I did not know how to do the same for us.

There were onlookers idly cheering Bao's victory. Sensing the rising tension in the air, their cheers faltered and fell silent. Without looking at me, Bao gestured to his second opponent. Nodding, the man helped his fallen fellow to his feet, slinging one arm over his brawny shoulders. Together they limped away. Everyone else kept a safe distance.

Bao lifted his head and for the first time, met my eyes. "Moirin."

"Aye," I whispered.

His dark eyes glittered—whether with anger or something else, I could not say. I could not read his expression. His body was still and rigid, but I thought mayhap there was a reluctant tenderness lurking in the corners of his lips. His throat worked as he searched for words, his eyes searching mine. "You could not wait for me to choose?"

"No." I took a sharp breath. "*No!* Gods bedamned, Bao! You speak as though you were the only one to have a choice in this matter. Well, you're not. You asked me to wait, and I did. I got tired of it. I *chose* to wait no longer."

He looked away. "I see."

Frustration rose in me. "Can you not at least *face* me, you infernally stubborn peasant-boy? Gods! If you weren't willing to do that much at least, you should have run away. You had to know I was coming!"

Bao's hand slid down his staff. "I knew," he murmured, his head averted. "I chose to stay."

"Why?" To my chagrin, I was crying. If his *diadh-anam* was burning half as brightly as mine, yearning to close the distance between us, I couldn't imagine how he was resisting its call. It was taking every ounce of pride I possessed not to go to him, but I was damned if I would take those last few steps. "Why did you stay?"

"Where is your Imperial entourage, Moirin?" Bao asked, not answering my question. He frowned toward the horizon. "You took me by surprise. I knew you were close, but I thought you would enter with fanfare. Did Ten Tigers Dai come with you? I would be pleased to see him."

"There is no entourage," I muttered, wiping at my tears. "No Imperial entourage."

"What?" Bao stared at me as though my words made no sense.

"There is no Imperial entourage," I repeated with irritation. "Forgive me, I did not know you were missing Ten Tigers Dai so badly. I came on my own. Well, that is not entirely true," I added. "I came with representatives of Batu's tribe, who gave me hospitality during the long winter. They have been very kind to me. But it is not exactly an entourage."

"Moirin..." The blood drained from Bao's face, leaving him ashen. He continued to stare at me in horrified disbelief. "Are you saying you set out in pursuit of me alone? Across the Tatar steppe? In winter?"

"Yes, Bao," I said with precision. "That is exactly what I'm saying."

The blood rushed back into his face, flushing his high, wide cheekbones. He began shouting at me. "Oh, you stupid, stupid girl, in the name of all that is holy—"

I overrode him, my voice rising as I shouted in reply. "What else was I to do, Bao? You needed me to find a way to prove myself to you. How else was I to do it? Was I to wait forever in Shuntian like some poor besotted fool jilted by her suitor, praying for his return? You said yourself you didn't know if you would come back! This was the only thing I could think to do! And if you don't—"

Without a word, he crossed the distance between us.

I felt his arms come around me, and I clung to him, shameless, my tirade forgotten. The twinned flames of our *diadh-anams* surged, and I thought the blaze must be visible to onlookers. I could feel people staring, could hear shocked whispers, but I didn't care; and it appeared that Bao didn't, either. Both of us were silent for a time. It seemed a moment too vast for words. At last, Bao pressed his cheek against my hair and spoke in a low voice. "Moirin, do you not understand that what I feel for you is so strong it terrifies me? It's unnatural. I needed time to try and make sense of it."

"Yes," I whispered against his bare shoulder. He smelled of clean sweat and his own underlying scent, like heated metal. "Believe me, I know. I feel it, too. But hiding from it will not make it go away."

He sighed. "No. I know."

I stole a glance at him. That was definitely tenderness lurking in the corners of his mouth, the hint of a reluctant smile. I lifted one hand to stroke the hard, chiseled line of his jaw. "Stupid boy."

"Stupid girl." Bao lowered his head and kissed me.

Higher and higher, the blaze within me climbed. Ah, gods! It was terrible and glorious all at once.

I sank both hands into his hair, returning his kiss with ardor. The desire that had begun to rise with the coming of spring burst its last shackle. Naamah's gift unfurled within me like an endless ribbon of gold, infusing every part of me. When Bao broke the kiss, I was dizzy and breathless with a need beyond longing.

"Is there someplace—" I began to ask.

Bao nodded, his eyes glittering. "Come with me."

He took my hand and I followed in his wake, half stumbling with the insistency of desire. I was vaguely aware of him ordering some fellow to secure my horse Ember, vaguely aware that the man obeyed with deference.

With only a brief hesitation, Bao led me to a small *ger*. Unable to pay heed to aught but my own need, I didn't hear what he said to its inhabitants, but whatever it was, they departed with alacrity, leaving us alone.

Bao undressed me with fierce urgency, his hands and mouth staking claim to every inch of skin he uncovered; and I did the same to him. We grappled with one another, waging love like war. He bit and sucked at my throat, his callused hands caressing my breasts, pulling at my aching nipples. I licked the fresh, salty sweat from his bare chest, sinking lower to take his firm, throbbing phallus in my mouth until he groaned and tugged me upward, rolling me over effortlessly and pinning me to the carpeted floor of the *ger*.

It was not a gentle coupling, at least not at first.

The need was too great; the need of our long-separated *diadhanams* yearning to be fully joined, driving the need of our willing bodies. What Master Lo Feng had done to us had erased the division between flesh and spirit.

And when Bao entered me...

I have no words to describe it. If our *diadh-anams* had shone like beacons before, now, reunited, they erupted like wildfire, blazing toward heaven. I felt as though my heart might burst the confines of my breast.

"Bao," I whispered, tears in my eyes.

"I know," he whispered in reply, wonder in his. "Moirin, I know."

For a long moment, we lay locked together without moving, marveling at the intensity of our joining.

Slowly, slowly, it faded.

In its place, Naamah's gift reasserted its presence. Desire—this time simple and carnal—nothing more. I surrendered to it gratefully, kissing Bao's throat, wrapping my ankles around his buttocks. He propped himself on his elbows above me, his eyes dark and distant with desire, thrusting slowly in and out of me.

Stone and sea, it felt good! Again and again, I came beneath him, each shivering climax a physical echo of what I had felt when our spirits merged. Intangible brightness blossomed behind my eyes like a thousand flowers blooming at once, like stars falling from the night sky, tracing incandescent arcs across the glittering darkness. The bright lady smiled, placing a shining kiss filled with love upon my brow. It had been too long, far too long, since I had felt Naamah's approval.

Bao's pace quickened.

I urged him onward, my hips rising to meet him, willing him to spend himself inside me. At last he did, his entire body shuddering.

I sighed, content.

Bao rolled off me. "I ran away from *this*?"

I laughed.

"Moirin." He raised one hand to his lips, kissing my fingertips. "Let us be serious, now. Truly, do you know what of this is real, and what is the result of Master Lo's art?"

"No," I admitted, stroking his chest. I felt at peace for the first time since he had left me. "But, Bao...we'll never sort it out apart.

Can we not figure it out together? At least the endless clamor of my soul has gone silent. Is it not the same for you?"

"Uh-huh," Bao agreed. "That part's nice."

I laughed again. "Well, mayhap in the silence, we'll be able to listen to our hearts again."

The wooden door of the *ger* banged open. I squinted against the sudden stream of ordinary sunlight. A small, sturdy figure stormed into the *ger*, haranguing Bao at the top of her lungs. He rose to his feet, clutching a blanket around him, and replied in an aggrieved tone, both of them speaking too quickly for me to follow. Having said her piece, the young woman stormed out in a huff, slamming the door behind her.

"Bao?" I asked. "Who was that, and why is she furious at you?"

"Ahh…" He ran one hand over his rumpled hair and gave me a sheepish look. "That was my wife."

TWELVE

I stared at Bao. "Your *wife*?"

"It was a long, cold winter!" he said in a defensive tone, yanking on his felted trousers. "Will you tell me *you* of all people slept in an empty bed, Moirin?"

"I . . . yes!" Even as the words left my mouth, I remembered that I would have been happy to spend the winter in Shuntian with Snow Tiger if she had permitted it, and my denial emerged with rather less conviction than I intended. Bao raised one eyebrow at me. "In fact, I did," I said indignantly. "Ask Batu, or any of his people."

Bao tugged on his boots. "Well, I'm sorry. But it's complicated."

I sighed. "Oh, gods bedamned! Fine. I'm the last person to deny you the right to take pleasure and comfort where you find it. But, Bao . . . a wife?" A pang squeezed my heart. "Do you love her? Is that it?"

"It's complicated," he repeated, shrugging into his woolen vest. "You see, she's the Great Khan's youngest daughter."

At a loss for words, I continued to stare at him. Now, belatedly, I remembered how folk in the campsite had deferred to Bao, how everyone in the *ger* had departed swiftly at his command. Insofar as I'd noticed, I'd assumed it was because General Arslan had acknowledged him, or even just because of his prowess as a fighter. Never in a thousand years had I thought it was because he was the Great Khan's son-in-law.

"I'd better go to her." Bao stooped before me, crouching on his heels. "Terbish is the name of the fellow I asked to see to your horse. He'll escort you to your tribe's camp."

"I don't need an escort!" I shouted at him.

"I don't love her," he said abruptly. The words lay between us in an uncomfortable silence. "But Erdene *is* the Great Khan's daughter, and I suspect you are not one of her favorite people right now. Accept the escort."

I closed my eyes. "Fine. I'll accept the escort."

"Thank you." Bao straightened, waiting until I relented and looked at him. "I am sorry, Moirin. I didn't do this to hurt you. I never wanted to hurt you."

"It's complicated," I said dully.

He nodded. "I'll come find you later. We have a lot to talk about." He tried a faint smile on me. "Somehow, I thought there would be time for talking first. I should have known better, huh?"

I didn't answer.

As soon as Bao left the *ger*, I dressed in a hurry. My body was still singing with the aftermath of long-denied pleasure and my *diadh-anam* was quiet within me, but there was a maelstrom of confusion and betrayal in my heart.

It wasn't entirely fair, of course. But...a wife?

True to Bao's word, the man Terbish was waiting for me, holding Ember's reins. I nodded my thanks to him. He walked beside me as I rode slowly back to Batu's camp. Now folk were definitely staring, and I heard a murmuring susurrus of gossip that was all too familiar. I gritted my teeth, refusing to feel embarrassed. It wasn't *my* fault that I'd just engaged in a very public display of affection, and what was doubtless an obvious bout of intensive lovemaking, with the Great Khan's son-in-law.

Back at the tribe's camp, a pair of Vralians with ornate chains around their necks were talking with Batu through an interpreter. Seeing me return, Batu dismissed them and hurried over to me, his kind eyes soft with concern. I could tell that the news had travelled fast.

"Are you well?" he asked me.

"No," I admitted. Although it was customary in Tatar culture to deny any troubles on first inquiry, I didn't have the heart for it. "Batu, I didn't know, I swear!"

"I know this to be true," he said firmly. "I have given you the hospitality of my roof. You are a truthful person."

It made me feel better. I gazed after the departing Vralians. "What did those fellows want?"

He shrugged. "Them? They always want to talk about their gods. But they were asking about you, too." A glint came into his eyes. "I told them you were a mighty sorceress who brought the Great Khan's son-in-law back from death, and that there is a powerful bond between you. Do not worry, I did not speak of Ch'in. It will not cause trouble. It will teach them to respect and fear you."

I smiled sadly. "I don't feel very fearsome."

Batu patted my arm. "You did nothing wrong. Blame the young man. *He* has been untruthful." His eyes widened. "They did not even know he was twice-born!"

"Bao has been hiding from many things," I murmured.

"So it seems," he agreed.

I tried to make myself useful around the camp, but most of the work of setting up had already been done, and I was restless once more. If Checheg had been there, she would have shooed me away. So instead, I shooed myself away, saddling the uncomplaining Ember once more.

No doubt Bao would have scolded me for riding out without an escort, but I didn't intend to make myself an easy target for any vengeful Tatar princess. I rode through the campsite with my bow held loosely in one hand, guiding Ember with my knees, gazing fixedly forward with my mother's best glare.

Many people stared, but no one troubled me.

On the outskirts of camp, I passed a group of men slaughtering a sheep in the Tatar manner. I'd seen it done only once before, for the festival of the New Year. Two men held the sheep down on its back. A third man made a small incision in the sheep's abdomen, then plunged his hand into the slit, reaching for the sheep's heart within the cavity of its body and squeezing it until it ceased to beat. It was done so swiftly, the sheep scarcely had time to struggle.

I felt as though Bao had done much the same to me.

As soon as I'd passed the sheep-slaughterers, I summoned the twilight, breathing it in deeply and flinging it around my horse and myself. The world softened and dimmed in the silvery-violet dusk, easing my troubled spirits. A few seconds later, I heard a soft gasp behind me, and the murmur of voices. My passage and my subsequent, abrupt disappearance had been noted.

Well and so, let them take heed. Batu had a point; it was better to be feared and respected than despised. I smiled grimly to myself and nudged Ember with my heels, setting out at a trot.

The campsite was situated alongside a wide, meandering river. I followed its course aimlessly toward the north, riding over the twilit grasslands until the tents and *gers* behind me looked as small as toys. I rode until I found a flat, windswept place where I could sit and watch the river.

There, I dismounted and turned Ember loose to graze.

I sat cross-legged and tried to meditate, but my thoughts were a jumble. I could not let one thought rise from another. So instead, I concentrated on breathing, cycling through the Five Styles, willing my mind to be empty.

In perhaps an hour's time, I sensed Bao's presence growing closer. In the twilight, I could see the silver spark of his *diadh-anam* coming toward me over the plains even before I could make out his form.

He couldn't see me, of course; but he didn't need to. Bao knew where I was as surely as I did him.

He turned his shaggy pony loose to graze with Ember and sat cross-legged opposite me without speaking, laying his staff across his lap and settling into a breathing rhythm that matched mine. We might have been Master Lo's magpie and his least likely pupil once more. Except that in the twilight, Bao looked different than he had before.

It wasn't just that the spark of the divine spirit of the Maghuin Dhonn Herself shone within him. The faint shimmer of darkness that surrounded him since his rebirth was deeper here, impossible to ignore, impossible to dismiss as a trick of the light. It flickered all around him—darkness made bright, a penumbra like an eclipsed moon. Gazing at it, I remembered that there was more at issue here than the fact that Bao had left me and ridden away to find his blood-father and wed some Tatar princess in the bargain.

He had died, and been restored to life. He was twice-born, and he was learning how to live with it. And although I was angry, mayhap I owed him the chance to explain.

With a sigh, I released the twilight, letting the daylight world return.

Bao's lips parted at my sudden appearance, but having known I was there all along, he showed no other sign of surprise. I tilted my head to indicate I was listening. He nodded in acknowledgment and cleared his throat. "First of all, it would have been a grave discourtesy to refuse such an honor from the Great Khan. Second, I did not seek it out, Moirin."

I stayed silent.

"You remember Master Lo's snowdrop bulbs?" he asked me. "Well, I took them. I made a tonic like Master Lo prepared."

"I know." I wasn't very good at holding my tongue. "I heard. That's how you bribed your way into General Arslan's favor."

"My father's favor, yes." Bao fidgeted with his staff, frowning a little. "It's true, you know. Although the truth isn't exactly what I expected it to be. I thought...I thought that mayhap that once I gained his trust, I would avenge my family's honor."

"But it's complicated," I said in a neutral tone.

"Yes." He straightened his back. "For now, it is enough to say that my father claimed me with pride, and I allowed it. When the Great Khan Naram visited his most loyal general, he was intrigued. He wished to see the fighting prowess of which my father boasted. He wished to sample my famed tonic. I obliged."

"And the Great Khan was pleased," I noted.

"Very pleased," Bao agreed. "So pleased that he insisted on giving me his youngest daughter in marriage."

I scowled at him. "Bao, you are the stubbornest person I've ever met, and now that Master Lo is gone, I do not think there is anyone under the sun who could make you do a thing if you did not wish it. You're a clever and skilled liar. Don't tell me you could not have talked your way out of it."

"I'm not," he said mildly.

I waited.

Bao sighed. "Moirin, you possess a gift the likes of which no one outside your strange bear-folk has ever seen. You possess a strange beauty the likes of which *no one* has ever seen. You are descended from three different royal lineages. And I'm nothing but a simple Ch'in peasant-boy—or at least I was. Do you think I don't know it matters?"

I looked blankly at him. "*You're* the one who insisted on referring to yourself thusly! What did I ever say or do to make you think it mattered to me?"

"You didn't need to say anything!" His voice rose. "Gods, Moirin! Do you know how much gossip I had to endure in Terre d'Ange? I know your history as well as my own. Better, maybe."

"So?"

"So there was that lord's son in Alba, the one who died." He began to recite a litany of my lovers, ticking them off on his fingers. "And I am sorry, because I know you cared for him, but he was a lord's son. High-and-mighty Lion Mane, that Raphael de Mereliot, what was he? Some kind of nobleman. His sister ruled a city, anyway. When you quarreled with him, you bedded the Crown Prince, didn't you?" Bao raised his brows at me. "That's what they all said. And when you quarreled with *both* of them, the White Queen herself."

I flushed. "Aye, but—"

He cut me off, lowering his voice to a fierce, hushed whisper as though someone might overhear us. "And I am not sure how to count the fact that a dragon decided you were a worthy mate for the heir to the throne of the Celestial Empire, but I am quite sure it *does* count, even if the Noble Princess was not particularly pleased with his choice. There is no place for peasants in your history, Moirin."

"You're not as clever as you think," I muttered. "You missed one."

It was Bao's turn to look blank. "Who?"

"No one important." I drew up my knees beneath my Tatar coat, wrapping my arms around them. "His name was Theo, I think. He drove the coach that brought me to the City of Elua. By the way, *I* have not kept count of the bored wives you claim to have bedded, although I am grateful for all they taught you."

"It's not the same." Bao eyed me. "A coach-driver?"

I nodded, resting my chin on my knees. "In the stables along our route, yes. It was after Cillian's death. I took comfort in it."

"But you spurned him in the end," he said uncertainly. "Right?"

I shook my head. "Not I, no. It was his choice."

"*He* spurned *you*?" Bao shot me an incredulous look. "What an idiot!"

Despite everything, I laughed. "You're a fine one to talk!"

"Moirin..." Bao leaned forward to take my hands in his, gazing intently at me. "All right, perhaps I was wrong about certain things. But this I know to be true. Before what happened, happened... it is as I told you, I was ready to ask Master Lo to release me from his service. I was ready to give up my life as his magpie for you. After his death..." He shrugged. "I could not bear to be herded into accepting my fate like some stupid, mindless sheep. I needed to find a way to make this choice my own. To make it meaningful, to make it a choice that counted for something larger."

"By finding something worthy of sacrificing?" I asked. I did not fully understand the way his fierce sense of pride goaded him, but I'd come to recognize its workings.

"Perhaps," he said simply. "I did not think of it so, but... perhaps."

I bowed my head over our joined hands, rubbing my thumbs over his callused palms. "So everything comes around full circle,"

I murmured. "The peasant-boy has become a prince. What do you want, Bao?"

"You."

The certainty in his dark, steady gaze undid me. I wanted to believe in it. I glanced at him, then away. "How can you be sure?"

He smiled wryly. "When I first sensed you coming after me, I'll admit, I was angry. Angry that you could not bring yourself to trust me long enough to wait. Angry that you would use all the resources at your disposal to hunt me down like a runaway dog." He shook his head. "Never, ever did I imagine you were not travelling with an Imperial entourage. The Noble Princess would have granted you whatever you had asked," he added. "I know she is a very private person who does not show her feelings easily, but despite the way things began, I think she came to be fond of you, Moirin."

A memory from those last few days in Shuntian arose unbidden: Snow Tiger, kneeling over me in a bed strewn with the cushions I had asked for. I'd never grown accustomed to the hard wooden or porcelain stands that passed for pillows among the Ch'in. *Are you* quite *sure this is enough cushions, my barbarian?* she had teased me, her eyes bright with affection, her hair hanging loose and unbound to curtain both our faces with black, shining silk. When she shook her head, it tickled. *Are you* quite *sure you are comfortable?*

It was a memory I did not intend to share with anyone, even Bao. That had been a time of grace, and it was Naamah's business.

I cleared my throat. "Ah...yes, I know. And yes, she begged me to accept an entourage. But, Bao, your anger proves it would have had exactly the result I feared—not to mention the possibility of provoking outrage among the Tatars. And unlike you, the princess respected me enough to believe me when I said I could take care of myself."

Bao gave me a skeptical look. "That is because you were always strong for her. You showed her every kindness and gave her a shoulder to lean on when she did not know she needed one."

That was true, and I did not argue.

"Anyway, it does not matter." His hands tightened on mine.

"Today, when I learned you came after me alone, I felt as though the earth had dropped away beneath me. Even though you were standing safe and whole before me, the thought of what could have happened to you terrified me. I do not ever want to feel it again."

"So?" I whispered.

"I love you." In a firm, steady tone, Bao said the words he had never before spoken to me, the words he had died without speaking. "There is a great deal we have to figure out together, but of that, I am sure. And if you will have me, it is my choice to be with you. Will you?"

"Yes." My *diadh-anam* blazed and my heart sang within me, not squeezed lifeless in my chest after all. I took a deep breath, willing myself not to cry. "Yes, my Tatar prince, I will have you."

His shoulders relaxed. "Good."

I pulled my hands from his, wiping my eyes. "What do we do now? What about this girl, Erlene? You said you did not love her; does she love you? If so, you've used her unkindly."

Bao hesitated. "Erdene. She thinks she does. She is very young, and jealous. You are right, I've wronged her. I will ask her forgiveness, but I do not think she will be quick to grant it. And . . . I do not know how one goes about setting aside the Great Khan's daughter. I do not think it will be easy."

Suspicion flared within me. "You're not suggesting taking me as a second wife!"

"No!" He raised his hands in denial. "No, Moirin." His mouth quirked. "Among other things, I do not think I would trust you with anyone's wife, my own included. You have too many strange desires."

I laughed.

Bao took my hand again, my right hand. With his left, he tapped his chest. "Listen."

"To my heart?" I asked uncertainly.

He shook his head. "I think we are in agreement for now. No. The other thing, the shining thing that binds us."

"My *diadh-anam*."

"Yes." He repeated the word carefully. "Our *diadh-anam*."

I closed my eyes and listened. Opposite me, Bao began breathing the Breath of Earth's Pulse, slow and deep. I fell into his rhythm. We were together, hands clasped. My divided soul was at peace. For the first time since my spirit had been sundered, I could sense my destiny calling to me, far, far away.

So far away, it might be home.

"West," I whispered, opening my eyes. "It's beckoning us westward."

Bao nodded. "I dream of bears, Moirin. I dream of a hollow hill with a wondrous, shining cave inside it. I dream of a doorway built of three slabs of stone. And I would like to go there with you."

I flung my arms around his neck, kissing him. "Then we will find a way."

THIRTEEN

———————◆———————

It wasn't easy.

By the time we returned, the campsite was abuzz with a fresh set of gossip, spurred by the tales Batu had told.

"Why do they stare anew?" Bao muttered.

"Ah..." I winced. "I daresay it is because Batu told them you were restored from death, and I am the sorceress who made it happen. Twice-born, they call you. Bao, why didn't you tell them?"

He sighed. "I sought to begin a new life. And I did not wish to stir trouble. I have not told anyone my story since I left a very small village in Ch'in."

"Tonghe?"

He gave me a startled look. "How do you know?"

"I followed in your footsteps," I reminded him. "I found the village. I met your mother and your sister—and your father, too."

Bao looked away. "He is not my father."

"No, I know." I fidgeted with the last remaining jade bangle on my wrist, the one the color of the dragon's pool. "But he is a man racked by guilt and sorrow. Anyway, I liked your mother and sister very much. I have a gift for you," I added. "A piece of your mother's embroidery."

"Truly?" For a moment, he looked young and vulnerable.

I nodded. "Truly."

Bao blew out his breath. "Yes. She is my mother. I should have asked for a gift to remember her by."

I did not say that I had bought the piece, paying Auntie Ai's best price because his mother could not afford to make a gift of it. Not to me, not even to Bao, her long-lost and much-beloved son. I did not tell him that I had given gifts of Imperial jade to his mother and sister—and aye, to his father who was not a father.

"It is enough that she remembers you," I said instead. "It is a square she embroidered after your visit. You spoke of your travels with Master Lo Feng to her. It has a pattern of magpies. She hoped that it would please you."

Bao's dark eyes shone, this time with unshed tears. "Thank you. Your kindness is not confined to princesses and dragons, Moirin."

Out of the corner of one eye, I caught sight of a small, stalwart figure surrounded by guards glaring at me.

Erdene, the Great Khan's daughter.

"Perhaps not," I murmured, tightening my reins, tightening the grip of my thighs. Ember stepped backward, picking up his hooves with precision, obedient to my touch. "But a kindness extended to one may be an unwitting cruelty dealt to another. I should go."

"We will talk on the morrow, then."

I nodded, turning my mount. "On the morrow. I'll bring your mother's gift."

I slept, deep and dreamless. Complicated though matters might be, for the first time since Bao had died, I was at peace.

The following day brought a request for an appearance—not from Bao, but from his father, General Arslan. I was reluctant to accept it, but Batu advised me that it would be rude to refuse.

"Oyun and I will accompany you," Batu said firmly. "I will make it clear that you are under the hospitality of my roof."

I was reluctant to endanger him. "What happens if the general chooses to ignore that fact?"

He shrugged. "If he harms you, it will be cause for a blood feud. I do not think he will be quick to do so."

It was not particularly reassuring, but when Batu pointed out that Checheg would have his hide if he didn't do his best to protect me,

I acceded. So it was that Batu and Oyun, one of the young men with whom I'd often raced and shot at targets, accompanied me to General Arslan's *ger*.

A burly fellow wearing a curved scimitar at his belt ducked inside to fetch the general when we arrived. We dismounted and waited until General Arslan emerged.

Bao's father.

I could see the resemblance in the strong line of his brows, and most of all, his eyes. They were set at the same angle as Bao's, and they held the same proud spark in their dark depths. Although an old scar bisected the general's right eyebrow and dragged down his lid, his eye glittered fiercely beneath the drooping lid. The men exchanged customary Tatar pleasantries about cattle while I waited nervously.

"This is Moirin," Batu said at length, speaking slowly for my benefit. "She is a guest under my roof." He nodded significantly at the blue silk scarf I wore draped around my neck. "My wife, Checheg, has given her a gift of kinship."

"So I see." General Arslan's gaze settled on me. "Moirin mac Fainche." He made a point of pronouncing my name with care. "I would speak with you. Alone."

"I will accompany her," Batu said.

The general raised his left brow in a familiar, sardonic gesture. "Surely you do not question the hospitality of *my* roof?"

Batu hesitated, then shook his head, defeated. "No. Of course not."

"Good." General Arslan beckoned to me. "Come."

I followed him into the *ger*. There was a youngish woman there who did not meet my eyes, and two girls no older than Sarangerel who stole curious glances at me. The youngish woman poured a bowl of salty tea and offered it to me, all the while avoiding my gaze. I accepted it with thanks. As soon as she had done the same for the general, she gathered her daughters and left.

"Let us sit." The general indicated the table and low chairs. I sat warily opposite him. He sipped his tea and studied me, taking my measure without speaking.

Suspecting I could not match his capacity for silence, I didn't bother trying. "You wished to speak to me?" I asked politely.

"Yes." He took another sip of tea. "First, I wished to see you. Having done so, I understand why my son is enamored."

I inclined my head. "You are kind to say so."

"Have you bewitched him?" he asked in a steady tone. "There is talk of it."

I flushed. The inquiry evoked painful memories of Cillian, my lost first love. His mother had accused me of bewitching him, too. And yet this time there was an element of truth to it. "No," I said slowly. "We are bound together, he and I. But it was not by my choice. I did not know it would happen."

General Arslan took a thoughtful sip of tea. "Then why are you here?"

"Because we *are* bound together," I said, adding, "And I love him."

He ignored my last comment. "If it is true that you are bound, it seems to me that until you arrived, my son sought to break that binding."

I shifted in my chair. "I do not believe that is exactly true, but I cannot speak for Bao. It may be that there are truths of his heart he has not shared with you."

He raised that eyebrow again. "Of course there are. I am not so foolish as to believe he came seeking me with an open heart. But he came seeking knowledge of himself, and he has found more than he expected."

"Yes," I said. "And now he is ready to leave."

The general folded his hands atop the table. "I do not wish to lose my son," he said in a formal tone. "When I lost my wife, I spent many long months searching for her, and many months avenging her loss."

"I know," I murmured.

"I did not take another wife for a long time," he continued. "When I did, she gave me nothing but daughters. I have yearned for a son."

"The Emperor of Ch'in is content to take pride in a daughter," I observed.

"Yes." The scar tissue on General Arslan's right eyelid tightened. "So it is said. The warrior princess who descended from heaven in a dragon's claw to reunify the Celestial Empire." His eye twitched. "It is rumored that you are more than passing familiar with the tale."

I held my tongue—and my breath, too.

"Of course, that means that there is a good possibility that the same holds true for my son," he mused. "So I will not pursue these rumors. You might wish to tell Batu that his young tribesmen are not discreet when their tongues are plied with *airag*."

I let out my breath in a sigh. "I am sorry for the loss of your first wife, for it seems you loved her very much. And I am sorry that your second wife has not given you sons. But Bao's choice is his own to make, and I swear to you, all the magic in the world could not sway him against his will. He is very, very stubborn."

"I know." Unexpectedly, General Arslan smiled. It lent his scarred face a sudden roguish charm, and I found myself smiling in response. "That is one of the reasons I know he is *my* son."

I laughed.

"Moirin mac Fainche." He leaned forward, his smile fading. Intensity returned to his eyes. "What offer can I make you that would persuade you to leave, and leave my son in peace?"

"None." I swallowed the laughter that died in my throat. "I'm sorry, but there is none. If Bao bade me go, I would go. But he carries half of my soul inside him, and so long as I live, I will yearn to be with him."

The general leaned back in his chair. "You claim this matter of his death and rebirth is true?"

"I do."

"Let me see it, then." He gestured. "Your magic."

I shook my head. "No."

His eyes narrowed. "Why?"

I took a deep breath. "Because it is a gift of the Maghuin Dhonn Herself, and a sacred trust given to my people to hold. Because I have let myself be used unwisely in the past. I will not perform tricks to satisfy your curiosity."

"Will not or *cannot*?" General Arslan eyed me speculatively. "The Vralians tell a tale about one of your kind, you know. He was either cursed or sainted. I am not certain."

"Both," I murmured.

"Can *you* take on the form of a bear?"

I didn't answer.

"I think not." He pushed his chair decisively away from the table. "I think that although there may be a kernel of truth to these tales, you are weaker than you pretend. And I will ask you one last time, Moirin mac Fainche. Will you go from this place and leave my son in peace?"

"No," I whispered. "I can't."

The general inclined his head. "So be it."

I rose to my feet, leaving my tea untouched on the table. "Is that all? Are we enemies, then?"

"No." He drained his bowl of tea noisily, then shoved it away as though it had offended him, his face stony. "But we are not friends, either."

FOURTEEN

Bao, your father is a bit...scary."

"Yes," he agreed, not sounding particularly displeased by it. "I think so, too."

I shivered. "He wants you to stay."

"I know." As we walked through the campsite together, Bao and I behaved in a circumspect manner, making sure to keep several feet of space between us. It didn't matter. He was near enough that our *diadh-anams* whispered together. It felt at once odd and familiar. "But I am going."

"How?"

"*How* is the problem." He paused to watch a pair of wrestlers engaging in a practice bout. I'd been wrong, the formal games had not yet begun. "The Great Khan has informed me that he has no intention of allowing me to leave his daughter. But if I won one of the contests, I would earn the right to ask him for a boon. He would not like it, but he would be honor-bound to grant it."

I felt relieved, remembering the ease with which he had dispatched his opponents the other day. "Well, then! Fighting is what you do best, right?"

"Fighting, yes." Bao looked somber. "But there is no fighting that suits my skill in the contests. Only traditional Tatar sports. Horse-racing, archery, and wrestling." He pointed at the two men grunting and straining for purchase as they grappled with one another. "They have been doing this all their lives. I do not think I can beat the best of them."

"No?"

He shook his head. "Armed with my staff, I would gladly take on any man here with any weapon he chose. Unarmed, I am very good in a brawl. But I'm not a wrestler, Moirin."

I believed him. Gods knew, Bao wasn't given to false modesty. He wasn't given to idle boasting, either. If he said he could do a thing, he could. If he said he could not, it must be true. I swallowed my disappointment.

Horse-racing was out—and archery, too. I'd seen Bao ride, and while he was skilled enough, I was a better rider. If I couldn't win against the young men of Batu's tribe, there was no way Bao could win against the best here. And he had become a stick-fighter because peasants were forbidden edged weapons in Ch'in. He had no skill with a bow.

I did, though.

I contemplated that fact in silence for a moment. It was a daring enough notion that it made me sweat with anxiety at the mere thought of it. "Bao . . . in the archery contest, do they shoot on foot or from horseback?"

"Both," he said. "There are three contests. Two for the short bow—one on foot and one on horseback at a full gallop. One for the long bow on foot. But, Moirin, I'm not—" He paused, gazing at me with a speculative gleam in his eye. "*You* are. Do you think you could outshoot a Tatar?"

I licked my lips, finding them dry. "Not on horseback, no. But on foot I held my own against Batu's folk."

"Against men?" Bao asked. "Because there are no contests only for women."

I scowled at him. "Aye, against men!"

"Peace, Moirin. For you, I am willing to swallow my pride. I only wanted to be certain." He flashed a grin at me. "I know you are a very good archer. Do you remember in Shuntian when that fellow interfered in my fight with Ten Tigers Dai, and you shot the hat clean off his head? Even a Tatar would think twice at taking that risk."

It made me smile. "Well, I was angry—and it was at close range. I don't know if I could beat the best here, Bao. Probably not. Do you think they would even let me try?"

He rubbed his chin. "Maybe. I do not think there is any rule forbidding a woman to compete against the men, it is only that women are not strong enough to draw a bow hard enough to shoot as far as a man." He glanced sidelong at me. "If you won, they would say it was magic."

"Like as not," I agreed.

Bao's gaze was candid. "Would it be?"

I opened my mouth to say no, then paused, frowning. "Truly? I don't know, Bao. I've been shooting for the pot since I was a child in Alba. My skill is fairly earned."

He followed my thoughts. "What about your bow? Is it charmed?"

"I don't know," I admitted. "My uncle Mabon made it for me. My mother said he had a gift for working with wood." I shrugged. "I don't know if she meant an ordinary knack, or a gift of the Maghuin Dhonn Herself."

"Your mother wasn't very talkative, was she?" Bao observed.

It was true, and I laughed. "No."

"It doesn't matter." He gave a dismissive wave. "They will claim it, but they cannot prove it. I have seen your bow, and there is nothing remarkable-looking about it, nothing to suggest it is charmed in any way. Actually, it looks quite primitive."

"Nonetheless, it is a very fine bow," I said with a touch of indignation.

"So it is." Bao's expression turned grave. "Moirin, this might be our best course. If you fail, the worst that will happen is that your opponents will gloat. And I think they might permit it in the hope of that outcome. Are you at least willing to try?"

I eyed him. "Are you *sure* you're not a wrestler?"

"Very," he said with regret. "Given a few more months' time, I might become one. I'm good at learning such skills. Now?" He shook his head. "As little as I like to admit it, I stand no chance of winning."

I sighed. "Then I will try."

"Good," he said simply.

We walked together in silence for a time, keeping our careful distance from each other. Folk in the camp steered away to give us a wide berth, no one willing to start trouble so long as we were discreet. Giving the lie to appearances, our *diadh-anams* twined with one another, flickering and teasing, rising and falling joyfully in a private celebration. It was a sensation in some ways more intimate than a touch, both pleasurable and unnerving.

"Strange as it is, I am learning to live with it," Bao said presently. "Now that you are here, it is not entirely unpleasant."

I did not need to ask what he meant. "Yes, I know. Bao..." I halted. "I would like to speak with her."

His brows shot upward. "Erdene?"

I squared my shoulders. "Yes. I would like to apologize to her. I owe her that much, at least."

His expression turned dubious. "Moirin, I think it is very wonderful that you always wish to do what you think is right and honorable. But it is not always what people want. Erdene is angry, very angry. Believe me, I have tried to apologize to her many times already. She is not ready to hear it."

"Mayhap she is ready to hear mine," I said.

"Mayhap," he said doubtfully.

She wasn't, at least not at first.

I called on the Great Khan's daughter later in the day, taking Oyun and one of the other young tribesmen as an escort. Erdene made me wait a long time outside her *ger* before deciding to honor the laws of hospitality and allow me to be admitted. She did not go so far as to offer me the traditional bowl of tea, for which I was just as glad. By the look on her face, it would have likely been poisoned.

It felt strange being in the dwelling she shared with Bao. Although

I hadn't known it at the time, the *ger* to which he had led me that first day belonged to another family who had vacated it willingly at the request of the Great Khan's son-in-law. It embarrassed me to think on it.

Here, I saw signs of Bao's presence. There was a string of dried snowdrop bulbs hanging from the framework, their number diminished since I last saw them. The square of embroidered black and white magpies I had given to him was unfolded in a deliberate display on a bed.

That, I thought, was Erdene's doing. Bao would not have flaunted it. She wanted to remind me they shared a bed.

Having granted me admission, Erdene sat stiffly on a chair, several attendants around her. She did not invite me to sit.

"Greetings, your highness," I said politely. "Do your cattle prosper?"

A flicker of irritation crossed her face. "What do you want, witch?"

So much for pleasantries. "I come to offer an apology," I said in a steady tone. "My actions have caused you pain. I am sorry."

Erdene's nostrils flared. "Then undo it! Undo your magic and give me back my husband!"

"I cannot undo it," I said softly. "And Bao is not mine to give. His choices are his own to make."

Her mouth hardened. "You lie."

"No." I shook my head. "My father once told me that the gods use their chosen hard. I believe it is true. I believe it is also true that the gods are careless of those whose fates are crossed by their chosen."

In a flash, Erdene rose from the chair and launched herself at me, plucking a dagger from her sash. It was so quick and unexpected, it took me utterly by surprise. She planted the tip of her dagger against my throat, grabbing my hair with her other hand. "I do not want to hear you speak! One more word, and I will cut out your tongue!"

I forced myself to breathe slowly and calmly—the Breath of Ocean's Rolling Waves, the most soothing of all the Five Styles. The Great Khan's daughter was a head shorter than me, but there was a great deal of strength in her small, sturdy figure.

Her grip on my hair tightened, the point of the dagger digging into my skin. "Do you understand?" she asked fiercely, her voice trembling. "Do you, o chosen one?"

I gazed at her without speaking. There were angry tears in her wide-set eyes. Gods, she was young! No more than sixteen.

Erdene pressed the dagger harder and I felt a warning pin-prick of pain as the tip pierced my skin. *"Do you?"*

"Yes, your highness," I said quietly, ignoring the trickle of blood at my throat and speaking to the hurt and anger within her. "Better than you know. I am a woman, too. I once loved a man who could not give his heart to me. I persisted in loving him well beyond folly. Bao has been cruel to you in his thoughtlessness, but I do not think he meant to be. This man used me badly on purpose, and I let him."

The pressure eased.

"I understand the pain, the sense of shame, the anger at the unfairness of it all," I continued. "But it is not your fault. There is no shame in loving, no shame in honest desire. You did nothing wrong. It is only that the gods have decreed otherwise."

The Great Khan's daughter blinked rapidly, her throat working. "It *hurts*!"

"I know," I whispered, my heart aching for her. "I know it all too well, which is why I am so very sorry."

She released me abruptly, turning to hurl her dagger across the *ger*. Her attendants flinched.

"Go." Erdene kept her back turned to me, her shoulders hunched and tight. "I have heard your apology. I do not wish to hear more."

I bowed, and went.

FIFTEEN

———— ❖ ————

The archery contest was set to take place three days later, and I was
to be allowed to compete in it.

All in all, spirits were running high in the campsite. There were
exceptions, of course. The Great Khan's daughter was miserable; the
Great Khan himself was disgruntled. His loyal general Arslan was
unhappy. I was torn between guilt and hope; and I knew Bao felt
much the same.

Everyone else was excited.

It was almost all Tatars, now. Whatever negotiations took place
among the northern Bhodistani and the Vralians had been concluded.
Most of them had departed, only a few lingering out of a mild curiosity, I supposed. No one but the Tatars truly cared about the contests.

And they cared very much. They were eager to see me humiliated,
or at least most of them were.

When I thought about it, I felt sick and scared inside. I was no
warrior, raised to take pride in my prowess with a bow. I was just…
me. I had only learned to shoot to help provide for my mother and
myself. It was a way of life, nothing more.

"That is the best reason of all, Moirin," Batu said firmly to me.
"Survival. Do not worry. Whatever happens, you will not embarrass
yourself."

"No?"

"No." His kind eyes crinkled. "I am aware of the games that were played in the deep of winter. It has always galled the young men of my tribe that they cannot defeat you in this sport. Do you think that we are so unskilled that we cannot hold our own with the best of the Great Khan's men?"

"No." I smiled at him. "Batu, with your kindness and generosity, I am quite sure you *are* the best of the Great Khan's men."

He blushed and averted his head, which I found utterly charming. I would have kissed his cheek, except I knew it would scandalize him. "I have asked everyone to cull their arrows to choose those with the straightest shafts and the finest fletching. We will do our best to make sure you have arrows that fly true."

I was touched. "I will try not to disappoint you."

"You could never disappoint me, Moirin," Batu said in a gentle voice. "I wish you well."

I spent many hours practicing away from the campsite, honing my skill. Alone, I was better able to concentrate, and I found that the discipline that Master Lo had taught me served me well.

On the day before the archery contest, Bao rode out to meet me. Although it was hard to be apart, we had continued to be circumspect. There had been little contact between us since it had been decreed that I would be allowed to compete. My heart and my *diadh-anam* leapt inside me at his approach, and I knew he felt the same.

We found ourselves smiling foolishly at each other, both of us self-consciously aware of it, yet unable to help ourselves.

"So," I said.

"So," Bao echoed, dismounting. "It is almost upon us. I will be glad when this is over, Moirin."

My anxiety returned ten-fold. "So will I, but, Bao, please don't count on me to win! Truly, I think the odds are very much against it."

"They are," he observed. "Almost no one is wagering on you. And yes, I know it is unlikely. It is only that it is our best chance of seeing the matter resolved peacefully."

I was relieved that he wasn't putting unreasonable expectations on me. "What happens if I *do* lose? Other than the gloating."

"I don't know," Bao admitted. "Erdene tells me that her father has promised to hunt me down like a dog and slit my throat if I leave without his permission."

That didn't do much to alleviate my anxiety. "I see."

"At least she is speaking to me, which is an improvement. Whatever you said to her, it helped." He gave me a curious glance. "What *did* you say to her?"

"I told her I understood how she felt," I murmured. "I told her I had once loved a man who could not give his heart to me."

Bao's eyes widened with indignation. "You compared me to that stupid ass Lord Lion Mane?"

"Aye, I did." I raised my brows at him. "I know you didn't intend to hurt Erdene. Nonetheless, you did."

"I know, I know!" He sighed. "And I am sorry for it."

"I know." I steered the conversation back to more pressing matters. "Bao, I'm serious. If I lose, what will we do?"

He smiled ruefully. "If the Great Khan's threat is sincere, I think there is only one way we can evade his pursuit. We can't outrace a Tatar hunting party. Have you seen them ride?"

"Aye." I nodded. "You mean for me to call the twilight."

"Yes." Bao's smile faded. "And I know you are concerned about your ability to shield both of us within it long enough. I am, too. I remember how difficult it was for you with the princess when we climbed toward White Jade Mountain. Believe me, I do not like to ask. It is a piece of irony, Moirin. Before... before I died, when I had decided I would offer to leave Master Lo's service, it was because I meant to protect you."

"Only that?" I asked.

"No, of course not." His eyes softened. "Also because of your noble instincts and generous heart, and yes, your beauty, and the way you revel in pleasure, and many other things large and small. But you're impulsive, too, and all these things combined make you a danger to yourself."

"I'm not impulsive," I muttered. "I have an inconvenient destiny, that's all."

"*And* you are impulsive," Bao repeated, ignoring my disclaimer. "Anyway...it is a piece of irony that I can do nothing to protect you here, but must rely on your skills and gifts to save us both from a dangerous situation I created." He looked unhappy. "I am not making a very good start as a heroic protector like the ones in your tales."

"Close your eyes," I said to him.

"Why?"

I blew out my breath. "Just do it!"

He obeyed, and I summoned the twilight, folding it around us both. Bao opened his eyes to a world gone silvery, dim, and lovely.

I touched his face. "I do not recall asking for a protector, my stubborn magpie. And before you take the entire blame for our troubles, I will remind you that I created the problem by coming after you."

Bao smiled. "Impulsively, yes."

"Oh, fine." I slid my hand around to the back of his neck, tugging his head down so I could kiss him.

Naamah's gift sang within me as he kissed me back, one arm around my waist. His other hand pressed against my back, claiming me firmly.

We made love on the twilit steppe, and it was gentle and magical.

Never before had I been able to surrender to pleasure without losing my grasp on the twilight. It was different with Bao. He carried the missing half of my divided soul within him, and I could hold us both in the twilight as easily as I could myself—as easily and naturally as breathing.

"Moirin." He whispered my name against my throat, his hand parting my thighs. "It is so beautiful here."

"Yes," I whispered in reply, my back arching as his fingers teased my slick cleft.

Bao lifted his head, his gaze intent on mine. "Is it like this beyond the stone doorway?"

Ripples of pleasure ran through me. "Even more so." I gazed back at him, seeing the flickering penumbra of his aura. "It is everything bright and dark all at once, everything in the world."

"Everything?" He moved over me.

I spread my thighs wider to welcome him, feeling the bonfire of the spirit as our *diadh-anams* joined in full. "Everything."

All through our lovemaking and beyond, I held on to the twilight, not losing it even in the throes of climax—not mine nor his. In the aftermath of love, I lay with my head on Bao's chest, listening to his steady heartbeat and watching the silvery grasses move slowly in the breeze. Everything seemed to move more slowly in the twilight.

Time passed differently in the spirit world, I remembered. When I had gone through the stone doorway, days had passed without my knowledge.

Bao's warm breath stirred my hair, and his arms were warm around me, strong with corded muscle.

It felt good.

I didn't want it to end.

"Moirin," he said at last, his voice reluctant. "We should go."

"I know." I forced myself to sit upright. After we donned our clothing, I took one last, deep breath of the twilight, and then let it out, releasing the magic.

The world returned in a rush. It was late—later than I had reckoned. The setting sun hovered over the horizon like a great orange orb, staining the grasslands with ruddy light, throwing our long, stark shadows before us.

For the first time in days, I felt calm.

"I can do this," I said to Bao. "If I fail on the morrow, we can escape into the twilight. I can hold it long enough."

He cupped my face in his hands and kissed me. "Yes, you can."

SIXTEEN

"Pull!"

I eased the bowstring back—gently, gently. The sturdy yew-wood bow my uncle Mabon had made for me bent obligingly. The fletching of the arrow I had nocked tickled my earlobe—vulture feathers, from one of the arrows borrowed from the members of Batu's tribe.

I eyed the distant target, gauging my angle. I did my best to ignore the fact that my heart was hammering inside my chest.

"Loose!"

I loosed the bowstring.

A puff of errant wind blew as my arrow arced into the sky—mine, and six others. Against all odds, I had shot well enough to reach the penultimate round.

Now, I sucked in my breath.

Six arrows thudded into six leather targets stuffed with wool. I winced, seeing I had missed the crudely painted red circle on mine. I had misjudged the wind and the angle.

Two had pierced the circle, one dead-center, the other slightly off. Three others had missed by a wider margin than I had.

The watching crowd of Tatars murmured. The judges conferred.

"You, and you." An officious fellow serving as the judges' liaison pointed at the two men who had shot best. When he came to me, his mouth tightened. "And you. Now, you will shoot one by one. Ten paces!"

I breathed a sigh of relief.

Ah, gods! If it hadn't been for the sense of calm I'd found yesterday, I was quite sure my nerves would have undone me. The riding archery contest had taken place earlier. I'd watched the competitors shoot from the saddle at a row of dangling rings while they raced at a flat-out gallop. They were incredibly accurate, and I resigned myself to the fact that there was no way I could truly compete against the best of the best here.

But so long as I had the knowledge that Bao and I could escape into the twilight, that I could hold it long enough to keep us both safe, it didn't matter.

As a result, I had shot fearlessly and well in the early rounds of the standing archery contest. Over a hundred men took part, shooting in groups of a dozen at a time. For each group to partake, half passed on to the next round and half were eliminated. With each successive round, we retreated ten paces from the targets.

Again and again, I found myself placing within the top half of my group. It wasn't until the number of competitors had dwindled to a mere dozen that I'd begun to wonder if I *could* win, and my anxiety returned in full force.

That was also when my opponents began to grumble and mutter about magic, and the officious liaison had come to inspect my bow.

Was it charmed? I truly had no idea. Mayhap my uncle Mabon had whispered some arcane charm into the very wood and sinew. I did not know the extent of the small gifts of magic the Maghuin Dhonn possessed. Mayhap there was some secret in the way he had seasoned the wood. Mayhap the secret lay in the powerful resilience of the wood itself, or the sinews or the glue.

Whatever the truth, Bao was right. It didn't look remarkable and there was nothing for the official to find. After testing my bow for himself and finding that it shot no more true than the archer's skill, he shrugged and handed it back to me.

Now...

Now there were only three of us, and I had begun to sweat. Oh aye, if I lost, there was still the twilight. But now that victory was actually within reach, I could not help but think how much better it would be if the Great Khan were forced to grant my boon, and let Bao and me go freely.

The steppe was a vast expanse of open land to traverse. I had no doubt that there were skilled trackers among the Khan's men. Even having discovered that I could ward Bao as easily as myself, it could be a long, long time to hold the twilight. And there would be no room for error.

The first of my remaining two opponents stepped up to the mark. He nocked an arrow and drew with the unique Tatar grip, using a ring on his thumb to pull the bowstring, the muscles of his heavy shoulders bunching. He was a strong, burly fellow, and if the contest were to be decided on distance alone, I had no doubt that he would prevail.

It wasn't, though. Accuracy counted.

With a grunt, he loosed the bowstring. His arrow sank into the distant target, landing on the outer rim of the red circle. His supporters cheered and shouted.

It was the second fellow who worried me the most. He was lean and taciturn, and he shot with great accuracy and ferocious concentration. It was he whose last shot had been dead-center. He took his place at the mark, drawing his bow with fluid precision.

Another gust of wind blew as he loosed his arrow, more lively than the first. Even so, his arrow pierced very close to the center of the target. My last opponent gave a little sigh, and an unexpected, courteous bow in my direction.

Holding my bow loosely, I toed the mark. The onlookers had grown quiet. I didn't dare look at them, not even my few supporters, fearful of losing my own concentration.

I had missed the circle on my last shot. This one could mean the difference between safe passage, no matter how reluctantly granted, and deadly pursuit.

I chose the straightest shaft in my quiver, the one I had left for the end, nocking it carefully. Gently, gently, I hooked my forefingers around the bowstring and drew it back beyond my ear.

My heart thudded in my chest, and my extended left arm trembled, my knuckles pale where I clutched my bow's grip. Beneath the thick Tatar coat I wore, trickles of nervous sweat trailed down my skin. A fitful breeze rose and fell, tugging at my hair.

I fixed my gaze on the distant target. Gods, it looked far away and small!

There were no official commands to be given in this final round. A handful of spectators took it on themselves to remedy the situation.

"Loose!" someone shouted; and scores of other voices took up the chant, seeking to unnerve me. "Loose, loose, loose!"

I ignored them.

I breathed the Breath of Wind's Sigh, drawing it up behind my eyes, remembering all that Master Lo Feng had taught me. I meditated on the calm I had found in the twilight. I willed my body to be still and quiet. I willed the *world* to be still and quiet.

The fitful wind died, and I loosed the bowstring.

My arrow arced into the blue, blue sky. Too high, I thought for the space of a heartbeat, my chest constricting. Once again, I had misjudged the angle.

And then my arrow completed its arc with consummate grace, falling to pierce the very heart of the red circle on my target.

I stood staring in disbelief.

The Tatar beside me, the taciturn fellow I'd reckoned my worst competition, clapped me on the shoulder. "Well shot, lady."

I swallowed. "I didn't . . . the wind. I was lucky."

He shrugged. "There is always luck. The gods favored you today, and you deserved it."

"Thank you," I whispered.

The others were not so gracious. There were jeers and boos, and cries of sorcery. But it was done. The judges confirmed it and the official announced their decision. For the first time since I'd reached the final dozen, I dared to glance in the Great Khan's direction.

Although the Great Khan Naram was a short, stocky fellow with bowed legs, he had a commanding presence nonetheless. His broad face was impassive, but his body language radiated disapproval, his bowed legs planted, his arms folded over his chest as he stood amongst his wives and children, watching the contest. Even as I wondered if I should approach him, he beckoned to one of his warriors and spoke to the man.

The warrior nodded and trotted over to me. "The Great Khan wishes to confer with his shamans," he said. "He will send for you tomorrow."

Given no choice in the matter, I bowed. "I await his summons."

The Great Khan clapped his hands, turning to depart. Bao left his entourage and came over to congratulate me. He halted some feet away from me, and I felt the familiar-strange sensation of intimacy as our *diadh-anams* intertwined. Although Bao was taking care not to gloat, his eyes shone with pride.

"Gods, that was well done, Moirin," he said in a low, fierce voice.

The victory didn't feel as sweet as I would have reckoned. "Why does the Khan want to confer with his shamans?"

Bao shrugged. "He knows what boon you will ask. I suppose he wants to talk to them about releasing me from my marriage vows."

"Oh." I relaxed a little.

"You should go celebrate with your tribe." He nodded toward Batu and the others. "They are nearly bursting with pride." He gave me a smile filled with rare, genuine tenderness. "I feel the same way, but I will wait until the Great Khan's boon is granted to show it."

I smiled back at him. "Tomorrow, I hope."

"I hope so, too," he agreed.

Due to the amount of resentment in the camp, our celebration was muted, but it was heartfelt nonetheless. Many, many bowls of *airag* were consumed, the frothy, fermented mare's milk all Tatars loved.

In the late hours of the night, Batu gave me a drunken, fatherly embrace. "If all goes well tomorrow, I hope you will be happy with your young man."

"Thank you, Batu." This time, I did plant a kiss on his cheek. "You have stood as a father to me, and I will always be grateful for it."

It had been a long time since I'd drunk spirits of any kind; and too, I'd been too nervous to eat much that day. Although I did my best to keep up with my adopted Tatar tribe, the celebration was still under way when I gave up and staggered to my pallet, my head swimming with *airag*.

I felt dizzy, drunk, and more than a little nauseated; but I felt good, too. The warmth of the tribe's response had let me savor my victory. As soon as the walls of the *ger* ceased the semblance of spinning around me, I fell into a deep, dreamless sleep.

It seemed as though only a few hours had passed when one of the tribeswomen shook me awake—Solongo, her name was. I propped myself up on one elbow and squinted at her through the haze filling my head.

"The Great Khan Naram sends for you, Moirin," she whispered. "He wishes to see you *now*."

"Oh." The inside of my mouth felt foul. I licked my dry lips and swallowed against a sudden surge of nausea.

Solongo shook her head. "You may shoot like a man, but you cannot hold your drink like one," she said, not unkindly. "I will bring you tea."

The hot, rich tea helped. I drank it down in gulps, willing it to settle my stomach. The *ger* was filled with snoring, slumbering men sleeping off the aftereffects of too much *airag*. Not wanting to disturb anyone, I washed my face in a bucket of clean water and went to answer the Great Khan's summons.

He had sent an escort of ten warriors. They greeted me with nods of acknowledgment, and we set off through the campsite. It *was* early. The sun had not yet cleared the horizon. In the east, faint streaks of gold lit the sky, but it was still dark in the west. The Khan's men set a brisk pace, and I stumbled as I tried to keep up with them. I felt disheveled, disoriented, and out of sorts, and irritated at the Great Khan for exacting such a petty revenge.

Inside a spacious *ger* with a splendidly painted door, the Great Khan Naram was waiting for me, flanked by a pair of somber, bearded Vralian men with gold chains around their necks, heavy medallions dangling.

I blinked, perplexed. The Khan's men crowded into the room behind me.

"Moirin mac Fainche." Like General Arslan before him, the Khan pronounced my name with care. There was no expression I could read on his face. "These fine men from Vralia wish to meet you."

Both of them inclined their heads.

I supposed they were among those few who had stayed out of idle curiosity. I couldn't imagine why they cared about the outcome of a Tatar archery contest, or why they wanted to meet me, but I inclined my head in polite reply. When one of them stepped forward and extended his hand toward mine, I gave it to him.

Instantaneously, his fingers tightened around mine in a crushing grip. His other hand came from behind his back, trailing a rattling chain. Before I could react, he had clamped a cuff of silver metal around my wrist.

I pulled back sharply, drawing breath to shout.

A hard hand covered my mouth from behind—one of the Khan's men. He twisted my head, wrenching it backward and sideways until my neck bones strained in agony.

Terror flooded through me.

Now the Great Khan's face came alive with righteous fury. "Struggle, and he will snap your neck," he hissed at me. "Do you understand?" Behind the warrior's hand, I made a faint, terrified sound of assent. "Good." He gestured at the Vralians to continue.

One of them produced a key, locking the silver cuff in place around my right wrist. I felt the beginning sensation of my spirit being suffocated, the way I still felt sometimes in man-made places. Panicked, I breathed hard through my nose.

Chains jangled. A second cuff was clamped on my left wrist, and then a larger circlet around my neck. The Tatar holding my head wrenched sideways moved considerately to make room for the Vralians, who worked gravely and dispassionately.

With each shackle, the sense of suffocation intensified—and my awareness of Bao's *diadh-anam* faded.

And then the Vralians yanked off my thick, felt-lined boots and placed shackles and a chain on my bare ankles, and the process was complete.

My spirit was bound.

My *diadh-anam* was a frantic blaze inside me, beating at the walls of my chest like a caged hawk. I could no longer feel Bao's presence in the camp. I could no longer sense the faint call of destiny in the west. I couldn't even sense all the familiar things I took for granted, like the whisper of grass growing.

Seeing the horror written on my face, the Great Khan smiled slowly. "The witch is contained, I think. Now you will listen." He raised one finger. "I will tell my man to release you. If you hold your tongue, I will honor my agreement with the Vralians. You will go with them, alive. If you cry out for help..." He plucked a dagger from his belt. "I will simply kill you here and now. Will you be silent?"

I nodded as best I could.

The Khan gestured to the man holding me. He let go of my head. I fell to my knees in a rattling tangle of chains, breathing hard, my neck aching.

"You cheated yesterday." The Great Khan stooped to grab a handful of my hair, yanking my head upright. "My shamans agree. You used witchcraft to still the wind."

I gave my head a faint shake of denial.

"Do not lie!" Clutching a hank of my hair, he gave my head a fierce shake. My scalp burned, bringing tears to my eyes. He narrowed his gaze at me. "I will not allow you to make a mockery of me, to bring shame and dishonor upon my family."

"Please..." I whispered.

The Khan struck me across the face—hard enough to sting, no harder. It was only a warning. "You will be silent." He released his grip on my hair, setting his hands on his belt and contemplating me. "Clearly, you possess magic. I think Arslan is right, and you are not so powerful as you pretend. Still, your tongue is a dangerous weapon. As much as he resents you, you charmed him to the point where he would not counsel violence against you." He raised his brows. "Batu's tribe is bewitched. Even my own daughter softened toward you. Should a daughter of mine accept her own humiliation?" He shook his head. "Never. I regret that she did not cut out your cursed tongue, but listened to it instead."

I swallowed hard.

He leaned over me. "What did you say to her? That it was not her fault, that she had done nothing wrong?" With a cruel smile, he quoted my words. "*It is only that the gods have decreed otherwise.* Perhaps you may take comfort in those words as you find your fate is not as you had imagined." Straightening, he nodded toward the Vralians. "It seems *their* gods have decreed otherwise."

My heart was hammering in my chest, competing with my frantic *diadh-anam*. And yet I had to speak, even if the Great Khan struck me again. "Bao," I whispered, flinching in anticipation. "He will know."

"Yes." Magnanimous in victory, the Khan withheld the blow I deserved. "I daresay he will when he wakes. Like you, he was plied with strong drink last night. If the magic of Vralia's gods is as strong as they claim, my son-in-law will be free of the ties that bind you to him. Perhaps he will choose to stay after all." He shrugged. "If not, for the sake of my soft-hearted daughter and my good general Arslan, I will show him mercy."

It gave me a glimmer of hope.

The Khan Naram saw it, and crushed it with pleasure. "In time, I will relent and tell him what befell you. I have a fine tale prepared."

Another cruel smile curved his lips. "One that will send him far, far away from where you are going."

I closed my eyes in despair.

The Great Khan gave an order.

Someone struck me hard from behind. Pain burst across my skull, and stars of spangled light burst behind my eyelids, flickering and fading.

I fell into darkness.

SEVENTEEN

I awoke in a covered cart, jolting over the plains.

At first I thought it was a bad dream, a nightmare brought on by strained nerves and too much *airag*, a jumbled mess of old fables and dire magic spun by my sleeping mind. But when I stirred, chains rattled.

Bound.

I was bound, well and truly bound. I remembered the shackles being clamped on to me and locked into place, the Vralians' grave, dispassionate faces. My head ached ferociously. My *diadh-anam* was a faint, defeated spark inside me. I couldn't sense Bao's presence anywhere. I couldn't feel a thing beyond the confines of my skin.

My stomach lurched, and I swallowed bile. Gods, I needed air! Frantic as a trapped animal, I scrambled blindly toward the rear of the cart, dragging my chains, bumping into obstacles I couldn't make out in the dim light.

It was a tarpaulin of oiled canvas that covered the cart, secured in place by ropes. It gapped at the far end, glimpses of the brightening blue sky visible between the rope lashings.

Rope could be cut. Ignoring my chains, I groped at the sash around my waist for the dagger that Snow Tiger had given me, with its ivory hilt carved in the shape of a dragon's coils.

It was gone.

Wheels creaking, the cart ground to a halt. Deprived of any sense beyond the ordinary mortal ones, I lay still and took quick, shallow breaths, listening to the faint sound of approaching boot steps. Unseen fingers fumbled with unseen knots. I willed myself to be calm, and sought to summon the twilight.

It was gone, too—or at least, it was beyond my reach. With my magic constrained by these bedamned chains, I could no more take a half-step into the spirit world than I could fly to the moon.

The canvas was folded back to reveal a bearded Vralian face peering at me. Filled with an unreasoning mix of panic and fury, I tried to hurl myself at him. Weighted down by shackles and chains, I merely fell over the tailgate of the wagon, the impact driving the air from my lungs.

"No good!" Retreating out of reach, the Vralian wagged a stern finger at me, speaking a limited version of the Tatar language. "We save you."

I heaved myself and my chains backward, huddling in the rear of the wagon, wrapping my arms around me until I caught my breath. "Why?"

The second Vralian, who looked to be a few years younger than the first, came to confer with him, speaking in an unfamiliar tongue. The first raised his medallion to his lips and kissed it. "God wills it," he said in a reverent tone.

"Then I am grateful to your god," I said slowly and carefully, unfolding one arm and extending it. "If you will take off these chains, I will go with thanks."

Free of the chains, I could summon the twilight and pass through the campsite like a phantom, taking Bao with me.

The Vralian smiled gently and shook his head at me, as though I were a child who'd said somewhat foolish. "We save you from *you*."

I stared at him, and then raised my voice. "Well, then, I bedamned well don't want to be saved!"

He shrugged. "God wills it."

"I don't care!"

He made a hushing sound, pointing backward toward the Tatar

campsite. "Not far yet. No trouble, or the young man..." He made a slashing gesture across his throat. "Khan say he kill."

Bao.

I weighed my choices. My head ached too much to think straight. If Bao was awake, he would know something had happened to me, for as surely as the chains kept me from sensing his *diadh-anam*, they would prevent him from sensing mine. Whatever their purpose, the Vralians didn't seem intent on harming me. They said we had not gone far yet, so I couldn't have been unconscious for long. If I screamed and shouted at the top of my lungs, it might be that Bao would hear me.

And what then?

I didn't doubt that the Great Khan would sooner kill Bao than allow him to rescue me. Skilled as he was, Bao couldn't take on all the Khan's men; and he surely couldn't outride them. It would be best to be patient. There was a key to these chains. All I needed was a chance to steal it, and a minute or two to undo my shackles.

I raised my hands in surrender, chains dangling from my wrists. "No trouble."

The Vralian nodded. "Good." He pointed at the floor of the cart. "Today, hide."

Forcing myself to be compliant, I lay down. They pulled the tarpaulin back in place, lashing it securely.

Hours passed, long, stifling hours filled with fear, nausea, and tedium. Every hour took me farther away from Bao, farther away from freedom, farther away from the hope that my destiny was calling me home.

What in the name of all the gods did the Vralians want with me?

Never in my life had I felt more alone, miserable, and helpless. At least in the face of the storm that had nearly killed me, I'd been too busy trying to survive to even know what I was feeling.

Although I tried not to, I wept.

My only comfort was the spark of my *diadh-anam*, alive and flickering inside me, a promise that the Maghuin Dhonn Herself had not forgotten me. I was Her child. These cursed chains could bind

Her gifts, but they could not kill Her divine spark within me. In the suffocating darkness beneath the tarpaulin, I prayed to Her; and I prayed to Naamah and Anael, who were my D'Angeline patron gods. Although I could not sense their presence, I prayed they had not forgotten me, either.

At last, the interminable cart-ride came to an end. The Vralians unhitched their horses, hobbled them, and turned them loose to graze, then untied the tarpaulin once more. With a strange, reluctant solicitousness, they helped me clamber out of the cart.

It wasn't easy.

In the early-evening light, I got a better look at the shackles that bound me. They were etched with sigils and inscriptions in a strange alphabet. The cuffs around my wrists were linked to the circlet around my neck by chains long enough that they didn't restrict the movement of my arms overmuch. That wasn't their purpose. The chain that linked the shackles around my ankles was another matter. It was short enough that I was forced to adopt a halting, mincing gait.

Clearly, running away was not an option.

In case the matter was in doubt, one of the Vralians—the one who spoke a bit of the Tatar language—produced yet another chain, looping it around the front axle of the cart, and lacing it through the chain on my left arm. Averting his gaze, he put down a pallet of furs for me, indicating that I could take shelter beneath the wagon.

"You're too kind," I muttered.

Deeming me safely secured, he studied me with deep-set eyes. "God wills this."

Already, I was perishing sick of his bedamned god; but I had the sense to hold my tongue. The other fellow set about erecting a tent well beyond the reach of my tether, which I was sorry to see. They had not been overtly cruel to me thus far, but what kindness they had shown me, chaining me like a dog, I misliked.

I was scared and alone, and if they had given me the opportunity to bash in their heads with a rock while they slept, I would have taken it.

They didn't.

Instead, they kindled a careful fire of dried dung-chips, heating a pot of water filled with strips of dried meat and root vegetables. They knelt in prayer before they ladled out servings, murmuring in sonorous tones.

The second fellow brought me a steaming bowl of stew and a spoon. Far from it though I felt, I resolved to try being pleasant.

"Thank you." I accepted the bowl, my chains rattling as I reached for it. I took a deep sniff, miming pleasure, then smiled at him. "It smells good."

He beat a hasty retreat, avoiding my gaze. Stone and sea, what was *wrong* with these men?

Whatever it was, I didn't learn the answer that night. When dusk fell over the steppe, they extinguished their fire with care, retiring to the safety of their tent. Huddled in my cocoon of furs, I watched the moon rise and spill its silvery light over the plains, thinking and thinking, my mind restless.

I wondered if I could shift the cart.

I tried. Scuttling underneath it, I found the wooden chocks that braced the front wheels and pried them loose. When I banged them softly together in my fists, it made a very satisfying sound.

Scrambling out from beneath the cart, I got to my feet and went to the end of my short tether. Throwing my weight into the effort, I tried to drag the cart toward the tent.

I failed.

There were chocks bracing the rear wheels, too, and those I could neither reach nor dislodge, no matter how hard I strained. My tether was too short, and the cart was too heavy. I could not do it.

In the end, I gave up. I was cold and tired and heartsick, and tomorrow was another day. Sooner or later, I thought, an opportunity would present itself. When it did, I would take it and flee.

Gathering my furs, I crawled beneath the cart.

There, I curled up like a dog, and slept.

EIGHTEEN

———◦———

On the morrow, my situation looked as bleak as ever.

The Vralians were careful not to give me any opportunities for escape or violence—not that I could have taken either easily, entangled in a clinking, rattling mass of chains as I was, unable to take a single full stride.

They gave me hard black bread and water to break my fast in the morning. When I explained to the older fellow that I needed to answer nature's call, he shook his head, not comprehending. Clearly, his limited Tatar vocabulary did not extend to encompass the mortal body's most basic requirements.

"I need to piss!" I said in frustrated Alban, using a vulgar slang term and knowing he wouldn't understand a word of it. I pointed at his crotch, and mimed a man holding his phallus and relieving himself. "Gods! Do you people lack bladders as well as hearts?"

He flushed to the roots of his hair, his face darkening with embarrassment and disgust. But at least he unlocked the chain that tethered me to the wagon and pointed toward the outskirts of the camp.

I made my clanking, mincing way over the plain. Whatever else the Vralians were, they weren't voyeurs. Both of them turned their backs on me as I concluded my business. And an awkward business it was, hovering in a narrow squat, trying not to let urine splash on my bare feet, my felt trousers, or the bedamned chain between my ankles.

The sheer misery of the experience nearly brought me to tears.

I breathed slowly until the moment passed, distracting myself with thoughts of flight. It was impossible, at least for now. I could barely walk, let alone run. Still, the thought of forcing them to chase me down held a certain grim satisfaction.

But there was no point in rousing my captors' ire for the sake of a foolish whim—and my body was stiff and aching from the wagon's jolting. So instead I hobbled back to rejoin them like an obedient dog.

For a mercy, they didn't force me to hide beneath the tarpaulin today, but allowed me to ride atop it, pointing out a spot where I could sit atop some covered bales of wool. As such things went, it was reasonably comfortable.

We set out once more, heading due north. The younger man drove the cart, his hands firm on the reins. The older sat beside him. Their backs were rigid and upright, and they exchanged few words. There was only the sound of the breeze and the steady clopping of the cart-horses' hooves.

I endured the silence for the better part of an hour, staring at the backs of their heads and despising them.

"May I ask *why* your god wills this?" I asked in the Tatar tongue, forcing myself to speak politely.

The older man turned his head in my direction without actually looking at me. "To save you."

"To save me, yes." I was as perishing sick of the phrase as I was of his god. "Why?"

He held up his gold medallion, which was shaped like a square cross with flared arms, and kissed it reverently. "Yeshua."

"Yeshua," I repeated. It wasn't much of an answer. "Yeshua ben Yosef? Are you his priests? Did he tell you to save me? Am I to save *him*?"

That the Vralian understood; he reacted in shock, drawing back as though I had struck him. His companion queried him in their own tongue. They spoke for a moment, and the first man took on a thoughtful look.

Gods, I didn't understand a thing about these men!

"No talk here," the older man said. He pointed toward the north. "There, in Vralia."

I sighed, collapsing onto my canvas-covered bales. If I didn't escape soon, it was going to be a very long, very miserable journey.

I occupied myself with studying my shackles and chains. Now that my head was no longer spinning and yesterday's vicious ache had dwindled to a tender, throbbing lump on the back of my skull, I realized I'd seen the like before.

When Raphael de Mereliot and the Circle of Shalomon had summoned the spirit Focalor, a Grand Duke of the Fallen, the silversmith Balric Maitland had wrought a chain to bind him—a silver chain with a silver lock, each link etched with sigils. These were much the same, and I thought the inscriptions on the shackles might have been written in the Habiru alphabet. I'd seen it before in the summoning invocations the Circle studied.

Well and so, I thought. Focalor, who had appeared in the form of a tall man with immense wings like an eagle's, had broken the chain with ease.

He had also killed Claire Fourcay, another member of the Circle, and breathed her life force into me, forcing me to keep open the doorway to the spirit world that had allowed him to be summoned. And he had very nearly succeeded in pouring his own essence into Raphael, taking possession of his mortal being and wreaking untold havoc on the world.

If it hadn't been for Bao and Master Lo, Focalor *would* have succeeded. But the important thing now was that the fallen spirit we summoned had been able to break the chain in the first place.

I racked my brains trying to remember how he had done it, recalling at last that the spirit had accused Claire Fourcay of mispronouncing two words in the spell of binding. That was no help, since the Vralians hadn't spoken at all when they bound me. If there was a spell, like as not it was written in the inscriptions on the cuffs.

There had been another thing, though. Focalor had told the

silversmith that a single drop of solder had obscured the sigil on one of the links.

That, mayhap, could be of use to me—although how the spirit had known it to be true, I couldn't say. I supposed a Grand Duke of the Fallen, able to wield power over wind and sea, had magical resources well beyond the ken of one frightened, lonely bear-witch. Still, I could examine the chains for myself. I set about examining the links one by one, starting with the chain that ran from my left wrist to the collar around my neck.

Hearing the slow, methodical rattle as I made a close study of each link, the older Vralian glanced behind him to see what I was about. I raised my brows coolly at him and kept at it. He watched me in that reluctant, sidelong fashion for a moment, then shrugged and turned back.

His lack of concern didn't bode well.

There was good reason for it. The chains that bound me were impeccably wrought. Every single bedamned link was a miracle of perfection, joined without the slightest gap or chink, burnished to immaculate smoothness. I couldn't find a single drop of solder that had fallen astray. Every perfect link was etched with a tiny, perfect sigil.

Insofar as I could tell, the chains were flawless. And to be honest, I wasn't sure what I would have done if I *had* found a flaw. Focalor had spread his enormous wings, and thunder had rolled. Lightning had flashed in his eyes. The chain wrapped around him had burst with a sharp crack and fallen to the floor.

I couldn't summon thunder and lightning, only the gentle twilight. I was good at the arts of pleasure and coaxing plants to grow, not commanding the sea to rise and fall.

At last, I gave up searching for a flaw that didn't exist, and that I wouldn't know how to exploit if it did. Instead, I began testing the chains' strength, gathering short lengths in my hands and hauling on them with all my might. Mayhap there was some weakness in a link not visible to the eye.

Again, the older Vralian glanced back at my strenuous efforts and the elaborate contortions that accompanied them.

I was short of breath, furious, and sweating beneath my thick Tatar coat. "Do you expect me not to try?"

He shook his head, his expression curiously gentle. "No."

I wore myself out with trying.

By the time we made camp that evening, I was too tired to despair. Chained to the axle once more, I ate my bowl of stringy stew-meat and stale roots, and retreated beneath the wagon to curl up in my nest of furs. The ground was harder and rockier than it had been. Shifting stones out of the way, I had another idea. Selecting an especially keen-edged shard, I fell asleep clutching it in my hand.

On the following day, I set about trying to destroy the integrity of my chains. I affected a docile appearance and hid the stone shard in my sleeve until we were under way. As soon as the cart-horses leaned into their traces and we resumed our plodding, jolting progress toward the north, I shook the shard into my palm.

Both Vralians gazed fixedly forward. I had begun to note that they had a marked reluctance to look directly at me, especially the younger one.

Fine.

This time, I took care to make my movements small and unobtrusive. Leaning back against the covered bales of wool, I drew up my knees. I braced my left wrist against my left knee, shoving my last remaining jade bangle higher on my forearm so it wouldn't rattle against the metal and give me away. I chose a link, the third closest to the cuff around my wrist, easiest to reach.

Its perfect little sigil gleamed.

With my right hand, I drew the sharp edge of my stone shard across it, timing my action to the dull, thudding fall of the cart-horses' hooves.

It didn't even make a scratch at first. But I kept at it, patient and deliberate, timing each careful stroke to hide the faint scraping sound, scoring the metal's surface over and over until the lines of the sigil were blurred and imperfect.

It *should* have worked. I don't know why it didn't, except that it didn't. Like as not there was some rule governing its magic. The chains had been made perfectly at their inception, and I could not unmake them by inducing a flaw after the fact.

And I hadn't been as discreet as I'd thought. When we halted for the evening, the older Vralian came around to the side of the wagon and put out his hand, looking like a reproving parent. "Give the stone."

I hesitated, fingering the edge of the shard. With sufficient force behind the effort, it was sharp enough to cut through flesh.

A trained warrior like Snow Tiger wouldn't even have hesitated. I'd watched the princess snatch an arrow from an enemy's hand and plunge it into his throat in a move as swift and deadly as a snake striking.

Of course, she hadn't been laden with chains.

A clever, cunning fighter like Bao would have found a way to use the chains to his advantage. He probably wouldn't even bother with the stone. I could imagine him vaulting over the Vralian's head, wrapping his chains around the fellow's neck in the process and throttling him on landing. By the time the second man had a chance to react, Bao would have plucked the knife from the first man's belt and armed himself.

But I wasn't a trained warrior or a skilled, clever fighter any more than I was a Grand Duke of the Fallen. With the element of surprise, I might, *might* succeed in slashing the first man's throat. Even if I did, I could barely climb out of the cart unaided. I didn't like my chances against the second fellow.

The Vralian watched me with his deep-set gaze, holding out his hand and waiting for me to make up my mind. Obviously, the element of surprise was gone.

With a heavy sigh, I put the shard in his palm.

His expression softened. "Good girl."

I lowered my gaze in a penitent manner, replying in vulgar Alban and a sweet, remorseful tone. "Go to hell, you miserable goat-fucking bastard."

We made camp that night within the sight of mountains. After I finished the bowl of barley gruel that they gave me for the evening meal, I sat with my back against one of the wagon-wheels and gazed at the distant range. Here and there, I could make out carpets of dark green on the slopes.

Trees.

As much as I'd come to be fond of the vast, wide-open expanse of the Tatar steppe and its immense blue sky, I'd never stopped missing trees. I'd never imagined that my first glimpse of them would be aught but joyful. Instead, it was a reminder that I was bound and helpless, cut off from my own inner senses, and headed in the opposite direction from everything and everyone I had ever loved.

It was not a joyful moment.

NINETEEN

The older Vralian's name was Ilya; the younger's was Leonid. I learned this through observation over the course of days, since neither of them deigned to tell me when I asked. It is more difficult than one might expect to pick out proper names in the midst of an utterly foreign tongue, especially among folk who speak seldom.

Beyond that, I learned nothing. By the time we had spent a week's time jolting our way through the mountain passes, I was just as puzzled and confused as I had been from the moment Ilya first clamped a cuff around my wrist. I could not for the life of me understand what it was they *wanted* of me.

Not pleasure, that was certain. They were as reluctant to touch me as they were to look at me or talk to me.

For that, I was grateful. If they had been intent on committing heresy on me, I would have been helpless to prevent it. But instead, it seemed quite the opposite. I had the sense that they regarded me as unclean, and not in a way that owed to my limited and unsuccessful attempts to maintain good hygiene, a difficult task rendered near impossible by virtue of being chained within my dirty clothing.

No, it was somewhat deeper and more profound.

Over and over, in a thousand different ways, I asked what it was they wanted, why they had taken me. The only answer I ever got was, "God wills it." Eventually, I gave up asking and pondered why Vralia's god wanted me.

What little I knew of Vralian faith came from Berlik's tale—Berlik the Oath-Breaker, who had fled to the snowy wastes, carrying his curse far, far away from his people. In the end, the Maghuin Dhonn Herself had accepted his atonement.

I knew that Berlik had fallen in with Yeshuite pilgrims on his journey, and that he had found a place of sanctuary in a Yeshuite monastery in Vralia. No one had clapped him in chains. No, the head priest had given Berlik his blessing, allowing him to retreat into hermitage and roam freely in an immense tract of pristine wilderness owned by the monastery. When Imriel de la Courcel came seeking vengeance for the life of his wife and unborn child, the priest begged him to spare Berlik.

Of course, we only know Prince Imriel's side of the tale, but the Maghuin Dhonn have always believed he told it fairly. Tales say that Berlik bowed his head to the sword willingly, and the prince fell to his knees in the snow and wept after he took his life. A man with every right to vengeance would not lie about such a thing.

I wondered what had changed in a hundred and some years that Yeshua's priests had gone from giving succor to a great magician of the Maghuin Dhonn, one with a dire curse on his head, to dragging me away in chains for the dubious sin of having been falsely accused of cheating in an archery contest.

It was madness.

Vralia had been a country at war in Berlik's time, that I remembered. The Yeshuite faith was not born here; indeed, it had far closer ties to Terre d'Ange. Mayhap I was approaching the matter from the wrong direction, and Vralia's gods were interested in me because of my D'Angeline blood.

I tried to think the matter through, looking for some thread of a clue woven into the tapestry of history.

"Yeshua ben Yosef was the only begotten son of the One God of the Habiru folk," I said aloud in my native tongue, addressing the back of Ilya and Leonid's heads. "And they acknowledged him as the long-awaited savior of their people. Is that not so?"

I could see both of them stiffen at hearing Yeshua's name coming from my lips. Although they understood nothing else, they did not like it when I spoke of him, but it helped me think and remember.

"But the Tiberians reviled him for sowing disorder. They took him prisoner, and killed him like a common criminal," I continued. "And as his true love Mary wept at the foot of the post to which he was nailed, her tears mingled with his dripping blood in the soil. From this joining, Blessed Elua was engendered, and Mother Earth herself nurtured him in her womb."

They didn't like hearing Elua's name, either, although I had the impression it was for different reasons.

I pondered what little else I knew. Of Yeshua ben Yosef, not much. The history of Blessed Elua and his Companions, I knew well. Ever since I had learned that I was half-D'Angeline, I had been curious about it.

The One God had turned his back on his Earth-begotten grandson, but a handful of his divine servants had abandoned their posts in Heaven and gone to Elua's side: Naamah, Anael, Shemhazai, Eisheth, Azza, Camael, and Cassiel. When the King of Persis put Elua in chains, Naamah offered herself to him in exchange for Elua's freedom. When Elua hungered, Naamah lay down with strangers in exchange for coin that he might eat.

Wandering the earth, they came at last to Terre d'Ange, where they were welcomed with joy. There, they made a home and begat thousands upon thousands of children.

Except for Cassiel, anyway. Although he stayed for love of Blessed Elua, he obeyed the One God's commandment that his servants remain chaste.

I'd never quite understood Cassiel.

When their descendants grew too numerous, the One God took notice at last. He sent his commander-in-chief to fetch Elua and his Companions back to Heaven, but Elua refused, saying his grandfather's Heaven was bloodless. In the end, Mother Earth intervened and struck a bargain with the One God, who had been her husband long, long ago. Together they created a new place beyond the mortal realm, which D'Angelines call the Terre d'Ange-that-lies-beyond.

Well and so, it seemed to me that the matter had been peacefully resolved. It had taken place over a thousand years ago. So far as I knew, Yeshuites and D'Angelines had lived peaceably together for those long centuries.

Mayhap the answer lay in more recent history. My thoughts circled back around to Berlik's tale. In his day, there had been a great exodus of Yeshuites around the world as they embarked on pilgrimages to Vralia. There was a prophecy that when Yeshua ben Yosef returned to the world, he would establish his kingdom in the north, and the Yeshuites believed the time was nigh.

That, I remembered, was because of the war in Vralia. Some royal prince named Tadeuz Vral had set himself up as the supreme monarch. He'd even named the place after himself. But his brother had rebelled against him. Tadeuz Vral had appointed a Yeshuite immigrant with a gift for military strategy to lead his army, and swore an oath that he would convert and rule the country in Yeshua's name if the fellow was victorious.

As it happened, he was.

That was how Vralia had become a Yeshuite nation, and that was the extent of my knowledge. I did recall that in Prince Imriel's tale, this Tadeuz Vral had been none too pleased with him for killing Berlik, as all Yeshuite pilgrims were under his protection and Prince Imriel had lied about his intentions. But it was the very same priest who had begged Prince Imriel to spare Berlik who convinced Vral to let the prince go, so I did not see how the incident could be the cause of a grudge that had festered for over a hundred years and led to my own half-breed D'Angeline self being taken into captivity.

Again, so far as I knew, it was the start of a diplomatic relationship between the nations, and I didn't recall hearing aught to suggest it was anything but cordial in the decades that had followed.

None of it made a damn bit of sense.

Of course, I had been gone for a long while. For all I knew, there had been some new incident that had Vralia in an uproar against D'Angelines or the folk of the Maghuin Dhonn, and I was paying the price.

It seemed unlikely, though. There were no great, shape-shifting magicians like Berlik left to my people, and I could hardly imagine thoughtful, steady-minded King Daniel of Terre d'Ange allowing a diplomatic outrage to take place on his watch. No, if anything, he was overly cautious. The only outrageous thing he had ever done in his life was marry Jehanne.

Despite everything, the thought made me smile.

Few folk had ever understood that match, but I did. Daniel's first wife, the one who died, had been the love of his life, gracious, noble, and kind. To this day, he grieved deeply for her. He had allowed himself to love the fickle, tempestuous courtesan that was my lady Jehanne because she was nothing like her predecessor—and Jehanne knew it full well.

That's why he tolerates my foibles, she had told me once. *We're unfaithful to one another in different ways.*

It was true, but not wholly so. Deep down, Jehanne was a great deal wiser and kinder than she pretended. I knew, because she'd let herself show it to me. And for all her fears and uncertainties, I didn't doubt that motherhood would bring out the best in her.

I only hoped I'd have the chance to see so for myself one day. Rattling my chains ruefully, I remembered gentle Checheg lying exhausted and calm in the aftermath of giving birth, assuring me of just that thing as she described my glad return to Terre d'Ange with Bao at my side—and little Sarangerel telling me that Jehanne's babe would be as big as her bright-eyed, toddling brother, Mongke, already creating mischief.

It had seemed possible then.

Now…

I fought down a wave of despair, stroking the blue silk scarf that Checheg had given me. I wore it knotted around my throat.

That, and one jade bangle the color of the dragon's translucent

reflecting lake were all that were left to me of the tokens I had col-
lected along the way, reminders that I had been loved once.

Everything else was gone.

My yew-wood bow, gone, left behind in Batu's *ger*. My ivory-
hilted dagger, gone or taken. Also left behind, my battered canvas
satchel that held items of little value to anyone but me. There was the
Emperor's jade seal, which I'd stashed there for safe-keeping. That,
I supposed, might be bartered for a considerable amount. The same
was not true of the other items. Not the signet ring my mother had
given me, proof that I was a child of Alais' line.

Not the square of cloth embroidered with flowering bamboo by
Bao's half-sister, Song.

And surely, surely, not the little crystal vial of perfume that
Jehanne had given me to remember her by.

No one but a D'Angeline would know what *that* was worth.

It shouldn't have mattered so much; they were only things, after
all. But they were things that had given me comfort.

And there was no comfort here.

None at all.

TWENTY

We began to pass through villages.

I had some mad idea that I might find help or allies within them. I called out to the staring villagers in the Tatar tongue, rattling my chains plaintively, clasping my hands and pleading, doing my best to convey that I was a captive in need of rescue.

They looked away.

Ilya spoke to them in his deep, sonorous voice, and they nodded in understanding. Some turned and spat as I passed. One little boy stooped, picked up a rock, and hurled it at me, his face contorted with disgust. He had good aim and a strong arm; although I jerked away, the rock grazed my brow in passing.

"What are you saying to them?" I asked in fierce frustration.

He eyed me sidelong. "God wills this."

God.

God.

God.

Oh, how perishing sick I was of hearing it! *Why?* It nagged at me.

If the answer didn't lie in the distant past, nor the recent past, mayhap it lay in the immediate past. The Vralians and the Tatars appeared to have an alliance of sorts, and it was no secret that the Tatars would gladly invade Ch'in if the opportunity presented itself. I knew Batu's men had been indiscreet regarding my role in resolving the civil war there. Mayhap I was being punished for it; or mayhap the Vralians believed they could use me as a bargaining chip in some way.

"Ilya?" I tapped his shoulder. Although he did not meet my eyes, his head turned in my direction. "Is it because of what I did in Ch'in?"

He didn't answer.

"Is it?" I persisted. "There were tales told, I know. Am I being punished?"

Ilya gave his head a faint shake. "No."

"Is it politics, then?" I asked. "If you imagine the Emperor of Ch'in will move heaven and earth to rescue me, you are mistaken."

Another shake of his head. "God wills this."

I had reached the end of my tether. Ilya was never going to give me a meaningful answer. I was never going to fathom his god's mysterious intent on my own. I couldn't think of any further way to break or compromise the chains that bound me, nor to overpower my captors and escape.

And no one, no one was going to aid me.

We passed through forests of majestic spruce trees and stands of graceful birch. I gazed at them with bittersweet longing, severed from my awareness of their slow, stately thoughts. I wished I were a great magician like Berlik. I wished I could take on the shape of the Great Bear Herself and burst my chains, vanishing into the wilderness where no one would ever find me unless I willed it.

My imprisoned *diadh-anam* flared in agreement.

I wished I knew what had befallen Bao. Despite what the Khan had said, I did not for an instant think that he would rest content among the Tatars with his hot-tempered princess now that the bond between us was broken—or at least blocked.

No, my stubborn magpie had made his choice; and Bao *would* move heaven and earth to rescue me. Of that, I hadn't the slightest doubt.

I suspected in truth the Great Khan didn't, either. That was why he had prepared a tale to send Bao far, far away.

The thought made my heart ache. Gods, it seemed so unfair! Bao and I had only just begun to make sense of our strange fate, sorting out the tangled threads of friendship, love, desire, and magic that bound us together.

I missed him, and this time it was a yearning that owed nothing to magic. Until we were reunited, I hadn't realized how much I simply liked being with him—even when he infuriated me, even when he told me true things about myself no one else saw.

After conceding that at least for the moment, my situation was hopeless, I allowed myself a full day to wallow in self-pity and despair.

I turned the jade bangle on my wrist, thinking of the dragon dreaming on the distant peaks of White Jade Mountain above his reflecting pool, and allowed myself to entertain a fantasy of rescue and revenge in which the dragon flew to my aid and descended from the sky in all his celestial glory, roaring in mighty fury while Ilya and Leonid cowered and begged forgiveness.

It was a pleasant fantasy.

But it was nothing more, and I knew it all too well. If I were not bound, mayhap it would be different. Snow Tiger had said once that no one in Ch'in would raise a hand to me for fear of the dragon's fury. If he had been able to sense my plight, mayhap he would have come to my rescue.

I doubted it, though. For all his celestial might and majesty, the dragon was very much a creature of his place, inextricably linked to his mountain and pool. I did not think his jurisdiction over the skies extended beyond the boundaries of Ch'in.

Anyway, so long as I was constrained by my chains, it didn't matter. After a day of wallowing, I did my best to set aside despair, self-pity, and useless fantasies.

For the first time since I had been taken captive, I willed my thoughts to be quiet and practiced the Five Styles of Breathing, returning to my original plan.

I would wait.

I would be patient. Sooner or later, a chance would come. When it did, I would be ready to seize it.

Such were my thoughts several days later when we emerged from the mountain passes and caught sight of the city of Riva, as I later learned it was called, built along the shores of an inland lake in a sizable valley.

It was the first settlement of any significance that we had encountered, and I knew within the space of a few heartbeats that it was our destination. Almost entirely deprived of conversation, I'd grown skilled at reading more subtle cues. Leonid's chin rose, and he gave the reins a brisk shake. Beside him, Ilya took a deep breath. The cart-horses pricked their ears and leaned into the traces.

"Home?" I murmured in Tatar.

Ilya turned his bearded head a few degrees in my direction. "Yes."

I gazed at the city as we approached. It wasn't large, but it wasn't insubstantial, either. There were farms on the outskirts, using up every bit of arable land in the valley. The city proper was compact, nestled against the shores of the lake.

It had one building of note, larger than the rest. It put me in mind of the palace of the Lady of Marsilikos, where Raphael de Mereliot's sister, who had once reviled me spitefully, held that ancient hereditary title. Like the palace, it sported a gilded dome that shone in the sunlight, a beacon to weary travellers. There was one difference, though. Unlike the palace, this dome ended in a spire, for all the world like a sprouting onion.

Atop the spire, a flared cross gleamed.

Ilya raised his medallion to his lips and kissed it.

I found myself tensing as we descended into the valley and entered the city. Folk going about their business on the narrow streets paused to stare. A few—men, always—called out questions.

Ilya answered in his deep voice.

In response, they shuddered with distaste and gazed at me with fascinated horror. I flinched, waiting for stones that were not thrown.

Not yet, anyway.

The promise was there. I saw it in the way the men clenched their fists, muscles knotting. I saw it in the hot gazes of small boys, ever unwittingly eager for mayhem. I saw it in the way modest Vralian women with scarves wrapped around their heads turned away, averting their eyes, blocking the sight of me with their bodies lest their daughters see.

It scared me.

Stone and sea! What in the world had I ever done that these people, total strangers, should hate and despise me? I thought I'd become accustomed to living with fear, but I was wrong. After the initial rush of terror, I'd come to rely on Ilya and Leonid's reluctant forbearance. This, this was different.

I huddled in my chains, breathing quietly, trying to cling to a sense of calm. It was not easy. I felt helpless and vulnerable, dirty, disheveled, and very, very alone.

When we reached the building with the gilded dome, Leonid reined in the cart-horses. They cocked their haunches, resting in the traces. Ilya dismounted and came around the side of the wagon to help me climb down, touching me as little as possible.

My bare feet struck the cobblestones, my toes curling.

I was scared, so scared.

"Come." Ilya beckoned to me. "Here, it is good."

I went with him, mincing awkwardly in my chains.

Inside the temple, there was a large space for worshippers to gather. There was an altar, and a vast mosaic on the wall behind it, an image of a bearded man I took to be Yeshua ben Yosef. His big eyes were hot and stern, and he held a disc that depicted the earth in the palm of one hand, a flared cross sprouting from it, his other hand raised in a foreboding gesture.

It seemed word of our arrival had already reached the temple. A bearded middle-aged man in embroidered woolen robes stood before the altar. Like Ilya and Leonid, he wore a flared cross medallion on a gold chain. Behind him were three other figures: two women, and a much younger man, taller than the other, his head averted.

"Welcome." The man in the front breathed the word with a startling reverence, addressing me in flawless D'Angeline. "Moirin mac

Fainche of the Maghuin Dhonn, be welcome to this place God has brought you."

I stared at him. "Excuse me?"

He came toward me, smiling. "Do not be afraid. My name is Pyotr Rostov, and I am the Patriarch of Riva. Let me have a look at you, child."

Since I didn't have a choice, I stood my ground as he lifted my chin with gentle fingers, peering at me.

I took his measure, too. He was ruggedly handsome in the Vralian manner, with weather-beaten skin and strong, prominent bones. His hair and long, thick beard were black, his eyes a dark, velvety brown. At the moment, they shone at me with surpassing warmth, so much so that I felt myself relaxing.

"Flawless!" Pyotr Rostov breathed with the same peculiar reverence. Releasing my chin, he lifted his medallion and kissed it, murmuring a prayer in Vralian. "Oh, child! I have been looking for someone like you for so very, very long, but never in my fondest dreams did I imagine God would grant my prayers with such perfection."

"Oh?" I whispered uncertainly.

"Oh, yes." He smiled at me with a father's tenderness. "Look at you! Every abomination of two sinful races combined in one flesh, trailing a history of foul magic and blasphemy—and all of it wrapped in a package of unholy temptation." He kissed his medallion again. "Truly, God is great."

I felt sick. *"Why?"* I asked for the thousandth time, trying not to break down in tears. "What do you and your god want of me?"

This time, I got an answer. The Patriarch of Riva spread his arms. "I am the servant of God and his son Yeshua, and I pray that they work through me." His eyes shone even brighter, taking on a hectic, avid quality. "If I can lead one such as *you* to salvation, surely I can change the world!"

My trapped *diadh-anam* surged in alarm.

I had my answer, and I did not like it. Not one bit.

TWENTY-ONE

W ith unctuous courtesy, the Patriarch of Riva introduced me to his family, my new jailors.

The older of the two women was his wife, Luba, a stern-looking woman with grey eyes and lips thinned with disapproval. The other woman, Valentina, was his sister. Although she was younger than her brother, she had the same velvety brown eyes and worn traces of beauty in her features. Both of them wore scarves wrapped around their heads.

Neither of them cared to meet my eyes, nor did the young man.

He intrigued me.

He hadn't lifted his head once since Ilya escorted me into the temple, keeping his face stubbornly averted. Tawny hair, bronze streaked with lighter gold, fell to curtain his features, reminding me uncomfortably of Raphael de Mereliot.

It wasn't just that, though. When I gazed at him, I felt the unmistakable stirring of Naamah's gift within me, recognizing its presence in another. Without ever looking at me, the young man flushed beneath my gaze, a tide of red blood creeping upward to stain his throat and cheeks.

"Aleksei," the Patriarch said in a somber voice. "She is a test and a trial of your faith as much as mine, and perhaps even more so. It is the only way you can ever redeem your mother's sin."

The young man nodded. "Yes, Uncle." Squaring his broad shoulders, he lifted his head and met my gaze.

I drew in a sharp breath. He was half-D'Angeline, no doubt. The stamp of Terre d'Ange was on his features, that keen, fearful symmetry wedded to the rugged Vralian bones to form a different kind of beauty. His full lips were made for kissing, and his eyes, gods! They were a vivid hue of blue tinged with violet, like rain-washed speedwell blossoms.

At the moment, they gazed at me with a mixture of fascination and morbid fear.

His mother, Valentina, made a choked sound and turned away.

I let out my breath. "Is that what this is really about?" I asked the Patriarch, trying not to let my anger show. "Some D'Angeline laid a cuckoo's egg in your sister's nest, and I must be punished for it?"

"No, child." Pyotr Rostov shook his head. "I spoke the truth. It is about sin and redemption—yours, mine, Aleksei's, Valentina's, and the whole world's. It is about the Rebbe Avraham ben David, and the struggle for the soul of Vralia's faith. It is about the prophecies of Elijah of Antioch...do you know of them?"

"No," I said curtly.

"You will," he said in a calm tone. "Have no fear, Moirin mac Fainche. I will teach you. Through Yeshua's grace, I will guide you to the light of the One True God."

"I would rather you didn't," I muttered.

The Patriarch laid a hand on my shoulder. "Child, you only think that because there are blinders on your eyes. I will remove them and teach you to see. What men call Hell is but the absence of God. When you learn to see, when you accept God's presence in your life, you will understand that you have been suffering needlessly for a very long time."

I jerked away from him, my chains rattling. "Will you remove *these* when I do?" I asked, holding out my shackled wrists.

"I will." He beckoned to Ilya, still loitering discreetly behind us. Ilya came forward, fishing the key from a second chain around his neck, hidden beneath his robes. It was one of the first places I would have looked if I'd ever succeeded in bashing his head in. I wished I had. He handed it over with ceremony. The Patriarch let it dangle from his fist. "On the day that you pledge yourself heart and soul to the One True God and his son Yeshua, I will unlock your chains, Moirin."

"I'll do it now," I offered, reckoning that under the circumstances the Maghuin Dhonn Herself would forgive me the lie.

He gave me a condescending smile. "True faith is hard won. I will know when you have won yours. You have not even made a beginning until you confess the full litany of your sins." He stroked his beard. "I suspect that alone will take a long, long time."

I was silent.

The Patriarch sighed. "There will come a day when you will thank me, but I do not expect you to believe me now. Now..." His nostrils flared. "I do believe you would be well served by a good scrubbing."

With that, I was dismissed.

Luba and Valentina led me away. I glanced over my shoulder to see Aleksei kneeling at his uncle's feet, the Patriarch's hand resting on his head in benediction as he spoke to the young man in hushed tones.

There were living quarters attached to the temple, modest and simply adorned. The bathing chamber was a stark affair—a room with a tin tub filled with water, and a wooden bench with a ball of soap and a wire brush. As I wondered exactly how I was meant to bathe while I was still chained into my clothing, Luba exited and returned with a pair of sharp shears and a grim smile.

It wasn't easy to cut through the thick Tatar wool and felt. She struggled, breathing hard, scoring my skin a number of times as she strove to find an angle that would give her leverage.

The third time it happened, I winced. "It would be a great deal easier if you just took off the chains for one bedamned moment."

She ignored me.

"It's not as though there aren't enough of you to overpower me," I added.

The tip of the shears dug into my spine. She gave a wrenching squeeze, and more thick fabric tore. I sighed.

"Luba does not speak your tongue," Valentina said in a low voice. "You cannot tempt her to folly."

"I was not trying—"

She gave me a sharp look. "Save your lies!"

At least she had looked at me. I breathed slowly and held my tongue, reminding myself to be patient. I needed some ally, any ally. I would not find one in this woman by insulting her intelligence.

It must have taken the better part of an hour for Luba to cut away the last of my filthy clothing. Avoiding my gaze, she gestured for me to climb into the tub. Naked and clanking, I did.

The water was cold, and although I would gladly have done it myself, Luba set about scrubbing me with relentless determination, as though the act were some kind of hateful duty. The lye soap was stinging and caustic, especially on the myriad nicks she had inflicted on my skin and the chafed welts that had begun to rise beneath my shackles. The wire brush was harsh and painful, taking off layers of skin. Unbidden tears came to my eyes.

"It is good to mortify the flesh," Valentina said unexpectedly, an edge to her tone. "The flesh is weak and sinful. Only the spirit is pure."

I sought her gaze. "Is that what you believe?"

She looked away. "You should not be here. My brother is a fool to bring you under his roof."

I raised my hands helplessly. "Steal his key and set me free, and I will go, my lady. I will go so swiftly, it will be as though I were never here."

Her shoulders tensed. "I dare not."

"Are you afraid of him?" I asked softly. "Your brother?"

"Pyotr? No." Valentina fixed me with a hard stare, pointing at me. "I fear you, and all you represent. I am afraid for myself, and I am afraid for my son. I am afraid of God's judgment upon us. But if there is a chance that I am wrong and my brother is right, I will take it. If you are the penance we must endure, I will accept it."

I was confused. "I don't understand."

She gave a short, harsh laugh. "You will in time."

Luba spoke to her in Vralian, words that sounded like a warning; and then the Patriarch's wife put her hand on the back of my neck, dunking my head forcibly beneath the cold water. When at last she allowed me to lift my head, I sputtered for breath. She scoured irritably at my long, tangled hair with the lye soap, then gave up and put out her hand for the shears, which Valentina gave to her.

I felt an unexpected pang. "Oh, please don't—"

The shears closed with a sharp, snicking sound. I felt cool air on the nape of my neck. My wet hair swung forward, chin-length.

"Vanity, vanity, all is vanity!" Valentina said bitterly. "How weak is a woman's spirit? How willing is she to succumb to the temptations of the flesh? How eager to tempt others into sin?"

"I am hardly in a position to tempt anyone," I muttered. "Nor am I to blame for whoever led you into temptation."

She shrugged. "We shall see."

They took no chances with me, no matter how much effort it entailed. Once I was scrubbed and shorn, the two women worked together to pick apart the seams of a coarse woolen dress, then draped it around my chained body and sewed it in place. It was drab, shapeless, and grey, and the unrefined wool itched and chafed against my raw, abraded skin. Valentina wrapped a woolen scarf around my head, tucking the strands of my wet hair beneath it.

"You will learn to cover your head like a decent woman," she said firmly. "Wear this at all times in the presence of men."

"Lest I tempt them with my dazzling beauty?" I asked in a wry tone. Never in my whole life had I felt so thoroughly miserable and unappealing.

Even so, Valentina's mouth tightened. She surveyed me with profound distaste and apprehension. "Yes."

From the bathing chamber, they led me to my cell—another simple, stark room. It contained a bed with a thin pallet and a single blanket, a chamberpot, a straight-backed chair, a wooden stool, a stand with a ewer of water, and a tin cup. There was one high, narrow window, far too narrow for anything larger than a cat to squeeze through.

Luba spoke to Valentina, who nodded and translated. "Here, you will stay. Today and tonight, you will fast and think on your sins. Fasting clears the mind. Tomorrow, the Patriarch will begin your instruction."

I unwound the head-scarf with a yank, shaking my damp, shorn hair loose in a defiant gesture. "Then I'll not need *this* until tomorrow."

"You would be wise to heed my advice and think on your sins." Valentina's gaze was bleak. "As my brother said, the path to salvation begins with confession. And he will demand a very full accounting."

Pity stirred in me. "As he did of you?"

Her gaze slid away. "Think on it."

The women left me, locking the door behind them with a firm click. I tried it anyway and found I couldn't budge it.

I was alone with my sins, whatever they were.

TWENTY-TWO

———◆———

As promised, the Patriarch came on the morrow, bringing with him sheaves of paper filled with writing in yet another unfamiliar alphabet. He smiled at me with unnervingly genuine warmth. "Good morning, Moirin."

I bowed my head, demurely wrapped in the woolen scarf. Left to contemplate my sins, I had taken Valentina's advice to heart, insofar as I had determined to wrestle my fear and anger into submission, and give the semblance of cooperating with Pyotr Rostov to the utmost of my ability. "Good morning, my lord."

He fixed me with a shrewd look, and I warned myself inwardly against overplaying my hand. "I expect you have many questions." He took a seat in the straight-backed chair, indicating the stool with a nod. "Let us see if I might answer some of them before we begin."

I sat obediently, wondering if this was some sort of trick.

The Patriarch saw the uncertainty on my face. "Allow me to speculate," he said gently. "Surely you must wonder how I knew of your existence, your nature, and your history. Is that fair to say?"

I nodded. "Aye, my lord."

He stroked the sheaves of paper in his lap. "Are you aware of the prophecy that Yeshua will return to establish his kingdom in the north?"

I nodded again.

"Very good." He gazed into the distance. "When I was a child,

I believed that Vralia had done everything possible to make ready for his return. Every day, I awaited it; and yet it did not come. As a man, I began to doubt. I sought answers. In my quest, I turned to men of great wisdom and discipline." His expression turned stern. "Are you aware that there was a schism in the Vralian Church of Yeshua?"

I shook my head.

"Yes, indeed." The Patriarch nodded, half to himself. "It came about after the death of Avraham ben David, the Rebbe who counseled the mighty Grand Prince Tadeuz Vral in the aftermath of his historic victory and shepherded the birth of the Church of Yeshua."

It struck a distant chord of memory within me. "Was he the priest who granted sanctuary to Berlik?"

"Exactly so!" His eyes shone, his gaze returning to me. "Berlik of the Maghuin Dhonn, Berlik the Cursed. Is he your ancestor?"

I shrugged. "All of the Maghuin Dhonn are kin in some way. We are a scarce folk."

"So you are," he agreed. "Scarce and secretive."

I was confused. "I don't understand."

Pyotr Rostov lifted a finger. "Patience, child. I am telling you a tale." A deep solemnity returned to his features. "In his last years, when he was old and ailing, Avraham ben David wrote a series of essays, memoirs of his life. One infamous tract centers around his encounter with Berlik the Cursed, and the many discussions they had."

"Oh?" I murmured.

He leaned forward, like a man uttering a confidence. "It is called *Conversations with a Heretic Saint.*"

I still didn't understand.

The Patriarch of Riva leaned back in his chair, obviously feeling he had made his point clear. "*That* is the tract that led to the Great Schism," he said in a satisfied tone. "For all that he was a great man, the Rebbe Avraham ben David faltered in the face of his mortality. The path to God's grace is a straight and narrow one. In his final days, the Rebbe expressed regrets for helping make it so in Vralia."

I blinked. "Because he was kind?"

He raised his voice like thunder. "Because he was weak and fearful!"

I forced myself to breathe slowly and deeply. "Forgive me, my lord. I do not understand why you are angry with this man."

"No." With an effort, he controlled himself. "No, of course not. Suffice it to say that from that day forward, the Church was divided. Tadeuz Vral's heirs embraced a broader path toward the faith. It is only in the far east of Vralia, where greater discipline was necessary to enforce order, that they remember it is not meant to be an *easy* path to tread."

"Why?" I asked honestly.

Pyotr Rostov ignored the question. "Thus began my interest in your mother's folk," he said in a conversational manner. "Your people. Berlik's folk. The bear-witches of the Maghuin Dhonn. I was intrigued by the fact that they had gone so deep into hiding. For three generations...nothing."

"We were not in hiding, exactly," I murmured. "It is the way we live. We are a reclusive folk as well as a scarce one."

"*You're* not," he observed. "But then, you're a half-blood. No matter." He waved the issue away. "I'll come to your father's people in time. You know, there is very, very little written or known about the Maghuin Dhonn. And yet one bear-witch managed to change the entire course of the Vralian Church."

Since I didn't know what to say, I held my tongue.

"For all their conversations, the Rebbe Avraham was never able to persuade Berlik to accept salvation through Yeshua's sacrifice," the Patriarch continued. "That is when it came to me that if I could succeed where he failed, it would restore the Church to its rightful path. I let it be known that I would pay traders or diplomats for any word of the Maghuin Dhonn resurfacing."

I met his gaze. "And they did."

"Not for many long years," he said ruefully. "It was during that time, when my sister succumbed to temptation and fell into sin, that

I turned my attention to Terre d'Ange. Now, about Elua ben Yeshua and the Fallen Ones, much is written. I began reading the lesser-known prophets. Do you recall I spoke of Elijah of Antioch yesterday?"

"Yes."

Rostov's eyes took on a hectic light. "Do you know what apostasy means, Moirin?" I shook my head. "It is the sin of abandoning one's faith in God." He steepled his fingers and touched them to his lips. "It is not uncommon to find scripture that names Cassiel of the Fallen Ones the Apostate whose return to God will bring about the return of Yeshua ben Yosef. Elijah of Antioch believed otherwise. He believed that it is Elua ben Yeshua himself who is the Apostate, that it is the Fallen Ones, and most especially the Great Whore Naamah, who led him astray."

"I see," I said politely.

"No, you don't. Not yet." He smiled at me. "But I am giving you the tools to understand, and in time, you will."

"I am trying, my lord."

The Patriarch shook his head. "You are dissembling in the hope of fooling me. Don't worry, child. God is patient, and so am I. I came to understand that my sister's disgrace was an opportunity in disguise. Like you, my nephew is afflicted by Naamah's curse, but I have taught him that it may be repudiated through prayer and discipline. Once you have accepted salvation, I will do the same for you."

Unable to hide my feelings, I looked away.

"You are angry." He gave me another indulgent smile. "Only consider this, Moirin." He tapped the sheaf of papers on his lap. "Long after I had begun to lose hope that the Maghuin Dhonn would ever resurface, *you* appeared. Not only a witch born to Berlik's folk, but the daughter of a priest of the Great Whore herself. And your deeds!" He fanned the pages. "Fornicating with men and women alike... well, that is no surprise in Terre d'Ange, bastion of depravity as it is. But wreaking false miracles and summoning demons?" He raised his brows. "Surely your presence is a sign that God is testing us to see if we are prepared for his son Yeshua's return."

"There were no false miracles," I said in a low tone. "The gift of healing was Raphael's, not mine."

Pyotr Rostov peered at his notes. "By all accounts, he was a skilled physician, but he credited your magic with allowing him to achieve miraculous cures. But we are getting ahead of ourselves. When you make your full confession, you may tell me how you used your dark arts to tempt him into the sin of hubris. Do you know that word?"

"Yes." I shifted on the stool, my chains rattling. "It is a Hellene word for excessive pride that leads to folly. Cillian taught it to me."

"Cillian…" He glanced at his notes again. I suspected it was just for show, and that he had my entire history memorized. Not for the first time, I cursed the fact that gossip was the life-blood of Terre d'Ange, and precious little I had done in my life was hidden from common knowledge. "Cillian mac Tiernan, son of the Lord of the Dalriada. That's a good place to begin your confession. He is the first man you ensorceled, is he not?"

"I didn't ensorcel him. He was my friend."

"It says here—"

"I don't care what it says!" I sighed. "How did you find me, anyway? The Tatar lands are a long way from Terre d'Ange."

"Indeed." The Patriarch nodded gravely. "I received these reports only last autumn, for they were many months on the road. It was in my thoughts to petition the Duke of Vralsturm to fund an expedition to Terre d'Ange in the spring to seek you out. Instead…" A look of awe settled over his features. "Before winter fell, traders from the east brought rumors of war in Ch'in, and a jade-eyed foreign witch who served the Emperor. I did not think there could be two such in the world. So I had these chains forged over the course of the winter, and come spring, I sent Brother Ilya and Brother Leonid eastward to investigate."

"Yes, I know," I said bitterly.

"Do you not see that it is a sign from God that they found you so swiftly, so near to this place?" he asked with the inexorable logic of his faith. "You were already on a path toward salvation, Moirin. You just didn't know it."

My palms were sweating, and I rubbed them against the prickly woolen fabric of my dress. "Are you so certain you know your God's will? Mayhap I was sent here for some other purpose."

"No." The Patriarch shook his head. "You were not. I am not immune to doubt, but in this, I am certain. There have been other signs that the days of conflict that will accompany Yeshua's return are nigh. I have sensed it ever since the King of Terre d'Ange had the temerity to raise a whore, an unrepentant *whore*, to the royal throne."

I flushed.

He ruffled his notes. "Yes, you knew her intimately, did you not? Take heed from her fate, Moirin mac Fainche, lest God strike you down, too."

A jolt of unexpected horror ran through me, and I found myself staring at him. "What fate?" I raised my voice. *"What fate?"*

"You didn't know." It was a statement, not a question. The Patriarch of Riva met my gaze without flinching. He didn't smile, not exactly, but his lips curled and his face took on a satisfied expression I would come to think of as his creamy look, the one that meant he was reveling in the pain he was about to inflict upon me for my own good.

It came and went in the flicker of an eye, but it was there, and already I dreaded the words that would follow it.

He spoke them. "The D'Angeline whore-queen Jehanne de la Courcel died in childbirth over a year ago."

It hit me like a fist to the belly. I wasn't aware of toppling from the stool, wasn't aware of falling. Only that there was cold stone pressed against my cheek, and I couldn't breathe. I lay curled around my misery and shoved my manacled hands against my stomach, gasping for air, my body punishing itself.

Jehanne! Ah, gods.

All this time.

No.

I wanted to weep, and couldn't. The grief was too vast, too unanticipated. Not Jehanne, my unlikely rescuer, my mercurial Queen.

I dragged a ragged gulp of air into my lungs, expelling it with a low keening sound.

I wanted to believe it was a lie.

I knew it wasn't.

Chair legs scraped. "You are upset," Pyotr Rostov said with regret from somewhere above me. "Forgive me, I should have realized it had been a very long time since you had news from your homeland, Moirin. I will leave you to your grief, and we will resume on the morrow."

He left.

TWENTY-THREE

———◆———

The days that followed were a blur.

I refused to eat, refused to talk, turning my face to the wall of my cell. There was no thought or strategy behind it, only the profound, endless ache of grief.

Jehanne. My lady Jehanne.

All this time...ah, gods! She had been frightened, so frightened. Frightened of impending motherhood, frightened of childbirth. And I had left her anyway, obeying the call of my bedamned destiny.

If I had stayed, I could have saved her. Raphael de Mereliot and I could have saved her.

It was a thought that haunted me, circling back upon me no matter how hard I sought to avoid it. We had done it before, Raphael and I. Together, with my magic channeling his gift for healing, we had saved a young mother bleeding excessively during the act of giving birth.

I wondered if he had been there at the end.

I suspected he had.

King Daniel would have sent for him. It was true, even without my aid Raphael was a skilled physician. In their own ways, they had both loved her, and Jehanne had loved them, too.

And me.

I tortured myself with imagining it. Jehanne, weakening, her exquisite face drained of blood. Raphael, rubbing his healer's hands together to generate warmth, laying them on her, trying in vain to staunch the bleeding. King Daniel hovering over the tableau in anguish, all his solemn poise undone.

And all the while, a thing unsaid lying between them.

If Moirin were here…

Folk came and went. The Patriarch tried to coax me into talking. Valentina and Luba took turns trying to coax me into eating, putting spoonfuls of hot broth to my lips. I ignored them, keeping my mouth stubbornly closed. For a mercy, no one tried to force me.

I ached at the unfairness of it. Even if I'd known what would happen, I couldn't have chosen otherwise. How many more would have died in the war in Ch'in if I hadn't been able to help free the dragon? Thousands, likely.

Or mayhap there would have been no war; mayhap Emperor Zhu would have surrendered, believing he had lost the Mandate of Heaven. Master Lo and Bao would have failed in their mission. My lovely princess Snow Tiger would have been put to death, and the dragon's splendid spirit would have died with her, ceasing to exist forevermore.

Black Sleeve and Lord Jiang would have been free to loose the dreadful weapons of the Divine Thunder on the world, and the world would have become a far more terrible place. I couldn't weigh Jehanne's life against such a fate.

But oh, gods! It hurt.

If it hadn't been for Aleksei, I don't know how long I would have kept my fast. It wasn't that I sought death, at least not consciously. But I hadn't much will to live, either. Everything I loved had been taken from me. This last blow was simply more than I could bear.

Every day, Aleksei came and read to me from the Yeshuite scriptures, beginning with the tale of the world's creation, and Edom the First Man and his wife, the All-Mother, Yeva. At first I ignored him, too, sitting huddled on the hard stone floor of my cell with my manacled arms wrapped around my knees and my face turned toward the wall.

He persisted, hunkering on the wooden stool that he might be closer to my level, reading in a pleasant, melodious voice.

I could ignore him, and I could let the words he spoke wash over me, but I couldn't ignore the presence of Naamah's gift in the room between us. Every time his voice faltered, I felt it.

In those brief moments of silence, I felt his gaze on me.

And I felt Naamah's gift respond within me. It was not desire on my part, not even close. My grief ran too deep. I hadn't even begun to cope with the shock and pain of being torn away from Bao's side so unexpectedly, so soon after being reunited with my stubborn peasant-boy and the missing half of my soul, before being struck with the news of Jehanne's death.

But it was a response to his desire, an instinctive urge toward life as simple and natural as a plant yearning toward the sun.

On the third day, or mayhap the fourth, Aleksei's voice faltered, and he let the silence stretch.

When it didn't break, I shifted, turning away from the wall to meet his gaze.

He flushed, and I saw his throat work as he swallowed hard. "Your queen...the babe was a girl. I thought you would want to know."

Grief caught in my chest. "Is she alive and well?" I whispered. "Jehanne's daughter?"

Aleksei nodded and looked away from me, fidgeting with the leather-bound book in his hands. "Before...before she died, the queen asked that the babe be called Desirée, so she would always know she was loved and wanted."

Something within me broke, and for the first time since I'd heard the news, I wept in great, racking sobs—a storm of sorrow, my head bowed against my knees, tears soaking the coarse wool of my dress. Ah, gods! Everything I had told Jehanne was true. She *had* been a great deal kinder, wiser, and more gracious than she pretended, and for all her fears, she *would* have been a good mother.

Even in dying, Jehanne had found a way to let her daughter know she was loved.

Aleksei waited awkwardly for my sobs to subside. It was a long while before I got myself under control, rubbing my tear-stained face.

"Thank you," I said to him. "It was kind of you to tell me."

He looked away, looked back at me. "I wish you would relent. My uncle feels terrible about telling you thusly." His color rose again, his fearful gaze skidding away. "He did not know you cared for her so."

I leaned back against the wall, resting my head on the cool stone. I felt tired and hollow, and weak with hunger. "That's not true."

His blue-violet eyes widened. "Of course it is!"

"No." I moved my head from side to side. "I saw his face, Aleksei. He heard the fear in my voice when I begged him to tell me what he meant by Jehanne's fate. He knew. He relished the pain it would inflict."

His flush deepened with anger, his voice dropping to a lower register. "You seek to sow doubt. I do not believe it."

I shrugged wearily. "Believe what you like."

Aleksei closed his eyes, his lips moving in a silent prayer. When he opened those glorious blue eyes again, they were luminous with the inner light of his faith. "I will not be swayed," he said in a firm tone. "You were sent to us as a test and a trial, and I will not fail. God loves you, Moirin, and his son Yeshua gave his life that you might know it. I am trying; we are all trying. Do you but open your heart and listen, and you will hear the call to salvation."

I studied him, studied the rugged planes of his young face, graced with that unmistakable D'Angeline symmetry. I tried to guess his age. Sixteen, mayhap; seventeen at most.

A year younger than me? Two years? Or mayhap three? Gods, I wasn't even sure how old I was anymore.

He had only just begun to grow into the newfound strength of his adult frame—broad-shouldered and rangy, with long, loose limbs and oversized feet and hands. I remembered Cillian at that age.

And I remembered Jehanne at Cereus House, where she had first seduced me as a ploy in her ongoing game with Raphael de Mereliot, her fair skin flawless in the sunlight, her blue-grey eyes sparkling like stars as she caressed my face, uttering one of desire's truths. *Do you know how long it's been since I let myself indulge in the headlong rush of youth's untutored passion?*

No.

She had kissed my lips, a kiss as sweet as a promise. *Far, far too long, my gorgeous young savage.*

And I had succumbed to her charms—oh so gladly!

The memory hurt. Neither of us could have guessed that that moment would lead us into a far more significant and complicated bond, one that I would never, ever regret. I had loved Jehanne, and I had loved her well. I took a deep breath, steeling myself against the pain, and contemplated young Aleksei, a tightly wound knot of desire and denial, sitting hunched on my wooden stool.

He was filled with youth's untutored passion, taught to consider it a curse. Perhaps Naamah had some purpose for me here after all. One thing was sure; I was in desperate need of an ally.

I loosed my breath. "Read to me," I said gently to him. "I will listen, I promise."

Aleksei bowed his head and read to me, his tawny-gold hair falling about his face.

I listened, and began to plot.

TWENTY-FOUR

Seducing Aleksei might well prove to be my best chance at finding an ally to help me escape, but if I had any illusions about how difficult it would be, they were shattered the following day when his uncle the Patriarch returned to bear witness to my confession.

"Can it not wait a bit longer?" I asked him. The prospect of laying my life bare for him repulsed me. "Aleksei's reading is very instructive, but I am only just beginning to learn to understand what God wants of me."

"No, child." Pyotr Rostov gave me a compassionate look. "Let me put it to you in a way you might understand. You have studied the healing arts, have you not?"

"A little." I knew enough to assist Raphael, and later Master Lo, though not enough to consider myself skilled.

He steepled his fingers, which meant he was in a lecturing mood. "Suppose you had a patient suffering from festering boils. Is it more important to lance the boils, or to serve the patient a nourishing broth?"

"To lance the boils," I murmured.

"Even so." The Patriarch nodded. "You are that patient, Moirin. The scripture that Aleksei reads to you is a fine, nourishing broth. But your unconfessed sins are boils festering on your soul. Left untouched, they will poison your soul, heart, and mind. Confession is the needle that will burst them, and repentance will heal the abscesses. Do you understand?"

I nodded reluctantly. I didn't like it, and I didn't agree with it, but I understood his meaning.

"Very good." He had a portable writing desk on his lap. Now he dipped a quill pen in the inkpot. "I will record your confession. I do not expect to succeed all at once. It may be that some boils are more stubborn than others, and must be lanced many times before they are fully drained. This document will be helpful, and I hope my notes will prove useful over the course of history."

"I'm so very pleased." I could not keep the bitterness from my tone. "All that was missing in my life was a written catalogue of my every folly."

The Patriarch's expression turned stern. "We are not speaking of mere *folly*, child. We are speaking of beast-worship, witchcraft, unholy fornication, demon-summoning, and blasphemy. These are things that are abominations in the eyes of God."

"Why?" I asked.

He blinked, startled. "Have you not been listening to the scripture Aleksei reads to you? Did you not just say you were beginning to gain understanding of God's will?"

"What he wills, aye, but not *why* he wills it," I said honestly. "Not always, anyway. Obviously, it is a very bad and foolish idea to summon fallen spirits, and if God wishes to call it a sin, I will not argue. I wish—" It was on the tip of my tongue to say I wished I had never taken part in it, but then I remembered the gift that the spirit Marbas had given me, the charm to reveal hidden things. Had it not been for Marbas' gift, the dragon's spirit would have remained trapped in the princess' mortal being.

Rostov was still staring at me with incomprehension. "Yes? You wish what?"

I took a different tack. "For greater understanding. Why does it matter who I bed, so long as we are both consenting?"

"Naamah's curse has a strong hold on you indeed," he murmured. "But do not despair, Moirin. No one comes to understanding without guidance. It is my role to help you understand the word of God and his son Yeshua."

I waited.

"Our goal in life is to join with God in a perfect spiritual union," he said patiently. "That is pure joy, and pure love. Anything that distracts from this goal is a trap, and the pleasures of the flesh is one of the greatest traps in existence. God allows us the sacrament of marriage that we might obey his command to be fruitful and multiply. To abuse the flesh in pursuit of carnal pleasure is an abomination to him, for it causes us to stray far, far from our true goal. Do you understand?"

"Yes, I think so." Again, I didn't agree, but at least the logic was clearer to me. "Thank you, my lord."

The Patriarch rewetted his pen in the inkwell. "Let us set aside matters of the flesh for the moment," he said in a judicious manner. "Let us begin at the very beginning. Is it true that the Maghuin Dhonn worship a *bear*?"

I did my best to answer his questions honestly, reckoning I had nothing to lose; and too, I was wary of his perceptive shrewdness. He could track a lie like a hound on the scent. The truth was a greater struggle for him.

It had always been difficult to explain the existence of a *diadh-anam* to folk who had none, and the Patriarch of Riva was no exception. And I had no words to describe the Maghuin Dhonn Herself.

The irony of it was that when he spoke of a perfect union with his God, of pure joy and pure love, I knew what he meant. Beyond the stone doorway, when the Maghuin Dhonn Herself had come to me, I had felt it. Half-blood though I may be, with my patron D'Angeline gods attendant on my life, She had claimed me as Her child, then and always. She had laid a grave destiny on me, but She had claimed me.

It had been a moment of perfect bliss, and if it had gone on forever and ever, I would have been content.

But I could not convey it—not the joy, not the immense, overwhelming nature of Her presence. Not the way the earth had trembled beneath Her tread, not the awe and humility I had felt as She dwindled willingly and shaped Herself to a mortal scale. Surely, surely, not the profound depth of sorrow and compassion in Her eyes.

No, to everyone but my people, She was a bear, only a bear.

Eventually, he gave up on that line of questioning, turning instead toward magic. "When did you begin to practice witchcraft?"

I shrugged, already weary of explaining myself. "My mother taught me to summon the twilight when I was some five years of age."

Pyotr Rostov's pen hovered over the page. "Summon the twilight?"

"Aye."

His eyes took on a gleam. "What is it? How is it done?"

I told him, but he didn't like that truth, either. It was too simple, too elemental. He did not want a gentle magic that came as naturally as breathing. He wanted charms, incantations, dire rites filled with chanting and blood sacrifices. It did not satisfy him when I said it was a small gift, meant to protect and conceal us. That in Alba I had only ever used it to hide, to catch fish with my bare hands, and to coax plants to grow.

"Is that a sin?" I asked.

The Patriarch set down his pen and pinched the bridge of his nose as though to alleviate the pressure of an aching head. "Plants."

"Aye, plants."

He sighed. "I do not believe it is addressed in the scripture. But this gift, how did you describe it? Taking a half-step into the spirit world?" I nodded. "In Terre d'Ange, you found other purposes for it."

I looked away. "It is more as though they found me. Is that what you wish to speak of next, my lord?"

"No." He took up the pen with grim determination. "Let us proceed in the proper order. I believe we have come to Cillian mac Tiernan, and the sins of the flesh."

So we had.

On the point of having ensorceled Cillian, I resisted stubbornly. It was a false accusation, and one that still pained me, inextricably linked as it was to the sorrow of his death. At length, the Patriarch relented, although only on that single point.

"But you *did* fornicate with him out of wedlock?" he persisted.

"Yes," I murmured.

His pen hovered. "How many times?"

I shook my head slowly. How many times? I hadn't counted. Cillian had come to me whenever he could. In the spring and summer, we had lain together in the Alban meadows, flowers and plumy grasses springing around us. I'd come to know his body as well as my own, reveling the feel of him between my thighs, his strong, young phallus plowing my depths. Afterward, I had counted the freckles on his fair skin, his long, muscled limbs tangled with mine. Once, I had coaxed a dragonfly with translucent wings to land on my fingertip, and he had marveled at it, asking if it was magic. Only the ordinary, everyday kind, I had told him.

Was that sin?

In hindsight, it seemed a profoundly innocent time.

The Patriarch dipped his pen, tapped it impatiently against the inkwell. "How many times?"

"I don't know," I said. "Many."

"And then he died."

"Yes." I closed my eyes, tears leaking from beneath my lids. Since the news of Jehanne's death, my grief was still very, very close to the surface. "Cillian died in a cattle-raid."

"Because of you?"

"No." I rubbed my face. "Yes. I don't know. It was foolish and unnecessary. He shouldn't have gone. Cillian was a scholar, not a warrior. But he felt he had somewhat to prove."

"To you?"

"To me, to his father, to the Dalriada. I don't know. I don't know." The tears wouldn't stop coming. "If I had loved him better, if I had agreed to wed him, mayhap he would not have gone."

I bowed my head against my knees, and wept.

There was a rustling sound as the Patriarch gathered his accounting, and then the scraping sound of chair legs as he stood. "Now you begin to see, Moirin," he said in a gentle tone. "Had you engaged in the holy sacrament of marriage, matters would have fallen out differently. Your sorrow stems from failing to obey God's will." He laid one hand on my shaking shoulder. "It is a good beginning. Tomorrow, we will continue."

He left me alone, locking the door behind him. After my tears had run their course, I rose and splashed cool water from the ewer on my face.

It didn't feel like a good beginning to me. I felt hot, flushed, confused, and miserable. I'd always felt a powerful measure of guilt for Cillian's death. At the same time, I knew in my heart of hearts that I could never have been the faithful wife he wanted me to be. It would only have led to a different kind of sorrow and acrimony.

Now...

Somehow, the confession the Patriarch had dragged from me had soiled every aspect of my relationship with Cillian. Was our lovemaking a sin? I didn't believe it, didn't want to believe it.

And yet the mere act of confessing it made it seem so. My memories had been violated—and it was only the beginning.

With beliefs so deeply ingrained, seducing Aleksei was going to be very, very difficult indeed.

Still, I meant to try.

TWENTY-FIVE

In Terre d'Ange, seduction is reckoned an art and a sport alike, and yet I'd never had cause to practice it, not really.

When I arrived in the City of Elua, I fell straightaway into Raphael de Mereliot's schemes—quite literally, from the moment his carriage struck me down unwittingly in the street and he found the signet ring around my neck identifying me as a descendant of House Courcel.

And from the moment Raphael made me a pawn in his complicated game with Jehanne, I became a target, a prize to be claimed.

I'd known it when I let Jehanne seduce me.

I'd known it when Prince Thierry courted me, and I bedded him in a moment of loneliness.

I'd been prey, not a hunter, albeit rather willing prey. Now that would have to change, and I would have to play a very subtle game with my oh so skittish prey.

Well and so, I knew how to hunt. Unlike D'Angelines, I had never practiced it as a sport. It was a means of survival.

So was this. And as Batu had said, survival was the best reason of all.

Any overt move on my part would send Aleksei fleeing, of that I was sure. I could sense it in the nervous tension in his body when he was alone in my cell with me, in the way his voice broke and faltered as he read to me, in the way he avoided my gaze. But a good hunter observes his prey, and a very good hunter makes the prey come to him. For now, I was content to wait and observe Aleksei.

I sat demurely on my stool and listened to him read, keeping my expression open and earnest. I learned to look away when he faltered, for those were the times when he allowed himself to steal glances at me.

In Terre d'Ange, one of the Thirteen Houses of the Night Court is dedicated to modesty—Alyssum House, whose motto is *With eyes averted*. When first I heard of it, I hadn't understood the allure. Jehanne had explained to me that there were two kinds of patrons drawn to modesty. The first kind simply reveled in the delicious sense of wickedness involved in coaxing a modest adept to a state of wanton abandonment.

The second, more sensitive kind was moved by the tender sense of protectiveness modesty aroused in them.

Young Aleksei was surely the latter.

So I played at being modest, feeling him relax a measure in my presence. When he finished his reading for the day, I thanked him for it.

"You're welcome." He gave me a shy smile. "Did you enjoy it?"

It had been a long, repetitive tale about the plight of the Habiru folk in the land of Menekhet in which their prophet Moishe dueled with the Pharaoh's magicians. I felt very sorry for the Habiru, enslaved in a foreign land and forced to labor, but I also felt sorry for the ordinary folk of Menekhet, forced to endure rivers of blood, plagues of flies and frogs, boils, hailstorms and locusts, darkness that lasted three days, and the death of their firstborn children, all because the ridiculously stubborn Pharaoh wouldn't grant the Habiru their freedom. It seemed to me that God was cruel to punish a whole nation of common folk for the whim of one stubborn man.

And I couldn't understand for the life of me why it was acceptable for this fellow Moishe to call down darkness across the entire land, while it was a sin for me to summon the gentle twilight. But I had a sense it would be better not to ask.

"It was very interesting," I said politely. "When do we begin to learn about Yeshua ben Yosef?"

"Not for a long while," Aleksei admitted. "The history of the Habiru is a lengthy one. Perhaps...perhaps Uncle would consent to allow me to read to you from the gospels that tell Yeshua's tale."

"I would like that, I think." I averted my eyes, smoothing the prickly grey wool of my dress over my knees. "Among my people, it is said that Berlik, who came here many years ago, said that if there were any god he might call a friend, it was Yeshua ben Yosef."

Aleksei drew in a sharp breath. "Berlik the Cursed?"

I nodded.

He was silent for a moment. "You should not take him for your example. I have read about him."

I glanced up in surprise. "You read Rebbe Avraham's memoir?"

Aleksei colored. "*Conversations with a Heretic Saint*, yes. My mother..." He looked away. "A year ago I came across a copy in her things, hidden beneath a false binding. I began reading before I knew what it was. I found it...dangerous."

The soft tone of his voice said otherwise, said he had found beauty in it. I kept my mouth shut on that observation, watching him.

He looked back at me, his brow furrowed with worry. "I shouldn't have said anything. Don't tell my uncle, please? He doesn't know she has it. It's a small thing, but it gives her comfort, and I cannot find it in my heart to begrudge her."

"I won't," I promised.

"Thank you." The worry lines eased from his face. "I will ask Uncle about reading from the gospels." He essayed another shy smile. "He said your confession yesterday went well. He is pleased with your progress."

I bit my tongue on a number of scathing responses, lowering my gaze modestly once more. "I am pleased to hear it."

Now that, I thought, was an auspicious beginning more to my liking. We shared a secret, Aleksei and I.

Trust was a beginning. The rest would come.

Far less to my liking was my second confessional session with the

Patriarch. As before, he came laden with notes and his portable desk, balancing it on his knees, dipping his pen in the inkwell and preparing to exhume every last private detail of my life, sullying each and every one in the process.

"Well, Moirin." His creamy look came and went, quick as the flick of a cat's tail. "Let us turn our attention to Terre d'Ange."

I sighed. "Where do you want to start?"

He shook a few drops of ink from the quill and poised it over the paper. "Raphael de Mereliot."

If I had a sin to confess, surely it was Raphael, and I knew it full well. I had let him use me. I'd committed follies I regretted, the worst of which was helping the Circle of Shalomon to summon Focalor.

Even so, it hadn't been *all* bad. There had been moments of brightness here and there, moments when I felt Raphael genuinely cared for me and desired me. The first time he kissed me and I felt his healer's gift entwine with my own magic in a way I hadn't known was possible... it had been glorious. We had saved lives together, Raphael and I, and even though the process proved too dangerous for me to continue, I had been proud of what we had done. He had introduced me to Master Lo Feng, for which I was grateful.

The act of confession tainted it all. Pyotr Rostov was merciless in his inquiry, already knowing many of the answers, but not content until I confessed them aloud.

Yes, I had engaged in fornication with Raphael de Mereliot. How many times? I don't know, mayhap a dozen times.

Yes, I had used my magic to help him heal others; and no, I did not understand why that was a bad thing, except insofar as it was an unnatural use of my gift that nearly killed me.

"Life and death are God's to command, Moirin," the Patriarch said sternly. "You have meddled in affairs beyond the mortal ken, and nothing good can come of it." His velvet-brown eyes darkened ominously. "We will speak more of this later."

Yes, I had helped Raphael and the Circle of Shalomon summon fallen spirits, and yes, I had consorted with these spirits.

No, I had not fornicated with them. Yes, I was sure.

"They spoke to me!" I said in frustration. "What was I to do? Stop my ears?"

"Better you should thrust bodkins in your ears than listen to the beguilings of demons," he said grimly. "Did they tempt you?"

"No—" I remembered Marbas.

Rostov was quick to seize on the slightest hesitation, the slightest opening. "Aha! What did they offer you?"

I met his gaze. "The gift of shape-shifting, the gift the Maghuin Dhonn Herself withdrew from us. I refused it."

He studied my face, looking for the lie, then gave a slight, genuine smile when he did not find it. "Well done, child."

Gods help me, I found myself grateful for his praise.

The summoning of spirits was a matter of great interest to the Patriarch of Riva, and he went back and forth over it, demanding that I relate each incident in ever-increasing detail. I obliged, talking myself hoarse while his pen hovered and scratched over the paper, recording my every word.

He didn't know about the gift Marbas *had* given me, the charm to reveal hidden things. I did not offer it. If there were any small secrets he was unable to exhume, I meant to keep them to myself.

Thus far, it was Marbas' gift, and the fact that I had bedded a coach-driver.

It wasn't much comfort.

"My lord?" I inquired when he paused to dip his pen. I raised my hands, chains dangling from my wrists. "It seems to me that these chains are very like the silver chain with which we attempted to bind Focalor, only they were wrought without flaws. Tell me, how is this *not* witchcraft?"

The Patriarch frowned. "Because it is done in the service of God's will and with the intention of saving your immortal soul. It is not even remotely the same."

"No?" I let my hands fall into my lap, chains rattling.

"No." He didn't like that question, I could tell. He began to gather up his things brusquely. "That is enough for today. We will resume your confession on the morrow." He hesitated, taking on a more compassionate tone. "What we must discuss will be difficult for you. But it is necessary, I assure you."

My chest tightened, and I looked away. "You mean to make me speak of Jehanne."

"I know it seems cruel," he said gently. "But you must make your confession in full, Moirin."

I couldn't bear the thought of it, knowing the covert pleasure he'd taken in telling me of her death, and that grief yet raw. "And if I don't?"

"God is patient, and so am I," Pyotr Rostov said. "I am prepared to wait a long time. And yet I am only mortal. If, in the end, you prove intractable..." He gave a sad, weary shrug. "If you do not repent, you will be stoned to death for your sins."

I stared at him, wide-eyed.

"I fear that is the punishment God demands," he said to me. "I do not wish to administer it, but I will. Think on it."

TWENTY-SIX

Aleksei began reading Yeshua's tale to me.

It was clear he took pleasure in it. I did my best to appear to listen attentively, all the while scheming ways to engage him. With the Patriarch's threat hanging over my head, it had become more urgent than ever.

All I had to guide me was Naamah's gift and my own instincts. I developed a finely honed sense of Aleksei's reactions, and the response of Naamah's gift within him.

So long as I looked away from him, he could not resist stealing glances at me. Swaddled in a shapeless woolen dress and draped in chains, a long scarf wrapped around my cropped hair, I hardly felt at my most alluring.

Still, he was a young man with a young man's appetites surging beneath his efforts to suppress them, and I found ways to tempt him. If I angled my body just so and clasped my hands in my lap in a demure pose, the chains that ran from the collar around my neck to the cuffs at my wrists pressed the fabric against my skin, showing the shape of my breasts beneath the prickly wool.

When I smoothed the fabric over my knees in another seemingly absentminded gesture, it pulled it taut for a moment, revealing the line of my thigh; and when I tilted my head a certain way, the trailing end of the woolen scarf fell away to bare my throat.

Such small enticements! And yet, to a starving man, they held all the promise of an extravagant banquet.

Once again, I thanked him for the day's reading. "I look forward to hearing more," I added. "Especially the love story."

Aleksei looked confused. "What love story?"

"The love between Yeshua ben Yosef and Mary of Magdala," I said. "Surely that is one of the best parts."

"Ah...no." He flushed, fidgeting with the book. "No, it is not reckoned so in the Church of Yeshua Ascendant."

"Oh." I was disappointed.

He gave me a yearning look. "Mary of Magdala took the blood that Yeshua spilled on the cross and used it to a corrupt end. God only allowed it that even Elua might learn to resist temptation in the end. Moirin, you must set aside the false beliefs you were taught in Terre d'Ange."

I shook my head. "There is no sin in love, Aleksei, nor in honest desire."

"Please do not say such things!" His face looked pale and pinched.

"Why?" I asked softly. "Because they are dangerous truths you fear to hear? Or because your uncle will have me stoned to death for saying them?"

Aleksei scrambled to his feet, once more avoiding my gaze, clutching the book before him as though it were a talisman to ward me off. "It's best that I go."

Still, he hesitated. I rose from my stool, crossing the space between us. Although it was difficult to move gracefully in shackles, I had been practicing. "Aleksei, I am trying," I said in a low tone. "But I am as the gods have made me. Naamah's gift is real. I have felt her blessing, and there is only grace and beauty in it. It is no curse, and I do not know if I can repent of it in earnest."

He was trembling, and I was standing close enough that I could feel the heat coming off him in waves. "I should go," he repeated.

I touched his cheek—oh so lightly. His pupils dilated, and the pulse in the hollow of his strong young throat beat hard and fast. "You feel it, too. I know you do."

If I pressed him any harder, I would lose him. I made myself turn away, bowing my head. Aleksei's breathing was ragged in the small cell.

"Moirin . . ." He whispered my name.

Whatever else he meant to say, he fell silent at the sound of a key turning in the lock. Valentina opened the door and entered the chamber, bringing a tray with my mid-day meal. Mother and son exchanged a long glance, and then Aleksei left, stumbling and banging his shoulder against the door-frame in his haste.

I sighed.

"I know what you're about with my son." Valentina set the tray down on the little table, hard enough to make it rattle. Her voice was grim. "God help me, I don't know if I'm praying for you to succeed or fail."

I extended my arms toward her in supplication, dangling my chains. "Believe what you will, my lady. My offer stands. Purloin the key, and I will go and take any dilemma I may pose from you."

Her mouth hardened. "Would you take him with you?"

"Aleksei?"

"Who else?"

"Yes," I murmured. "If he wished to go, yes, of course. Your son was not meant to live this way."

"Would you love him?" Valentina appraised me with a mother's shrewdness.

I found myself unable to lie to her. For all I knew, I could come to love him. As Bao had observed, I had a tendency to give my heart away quickly. But at the moment, Aleksei was but a means to an end; and no matter what else transpired, it was Bao who held the missing half of my soul.

So I stayed silent.

"As I thought," Valentina said bitterly. "You do but ply him with a whore's cheap wiles."

I sank onto my narrow bed, unwinding my head-scarf and shaking my shorn hair loose, weary of playing games. "Forbid him my company if you fear for him so."

Her voice dropped. "I dare not."

"Why?" I glanced at her. "God's judgment?"

She looked away from me. "It is a test and a trial. Aleksei's, not mine. I should not even speak to you."

"Do you fear I'll seek to seduce you instead?" I asked wryly, giving my chains an enticing jangle. "I'm willing to try, but I'm not at my best."

Valentina shook her head. "Even if I were inclined to such depravity, do you think I would not know it for a lie, old and haggard as I have grown?" Unexpectedly, her voice cracked. "Do not mock me."

"I'm not mocking you." There were tears on her cheeks and the pain in her voice tugged at my heart, making me relent. "I'm sorry, my lady. I'm alone, scared, and desperate." I paused, addressing her in a more gentle tone. "Who was he? Did he break your heart?"

She didn't pretend not to understand. "Aleksei's father?"

I nodded.

"Just a man." Valentina dabbed at her eyes. "He was a young D'Angeline diplomat in Vralgrad. I was a young bride wed to an elderly groom, a match meant to bring prestige to the Rostov family."

"This man tempted you?"

Her shoulders rose and fell. "I let it happen. I wanted it to happen, wanted *him*. All that youth and unholy beauty. Aleksei's father told me no lies, made me no false promises. Nonetheless, I fell in love and broke my heart against him."

"Men can be careless," I murmured, thinking of Raphael de Mereliot, thinking of Bao and his Tatar princess.

"Yes, they can." We regarded each other.

"Give my brother whatever he wants," Valentina said softly. "He is not given to making idle threats. I don't know how much time you have."

"Will you not help me?" I asked. "Please?"

She shook her head from side to side, slow and deliberate. "I am sure of nothing. I have made mistakes. Forgive me, Moirin. God has decreed your person a battleground. I dare not intervene."

"My lady Valentina!" I called after her as she made for the door. She paused, raising her brows in inquiry. I smiled at her, a genuine smile. Even though she had refused me, I could not help but pity her. "Not so very old, nor so careworn that I do not see the beauty your young D'Angeline diplomat saw in you. Careless or no, he must have accounted himself a fortunate fellow."

Tears shone in her velvet-brown eyes, and she gave a harsh laugh. "I'd rather you weren't kind."

I shrugged. "That is your burden to bear."

That afternoon, the Patriarch of Riva returned to hear my continuing confession.

I dreaded it.

I didn't want to speak of Jehanne to him. Against all odds, it had become one of the purest and best things in my life.

He would taint it, of that I was sure.

He settled into the straight-backed chair, settling his portable writing desk on his lap. His dark eyes gleamed at me, his pen hovering over the virgin pages.

"So," he began in a conversational manner. "Tell me of the whore-queen, Jehanne de la Courcel."

I held back only what I dared. The Patriarch did not know how early in our acquaintance Jehanne had seduced me—no one did, save the Dowayne of Cereus House. He knew what the rest of the world knew, that Jehanne had stolen me away from Raphael de Mereliot at a dinner party.

"You became her..." He glanced at his notes. "Royal companion? Tell me of this practice."

"It was a jest of sorts at first between us," I said candidly. "I was all wrong for it. A royal companion is meant to be someone older and wiser. Skilled in Naamah's arts, aye, but willing to offer loyalty above all else."

He studied me. "And you come from a long line of these... royal companions, is that not true?"

"Yes." My palms were itching and sweating. "The tradition began with my great-great-grandmother, who served as royal companion to the Dauphine Sidonie. My father served as royal companion to the Duc de Barthelme."

"Fascinating," the Patriarch murmured. "Is a royal companion always of the same sex as his master or her mistress?"

"As far as I know, yes."

He stroked his beard. "Very cunning. So Naamah's Order seeks to corrupt and debauch the flower of D'Angeline nobility from a youthful age, enticing them into unnatural perversions."

"No." I rubbed my palms on my dress. "It is only because a royal companion is meant to be a friend, and it is easier to forge a friendship with someone of the same sex, especially at a young age. Men and women take different paths to adulthood."

Pyotr Rostov scowled. "It is a pretty argument to hide an ugly, sordid truth."

I shook my head, unwilling to relent. "My lord, I have not lied to you. Loyalty is the most important aspect—the ability to give them one person they can trust without fear, one friend who will keep all their confidences. That is the one gift I had to offer Jehanne, and the one gift she accepted from me."

He wetted his pen, tapping it on the edge of the inkwell. "But it was part of your job to service the queen in a sexual manner, was it not?"

Give my brother whatever he wants.

He would not listen; he would never listen. These Yeshuites accused me of closing my ears to God, but at least I was trying to understand what they wanted and why. The Patriarch of Riva would never hear aught but what he wanted to believe from my lips. To *service*, gods! As though anyone in their right mind wouldn't rejoice at the chance to share Jehanne de la Courcel's bed, as though anyone could consider it a *job*, and not an honor and a privilege. It was an ugly, sordid term to describe something lovely.

"Yes," I said wearily, leaning back on my stool and resting my scarf-wrapped head against the wall. "It was part of my job."

The Patriarch's pen skated avidly across the page. "How?"

"What do you mean?"

He gestured impatiently at me. "These are sins against nature, child. You must confess them in full. What acts did you commit?" He lowered his voice. "I have heard that D'Angelines sculpt vile semblances of a man's generative organ through art and artifice. Did you play the man's role with her? Or did you take turns at it?"

I closed my eyes, remembering Jehanne in Cereus House, showing me the ivory *aide d'amour*, cradling it in her palm and promising with a wickedly sweet smile to demonstrate all its uses to me. It had been one of the only times. "Not usually, no."

"Did you perform unclean acts on her?"

"Unclean acts?" I opened my eyes.

The hectic sheen had returned to his gaze. "Did you pleasure her with your mouth?"

"Oh." It wasn't a topic that had arisen before. I wondered if it was because the act of the *languisement* was less unclean when performed on a man, or if the confession of fornication had sufficed, or if the Patriarch had been saving the accusation for the moment when it would hurt me the most, knowing my grief was still fresh. All three, mayhap. "That, yes."

He muttered to himself in Vralian, recording my confession. "How many times?"

"Many. But it is not listed among the things that God finds an abomination, my lord," I observed. "Why is it reckoned unclean?"

His head jerked up, outrage written on his features. "Need you ask?"

I shrugged. "Apparently so."

Pyotr Rostov's face darkened, and he leaned forward in his chair.

"God gave you lips and a tongue that you might give praise to him, Moirin. Not that you might pollute them by placing them where the body's foulest excrescences emerge. It should be obvious. Is it so hard to understand?"

I flinched away from him, my chains rattling.

Give my brother whatever he wants.

I couldn't, not this. "You speak of the very font and wellspring of life, my lord," I whispered, tears stinging my eyes. "And no, I do not understand."

My memories blurred.

There was my lady Jehanne, lying indolent and languid in the bower she'd had created for me, her arms stretched above her head, her thighs parted so I could kneel between them, her pink nether-lips already glistening with desire. She had smiled at me, her eyes sparkling with unremitting delight, the overhanging ferns painting intricate green shadows on her oh so fair skin. And Checheg, grunting and straining in the *ger* in the throes of labor, the babe Bayar's head crowning, tearing delicate flesh. It was all part and parcel of the same thing.

My voice shook. "How is that not a sacred thing to worship?"

The Patriarch did not answer, not right away. He sat very still, gazing at me with fixed intensity, until I had to look away. "It is not your fault that you were born into sin, Moirin," he said at length. "But your actions are your own. If you cannot learn to acknowledge them for what they are, I cannot help you."

"I am *trying*!" I said in frustration.

"Not hard enough." He took his line of questioning in a different direction. "Let us move forward in time. You spent a great deal of time travelling with the Emperor of Ch'in's daughter. Did you serve as a royal companion to her?"

It caught me unaware, and I felt the breath go out of me. Pyotr Rostov's lids drooped and his lips curved in the beginning of his creamy look, sensing he had landed a blow.

A cold, hard anger settled over me. He could tell himself whatever he liked, but deep inside, this confession he was forcing from me titillated him.

"Yes," I said coolly, watching his creamy look deepen. "I had the honor of serving as her confidante on several occasions."

That drove the smirk from his lips. "That is not what I asked."

"It is exactly what you asked, my lord," I retorted. "You were not listening when I spoke of trust and loyalty."

His brows rose. "You deny a physical relationship with her?"

"Physical?" I shrugged. "Not entirely, no. I offered such comfort as she would accept. The princess suffered from night terrors, memories of her bridegroom's death. When it was very bad, when she would awaken shaking and trembling, sometimes she would let me hold her until she fell asleep."

The Patriarch studied me with a hooded gaze. "But that is not the whole truth, is it, Moirin?"

"It is!" I protested.

His lips curled. "Do you think you can lie to me? I am a servant of God, and I hear the lie in your voice. I see it festering on your soul. Tell me, did you debauch the Emperor's daughter under the guise of giving comfort to her?"

Gods, I hadn't been prepared for this. Too much of my life was an open book. I'd known I couldn't protect my memories of Cillian, of Raphael such as they were, of Jehanne, or Bao when it came his turn. I'd conducted my affairs in far too public a manner.

But it should have been different with Snow Tiger, my fiercely private and reserved princess.

What had passed between us in the beginning at the dragon's insistence, neither of us had chosen—and only Bao knew about it. What had passed between us at the end was another matter altogether. She had blushed to the tips of her ears when she had asked me to invoke Naamah's blessing for her, charming me beyond words. She knew how deeply she was wounded, but she was proud and it had not been easy for her to ask.

And Naamah . . . Naamah had granted her blessing when I prayed for it, placing words in my mouth that took the fear away, every last bit of it. Snow Tiger had laughed out of sheer wonder—laughed, and kissed me. I had laughed, too, pulling her down atop me.

I wasn't willing to give up that memory, either. The Patriarch was merely guessing in his ungodly perceptive way, probing at my vulnerabilities. I couldn't bear to have him sully it with his vulgar accusations. He didn't know. No one knew, except mayhap a few discreet servants who loved their mistress too well to gossip. I had gladly given the princess every ounce of pleasure I had to offer, gladly accepted it in return, delighting in the healing she found in it, delighting in *her*.

But I had not sought it out.

And I hated the Patriarch for trying to make it something vile. He awaited my answer with infernal patience.

I remembered how the fallen spirits had tricked the Circle of Shalomon over and over, finding loopholes in the commandments given them even as they obeyed to the letter, and I parsed my words with care.

"You are asking if I seduced her, and the answer is no." I met his gaze steadily, my anger a cold blaze within me. "Do you need to hear truth in my voice, my lord? Very well, I will swear to it." I uttered the sacred oath of the Maghuin Dhonn, each word precise. "By stone and sea and sky, and all that they encompass, by the sacred troth that binds me to my *diadh-anam*, I swear I did not seduce the Emperor's daughter."

My chains shivered, the sigils and inscriptions etched on them flaring briefly. This time, it was the Patriarch who flinched.

"Witch!" he hissed.

The spark of my *diadh-anam* was undiminished. Although I had pared it to the bone, I had spoken the truth. "It is the sacred oath of my people," I said coldly. "The one Berlik the Cursed broke. I do not swear it lightly."

Pyotr Rostov mastered his unease, resuming his study of me. "And yet you are angry," he observed. "Angrier than the question warrants. Even under oath, you withhold the greater truth." His creamy look returned. "You say you did not seduce the princess, but you do not deny making the attempt."

I looked away, willing him to believe it.

"Yes." He nodded to himself in satisfaction. "I think it is so, child. You tried and failed. Is it not so?"

"Must you humiliate me as well?" I muttered.

"It is for the good of your soul," he said sternly. "You must confess it."

It seemed I *could* lie to the Patriarch after all—so long as it was a lie he already wished to believe.

I let my shoulders slump. "Yes, my lord," I lied in a defeated whisper. "In the small hours of the night, when she was lonely and frightened, I sought to entice the Emperor's daughter. I failed."

"Good, very good." His pen skated over the page. "The Ch'in are a heathen folk, but they have a great respect for custom and propriety," he said in an absent tone. "Take heed from the lesson of the Emperor's daughter, Moirin. The temptations of the flesh *can* be resisted. All it takes is discipline."

I bowed my head. "Yes, my lord."

TWENTY-SEVEN

When Aleksei came to read to me the following morning, he was moving stiffly, as though he were in pain.

I eyed him. "Are you hurt?"

Predictably, he flushed. "No . . . *no!*" He shrank away from me as I ignored his protestations, stooping beside the stiff-backed chair and unlacing the ties of his linen shirt, peeling back the lapels. "Moirin, please don't."

"Let me see."

"*No!*"

I did, though. I caught a glimpse of the garment he wore beneath the outer layer of his clothing, a crude goat's-hair vest.

My nostrils flared. "Stone and sea!" I gagged. "Aleksei, this thing is crawling with lice. How is *that* not unclean?"

"It helps me ignore the distraction of temptation." He pulled away from me, lacing his shirt. "Even the lowest of the low is part of God's creation, and may serve his purpose. Do you not see the beauty in it?"

"No." Yesterday's anger lingered in me. I paced my cell, taking precise, mincing steps. "No, Aleksei. I do not. I am sick unto death of hearing about your God and his everlasting fascination with things he has decided are abominations. Apparently, that includes everything in my life I have ever done that brought me joy."

"False joy," he whispered.

I rounded on him. "How in the name of all the gods would you know? Filled with abject terror as you are?"

He shuddered away from me.

That, and the sight of that crude, stinking vest seething with lice, broke something inside me.

I sank to my heels, covering my face with my hands. "I'm sorry. I'm *sorry!*" I forced myself to breathe slowly, fighting a losing battle with tears.

Aleksei hovered anxiously in front of me, undone by my tears. "Don't cry! Moirin, please." Greatly daring, he knelt and held out his hands. "Come, pray with me. It will help, I promise."

His glorious blue eyes were filled with genuine pity and compassion. Unlike his uncle, I'd never seen anything less in him. I took one of his hands in mine, rubbing at my tears with the other.

His breathing quickened, and his long fingers stirred in mine. I stroked them gently. "Sweet boy, do you know what I see when I look at you?" I whispered. He shook his head, tawny locks shining in the sunlight that slanted through my narrow window. "I see a bird raised in captivity, taught that his wings were a curse and flight a sin. A beautiful bird taught from birth to love his cage and fear the open sky."

Aleksei's lips parted. "You must not say such things!"

"It's true." I lifted my free hand, chains dangling. "Your uncle has clipped my wings. But he will not be content until he has broken every bone in them."

"It's *not* true!" He wrenched himself away from me, fumbling back toward the chair for his book. "I will read to you. Only... be still, and listen. I keep telling you, you must open your heart and listen, Moirin!"

"I *have* listened," I said wearily. "And yes, there are moments of glory and wonder in your tales. Yes, your Yeshua sounds like a decent fellow for a god, filled with love and kindness toward mankind. But there are also great, long boring bits about the genealogy of the

Habiru, which holds little interest for me, and there are tales that make no sense at all, and other parts that are simply harsh and cruel."

He looked aghast. "Only because you do not understand them yet!"

"Do you think so?" I shook my head. "No, I think I am beginning to understand. These scriptures, they were written by mortal men. And mayhap some of them were moved by divine grace, but others were petty, jealous fellows moved by the ordinary concerns of everyday life, like being cuckolded by a straying wife."

"Now you throw my mother's sin in my face?" For the first time, he sounded angry. "I have spent my life trying to atone for it!"

I winced. "No. I'm sorry, I forgot."

"I suppose your D'Angelines would not reckon it a sin," Aleksei said bitterly. "I suppose it's just *fine* for a woman to betray her husband, to give a man a bastard son and expect him to call it his own."

"No, it's not." That brought him up short. "For all her infidelities, my lady Jehanne knew full well that was the one betrayal the King would not tolerate. But unlike your mother, I suspect, she loved her husband."

"That's a cruel blow," he said in a low voice.

"Yes," I agreed. "It is. And yet if your mother had been allowed to wed for love instead of prestige, would she have strayed?"

"D'Angelines do."

"Many, aye. Within their culture, it is permitted. Blessed Elua allows what God and Yeshua forbid." I shrugged. "And it *is* possible to love more than one person."

Aleksei swallowed hard, the words evoking a yearning in him that he could not hide. "Have you?"

I held his gaze. "Yes."

Gods, I could almost *taste* the ache of desire in him! And not only for sex, no. He was Naamah's child, as surely as I was. His poor, caged spirit longed to love freely. To share Naamah's gift within him, to delight in pleasures ranging from the sheer carnal bliss of pleasure to all of love's myriad tendernesses. Oh, he hungered for it so.

He turned away, his shoulders hunched. "I will read to you."

I sighed. "As you will."

Later that day, the Patriarch returned with his hateful desk and his hateful quill to resume the hateful process of hearing my confession.

"So, Moirin," he said when he had everything in readiness, pen poised above his account of my sins. "Let us speak of this young Tatar prince."

I almost laughed, picturing Bao's insolent grin at hearing himself described thusly. "Bao?"

"Bao, yes." Pyotr Rostov frowned. "I must confess, I am confused. Is he Ch'in or Tatar?"

"Both," I said. "His mother was a Ch'in woman, ravaged by a raiding Tatar warlord. Although to be fair," I added, "Bao's father sought to avenge the loss of his own wife, taken by the Ch'in. It is a complicated matter."

He stared at me. "And this Bao, who is the Great Khan's son-in-law, is also the companion of the physician Lo Feng?"

I nodded. "Yes."

"You travelled from Terre d'Ange to Ch'in in his company?"

"Yes, my lord." Although I had dreaded this moment, too, now that it had arrived, it was not as awful as I had feared. It was different from the others. My *diadh-anam* shone within me, a reminder that there was a powerful magic about the bond between Bao and me that not even Pyotr Rostov could sully. And, too, the thought of Bao's cocky grin made me smile inwardly. I could guess what he would say if he knew, could almost hear the cheerful cynicism in his voice. *Tell the stunted old pervert whatever he wants to hear, Moirin, and I will bash his head in when I have the chance.* "Do you want to hear about the fornication and unclean acts?" I asked politely. "It was a very long journey."

"Ah . . . yes, of course." The Patriarch glanced at his notes. "For the moment, let us take it as a given fact."

"All right." Bao, I thought, would be obscurely disappointed. He was proud of his prowess in bed—and rightfully so. As usual, he made good on his boasts.

Rostov gave me a sharp look. "Brother Ilya gathered extraordinary reports from the Tatar gathering. It seems that you claimed that this young man, this Bao, died and was restored to life."

"Yes," I agreed. "So he was."

"By *you*."

"No, not exactly." My moment of private mirth faded. This was another trap I hadn't seen coming, one I didn't begin to understand. Gods, it seemed there was an unintended sin lying in wait around every corner of my life! Once again, my palms were sweating. "It was Master Lo Feng's doing. He was grieving. He gave his life to restore Bao's, and required my magic and half my *diadh-anam* to do it, although I did not know what he was asking at the time." I shook my head. "And if you are asking me to tell you how it was done, I cannot."

"I am asking nothing." The Patriarch's expression had gone stony. "I am telling you it cannot have been done."

"But it was," I said, bewildered.

"No." He raised one finger. "Only Yeshua ben Yosef rose from the dead, and lived. No other. You are mistaken."

"I do not claim to explain it, my lord," I said. "But I assure you, Bao *was* dead. I felt for a pulse myself. There was none."

His face was implacable. "You are mistaken."

"For over an hour!" I shook my head again. "No. I tried to suck the poison from his flesh, tried to breathe life into his lungs. Bao died, and lived. Believe me, my lord, he was none too happy about it."

"You are mistaken."

Why it mattered to him so deeply, I could not begin to guess; I could only see that it did. He demanded truth from me, but only when it agreed with his beliefs, and I did not understand the intricacies of his faith. All I knew was that I would not win this argument; I would never win this argument or any argument with the Patriarch of Riva.

Never, ever, ever.

There are ways and ways of betraying memory, of betraying the truth. I hadn't expected this one. In my mind's eye, I saw the amusement fade from Bao's face. The fierce determination and stubborn pride lingered. Bao would not care what lie I told, what truth I betrayed, so long as I lived.

Tell the stunted old pervert what he wants to hear.

I took a deep breath. "Mayhap ... mayhap I was mistaken. Mayhap I let my fear master me. And Bao was never dead, only stunned."

The Patriarch smiled his creamy smile, his eyelids drooping with satisfaction. "Yes. Yes, indeed. Good girl."

TWENTY-EIGHT

❦

I had begun to think the hellish cycle of confession would never end, but the next day, the Patriarch surprised me.

He came in the morning, instead of the afternoon as he was usually wont to do. I wondered if it meant Aleksei would not be reading to me anymore, but I was reluctant to ask, wary of showing too much interest in the lad. I hoped I hadn't driven him into a full-blown retreat the other day.

I had to own, it galled me that I'd had so little success seducing a young man at the apex of his transition to adulthood, a young man so desperately starved for love. I'd lain awake for hours berating myself for it, convinced that a skilled adept like Jehanne would have had Aleksei eating out of the palm of her hand in a matter of minutes.

Then I would remember the lice, and think again.

I'd known it wouldn't be an easy task, but I was still struggling to grasp the scope of the damage done to him. It wasn't just the deeply ingrained strictures of his faith. Aleksei had been raised his entire life to believe he was the product of his mother's sinful downfall, tainted with a foul curse. He was determined to redeem them both through this trial—and, I sensed, to redeem me, too.

I was no mere mortal temptation, oh, no. As Valentina had said, God had decreed my person a battleground.

Stone and sea, it surely felt that way.

For two hours, I endured another assault as the Patriarch questioned me, exhuming another batch of sins and false beliefs.

First, it was the dragon.

Pyotr Rostov was convinced it was a demon that had possessed the princess. I could not entirely blame him, since everyone in Ch'in had believed it, too, including Snow Tiger herself. She had only believed otherwise when I had summoned the twilight and shown her the dragon's reflection in the mirror.

I could still see the wonder on her face.

The rest of Ch'in had come to believe after we succeeded in freeing the dragon, when he came arrowing through the skies over White Jade Mountain, silver coils shimmering, calling down rain and lightning.

Pyotr Rostov refused to believe, refused to accept the dragon's nature as a celestial being of elemental magic. No, nothing would do but that it was a fallen spirit bent on wreaking havoc and harm in the world.

"You said yourself that the fallen ones took strange and fantastic forms, Moirin," he pointed out to me. "That they liked speaking to you, that at least one wielded power over the elements. Can you not see that this is exactly the same?"

"But it's *not*, my lord." I turned the jade bangle on my wrist, agitated. "The dragon is a creature of his place. He wanted nothing more than to drowse on the peaks of White Jade Mountain, gazing at his reflection and guarding his pearl."

"And yet he caused the Emperor's daughter to tear her bridegroom from limb to limb," he said sternly.

"He awoke trapped in her flesh! He was in a blind panic. It drove him mad not to be able to *see* himself."

"You excuse the deed?"

"No! Of course not. I understand it, which is not the same. When the dragon understood what he had done, when he understood what had befallen him, he regretted it very deeply."

The Patriarch shook his head with sorrow. "Child, have you learned nothing from your experience yet? Nothing of the lies unclean spirits will offer to tempt you? You of all people should know better."

Around and around we went. I was fighting another losing battle, and I knew it. In the end, I would acquiesce. I was alone and scared, and I did not want to be stoned to death. I would betray the dragon's memory as surely as I had betrayed Cillian's, Jehanne's, Bao's...even Raphael's, as much as he deserved it. Unless one counted the coach-driver, Snow Tiger's memory was the only one I'd been able to protect. I couldn't save the dragon's.

But I would not surrender without a fight.

During the long, losing argument, I thought about a woman I had known in the City of Elua, Lianne Tremaine, the King's Poet. She was the youngest ever to have been appointed to that post.

And she was good, very good. I heard her recite a poem about a man mourning the death of his beloved. It had moved everyone in the room to tears, including me.

Even so, she had been a member of the Circle of Shalomon, longing for gifts the spirits they summoned could bestow. When I asked her what more a poet of her stature could possibly want, she had replied that there were always further thresholds to cross.

I seek words of such surpassing beauty that they might melt the hardest heart of stone, she had said to me.

I hadn't understood the hunger at the time, but I was beginning to. If one of those fallen spirits had appeared in my cell and offered to gift my tongue with words that would melt the Patriarch's heart, I would have accepted it in a heartbeat and damned the consequences.

Of course, the King's Poet had been driven by excessive ambition, not fear and desperation. Still, I did not think this business of forcing me to betray my fondest memories was teaching me to resist the temptation to sin.

Quite the opposite, in fact.

When I saw the Patriarch's face begin to darken with frustration and impatience flickering in his eyes, I gave up.

"I'm sorry, my lord," I whispered, bowing my head and gazing at the translucent jade bangle, apologizing in my heart to the dragon above his reflecting pool. "I do not mean to be so stubborn. It is only...it is hard to admit one has been so foolish as to be taken in by the same lies twice."

"Well done, child." Leaning over his portable desk, Pyotr Rostov reached out and lifted my chin. At least he didn't have his creamy look. Apparently, the confession of sins that didn't involve fornication, unclean acts, or blaspheming against Yeshua weren't quite as delectable. "Remember, pride is also a sin."

I nodded. "Yes, my lord."

Having stripped that away from me and besmirched it to his satisfaction, he moved on to further acts of iniquity on my part—namely, my role as Emperor Zhu's jade-eyed witch, the Imperial swallower-of-memories.

It was a gift of the Maghuin Dhonn Herself, the ability to take away memories.

Among my folk, it had a purpose. It hid the hollow hill and the stone doorway that I had passed through after Cillian's death, that Bao had seen in his dreams since he'd held half of my *diadh-anam*. Those of us whom the Maghuin Dhonn Herself acknowledged as Her own kept the secret of Her sacred place. Those She did not accept surrendered it, giving unto the keeping of Old Nemed, who was the only one of us to wield that particular gift until I had discovered it within myself at a time of extreme need.

It worked only if the memory was offered freely and willingly. Old Nemed had said no one the Maghuin Dhonn Herself did not acknowledge ever, ever failed to consent to have her take their memory.

I believed it.

The memories I had taken in Ch'in were those of every soldier, engineer, and alchemist with knowledge of the workings of the Divine Thunder, those terrible bronze tubes and fire-powder that belched foul smoke and spat death across an impossible distance. I had seen firsthand the horrible carnage they wrought on the battlefield.

Tortoise...

Tortoise had been one of the stick-fighters who had accompanied us, a member of Bao's old gang of thugs and ruffians. For all that, he'd been a loyal companion with a generous heart, the first to pledge himself to the quest to free the dragon and the princess. In my last memory of him, he had been hurrying across the battlefield to aid me, jouncing in the saddle, his homely face determined.

And then the Divine Thunder had boomed, and Tortoise was no longer there. There was only a smoldering crater with his unrecognizable remains.

"Why did you do it, Moirin?" the Patriarch asked in a gentle tone. Lost in my reverie, I looked blankly at him. "Why did you use witchcraft to steal men's memories on the Emperor's behalf?"

"Oh..." I rubbed my hands over my face, remembering the acrid taste of sulfur, saltpeter, and charcoal permeating my awareness. Too weary to argue, I tried a different tack. "Is that what folk are saying? I fear it is but a fanciful tale spread by the Emperor's men to explain his clemency."

Pyotr Rostov regarded me in silence.

Beneath my head-scarf, sweat gathered along my brow. "Surely you do not believe me capable of such a dire thing."

"I do," he said soberly. "Make no mistake, Moirin. I do not underestimate your foul magics, bound though they may be." His voice took on an edge. "Do you think I do not know your folk have the ability to cloud men's minds? Your ancestor Berlik swayed the thoughts of Rebbe Avraham ben David, a great and devout leader, one of the greatest thinkers of his day; swayed him from the path of righteousness and discipline to a soft-minded tolerance of sin. By what dire magic was *that* done?"

I shook my head. "None that I know of, my lord."

"You are lying again." A note of sorrow returned to his voice. "Ah, Moirin! God cannot save you if you will not let me help you." Behind his veneer of compassion, the threat of stoning lurked. He dipped his pen in the inkwell. "Now, why did you use witchcraft to steal men's memories?"

My eyes stung with defeat. "I did not steal them, my lord. Every single one was offered to me."

That made him pause. "But you did not have to take them."

"No," I murmured. "But if I had not, the Emperor would have put to death every man with knowledge of the Divine Thunder's workings. It was an act of mercy on his part to allow me to take their memories instead."

He was silent.

"That was the choice, my lord," I added. "You will have to explain to me how what I did was a sin."

"It was witchcraft," he said simply.

"Aye, but—"

"Moirin..." Pyotr Rostov sighed. "Oh, child! I do not deny that this was a very difficult choice. But the choice Emperor Zhu laid upon you was a false one, based on a false premise." He steepled his fingers. "He did not have to kill those men, did he? That was *his* choice."

"Aye, but—" My voice faltered. How could I make him understand that the weapons of the Divine Thunder had been *that* terrible? That it was worth almost any cost to suppress that knowledge, even the cost of innocent lives? Although I lacked a poet's words, I had glimpsed a future more dreadful than I could begin to articulate. The smoking crater that housed Tortoise's remains was only the beginning. It led to a far, far worse place.

"You took this sin upon your head that the Emperor's hands might remain clean," he said firmly. "It is enough that you repent of it."

I bowed my head. "Yes, my lord."

"Moirin."

I looked up at him. "Yes, my lord?"

His fingers were still steepled. "Understand, child. The scripture is very clear in places. In the earliest writings, it tells us that we must not allow a witch to live." His velvet-brown eyes were warm and earnest.

"Based on what you have confessed from the first day to the last, I would be justified in putting you to death. But I believe that God's grace is truly infinite, and even one such as you should be given the chance to repent. Do you understand?"

I shivered involuntarily, huddled on my stool, my chains rattling. "I am trying. I am always trying."

"No." Pyotr Rostov smiled at me. "Mostly, you are still trying to defy me, still trying to find some way to escape. I know. But God and I have not given up on you, Moirin. Here and there, we catch glimpses of the truth, and it is the truth that will free you in the end." He paused, contemplating me. "Have you anything left to confess?"

I shook my head. "No, I don't think so."

He put away his things, straightened his papers, and corked his inkwell. He stood and laid a hand on my scarf-wrapped head. "My child, you have made your confession to me. I, a mortal man and a lowly sinner myself, do not have the power to absolve you. This, only God can do. These sins you have confessed to me, and any you may have neglected, either through ignorance or forgetfulness, may God forgive you for them, in this world and the next."

I wondered if I was supposed to feel any different. I didn't feel much of anything, except a vague sense of relief that the process of confession appeared to have reached an end, and apprehension about what came next.

The latter was well placed.

The Patriarch removed his hand from my head. "I am satisfied with your progress, Moirin. I am willing to pronounce you ready for the next stage of your penance."

"Oh?" My heart sank. "What is that, my lord?"

He gave me another smile. "Come, and see."

TWENTY-NINE

For the first time in days, I was allowed to leave my cell.

That was the one good thing about this second stage of my penance. To be sure, it was the *only* good thing about it.

Pyotr Rostov led me through the modest living quarters back to the temple where I had first arrived, passing through a curtained doorway in an alcove behind what I would later learn was a stand for chanters during the liturgy.

We entered the temple proper. Yeshua ben Yosef was there in the presence of the immense mosaic on the wall, holding the world cupped in his hand, looking stern and imposing and not at all like the kind fellow from Aleksei's readings. *That* Yeshua had prevented an adulterous woman from being stoned. This one looked like he would give the order himself, and look on with an impassive gaze.

The Patriarch's wife, Luba, was there waiting for us at the foot of the altar, a wooden bucket on the floor beside her. They exchanged a few words in Vralian.

"Very good," Rostov said, switching back to D'Angeline for my benefit. "Now, Moirin. It is important that you understand this is not a punishment. To do penance is to seek redemption, to purge one's sins. It is a time to reflect and meditate."

"Yes, my lord," I said obediently when he paused.

Luba's upper lip curled. A few times, she had brought food to me; otherwise, I'd seen very little of her since I'd been brought here, and

I suspected that was by her choice. On no occasion had she spoken a single word to me. But although she did not like me and did not want me here, based on their interactions, I was certain she would sooner cut out her tongue than defy her husband.

"As an act of penance, you will wash the floor," the Patriarch said.

"Oh, I see." I relaxed a bit. No doubt he thought it was a fitting humiliation for the descendant of three royal houses, but I had been raised in a cave in the Alban wilderness. From the time I was old enough to hold a broom, I'd swept our hearth every day. I wasn't afraid of hard work, nor did I think it beneath me.

I glanced at the bucket, looking for a mop.

With a satisfied look on her face, Luba held out a very, very small scrub-brush.

"You see the squares, Moirin?" Her husband pointed at the floor. Until this moment, I hadn't bothered to take it in. The floor was also a mosaic, this one formed of pebbles in contrasting hues. The pattern was an abstract one of small squares, each one a box containing a flared cross.

Any sense of relief I had vanished. "Yes, my lord."

"On your knees, you will scrub each one in order," he said, pacing to the far right of the altar. "Beginning here." He raised a finger in caution. "You are not to touch the altar, or anything on it. You are not to venture past it into the sanctuary. Is that understood?"

I sighed. "It is."

"This is *not* a punishment," the Patriarch repeated. "It is an opportunity. Focus your thoughts on each square. Contemplate the sign of the cross, that vile instrument on which Yeshua suffered for your sake. Think upon his suffering. Think upon your sins, and beg his forgiveness. Will you do this?"

As if I had a choice. "Yes, my lord," I muttered.

"Moirin." He said my name sharply. I looked reluctantly at him. "Over each square, you will utter this prayer. 'Yeshua the Anointed, Son of God, have mercy on me, a sinner.' Say it."

"Yeshua the Anointed, Son of God, have mercy on me, a sinner," I echoed.

He spoke to his wife in Vralian, then addressed me in D'Angeline. "Very good. Say it again."

I repeated it, while Luba listened intently.

The Patriarch nodded in satisfaction. "She will be listening to make sure you do not err." His face softened. "I know you do not mean the words, not yet. But repetition is a powerful tool. If you say a thing often enough, it may become true."

I blew out my breath, glancing over the vast expanse of squares and crosses. "Do you expect me to finish it today, my lord?"

"No." He smiled at me. "I do not think that is humanly possible. But it matters not when you finish, for you can always begin again."

Helpless tears stung my eyes, and I bit the inside of my cheek to try to keep the tears from spilling. I didn't want him to see.

He knew, anyway. "God's work is endless, Moirin," he said, and took his leave.

Luba handed me the scrub-brush and addressed me for the first time, pointing toward the corner and speaking three curt words in Vralian. They didn't need translating.

Get to work.

Scrub-brush in hand, I hauled the wooden bucket to the far right of the altar and knelt on the pebbled floor, my chains clanking and rattling around me.

It hurt; of course it hurt. If the mosaic floor had been comprised of smooth bits of tile like the one on the wall, it wouldn't have been so bad. But the inlaid pebbles were raised, digging into my knees. Right now, the pain was a minor annoyance. Over the course of hours, or gods, days, it would grow much, much worse. Gritting my teeth, I contemplated the first square. It was a bit larger than the palm of my hand, mayhap four inches by four.

It was the first of more than I could count.

Hovering behind me, Luba repeated her curt Vralian injunction. I dipped the brush into the bucket, into cold water that smelled strongly of lye. Water sloshed onto the floor as I withdrew the brush, scrubbing the pebbles.

"Yeshua the Anointed," I said grimly, "Son of God, have mercy on me, a sinner."

I moved the brush to the adjacent square. Luba made a disapproving sound, leaning over to tap the bucket, indicating that I was to dip the brush anew.

I sat back on my heels. "Every single bedamned square?" I pointed, miming. "Each and every one?"

She nodded and tapped the bucket again.

I eyed her, remembering the fantasies of violent escape I had entertained on my journey here. We were alone in the temple together. If I rose right now and wrapped my chains around Luba's neck, throttling her, there was no one to stop me. I was young and strong, and I was fairly confident I could overpower her.

And go . . . where?

Alarmed by the unspoken menace in my face, Luba retreated a few cautious steps, fixing me with a seething gaze. She pointed toward the temple doors far behind us, interlacing her fingers with a sharp gesture. She pointed at my chains, and mimed rattling them, mimed stones being thrown. She shook her head slowly at me, pointing at the bucket and the floor.

In the Tatar lands, I had come to recognize how easily two people of like minds could converse without a common tongue. Checheg with her gentle, unremitting kindness and hospitality had taught it to me, long before I had mastered the rudiments of her language.

This was the other side of the coin.

And I understood it full well. The meaning of Luba's gestures was clear. The temple doors were locked, inside and out. Even if I could escape, my chains marked me as a witch, singled out for death in eastern Vralia.

Here, I would be stoned.

I dipped my brush into the harsh lye and scrubbed at the second square, intoning the prayer the Patriarch had taught me.

"Yeshua the Anointed, Son of God, have mercy on me, a sinner."

Again.

Again.

Again.

I kept count during that first row. There were one hundred and fifty squares in it. Each and every one, I scoured. Over each and every one, I uttered the same prayer.

I reached the end of one row, moved on to the second one. The temple was at least twice as long as it was wide, which meant there were at least three hundred rows. I was no mathematician, but by my calculation, that meant I had some forty-five thousand squares in total.

I drew a long, shaking breath, trying once more not to weep.

Luba smirked.

I shuffled on my bruised, aching knees, bowing my head to the task. I was sweating and itchy beneath the coarse woolen dress. My back began to ache from bending. The words of the prayer began to blend together into one long stream of meaningless syllables.

Yeshuatheanointedsonofgodhavemercyonmeasinner.

Although she did not speak D'Angeline, Luba had a good ear. When my prayer degenerated into an inarticulate mumble, she tapped me on the shoulder and made a gesture with both hands as though stretching a rope, telling me without words to slow down and do a proper job of it.

"Yeshua the Anointed, Son of God, have mercy on me, a sinner," I said with fierce precision, dipping and scrubbing. "Yeshua the Anointed, Son of God, have mercy on me, a sinner."

The only small mercy that Yeshua the Anointed saw fit to grant me was that by the time I had finished the second row, Valentina came to replace Luba on sentinel duty. Her, at least, I could bear.

And she did not badger me when I paused to wipe my sleeve over my sweating brow and stretch my aching back. My spine made unpleasant crackling sounds. I shifted on my sore knees, trying to find a position in which the pebbles didn't dig into my flesh so.

"He assigned me this penance, too," Valentina said in a low voice. "For sins committed with Aleksei's father."

"Did you find redemption in it?" I asked wearily.

"Yes," she said simply. I gave her a sharp look, and for once she did not look away. "There is peace to be found in surrendering to God's will and begging his forgiveness."

I shook my head. "For his children, mayhap. I am not one of them."

"We are all God's children," she replied.

I smiled bitterly. "Tell that to the Maghuin Dhonn Herself, who claimed me as Her own."

"Where is she, then?" Valentina gestured around. "You are here in the temple of God and his son Yeshua, Moirin. Where is your bear-god? Where is your D'Angeline whore-goddess Naamah? They have abandoned you."

"No." I touched my chest. "Perhaps they cannot find me, with my spirit shrouded in chains and charms. But I carry the divine spark of the Maghuin Dhonn Herself within me. I carry Naamah's gifts in my blood. So long as that is true, I do not believe they have abandoned me."

There was sympathy in her gaze. "It would be better for you if you did."

"I know." I picked up the brush, dipped it in the bucket, and began scrubbing anew. "Yeshua the Anointed, Son of God, have mercy on me, a sinner."

I had completed a grand total of four rows when Valentina bade me stop—not out of any sense of pity, but because it was time to prepare the temple for the afternoon liturgy.

I got gratefully to my feet, pain shooting through my abused knees and stiff, aching back. I felt a hundred years old. "Does it get any easier?"

"No," she said. "Harder."

I'd assumed as much. I wiped my tired, stinging hands on the woolen dress. I stank of lye and sweat. "My lady, is it possible to have a bath?"

She hesitated.

"I do not ask with an eye toward seducing your son, who seems to be avoiding me anyway." Even my voice was tired, my throat raw from endless prayer. "I've been chained in the same garment for many days. Whatever else you may think of me, I do not like being unclean."

For a mercy, another small mercy, Valentina relented. She even let me scour myself, although I suspected it was due to a reluctance to get anywhere close to touching my skin. I could feel the tension in her haste as she sewed me into a fresh, sack-shaped woolen dress just as drab, prickly, and hateful as the first one.

Still, it was something.

My soul might be black with sin, but my flesh was clean.

THIRTY

I was wrong about Aleksei.

To my surprise, he came in the early evening to read to me. I hadn't expected him, and I was in a morbidly foul mood. My entire body was sore and aching. In something like three hours of scrubbing, I'd gotten through four rows.

If my rough calculation was remotely accurate, that left at least two hundred and ninety-six to go.

And then I could start over.

I didn't bother rising from the narrow bed where I had flung myself, greeting Aleksei with silence and a sullen glare.

It took him aback. "What is it?"

"What do you think?" I asked in a cool tone. "Have you ever knelt on that bedamned floor?"

His blue eyes were wide and earnest. "Many times, yes."

"For three hours?"

"No." He flushed a little, looking away from me in that skittish way. "Moirin . . . your head is bare."

I hadn't put on the head-scarf when I heard the key in the lock, expecting Valentina or Luba. "Oh, for the love of all the gods! My hair is cropped like a twelve-year-old boy's. How tempting can it be?"

Aleksei shivered. "It's . . . very shiny."

"It's clean," I said rudely.

"And soft-looking," he whispered.

"Oh?" I hauled myself upright, tilting my head. My hair fell forward in a short, glossy curtain. "You may be interested to learn that there is an act of love in Terre d'Ange called Winding the Spindle," I said in a conversational tone. "One twines one's hair around a man's erect phallus, then pulls it away slowly. To be done properly, it is done without using one's hands, only swirling one's head gently around the phallus."

He stared at me in shock. I'd never spoken to him thusly before.

"My lady Jehanne says that the technique is a tricky one," I said sweetly. "But she assures me that men find the sensation subtle and exquisite, and the sight most provocative. I fear it will be some time before I'm able to attempt it, since your aunt Luba saw fit to shear me like a sheep."

"Why—" Aleksei's voice cracked. "Why are you saying such things?"

"Don't you like it?" I raised my brows. "Your uncle does. Nothing brings him greater pleasure than hearing me confess to unclean acts."

"That's not true!"

"Aye, it is." I gave him a pointed look. "Do you think I cannot tell when a man is aroused?"

"I...yes. No." His chest rose and fell as he took a deep breath, struggling for self-control. "You're being cruel, Moirin. That's unlike you."

"True." I rattled my chains with a theatrical gesture. "Today, I entertained the notion of throttling your aunt. A wolf in the wild will leave you alone. If you capture it and put it in chains, do not be surprised when it tries to bite your hand off."

"This is not you," Aleksei said stubbornly. "It is only Naamah's curse talking, trying to sway me."

"There *is* no curse!" I shouted.

He ignored me, pulling up the stool. "I will read to you. What would you like to hear today? I'll let you choose."

"I don't care." I sighed, losing my will to antagonize him. "Do you know, the Maghuin Dhonn have no written language?"

He frowned. "Why not?"

"Because knowledge is a living thing." I leaned against the wall of my cell, rubbing my sore knees. "I knew the name of every plant and tree that grew in our woods. I knew which were good to eat, which were good for other purposes, which were to be avoided. I knew when they came into season, and how to recognize signs of rot or taint. I knew the habits of every creature that shared our woods, how to track and hunt them, or merely to spy on them with delight, like a fox playing with her kits. It is a living knowledge that changes with the seasons. The whole of it could never have been confined to writing."

"But a written record could be a useful tool, could it not?" Aleksei asked with genuine curiosity.

I shrugged. "Yes and no. When I first learned such a thing as writing existed, I thought it a fine kind of magic. But folk come to rely on the record, and ignore the living truth before their eyes." I pointed at the book in his hands. "What happens when there are errors in the record?"

His color rose. "Now you are baiting me again. Come, Moirin. If you won't choose, I will."

I closed my eyes. "Read what you like, Aleksei. I don't care. I'm tired. I hate this place. I hate your uncle. I hate your aunt. I hate your mean-spirited God and his precious son Yeshua."

"You don't mean that!"

"Today, I do." I shrugged again. "Why shouldn't I? Everything I am is hateful to them."

Aleksei was silent long enough that I opened my eyes again and glanced at him. He wore an uncertain look that gave way to one of determination. "Wait," he said to me, getting to his feet. "I'll be right back."

Since I had no choice, I waited.

He left and returned a few moments later with another book in his hands—a different one, a slender volume.

"Here." He presented it to me.

I glanced at it without interest. The title was etched on the leather binding in the Vralian alphabet. "I cannot read it."

"It's not what it says it is." Aleksei hunkered on the stool, watching me with a grave look. "Inside, it's written in D'Angeline script. You... ah, can you read your native tongue, Moirin?"

"Yes." I scowled a bit. "I am no scholar like Phèdre nó Delaunay, who could likely recite your bedamned scriptures to you backward and forward in the original Habiru, but I can read. And D'Angeline is not my native tongue, by the way."

"I'm sorry." He flushed. "Who is Phèdre nó Delaunay?"

"The D'Angeline courtesan who sought out and found the Name of God? You don't know that story?" I asked. He shook his head. "I'll have to tell it to you," I said absently, opening the book he had given me. "Among other things, it suggests that perhaps you do not know your God as well as you think." I glanced at the inner title page. "This is the priest's book about Berlik."

"Yes," Aleksei murmured. "I took it from my mother's hiding place."

I was intrigued, especially given the Patriarch's aversion to the book. "You said you found it dangerous."

"Yes." Although his rangy, long-limbed figure was hunched and awkward, his blue gaze was clear and steady. "But... I think what you are feeling now is dangerous, too. You are giving in to hatred and anger, straying farther and farther from grace. And though I am loath to question my uncle's judgment in any way, I do not think he understands your need for, um..." His voice dropped to a whisper. "Love."

"Love," I echoed.

Aleksei nodded. "The Rebbe Avraham ben David found much to love in your people, Moirin. Both in the magician Berlik and the D'Angeline prince Imriel who delivered him into martyrdom. I hope... I hope that perhaps his words will find a path to your heart, and you will allow yourself to accept God's love, and learn to love him and his son Yeshua in return."

I contemplated him thoughtfully. "You're an interesting young man, Aleksei."

He looked away. "Will you at least read it?"

"I will."

THIRTY-ONE

The Rebbe's memoir was beautiful, so beautiful in places that it made my heart ache.

He was a wise, compassionate, eloquent, and profoundly conflicted man, who had seen his deepest-held desire come to pass, and feared he did not welcome the form it had taken, even though he had helped to shape it.

At the center of the book was his struggle to reconcile the two Yeshuas: Yeshua-that-was, the gentle philosopher whose teachings formed much of the long-held faith of the Habiru, whom he called the Children of Yisra-el; and Yeshua-who-comes, the fierce warrior in whose name a new faith arose in Vralia.

It was during his long conversations with Berlik that doubt had arisen. Here was a man who had committed a terrible deed to save his people, who had taken on his shoulders the price of breaking an oath sworn in their name. If ever there were a man in need of Yeshua's salvation, it was Berlik.

And yet he refused it.

"Gently, sorrowfully, and steadfastly, he refused it," the Rebbe wrote. "Insisting that the burden was his own to bear, he refused it; and with consummate and relentless kindness, he pointed out the discrepancies between my own beliefs and events transpiring in war-torn Vralia. Yet it was also true that Berlik found his own grace through

Yeshua, whose compassion made him believe that the gods themselves were capable of forgiveness."

There were things the Rebbe had not fully understood, but I did. When Berlik broke the oath he had sworn on his *diadh-anam*, the Maghuin Dhonn Herself had turned Her back on him. The divine spark within him had been extinguished.

In distant Vralia, where Berlik had resigned himself to death at the prince's hands, She had forgiven him and it had been rekindled.

Accepting sanctuary, Berlik had vanished into the wilderness. And then Prince Imriel had come, and in time Berlik had surrendered himself willingly to his justice, bowing his head for the sword.

Before he died, he spoke of Yeshua ben Yosef.

I had known part of it, but the Rebbe had recorded Berlik's words in full—at least as related to him by the prince. "I came to see that he is the one god who understands what it is to fall low. That when every other face is turned away from you, he is the friend who is there, not only for the innocent, but for the guilty, too. For the thieves and murderers and oath-breakers alike, Yeshua is there."

It made me want to weep. I could pray to *that* Yeshua, if he had not seemed so very, very far away.

Such was the argument the Rebbe Avraham ben David made, that until such a time as Yeshua-who-comes returned to make his will manifest, an hour that Yeshua himself had declared unknowable, those who worshipped him should obey the teachings of Yeshua-that-was, who turned no one away.

"Against the backdrop of war, of great and awesome change, I witnessed a profound mystery take place," the Rebbe wrote. "Even now, I cannot claim to understand it. As I reflect upon those events, I am reminded that the will of Adonai is vaster and more wondrous than any mortal mind can encompass, and that the world is filled with marvels and terrible beauty. To those who will shape Vralia's future, I say this. You are mortal, and you will err. It is inevitable, as inevitable as the rising of the sun. I beg of you, have compassion in all your doings and always err on the side of love, for that is the greatest gift of all."

Reading that, I *did* weep.

Aleksei's gift had accomplished its purpose.

I tried, I truly did. After reading the Rebbe's book, I thought that mayhap if Berlik could find his way back to grace through Yeshua, so could I. Mayhap the Maghuin Dhonn Herself *was* wroth with me. I had done some very foolish things, especially allowing the gifts She had given me to serve Raphael de Mereliot's ambitions.

For four days, I was good.

Day after day, I did my slow, exacting penance, row by row, shuffling in my chains, kneeling on the hard pebbles, and dipping my scrub-brush into the bucket that I might scour each and every square.

"Yeshua the Anointed, Son of God, have mercy on me, a sinner," I murmured, speaking to the gentle Yeshua-that-was, and not the hot-eyed warrior on the wall, holding the world in his palm. "Yeshua the Anointed, Son of God, have mercy on me, a sinner."

The Patriarch of Riva approved.

"I have a mind to reward you, Moirin," he said to me in a jovial tone, visiting me in my cell after I had completed my fourth day of flawless penance.

"Oh?"

He nodded. "I will be conducting the morning service tomorrow. Would you care to attend?"

"Of course, my lord," I said politely. It was a lie. I wanted nothing to do with him. I still hated Pyotr Rostov. I would always hate him.

"Very good." He smiled at me. "Since you are unbaptized, you will have to observe from the narthex, but I think you will benefit from the experience. Luba will escort you."

Doubtless that would be a pleasure for both of us. "Thank you, my lord."

The Patriarch laid one hand on my head. "You're welcome, Moirin."

Despite everything, I had to own that I was curious—and more than a bit apprehensive, too. Since the day I arrived, I hadn't seen another living soul save Pyotr Rostov and his family. I would see them in the temple, all the fine folk of Riva who would take part in stoning me to death if I didn't find a path out of this mess one way or another.

Scowling Luba came for me at daybreak, the ferocity of her expression letting me know just exactly how little she welcomed this chore. At least her dislike was honest and genuine. I preferred her heartfelt scowls to her husband's unctuous smiles. Since I was still trying to be good and open myself to the possibility that there *was* some purpose in my presence here, I met her glare with a calm, steady gaze.

It didn't impress her.

She led me on a different course through the living quarters. It seemed we were to exit onto the street, and enter the temple through the main doors.

I hadn't been outdoors for days—weeks, by this time. If it hadn't been for the magic of the bedamned chains stifling my senses, like as not I would have lost my mind by now, confined in a man-made structure for so long.

Even so, the sight of the blue sky above me and the feel of open air around me was a powerful tonic. I drew a long, shaking breath, every fiber in my body urging me to run, to flee, to get away.

But there were the shackles on my ankles, limiting me to mincing steps. There was Luba at my side, taking a fierce grip on my elbow. There were streams of Vralian worshippers heading for the temple, eyeing me with avid curiosity.

I let out my breath and allowed Luba to steer me into the temple.

Vralians stood to worship—men on the right, women on the left. Most of them passed beyond the outermost chamber of the narthex to enter the inner chamber of the nave. I winced to see dirty shoes and boots trampling the pebbled floor.

A few lingered in the narthex, staring and whispering. I did not see kindness or pity in any of their faces. At best, curiosity; at worst, revulsion. I made myself meet their eyes, willing my expression to give nothing away. When I did, they averted their eyes. It was altogether too easy to picture the stones in their hands.

It was better when the service began. Since it was conducted in Vralian, I understood none of it. Pyotr Rostov had been careful to ensure that precious little was spoken in my presence so I had no chance to learn to communicate with anyone else, keeping me as isolated as possible. But there were long prayers chanted in deep, sonorous tones, and at least the sound of it was pleasing. The Patriarch stood before the altar wearing a fine embroidered stole over his robes and swinging a censer from which sweet-smelling smoke trickled.

I let the sounds wash over me, lifting my gaze to contemplate the image of Yeshua on the wall above the altar.

I tried to envision him as Yeshua-that-was, willing his stern visage to soften into the gentler one Rebbe Avraham described.

"What is it you will of me?" I whispered under my breath, asking the question in earnest for the first time.

A vision unfolded behind my eyes: Yeshua ben Yosef as savior and intercessor, coming to my aid as he had come to the aid of the adulterous woman in one of the tales Aleksei had read to me.

And truly, his face was oh so very kind.

And as in the tale, Yeshua stooped and traced an unknown word on the ground. Then he stood and touched my chains one by one, and one by one my chains fell away. He reached out his hand to me, beckoning for me to take it.

I gazed into his eyes.

They were dark, dark and wise and fathomless. There was an entire world behind them, a night sky filled with stars, vast mountains blotting out sections.

No.

The mountain moved forward and dwindled, taking on a familiar shape, taking on mortal dimensions. I gazed through the eyes of Yeshua into the eyes of the Maghuin Dhonn Herself, and they were filled with infinite sorrow.

With infinite regret, She turned away from me. I felt the divine spark of my *diadh-anam* go out like a blown candle and gasped, my soul suddenly empty and hollow.

There would be no more twilight, no more gifts, no more magic. Never again would I sense the slow thoughts of trees growing, the flickering awareness of animals in the field. Never, ever, would I pass through the stone doorway. That was the price of accepting Yeshua's salvation.

"*No!*"

The world, the real world came crashing back as though I had released the twilight. I hadn't known I'd shouted aloud until I heard the echoes of my own voice in the sudden, shocked silence. My chains were shivering, the sigils on them glowing.

My *diadh-anam* blazed within me. It had only been a vision—a true vision, mayhap, but a vision nonetheless.

I had not taken Yeshua's hand.

I gasped again with relief, and then a third time as Luba fetched me a great, ringing slap across the face, knocking me sideways, staggering in my shackles. Without giving me a chance to recover, she grabbed the chains that ran from my collar to my wrists, hauling me out of the temple unceremoniously.

I stumbled in her wake, scarce able to keep my feet, my wits addled and my face stinging. The anger that Aleksei's compassion and the Rebbe's book had softened returned full force. Halfway to the door to the living quarters, I got my feet beneath me, planted my heels, and yanked the chains out of her grasp.

Luba reached for me. I grabbed her arm first, pivoting on my heel to swing her against the outer wall of the temple.

Her grey eyes went wide and shocked.

I leaned my right forearm across her throat. "I am not a dog, and you will not treat me like one!"

And then there was the sound of running feet and shouting, and there were hands dragging me off her, many hands. I didn't fight. Three Vralian men held me uncertainly, waiting for the Patriarch, who came striding down the street, his fine vestments swinging, his face filled with anger.

"You disappoint me, Moirin," he rumbled. "You disappoint me sorely!"

Behind him, I could see Aleksei shaking his head in frantic warning, urging me not to further anger his uncle.

I gazed at the sky and breathed the Breath of Ocean's Rolling Waves, willing myself to find the still, calm place within me that Master Lo had taught me to seek. It had been too long since I had practiced the discipline of the Way.

It helped.

"I'm sorry, my lord," I said to the Patriarch. "A kind of fit came over me."

It was an answer he could understand, and the worst of his anger abated. "It is Naamah's curse within you struggling against the forces that would contain it," he said in a judicious tone. "In my eagerness, I fear I misjudged your progress, as well as the tenacious nature of the curse. I should have allowed you to finish a full cycle of penance before exposing you to God's holy liturgy."

I sagged a bit in my captors' grip. "Thank you, my lord. I'm very sorry."

Pyotr Rostov said somewhat in Vralian to the men holding my arms. They let me go with alacrity. Luba coughed and massaged her throat in an ostentatious manner, malice in her gaze. Rostov turned back to me, his face grave. "You understand, of course, that you will have to be punished. It is for your own good. I fear the demons that possess you will only respond to strong discipline."

"Of course, my lord." I met his gaze. "For my own good."

He smiled with gentle regret. "I'm glad you understand."

THIRTY-TWO

M y punishment was a whipping, and the Patriarch administered
it himself.

Of course.

It took place in a small inner courtyard I hadn't even known
existed. There, I was made to kneel on the slate, my chained wrists
draped over a hook on a large post. With great delight, Luba took her
shears to the back of my dress, cutting downward from the neckline
and parting the flaps of fabric to lay my back bare.

Pyotr Rostov beat me with a knotted rope, administering twenty
firm lashes, counting out each one in a solemn voice.

It hurt.

I'd only ever been struck thrice before in my life. Once, when I told
Jehanne I was leaving. She had slapped me with surprising strength,
and fallen weeping at my feet. That was one blow I didn't begrudge
her. The second time was in the Great Khan's *ger*. To be fair, he hadn't
hit me hard. It had only been a warning.

The third time was Luba, and that, I *did* begrudge her.

This was much worse.

The rope was heavy, and the knots struck with bruising force. I
managed not to cry out loud, but I flinched in anticipation of each
blow. My breath grew ragged and helpless tears filled my eyes. There
are those who find pleasure in pain and in Terre d'Ange, it is one of
Naamah's arts, but it was not one I had ever relished.

After ten blows, my back was a welter of pain. By fifteen, I was biting my lip and squeezing my eyes shut, willing it to end.

"...eighteen."

Thud.

"...nineteen."

Thud.

The Patriarch was beginning to breathe hard, too. Through the haze of pain, I sensed that there was more than exertion in it. Although he might deny it to himself, he took pleasure in administering this punishment to me, as surely as he did in forcing my unwilling confessions. The exercise of power aroused him.

"...twenty."

Thud.

It was finished. He unhooked my chains from the post and helped me to my feet. I stood unsteadily, my back throbbing in agony. My violated dress hung low on my shoulders, baring the upper swell of my breasts. He looked away, but not before his gaze had skated oh so briefly over my exposed flesh. A dark flush suffused his face, further betraying him.

Valentina hurried to my side, a needle and thread in her hand, yanking my dress in place and beginning to stitch.

"Very good," Rostov said brusquely. "Sister, see Moirin to her chamber. She is to fast for two days. Luba, Aleksei, come."

Oh yes, the entire household had been required to bear witness to my punishment. I glanced at Aleksei, who was staring fixedly at his feet. He went with his aunt and uncle without a word, without ever looking in my direction.

"*Why* do you persist in defying him?" Valentina whispered behind me, stitching furiously.

I turned my head in her direction. "I didn't mean to, not this time. I had a vision in the temple. It caught me unaware."

Her voice was low. "And assaulting Luba?"

I rolled my shoulders, testing the depth of my pain. It was considerable. The Patriarch was a fairly strong fellow, and he had not held back. "Ah, no. That I meant to do. And it was almost worth it."

A shocked sound escaped Valentina. It took me a moment to recognize it as a stifled laugh. Her hand flew up to cover her mouth. "I have entertained similar thoughts on occasion. But, Moirin, you *will* get yourself killed if you continue this way."

"I know."

She lowered her hand from her lips and touched me lightly, ever so softly, her fingertips grazing the sore skin between my shoulder blades where my dress yet gaped. It made me shiver. There was something of a mother's tenderness in it, and something else, too. It seemed a very, very long time since anyone had touched me with kindness. Despite everything, I yearned for it. "I would rather you didn't die," she murmured. "Still, I owe everything to my brother, and I have nowhere else to go. You know I dare not intervene?"

"Aye," I said wearily. "And I do not blame you. I am learning. This is a harsh place for a woman, especially one judged and found wanting. But your son is proving stubbornly incorruptible, my lady."

Valentina bent her head to the task at hand, finishing sewing my dress. "Oh? And yet he stole my book for you."

"You knew?" I asked.

She tied a knot in the thread and broke it. "Yes, of course. Offer Aleksei what he craves."

"Love?" I guessed. "Pleasure?"

Valentina shook her head. "Truth."

So I did.

Two days passed before Aleksei came to me again. In accordance with the Patriarch's orders, I was given no food, only water. I was not even allowed to continue my penance, which I did not mind a bit. It gave my aching body a chance to heal. My lower back hurt from kneeling and bending; bruised to the bone, my upper back hurt from the lash. The pain in my knees was chronic.

I spent the time returning to the discipline that Master Lo had taught me. I sat cross-legged and half-starved on my narrow berth until Aleksei came back, cycling through the Five Styles of Breathing.

I prayed, too. Not to God and Yeshua, but to the Maghuin Dhonn

Herself, and to Blessed Elua and his Companions, and most especially among them to Naamah. In this, too, I had been neglectful.

When Aleksei returned with his book of scriptures, I could see the trepidation in every line of his body. His broad shoulders were hunched and tight, and I suspected he was wearing that vile goat's-hair vest beneath his shirt again. His uneasy gaze skidded toward me.

I sat cross-legged on my bed, my mood and my face calm. "Hello, Aleksei."

"Moirin." His hunched shoulders relaxed by an inch or two. He met my eyes, frowning a little. "I thought to find you angry."

"No." I shook my head. "I have gone beyond anger, at least for the moment. I do not promise it will not return." I nodded at the chair. "Will you sit? I'd like to speak to you."

Aleksei pulled the stool over instead, hunkering on it with that combination of awkwardness and grace unique to young men. He turned the book over in his hands, his glorious blue eyes wide and uncertain. "I'm supposed to read to you."

"I know, and in a little while, you may," I said. "Are you willing to listen to me first?"

Unexpectedly, he smiled. "Yes, Moirin. I do like listening to you, and I *am* trying to understand, too."

"Thank you." I smiled back at him, and took a deep breath. "Aleksei, I had a vision in the temple. That is why I cried out."

I told him what I had seen, my vision of Yeshua and the Maghuin Dhonn beyond him, and the spark of my *diadh-anam* extinguished.

Although he didn't understand it, not wholly, he listened attentively and he understood as well as any Vralian could.

"It has made one thing clear to me," I said gently when I had finished. "No matter what else, I cannot accept Yeshua's salvation without betraying the Maghuin Dhonn Herself and losing my soul in the bargain. I can't do it, Aleksei. I do not want to die, not at all, but I would rather die than lose my *diadh-anam* and live without it."

There were tears in his blue, blue eyes. "You're sure?"

"Yes." I nodded. "More sure than I've ever been of anything in my life. And if you do not help me, sooner or later, your uncle *will* kill me."

"You want me to help you escape," he murmured. "To betray my uncle and everything he holds dear."

"He seeks my redemption as a means to an end," I said. "A sign from God that it is time to launch a crusade to convert the D'Angelines, to bring the apostate Elua and his Companions back to the fold." I shook my head. "It will not happen, not here and now. Not beginning with me."

"What did he write?"

I blinked at him. "Who?"

Aleksei rubbed his hands on his knees. "Yeshua. In your vision. You said he wrote a word on the floor. What was it?"

"I don't know," I admitted. "What was the word he wrote in his encounter with the adulterous woman? Mayhap it was the same."

"No one knows." He looked somber. "Sometimes I think the entire mystery of Yeshua must be contained in that word."

What he was thinking, I couldn't begin to guess. I put out my hands, palms upward. "If I were free, I would invoke Naamah's blessing for you, Aleksei. You think you understand what that means. You don't. There would be healing in it for you."

He glanced at me, unable to hide the hunger and the yearning in him. "You seek to tempt me."

I smiled wryly. "For quite some time now, yes. But this is an honest offer. You need not accept it. I am asking you to free me out of the kindness of your heart. And," I added, "because I do not think you wish to see me cut down in a hail of stones, my skull cracked open and my brains leaking onto the cobbles." Aleksei jerked as though I'd struck him, then winced in obvious discomfort. I narrowed my eyes at him. "Are you wearing that bedamned goat's-hair vest again?"

"No," he murmured, bringing his shoulders forward. "I...after your punishment, I thought it only fair I endured the same. If I had been a better teacher, you would not have been punished."

I drew a sharp breath. "Your uncle beat you?"

Aleksei shook his head. "No. Oh, no. I administered it to myself."
He gave me an earnest glance. "Mortification of the flesh is good for
the soul."

I wanted to cry. "Aleksei..."

"It's all right, Moirin," he said quietly. "I don't mind."

"*I* do!" I wrestled myself back to calmness, breathing slowly and
trying to find words that would reach him. "You know, I do believe
your mother would do it if she dared. Set me free."

"Nooo..." He drew out the word, uncertain.

"I understand her fears," I said. "I didn't at first. But she is a woman
shunned by her society, always and forever paying for her youthful
mistake. It is a cruel world for one such as her, and she has nowhere
else to go. It would be different for you. You're a young man, healthy
and strong. You could apprentice yourself, learn a trade."

Aleksei squared his shoulders. "I have a trade. A calling. My uncle
has raised me—"

"To convert D'Angelines," I finished for him.

He flushed. "Yes."

"That is *his* dream, *his* interpretation of God's will." I eyed him
speculatively. "What is *yours*? With your fluent tongue, you could
find work as an interpreter in the D'Angeline embassy. With your
training, you could go west and study with those priests who took
Rebbe Avraham's words to heart, those on the opposite side of the
Great Schism."

That hit home.

Aleksei's fists knotted, his raw-boned knuckles turning white, the
book of scriptures forgotten in his lap. The hot flush on his rugged
cheekbones deepened, and his blue eyes darkened with anger and
despair. "You seek to tempt me!"

"No," I said simply. "I seek to live. And I am only telling you the
truth, whether you welcome it or not."

He surged to his feet with fluid grace, all awkwardness forgotten
in the heat of the moment. The book of scripture fell to the floor. He

paced the confines of my cell, muttering to himself in Vralian, his fists clenching and unclenching.

I watched him, fearful and fascinated.

At length, Aleksei fetched up before me, looming over my narrow bed, wild-eyed and grim-faced, his tawny hair tousled. "I cannot do it, Moirin. After so long, I dare not succumb to temptation. I cannot set you free. I cannot betray my uncle. Everything I am, I owe to him. Everything! Do you understand?"

"Aye," I murmured with regret.

He wasn't finished. "Nor can I watch you die and believe it God's will in truth. So..." His chest rose and fell. "Instead, I will teach you."

"Teach me?" I echoed. "Were you not listening when I said—"

"Yes." Aleksei cut me off. "I was." He picked up the fallen book, kissing it reverently.

I was confused. "I don't understand."

He settled onto the stool. "In a little more than two months' time, the Duke of Vralsturm will come to Riva to attend the midsummer festival. It is my uncle's hope that he might present you as his greatest success, and gain the Duke's patronage. If he succeeds, the Duke might petition his kin in Vralgrad on behalf of his D'Angeline crusade. It is my uncle's fondest dream, to see the prophecies of Elijah of Antioch bear fruit," he added.

"I know," I said. "And I told you, it will not begin with me."

"Yes, but my uncle does not know that." Aleksei opened the book. "Are you willing to lie?"

I nodded. "Yes, of course. But, Aleksei, even when I am telling the truth, he does not always believe me. I do not know how to make him."

"I do." He nodded, too, turning the pages. "And I will teach you what lies you must utter to save your life."

THIRTY-THREE

Playing the role of a lifetime, I lied.

For two months, I lied through my teeth. I memorized the creed and the lengthy catechism Aleksei taught me, until I could recite it in my sleep. I kept my temper in check. I gave no one cause to doubt me.

I resumed my penance, scouring squares. I uttered the prayer that the Patriarch had given me.

In time, I was allowed to attend another service. I had no visions or fits. I did not assault Luba.

It was without a doubt one of the most excruciating things I'd been called upon to do in my young, but eventful, life. I was not a patient person by nature, but it seemed the gods were hell-bent on teaching me to become one.

Betimes I thought of my restlessness during the long Tatar winter when I was frustrated by the knowledge that Bao was so very near, and I could have laughed in despair at the irony. I would have traded this hardship for that one in a heartbeat.

Then I'd had the kindness of Batu and Checheg and their family to sustain me, the innocent ardor of the children to fulfill my yearning for the warmth of human contact. I'd had chores that made me feel useful and welcome, not pointless ones that left my body sore and aching.

I'd had the escape of the vast, wide-open steppe, the immense blue sky. I'd had the distraction of horse races and archery contests. And ah, gods! I'd had the solace of being able to summon the twilight.

Now I was a prisoner wrapped in chains, condemned to harsh labor and the tedium of memorizing the tenets of a faith I would never embrace. I had a captor I despised. My senses and my magic were stifled.

And Bao...like as not Bao was a thousand leagues away from me by now, heading determinedly in the wrong direction, taking the missing half of my soul with him. I wondered what would have befallen him if I *had* taken Yeshua's hand in my vision, if I *had* lost my *diadh-anam*.

Would his be extinguished, too? Would he survive it?

Somehow, I didn't think so. Master Lo had given his life that Bao might live, but it hadn't been enough. It had required the divine spark of the Maghuin Dhonn Herself to rekindle his life. If that were gone...I feared death would reclaim Bao.

It was a terrifying thought.

I wondered, too, what would happen to Bao if I were to die. I didn't *think* it was the same. If I died with my *diadh-anam* alight, it would not be extinguished. I would pass through the stone doorway to rejoin the Maghuin Dhonn Herself.

But I wasn't entirely sure, and that thought terrified me, too. So I applied myself diligently to my scrub-brush and my studies, and I became far more skilled than I had ever been at lying and deception in the service of my purported redemption, pretending to be humble and earnest in my desire for God's forgiveness.

Even so, had it not been for Aleksei, I would have lost my wits. To be sure, he was a very peculiar young man and there were times when I couldn't understand him in the slightest. But since he had compromised his conscience and agreed to help me on his own terms, he was a bit easier in my presence.

For my part, I abandoned the myriad small ways in which I'd sought to tempt him. Of course, the matter lay between us nonetheless. Naamah's gift could be suppressed, but it could not be extinguished.

It was no ephemeral spark like my *diadh-anam*. It was written in flesh as well as spirit, written in the quickening of the blood, the gladdening of the heart, the language of desire.

I had to own, the boy had a formidable will to resist it. I didn't doubt that much of it was due to having a lifetime's worth of repression and discipline drilled into him. Still, in his own way, Aleksei was as stubborn as Bao.

Unlike my stubborn magpie, who had once posed rather unconvincingly as a travelling monk sworn to celibacy, I thought Aleksei *would* make a good priest...if he were ever to free himself from the shackles of the Church of Yeshua Ascendant and its harsh strictures and embrace the kinder tenets Rebbe Avraham had espoused, as he so clearly longed to do in his heart of hearts.

He liked the role of teacher, and he was good at it. When I pleaded with him, he relented and began teaching me a few words of Vralian along with the Yeshuite scriptures. When I escaped, I meant to vanish into the twilight and stay there as long as possible, but there might be times when I would need to communicate.

But Aleksei listened, too. True to my word, I told him the tale of Phèdre nó Delaunay de Montrève and her quest to find the Name of God. Fascinated and horrified, he hung on my every word. He thought about it for days, although the things he pondered were often issues that never would have occurred to me.

"This lost tribe, the Tribe of Dân. Did they embrace Yeshua as the *mashiach* once they learned of him?" he inquired.

"The *mashiach*?"

"The Anointed One," he clarified. I had learned that along with the D'Angeline tongue Aleksei had learned that he might one day use to convert us all, he spoke and read fluent Habiru.

"No, I don't think so." I knew only a little about the matter, having overheard discussions among members of the Circle of Shalomon regarding various Habiru scholars.

Aleksei looked astonished. "Why ever not?"

I shrugged. "I think they believe the true *mash*...Anointed One is yet to come."

He couldn't stop gaping. Clearly, the notion rocked the foundations of his world. As intelligent and well studied as he was, he had led an extremely insular life.

"The world is a vast place, Aleksei," I said softly. "I know you are very sure that your God is the One True God, but...I do not believe it. If there is a truth beyond all other truths, I think Master Lo has the right of it. The Way that can be told is not the eternal Way. It comes before all else, and everything comes from it. Even gods."

Aleksei shook his head at me. "You *are* a heretic!"

"To you, aye." Deciding it had been too long since I'd seen his blush, I gave him a wicked smile, letting it linger on my lips. "But decidedly not a saint."

His color rose; but he'd found his own ways of dealing with me. A muscle in his jaw twitched. "If you bait me, I will not teach you Vralian, Moirin."

"Oh, fine." I let my smile fade.

"Anyway, I am not so sure," Aleksei said unexpectedly, once again taking the conversation in a direction I couldn't have anticipated. He bowed his head, his tawny hair falling over his brow, bronze locks shot through with gold. I longed to run my fingers through it. "I wonder...I wonder, why *has* God sent you to tempt me? Surely, you have suffered in the bargain. Are you *my* heretic saint? What am I meant to learn from this?"

"I don't know," I murmured.

"It is hard, so hard," he said, more to himself than to me. "I wish I knew."

I did, too.

And because I had come to care for Aleksei, compassionate, damaged soul that he was, I wished I could comfort him. I wanted to go to him, put my arms around him, offer the solace of human warmth and kindness.

I didn't dare.

He might have accepted it—*might* have. Or he might have pushed me away and fled, fearful that I meant to seduce him. The stakes were too high, and I was too afraid. So I remained where I was and stifled my urge to give comfort, reckoning it was but one more casualty in the ongoing war for my soul.

THIRTY-FOUR

B eneath the Patriarch's stern gaze, I dipped my brush in the lye
bucket and scrubbed the last square of my penance.

"Yeshua the Anointed, Son of God, have mercy on me, a sinner."

It was done, twice over. Over the course of weeks and months, I
had finished one complete circuit and begun anew.

Now that was done, too.

I clambered wearily to my feet, my stiff back and bruised knees
protesting. "Again, my lord?"

"No." Pyotr Rostov placed both hands on my shoulders. "No,
child. You have done well, so very, very well, and I am proud of you."
His velvet-brown eyes shone with genuine warmth. "Moirin mac
Fainche of the Maghuin Dhonn, are you prepared to be baptized into
the Yeshuite faith?"

I would have danced naked in the village square if it meant getting
rid of these hateful chains.

I lowered my gaze. "Do you think me worthy?"

He embraced me. "I do."

I made myself glance shyly at him beneath my lashes. "Then it
would be my honor, my lord."

"Good, good!" The Patriarch embraced me again. I managed not
to shudder with revulsion. After a moment, he let me go, regarding
me and steepling his fingers. "The Duke of Vralsturm comes next
week for the festival. I shall arrange for your baptism and chrismation

to coincide with his visit, that he might see God's glory at work. I trust you do not mind?"

I shook my head. "No, my lord. I am privileged to serve as an example."

His creamy look came and went, replaced by one of solemn gravity. "And I to serve as the vessel of your redemption."

"Yes, my lord."

In the privacy of my cell, I wondered if he believed it. I daresay he did. Like Raphael de Mereliot, he was a man of great ambition. Unlike Raphael, I had no idea what forces had shaped the Patriarch's nature. I only knew he had a profound hunger to believe himself the conduit of his God's will.

Well and so, I would let him.

Like Aleksei, I did not feel wholly good about our endeavor. Alone in my cell, I addressed Yeshua ben Yosef in quiet prayer.

"Forgive me," I whispered. "I do not wish to lie. But I do not wish to die, either. So when the time comes, I will lie. If Berlik was right about you, you will understand and forgive me, along with the oath-breakers and the murderers, and everyone else who has fallen low. Will you?"

Yeshua did not answer me—but then, gods seldom did.

The following week, the Duke of Vralsturm arrived in Riva, where he was received with great fanfare. I was not permitted to take part in any of the celebrations, but I could hear them through the narrow window of my cell. Hard as it was for me to imagine them rejoicing, the folk of Riva sounded merry.

My baptism was to take place the following day on the shores of Lake Severin, for one of Yeshua's apostles had decreed that it was best done in living water. There was to be a solemn procession through the town wherein the Patriarch and a coterie of lesser priests led me in my chains to the lake. There I was to be submerged in water three times, and then led in procession back to the temple, where the final ceremony of the chrismation was to be performed.

I was not looking forward to it.

But Pyotr Rostov had promised that once I was baptized and anointed, once he had pronounced me born anew in the Yeshuite faith, he would unlock my chains and set me free; and Aleksei claimed his uncle was a man of his word.

Stone and sea, I hoped so.

For two days before the ceremony, I was made to fast. I would have reckoned it yet another punishment, but the truth was, these Yeshuites were mad for fasting. Aleksei regularly fasted for days at a time. I wondered if they would be quite so keen on the practice if they'd ever had to endure a long, lean winter.

Probably. In Aleksei's case, definitely. He would welcome the opportunity to offer his suffering up to God. Me, I could not help but think that there was more than enough suffering in the world without adding to the balance.

The morning of my baptism, Valentina came to fetch me. I was to be given a thorough bath and dressed in a clean garment of white wool. Gods willing, I thought, it would be the last time I had to be sewn into my clothing.

Although she had shown me occasional small gestures of tenderness since my whipping, today Valentina handled me with impersonal efficiency, draping the shapeless robe of white wool over me once I was scrubbed clean. Her face was more careworn than usual, and she looked unhappy.

"What is the matter?" I asked softly. "Is this not the very outcome you desired upon my arrival, my lady?"

She gave me a sharp look. "Is it?"

"Your son has helped guide me on the path toward redemption." I'd developed a certain fondness for poor Valentina, forever punished for her transgression, unable to help yearning for beauty nonetheless— but not enough to trust her with the truth. "Is that not pleasing in God's eyes? Does it not suggest he has forgiven you?"

Valentina laughed, a broken sound. "It begs the axiom, does it not? Beware what you pray for, lest God grant your prayers."

I was silent.

She paused in her stitching, gazing into the distance. "Do you know, in the western Church, they venerate Yeshua's mother, Marya. We do not do that here in the east. Women are not venerated, not even the Mother of God. After all these years, I still miss it." She continued stitching. "Would that I had appreciated such grace when I had it."

"I understand," I murmured. I did, all too well.

A single bitter tear trickled down her cheek. "God help me, I'd come to hope..." She did not finish the thought.

I knew, though. Valentina had come to hope that I would succeed in seducing her son, that I would persuade him to leave this place and find his wings. I wanted to tell her that I had tried my best, that one cannot free someone who doesn't wish to be set free. Two months ago, I would have done it without hesitation.

Moirin the unrepentant sinner would have said it. Moirin the penitent catechumen didn't dare.

Even so, I reached out and wiped the tear gently from Valentina's face, trying to tell her without words that I was sorry for failing. She shook her head at me, and finished stitching me into my white robe, then winding a white woolen scarf around my head.

And then it was time.

My nemesis Luba came to fetch us. Once again, I was led outside so that I might enter the temple properly. It was a fine, bright summer day. If I'd actually wanted to be baptized, I couldn't have asked for a more auspicious day.

Inside the temple, there was a considerable crowd. Scores of villagers were present. Aleksei was there, and gave me a slight, encouraging nod. The Patriarch was there before the altar in his vestments, flanked by a handful of priests including my former captors Ilya and Leonid. There was a wide-set fellow with a greying beard and keen blue-grey eyes. He wore fine clothes and was surrounded by soldiers, and I took him to be the Duke of Vralsturm. He eyed me with intense interest as I approached the altar, breathing the Breath of Ocean's Rolling Waves to calm my nerves.

"Moirin mac Fainche of the Maghuin Dhonn," Pyotr Rostov addressed me in a deep voice, speaking in D'Angeline for my benefit. "Is it your will this day to be baptized into the faith of the One True God and his son Yeshua?"

"It is, my lord," I said firmly, willing myself to meet his eyes without a trace of guile.

He asked me the first question of the catechism. "What is our church called?"

"The Church of Yeshua Ascendant."

"Why is it called the Church of Yeshua Ascendant?"

These were the easy questions. "Because it is dedicated to building the Kingdom of Yeshua on earth and preparing for his return."

The Patriarch nodded in approval. "State its teaching briefly."

I took a deep breath, reciting the words Aleksei had taught me. "God made the world and created Edom the First Man and his wife, the All-Mother, Yeva. Although our first parents were fashioned to be good, they succumbed to temptation and disobeyed God. Through the sin of disobedience, their minds were darkened. Their hearts were made evil, and they fell into wickedness and death. Their descendants suffered for their sins. But God in his infinite love sent his son Yeshua ben Yosef to redeem them..."

On and on it went.

I made a few mistakes, faltering here or there. Aleksei and I had agreed it would be more believable if I didn't have the catechism down letter-perfect. But on the whole, I performed to Pyotr Rostov's satisfaction.

The Duke of Vralsturm appeared impressed. I wondered if he spoke D'Angeline, but then I realized Aleksei was translating for him in a quiet murmur.

The Patriarch was pleased. On the surface of it, his expression remained grave, but I could sense his creamy look hovering just beneath his solemnity. This was the beginning of his great moment of triumph.

I let him bask in it.

He stepped down from the dais, swinging his censer about me, enveloping me in a cloud of fragrant smoke, laying a hand on my head and speaking in sonorous Vralian. The crowd murmured, ascertaining that I had passed the first test.

From thence, the processional to the shores of the lake.

It was a slow process, the pace dictated by the mincing steps I was forced to take, constrained by the shackles around my ankles and the short length of chain joining them, my bare feet shuffling on the sun-warmed cobbled streets. Pyotr Rostov didn't mind. He would be happy for this moment to stretch into eternity.

I saw the Duke of Vralsturm gesture at my chains, leaning in to ask the Patriarch a question.

Rostov made him a somber reply. I'd learned enough Vralian to catch the gist of it.

Yes, yes, it is necessary.

We reached the shores of Lake Severin. They were stony and harsh beneath my bare soles. I'd gone unshod since the day Ilya and Leonid had wrenched off my thick Tatar boots in the Great Khan's *ger* and clamped the shackles onto me.

That seemed a very long time ago.

The sun was high overhead, sparkling on the lake's surface. I felt a touch lightheaded, no doubt from fasting. The villagers fanned out along the rocky shoreline, watching with avid interest. The Duke took a good vantage point for himself and his men, watching, his expression curious and interested.

The Patriarch waded into the lake and beckoned to me.

I wallowed into the cold water, my white robes billowing around me, my chains weighing me down.

"Moirin, recite the creed."

"We believe in one God, the Father Almighty, Maker of Heaven and Earth, and all things visible and invisible," I said in a breathless rush. "And in Yeshua the Anointed, the only-begotten son of God, light of the light, being of one substance with the Father, by whom all things were made. Yeshua, who came down from Heaven and was made man, who suffered and was buried and rose again. Yeshua, who will come again in glory to judge us all, whose kingdom shall have no end."

Pyotr Rostov smiled, laying his hand on my head. Gods, I hated that gesture.

"Verily, verily I say unto thee," he quoted. "Except a man be born of water and the spirit, he cannot enter the Kingdom of Heaven. Moirin mac Fainche, be you born anew this day in the faith of God and Yeshua, his son."

He pushed my head underwater.

Once...

Twice...

Thrice.

I came up dripping, my wet robe plastered to my body, my headscarf askew. The wool was thick enough that it didn't become sheer, but I doubted it left much to the imagination otherwise. Onlookers murmured once more, and I made an extra effort to keep my expression earnest and guileless.

"Well done, child." The Patriarch extended his hand to me, and I took it, letting him help me out of the lake's chilly depths. "Only the final step remains."

I nodded. "Yes, my lord. I am ready for it."

Dripping, we returned to the temple in another slow, mincing procession. I was acutely aware of my own sodden discomfort and the gaze of others on me.

I was ready, so ready, for this to be over.

To be free.

I had entertained fantasies of defying the Patriarch the instant my chains were loosed, but I had decided against it. Better to be circumspect and keep up the charade until the Duke had departed.

Once more, I stood before the altar. Pyotr Rostov swung his censer, sanctifying the dish that held the holy oil, then took up the dish, dipping his fingers into the oil. He offered another prayer in Vralian, then turned his attention to me. "One last step, Moirin," he repeated, his fingers glistening with oil.

"Yes, my lord." I raised my face obediently, ready for him to anoint me.

But that wasn't what he meant. "Very good. Before God and all here assembled, pledge yourself to the Yeshuite faith on the sacred oath of your people."

I stared at him, my mind a blank.

It felt as though the ground had crumbled beneath me, leaving me teetering on the edge of a precipice. This wasn't part of the chrismation ceremony. I knew it backwards and forwards, Aleksei had gone over it with me a hundred times. This was not part of it.

"The oath Berlik the Cursed swore and broke," the Patriarch reminded me. "The one you uttered to me once before. Swear it now."

Oh, gods.

I couldn't.

If I swore it and broke it, I would lose my *diadh-anam*. If I swore it and *kept* it, I would lose my *diadh-anam*.

I swallowed hard. "I can't, my lord."

THIRTY-FIVE

The Patriarch of Riva had not expected defiance. He frowned at me, holy oil dripping from the tips of his fingers. "What do you mean you can't?"

It had gotten very quiet in the temple. I could hear the low murmur of Aleksei translating for the Duke of Vralsturm, and faint whispers as those around him eavesdropped and passed on his words.

I'd gone ice-cold beneath my damp robe. My mind worked frantically. "I...It would be blasphemy, my lord. I cannot swear an oath to Yeshua on the troth that binds me to my *diadh-anam*." My voice trembled. "You may as well ask me to swear it by the Maghuin Dhonn Herself! That cannot be right!"

Over the course of months, I'd gotten good at lying, good at dissembling. Not good enough. Not here, not now. He could see the panic in my eyes.

"*I* will be the judge of what is blasphemous or not, Moirin," Pyotr Rostov said in a smooth tone. "Not you, a lowly catechumen. Will you swear the oath or not?"

I shook my head slowly. "No."

He lowered the dish of holy oil. "Then I will cancel the ceremony."

"My lord..." My mouth had gone dry. "Please, no. I've worked so very hard to obey you. This is your moment of triumph. Will you spoil it?"

The Patriarch's eyes narrowed. I watched him weigh the decision. If he acceded, he would have his moment of mortal triumph intact and unspoiled, but it would be a lie, a holy rite violated in the temple of God. In the struggle for my soul, he would be acknowledging his failure.

All I could do was pray that his ambition outweighed his fanaticism. It didn't.

"I'm sorry, Moirin. More sorry than you know. I take no pleasure in what must follow." He returned the dish to its stand, addressing the congregation in sonorous Vralian, his voice heavy with regret.

Shocked gasps rippled through the crowd. I didn't know enough Vralian to follow everything he said, but I didn't need to. Here and there, I caught words I knew. The reaction of the crowd and the look of dawning horror on Aleksei's face told me everything I needed to know. All my hard work, all my patience, everything had unraveled in a matter of heartbeats. All for one oath unsworn.

"You're condemning me to death, aren't you?" I whispered.

Rostov didn't look at me. "You leave me no choice."

"No choice!" My long-repressed anger returned ten-fold, fueled by mindless terror. "Oh, please, *my lord*! You have chosen everything! Everything! You have chosen which of the prophets you will heed, and which you will ignore! You have chosen to elevate the harshest strictures over the kindest of Yeshua's teaching!" I yanked off my sodden head-scarf, hurling it away from me. "*You* have chosen this endless fascination with sins of the flesh!"

His face darkened. "Moirin, be silent!"

"No!" I shouted at him. "I have been silent long enough! Do you think I do not know how it aroused you to hear my confession? *How many times did you fornicate with him? Did you pleasure her with your mouth?*" I asked, mimicking him. "Do you think I did not know it made your rod harden and swell to hear it?"

"You *will* be silent!" The Patriarch strode down from the dais and struck me hard across the face, knocking me to the floor in a tangle of chains and wet robes.

I scrambled backward, my head ringing, but I did not cease taunting him. "Does it harden even now, *my lord*?"

He strode after me, reaching down to grasp my chains and haul me to my feet, raising his hand to strike another blow.

And then the Duke of Vralsturm and his men were there to intervene, easing us apart. I gasped with relief at the reprieve and gazed at the Duke's weather-beaten face, a spark of hope coming to me. I tried to think of a single word of Vralian, and failed. My wits were too scrambled. "Aleksei!" I looked frantically for him, found him and caught his arm. "Aleksei, I need your help."

"Moirin..." Aleksei wouldn't meet my eyes.

"Just translate for me!" I said. He nodded reluctantly. Collecting myself as best I could, I turned to the Duke. "My lord, forgive me this scene. But I have been held prisoner here against my will for many months. I am a citizen of Terre d'Ange and Alba, and descended from the royal houses of both nations."

Aleksei translated. The Duke listened and nodded, appraising me with his sharp blue-grey eyes. He asked a question, and Aleksei relayed it. "Descended how so?"

"I will give him my genealogy if he wishes," I said. "Daniel de la Courcel, the King of Terre d'Ange, acknowledged me as kin. Ask the Patriarch himself; his own notes confirm it. I have no doubt his highness would reward my rescuer, as I have no doubt he would be most wroth if I were put to death here."

It was a gamble, but King Daniel had always been fond of me. I wished now I had presented myself to the Cruarch before I'd left Alba.

Once again, Aleksei translated; once again, the Duke asked questions of him. These, Aleksei answered himself. The Duke bowed his head toward me and spoke at length, and there was regret in his voice.

"What did he say?" I asked dully.

"He said..." Aleksei cleared his throat and stared at the pebbled floor. "He said what you say may be true, but you have sinned against the Church nonetheless. You are far from home. No one knows you

are here, and no one will know if you die here. And although...
although it is a shame to destroy such exquisite beauty, any woman
who can tempt the Patriarch of Riva to lose control of himself in the
temple of God is too dangerous to live."

"Oh." My last spark of hope guttered and died.

The Duke of Vralsturm spoke to the Patriarch briefly, then beckoned to his men. Together, they exited the temple.

In the wake of their departure, the crowd began to surge forward.
They may not have understood all that had transpired, but they were
ready to drag me to the town square and stone me here and now.

"Aleksei..." My voice was high with fear.

With only a moment's hesitation, he put himself between me
and the crowd, reaching out his hands in a pleading gesture.

What would have happened if Pyotr Rostov had not addressed
the crowd, I cannot say. But he did, and it quieted them. One by one,
they began to file out of the temple.

I did not think it was much of a reprieve.

I was right.

The Patriarch turned to me. "Moirin mac Fainche of the Maghuin
Dhonn," he said with velvety malice. "For sins of the flesh, witchcraft,
and blasphemy against the Church of Yeshua Ascendant, you will be
put to death by stoning at dawn tomorrow. I recommend you spend
the night meditating on your sins."

"Go to hell, you stunted old pervert," I muttered.

He gave me a creamy smile, not trying to hide it for once. "Nephew,
I think it best if you have no further contact with the witch. Luba,
Valentina, escort her to her cell."

I glanced over my shoulder at Aleksei as we left. He was staring at
the floor again, which didn't bode well for me.

Luba was smiling, broadly and openly. For a piece of irony, it made
her look pleasant and kind for the first time since I'd known her. I
wouldn't have been surprised to hear her burst into song.

Valentina was silent, her face shuttered and averted. When they
made to leave, I caught her sleeve.

"Thank you, my lady," I said softly. "For such small kindnesses as you have shown me. My mother..." My voice broke. "If she knew, my mother would be glad that her daughter did not die entirely friendless."

She did not answer or meet my eyes, only freed my hand gently from her sleeve. They left, and I heard the key turn in the lock.

I was alone.

Tomorrow, I was going to die—and quite horribly.

It took some time for the enormity of that notion to settle over me. I had faced death before, more than once. I wasn't afraid of death, not exactly. I had made peace with it. I knew what awaited me on the far side of the stone doorway. The precious spark of my *diadh-anam* shone inside me, a promise that the Maghuin Dhonn Herself would welcome me home, and I would be free at last.

The dying itself was another matter.

I wondered how long it would take, and how much it would hurt. A lot, I thought. The bones of my face ached where the Patriarch had struck me, and my cheek was bruised and swollen.

I prayed.

I cried.

I thought about all the people who would never know that I had died here and would always wonder what had befallen me. I wished I could speak to them. My mother, most of all—and Bao, a close second.

What would become of him? If I were right and I died with my *diadh-anam* unextinguished, he would live, condemned to wander the earth in search of the missing half of *his* soul, never knowing for sure.

Mayhap it would be better if I were wrong.

I thought about everything I had done here in Riva, wondering what I could have done differently. Something. Nothing. If I had not lost my temper and sworn the sacred oath of the Maghuin Dhonn earlier, mayhap the Patriarch would not have sought to bind me with it—or mayhap not. He had known of Berlik's oath. Mayhap if I had not baited the Patriarch in the temple, the Duke of Vralsturm would have relented and aided me.

Mayhap.

Bao had accused me of being impulsive. He was right; he was usually right. But I had been patient for so very, very long; and Pyotr Rostov had already condemned me to death. I didn't know if it would have made a difference if I had held my tongue.

I leaned my head against the wall and watched the light change in my narrow window, mellowing to an afternoon glow, fading slowly to dusk, a painful reminder of the twilight that was forbidden to me.

Come dawn...

They would gloat, those bedamned villagers. Hurling stones that broke my bones and tore my flesh, eking out a slow, painful death; oh yes, they would gloat, glorying in their almighty self-righteousness.

It was going to hurt a lot, for a long time. It was a bad way to die.

I closed my eyes, slow tears leaking beneath my lids. I wished I could be brave and defiant on the morrow, but I was fairly sure I would just be terrified. And I was fairly sure the Patriarch had granted me this day's reprieve only that I might fully experience the depth of my terror.

No, I *was* sure.

When I heard the sound of a key turning in the lock of my cell door, I thought at first that I was dreaming.

I wasn't.

My narrow window was dark. I sat upright on my narrow bed, watching a gilded wedge of lamplight enter my chamber as a lone figure slipped through the door, tall and rangy.

"Aleksei," I breathed. "You've risked everything to free me after all?"

In the lamp-lit darkness, he shook his head. A silver key dangled from his fist on a chain. "Not I, no. My mother."

THIRTY-SIX

Valentina; oh Valentina! "How?" I whispered.

Aleksei knelt at my feet, busying himself with the key, unlocking the shackles around my ankles. "My uncle takes tea after supper. From time to time, Mother puts a sedative in it to ease his rest and give the rest of us a measure of peace. A tincture of valerian. He's never known about it." He eased the cuffs from my ankles. "Better?"

"Yes." I wanted to leap to my feet and dance. "But . . . you?"

"She stole the key and gave me a choice," he murmured, his head bowed. "To do this myself and see you to the border, and take my own freedom. Or to let her free you, and watch her suffer the punishment for it. I chose. Hands, Moirin."

I held them out to him. "You chose this?"

Aleksei gave me a pained, fleeting smile. "What is the fifth commandment that God inscribed on Moishe's tablets?"

This, too, I had memorized. "Honor your mother and father."

He nodded. "Even so."

One shackle opened. I raised my left hand, shaking it. I didn't feel any different yet, and a creeping fear filled me. I tried to take comfort from the spark of my *diadh-anam* inside me, but I was scared. What if that were the most I would ever feel? What if the damage done to me were permanent? What if God and Yeshua were punishing me after all? I *had* lied, I *had* violated the sanctity of their rites. I whispered a soft prayer for their forgiveness as Aleksei unlocked the second wrist cuff.

"That almost sounded genuine," he murmured, moving behind me to unlock the collar around my neck.

"It was."

"I'm pleased." Aleksei got the lock undone and removed the silver collar, the chains coming away with it.

My *diadh-anam* blazed riotously as my senses opened and expanded in a hectic rush, my awareness surging outward to embrace the world. All of my senses were suddenly keener, sharper, more alert.

I laughed aloud for the sheer joy of it. "Aleksei, Aleksei, I can *see* again! I can *feel*!"

"Hush," he cautioned me, looking perplexed. "But you weren't blind, Moirin. Were you?"

Bao. Where was Bao? I stood and turned instinctively, seeking the beacon of his *diadh-anam*.

It was far away, far to the south, and fainter than it ought to be even at such a distance. I frowned, wondering what that meant. Was he ill? Injured? It seemed I should have felt some flare of recognition in his *diadh-anam* at sensing mine unveiled after so long. But mayhap I was wrong. After all, this was uncharted territory. Insofar as I knew, no one had ever had the divine spark of the Maghuin Dhonn Herself divided and shared with another living soul.

"Moirin?"

I glanced at Aleksei, still looking perplexed. Fretting over Bao would have to wait. I had a long way to go before I was safe. Wherever he was, my magpie could take care of himself. "Not blind, no, but something akin to it. The chains blocked my sense of magic in the world."

"I see." Now he looked uneasy.

"You will," I said to him. "Close your eyes a moment." Although he didn't like it, he obeyed. I took a deep breath, let it out, took another and summoned the twilight, breathing it out over both of us.

It settled over me like an embrace, soft and gentle, drenching the lamp-lit cell in silvery-violet dusk, turning it into a magical place. It felt like a homecoming, like being reunited with a long-lost love.

I smiled. "Now, see."

Aleksei opened his eyes. "Oh!" Wonder dawned over his features. "It's...it's so beautiful!"

"Aye." I breathed it deep into my lungs, along with the scent of pine-trees growing on the outskirts of town. I longed to touch their rough bark, listen to their slow thoughts. "Now you've seen the great and terrible sin of witchcraft at work."

"It's beautiful," he repeated. "And you...you're beautiful in it." He smiled shyly at me. "Even more so, I mean. And it doesn't *feel* like a sin."

I touched his cheek. "Thank you, my sweet boy. Now, how do we get ourselves safely away from here?"

"Oh!" Caught up in the twilight's charm, he'd nearly forgotten our plight. "Here." He fetched a bundle from the floor and thrust it at me. "From my mother. Clothing, shoes, a head-scarf. Bread and cheese, as much as she could get on short notice." He jingled a purse at his belt. "She had a little money. Not much."

"Blessed Valentina," I murmured, shaking out the drab woolen dress. It was a good deal less conspicuous than my catechumen's white robe. "Do we have waterskins? A striking kit? Bow and arrows?"

"No." Realizing I was preparing to change my clothes, modest Aleksei turned his back on me. "I'm sorry, Moirin. I've never done anything like this before."

"No matter." I shed the robe, donned the dress. Shoved my feet into the shoes, and wrapped the scarf around my head. "We'll find what we need along the way. You can turn around," I added.

He did, looking dubious. "We haven't much coin, truly."

It was on the tip of my tongue to say I'd gladly steal whatever was needful when my gaze fell on the hateful, discarded chains. "Actually, we do." I picked up the chains. "These are nearly solid silver. They must be worth a small fortune."

Aleksei frowned. "You mean to steal them?"

"Aye, sweet boy, I do," I said. "As fair exchange for the months of my life stolen from me. They were made for me, were they not? And I mean to sell them to a smith who will melt them down and ensure they are never, ever used again to bind someone against their will."

He was silent a moment.

I raised my brows at him. "Aleksei, whatever sins must be committed in the pursuit of freedom, I will gladly take on myself. If you are going to scruple at it, stay. Stay and take your punishment, and break your mother's heart. Only tell me first where I might find a smithy south of Riva."

"Moirin, you can't go south."

I glanced in the direction of Bao's distant *diadh-anam*. "Oh, but I am."

"Not right away," Aleksei said in stubborn tone. "That's exactly where my uncle will look for you. And he will look, believe me."

I shrugged. "He cannot find me in the twilight."

"Can you work your magic while sleeping?" he asked shrewdly. "Can you be on guard every minute of every day? Do you imagine there's a single village between here and the border that doesn't remember you passing through it in those chains? It's not a sight one forgets. Any smith you approach would know you in an instant for the Patriarch's witch. Any baker in the market, any...anyone!" He shook his head. "I may not have thought this through, but this part, I have. It's too dangerous to do exactly what my uncle will expect."

I didn't like it, but he had a point. "Where, then? We haven't much time to debate this."

"Udinsk," Aleksei said promptly. "It's a city some days away to the northeast. It's a trade center. I thought I could find work there. I'm sure we could find a smith willing to ask no questions, and aught we need to purchase for the journey."

"The journey south," I said.

He nodded. "In two weeks' time, my uncle will realize his mistake and begin searching farther afield. Then we can slip through, amply provisioned, hidden by your magic when need be."

I hesitated.

Every impulse in me yearned to go south, toward Bao, to flee. To trust to my magic to conceal me, to my hard-won skills to allow me to survive. But I'd ventured into Tatar territory alone despite being warned of the danger and nearly died because of it; and I'd had all the supplies I thought I would need there. If I'd learned nothing else from this ordeal, I'd learned a measure of patience.

And, too, there was Aleksei to consider. He was betraying everything he held dear to help me. I owed it to him, and especially to his mother, Valentina, not to do anything rash and impulsive for once in my life.

"So be it," I said. "Let's go to Udinsk."

Cloaked in the twilight, we stole through the Patriarch's living quarters, Aleksei carrying bread and cheese and a few weighty yards of bespelled silver chains knotted in a worn woolen blanket.

My senses heightened in the twilight, I let my awareness roam through the quarters, touching on its inhabitants.

Stone and sea, it was good to feel wholly myself once more!

Pyotr Rostov slept deep and hard, and the acrid taste of his dreams reminded me of the sulfur and saltpeter of the Divine Thunder. Even in his sleep, he was angry. I shuddered, and looked elsewhere.

His wife, Luba, slept beside him, more lightly. She was smiling in her sleep, no doubt dreaming of selecting the perfect stone to hurl at me come dawn.

Valentina...

She was awake, kneeling in the antechamber by the outer door, her head bowed and her arms wrapped around herself, filled with a despairing mix of hope and fear.

"Aleksei." I touched his arm. "Your mother is waiting for us. I think she wishes to say farewell."

His eyes widened. "How do you know?"

"I just do."

A moment later, he saw her huddled figure. A faint sound escaped him. Valentina didn't hear it, didn't raise her head. Aleksei glanced at me in alarm. "Moirin..."

"It's all right, sweet boy." I brushed his cheek with my fingers. "I told you, they cannot see or hear us in the twilight. I will try to bring her into it."

I breathed it in deeper, blew it softly over Valentina, spinning it around her like a gentle cocoon.

Her head came up. "How——?" She glanced all around her, eyes stretched wider than her son's. "What is this? Am I dreaming?"

I smiled at her, helping her to her feet. "No, my lady. It is only a small piece of magic. I will release it if you like, but I think it is better if I don't. Your sister-in-law sleeps lightly, dreaming of cracking my skull open."

Valentina gave her broken laugh, hands rising involuntarily to stifle it. "Moirin. It is you. So Aleksei...he did it. He did it. Oh, God. God have mercy on me. I was afraid he wouldn't. Will you...?"

I nodded. "I will try."

She glanced at her son. In the twilight, the tears in her eyes shone like stars. "Aleksei..."

He embraced her. "Mother."

Valentina clung to her tall, broad-shouldered son like a drowning woman—and mayhap she was. My heart ached for the both of them. She tugged his head down to her shoulder and whispered somewhat in his ear. What she said to him, I could not say. Even if I could have heard it, I would not have listened.

Aleksei nodded, tears streaking his cheeks.

I peered through the small window set into the outer door. It was hard to gauge the hour in the twilight, but the summer nights were short, and every hour of darkness was precious. "My lady, I'm sorry, but we have to go."

"Go." With an effort, she released her son, turning him loose. "Go. For what it is worth, go with my blessing."

"A mother's blessing is worth a great deal," I murmured. "I will not forget this." I kissed her cheek. "Thank you, a thousand times over. Thank you."

Valentina nodded. "You are a mother's child, too, Moirin. I can only begin to imagine how much she is missing you. For her sake, I pray you come home to her someday."

Oh, it hurt.

"So do I." It was all I could say, all I had to say. Valentina gave her son one last, long embrace, and then opened the door for us.

The street was empty and quiet. Aleksei squared his shoulders and began walking purposefully.

I ran after him. "Wait! Aleksei, you mean to go on foot?"

He gave me a blank look. "How else?"

"I was brought here in a wagon. I know cart-horses are not ideal for riding, but it's faster than walking." I cast around with my senses. "The stable's over there, is it not?"

"Moirin, you can't steal the Church's horses!"

"Oh, yes, I can. Your precious Church didn't hesitate to steal *me*." Aleksei's delicate sensibilities were beginning to grate on my nerves. I set out in the direction of the stable. "You'd best stay close to me," I said over my shoulder. "Else you'll lose the cover of the twilight. I can only extend it so far, for so long."

He followed, silent.

The cart-horses were drowsing in their stalls, heads nodding low. I glanced around and quickly determined there was no riding tack, only the wagon and harness gear.

"That's because they're not for riding," Aleksei murmured. "Moirin, can we please go now?"

Ignoring him, I spun the twilight over one of the horses. He lifted his head, lambent eyes open and gleaming. I blew softly into his nostrils, touching his thoughts. "You're a big, strong fellow, aren't you?" I whispered. "Strong enough to carry us both." The cart-horse pricked his ears in agreement and lipped at the trailing ends of my head-scarf. I smiled and unlatched the door to his stall.

"Moirin!" Aleksei sounded near to panic.

"It's all right." There was no mounting block, but the wagon would serve. I clambered onto it. The cart-horse moved obligingly into place for me. I grabbed a double fistful of his mane and swung myself astride. "Come on," I said to Aleksei. "You'll have to ride behind me."

He gazed uncertainly at me.

I sighed. "We'll turn him loose at the end of the day. Like as not, he'll find his way home."

"It might give our direction away."

"It might," I agreed. "But not our destination, and we'll have gained a sizable lead. Aleksei, I haven't eaten in three days. Thanks to your uncle's penance, I have shooting pains in my knees. I'm not even used to taking full strides. I won't get far on foot. So are you coming with me or not?"

Without a word, he climbed onto the wagon, then scrambled awkwardly astride behind me while the patient cart-horse stood motionless.

"Ready?" I asked when Aleksei was settled. Although he'd wedged the bundle of supplies between us, his entire body was rigid at the forced contact with mine.

"How...how are you controlling it?" His voice sounded small.

"I'm not," I said. "I asked him if he's willing to carry us, and he is." I patted the horse's sturdy neck. "So hold on, because we're on our way whether you're ready or not."

The horse clopped steadily out of the stable, his abandoned stable-mate giving a low whicker. I wished we could have taken both of them, but it would have been too much effort to maintain a bond with both of them and keep my hold on the twilight. As it was, I was spreading myself thin.

On the street, I asked the cart-horse to pick up his pace. Once again, he pricked his ears in willing agreement and began walking at a good clip.

Behind me, Aleksei slid and jounced, nearly losing the bundle, grabbing for it and almost falling off in the process.

"Pass it to me." I reached backward. "I'll hold it, and you can put your arms around my waist."

"I don't..." He sounded miserable. "It's just that his back is so very broad."

"I know." I struggled for patience. "Aleksei, give me the bedamned bundle and put your arms around my waist."

Tentatively, he did.

I settled the bundle of chains and supplies on the cart-horse's withers, holding it in place with one hand and knotting the other in his mane, then asked him again for a swifter pace. He answered by breaking into a brisk trot.

Aleksei exhaled sharply, his arms tightening around my waist. Now I felt the entire length of his body pressed against me, his thighs firm against mine. Despite everything, it felt very good.

"You might as well enjoy it," I said to him. "*I* am."

"Moirin!"

"Hmm?"

"This is serious business we're about," he protested. "Please don't try to scandalize me in the midst of it."

"I'm sorry." I let go the cart-horse's mane and touched Aleksei's knee lightly. "I cannot begin to imagine what it's costing you to do this. I'm very, very grateful, and I don't mean to bait you. In times of mortal danger, people often make jests. We'd lose our wits if we didn't."

"Oh." He relaxed a little. "So...you were jesting?"

Now he sounded disappointed. "No," I said gently. "Only teasing. It feels very good to have your arms around me, Aleksei."

"Oh."

We rode in silence for a time while he contemplated that. The outskirts of Riva came into view and fell away behind us. The cart-horse continued at a steady trot. I glanced at the sky overhead, trying to determine if the moon was bright enough to see by if I released the twilight. Gauging it was, I let it go.

The gentle twilight faded, the world turning darker.

Behind me, Aleksei stiffened. "What—?"

"I let the magic go for now," I said. "Now that we're out of town, we're safe enough under cover of darkness. In daylight, we'll need it more." I yawned. "I have to conserve my strength."

"So you *can't* do just anything you wish."

"No." I shook my head. "Not at all."

He was quiet for a while longer. I breathed the Breath of Trees Growing, reveling in the presence of pine-trees along the road, listening to them dream of the sun's return. Gods, it felt good to be free! Never, ever would I take it for granted again.

I only wished I wasn't headed in the opposite direction from Bao. It worried me that the spark of his *diadh-anam* felt so far away and dim.

I pushed the thought away. Later. Survive first, worry later.

"Moirin?" Aleksei's voice was low by my ear.

"Aye?"

"I like it, too." His arms tightened a bit. "And you smell good."

"It's the odor of sanctity," I said, referencing one of the signs by which saints were known.

"Moirin!"

I laughed.

"That was a jest, wasn't it?"

"Yes, sweet boy." I patted his knee. "It was a jest."

There was a hint of a smile in his voice. "So says my heretic saint."

THIRTY-SEVEN

We rode through the night and into the day, alternating between trotting and walking. For a mercy, we were following the curve of the vast lake and were able to pause from time to time to water the cart-horse and ourselves.

Willing soul though he was, I felt our unlikely mount's strength begin to flag by midday, his steps beginning to plod. He was unaccustomed to carrying such a burden on his wide back. My own strength was failing, too. I was hoarding it as best I could, straining my eyes to catch sight of fellow travellers on the road so that I might shield us at need, but I was tired and hungry, and I began to find myself getting careless.

I daresay Aleksei felt it, too. When I suggested that we turn off the road, conceal ourselves in the pines, and catch a few hours of sleep, he agreed readily.

He watched in perplexity as I borrowed his little belt knife and cut a few long, narrow strips from the blanket in which we carried our supplies. "What on earth are you doing, Moirin? Making some sort of charm?"

I concentrated on braiding the strips together. "Hardly. I'm making a hobble for this big fellow." I nodded at the cart-horse, who leaned down to lip at my head-scarf again. "I think he's done in. We'll turn him loose before we go, but this way he'll rest without straying far, and we'll gain a few hours before his return is discovered."

"Oh. I'd never have thought of such a thing."

"You might if you'd spent three months in shackles," I said absently, knotting the makeshift hobble around the cart-horse's hairy fetlocks. "Sorry about this," I added to the horse, who responded by pulling the scarf clean off my head with his dexterous lips. I laughed and tugged it away from him, then kissed his velvety muzzle. "What, do you think you're a goat now? Rest, great heart. I'm sorry I've nothing to feed you." I turned to find Aleksei gazing at me in wonder. "What is it?" Realizing my head was bare, I touched my hair. "This? Aleksei, I will wear the scarf in public, I promise, but is there any chance you might endure it otherwise? It's very itchy."

He shook his head. "It's not the scarf. It's just...you, Moirin. You're not like I expected."

"How so?" I sat cross-legged beside the blanket of supplies and cut myself a hunk of bread and cheese before passing them to him.

"I don't know if I can put it into words." He took a modest portion of food for himself. "For all that you tease me, for all the sins you've confessed to committing, there's something oddly...innocent... about you."

I laughed. "Innocent?"

Aleksei nodded. "Seeing you like this, yes."

I shrugged. "Mayhap it's just that you're seeing me happy and free for the first time since you've laid eyes on me."

"No, it's something more." He rolled a hunk of brown bread in his hand, then whistled softly to the cart-horse, who came over to accept it gratefully, his lips nibbling Aleksei's palm. "They like bread, especially if you roll it like that," he added. "I expect it's the salt from one's sweat. When I was a boy, I used to hide in the stables sometimes."

I chewed and swallowed a bite of my own. "Oh, aye? So did I when I was younger, when I visited Cillian at Innisclan."

"Who is Cillian?"

I forgot that unlike his uncle, Aleksei didn't have knowledge of the vast litany of my sins. He knew I had confessed to them, but he wasn't privy to all the salacious details. "My oldest friend, and my first lover."

Aleksei flushed, but he didn't look away. "Are you trying to shock me because I called you innocent?"

"No." I shook my head. "I don't mind it. Only do not mistake me for something I'm not."

He rolled another pellet of bread. "I don't think I am."

I watched him feed it to the cart-horse. "You remind me of him a little. Cillian, that is."

His flush deepened. "Oh? How so?"

"You've a similar build," I said. "Tall, long-limbed. And Cillian was a scholar, too, although it was tales of adventure and magic he loved." I smiled sadly. "And he was only a little older than you when he died, I think."

Aleksei's face softened. "I'm sorry; I didn't know. How did he die?"

"On a cattle-raid," I murmured. "He was thrown and trampled."

"I'm sorry," Aleksei repeated.

"Thank you." I was grateful for the simple gift of his sympathy, grateful that unlike his uncle, he was willing to allow me the privacy of my memories. I hadn't forgotten his kindness when I was dealing with the worst of my grief at hearing of Jehanne's death.

We ate together in companionable silence. When I had finished, I folded my head-scarf into a pillow, preparing to settle onto the pine-mast.

"Sleep for a few hours," I suggested. "We'll set out before dark, and walk through the night. It ought to be clear enough to see again, and it's safer."

He nodded. "If we do, we ought to reach the Ude River by noon tomorrow. I'm hoping we can buy passage on a barge."

I smiled at him. "Ah, so you have thought this through, my hero."

Aleksei returned my smile wryly. "It's a poor excuse for a hero that has to be pushed by his mother into rescuing the maiden, then rely on the maiden to make their escape. But I am trying."

"Heroes are not made overnight," I murmured, curling up on the pine-mast and cushioning my head on the folded scarf and closing my eyes. "I think you're doing very well."

Worn out by exertion and fear, I fell asleep almost immediately, although it was a restless sleep. I dreamed I was back in Riva, back in chains, scrubbing the temple floor under Luba's merciless gaze. Every time I thought I was finished with a mosaic square, she would point out ingrained dirt I had missed, forcing me to dip the scrub-brush back into the bucket of lye and begin over again, and it seemed to me in my dream that if I did not finish before the Patriarch came to inspect my work, I would be hauled to the town square and stoned.

I awoke to low, slanting sunlight, the scent of pine-trees, and bird-song, and I laughed aloud for the sheer joy of it.

"What is it?" Aleksei mumbled, pushing himself upright. His tawny hair was disheveled with sleep and stuck about with pine needles. "Moirin?"

"Nothing, nothing. Everything's fine." I stretched luxuriously, arching my back and stretching my limbs as far as I could, free and unfettered. "I'm happy to find myself free, that's all."

Aleksei gazed at me, his blue, blue eyes wide, his lips parted. Naamah's gift swirled between us. There was a question behind his eyes, and it was one that made the bright lady smile.

"Ah." I smiled, too. "Yes."

He ducked his head. "What do you mean, yes?"

I ran my fingers through my hair, dislodging pine needles of my own. "You are wondering if I mean to honor my offer. I do. Only not here, not now." I probed my cheek with my fingertips, wincing at finding it still sore and swollen where Pyotr Rostov had struck me. "Later, when we are safer, I will honor it."

"Naamah's blessing?"

"Yes, my sweet boy." I examined the raw, chafed marks the chains had left on my wrists and ankles. "Only if you wish it."

"You don't love me, though." Aleksei's head came up. "Do you?"

"I care for you," I said honestly. "It is a gift I would like to give you, if you're willing to accept it. It is a gift I would gladly accept from you, if you are willing to offer it." I frowned, searching for words he would understand. "It is a sacrament, Aleksei. I could not offer it without love, although I do not know if it is the kind of love you mean when you ask if I love you."

He met my eyes. "It's not. Do you think you could, though? Come to love me?"

A vision unfolded.

I'd caught involuntary glimpses of others' memories before, but never of their dreams of what might be. Now, here, I *saw* Aleksei's—and it made me catch my breath. Aleksei and I, together as man and wife, forging a new path in eastern Vralia, preaching a doctrine of love in which desire and innocence walked hand in hand. Aleksei and I, a new Edom the First Man and Yeva the All-Mother, sanctifying a new Garden of Eden.

No, my *diadh-anam* whispered. *No.*

My eyes stung and watered. "No," I murmured, wiping at them. "No, Aleksei. Not like that. I'm sorry."

His throat worked. "You *saw*?"

I nodded.

Aleksei's head dropped to his knees, his arms encircling them. "I thought...maybe. Maybe my uncle was wrong and this was what God and Yeshua willed after all. I have feared it, yearned for it, struggled against it for so long. Now, now that this has come to pass..." His broad shoulders rose and fell. "I thought if I accepted it...maybe."

I went to him, held him as I had longed to do before. "Sweet boy," I whispered against his temple. "Why do you struggle so hard to discern your God's will? Stop fighting, and let him reveal it to you. All will come clear in time."

Nearby, the cart-horse whickered as though in agreement.

"Truly?"

I kissed his brow. "Truly. Now, please, can we gather ourselves and take to the road?"

After Aleksei went to scout to see that the road was clear, I cut the cart-horse's hobbles and we set out north on foot. The horse followed us for a while, peering after us through his forelock with great, liquid-dark eyes. I had to shoo him away, reminding him that his stable-mate would be missing him.

"He likes you," Aleksei commented.

"Animals usually do," I said. "Though I suspect it had as much to do with the bits of bread you fed him."

"Can you really talk to them?" he asked.

"After a fashion," I said. "Not with words, not really. But I can touch their thoughts and feelings."

"Like you read mine," he murmured.

I shook my head. "That's never happened before. Only with memories. I'm sorry, I didn't mean to intrude. I don't always know what form the Maghuin Dhonn's gifts will take. It seems to change and grow as I get older."

He processed that in silence. The sun sank low in the west, gilding the surface of the lake and sending our shadows stretching sideways. I didn't relish the prospect of a long night's walk, but at least it was peaceful here, and I felt a great deal better after some food and a few hours of sleep.

I was young, and gods willing, the various aches and pains my ordeal had inflicted on me would vanish in time. The bruises would fade, the welts would heal, the stiffness would pass. In time, I hoped, the memory of the Patriarch's creamy smile as he heard my confession would fade, too, and the treasured memories he had violated would regain their luster.

I toyed with the jade bangle on my wrist as we walked, thinking about Aleksei's plight, thinking about invoking Naamah's blessing on Snow Tiger's behalf. It was a piece of irony that my effort to protect *that* memory had nearly gotten me killed. If I hadn't sworn the sacred oath in the Patriarch's presence, he might never have known what form it took. No one had ever recorded the exact wording, not even Rebbe Avraham. I could simply have lied in the temple and sworn a false oath.

And what if I had?

Mayhap Pyotr Rostov would have kept his word and freed me. And the moment I fled, I would have been in exactly the danger Aleksei had described—alone, utterly dependent on my magic, conspicuous and vulnerable when my strength failed, sure to be pursued.

Instead, I had my awkward, fledgling hero to guide me, and the rudiments of a plan. Mayhap matters had fallen out for the best after all.

"What is that?" Aleksei broke the silence, nodding at the bangle. "Some sort of charm?"

"What is your obsession with charms?" I smiled to take the sting out of my words. "No, Aleksei. It's a bracelet. It was a gift from the Emperor of Ch'in's daughter." I held out my wrist. "Do you see the color? It is the exact hue of a pool beneath the peak of White Jade Mountain, where the dragon gazes at his reflection. We jumped into that pool together from a very great height, the princess and I, and it was there that the dragon's immortal spirit was freed."

He eyed me. "Are you teasing me again?"

"Not in the least. You could ask your uncle if he were here; he's got it all written down. Only he made me say the dragon was a fallen spirit."

"Was it?"

"No," I said. "He was a dragon." It felt good to say it aloud, as though I were reclaiming the first of many truths the Patriarch had stolen.

The sun dipped beneath low mountains on the far side of the lake, and dusk, true dusk, settled over the empty road. Aleksei and I walked side by side, the only sound our steady footfalls and the faint jangling of the chains he carried in our bundle. I listened to the pine-trees murmur in the growing darkness.

"Moirin, why not?" Aleksei asked in a low voice. "Why are you so sure you couldn't love me? Is it that you're still mourning the young man you told me about?"

"No, my sweet boy," I said with regret. "That was a long time ago.

The grief never goes away, but it gets easier to bear. And if it were because I was in mourning for a lost love, it would be my lady Jehanne I was grieving for, since that loss is fresh and the ache of it far from fading."

He stopped stock-still. "The D'Angeline *Queen*?"

I glanced at him in surprise. "I thought you knew. You were so kind to me."

"That you cared for her, yes, but..." Words failed him. "Did my *uncle* know?"

I sighed. "Yes, Aleksei. What did you think I was shouting about in the temple? He took great pleasure in extracting every detail, twisting, perverting, and tarnishing my happiest memories."

Aleksei just stared at me.

"You see?" I said to him. "*This* is why I could never be the wife and helpmate you envision. You're not seeing me as I am, Aleksei. Not yet. You're seeing me as you think I ought to be."

"What is wrong with wishing to see you perfected in God's eyes?" he whispered. "A God of love, not punishment?"

"Nothing." I set out walking again, forcing him to come after me. "Except that it will not happen. I told you before, I am a child of the Maghuin Dhonn, and I will die before I betray Her. And," I added, "I am a child of Naamah and Anael, too. I cannot swear a sacred oath to serve them over the Maghuin Dhonn Herself, but I am grateful to allow Naamah to use me as her vessel when she sees fit. And when Anael the Good Steward makes his will known to me, I will obey that, too."

With his long legs, Aleksei caught up to me easily. "So that's why you cannot love me? The gods will not allow it?"

"No." I shook my head. "I am sorry, Aleksei, truly. I didn't know how you felt. And I thought you knew, I thought your uncle had shared the catalogue of my sins with you. It isn't only a question of faith. There's someone else."

His voice took on a savage note. "*Other* than this Cillian, *other* than the D'Angeline Queen."

"Aye," I said coolly. "*Other* than Raphael de Mereliot, *other* than the carriage-driver not even your uncle knew about. Would you have me make my confession to you?"

"No! No, it's just..." His voice trailed away.

I sighed again. "I know, I know! You had a dream, and I dashed it. You took me by surprise, you know. I didn't expect you to entertain such heretical fantasies."

"Why do you think I struggled so hard against it?" he asked. "Why do you think I went to such extreme measures?"

I shrugged. "Ordinary mortal desire was enough to terrify you. How was I to know it was more than just that?"

"I suppose you weren't," Aleksei admitted. He walked without speaking for a while. "So who is he? This *other*?"

Unable to help myself, I glanced over my shoulder toward the south where Bao's *diadh-anam* guttered so disturbingly low. "It's a long story, and it's difficult to explain. There are parts of it you will find blasphemous. And I will tell you one day, but I don't feel like it tonight. He's very far away, looking for me in the wrong place, and I'm worried about him."

"You know where he is?" he asked.

"Always, except when I was in chains." I rubbed my face wearily. "We're joined together, Bao and I."

Mercifully, Aleksei didn't press me. The dusk deepened, stars and a ghostly half-moon emerging in the soft violet-blue sky. The sound of bird-song faded. Dusk gave way to true darkness, the moon and stars brightening to light our way. Slowly and steadily, step by step, we made our way north.

An hour or so before dawn, I suggested that we break once more for sleep. I would need more rest if I were to be able to summon the twilight in daylight tomorrow. Aleksei nodded in agreement, and we left the road, stumbling through the pine-scented darkness until we found a good place to make camp.

Once again, I curled gratefully onto the pine-mast, half-asleep by the time I pillowed my head on my scarf.

"Moirin?"

Aleksei's voice jolted me awake. "Aye?"

"If you truly love this other man, how can you offer to invoke Naamah's blessing for me?" he asked.

"Oh . . ." I yawned in the darkness. "It *is* possible to love more than one person, Aleksei. But that is one of Naamah's mysteries, and you will never understand it if you do not seek her blessing."

He was silent for so long I almost fell asleep again. "I will pray on the matter."

"You do that," I murmured.

THIRTY-EIGHT

True to Aleksei's prediction, we reached a settlement along the Ude River by mid-day.

Setting aside our differences, we worked together to hone our plans. He estimated it would take two days to reach Udinsk. I couldn't hold the twilight for both of us that long, not even close. But it was most important that the villagers in the settlement didn't see me, that we didn't leave behind rumors of a green-eyed witch.

So I would conceal myself while Aleksei sought to book passage for us. He was conspicuous too, but not as much as I was, with his half-Vralian features and his fluent tongue. When the time came to board the barge, I would swaddle myself in my scarf as best I could, keep my head low and myself largely silent. Aleksei would pass me off as his pilgrim bride, recently arrived in Vralia, unable to speak the language.

If the barge-hands suspected otherwise, so be it. At least we were carrying any rumors upriver, away from pursuit.

Gods be thanked, it worked.

Aleksei was beaming with pride when he came to fetch me out of concealment on the outskirts of town. "Moirin! Moirin?"

I let the twilight go.

He startled. "Yeshua have mercy! It's unnerving when you do that. Moirin, I did it! I booked passage for us on a fur-trapper's boat. It's a bit smelly and it took every coin I had, but I did it."

I smiled at him, genuinely pleased at his sense of pride. "Well done, my hero. See, you've a knack for this after all."

Color crept into his cheeks. Stone and sea, I'd never known a man who blushed so easily! "It's a foolish thing to be proud of, I know."

"Aleksei, I wasn't teasing." I laid my hand against his warm cheek. "It's a good plan, and I would never have thought of it. You were right; without you, I'd be in dire trouble."

It wasn't a pleasant journey. The boat was low and narrow, piled high with furs; and yes, they smelled, being scraped but uncured. The fur-trappers were taciturn fellows who concentrated on paddling, content to leave us alone except for stealing speculative glances at me from time to time. I strongly suspected Aleksei could have driven a harder bargain than he did, leaving us without coin.

I didn't care.

We were on our way, headed east, outpacing any rumor of our presence. We had a little bit of bread and cheese left, and river water to drink. It wasn't the cleanest, but neither of us took sick from it. We had the silver chains of my captivity hidden in our bundle, and I was hopeful that we could dispose of them in Udinsk.

I had to wear that bedamned head-scarf at all times and pretend to a modesty I didn't possess, but I'd had a great deal of recent practice at it.

We were two and a half days on the river, and on the second day, Aleksei asked me about Bao. "I do not mean to pry, Moirin," he said in a low, earnest voice. "But you're the most unusual person I've ever met, and I cannot help but be curious what manner of man won your heart."

"Oh..." I sighed. "A rather infuriating one. And whether or not he's won my heart is a matter of debate. We're still working on that part. What is certain is that he carries half of my *diadh-anam* inside him."

Aleksei's blue eyes widened. "Your soul-spark from your bear-goddess?"

"You *were* listening!"

He smiled faintly. "You were willing to die for it, Moirin. Yes, I was listening. I *am* trying to understand."

So I told him about Bao—not the sordid details his uncle would have extracted, but the deeper truth. How Master Lo's magpie and I had forged a friendship that had begun tipping toward love, stymied by the dragon's jealousy. How Bao had died, and how Master Lo had given his own life and taken half of my *diadh-anam* to restore him. How he had left, and I had gone after him, crossing the vast steppe to find him.

Unlike his uncle, Aleksei listened without judgment. "And then we took you away from him," he said when I had finished.

"Aye," I murmured. "And the Great Khan sent him off in the opposite direction."

He touched my cheek, brushing away tears. "I'm sorry, I didn't know. It's a very sad story." He offered me another faint smile. "No wonder you were looking forward to a great love story in the scripture. You're living in one, Moirin."

I wiped my eyes. "Oh, I don't know. You would probably not say that if you ever met Bao."

"I'd like to," Aleksei said, surprising me. "He sounds...fearless. Interesting. Maybe even a match for you. You said you were worried about him. Why?"

My gaze turned unerringly south, drawn as though by a lodestone. "I don't know. Something's wrong. His *diadh-anam* burns too low. And he hasn't moved since you took my chains off," I added. "He should have been able to sense my presence for days now. If he isn't coming toward me, something's keeping him from it."

"You're that sure of him?"

I nodded. "Bao had made his choice, and he's infernally stubborn. I'm sure."

Aleksei laced his hands around one knee. "That's why you were so determined to go south."

"Aye."

"I'll see that you do," he said in a firm voice. "I'll do my best to make good on the debt you're owed for the suffering we caused you. And I swear...I swear on my honor, I will *not* accept your offer."

I stared at him. "Naamah's blessing? Why ever not?"

He blinked. "Well...it would be dishonorable, obviously."

"No. Oh, no." I shook my head. "Naamah's blessing is a separate matter, and it has nothing to do with my relationship with Bao. Refuse it if you wish, but not on those grounds. I do not accept your promise."

"Yes, but—"

"Besides," I added, overriding him, "Bao is the one who ran off and married a Tatar princess, so he hardly has reason to object."

It was Aleksei's turn to stare. "He *what*?"

I'd skipped over that part. "Oh, yes. That's why the Great Khan was so eager to sell me into captivity and send Bao in the opposite direction. He was avenging a slight to his daughter's honor. And I do not blame him for being angry, but it was a rather extreme response if you ask me."

Aleksei gave his head a bewildered shake. "Moirin, I swear, the more I try to understand you, the less I do."

"I know, sweet boy." I patted his hand. "I told you, if you choose to accept Naamah's blessing, you will understand a great deal more." Regarding his troubled face, I softened my voice. "It is more than carnal congress, Aleksei—so much more. We are both Naamah's children, you and I. It is a sacrament I offer to you. Whether or not you wish to accept it is entirely up to you."

"It just seems so messy and complicated." He sounded dubious.

"It is." I leaned back against a bale of fur. "The affairs of humanity tend to be messy and complicated. And at the same time, it's the simplest thing in the world." I remembered the look of wonder that had dawned on Snow Tiger's face when Naamah had taken her fears away, and smiled to myself. When all was said and done, I was glad I had kept that memory private. "It is a wondrous grace."

"What do *you* want me to do?"

I let my gaze linger on Aleksei's face, on his rugged cheekbones and full lips, on his eyes the color of rain-washed speedwell blossoms. "I spoke the truth when I said it is a gift I would like to give you. But you cannot do it for my sake, Aleksei, no more than you can refuse it for Bao's. We are speaking of divine grace. It is your birthright as a child of Naamah's line, and it is her blessing that you refuse or accept."

He did understand then. "Just as you refused Yeshua's blessing."

I nodded. "Even so."

We spoke no more of the matter that day. The choice facing Aleksei had been cast in stark terms at last. At last, he had begun to understand that I was what I was, that I would never be what he wanted me to be. He understood that I offered what I could, no more and no less, and that I would leave him to seek Bao as soon as possible.

Usually, my instincts were good, but I had no idea what Aleksei would choose. He had been raised from birth to believe Naamah's gift was a curse, and Naamah was the whore-temptress who led Blessed Elua into apostasy.

There was nothing I could say to him to counter that belief. Faith cannot be proved, else it would not be faith. It can only be experienced. Whether or not Aleksei would allow himself to experience it, I could not say.

In truth, I did not even know which choice was right for him. He was a child of Naamah's line and he carried her gifts in his flesh and blood; but in his soul, he was a child of the One God and Yeshua, and no mistaking it. What I thought would bring healing to the damaged part of his spirit might well prove damaging in a different way if it strained and broke the covenant he knew so well and loved so deeply.

I hoped not, but it was possible.

In the scripture, the One God makes it clear that he is a jealous god; indeed, it is the first commandment he inscribed in stone on Moishe's tablets: I am the Lord your God, and you shall have no other gods before me.

And yet was that so different from the truth the Maghuin Dhonn

Herself inscribed in the very souls of Her children, written in the living fire of divinity? I didn't know, but I didn't think so.

In every part of me, I knew it was true; I could set no other gods above Her, not without killing the divine spark within me. But nor did She begrudge me my heritage as Naamah's child. So long as I knew myself a child of the Maghuin Dhonn, She was content to allow me to worship others alongside Her.

If Aleksei chose to accept my offer, I hoped he would find that when freed from the tyranny of mortal men, their ambitions, and the harsh strictures they sought to set upon the nature of love and pleasure, the love of God and his son Yeshua was as vast, generous, and all-encompassing as that of the Maghuin Dhonn Herself, my infinite bear-goddess whose worship was so often met with incredulity.

But I wasn't sure.

THIRTY-NINE

———◆———

The following day, we arrived in Udinsk.

Although it wasn't a very large city, it was bustling with traders and activity. I was glad to see it wasn't all Vralians. There were Tatar faces here and there, trading sheep, cattle, and goats for furs and timber. Any sort of diversity made it easier to blend into the crowd, and their brown skin made the honey-colored hue of my own less noticeable.

There were vendors selling food-stuff along the wharf where we disembarked, leaving behind our taciturn fur-trappers. I wished to all the gods that Aleksei hadn't spent our last coin on the passage. The smell of food—ground, seasoned meat grilled on a stick, cooked cabbage stew with dumplings floating in it—made my mouth water and my belly growl. Blessed Valentina had done her best, but it had been a long journey coming on the heels of three days' worth of fasting, and we'd eaten the last of her bread and cheese yesterday.

I was starved for food, real food. I couldn't help but eye the vendors' fare longingly, breathing the savory aroma deep into my lungs.

"Moirin." Aleksei cleared his throat. "You're not exactly looking demure."

"I'm *hungry*!" I said plaintively. "I'm hungry and tired, and I would like a hot meal, a bath, and a clean place to sleep."

"I know, I know," he said soothingly, jingling the bundle of chains.

"Let's find a place where you can call your magic safely, and I'll look for a smith willing to pay good coin for silver."

"No. Oh, no." I shook my head. "No, I want to watch them melt. I need to see it done myself. I need to know for sure no one else will ever be forced to wear those chains."

"Moirin, be reasonable!" he pleaded with me. "Once we've gotten rid of the chains, I won't worry so much. Until we do, the less you show yourself, the less chance there is that word will get back to Riva."

"You're not all that inconspicuous yourself, my blue-eyed boy." I pointed at the bundle. "Not peddling those."

In the end, we struck a compromise. I would summon the twilight and accompany Aleksei cloaked in its concealment.

We found a narrow alley and ducked into it. Aleksei turned his back on me, shielding me from view, and I called the twilight. It was still a blessed relief to feel it settle over me, to watch the world turn soft and silvery.

"Moirin?" Aleksei turned around.

"Aye," I said, willing him to hear me. I reached out and touched his hand. "I'm here."

He shuddered. "Don't do that, please. It's unnerving. It feels like I'm being touched by some unholy spirit."

"No, just me," I murmured. "Lead on, my hero."

There were three smithies in Udinsk, easily located by the smoke and clatter. The first smithy dealt only in weapons, horseshoes, tools, and the like, and sent us—or at least, Aleksei and my invisible self—on to the others.

The master smith at the second place gauged the chains with an appraising eye and asked questions. Too many questions. Aleksei flushed and stammered out the tale we had concocted about the chains being his wife's dowry, an heirloom from her mother, who was freed from vile servitude in a D'Angeline pleasure-house. Even with my limited Vralian, I could tell he was doing a bad job of it. It wasn't a very convincing tale, and my earnest Yeshuite scholar lied very, very badly.

"Aleksei," I whispered in his ear, making him jump. "Not here. Let's try the third smithy."

He twitched and bit back a reply, stuffing the chains back in the makeshift satchel and bidding the second smith a curt farewell.

To my everlasting relief, the thick-set master smith at the last place was every bit as taciturn as our fur-trappers. He examined the chains, bit into a link to test the quality of the silver, and made a gruff offer.

Aleksei countered.

He didn't haggle any better than he lied, but I was proud of him for making the effort. When he told the smith that he had promised his wife he wouldn't leave until the chains had been rendered molten silver, the fellow merely nodded without a trace of curiosity and placed a crucible on the forge, ordering an apprentice to feed the forge and pump the bellows.

It was a tedious process, but I didn't mind. It was worth it to see those bedamned chains destroyed.

While the crucible heated and Aleksei hovered nervously, I wandered the smithy unseen, examining a tray of wares on display. Some of the work was surprisingly lovely and delicate—brooches and necklaces set with gems. Amber, I thought, although it was hard to tell in the twilight. I glanced at the master smith with his bushy beard and thick, blunt fingers, wondering what inspired him to create such delicate beauty.

I touched his work lightly, thinking of Terre d'Ange and all the careless riches that had been bestowed on me there.

Of Jehanne, commissioning her former adversaries at Atelier Favrielle to make a sensuous gown and an elaborate headpiece with gilded branches and garnet berries for me to wear on the Longest Night.

Of how she had smiled and stroked my cheek. *I've no objection to you looking as stunning as possible now that you're mine, Moirin.*

It made my heart ache, but it was a good memory, too. It had surprised and delighted me to find such an unexpected streak of generosity in Jehanne. On the Longest Night, she'd had living pine-trees brought in to decorate the great hall in the Palace; immense evergreen trees in huge pots, their tops reaching for the ceiling high overhead, releasing their fragrance into the hall, their branches hung about with sparkling glass icicles. No one had ever conceived of adorning the hall on that scale before. She had done it just to please me.

I looked across the smithy at Aleksei, the forge-light flickering over his features. I wondered if he could ever understand that it was a blessing, not a sin, to be graced with more than one love.

It could be complicated; of course it could be complicated. And it opened one up to the possibility of more pain and loss.

Still, it was a blessing I would never relinquish. Love, genuine love, was always a cause for joy.

At last the crucible reached the proper temperature, glowing bright silver in the twilight. The smith began feeding the chains into its maw, and I drifted over to observe the process, standing unseen at Aleksei's shoulder and peering into the crucible. Slowly, slowly, the chains and shackles began to glow with heat, the perfect links softening, the cursed lines of each perfectly etched sigil and inscription beginning to blur.

It was profoundly satisfying.

Once or twice, Aleksei shifted restlessly, glancing around as though to ask if I were ready to leave, but I wasn't content until those chains were altogether gone forever, reduced to a seething mass of molten silver. Then, and only then, did I whisper in his ear that I was ready to go.

Outside in the cool air, it was hard to contain my exhilaration. Those hateful chains were gone, gone, gone. Oh, I knew they could be forged anew, but for now, they were *gone*. Even if the Patriarch found me, he couldn't bind my spirit. Those chains would buy my passage out of Vralia. I laughed and spun around Aleksei in circles as he led us back to the narrow alley where I could release the twilight safely.

He smiled wryly when I did. "You look positively giddy, Moirin."

"I am," I admitted. "I'll try not to look it."

"Yes, do. It's nice, though," he added. "You're right. Until we fled,

I'd never seen you happy. I imagine..." He cleared his throat. "I imagine it would make a person want to go to any length to coax such a dazzling smile from you."

I raised my brows. "Are you turning romantic on me after all?"

"I don't know." Aleksei frowned a little, nodding to himself. "Mayhap I am. It's a bit like trying on a strange garment. I'm not sure how I feel about it yet."

"It looks well on you," I said. "But if the fit doesn't suit you, you needn't keep it. However, since we're posing as husband and wife, you may as well wear it a while longer." I took his arm, resting my fingers lightly on his forearm. He gazed at my hand as though it were a foreign object. "Here." I adjusted the angle of his elbow. "This is how you would escort your beloved, at least in Terre d'Ange."

"Like so?"

I smiled at him. "Aye, perfect."

Naamah's gift stirred between us, coils as hot and bright as the molten silver roiling in the crucible.

Aleksei tensed, but he didn't pull away from me. He returned my smile, and there was yearning in his eyes, but there was sorrow and regret, too. "Let's find an inn, and a hot meal for you."

"And a bath," I reminded him.

"And a bath," he agreed.

There were several inns to choose from in Udinsk. We found a quiet one on the outskirts of town run by a devout Yeshuite couple. They regarded me warily at first, but I kept my eyes modestly downcast and Aleksei's earnestness soon won them over. It was too late for a bath that day, but they offered us an ample supper and a private room, with the promise of a bath on the morrow—a hot bath, if we were willing to pay extra.

"Can we, please?" I begged Aleksei. "I know we can't afford to be wasteful, but just this once?"

He hesitated, then nodded. "All right."

"Thank you!" I kissed his cheek, making him blush. "Thank you, thank you, thank you!"

It won a smile from the innkeepers. So they were not so dour after all that they could not be touched by a pair of young newlyweds in love, the shy husband indulging his foreign bride in a small luxury.

It was such a pleasant fiction, I almost wished it were true.

That evening we dined on roasted chicken generously basted with butter, the skin a crisp golden brown, with stewed cabbage and dumplings on the side. It tasted like the best thing I'd ever eaten, and when I complimented our hostess in my halting Vralian, she seemed genuinely pleased.

Even Aleksei relaxed over the meal, setting aside his abstemious discipline to eat with rare gusto. I was glad to see it. I knew what young men's appetites were like. If I was hungry, he had to be ravenous. He was too young for the ascetic lifestyle he led. The hollows of his cheeks were too gaunt beneath those rugged cheekbones with their perfect D'Angeline symmetry, his rangy, long-limbed body too rawboned.

If he *were* my husband, I thought, I'd take better care of him. The thought filled me with unexpected tenderness.

"Moirin, why are you looking at me that way?" he asked.

I bent my head to my plate, knowing it was unfair to give him even a hint of false hope. "Oh, no reason."

Once our hosts escorted us to our chamber and the door closed behind us, the pleasant fiction ended. There was one bed in the chamber, big enough for two, but with little room to spare. Aleksei eyed it sidelong, nervous as a green-broken colt shying at a fence, fidgeting with the worn blanket that had served to carry our possessions. "I . . . I will sleep on the floor. I don't mind. I'm used to it."

"Mortification of the flesh?" I asked.

He nodded.

I was sorry, but not surprised. "As you wish, sweet boy," I murmured, turning back the bed-linens. "Sleep well."

FORTY

⟨ ✦ ⟩

I slept.

I slept without dreams, long and hard and deep. I slept the sleep of finding respite after profound fear and exhaustions—luxurious sleep, healing sleep. I slept well past dawn and awoke to slanting sunlight and a sense of being watched.

Opening my eyes, I found Aleksei sitting awkwardly on the foot of the bed, his hands clasped in his lap.

"How long have you been watching me?" I asked sleepily.

"Hours," he murmured.

I propped myself on my elbows. "Did you not sleep well?"

He shook his head. "No."

"Oh." Half-awake, I yawned and ran a hand through my hair, untangling the silken strands. It had grown a few inches since Luba had cropped it, long enough to fall over my shoulders. "I'm sorry. Tonight, you will take the bed, and I the floor. You'll sleep better for it, I promise." I paused. "Is there some reason you're staring at me, Aleksei?"

"Yes."

It was one word, one syllable, but something in the way he spoke it caught my attention. That, and the way he was sitting—awkwardly, aye, and yet as still and grave as a carved saint.

I hauled myself upright, rubbed my eyes, and shook my head, trying to dispel the last dregs of sleep. "I am listening."

"Moirin…"

I waited. "Aye?"

Aleksei took a deep breath. "I have been thinking. And praying. And yes, watching you while you slept. Watching you at your most vulnerable, with no magic to protect and conceal you, no teasing to bait and entice me. No tales of depravity to shock me. I have been trying to see that unclean spirit in you which seeks to tempt me and lead me astray."

I opened my mouth to speak.

"Wait." He raised one hand, his face solemn. "I don't see it, Moirin. I don't. Only you, mortal and fallible, and…yourself. Beautiful, yes. Impetuous. Uncanny, to be sure. But a girl, only a girl, too— one apt to kiss a horse on the nose, and quick to delight in a meal of roasted chicken and dumplings. A mother's child far from home. And I have been asking myself, if it is not to fulfill my uncle's dream, why has God set you in my path?"

"To test you?" I murmured.

Aleksei spread both hands. "If that is so, I have already failed. I have betrayed my uncle to aid you. Does it matter how much farther I fall?"

"I don't know."

"Neither do I." His chest rose and fell as he took another sharp breath. "And so…so I am thinking, I will never know if I do not accept what you offer. And I believe strongly enough in Yeshua's forgiveness that I am willing to risk damnation in pursuit of truth."

I laughed.

I couldn't help it, I laughed aloud for the sheer joy of it; and I flung myself forward, putting my arms around Aleksei's neck, kissing his face. "You mean it?"

"Yes!" He pushed me away, blushing furiously. "Only not this very moment, all right? Give me some time to grow accustomed to the notion."

"All right." I sat back on my heels, beaming at him.

He scowled. "You needn't look so pleased."

"Why ever not?" I asked. "I *am* pleased."

"To have won?"

"No!" Gods, he was as infuriating as Bao in his own prickly way. "No, of course not." I took one of Aleksei's hands and kissed it. "Your choice makes me happy, sweet boy. That's all. I pray it will make you happy, too."

It mollified him, and restored a sense of brightness to the day. In the common room, we broke our fast with brown bread and fresh-churned butter. Our hostess promised a hot bath would be made ready in a few hours' time, so we set out for the marketplace to begin purchasing supplies for the journey south.

I was happy, happy with Aleksei's choice, happy that he wasn't fussing about me needing to conceal myself today. Those bedamned chains had been a weight on both our minds. And in truth, he needed my counsel to provision us for the journey. I saw to it that we spent our coin wisely.

In a rag-merchant's shop, we bought a canvas satchel, a spare blanket, and a change of clothing for both of us. A leather-worker sold us a pair of generous waterskins, and also a pair of well-made boots for me to replace the shoes Valentina had given me, which pinched my feet and gave me blisters. We purchased several tallow candles and a flint-striking kit from a chandler.

Other than a sack of barley we bought, we decided food supplies could wait a few days. Aleksei reckoned it best if we gave it a week before heading south. Still, we identified a smoke-house where we could purchase dried meat, and a baker and a cheese-maker for additional, fresher fare.

Our greatest expense would be horses and tack, and both of us were eager to have the matter settled and our escape secured. There was one horse-trader in the city, a squinty-eyed fellow. I didn't like the look of him, and I liked him less when he offered to sell us a sway-backed mare, an elderly gelding, and a spavined pack-horse for an outrageous price.

When Aleksei glanced at me in inquiry, I shook my head. "Walk away," I murmured in D'Angeline. "Don't argue, don't haggle. Just walk away in disgust."

He did, me at his side.

The horse-trader ran after us, protesting and apologizing, claiming that he had merely been testing us to see if we were any judges of horse-flesh.

It took the better part of an hour to conclude a deal with him, but in the end, we struck a bargain to purchase a trio of sturdy little horses, as well as tack and grain. After living on the steppe, I could tell that these horses had Tatar stock mixed in their lineage, and I knew full well how swiftly and willingly they travelled. After some more haggling, the squinty-eyed fellow agreed to board them for another week for an additional fee.

"Well, that's done, then," Aleksei said after we left the horse-trader. He looked pleased with himself. "Are we finished?"

I shook my head. "We'll want a tent. Mayhap there are sail-cloth merchants along the wharf who make such things. And a pot...it might be best if you returned to the smithy alone. We don't want him linking my face to those chains. And a bow and arrows, if we can find a fletcher."

"Ah..." He hesitated. "I've never shot a bow, Moirin."

I smiled. "I have."

"You?" Aleksei looked dubious.

"I've shot for the pot since I was ten years old," I told him. "Believe me, after days of dried meat, you'll be grateful for fresh when we can get it. Besides, I'll feel safer with a bow at hand. One never knows what one might encounter on the road."

It seemed there was no fletcher in the city of Udinsk, but our inquiries led us to a camp of Tatar traders on the outskirts of town. Given my history with the Great Khan, I was reluctant to approach them; but Aleksei didn't speak the Tatar tongue, and I was determined to procure a bow for myself.

The sight of felted *gers* with smoke trickling out of the holes at the apex of their domes made me feel nostalgic. A young woman at the first *ger* we tried greeted us politely and directed us to seek out a fellow named Vachir, a renowned archer.

"He may have a bow to sell you, or he may not," she said. "I do not know."

I thanked her. "May your herds prosper, my lady."

We found this Vachir some distance away, squatting outside his *ger* and working on the very thing I coveted, a fine-looking bow. I began to greet him in the Tatar tongue when he glanced up, and my heart skipped a beat.

I knew him.

His eyes widened, and he rose to his feet. "You!"

"Moirin?" Aleksei said behind me. "What is it?"

"I know him," I said helplessly. "Or at least I've met him. More to the point, he knows who I am."

Another man would have sworn; Aleksei's voice tightened. "I knew this was a bad idea!"

The fellow came forward, unfinished bow in one hand. I took a step backward, bumping into Aleksei. The renowned Tatar archer Vachir, who happened to be the last man I'd defeated in an archery contest, smiled quietly and clapped his free hand on my shoulder. "I am pleased to see you alive, lady," he said with a gentleness that reminded me of Batu and Checheg.

I blinked. "You are?"

He blinked back at me. "Yes, of course! It was a fair contest. I have no quarrel with you. Many wondered what befell you when you vanished. I would hear your tale. Will you accept the hospitality of my roof?"

I relaxed. "It would be an honor."

With a bewildered Aleksei trailing behind me, I followed Vachir into his *ger*. He introduced us to his wife, Arigh, who served us bowls of hot, salty tea, the steaming liquid's surface slick with butter-fat.

Beneath the felted dome, I told them how the Great Khan Naram had betrayed me to the Vralians. It was impulsive, aye, but all my instincts told me I could trust them. They listened with disapproval, shaking their heads.

"Batu's tribe had acknowledged you as kin," Arigh said firmly. "Not even the Khan himself had the right to do what he did."

"Moirin, you *will* explain all this to me, will you not?" Aleksei asked in a low voice.

I nodded. "My lord, my lady, do you know what happened to Bao? General Arslan's son who wed the Khan's daughter?"

They exchanged a glance and shook their heads. "That young man vanished, too," Vachir said. "No one knows where or why. Only that the Great Khan's daughter Erdene was very angry at her father."

I sighed.

"Are you seeking the young man?" Arigh asked in a gentle voice.

"Aye." I spared a guilty glance at Aleksei. "He's nowhere close, though. Far away. Right now, I come seeking to purchase a bow for the journey. My quest led me to you."

Husband and wife exchanged another look. Arigh rose and went to the back of the *ger*, returning with a Tatar-style bow smaller than the one Vachir had been working on outside, as well as a quiver of arrows.

"For you," she said simply. "My husband made it for me. I wish you to have it."

"Your own?" I shook my head. "No, I cannot accept it."

She thrust it at me. "You can."

"Take it, please," Vachir added. "I will make her another. It will go a little way toward settling the debt you are owed."

I closed my fingers around the bow. "You're sure?"

Vachir smiled, his eyes crinkling. "Would you have me set a price on it? I will, then. Give me a chance to reclaim my honor. Grant me a rematch, here and now." He saw me hesitate. "You are fearful. I promise you, no one among us will endanger you. I have granted you hospitality. I swear by the sky itself, we will protect your secret as our own."

"All right, then." I smiled back at him. "A rematch."

It being a Tatar encampment, naturally there was an archery range with targets already established. Word swept through the camp as we ventured out to the range, and folk abandoned their chores to watch.

"Moirin, this is foolish!" Aleksei pleaded with me. "Whatever you're doing, I wish you wouldn't."

"It's all right," I said. "I trust them."

He shook his head in mute dismay.

Vachir and I agreed to a simple contest—the best of three shots at the distance at which we had last competed. He let me take a couple of practice shots to accustom myself to the feel of a new bow. It was different, very different, from the yew-wood bow my uncle Mabon had made me. It was shorter and stiffer, and the ends curved sharply outward, making for a tighter, more concentrated draw, the bow recoiling sharply when the string was loosed.

On my first shot, I missed the target altogether, provoking good-natured laughter from the onlookers. But I got the feel of it and adjusted quickly, acquitting myself well enough with my three official shots.

And then Vachir stepped up to the mark, drawing and releasing three times in quick succession, clustering three arrows in the center of the crude red heart painted on the stuffed target.

I laughed and bowed to him in the Ch'in manner, one hand clasped over the other. "Your honor is restored."

He smiled his quiet smile. "I suspect we would be closer matched if you had more time to practice with an unfamiliar bow. May it serve you well, lady archer."

After I had thanked Vachir and Arigh for their generous gift one last time, Aleksei and I took our leave of the Tatar camp. I gave him the bow and quiver to carry, reckoning it would look less conspicuous on the streets of Udinsk. He listened silently to my explanation of how I had come to compete against Vachir in the archery contest at the spring gathering.

"Are you angry?" I asked when I had finished. "Truly, I wouldn't have done it if I didn't think we could trust them. The laws of hospitality are sacred among the Tatars."

"Not angry, no," Aleksei said slowly. "You lived among them, you know their ways. It was just...strange...seeing you thusly. Strange, and beautiful. It made me understand why the old Hellenes gave one of their goddesses a bow. Every time I think I am coming to know you, Moirin, I discover a new you. It's as though I turned a corner I thought was familiar, and found myself in a hallway I hadn't known existed."

"Oh." I wasn't sure how to respond.

He gave me a sidelong glance. "Are there many more of you?"

I thought about it. "Well, there is the Moirin of Terre d'Ange who served as royal companion to the Queen, who went about in jewels and finery, attending balls and concerts and poetry recitals. And there is the Moirin who was Master Lo Feng's pupil, and learned to master the Five Styles of Breathing and studied the Way. But they are all me, Aleksei. Does it trouble you?"

"No." He frowned. "It's just that I've only ever been one person, I suppose."

I took his arm. "You're an uncut gem, sweet boy. Time will reveal your facets. The Aleksei I met three months ago is not the Aleksei who offered to teach me to lie to his uncle, and that young man is not the Aleksei who plotted our escape. Of a surety, none of them are the Aleksei who consented this very morning to accept Naamah's blessing." I raised my brows. "Or had you forgotten?"

"No." Aleksei flushed and looked downward, his dark lashes shuttering his eyes. "Oh, no."

"Good." I squeezed his arm. "Now let us see if that bath is ready."

FORTY-ONE

The bathing-chamber was small and steamy, the tin tub was small and cramped—and the bath was altogether a glorious thing. It was the first hot bath I'd had since leaving Shuntian, and the first time in months I'd been able to bathe without chains rattling and clanking around me, and shackles chafing my skin. If I hadn't had to share it with Aleksei, I'd have stayed in that tub until the water cooled.

It was worth every cent it cost.

Such a simple thing; and yet it felt as though I'd taken a step further toward reclaiming myself, washing the taint of the Patriarch's touch from my soul even as I washed the grime from the journey from my skin.

Afterward, I found myself humming. To be sure, all was not right with the world. Distant Bao and his low-burning *diadh-anam* were never far from my thoughts; and I was a long way from being safely out of Vralia.

But yesterday I had been penniless, tired, and hungry, with scarce a possession in the world. Today, I had nearly everything I would need to set out on a long journey. I was well fed, well rested, and clean.

And today I was on Naamah's business, which made me happy.

I had assumed my modest, blushing boy would want to wait for nightfall and the cover of darkness to invoke Naamah's blessing, that I might even have to coax him into letting me light a candle.

Much to my delight, I was wrong.

I sensed it in the common room where our hostess, whose name was Polina, served us leftover chicken and dumplings for a midday meal. Clean and damp from his bath, Aleksei stole covert glances at me as we dined, and I could sense the yearning rising in him, an aching hunger I longed to assuage.

"You don't want to wait for nightfall, do you?" I asked softly.

"No." His voice was low and steady; and although he blushed, he held my gaze without flinching. "I want to see you, Moirin. All of you."

I nodded, rose, and held out my hand to him. "Let us go, then."

He took a deep breath, nodded in agreement, and took my hand. As we left the common room together, our hostess Polina gazed after us with a maternal look of habitual disapproval mixed with indulgence.

In the bedchamber, I closed the door and latched it. Aleksei glanced around the sunlit room. "It does seem very bright."

"Too bright?"

He shook his head. "No. I will not hide from this."

I fetched one of the tallow candles we had purchased earlier that day. It took several tries to kindle it with the flint striker.

"What's that for?"

"An offering to Naamah." I smiled at him. "It should be incense, but I thought you'd take it amiss if I stole some from a temple."

"Like as not." Aleksei tried to smile back at me, but it came out as an anxious grimace, tension beginning to war with desire in him. He took another deep breath, shuddering as he exhaled. "What...what am I supposed to be doing, Moirin? You will have to tell me."

"Nothing, sweet boy." I laid one hand on his chest. "I am going to pray to Naamah. If you like, you may pray with me."

"I don't think I can," he said earnestly. "But I will keep you company if you like."

"That would be nice." After removing my shoes, I knelt on the wooden floor, sitting on my heels and fixing my gaze on the candle-flame, barely visible in the bright daylight. Aleksei knelt beside me, quiet and still, doing his best to contain his nerves.

I prayed.

As strongly as I felt Naamah's presence in the gift that Aleksei and I shared, it took a long time before I was able to sense her will. I had sought to seduce Aleksei toward my own ends; I carried a burden of resentment that I had failed, a burden of resentment toward his uncle and his aunt; and aye, a lingering burden of resentment toward God and his son Yeshua.

I had to let go of those things, offer them up.

I did.

The bright lady smiled, but she remained silent. I concentrated on the flickering candle-flame, willing my heart to be open and my ears to hear.

"You wished this, O brightest of goddesses," I whispered in Alban, reverting to the tongue of my birth. "Will you not grant your blessing to this hurt and damaged child of yours? I offer myself as your vessel."

When it came, it came in a rush, a sense of Naamah's grace settling over me like a cloak of sunlight, like an embrace, like the tenderest of kisses, making my heart ache, setting the doves to fluttering in my belly. She was here, present between us. I drew a shaking breath, tears filling my eyes, words filling my mouth.

"Aleksei…"

He nodded, wordless.

I laid my hand on his chest again, spreading my fingers, feeling his strong, young heart pounding beneath my touch. "What you carry is no curse, but a gift. Like any gift, it can be used for good or evil. If you use it wisely and kindly, it will bring only joy, and never sorrow. Trust your heart to guide you. Take your shame, and offer it to God. Let him burn it away until only what is pure remains."

Naamah's grace expanded, encompassing Aleksei. He caught his breath, a single, gasping sob escaping him.

I didn't understand, not wholly. But her words were meant for him, not me. "Is all well?" I asked.

"Yes." Wonder dawned in his blue, blue eyes. "Oh, yes!"

"Good." I shifted, straddling his knees. "I am going to kiss you now."

Aleksei smiled through his tears. "Do you think you need to warn me?"

I nodded. "I do."

Leaning forward, I cupped his face in my hands. He closed his eyes, tears trickling beneath his lashes. I brushed them away with my thumbs, kissed the salty trails they left behind on his skin. I kissed his warm, firm lips until I felt them soften, and parted them with the tip of my tongue, letting it touch his.

He jerked back, eyes open and wide. "Is that...customary?"

I laughed softly. "Yes. Did you not like it?"

"I...don't know." Aleksei looked at me with that extraordinary earnestness. "Will you do it again, please?"

I kissed him again. This time, his lips parted more readily. I let my tongue slip between them, finding his and teasing it, coaxing and retreating. I let my hands slide upward into his damp, tawny hair. Let myself lean farther forward, pressing my breasts against his chest. Gods, it felt good.

Aleksei groaned into my mouth, his arms encircling my waist hard, his hands pressing against my back. In the bright sunlight, he pulled me down atop him, kissing me fervently.

"No sin?" I asked, breathless.

He shook his head. "No sin." He tugged away my head-scarf. "Why are you wearing this? You hate it."

"True," I agreed.

He stroked my hair. "It *is* as soft as it looks."

"Oh, aye?" I kissed his throat, biting softly at his skin.

He groaned again, his back arching. "Moirin, don't...don't. It's too much. I want to see you. I *need* to see you."

I sat back on my heels. "Then do."

Aleksei rose. I let him pull me to my feet. His big hands clutched folds of my drab woolen dress, lifting it and easing it over my head, discarding it. His hands tugged down my undergarments, and I stepped out of them.

"Oh, God." With profound reverence, he took his deity's name in vain, his voice shaking as he gazed at me. "Oh, God! Moirin. You are so very, very beautiful."

"So are you." I unlaced his shirt and removed it deftly. "So are you, sweet Aleksei." His pale skin gleamed in the sunlight, stretched taut over his angular bones. I trailed my fingertips over the jutting ridges of his collarbones, over his hard chest and his lean belly. I slid one finger along the waist of his breeches, glancing up at him. "May I?"

He swallowed. "Yes."

Kneeling, I unlaced his breeches and eased them down over his narrow hips. His erect phallus sprang free, straining so hard it looked as though it must hurt. I blew softly on it, and Aleksei groaned at the touch of my warm breath.

"Don't...don't..." He breathed raggedly.

"Do you think it unclean?" I stroked his phallus lightly, feeling the silken skin sliding over the rigid core, and swirled my tongue gently around the swollen head. "It is the staff of life, Aleksei."

"No, I know." He took a step backward, stumbling in the breeches I hadn't finished removing, and sat down hard on the edge of the bed. "It's just too much! Just the sight of you doing it. I don't want to—"

"Ah." I hid a smile. It had been a long time since I'd been with a man as young and inexperienced as Aleksei, fearful of spilling his seed too soon. "Don't worry, sweet boy," I said, pulling off his breeches. "We have all the time in the world."

He didn't protest when I took him into my mouth, only made a strangled sound deep in his throat and clutched my head. I performed the *languisement* as an act of worship—albeit a brief one, to be sure. Aleksei's hips jerked forward as he poured his seed and years upon years' worth of repressed desire into my mouth.

"God!" he said in a hoarse voice. "Oh, God!"

I sat back, smiling.

Aleksei eyed me, flushed for once with pleasure and not shame. "You *are* a witch," he murmured, reaching down to take my hands. "Come here."

I let him tug me onto the bed beside him, where he kissed me without reservation, his tongue exploring my mouth, his hands exploring my body. He was Naamah's child, and he had found his element. He kissed my throat, hands cupping my breasts, then gave me an inquiring look.

"Yes," I whispered. "Oh, yes."

His tawny head moved lower, his mouth closing over one nipple, suckling hard. Stone and sea, I had been too long deprived! I shivered with pleasure and ran my fingers through his hair, encouraging him.

"You like that." Aleksei lifted his head, eyes bright.

"Oh, yes," I said languidly.

"What else?"

I took his hand, guiding it between my thighs. "Touch me. Stroke me."

He did, propping himself on one elbow, gazing at the cleft of my nether-lips with intense interest. "So soft! And so hot and so wet. I didn't know."

"It means you're arousing me," I murmured.

With one fingertip, he circled Naamah's Pearl, caressing my tender, sensitive bud. "And this?"

I jerked involuntarily. "Is the seat of a woman's pleasure, my hero," I said breathlessly. "Your instincts are true."

Aleksei smiled. "Shall I kiss you there?"

"If you wish." I hoped he did.

"I think I do." Kneeling between my thighs, he studied me, looking like a scholarly angel. "Even here, you are beautiful, Moirin." Lowering his head, he kissed me—kissed and licked me with ardent desire. And although there was neither art nor skill in it, there was passion, and Naamah's blessing hovering over us.

I climaxed beneath his mouth, moaning shamelessly and clutching his broad shoulders.

"I pleased you?" Aleksei looked startled and glad.

I laughed softly. "Yes, my hero. Would you like to please us both further?" I pulled him down atop me, reveling in the weight of him, reveling in the warmth of his skin against mine, wrapping my legs around him. "Come here."

Aleksei was fully hard and erect again, the blunt head of his phallus nudging at my nether-lips in a tantalizing manner. His blue, blue eyes gazed earnestly into mine. "I won't hurt you?"

"No." I shook my head. "You would need to have greater care with a virgin," I added. "But you will not hurt me."

He nodded as though I'd given him a gift.

I reached between us, grasping his phallus and shifting my hips. The swollen head slid into me.

Aleksei caught his breath, thrusting; and the whole thick length of him filled me. His blue eyes widened. "It's so..."

"I know." I kissed him, hard and deep, Naamah's blessing like honey on my tongue. "I know, sweet boy. I know."

FORTY-TWO

❧

I liked the aftermath almost better than the love-making.

For the first time since I had known him, Aleksei was content in his own skin, calm and happy.

Fading sunlight filled the room. The candle I had lit burned low on the windowsill.

Naamah's blessing lay over us like a blanket.

"You are so very well made, Moirin," Aleksei murmured, stroking the curve of my hip. "As though your disparate gods conspired to combine all the best aspects of their folk in you. Tell me, how did you know the right words to say to me?"

I shook my head. "I didn't."

"You did, though."

"No," I said. "Naamah put them in my mouth." I hesitated. "What did they mean to you?"

Aleksei touched my face. "I cannot explain it, not entirely. But she told me to trust my heart. And I realized that it does not matter that you cannot love me as I wish. It matters that *I* love *you*."

"I'm sorry," I whispered, my eyes stinging.

He wrapped his strong, young arms around me. "Don't be. I'm not."

I laid my head on his chest. "I'm glad."

"I think this is what it must have been like for Edom and Yeva in the Garden before the fall," Aleksei mused. "To take pleasure in the light of day without fear of sinning, to be naked and unashamed. I think this is what I was meant to understand, Moirin. That state of grace is not lost to us after all; it is only that we have lost our way. Perhaps that is why God granted a measure of license to his errant grandson Elua and his disobedient servants. Perhaps their message is one we need to hear."

"Gods have mercy, I've made a heretic of you," I murmured.

He laughed, his breath stirring my hair. "Maybe. But I think rather that you've led me to the beginning of a deeper understanding of my faith."

I lifted my head. "No more mortification of the flesh?"

"No more," Aleksei promised. "At least not the kind meant to punish for desires that are natural and beautiful in their own right. I still believe there is merit in discipline such as fasting. As you said, this is a gift, and like any gift, it can be used for good or evil. I needed to hear that, too. Needed to hear it acknowledged."

I smiled at him. "I suspect you'll use it for good, sweet boy. You're too gentle a soul to do otherwise."

"I hope so," he said earnestly. "But my father used it carelessly, and ruined my mother's life because of it . . . Oh!" His expression changed, half-stricken and half-hopeful. "Moirin. What if I've gotten you with child?"

"You haven't," I said gently. "It's a gift Eisheth granted to the women of Terre d'Ange, and I'm D'Angeline enough to have inherited it. I'll not be fertile until I pray to her to open the gates of my womb."

Aleksei's face fell. "Oh."

I sat upright, taking his hand and stroking it. "You'll find her someday, Aleksei. A helpmate to share your vision and your dream, who will love you and only you with all her heart."

"I do love you, though," he said. "And I suspect there is a part of me that always will. I cannot imagine I won't."

"Probably," I agreed, thinking of my own lost loves. "But I think you will be surprised to find how much room there is for love in your heart."

He reached up to touch my hair, running strands of it through his fingers. "Like you? Have you made a little space in your heart for me, Moirin, that my memory might exist alongside that of the princes and queens and peasant-boys you've loved?"

"Aye, a little." I smiled at him again. "I will always be grateful for the gift you've given me today."

"Me?" Aleksei looked startled.

"Yes, sweet boy." I leaned down to kiss him. "You."

"How so?"

Stone and sea, no one in the world could look as bemused and earnest as Aleksei! I drew idle circles on the bare skin of his chest, gazing at him and wondering what manner of man he would become. A strong one, I thought; a good one. Right now, he was like a half-grown lion, only just beginning to come into his strength.

One day...

One day he might become a priest such as the Rebbe Avraham ben David, swaying the course of Vralian history with his eloquent passion and his faith, swaying it away from judgment and punishment, toward love and compassion and joy. Always, always seeking a deeper understanding of what the gods want of us.

Always seeking to divine the unknown word that Yeshua had written in the dust, that Yeshua had written in my vision.

Always deciding it must be *love*—over and over again.

I shivered.

"Moirin?"

I hadn't answered Aleksei's question. I came back to myself, smiling into his blue, blue eyes. "You gave me your trust," I said. "And that is the greatest gift anyone can give. You allowed me to invoke Naamah's blessing on your behalf, and you accepted it with grace and gladness, and an open, willing heart. And for the first time, I do believe there was a purpose in my presence here."

He smiled back at me. "Oh?"

I kissed him again. "Aye."

When the low afternoon light began to dim toward dusk, we

donned our clothes and left our bedchamber for the common room, entering it hand-in-hand. It seemed to me as though Naamah's blessing had graced the entire establishment.

Polina shook her head at us knowingly, disapproval giving way to pure indulgence. Her husband, Rodya, grinned and winked, setting deep bowls of cabbage stew simmered with seasoned balls of ground spiced meat before us.

The other four patrons of the inn watched us with envy and yearning.

"I feel so strange, Moirin," Aleksei murmured. "I feel as though I want to embrace them all, share this moment with them. Is that not strange?"

"Not to me, no," I said. "You know my father is a Priest of Naamah?" He nodded. "I think he sees the world this way all the time. I used to walk with him through the City. It made people glad just to see him. And when he smiled at them, they became beautiful."

He gazed around the room. "They're *all* beautiful, aren't they?"

I nodded. "Yes, they are."

"How do you stand it?"

"Oh..." I shrugged. "You just love them, I suppose. After all, you can't take the whole world to your bed."

Aleksei glanced at me. "*You* would if you could."

I laughed.

He laughed, too.

"Sweet boy," I said fondly. "I do believe you *have* begun to understand me."

Aleksei spooned stew into his mouth, eating with a good appetite. "Do you suppose other women have the same capacity for pleasure?" he asked, only flushing a very little bit at the question. "Non-D'Angeline women, I mean."

"Oh, yes," I said without thinking. "Of course."

"Well, but you can't know for sure unless..." His voice trailed off, his flush deepening. "Oh."

I laughed again at his expression. "It's not the same as possessing

Naamah's gift, no. Of understanding pleasure as a birthright, of reaching for it as simply and naturally as breathing, of swimming in it like a salmon in a stream. But it's there, it's always there. It may need to be coaxed a bit, that's all."

He took another bite. "You'll note I'm not asking who you may have been coaxing."

I smiled sweetly at him. "Which is to the good, since it was a piece of Naamah's business that does not concern you."

Aleksei shook his head. "That's an aspect of D'Angeline culture I cannot embrace. It is unnatural, and a point on which the scriptures are very clear."

"Oh, aye." I dipped a piece of brown bread into my stew. "I recall. A man shall not lie with another man as with a woman, or he shall be put to death. I expect that was written by a man who was used badly in his youth. But that is why there must always be consent on both sides of a union. You understand that is a sacred tenet in Terre d'Ange?"

"Yes, but—"

"But what?" I ate my bread. "No doubt sodomy is a vile and painful experience if it is forced. That does not make the act sinful in and of itself, nor does it mean it cannot be pleasant if done willingly and properly...Aleksei, your mouth is agape."

"Are you trying to find some further means of shocking me, Moirin?" he asked uncertainly.

"No."

He exhaled hard. "Every time I think I've begun to understand, there seems some further goal on the horizon. And I will say again, this is one I will not pursue. Not with a woman, and most assuredly not with a man."

"It's not a requirement, sweet boy." I toyed with my spoon. "There are D'Angelines who find pleasure in acts even I would shun; and there are D'Angelines who find the deepest abiding joy in remaining faithful to their chosen loves. So long as Blessed Elua's precept is obeyed and the sacred tenet of consensuality is honored, Naamah's blessing is on all of them." I took a bite of stew, and swallowed. "I would have you be mindful of it as you seek to bring new understanding to your faith, that's all."

Aleksei was silent a moment. "I will try."

"Some of it shocked me, too," I added. "At least at first."

He looked relieved. "I confess myself glad to hear it."

"I can teach you some of Naamah's arts if you wish," I offered. "Only the parts I think you will like."

His expression turned confused. "But you already have."

I hid a smile. "Ah, no. That was love-making as a simple act of benediction. There are a hundred different kinds of kisses and caresses one can use to coax and please a lover, and that is only the beginning."

Aleksei paused, then nodded. "I would like that, if you are willing. I think…" He smiled wryly. "I think perhaps one day my bride will be very glad I said yes."

I couldn't help but think of my lady Jehanne teaching me at Cereus House, naming and demonstrating until I had to beg her to stop; and Jehanne months later, giving me one of her sparkling looks in the enchanted bower she'd had made for me. *Oh, I've got you well on your way to possessing an adept's skills, Moirin.*

Gods, it hurt to think of her being gone. I wondered what she would make of the uses to which I'd put the arts she had taught me.

I thought she would approve; mayhap even laugh with delight. She was Naamah's child through and through. And ever since I had first laid eyes on Jehanne, Naamah's face had come to resemble hers in my thoughts.

"I was taught by the foremost courtesan in Terre d'Ange, Aleksei," I said to him. "Trust me, your bride will be glad of it."

FORTY-THREE

Several days of pure indolence followed.

In truth, we had little else to do in Udinsk while we waited for the Patriarch to turn his attention away from the south. We listened to gossip in the marketplace, hoping in vain to hear rumors of his movements. Aleksei returned to the smith who had bought my chains and purchased a cooking-pot and a small belt knife for me. We found a sail-maker and commissioned a tent of tough canvas that was done in a day's time.

Beyond that, our time was our own.

And Aleksei proved an apt pupil.

Betimes I was hard put not to laugh, as determined and earnest as he was. He was Naamah's child, aye; but he was a scholar by nature and training alike, and he applied a scholar's discipline to learning Naamah's arts.

"Tracing the nautilus," he breathed in my ear, echoing the latest term I had taught him. The tip of his tongue described a dwindling spiral and probed my inner canal rather too insistently. "Moirin, stop giggling!"

"It tickles!"

His blue eyes were wide and sincere. "Isn't it supposed to?"

"Not exactly, no." I showed him again, beginning with a line of soft kisses along his jaw, nipping gently on his earlobe, sucking it into my mouth. "Softly," I whispered into his ear. "Slowly. Delicately; oh so delicately." I traced circles with my tongue, darting and flickering it until Aleksei shuddered and groaned. I pulled back. "Listen, and pay attention to your lover's response. After all, that is the most important thing. Let her body's response tell you what pleases her."

Letting out a growl, Aleksei pinned me to the bed. "I know what pleases *you*!"

"Some things, aye." I wound my arms around his neck, kissing his lips. "Not all, sweet boy. Not even close. And you do not know what pleases this wife you have not yet met, who will no doubt be far less licentious than I. So I suggest you heed my advice."

By and large, he did.

And by and large, Aleksei blossomed under my tutelage. The sense of grace that Naamah's blessing had bestowed lingered over us. He remained comfortable in his skin. He walked differently, even stood differently. He held his head higher, no longer ducking it modestly under the slightest scrutiny, blushing less.

His taut, hunched shoulders straightened and squared. The movement of his long, rangy limbs acquired a loose grace. He ate heartily, loved freely. He began to laugh more easily and readily, even at himself.

It was beautiful to see.

I thought often of Aleksei's mother, Valentina, in those days, wishing she could see her son as I did. It was what she had wanted for him—her caged bird set free, free to stretch his wings and fly, finding his true element. I liked teaching him, but I liked best those times when lessons were over, and Aleksei gave himself over to sheer passion, rocking between my thighs and thrusting deep inside me, whispering blasphemous prayers into the crook of my neck.

But by the fourth day, I was restless, too long confined indoors.

"Let's go for a ride," I suggested.

He paused. "Why?"

I shrugged. "Why not? It will be good to acquaint ourselves with our mounts—and to make certain that dealer hasn't sold them out from under us," I added. "I don't trust that fellow."

That swayed him—that and the picnic lunch that Polina kindly offered to pack for us. Having discovered his appetite, Aleksei was constantly hungry, and I was pleased that he wasn't yet inclined to resume the discipline of fasting.

I took my Tatar bow with me, or at least, I had Aleksei bring it. I had in mind to practice with it. Taking note of it, Polina suggested that we might find grouse or pheasant in the meadows upriver, and that game-birds would be a welcome addition to supper. The thought of shooting for the pot made me homesick, missing my own mother, but it brought good memories, too.

For a mercy, our sturdy little horses were awaiting us safely in the dealer's stable. We rode out of town, past the Tatar encampment, and set out upriver in search of the meadows Polina had mentioned.

I was in good spirits. All had gone well in Udinsk, and in two days' time, we would take our leave.

And at last I would be travelling in the direction of Bao and the missing half of my *diadh-anam*. I'd managed to keep myself from constant worry, but it would be a relief to be moving toward him.

We found the meadows, filled with bright yellow flowers blossoming beneath the blue sky. I asked Aleksei what they were called, but he didn't know. After we tethered our mounts and spread a blanket for our picnic, I let myself stroke the blossoms, taking in their quick, joyous thoughts.

This, too, reminded me of home. I couldn't resist coaxing one unopened bud to blossom, breathing softly over it.

Aleksei watched wide-eyed as the bright yellow petals opened to the sun. "More magic?"

"Aye." I smiled. "A small gift, nothing more. If there's some greater purpose in it, it's not yet been revealed to me."

He shook his head. "You're full of surprises."

We ate the lunch of sausages, cheese, and brown bread that Polina had packed for us, and afterward, I introduced Aleksei to the pleasure of making love outdoors, with nothing but earth and sky around us.

"Now I truly do feel like Edom and Yeva in the Garden," he whispered to me. "I only wish—"

I stopped his mouth with a kiss. "I know. But I cannot stay here."

"I know," Aleksei said softly, brushing the hair back from my face. "But I do wish it, Moirin."

I kissed him again. "Let's see if I can get a brace of grouse for Polina, shall we?"

He accompanied me as I walked along the piney woods that lined the meadow, an arrow nocked loosely. It took half an hour before I flushed a lone grouse, rising out of the underbrush with a startling clatter of wings.

That bird, I missed; and it took us another half hour to find the arrow I'd loosed. But after that, I flushed and shot two birds in quick succession, wringing their necks swiftly so that they did not suffer. By then it was late enough in the afternoon that we decided to return to the inn.

"It's passing strange," Aleksei mused as we rode. "In Riva, you seemed so very different to me."

"One of the many Moirins," I said lightly.

"No, it's not just that. I saw you as I was taught to see you," he said. "When you were angry and bitter and resentful, I thought it was the badness in you, Naamah's curse, the unclean spirit fighting against God's efforts to redeem it. Even when I gave you my mother's book to read, it was because I hoped you would respond better to a message of love and compassion."

"You weren't wrong," I murmured.

"No, but...seeing you now, in your own element, I realize you were angry for the exact reason you said." Aleksei glanced at me. "You were a wild creature meant to live free, and we cast you in chains."

I raised my brows. "You're only just now realizing this?"

"Day by day, I realize it more." He smiled wryly. "Today, I am realizing that you would have every right to hate me for the role I played in your captivity." He paused. "Do you? At least a little?"

"No." I drew rein and leaned over in the saddle to touch his arm. "You were in a cage, too, Aleksei, only you could not even see the bars. I don't hate you. Even in my worst moments, I never hated you."

He took a deep breath. "I'm sorry, Moirin. I've never said it, have I? I should have said it days ago. I'm sorry for what my uncle did to you. I'm sorry for what you have suffered. I'm sorry for being a part of it. I'm sorry we took you away from…" His voice faltered, then continued. "From that Bao you spoke of, and your soul-spark he carries. No matter what I may wish, I can tell that you love him and fear for him." His blue eyes shone, guileless and remorseful. "I'm very, very sorry."

It touched me more than I could have reckoned. Until Aleksei gave me one, I hadn't known part of me yearned for an apology, any apology.

"Thank you," I said simply.

Aleksei nodded. "You're welcome. For all the many kindnesses you have shown me…" His color rose. "I owe you a great deal more than an apology."

I smiled. "Oh, I have enjoyed the kindnesses, sweet boy. Do not think I haven't."

"I don't." He smiled back at me. "You've taught me that much. But do not think I am not grateful for them, or for the generosity and forbearance you have shown me."

"I don't," I assured him. "You have a good heart, Aleksei."

Thus in accord, we resumed our journey back into Udinsk. Passing the Tatar encampment, I caught sight of Vachir's wife, Arigh, milking a goat and waved to her, hoisting the brace of grouse that she might see I'd put her bow to good use. She smiled and raised a hand in reply.

We entered the city proper, our stalwart horses jogging steadily beneath us. I bowed my head and touched the thoughts of my mount lightly, stroking her withers, trying to think of a name that might suit her now that we had spent an entire day together. The squinty-eyed trader hadn't bothered to name his wares.

Something calm, I thought, something hardy.

Somewhere, someone shouted.

My head came up sharply.

"Moirin..." Aleksei's voice shook. He pointed ahead of us.

There were men in the city square—too many men. Armed and mounted men, not merchants and traders. I recognized the wide-set figure and grizzled beard of the Duke of Vralsturm, and the attire of his soldiers.

And beside him...

I swore under my breath at the sight of the Patriarch of Riva, wearing black robes, seated astride a rather good-looking chestnut saddlehorse—swore and reached for my bow, glad that I'd forgotten to give it back to Aleksei for appearances' sake.

"Moirin, no!"

I ignored Aleksei, nocking an arrow. The Duke's men rode forward slowly, fanning out to create a semicircle. I willed my mount to be still, and she stood like a statue beneath me. Beside the Duke of Vralsturm, Pyotr Rostov smiled his creamy smile, raising one hand to stroke his beard in a thoughtful gesture.

"Moirin mac Fainche," he said in a deep, resonant voice.

I leveled my arrow at his chest. "One and the same, *my lord*. How did you find us?"

His smile broadened. "A suspicious smith offered an unusual set of chains for sale made certain inquiries. Pity about the chains, but that's a moot point now."

Ah, gods! It was the fellow at that second smithy, the one who had asked too many questions. I glanced around the square. Some folk were pelting off in different directions, spreading the news of the brewing confrontation. Others gathered at a safe distance to watch, curiosity written in their faces.

All too well, I knew how quickly it could turn to hostility.

Even now, the Patriarch was addressing them in Vralian, and I'd learned enough to grasp that he was explaining that I was a sinful witch possessed by unclean spirits, that I was sentenced to death, and that the Duke and his men had come to take me into custody and administer the sentence.

"That's not true!" Aleksei raised his voice, speaking slowly and distinctly in Vralian so that I could follow. "Uncle, I *know* Moirin. She has unusual gifts, yes, but there is no unclean spirit in her!"

"You are bewitched, boy," his uncle replied, his brows drawing together in a scowl. "We will pray together."

Aleksei shook his head stubbornly. "I'm telling the truth. I would stake my life on it!"

The Patriarch's voice dropped to a low rumble. "And you just might if you insist on this course. You've been like a son to me, Aleksei, but I cannot protect you if you will not renounce the witch."

Aleksei blanched.

"He can't," I said quickly. "You are right. I bewitched him so thoroughly he does not know it himself."

"She's lying!" Aleksei shouted. "She's trying to protect me! Moirin, I won't let you. I won't lie." There were tears in his blue eyes. "I felt Naamah's blessing myself. It is real, it is true and beautiful, and there is no curse in it. None!"

The Duke of Vralsturm gestured curtly to his men. "Take them both."

"Hold!" I drew the bowstring back two more inches to its fullest extension, keeping my arrow trained on Pyotr Rostov's chest, and my gaze fixed on his face. No one moved. "Let us go, or I will kill him."

"Moirin, don't!" Aleksei murmured. "Please, don't do this. You're not a killer."

"I have killed men before," I said with a calmness I did not feel. "And I will kill your uncle if he does not recant his order."

The Patriarch returned my gaze steadily. He had courage, I'd grant him that. Courage, ambition, and a fanatic's belief in the rightness of his cause. It was all written in his face. And I saw, too, that he believed in his heart that I was bluffing. I saw a vision of a future unspooling between us, a future in which my corruption of his golden nephew Aleksei became a rallying point for the Church of Yeshua Ascendant.

Here in this square, Aleksei would be slain for the sin of loving me, martyred for his uncle's cause—and my death would be but the first in a long crusade against the sinful D'Angelines and the unnatural bear-witches of the Maghuin Dhonn.

A future of banners and bloodshed, preparing the world with fire and steel for Yeshua ben Yosef's return; and in the center of it all, the Patriarch of Riva stoking the fires with his splendid rhetoric, causing it all to happen.

I sucked in my breath, shaking at the vision, my arms trembling from the strain of holding the drawn bow.

Pyotr Rostov smiled in triumph. "Take them."

Steadying my grip, I loosed the bowstring.

"Moirin, no!" Aleksei cried a second time, hurling himself from the saddle and crashing into me, dragging me from my mount. I fell hard onto the cobbled square, striking my head on the stones, Aleksei falling atop me.

The world went black for a moment—pitch-black, with starbursts of light spangling the darkness. My head hurt. Everywhere around us, there was shouting and clattering, sounds like an avalanche of rocks falling.

In the sparkling darkness, I wondered if the folk of Udinsk had begun to stone me already, wondered how they'd armed themselves so quickly. I shoved frantically at Aleksei's weight, pushing him off me.

The clattering got louder, and so did the shouting.

I scrambled to my feet, shaking my head to clear it. There seemed to be a sea of surging horse-flesh between me and my adversaries. In between the churning legs, shaggy flanks, and thick, arching necks, I caught a glimpse of the Duke's men retreating to regroup and the Patriarch kneeling on the cobblestones, grimacing, his fingers clutching at the shaft of an arrow protruding just below his collarbone.

"Lady archer." Vachir's face hung above me, silhouetted against the bright blue sky as he leaned down from the saddle. I squinted, seeing two of him. "Are you well?"

Tatars.

The Tatars from the encampment had come to my rescue.

I laughed, a short, wondering laugh. "Not exactly. But, Vachir... why?"

He smiled his quiet smile. "I offered you the hospitality of my roof."

There was more to it, but I understood. Vachir and his fellow traders were settling the balance of debt the Great Khan Naram himself incurred when he violated the sacred laws of hospitality. "Thank you," I said softly.

Vachir nodded. "You should come with us. Now."

I rubbed my hands over my face, gave my aching head another shake, and took stock of the situation. Beside me, Aleksei got to his feet, trembling.

It was a standoff. The Duke of Vralsturm and his men were in a cluster around the kneeling Patriarch, hands on their sword-hilts. Mounted Tatar warriors milled around them, bows drawn, arrows nocked and poised. The younger men among them had dark, glittering eyes and fierce battle-smiles that reminded me of Bao.

Vachir spoke.

One of the younger men translated his words into Vralian. "We are taking the lady archer and her companion," he said cheerfully. "If you do not wish to provoke a war, you will let us."

Pyotr Rostov drew a ragged breath, his voice hoarse with pain. "Your Great Khan *gave* her to me!"

The Tatars conferred.

"Oh, yes," their spokesman agreed. "That was a mistake. And the Great Khan will thank us for fixing it... one day." His battle-smile widened, his eyes bright. "Today, do you wish to make war?"

The Patriarch did.

The Duke of Vralsturm did not. He was a practical man. I watched resignation settle over his broad features, watched him signal his men to stand down.

I hoisted myself astride my mount, glancing at Aleksei. "I think it is best we go with the Tatars. Will you come?"

He hesitated.

"Aleksei, *no*!" his uncle grated. "It's not too late for you, boy!"

Aleksei squared his shoulders. "It is, actually," he said quietly. "I'm sorry, Uncle. All my life, I have tried to conform to your vision of what I should be. I have tried to redeem my mother's sin. But I think… I think you were wrong. I think you have tried to force God and his son Yeshua alike into a mold that is too small and narrow to contain them." He shook his head. "I did my best to honor you. I did my best to save your life. But I will not allow you to lessen the myriad wonder of God's infinite grace for me."

My heart and my *diadh-anam* sang within me.

"Aleksei…" The Patriarch of Riva repeated his name. "Aleksei, listen, only listen to me!"

My sweet, scholarly boy turned away from him, refusing to hear him.

I kneed my unnamed mount gently, and she stepped forward, ears pricked. From my vantage point, I gazed down at Pyotr Rostov, who knelt on the cobblestones and clutched the protruding shaft, staring at me with hot, angry eyes, as hot and angry as the image of Yeshua on the wall of his temple.

He would live, I thought. Aleksei had done that much for his uncle, sending the arrow I had loosed astray by mere inches.

But his dream, his hateful dream, would die. Neither Aleksei nor I would die here today at the hands of an angry mob. The future the Patriarch had envisioned would no longer come to pass.

And for that, I was grateful. Alive, and grateful.

"You lose," I said in Vralian, loud enough for everyone nearby to hear. "And I win."

FORTY-FOUR

We returned to the Tatar camp, Aleksei and I, protected by a guard of Vachir and his fellow traders.

They were in good spirits, having enjoyed the confrontation immensely, especially the younger men. I learned that it was a young fellow named Chagan, the one who had served as Vachir's translator, who had witnessed the beginning of the conflict and gone racing to rouse the camp, having recognized me from the archery rematch.

When I thanked him for it, he laughed, showing strong white teeth. "It was a matter of honor, lady archer! Anyone who shoots as well as you do must have Tatar blood in her somewhere."

Aleksei was quiet and withdrawn. Sensing he wished to be left alone, I didn't try to draw him out. When he suggested that he should return to the inn with an armed escort and fetch our things, I didn't argue, even though I had reservations.

I could not blame him for not wanting to be around me at the moment. After all, I had just attempted to kill his uncle in cold blood. The man might have been a monster to me, but for all his faults, he had been like a father to Aleksei; and Aleksei had no way of knowing the vision I had seen unfold.

Despite my reservations, he and his Tatar escorts returned safely with all the possessions we had purchased so painstakingly, even the pack-horse.

"What's the mood in the city?" I asked in an effort to gauge his own mood.

"Tense," he murmured without meeting my eyes. "But they are afraid of the Tatars. No one will make trouble."

I left him alone a while longer, busying myself with helping Arigh with chores around the *ger*. It felt oddly familiar, except for the absence of children. When I asked Arigh about it, she shook her head with regret, laying one hand over her belly. "No children, no."

"I'm sorry," I said.

She glanced at Vachir, conferring with a handful of traders on the men's side of the *ger*. "He is a good husband, though. And I think..." Her eyes crinkled. "I think if he had a daughter, he would like one like you. Spirited, and skilled with a bow."

I smiled at her. "You're very kind."

It was a strange thing indeed, I thought, how much cruelty and kindness existed side by side in the world. The great magician Berlik had found sanctuary and redemption among the Yeshuites in Vralia; save for Aleksei and Valentina, I had found only condemnation.

I thought about the D'Angeline Prince Imriel, who had pursued Berlik into the Vralian wilderness to avenge his wife's death. He had been used cruelly in his youth, stolen away into slavery, a captivity far worse than aught I had endured. There had been a Tatar warlord who hurt him badly, even branding him with a hot iron.

And yet when the adult Prince Imriel had been imprisoned with a young Tatar horse-thief in Vralia, he'd set him free when he made his escape. I wondered if that act of compassion resonated over generations in some mysterious way, leading to this moment, and my salvation at the hands of Vachir and his fellows.

There are things no one can ever know, I supposed.

For the first time in a while, I found myself missing Master Lo Feng, feeling his loss acutely. He'd always had a way of putting everything into perspective. I pictured him smiling, folding his hands into his wide sleeves.

All ways lead to the Way, Moirin.

"Moirin?"

"Aye?" I was startled out of my reverie by Vachir's voice, realizing I was standing and gazing into space, my hands sunk deep into floury wheat-dough. Arigh and I had been making meat-filled dumplings.

He gave a low chuckle, reaching out to rub a smudge of flour from my cheek; and indeed, there was a father's tenderness in his touch. "We were planning to return to Tatar territory in a week's time, but if we conclude our bargains swiftly, we can be on our way the day after tomorrow. Will you and your young companion accompany us? It will be safer for you," he added.

"I will," I said without hesitating, glancing at Aleksei.

Vachir followed my gaze. "And the boy?"

I shook my head. "I don't know."

Arigh laid her hand on my shoulder, squeezing it in gentle sympathy. "Talk to him."

After supper, I did.

It was hard, harder than I had reckoned. Everyone else in the *ger* gave us a wide berth. I sat cross-legged opposite Aleksei, drawing a deep breath.

"Are you angry at me?" I asked without mincing words. "I do not blame you if you are."

"Angry?" he echoed, his voice soft. "No...not angry, Moirin."

"Disappointed?"

Aleksei frowned in thought. "No, I'm...I don't know. I understand, I do. And I cannot blame you, not really. After all, he *was* sentencing you to death. All you wanted was to be left alone. It's just..." He shook his head. "It shocked me nonetheless. Are you angry at *me* for trying to stop you?"

"No." I took his hand, holding it lightly. He tensed, but he didn't pull away. "You would not be who you are if you hadn't, sweet boy. Only I would have you know, I did not do it solely out of hatred or a desire for vengeance."

His brows knit. "No?"

I stroked his palm. "Long ago, my ancestors among the Maghuin Dhonn had the gift of scrying the future in the stone circles, seeing all the different paths that might come to pass and trying to choose among them. It is a gift we abandoned voluntarily after choosing unwisely, after Berlik was cursed."

"I know," Aleksei murmured.

"It's not a gift the Maghuin Dhonn Herself withdrew from us, Aleksei," I said softly. "And I have seen visions of the future I did not seek. I saw one in the temple that day, do you remember?"

He nodded.

"It happened once before, too. On the battlefield in Ch'in." I kept my voice low and steady, realizing he was listening. "I saw a vision of a terrible future, one that should never be allowed to come to pass. I saw another one today, written in your uncle's eyes." Pausing, I debated whether or not to tell him that his uncle would have been willing to sacrifice Aleksei to his cause. "Your uncle's threat wasn't an idle one, Aleksei. I saw our deaths give rise to a future of war and bloodshed in Yeshua's name, in which D'Angelines and the Maghuin Dhonn alike were persecuted for their nature. And that is what I sought to avert."

Aleksei swallowed, his throat working. "Even so . . . you didn't even hesitate, Moirin!"

"I warned him," I said. "Beyond that, I didn't dare."

He looked away, and then looked back, gazing at his hand resting loosely in mine. Gently and regretfully, he extricated his hand. "I believe you," he said in a quiet voice. "I do. But I think our paths part here."

"You're sure?" I asked.

"Yes." Aleksei smiled with sorrow; and it was a man's smile, not a boy's. "You'll be safe with Vachir and his men. You have given me so much, Moirin. I suspect I will spend a lifetime contemplating its purpose in God's plan. But you are not for me, and I am not for you. I will free you to seek out this stubborn peasant-boy Bao, who carries half of the soul-spark of your unknowable bear-goddess within him."

"What will you do?" I whispered. "Where will you go?"

His wide shoulders rose and fell in a faint shrug. "I will stay here in Vralia, where I am meant to be, and try to determine what God and Yeshua will of me. Mayhap I'll make my way west to seek out a yeshiva where the wisdom of Rebbe Avraham ben David is taught. Once I know I can care for her, I'll send for my mother."

My eyes stung.

"Don't cry, Moirin," he pleaded with me.

"I'm not!" I lied.

Aleksei shifted, kneeling, and cupped my face. "You are," he said softly, tenderly. "And it's all right. I do love you. I will always love you." He smiled again, his expression transcendent, his blue, blue eyes filled with light. "And I will convince the world to do so, too; or at least my small corner of it."

He kissed me.

I kissed him back, and sniffled. "I will miss you."

"So will I."

FORTY-FIVE

＊

Two days later, Aleksei and I parted forever.

It hurt.

It always hurts, leaving a loved one behind. I hadn't meant to love Aleksei. Until the moment I knew I had lost him, I hadn't realized I *did* love him.

Naamah's curse, indeed.

Gods, he was such a gentle soul! He watched me depart amid Vachir's company of Tatars, following a southern tributary of the Ude River. He smiled in farewell, tall and broad-shouldered, raising one hand in a salute.

Our destinies tore and parted.

"May you find yours, sweet boy," I murmured under my breath. "May you reshape your Church in a kinder, gentler image."

I hoped he would be safe and well. I didn't like leaving him with the Patriarch's threat hanging over him. Aleksei had helped me escape, and he had refused to renounce me. On the other hand, he had saved his uncle's life, and all of Udinsk had watched him do it. And I couldn't protect him. Even if he had been willing to come with us as far as the Tatar lands, he would have returned to Vralia afterward. It was his home.

Over his protests, I'd left him one of the saddle-horses and half the remaining coin from selling the chains, along with a few supplies. Left to his own devices, Aleksei would have preferred to accept nothing, venturing out into the world like an itinerant wandering monk. I was glad I'd been able to convince him to accept what he had. Still, he was so naïve and inexperienced. I hoped it would be enough, and that the world would treat him kindly.

I wondered if I would ever know, and knew it was possible that I wouldn't.

But mayhap I would; mayhap one day I would hear of a half-D'Angeline priest in distant Vralia who preached a doctrine of compassion and acceptance that attempted to reconcile different faiths, who had written a tract regarding his encounter with his own unlikely heretic saint.

The thought cheered me during our journey.

And I was profoundly grateful to be travelling with the Tatars, profoundly grateful for their protection. The first leg of our journey was a tense one. Gossip had spread before us, and within days, we were passing through villages where Pyotr Rostov and the Duke's men had sought me.

In every village and settlement, people came out to stare and point, trying to pick me out among the Tatar throng.

A few times, they threw stones—small boys too foolish to be afraid, for the most part. When it happened, Chagan and the other young men dashed after them on horseback, instilling in them the fear the boys lacked.

At night when we camped, Vachir posted guards. No one came to molest us, too wary of the Tatars' reputation for ferocity, unwilling to provoke a conflict that might escalate. Still, I was glad when we passed the last settlement and entered the wilderness of the mountain range along the southern border.

For the first time in months, I truly felt I could breathe freely.

As the days passed, my worry over Aleksei began to fade into the background of my thoughts. He had chosen his path, and there was nothing I could do to aid him in a land where my very nature was despised. He had grown so much since first I met him, and he would continue to grow and change as he made his way alone in the world, preparing to meet whatever destiny awaited him. All I could do was pray for his safety.

My worry over Bao was another matter, growing stronger as I travelled in his direction. At least he was alive, I knew that much. Since first I'd been freed from my chains, I'd sensed no change in his *diadh-anam*. It continued to burn low—alarmingly low, but burning nonetheless. If he was ill or injured, his condition was a stable one.

He wasn't moving, or at least not much. The distance that separated us was great enough that I wouldn't be able to detect small movements on his end. To be sure, he wasn't journeying toward me.

It could simply be that Bao had fallen ill with a lingering sickness. It had happened to my father. He'd contracted an infection in his lungs and lain ill for long weeks without my knowing.

The thought made me shudder. If Raphael de Mereliot hadn't consented to aid me, albeit for a terrible price, my father would have died.

Raphael was ten thousand leagues away. If Bao was mortally ill, there was nothing I could do to save him even if I arrived in time.

But if it wasn't illness or injury, what could cause his *diadh-anam* to gutter so low, to burn so dim? Whatever it was, it was nothing good. I'd learned firsthand that there were magics capable of constraining the divine spark of the Maghuin Dhonn Herself. Who knew what other magics existed that were capable of binding or poisoning it?

I didn't spend all my time fretting over him, of course. I'd have driven myself mad if I did. Bao was simply too far away, and there was nothing I could do.

Still, I worried.

Riding with the Tatars, we passed more swiftly through the Vralian mountains than I had with my abductors. Vachir and his folk were travelling fairly light, having traded cattle and sheep for furs and amber, which they would trade in turn for more livestock once they reached Tatar lands. The weather was fair, and when we made camp, we slept in the open. *Gers* were only to be erected at more permanent campsites. We made good time, and it wasn't long before the mountains gave way to the vast, wide-open expanse of the steppe.

"Ah!" Vachir took a deep breath as we rode from the foothills onto the grassy plain, smiling with rare effusiveness. "Home."

I envied him; I envied all of them.

It wasn't that I wasn't glad to be back in Tatar lands. I was. I'd come to love the steppe despite its absence of trees, and the kindness and generosity I'd found here outweighed the sting of the Great Khan's betrayal.

But stone and sea...*home*! I was so very, very far away from mine, wherever my home even was anymore. The word was every bit as painful and bittersweet as it had been when I set out from Shuntian so long ago in pursuit of the missing half of my soul. And in all that time, I'd done naught but travel in an immense circle that had brought me back to the exact same plight: setting out to cross a vast land in search of Bao.

"Stupid boy," I muttered to myself. "Why did you have to go and wed the Tatar princess? We'd be together and halfway home if you hadn't."

In my heart, I understood, though. Bao had told me his reasons. Aside from the fact that one does not refuse the Great Khan, it was Bao's way of making himself my equal in status and rank, of giving himself a choice that entailed a sacrifice to make the choice meaningful. It didn't make sense, not really; but truths of the heart owe nothing to logic. Master Lo had laid a heavy burden on his magpie's shoulders when he gave his life to restore Bao's. This was Bao's way of accepting it.

Unfortunately, he hadn't reckoned on the consequences: the princess' injured pride and her father's wrath.

"Stupid boy," I said again.

The heart is a strange thing. Bao wasn't stupid, of course; in fact, he was quite clever. But he could be thoughtless with the feelings of others. He had a prickly sense of pride that was too easily rankled, and he was infernally stubborn. He was insulting and boastful, and he reveled in fighting.

And yet...

I loved him in a way I could never have loved Aleksei. My sweet, innocent Yeshuite boy had certainly found a place in my heart after all. I'd come to love him for his innate goodness that not even a lifetime of discipline and repression could extinguish, for the sense of wonder with which he viewed the world. But he had never made my heart soar, only ache at leaving him.

It was different with Bao.

When I tried to put my finger on the moment I *knew*, I couldn't. There wasn't one. There were myriad small moments, like the first time I'd seen the tenderness Bao extended to Master Lo. The first time he had lowered his guard with me on the greatship, confessing the less than savory details of his past.

There was the moment in a garden in the Celestial City, when he bade me farewell and left me alone with the dragon-possessed princess, worry in his eyes, knowing what I was about to do and not trying to dissuade me, only telling me not to get myself killed.

For better or worse, Bao understood me.

And when the Emperor of Ch'in had refused to heed Master Lo's advice, when he had accepted his fate and his daughter's fate as the will of Heaven, Bao hadn't hesitated to reject the Emperor's edict without a second thought. He had fetched a jar of rice-wine from the kitchen of our lodgings and sat us down in the courtyard, pouring three cups for us.

I smiled, remembering.

There is a time for strong spirits, Master, he had said. *This is one of them. Now, how are we going to save the princess and the dragon?*

I had choked on a sip of wine, startled at the fact that Bao was laying the matter bare before us. Bao had turned his dark, cynical gaze on me, that ironic look that masked his romantic and courageous heart.

You had other plans?

I hadn't; of course, I hadn't. In fact, I had already pledged to aid the princess in defying her father if it was necessary, promising to help her journey to White Jade Mountain to free the dragon by any means possible.

Somehow, Bao had known.

And he hadn't hesitated.

The phrase struck a chord. I thought of Aleksei's voice raised in anguish as he wrestled with the fact that I had tried to kill his uncle. *You didn't even hesitate, Moirin!*

He was right, I hadn't. Nor would I if I had to do it again. Confronted with the hateful future the Patriarch envisioned, I would loose that bowstring a thousand times over without hesitating.

And confronted with the vision of the dragon in all his celestial majesty gazing at his reflection in the twilight, filled with sorrow and regret, and my grave, lovely princess fighting so hard to maintain her sanity in light of what had befallen her, I would pledge my aid without hesitating another thousand times.

That, Bao understood.

Aleksei didn't.

One day, he might. He had the potential for greatness in him. I had seen it, and I hoped he would fulfill it. But whatever else might have come to pass between us, I would never be able to forget that in my hour of greatest need, Aleksei *had* hesitated, any more than he would be able to forget I had tried to kill his uncle. My sweet boy would never have set me free in the first place if his mother, Valentina, had not pushed him into it.

Bao...

Bao would not have hesitated.

I remembered another of the myriad moments. It was in the abandoned farmstead outside Shuntian where our small band of conspirators had first taken shelter with the escaped princess, and Bao and Master Lo were late in coming to join us. I had been worried, so worried.

They'd come, though.

Did you think we would not? Bao's dark eyes had gleamed beneath the broad-brimmed straw hat he wore. He had slid one arm around my waist, holding me close, and come as close as he'd done to a declaration of love, his voice a soft whisper in my ear. *I would not let that happen, Moirin.*

"You did, though," I said aloud to my memories. "Although I know it is not your fault, you left me alone in a very bad place. Where are you? Where did the Great Khan send you? Gods bedamned, Bao! Where are you, and what's happened to you?"

No one answered me.

I sighed, and kept riding.

FORTY-SIX

Two days into the steppe, my path diverged with that of Vachir and his folk.

He offered to send a couple of the young men of his tribe with me, an offer I declined with reluctance.

"You've given me so much already," I said to Vachir. "I cannot accept further aid. It would leave too great a balance of debt between us. Besides," I added, gazing south toward the faint, distant spark of Bao's *diadh-anam*, "I suspect I am going far beyond the boundaries of Tatar lands."

Vachir didn't argue with me, only smiled his quiet smile, this time tinged with sadness. "I wish you well, Moirin."

I hugged him. "And you, lord archer. May your cattle ever prosper."

His wife, Arigh, hugged me, too, and presented me with a blue silk scarf. "A small gift to replace the one that was lost to you. Now you are kin to our tribe, too."

"Thank you so very much, my lady." It brought tears to my eyes. I wrapped the scarf around my neck and kissed her cheek. "May I ask one last kindness of you?"

"Of course." Arigh smiled, her eyes crinkling. "You are kin now."

"When next you encounter Batu and his folk, will you tell them I am well?" I asked. "That I think of them with great fondness, and that the honor of their hospitality has been restored through your generosity."

Both of them nodded. "We will do this gladly," Vachir added.

I watched them ride eastward, watched until their company began to dwindle in the distance.

Once again, I was alone, save for my horses. "Well, my friends," I said to them. "Are you ready?"

They agreed they were.

And once again, I set out across the steppe.

At least this time the journey was easier. I was familiar with the terrain. The weather was temperate and mild, the skies largely cloudless. Most nights, I didn't bother pitching my tent, but slept in the open as I had been doing with Vachir's folk. The grazing was rich and my Tatar-stock horses were hardier than those the Emperor had given me, requiring less time to feed.

I was able to augment the stores of dried meat and hardened cheese that Vachir had given me with fresh game, mostly groundhog. I'd had the sense to gather as much timber as my pack-horse could carry before we left the mountains, and I parceled it out carefully, allowing myself a small fire to cook with when I had fresh meat.

The gamey, greasy groundhogs were no tastier than I remembered, but I came across wild onions from time to time. With those and a handful of barley from a sack Aleksei and I had purchased in Udinsk, groundhog made for a tolerable stew.

One good thing about the wide-open steppe was that one could see for leagues beneath the immense blue sky. I had no trouble spotting encampments and giving them a wide berth, nor avoiding travellers and herdsmen, summoning the twilight if necessary.

All in all, I made good progress.

Despite it, Bao's *diadh-anam* remained dim and distant.

I'd been travelling alone for over a week when I spotted a Tatar camp larger than any I'd seen since the spring gathering on the horizon. Out of habit, I began to veer well away from it, but curiosity niggled at me. One *ger* amidst the camp dwarfed the others, a mighty dome of white felt. I'd seen one that large only once before, and it had belonged to the Great Khan Naram.

Impulse warred with common sense within me.

I had no desire to confront the Great Khan himself, suspecting he wouldn't hesitate to clap me in chains and send me back to Vralia.

And yet...

The Great Khan Naram had sent Bao toward whatever fate had befallen him. If the Khan knew, mayhap others did, too.

Others, like his daughter, the Tatar princess Erdene, who was said to be angry with her father.

I breathed the Breath of Earth's Pulse, centering myself and thinking. I was riding toward the unknown, and like as not, danger. The D'Angelines of Siovale province, Shemhazai's folk, had a saying: *All knowledge is worth having.* And now when I thought of Shemhazai, the most scholarly of Blessed Elua's Companions, I pictured Aleksei's face—grave, ascetic, and beautiful.

"What do you think, my friends?" I asked the horses. "Is it a sign?"

They flicked their ears, not understanding. The pack-horse lowered his head and cropped at the grass.

It would be good, very good, to have some idea what I was getting myself into, to have some idea what had already befallen Bao. I made up my mind, choosing impulse over common sense.

Even so, I did not intend to be foolish about it. I studied the Great Khan's encampment and its movements, then stuck to my original plan, veering east to pass it, then veering back west to set up my own small camp alongside a bend in the river I had been following, well to the south where herds had already been pastured.

I watered the horses and turned them loose to graze, apologizing to them for the sparse fare. I gnawed on strips of dried meat for my supper. And when dusk began to settle over the plain, I saddled my mount, summoned the twilight, and backtracked toward the Great Khan's camp.

It was almost dark by the time I drew near, although I could see clearly in the twilight. At a hundred yards out, I dismounted and tethered my mare to a stake.

"Be silent, great heart," I whispered to her, touching her thoughts. I stroked her thick, coarse forelock and scratched the base of her ears. "The darkness will hide you, but I cannot shield us both."

She bent her neck and turned her head to lip softly at my palm, huffing through her nostrils.

I kissed her muzzle. "Good girl."

The last hundred yards, I crossed on foot, my Tatar bow held loosely in one hand, the quiver slung over my shoulder.

It was a familiar scene, albeit one rendered strange by the twilight. The Great Khan and his folk were celebrating and the *airag* was flowing freely, the pungent scent of fermented mare's milk riding the night air. Fires of dried dung burned, silvery in the twilight, folk gathered around them.

Unseen, I prowled through the camp until I spotted Erdene.

Bao's wife.

In so many cultures, this would have been unthinkable, that a princess should be so accessible and ordinary. But the Tatars, like the Maghuin Dhonn, live close to nature. I waited until Erdene excused herself, made her unsteady way to the latrine alone.

I followed her.

I waited until she had finished.

And when Bao's Tatar princess began to make her way back to her father's great *ger*, I drew the twilight deeper into my lungs and blew it softly around her, spinning it around her like a web, drawing and nocking an arrow as I did.

Erdene shrieked.

"Hello, my lady," I said softly.

Her almond-shaped eyes were stretched wide, showing the whites. "Are you a ghost? Have you come to haunt me?" Her chest rose and fell in a panic. "I swear, I did not know what my father intended!"

"I know." I kept my voice gentle, but I also kept my arrow trained on her. "I am no ghost, my lady. You are encompassed in my magic, nothing more. It will not harm you. Nor will I, if you are truthful. Tell me, where did your father send Bao, and what has befallen him?"

"No ghost?" Her voice trembled.

I shook my head, hoping to coax a measure of trust from her. "Flesh and blood, I promise you."

She wasn't convinced. "How did you escape from the Falconer's men if Bao did not find you? No one escapes."

"The Falconer?" I was puzzled. "Is that what you call the Patriarch?"

Erdene looked blankly at me. "Who is the Patriarch?"

"Pyotr Rostov, the Patriarch of Riva. Your father betrayed me to a pair of Vralian priests in his service..." I could see that the words meant nothing to her. "You didn't know."

She shook her head. "No. He said the Falconer had sent for you."

"Who is this Falconer? Is that where Bao's gone?" I lowered the bow a few inches. "He's in trouble, my lady. Far away, and in trouble. Mayhap injured, mayhap ill, mayhap imprisoned—mayhap all three, or worse. I don't know. If you care for him at all, I beg you to tell me the truth."

After a moment's hesitation, Erdene gave a curt nod. "For Bao's sake, I will help you, even though he does not deserve it. But not here. There is too much to tell. If I don't return soon, someone will come searching for me, and it's not safe for you to be here."

"They will not find us unless I release the twilight," I assured her.

She shook her head again, stubbornly. "I need to see you in daylight, to be certain you are flesh and blood. Tell me where to find you. Tomorrow at dawn, I will ride out to hunt alone."

It was my turn to hesitate.

"It's not a trick." Erdene read my thoughts and gave a grim little smile. "I swear by the sky itself, I will not lead anyone to you. And I have your things," she added. "I can bring them to you."

"My things?" I echoed.

The Great Khan's daughter nodded, plucking a dagger from her belt. I raised the bow automatically, but she only showed the blade to me. It had a hilt of white ivory carved in the shape of a dragon's coils. "See? This my father gave to me after it was taken from you. The rest

I had fetched from Batu's *ger* before they knew you were missing. Your bow, your satchel of trinkets."

"Why?" I felt bewildered. "Were they trophies?"

"Trophies?" Erdene gave a forlorn laugh. "No. Oh, perhaps at first. But after Bao left..." She lifted her shoulders in a faint, weary shrug. "In a strange way, they were all I had to remember him by." Reversing the dagger, she held it out to me hilt-first. "Take it. It's yours, as surely as he was. I'll bring the rest tomorrow."

Warily, I eased my drawn bowstring and reached out to take the blade. I had not forgotten that Erdene had held a dagger to my throat and threatened to cut out my tongue during our only previous conversation, nor that she was quick and strong.

But she only smiled sadly and let go of the hilt. "Tomorrow, then?"

I took a deep breath and nodded. "I'll be camped along the river in the southern pastures. And if you've sworn falsely, I *will* kill you."

With that, I unspun the twilight around her, leaving only myself cloaked in it.

Erdene blinked at the return of true darkness and my sudden absence. "Tomorrow," she said to the seemingly empty air, an edge of defiance in her voice. "And you will see! I am no oath-breaker."

I hoped it was true.

FORTY-SEVEN

D awn came, breaking golden over the steppe.

It did not bring a Tatar princess with it.

I waited restlessly, torn between staying and going. I'd slept poorly, anxious that I'd made a bad decision once more, wishing I had pressed Erdene harder to tell me about this mysterious Falconer fellow.

Why, oh why, had I trusted her?

I was an idiot. Oh, I could cloak myself in the twilight when I saw the Khan's hunting-party come searching for me, and like as not I'd get away; but they would know I was there. They would pursue me. And sooner or later, I would have to sleep—and my campsite and I would be vulnerable.

I thought wistfully of home. I'd not had time to learn all the myriad possibilities that the gift of the Maghuin Dhonn Herself possessed, but I remembered that when my mother had taken me to attend the vigil at Clunderry, where we remembered Morwen's folly and Berlik's cruel sacrifice, there had been a celebration in a glade afterward, and the entire glade had been wrapped in the glimmering twilight.

It must have been a ward of some sort, for no one was minding it, no one was concentrating on holding the cloak in place. No, they had been reveling in the aftermath of the grave vigil, drinking *uisghe*, feasting, playing music, and dancing—a rare party for my folk, who seldom gathered in numbers.

I wondered how it was done.

My mother hadn't taught it to me. Mayhap it was a gift she didn't possess, or mayhap she hadn't thought it necessary. I didn't know.

Trying to distract myself as the sun inched higher above the horizon, I breathed through the cycle of the Five Styles and pondered the matter. I drew the twilight deep into my lungs, and flung it out as far as I could, encompassing the whole of my campsite, my neatly laden packs and gear.

Pushing myself, I extended it farther, encompassing my grazing horses, doing their best to find fodder in the abandoned pasture. To be sure, I had grown stronger; but I had to hold it, mindful and conscious. The moment I let my awareness lapse, it faded.

So how did they keep it in place?

Remembering Master Lo's teaching, I forced myself to stop thinking about it, to stop worrying at it. To let my thoughts arise one by one, one thought giving birth to another. Once again, I sat cross-legged and breathed the Five Styles, accepting what thoughts came.

I would figure it out, or I would not.

Erdene would betray me, or she would not.

I would find Bao, or I would not.

A sense of calm settled over me; and strangely, it was Aleksei's voice that nudged at my thoughts. A memory of a passage from the endless scriptures he had read to me merged with an image in my mind, an image of a compass rose etched on a map, the four cardinal points clearly marked.

Aleksei's voice persisted, hesitant and faltering, but persistent nonetheless. *For the life of the flesh is in the blood, and I have given it to you on the altar...*

A compass rose, four cardinal points.

A dragon-hilted dagger, lost and restored.

All these things converged in my thoughts. "Is it that simple?" I said aloud. I opened my eyes, startled and chagrined to realize I'd had them closed for so long. A quick glance assured me that the horizon was still empty. If Erdene had betrayed me, her father's men were not coming yet—although neither was she.

I turned my hands palm upward on my knees, gazing at them. Gazing at the blue veins in my wrists. I breathed the Breath of Earth's Pulse.

Mayhap it *was* that simple.

Well and so, there was one way to find out. Rising, I called in the horses, tethering them close. I paced around my camp in a circle, glancing at the sun and marking the cardinal points of the compass in my mind.

I needed anchors.

Where that thought came from, I could not say; but it arose unbidden in my mind, the image of the compass rose now linked with that of an anchor rising from the deep, dripping with saltwater and seaweed.

Stones in the river called to me.

"All right," I murmured. "All right, then. Stone and sea and sky, and all that they encompass. The life of the flesh is in its blood. Let us see, shall we?"

The horses watched with pricked ears and curious eyes as I shucked my boots and waded into the river, hoisting my skirts. I selected four smooth, fist-sized stones, carrying them in the apron of my skirt as I waded back to shore.

I spared another glance toward the horizon.

Still empty.

Drawing the dragon-hilted dagger that my princess Snow Tiger had given me and Bao's princess Erdene had restored to me, I set the sharp point against the ball of my left thumb and pushed, grimacing at the sting as it pierced my skin. A bead of blood welled and gathered there. I dabbed it on one of the river-stones. Another rose to take its place, another and another, until all the smooth stones were anointed.

I stuck my thumb in my mouth, contemplating them.

Anchors.

The word felt right, the stones felt right. Beneath the mildly curious gazes of my horses, I retraced the steps of my circle, placing one blood-smeared stone at each of the four cardinal points of the compass.

I retreated to the center, and summoned the twilight.

The anchor-stones flared to life, setting and holding the cloak of the twilight within their compass. Even when I released my conscious hold on it, it remained in place.

"Ha!" I felt a fierce grin split my face. "I am learning, Great One," I said, bowing toward the west where the Maghuin Dhonn Herself resided. "I am Your child. Always and always, I am trying to do Your will, no matter how hard I find it. And always and always, I am grateful for Your gifts. I will try..."

I heard hoofbeats.

Glancing toward the east, I saw a rider approaching, a lone rider, small and sturdy in the saddle.

Erdene.

Late though she was, she hadn't lied. She had come alone. I saw the familiar shape of the yew-wood bow my uncle Mabon had made for me slung over her shoulder, the battered canvas satchel I had carried for so long tied to her saddle. I watched her slow her mount, gazing about nervously as she neared my campsite.

I blew out my breath, deliberately banishing the twilight and extinguishing the anchor-points.

A sharp gasp escaped her. "Moirin!"

"Aye, my lady."

"I'm late," Erdene said simply, dismounting in the bright sunlight. "I'm sorry. And you're... real."

"So I am," I agreed. "And you are no oath-breaker. I apologize for doubting you."

She handed over my bow and quiver, and set about untying the satchel. "I cannot say I blame you."

I ran my fingers over the well-worn wood of my bow, reveling in the smooth feel of it. "Tell me about this Falconer."

"His kingdom lies in the Abode of the Gods." Erdene tugged the satchel free and hauled it over to sit cross-legged opposite me.

I took the satchel and gave her an inquiring look. "Oh?"

"It's the name of a mountain range to the south," she said. "A very, very large and deadly mountain range."

"I see." I untied the mouth of the satchel and began removing and examining its contents.

"Everything is there." Erdene's tone was stiff. "I didn't steal anything."

"I didn't think you did," I said mildly, smoothing the square of silk embroidered with bamboo that Bao's half-sister had sewn. "I am taking stock and reuniting with old friends, that's all. Tell me more. Why is he called the Falconer?"

Erdene watched me lay the other items on the cloth square. "His stronghold is high in the mountains, inaccessible to anyone who does not know the secret path. Many have tried seeking it, and all have died. Only the Falconer, the Spider Queen, and their stable of assassins know the path."

I raised my brows. "Spider Queen? Assassins?"

She nodded, her round face grave. "The Spider Queen is his wife. Together they train the finest assassins in the world. His falcons, you see."

"I see." I felt a little ill. "And who do they kill?"

"For a price, anyone." Erdene watched me peer into a small purse, counting coins. "*That's* the most valuable thing you own, you know." She pointed to the Imperial jade seal medallion I'd laid on the embroidered square. "You could trade it for almost anything to someone seeking guaranteed safe passage across Ch'in."

"I'd rather not," I said.

She shrugged. "Think on it. There is but one passage south through the Abode of the Gods—the Path of Heaven's Spear. And you do not have coin enough to purchase the services of a caravan."

I set down the purse and examined my mother's signet ring with a pang, reminded once more how far from home I was. "I'll manage."

"No, you won't." Erdene shook her head. "You have your magic, and it is clear you have skill at living in the wild. It is not enough. Believe me when I tell you you will die in the mountains without guides."

"All right. Tell me more," I said. "Why would this Falconer have sent for me? And why is his wife called the Spider Queen?"

"He demands things that catch his fancy," she said. "Sometimes famous jewels for his queen." Her mouth twisted. "Sometimes legendary beauties for himself. If they are not given to him, he sends his assassins—and his assassins never fail. They are all fiercely loyal, for the Spider Queen has some magic that keeps them in her thrall."

"Like a spider in its web," I murmured. Erdene nodded. Now I felt more than a little ill. "Do you think that's what happened to Bao?"

"I don't know." She looked sick, too. "When he left...when he set out after you, I was certain he would catch up to the Falconer's men long before they reached his stronghold, and that he would find a way to free you. He's very clever and very stubborn, you know."

"I know." My throat felt tight. "But I was on my way to Vralia instead, and there were no men for him to catch up to, so he must have gone all the way to the Falconer's stronghold..."

"And the Spider Queen's lair," Erdene finished my thought.

We gazed at one another in silence.

"Do you really mean to go after him?" she asked at length, looking and sounding terribly young.

"Aye, I do."

Erdene took a deep breath. "There is someone who may be able to help you. The Lady of Rats."

"Rats," I repeated.

She gave me a wry smile. "I'm sorry, I cannot remember their names properly. They are all foreign, and until you vanished, these were but tales told on a long winter's night, brought by northern Bhodistani traders and repeated to pass the hours. But she is real. She is a widowed queen whose husband was killed by the Falconer's assassins when he refused to surrender her. Her kingdom is in a valley below the Falconer's, and she is his enemy."

"Why rats?"

"It is said they follow her."

I ran a hand through my hair. "Falcons, spiders, rats... my lady, how much truth do you reckon there is to these tales?"

"I don't know," Erdene said steadily. "I have heard tales of a jade-eyed witch who freed the Emperor of Ch'in's daughter from a dragon's curse, brought a dead man back to life, and dazzled a thousand others into losing their memories. How much truth do you reckon there is to that tale?"

"Some." I smiled ruefully. "The memories were offered freely. The curse wasn't the dragon's doing, and it was Master Lo Feng who restored life to the dead man."

She swallowed. "Bao truly died?"

I nodded. "Bao truly died."

Her face was vulnerable. "I didn't know."

"He should have told you," I said quietly. "And I will say again, I apologize to you. I didn't know about you, either."

"No, I know." Erdene sniffled. "Stupid boy!"

I laughed.

Through her tears, she summoned a faint smile. "You must love him very much. I thought I did, but I would never undertake such a quest."

"Oh..." I glanced toward the south where Bao's distant *diadh-anam* guttered, still and always calling to mine. "You might if your bedamned destiny insisted on it." Rummaging in my satchel, I found the last item I was missing—the crystal vial of Jehanne's perfume, her parting gift to me. Tilting it, I could see that a bit of liquid remained. The cut facets caught the bright sunlight, refracting it into tiny rainbows. My heart ached anew at the loss of her. "And where last I called home, nothing but grief awaits me."

"It's pretty, that bottle," Erdene offered in a soft tone. "And the scent smells so very, very nice."

"Yes, it does." I put it away, back in the satchel. "Thank you, my lady. You didn't have to do this. I am grateful."

"I didn't do it for you."

"I know." I busied myself repacking everything. "But I am grateful nonetheless. Is there more you can tell me about this menagerie of enemies and allies I face?"

Erdene shook her head. "Nothing useful."

"I should be going, then."

"How do you plan to cross the desert?" she asked.

I blinked at her. "Desert?"

"Yes, Moirin." She gave me an impatient look. "Beneath the shadow of the Abode of the Gods, no rain falls. It is all desert. Do you know the route to the caravanserai?"

"No," I admitted.

She sighed, scraping a patch of overgrazed earth clear. "I will draw you a map. Fix it in your mind, and do not wander into the desert alone, or you will die before you reach the mountains."

We knelt and leaned our heads together over the map Erdene sketched in the dirt. She laid out the route clearly, describing and indicating landmarks, and I did my best to fix it in my memory.

"You describe it well," I said when she had finished.

Erdene straightened and rested her hands on her thighs. "I studied the map with Bao before he left."

"You aided him?" It surprised me.

"Yes." She looked away. "I was angry at him, but what my father did was wrong. And I suppose..." She gave a little shrug. "You belong together, you and Bao. No matter how much it hurts to admit it, it is true. For whatever purpose, the gods have joined you. When you came, I saw a fierce passion in him I had never seen before. He loves you, not me." A wry smile curved her lips. "As you see, I am no thief, to keep what does not truly belong to me. I would rather know Bao was happy with you than miserable with me." She looked back at me. "I did not know my father had sent you to Vralia, I swear it."

"I know," I said.

"Was it terrible there?"

"Yes." I couldn't read her expression. "Terrible in its own way. I was lucky to escape alive. If it would please you to know that I suffered, I did." I glanced at the map. "Although I suspect there is more suffering in store for me."

"It doesn't please me." Bowing her head, Erdene fidgeted with the sash wrapped around her long coat. "Once upon a time I thought it would, but it doesn't. What you said to me before about not being ashamed of love and desire...Before all this happened, before my father betrayed you...it helped. And it helped to know you had once loved a man who did not love you in return, too. It made me feel less of a fool."

"I'm glad," I said. "And I do not think you are a fool at all, my lady."

Lifting her head, she smiled a crooked smile. "Even though I still love him?"

"Especially so," I said firmly. Getting to my feet, I extended my hand to her. "It takes courage to love."

Erdene took my hand and rose. Her gaze was clear and earnest. "I don't want Bao to die, Moirin. You'll do your best to find him?"

"I will," I promised.

Surprising me again, she gave me a hard, fierce hug. I returned the embrace, wrapping my arms around her small, stalwart figure. Short as she was, the top of her head barely came to my chin.

And I understood why she had kept my things as a reminder of Bao. We shared a connection to him. This was as close as I would get to my stubborn peasant-boy for a long, long time.

And I had a long, long way to go.

With a sigh, I released her. "Unless you have more wisdom to impart, I should be going."

She shook her head. "No, no more."

I bent and kissed her cheek. "Thank you."

"May all your gods be with you, Moirin," Erdene said soberly. "I fear you will need them."

So did I.

FORTY-EIGHT

For once, my impulsiveness had not led me astray. Without Erdene's directions, it was very possible I would have wandered into the desert, underestimating its rigors, and found myself trapped there. Wary of the Great Khan's enmity, I'd become accustomed to avoiding people. I felt safer alone, especially since I had discovered the secret of fixing anchor-stones to conceal my campsite beneath the twilight while I slept.

But when at last I reached the far verges of the southern steppe, my first glimpse of the stony, barren expanse of the empty desert that lay beyond the grasslands convinced me that Erdene was right.

I turned eastward, riding along the edge of the barren desert, following my memory of the map that Bao's abandoned Tatar bride had sketched in the dirt.

Erdene had guided me well; I had been right to trust her.

So it was that many days after our encounter, I found myself amidst a sprawling caravanserai on the outskirts of the desert, where traders from Ch'in, the Tatar territory, Bhodistan, and even Khebbel-im-Akkad bartered and traded, arranging for passage in a babble of competing tongues.

As used as I'd become to solitude, it intimidated me; and too, there was the lingering fear that someone loyal to the Khan would recognize and betray me. There weren't many women among the caravans, and my green eyes and half-D'Angeline features marked me. I thought of summoning the twilight to hide me while I took the measure of the place, but it was difficult to navigate through dense crowds unseen. And, too, it would only be delaying the inevitable. So I made camp some distance from the vast city of tents and *gers*, and entered it warily on horseback.

People, so many people! And there were milling horses, and tall camels with two humps on their backs, an animal I'd only ever seen before in a royal menagerie. Scents from scores of cook fires filled the air, and there was a steady stream of folk watering animals and filling skins and barrels at the river that seeped sluggishly into the barren desert.

I had to own, it was all a bit overwhelming; and now that I'd seen the desert, the task ahead of me seemed more daunting than ever. There was a part of me that yearned to turn tail and flee.

It *was* possible. I wasn't far from the Ch'in border. I still had the Imperial seal in my possession. I could travel east to the nearest gate in the Great Wall and present it, and all my difficulties would be over. To be sure, the Divine Emperor was a pragmatic fellow who thought of his country first. Having survived a civil war that could have torn his empire apart, I knew he would not risk sparking a fresh conflict by launching a quest into Tatar territory and beyond to retrieve one errant peasant-boy—but he *would* see me safely home.

That much at least, he owed me.

All I had to do was abandon Bao.

The Imperial army would grant me an escort to Shuntian. It would be a great pleasure to see Snow Tiger again. She was more than a friend, and she would understand the profound sense of loss I would feel better than anyone else in the world. And I had no doubt that for my services rendered to the Celestial Empire, her father, Emperor Zhu, would commission a greatship to take me home, carrying me thousands and thousands of leagues across the sea.

And, yes, Jehanne was gone; but at least in Terre d'Ange I would be reunited with my lovely, gracious father.

And across the Straits, in Alba, my mother. My private, taciturn, much-beloved mother, who had sent her only child off to an unknown destiny. If I died in the desert or the mountains, she would never know what had become of me.

If I gave up, I would see her again. See her face alight with joy, hear the lilt in her voice as she called me by the old, familiar endearment in my birth-tongue, a tongue I'd not heard spoken since I left.

I've missed you so much, Moirin mine.

Just the thought of it brought tears to my eyes—and yet my *diadh-anam* flared in violent alarm.

Far, far to the south, its missing half flickered feebly.

I couldn't give up. As appealing I might find the notion in a moment of weakness, I couldn't. I couldn't turn away from the call of my *diadh-anam*. I couldn't leave Bao to suffer and die at the hands of this bedamned Falconer fellow and his Spider Queen.

So I gave myself a moment to wallow in self-pity; then I wiped my eyes and summoned my resolve.

Emerging from my reverie, I realized there was a Tatar boy some twelve years old staring at me with disturbing intensity, his dark eyes scrutinizing every detail of my person. When I returned his gaze, he turned around and raced away, dashing through the corridors of tents.

That didn't bode well.

My thoughts were a jumbled mess. I glanced around, spotting the nearest encampment of Ch'in traders, wondering if it would be wiser to flee, or to ask them to grant me sanctuary based on the Imperial medallion. Technically, I was still in Tatar territory, but this was land that had been often disputed and currently existed in a state of uneasy truce for the purposes of trade.

If I fled...

I could summon the twilight and conceal my camp, but for how long? And how would I ever cross the desert if I did?

Torn between bad options, I hesitated too long. Quicker than I thought possible, the boy returned, tugging a much older Tatar man by the hand. Sighing inwardly, I unslung my bow and nocked an arrow. "If you mean to betray me to the Great Khan, I am warning you, I will go fighting!" I said in a fierce voice.

Both the boy and the old man raised their empty hands in a peaceable gesture, shaking their heads hard. The old man clicked his tongue and made the "Ha, ha," sound the Tatars used to soothe animals.

"No, no, no!" the boy said. "You don't understand!"

I lowered the bow a fraction. "What do you want?"

The old man peered at me, his eyes rheumy. "I do not see colors so well anymore, but my grandson says you have green eyes, as green as grass, and a blue-green jade bangle around your wrist. Some months ago, we escorted a rather desperate young man across the desert. He was looking for a young woman of your description."

My heart gave a leap. "Oh?"

They nodded. "He described her to every trader we passed," the boy said. "No one had seen her. But it sounded just like you. Was it? Are *you* looking for *him*?"

"Why do you want to know?" I asked.

The elderly Tatar rubbed his hands together. "He paid very well for a swift passage, the swiftest we could manage. Instead of coin, he paid with a tonic made from a dried root worth more than gold or gems. I was able to sell it at great profit, after I tried it myself to see how potent it was." A gleeful grin split his wrinkled face. "My wife was very surprised!"

I couldn't help but smile a little in response. "I believe it."

"Do you have more?" he asked hopefully.

I shook my head. "No. But I do have coin, and I am seeking passage across the desert, the swifter the better."

"Eh." He looked disappointed.

The boy tugged at his sleeve. "It's for Bao, grandfather!" There was a clear note of hero-worship in his voice. "We have to help her. She's Bao's Moirin! You are, aren't you?" he added, glancing at me.

"Aye," I said ruefully. "I suppose I am."

The old man sucked his teeth. "Eh, come along, then. If you're willing to put your bow away, I'm willing to discuss the price of passage."

I hesitated.

"We're not going to betray you to the Great Khan!" he said in an irritable tone. "My grandson says you wear the blue scarf of kinship, and I am offering you the hospitality of my roof. We're desert folk; we honor the sacred laws."

"Batu's tribe, right?" the boy asked, his eyes gleaming. "I remember!"

"Vachir's tribe," I said softly. "But you're right, I did wear a scarf given to me by Batu's wife. It was taken away from me in Vralia."

"Vralia!"

I nodded. "Bao was misled. The Great Khan sent us in opposite directions. And now I fear Bao is in trouble."

The boy caught his breath. "The Falconer and the Spider Queen?"

"You know of them?" I asked.

"Everyone knows!"

The old man cuffed the boy's head without malice. "Everyone knows tales," he said absentmindedly. "No one knows the truth. Well, child?" He turned his rheumy gaze on me. "Are you willing to trust my word, or do you doubt me?"

I paused a moment longer, then returned the arrow to my quiver and slung my bow over my shoulder. "No, Grandfather. I do not doubt your word."

"Good." He sucked his teeth again in a meditative manner, eyeing me beneath wrinkled lids. "You're *sure* you've none of the dried root to barter with?"

"Very sure," I said.

"Pity," he said with regret. "I should have saved more for myself."

FORTY-NINE

The old man's name was Unegen, which meant fox—and he was indeed an old fox. The boy's name was Dash, which meant good luck.

It was appropriate.

It was a piece of luck that he had spotted me, a piece of luck that he recognized me from Bao's oft-repeated description. A piece of luck that he had developed a boy's hero-worshipping attachment to Bao and begged so strongly on my behalf.

The bargain we concluded wasn't a perfect one. I didn't have enough coin to purchase the sort of exclusive, swift escort Bao had bought with the aphrodisiac tonic of dried Camaeline snowdrop bulbs.

No, I would be travelling across the Tatar desert with a larger, slower caravan under Unegen's supervision, a group of northern mountain-folk called the Tufani who had concluded a successful trade and were returning home laden with Ch'in silks.

Still, it would get me across the desert.

"After that, you're on your own," Unegen warned me. "Just like your young man. You'll need to find someone else to get you across the Path of Heaven's Spear."

"Who did Bao find?" I asked.

Unegen shrugged. "Not my concern."

So be it, I reckoned. I would deal with the next step when I came to it. For now I would cross the desert.

It was *not* a pleasant journey.

To spare the horses, we rode on tall camels, which also carried the bulk of the Tufani's cargo. That part I didn't mind once I grew accustomed to the strange, swaying gait of the camels. They weren't the friendliest creatures I'd ever met, but I had a good rapport with animals, and mine carried me willingly enough.

But I was not a child of the desert, not by any means. I was a child of the woods and forest. So very, very little grew here, it made the grasslands of the steppe seem lush by comparison.

And it was dry, so dry.

During the day, a hot, dry wind blew endlessly, scouring the barren rock and coating everything with dust. If there is one memory that defines that harsh passage for me, it is the memory of dust. Dust in every fold of my clothing, dust in my hair, dust making my eyes gritty, the taste of dust on my tongue, gritting between my teeth.

Washing was seldom an option. There was no water to spare. The river we followed at the outset quickly vanished. From time to time, it would resurface, and when it did, it was cause for rejoicing. We would water our animals and replenish our stores, and wash the ever-present dust from our hands and faces, even though we'd be coated anew within half an hour's time.

Mostly, though, when we came upon water, it was brackish little pools seeping to the surface. Sometimes it was fit for the camels to drink, for they were built to survive in the desert and had hardier systems than most creatures, but neither horses nor humans could stomach it. I tried washing in one once, and once only. The foul, brackish scent that clung to my skin wasn't worth a few dust-free minutes.

It wasn't entirely devoid of life. In places wild onion grew, and a kind of low scrub-grass. There were birds, little plovers that ran on long legs and hunted for insects on the desert floor.

My young companion, Dash, took great pleasure in telling me

about a legendary worm that inhabited the desert, a bright red segmented creature that resembled a cow's intestine. He cheerfully
informed me that it could grow up to five feet in length, and spat acid
that would eat one's skin.

That had me in a state of trepidation for days. Even after Dash
admitted that no one he knew had ever seen one of these fabled insects,
I kept a wary eye out for the sight of anything creeping and scarlet.

As we travelled, I did my best to make use of the time and learn
what I could about the Falconer, the Spider Queen, and the Lady of
Rats.

The Tufani traders were my best source of information, and I
found them a cheerful, friendly folk. During the day, it was too hot
and dusty for conversation—only Dash managed to find the energy
to chatter—but we spoke at night around campfires of dried camel-
dung gathered along the way, gnawing on strips of dried meat and
hard cheese, softening both with judicious sips of water.

"Oh, yes." Dorje, one of the traders who spoke fluent Tatar, nodded when I first inquired. "The Falconer in his eyrie, he is real. Ten
years ago, he stole a great jewel from Tufan."

"What kind of jewel?"

Dorje smiled with sorrow. "The human kind. A young woman
named Laysa who was born to a family of yak-herders. She was very
beautiful, and so gentle that it seemed as though a light shone from
her face. Everyone who saw her said she must be a reincarnation of a
great saint, one of the Enlightened Ones come back to guide us."

"Did you ever see her?" I asked him.

"I saw her," he said quietly. "It was true. She had a grace that one
cannot put into words. Surely, she was meant to accomplish much
on the Path of Dharma. But the Falconer heard of her, and sent his
messengers to fetch her. She refused to go, and her father and brothers
said that they would fight anyone who tried to take her."

One of the other traders, following the conversation, drew a hand
across his throat in a slitting gesture.

I winced. "They were killed?"

Dorje nodded. "One of the Falconer's assassins came the next night, a dark-skinned southern Bhodistani warrior. He fought with a battle-axe in each hand. He killed all the men, and took Laysa away. No one has seen her since."

"He takes real jewels, too," the second trader offered. "Did you hear of the famous Phoenix Stone?"

I shook my head.

"A ruby the size of my fist." He held out a clenched fist to illustrate. "Flawless, with a heart of fire. It belonged to the Maharaja of Chodur, who gave it to his bride on their wedding night. When the Falconer's spider-wife heard of it, she wanted it. He sent his messengers to demand it. The Maharaja laughed, sent them away, and doubled his palace guard. The next morning..." He made another throat-slitting gesture. "The Maharaja and his bride were dead in their beds, and the Phoenix Stone was gone."

"That may only be a traders' tale," Dorje said cautiously. "We do not know if it is true."

The other shrugged. "We do not know it is not. And there are others like it, too many for all to be lies."

I sighed. "Does he have a name, a real name, this Falconer? Where exactly does he live? What about his wife, the Spider Queen?"

"Oh yes, he has a name," Dorje confirmed. "Tarik Khaga, the Raja of Kurugiri. That is the name of his eyrie, his stronghold in the mountains. It is south of Tufan, looming above the Path of Heaven's Spear. His Spider Queen wife..." He shrugged, too. "She is called Jagrati. It is a Bhodistani name. But no one knows where she came from, not for certain."

Hearing the name Jagrati spoken, one of the other Tufani traders ventured a comment in his own tongue. They conferred amongst themselves, and for the thousandth time in my life, I wished humankind didn't have so many bedamned languages.

"Pemba says he heard that the Spider Queen Jagrati was born to the lowest of the low among her people," Dorje said in a hushed whisper. "She is what the Bhodistani call an untouchable."

I was confused. "I don't understand."

He studied me gravely. "You know nothing of Bhodistani society and religion?" I shook my head. "It is all very complicated. Everyone is born into a caste that determines their role in life, based on the life they lived before this one. The priests are the highest. Second are the rulers and warriors, and merchants are third. Fourth come the workers, who toil to serve the higher castes. The lowest of the low, the untouchables, they do not even have a caste. They perform tasks that are unclean."

The word *unclean* stirred an uneasy memory of the Patriarch and his creamy smile within my memories. "Such as?"

"Such as handling corpses and gathering night-soil. Tasks so unclean that even the shadow of an untouchable can pollute one's food, so it must be discarded." Dorje stretched out his hands and regarded them. "That is not the belief of those of us who follow the Path of Dharma and Sakyamuni's teaching. But it is the belief in Bhodistan, where they worship many different gods."

It was enough to make my head spin.

Stone and sea, the folk of the world hold a great many peculiar beliefs! That night, I was glad when Unegen bade us in an irritable voice to cease our yammering, extinguish the coals, and take to our bedrolls.

And in the morning...

More desert.

More dust.

"What about the Lady of Rats?" I asked Dorje on the second night into our journey. "Can you put a name to her?"

"Rats?" he echoed in an inquiring tone.

I nodded. "I was told she is the Falconer's enemy. Tarik Khaga's enemy," I said in clarification. "He sought to acquire her, and her husband refused. He was killed by Khaga's assassins—and yet she remains to defy him."

A heated discussion ensued among the Tufani.

"Yes," Dorje said at length. "There is such a woman, a widow. The

Rani of Bhaktipur, who rules in the valley kingdom below the Falconer's eyrie. The Raja hid her away when the Falconer sent for her. The Falconer's assassins slew him, but they did not succeed in taking his widow." He shuddered a little. "Why, no one knows for sure, except that the men who guard her are also fiercely loyal. And there is a temple there, a very famous temple among the Bhodistani, where rats are worshipped as an aspect of one of their goddesses."

"So it *is* true," I mused. "Rats."

He nodded. "Rats."

It was a long journey. Over the course of weeks, I must have heard a hundred tales of the Falconer and the Spider Queen, of his acquisitive nature, of her unholy wiles. Of the myriad assassins they employed, and the myriad ways in which they dispatched their targets. Dash listened to them with a boy's morbid delight, contributing details he had heard. Unegen shook his head in disapproval, but he held his tongue more often than not.

I tried to sort through it all and cling to what was real.

The Falconer was real; so be it. He had a name, Tarik Khaga. He lived in a place, a real place, called Kurugiri.

The Spider Queen...

Well, at least she had one name. Jagrati. Where she came from and what mysterious thrall she wielded were much in debate.

The fact that she *did* wield a mysterious thrall, wasn't.

FIFTY

Midway through the journey, I saw the mountain range on the horizon.

The Abode of the Gods.

It stretched east and west as far as the eye could see, but at first glance, I didn't think its snow-capped peaks seemed all that imposing. In a few days' journey, I thought, we would reach the base.

I was wrong.

It took us two more weeks of slogging across the barren desert, the mountains remaining tantalizingly distant. By the time we were travelling beneath their shadow, I was well and properly in awe of their scale.

I was also profoundly grateful that I hadn't had sufficient coin to book Unegen's caravan for an exclusive passage across the desert. I'd grown fond of the good-natured Tufani traders, and Dorje had seen fit to take me under his wing. He promised me that I might travel with them through the first series of passes into the trade-city of Rasa in Tufan. There, he assured me, I would be able to find an escort to guide me through the Path of Heaven's Spear, to the distant valley kingdom of Bhaktipur.

The day we reached the base of the Abode of the Gods, we made camp beneath their looming presence. In Alba, the foothills alone would have been reckoned formidable mountains. I gazed beyond the foothills at the narrow crease of the first great pass, ascending sharply into the unknown heights. The late-afternoon sun drenched the eastern half of the pass in golden light, plunging the western half in stark shadow.

"This is where you left Bao?" I asked Dash.

He nodded. "In the morning, he set out alone, and Grandfather and I turned back to cross the desert." He paused. "How is Bao?"

Dash knew I had a sense of Bao's presence. Over the course of the journey, there had been ample time for me to tell my half of our story, which the boy had been eager to hear. I consulted our *diadh-anams*. Mine burned strongly within me, a clean, blazing spark urging me into the dizzying heights.

Bao's was motionless and unchanged.

It was as it had been from the moment Aleksei had unlocked my chains—dull, sullen, and guttering.

"The same," I said soberly.

Young Dash knitted his brows. "That's not good, is it? Moirin... let me come with you. I can help. I'm sure I can."

His grandfather's head jerked up in alarm.

I didn't know whether to laugh or cry. I settled for bowing gravely to Dash in the Ch'in manner, hand clasped over fist. "Thank you, young hero. Your heart is wise and courageous beyond its years. But this task was set before me by the Maghuin Dhonn Herself, and I cannot allow you to risk yourself; nor can I risk depriving Grandfather Unegen of his pride and joy, the light of his heart."

The elderly Tatar grunted, relaxing.

Dash flushed, his cheeks reddening. "But I *want* to help!"

"And so you have," I said gently. "You are my piece of good luck, Dash. You found me when I did not think I wanted to be found, and because of you, I have reached the mountains safely, with good companions to continue the journey. I will carry the hope of that moment forward with me, always."

He looked away. "It's just..."

"I know." I knelt and hugged him. "You will find your own story, young hero. This is only a piece of it."

Dash returned my embrace, his wiry young arms flung tight around my shoulders, his face pressed against my neck. And there beneath the shadow of the Abode of the Gods, I could not help but think that Master Lo was right. All ways led to the Way. From one thing, all things arise.

Son, brother, lover, stranger... it was all part of the same river of life.

My heart ached.

"You will find Bao?" Dash's dark eyes searched mine. "Find him and save him? He told me things and taught me—oh so many things! I know it was only a short time, but he became as a brother to me, an older brother. I always wanted one. Promise me, Moirin! You'll save him, won't you?"

I leaned my brow against his. "I will do my best, little brother. Nothing is certain. I can promise no more."

Unegen coughed.

I kissed Dash on the cheek and stood. "Yes, Grandfather?"

"Eat and sleep," he said with rough gentleness. "No time for stories tonight. You will need all your strength tomorrow, and the next day, and the next. You will not find it easy in the heights where the air is thin."

I inclined my head toward him. "Thank you. I will heed your advice."

The following day, I saddled my mare and loaded my pack-horse for the first time in weeks. The Tufani supervised the transfer of cargo to their own string of pack-horses. After all of us had checked our goods and supplies one last time, there was nothing left to do but say farewell.

Dash gave me one last hug, and so, to my surprise, did his grandfather. I was touched by the gesture, at least until the old fox reached around and gave my buttocks a firm squeeze, startling a squeak from me.

"Heh." Unegen released me with a sly grin. "A man wouldn't need dried root tonic with the likes of you."

I shook my head at him. "You're a bad man, Grandfather."

His grin only widened. "I'm not your grandfather, girl, and that memory will keep me warm at night come winter."

I didn't mind, not really. There had been no malice in it, and if Unegen or any of the others had intended me harm along the way, they would have had ample chance to act on it. And it brought a moment of levity that made the parting easier.

All was in readiness.

On Dorje's word, our company set out to begin the long climb over the foothills. At the top of the first, I paused to look backward. Unegen and Dash led the caravan of camels across the desert plain. Already, they looked small and distant.

"You grew fond of the boy," Dorje observed.

"Aye, I did," I agreed. "It's just that my life seems to be filled with so many partings. It saddens me to think of how many good folk I've met that I'll never see again."

He leaned over in the saddle and laid a hand on my shoulder. "Do not let it sadden you, Moirin. You are blessed to have met so many worthy souls. It should gladden your heart to think on it."

"Oh, I've met my share of unworthy ones, too," I said.

"I do not doubt it." Dorje's expression was grave. "But I think the good ones outnumber the bad, do they not?"

I thought about my experiences among the Tatars, and nodded. Despite the Great Khan's betrayal, I had found a great deal of kindness and generosity among his folk. "Yes." I smiled at him. "And you are surely numbered among the good ones, Dorje. I will be sorry to part from you, too."

He smiled back at me. "Everyone loves a tale of great romance, but it is seldom that one gets to play a part in one. I am happy we can help you on your quest to find your young man." His expression turned grave again. "What will you do if you find he is well and truly under the Spider Queen's thrall? Have you a plan?"

I shook my head. "No."

It was a worry I had pushed to the back of my thoughts. I had to survive the desert and the mountains before figuring out how to free Bao from the clutches of a sinister queen abiding in an impregnable fortress ruled by her equally sinister husband.

The naïve, hopeful side of me wanted to believe that it would be easy, that all I had to do was find Bao, that once I did, the irresistible force of my *diadh-anam* calling to his would bring us together as simply and effortlessly as it had during the Tatar gathering that seemed so very, very long ago.

But since that time, I had been forced to confront my limitations. My *diadh-anam* was a symbol of living proof of the divine grace of the Maghuin Dhonn Herself, of Her love for Her children, of the gifts She had given us.

And yet it was fragile and vulnerable, too.

As I had experienced all too vividly, it could be constrained by foreign magics. Never in my life had I felt more helpless than I had during my captivity in Vralia.

If it was magic that held Bao captive, it must be at least as powerful. More, mayhap. He was a skilled, clever fighter. I had no doubt that in my place, Bao would have found a way to escape his captors long before they crossed the mountains into Vralia, throttling them with his own chains.

But he hadn't found a way to escape this.

By now I thought it unlikely that Bao was injured or ill, as I had first suspected. It had been too long. His condition would have improved or worsened, not remained in the same unchanging state for months.

Well and so, that was a good thing, wasn't it? My new friend Dorje would say so. I made myself believe it, pushing my worries aside once more. When the time came, I would find a way. For now, it was enough to concentrate on the journey.

Our small caravan descended the far side of the first foothill, and began ascending the second. Although I was glad to leave the desert, the terrain was still harsh and barren. Dorje assured me that there would be lakes and pastures along the way, pockets of green, growing life.

I hoped so.

On the first day in the mountains, we crossed three enormous foothills and made camp at the base of the third.

On the morrow, we would enter the first great pass. After tending to my horses, I sat and breathed the Five Styles, watching swift dusk fall over the tall peaks on either side of it, blue shadows turning to darkness.

Bao had set out on this path alone.

I wondered if he had been scared.

I was.

FIFTY-ONE

On the second day, we entered the first pass.

We climbed upward, ascending into the Abode of the Gods.

Upward.

Upward.

Upward.

And although I was riding, and my poor, laboring mare—whom I had named Lady, for lack of a more creative inspiration—was doing all the work, still, my breath came short as the air grew thin.

I felt pressure building behind my eyes, making my head ache fiercely. Betimes, my vision grew dark and spangled.

Stubbornly, I refused to succumb to it. I focused my gaze on Lady's bobbing ears and breathed the Breath of Wind's Sigh, calling it into the space behind my eyes, embracing the height and the thin air.

When I did, the pressure eased. Once again, I was indebted to Master Lo's teaching. The thought made me wistful, but it also served to increase my determination to find Bao and rescue him. It was unacceptable to think that Master Lo Feng had given his life to restore his magpie's in vain.

The Tufani were at ease in the mountains, bright-eyed and cheerful, reveling in the heights. Throughout the long, arduous climb, their spirits rose. All along the caravan, they called back and forth to one another in their own tongue, laughing and jesting.

I envied and admired them, forcing myself to concentrate. The path through the pass was steep and narrow. Sure-footed though she was, from time to time, Lady's hooves slipped and scrabbled on loose rocks. And I had my pack-horse, whom I called Flick, on a lead-line, and must not hurry him, letting him pick his way with equal care.

By the time we reached the path's summit, the sun was beginning to set—or at least, so it seemed in the gorge, stark shadows settling over us.

And then we *did* reach the summit.

"Oh!" I blinked, startled. A shallow descent led to a green, sun-gilded valley. There was a small lake nestled there as though within a cupped palm, its waters a startling turquoise hue. To the east and west of us, immense snow-capped peaks soared skyward with untouchable majesty.

I could not help but think of White Jade Mountain and the dragon. I thought that had been a vast peak, but these dwarfed it. And I understood, truly, why they called this range the Abode of the Gods. Surely nothing less than the gods themselves must dwell in those incredible heights.

Dorje smiled at my awe. "Now you see, Moirin. These are sacred places."

I didn't need to be told; I could feel it prickling against my skin. Even so, I smiled back at him. "I do see. It's very, very beautiful here."

We made camp in the valley beside the lake, turning the grateful horses loose to graze their fill. Once again, I watched dusk settle over the mountains. At this height, it was even more spectacular, vivid gold and ruddy pinks slowly giving way to shifting hues of blue and deep indigo darkening to pitch-black in the crevasses. I didn't think one could ever tire of the sight, and I found myself looking forward to dawn that I might see the entire process in reverse, the shadows retreating up the white-mantled glory of the peaks.

It was cold, though. Once the sun was altogether gone, I realized how much colder it was in the heights. And it was only going to get colder as winter drew nigh.

In my tent, I wrapped myself in my blanket and shivered myself to sleep. I would need warmer clothes and blankets if I was to survive this journey.

Come morning, the matter preyed on my thoughts. I would have to act swiftly in the trade-city of Rasa. If I didn't, I'd get caught out by winter once more, and Dorje had warned me that the Path of Heaven's Spear would be impassable for months.

I thought it very possible that I might die of impatience if I were forced to delay my quest for months.

Dorje was confident that so long as we met no trouble along the way, we would arrive in Rasa in time for me to join one of the last Bhodistani trade caravans going south. What troubled me was the matter of payment.

I'd given well nigh the last of my coin to Unegen, and while I didn't think the old fox had cheated me, it meant that Erdene was right, and the last item of great value I had was the Imperial jade seal.

It was a precious gift, and one that spoke of the great trust that Emperor Zhu had placed in me. I felt profoundly guilty at the notion of bartering it, although I would do it if necessary. At the same time, I was unsure if it would be as valuable as I needed it to be to Bhodistani traders going in the opposite direction from Ch'in. As an added difficulty, I would be facing a considerable language barrier.

As we made our way along the narrow trail, through gorges, along mountainsides, I weighed the matter, breathing the Breath of Wind's Sigh to clear my head of the aching dizziness that came with the thin air.

Toward the end of the day, our path intersected with one of the great rivers that carved its way through the Abode of the Gods. We made camp alongside the river in a broad, shallow gorge, pounding tent-stakes into the loose scree and anchoring them with heavier stones. While there was still light, I fetched my satchel and took stock of my possessions once more, sitting cross-legged before my tent, laying each item out on the square cloth embroidered with bamboo.

A handful of coins, no more than a pittance.

An ivory-hilted dagger.

The Imperial medallion.

Arigh's Tatar bow, superfluous now that I had my own yew-wood bow. The latter, I had no intentions of parting with. At some point, my survival might depend on it.

The last three items were dear to my heart for different reasons, and I would hate to part with any of them—but none of them would save my life.

A crystal bottle with a few drops of perfume.

My mother's signet ring.

Reluctantly, I worked the blue-green jade bangle loose from my wrist and added it to the array.

"Dorje?" I called to him. "Would you be willing to counsel me?"

He came over cheerfully, squatting across from me. "Yes, of course. What is it?"

I pointed. "I've almost no coin left to me. Along with passage to Bhaktipur, I will need warmer clothes and blankets. These are the items I have to trade, but I do not know how to value them."

Dorje clicked his tongue. "You should not trust a trader!"

"I am not trusting just any trader," I said steadily. "I am trusting *you*. Will you not advise me?"

He cast a shrewd eye over my belongings, reached out and touched Arigh's bow. "This you could easily trade for a blanket or clothing. It is the best Tatar workmanship, I can see. Such a bow is always of value and use."

I nodded, grateful.

"This, maybe also." He touched the dragon-hilted dagger. "It is very finely made. But you will not get full value for it. Or for this." He indicated the jade bangle. "It is of peerless quality, but no one values jade as much as the Ch'in."

So such a bangle was enough to provide Bao's sister, Song, with a dowry, but not enough to buy me passage across the Abode of the Gods.

I sighed.

Dorje examined the signet ring, its seal etched with the twinned insignia of House Courcel and the Black Boar of the Cullach Gorrym.

"I suspect this has value in your own country," he said. "But it is not wrought in a pleasing manner to my eye, and is worth no more than its weight in gold."

"Not enough?" I said glumly.

"No." Dorje picked up the crystal bottle, tilting it this way and that. Its facets flashed in the lowering light. I stifled a protest when he drew the tight stopper, sniffing at its contents. The scent of Jehanne's perfume brought a dreamy look to his face. "Does it possess some magical potency?" he asked. "Like the tonic Unegen spoke of?"

"No," I murmured. "It just smells nice."

He replaced the stopper carefully and set the bottle down. "I do not know, Moirin. It is very pretty, but I do not know what it is worth. Not passage through the Path of Heaven's Spear."

That left the Imperial medallion.

Dorje gave me an inquiring look as he plucked up the silk cord on which it was strung, studying the dangling medallion. "Is this what I think it is?"

I nodded.

He blew out his breath in a long, soft sigh. "This! Yes, to the right person, this would be worth a fortune."

"So I have been told." I swallowed. "Dorje, it was given to me in trust by the Emperor of Ch'in. I am reluctant to betray that trust, but I find myself with little choice. Although..." The memory of Unegen reaching around to squeeze my buttocks came to mind unbidden. "That's not true, I suppose," I said slowly. "Naamah lay down with strangers in the gutters of Bhodistan to get coin that Blessed Elua might eat. There is no reason I could not do the same for Bao's sake."

Dorje looked at me in horror. "Moirin, you mustn't!"

"Why not?" I shrugged with a nonchalance I didn't feel. It had seemed a much more romantic notion in tales than it did in the cold, gritty light of reality. I was no goddess whose very nature sanctified any union of her choosing, only a young mortal woman, tired and dirty and far from home. "Surely it would be worth the cost of passage, and I would not need to betray the Emperor's trust."

"No, no, no, no!" He shook his head in violent disapproval. "That is not acceptable." He rocked back on his heels, thinking. "Let me confer with the others."

"All right." I watched him rise with alacrity and trot over the scree to discuss the matter with the other Tufani traders. Two of them nodded in eager agreement; the others appeared to accede with varying degrees of enthusiasm.

Dorje returned beaming, dropping into a careless squat. "As soon as we have been paid for delivering our goods in Rasa, we will buy the Imperial medallion from you."

"You?" I stared at him.

He looked offended. "You said that you trusted me, Moirin! Why not? We would buy it from you in return for negotiating passage to Bhaktipur, and all that you require. Blankets and clothing and coin to spare. And I can promise you, it will not fall into the wrong hands." His voice took on an indignant tone. "I will not let that happen, not ever. We may even use it ourselves. So. Is it a bargain you can accept?"

I laughed with relief. "It is."

"Good." Dorje looked as relieved as I felt. "Shared journeys forge connections. You became as an older sister to the boy Dash, and you have become as a younger sister to me. I could not let you do such a thing."

I felt an obscure need to defend the notion. "It is a sacred calling among my father's people, you know."

Dorje raised his brows. "Are you called to it now?"

I paused, then shook my head. "No," I admitted. "I have been called to serve Naamah in different ways before. Not this way."

He nodded, satisfied. "Then it is decided."

I gave him an impulsive hug. "Thank you, Dorje."

He extricated himself and patted my head in a tentative manner. "You are welcome, Moirin. I hope it will help you to remember that there are more good people than bad in the world."

I did, too.

FIFTY-TWO

D ays later, we arrived at Rasa.
       It had been a harsh, grueling journey and it ended in a city atop a wind-swept plateau, an arid, dizzying place of dun-colored rock and cutting winds, ringed about with snow-capped mountain peaks.

Even so, it was not without beauty.

I had come to love the thin air and the heights, the hardy cedar and poplar that grew beneath the treeline of the mountains, with their stubborn, insistent thoughts. I had come to admire the tough yaks and sheep that found pastures in the valleys where village folk tilled the rocky soil and planted barley.

I had grown fond, very fond, of Dorje and his fellow Tufani traders.

Even so, it was difficult to place my unstinting trust in them. And yet I did, praying silently to the Maghuin Dhonn Herself that it was not misguided.

While they concluded their bargaining, I stayed with Dorje's family—his wife and two bright-eyed daughters, and also his elderly father. The houses in Rasa were two-story affairs, built that animals might shelter below, while humans lived on the second floor. The buildings were white with brightly colored trim, defiantly cheerful against the bleak landscape.

It was a holy place, I learned, and many followers of the Path of Dharma came here on pilgrimages. In Rasa, commerce and sanctity lived cheek by jowl, and it was strange to walk the streets and see shops selling all manner of goods, while colorful prayer flags fluttered overhead and pilgrims completed a circuit around the city, prostrating themselves every few steps.

Dorje's wife, Nyima, was a generous hostess, a sweet woman who was reduced to infectious giggles by my efforts to communicate with her. I let her daughters braid my hair in the Tufani style, weaving beads of coral and turquoise into the strands.

It took a day for Dorje's company to sort out their own business, and another day for him to see about arrangements for my journey.

And as it transpired, my trust wasn't misplaced, but it could only carry me so far. Dorje wasn't pleased with my options, and refused to finalize the arrangements before discussing it with me.

"There is only one caravan travelling to Bhodistan yet," he said unhappily. "And I do not like the look of the caravan-master."

"Has he a bad reputation?" I asked.

Dorje shook his head. "He has the name of an honest trader. But he does not follow the Path of Dharma, and he has hard eyes."

"There are a great many folk in the world who do not follow the Path of Dharma," I said philosophically. "Myself included. It does not make us bad people, Dorje."

He sighed. "I know this, Moirin. Still…why not wait and pass the winter here? You will be my guest. Come spring, I will put together an expedition myself."

My *diadh-anam* flared in a protest so violent, I winced. "I don't dare," I said softly. "As many lessons in patience as fate has taught me, I don't think this is one of them. Why don't you let me meet the fellow and decide for myself?"

With reluctance, Dorje agreed.

I had to own, I didn't exactly like the look of the man myself, either. His name was Manil Datar, and he had the preening, satisfied look of a man who thought very well of himself. To be fair, he was a handsome enough fellow with a quick, flattering smile, but Dorje was right, it was a smile that did not reach his eyes. Also, he had doused himself with a heavy, musky scent I did not care for.

Still, he spoke courteously and seemed professional enough, assuring me through Dorje that it would be his pleasure to see me conducted to Bhaktipur, that he would take personal responsibility for my safety, and vouch for the good character of all his men. And he came to Tufan to trade for glands of a musk-deer that was used in the making of perfume, so I supposed perhaps the scent he wore was an advertisement for his trade. It wasn't his fault I didn't care for it.

And, too, I had touched on the thoughts of his animals, the horses and yaks penned at the inn where Manil Datar's company was lodged, and found them to be glad and contented, well fed and well cared for. As much as anything, that decided me. A man who was good to his animals could not be so bad after all.

"I wish to do this, Dorje," I said firmly to him.

He sighed, and translated my agreement. Manil Datar smiled and placed his palms together in a Bhodistani salute, inclining his head and speaking.

"He says it will be his pleasure to escort such a beautiful young woman through the most beautiful mountains in the world," Dorje said in a glum tone. "And if you are interested, it will also be his pleasure to teach you to speak the Bhodistani tongue. No extra charge," he added. "Only for the pleasure of your company."

I pushed away any misgivings and returned the man's smile. "That's very kind. I would appreciate it."

Dorje translated my words and Manil's reply. "Come the day after tomorrow at sunrise and we will depart."

So it was decided.

I was glad to have it done. With Dorje's assistance, I acquired warmer attire, bartering Arigh's Tatar bow for a long coat and trousers of densely woven wool and a heavy sheepskin blanket.

Already, I felt better; and considerably warmer.

"Look at you, Moirin." Dorje smiled a little and brushed my braided hair with his fingertips. "A green-eyed Tufani girl. Who would ever have thought of such a thing?"

Unexpectedly, I sneezed. The coral and turquoise beads woven into my hair shook and rattled against one another. "Blame your daughters," I said. "And remind me to return all their pretty trinkets before I go."

"No, no!" He shook his head in refusal. "Those were a gift." He touched his chest, where the Imperial jade medallion lay hidden beneath his own woolen coat. "I am their father. I will buy them more beads." He paused, his expression earnest. "There *is* one thing I would ask of you."

"Oh?"

Dorje nodded. "Come to the temple with me," he said. "And ask for Sakyamuni's blessing. I know it is not your path, but I will feel better for it."

"It would be my honor," I said truthfully.

The temple of Sakyamuni the Enlightened One in Rasa was like and unlike temples I had seen in Ch'in. It was a pagoda, but built on a sturdier scale, built to endure against the harsh elements. In the courtyard outside, there were great, gilded bronze urns that rotated on tall spindles. Dorje told me that there were prayers written inside them, that with each turn of the urn, it sent a prayer up to Heaven. I had seen pilgrims carrying smaller versions, spinning them as they prayed.

"Turn them, Moirin. All of them."

I did.

They were surprisingly heavy, although they turned smoothly. One by one, I spun each urn, placing my hands on their etched surfaces and pushing.

"Maghuin Dhonn, forgive me," I murmured. "Naamah, too. But I am alone in a strange place. I will accept the aid of any god willing to offer it."

The urns turned, rattling.

Prayers arose, fluttering.

It felt so very real—the prayers arising, the prayer-flags fluttering here in the Abode of the Gods. I gazed upward into the blue sky, my spirit soaring. Dorje's hands tugged at me.

"Inside," he said. "Come."

Inside the temple, it was smoky and dense, the air thick with incense. I stifled a cough, breathing shallowly. At Dorje's insistence, I put money in a coin-box to purchase a bundle of incense, lighting it and thrusting it into the ornate offering tray before the altar. The altar held an effigy of Sakyamuni, and a smaller effigy of a woman, both with expressions of profound peace on their faces.

"Guanyin?" I asked, indicating the female effigy. In Ch'in, she was known as She Who Hears Our Prayers. Dorje shook his head.

"Tara," said a new voice, high and youthful. I glanced over to see a young monk—a boy, really, scarce older than Dash, his head shaved, his slender figure draped in the crimson and saffron robes of his order.

Dorje bowed to him, and I followed suit. The boy bowed in response, addressing Dorje in his clear voice.

"This is Tashi Rinpoche." Dorje sounded awed and nervous. "He is one of the *tulkus*, Moirin. A great teacher who has been reborn."

"He's just a boy," I whispered.

"Yes." He licked his lips as though they had gone dry. "But he has lived many lives. He says he has a message for you."

"Oh?"

The boy monk smiled and approached me. Despite his youthful features, his wide-set eyes had an extraordinary depth. There was a gentle wisdom in them that reminded me of Master Lo, and too, a purity of faith and trust that reminded me of Aleksei, although they followed very different paths. He spoke at length, never removing his gaze from mine.

"Tashi Rinpoche says you are not wrong," Dorje murmured. "Tara and Guanyin are different names for the same soul, an Enlightened One who has been born many times since, always returning to help others. In her last incarnation, it was his privilege to serve as one of her earliest teachers, before the pupil surpassed the master. He says—" He broke off to question the boy.

I heard the word "Laysa" repeated several times. It tugged at a thread of memory, but I couldn't place it.

"Laysa," the young monk agreed, smiling like the sun.

Dorje licked his lips again. "Tashi Rinpoche says that when you find her incarnation and free her, be sure to tell her that he is here in Rasa waiting for her. He did not mean to be born younger than her this time, but now it all makes sense. She has lost ten years of her life. Although he is still a student himself in this lifetime, he is eager to be reunited with her and resume the studies of their past lifetime."

"Laysa." I repeated the name, bewildered. "But I don't—"

"Remember, Moirin?" Dorje interrupted me. "I told you about her when you first asked about the Falconer."

I remembered. "The yak-herder's daughter, the one who was taken."

"Yes!" He gave me a happy smile. "Tashi Rinpoche says you are the one who must rescue her. Isn't that wonderful?"

It didn't feel it.

It felt like a new burden of expectations settling onto my shoulders, heavy enough that I sank to my knees beneath the weight of it, burying my face in my hands. I hadn't given any thought to the other victims of the bedamned Falconer and his mysterious Spider Queen. All I wanted to do was find my stubborn peasant-boy, free him, and go home, wherever that was. It was more than enough responsibility to carry.

I didn't want any more.

Tashi Rinpoche was patting my arms and shoulders, trying to comfort me, speaking in a voice as clear as a mountain stream. I gazed up at him. He touched my cheeks, wiping away tears with slender fingers, smiling encouragingly at me.

"He says not to be afraid," Dorje said softly. "He says that although you are very young in this world, you have a great heart."

I sighed.

They say the gods use their chosen hard. Apparently, the gods are part of a vast conspiracy to share their chosen, too.

"I will try," I said to the boy-monk. "If I can find a way, I will do it. But I beg you, do not depend on me."

He smiled again, replying without waiting for a translation.

I glanced at Dorje. "What did he say?"

Dorje looked grave. "Tashi Rinpoche says he is depending on you. That before your journey is done, many, many people will depend on you. And that it is still only beginning, Moirin. You have a long way yet to go, and many oceans to cross."

I closed my eyes briefly. "Lucky me."

FIFTY-THREE

I had a day of grace.

One day before I was scheduled to depart with Manil Datar's caravan, one day to spend as I wished.

Contrary to what one might expect, I spent it indoors. As much as I loved the wild places of the world, I'd had a surfeit of them—and there was more to come. I passed the day playing with Dorje and Nyima's daughters, indulging in the kind of revels I'd never known as a young child.

I taught them the Tatar counting word-game I'd learned from my young friend Sarangerel, and they taught me Tufani words in turn.

I let them unbraid and rebraid my hair, winding even more beads into the plaits.

We played at being animals—placid, long-horned yaks, prancing ponies, stalking snow leopards, and even slow-pacing bears.

Nyima watched over us with an indulgent gaze.

Dorje shook his head. "Is this the way great heroines are supposed to behave, Moirin?" he asked me.

"No." I caught his youngest daughter around the waist, settling her on my lap. She nestled against me, content to toy with my braids. "Not in the slightest. But I did not ask for this. And I cannot be otherwise."

"I wish you would stay the winter," he said quietly.

I hugged his daughter, mindful of the insistent call of my *diadh-anam*. "I wish I could, my friend."

Come the following day, dawn came bright and clear. I'd said my good-byes the night before. The girls had wailed, but they would forget me quickly enough. At such an age, children do. Nyima rose sleepily to brew salty yak-butter tea in the predawn light. I drank it down deep, grateful for its warmth.

Dorje escorted me to join the caravan, fussing over me all the while. "You have the purse I gave you?" he asked for the third time.

"Yes, Dorje." I patted the folds of my long coat. "Safely hidden."

"I hope it is enough," he said in a worried tone. As he had promised, in addition to paying the fare Manil Datar had demanded, Dorje had given me coin he deemed sufficient for a lengthy stay in Bhaktipur. "None of us were certain what value to place on the Imperial medallion. I do not want to think we cheated you, Moirin."

"I'm sure you didn't," I said. "And I am just grateful to know it will not be used in a way that betrays the Emperor's trust."

He shook his head vigorously. "No, I will not allow it!"

We found the caravan assembling for departure, an array of men, horses, and heavily laden yaks, breath rising in frosty plumes in the clear dawn air. Manil Datar strode around briskly, making sure all was in readiness. He greeted me with a courteous smile and a Bhodistani salute, which I returned. The porters eyed me with open curiosity, which earned one of them a casual cuff from Datar.

"I do not like the way they look at you, Moirin," Dorje fretted.

I shrugged. "Men do, Dorje. It looks as though Manil Datar runs his caravan with a firm hand."

He ignored me. "Look at *that* fellow!" With a subtle jerk of his chin, he indicated a hulking, broad-shouldered man with terrible scars disfiguring his face. "Surely, he means no good."

The scarred fellow was tending carefully to a yak's pack-harness. "Why?" I asked. "Because the poor man was injured once?"

Dorje sighed, exhaling a frosty cloud. "I am being foolish, I know. If Tashi Rinpoche is not afraid for you, I should not be. But a monk is not a man with daughters. A man with daughters knows what it is to be afraid. And after seeing you playing with mine, I am afraid for you."

"I'm afraid for me, too," I said. "But I still have to go."

"I know." He handed me a soft, cloth-wrapped bundle. "*Tsampa*," he said, referring to a roasted barley-grain mixed with lumps of butter that was a Tufani staple. "Nyima packed it for you in case Manil Datar does not feed you well enough. It is enough to last a few days." He smiled ruefully. "For a trader's wife, she does not understand the distances between places very well."

I tucked it in my pack. "Thank her for me."

"I will."

And then Manil Datar gave a sharp whistle and a gesture, indicating that we were ready to depart. He beckoned to me with a pleasant smile, indicating that I should ride beside him. Before I mounted, I gave Dorje a warm hug. "Thank you, my friend. Whenever I need to remember there are good people in the world, you and your family are among those I will surely recall."

He returned my embrace. "Be safe, Moirin. I hope you find your young man, and if fate wills it, our Laysa, too."

And with that, I was off once more.

Although the journey would grow more arduous in the days to come, the road leading southward out of Rasa was easily wide enough for two to ride abreast. True to his word, Manil Datar set about teaching me to speak Bhodistani, pointing at objects and naming them in his native tongue, making me repeat the words until I got them right. Horse, yak, saddle. Eyes, ears, nose, mouth. Sky, mountain, path. I had learned a bit of Tufani, which he spoke fluently, and it made the process easier.

I was grateful for his kindness, and he seemed pleased to offer it, although truth be told, given my preferences, I would rather have ridden alone, left to my own thoughts. The encounter with the boy monk Tashi Rinpoche had unsettled me.

When I had set out from Shuntian a year ago, my quest had seemed a simple one. All I wanted to do was cross the steppe and find Bao. And although I'd vastly underestimated the rigors of a Tatar winter, in a way, it *had* been that simple.

Now…

Now I felt like a pair of dice, swept up and shaken in a cup, cast on the gaming table over and over, the stakes growing higher each time.

It seemed like it never ended.

The quest I had undertaken in Ch'in to free the princess and the dragon should have been enough for anyone's lifetime. But oh, no! Not for Moirin. The Great Khan had betrayed me, the gods had scooped me up and tossed me back onto the gaming table, sending me to Vralia, where the Patriarch of Riva dreamed of destiny, dreamed of a Yeshuite empire built on bloodshed and loathing.

I had put an end to his dream.

I had armed my sweet boy Aleksei with the courage of his convictions that he might continue the fight against his uncle's vile legacy, raising a voice in favor of love, compassion, and understanding, altering the course of his world.

And yet it wasn't enough.

No, now I must be shaken and rattled and tossed once more, hurled back into the fray, pitted against this legendary Falconer and his bedamned Spider Queen with her unknown charms that held grown men in thrall. And it was not enough that I find the missing half of my soul, no. A boy-monk with kind, gentle, ancient eyes was depending on me to rescue the reincarnation of one of the Enlightened Ones.

And that, he had informed me, was only the beginning of my journey.

I had further oceans to cross.

It was a considerable weight to carry, a considerable weight to place on the shoulders of a young woman who had grown up in a cave in the Alban wilderness. And I felt very, very alone beneath my burden.

It wasn't that I failed to recognize the aid I'd found along the way. I did. And I was grateful to all of them: to kindhearted Batu and

Checheg, to poor Valentina and my sweet Aleksei, to steady Vachir and his wife, Arigh, to stormy Erdene, to my young friend Dash, to gentle Dorje and Nyima.

And yet...

Again and again, the dice were cast. Swept up on the tide of my fate, I left them behind and carried on alone.

"Moirin?"

I realized that Manil Datar had spoken my name several times over, and blinked at him. "Aye?"

"You were far away," he said in Tufani, and then repeated it in Bhodistani, slowly and carefully. "You were far away."

I echoed it back to him, memorizing the words. "Yes. I was far away."

"Where?" Leaning over in the saddle, he stroked my braided locks, setting the coral and turquoise beads to rattling.

Lacking words, I shrugged. "Far."

His fingertips brushed my cheek. "Do not go so far."

I felt a tickle of alarm at the base of my spine. I made myself smile at him. "Not so far, no. I am sorry."

Manil Datar smiled back at me, a smile that did not reach his eyes. "Good."

FIFTY-FOUR

———◆———

I did not like Manil Datar.

It was not that he wasn't a good caravan-master. He was. He was as solicitous of me as he had promised. When we made camp, he ensured that my tent was erected securely, that I had ample food to eat and my mounts were provisioned and watered. He listened to his porters, who knew the terrain better than he did. He insisted that they escort me on foot through the worst passes, through the narrowest defiles, where all of us stretched our ears, listening for the fearful sound of ice cracking, portending an avalanche of snow and rock.

It happened more than once.

The scarred fellow who had disturbed Dorje seemed to have the keenest senses. Twice, he called for a halt moments before an unholy cascade broke loose from the mountains, barring our path.

While the porters dug us out, Manil Datar further instructed me in the Bhodistani tongue.

Snow, ice, avalanche.

Coat, hat, mittens.

Even though I did not like him, I listened and learned, repeating words back to him. In Vralia, the Patriarch had kept me ignorant and unable to communicate. I never wanted to be that helpless again.

Slowly, slowly, we crept our way across the Abode of the Gods. Beneath the ever-present shadow of mountain peaks, we scaled heights where little grew save tough juniper shrubs. I learned to string simple sentences together in Bhodistani. We descended into forested valleys where cedar, blue pine, and larch grew with hardy exuberance, and Manil Datar began teaching me more abstract terms. We traversed narrow paths clinging to the side of a mountain gorge above fierce, rushing rivers. We crossed unexpected meadows, where we sometimes encountered nomads pasturing their yaks.

It was in one of the meadows that Manil Datar revealed his true colors.

Between Dorje's distrust and my own unease, I'd never fully trusted the man—all the more so when I realized that it was largely due to the scarred porter, whose name I had learned was Sanjiv, that the caravan's animals were so content and well tended. But I had passed many days in Manil Datar's company, and although he took the liberty of touching my hand or my cheek from time to time, he offered no further impropriety.

That changed in the meadow.

I was asleep in my tent, swaddled in woolen blankets with the heavy sheepskin atop them. I was awakened by an additional weight pressing on me, a hand clamped hard over my mouth, and a sharp edge against my throat.

A jolt of terror ran through me as I lurched from deep sleep to full wakefulness. Dim lantern light and the musky scent of perfume filled the tent. Manil Datar's face hovered inches above mine.

"Moirin," he whispered. "It is time." I struggled ineffectually, but he had me pinned beneath my blankets. He leaned harder on the knife against my throat. "Be still. I will not hurt you if you are good. Do you understand?"

I blinked in agreement, too terrified to move.

"Good." The knife's pressure eased a fraction. Datar smiled at me as pleasantly as though we were discussing the day's journey. "I wanted to wait until you understood. Some things are worth waiting for. I have heard stories of the bed-arts of D'Angeline women. I want you to show them to me. Do you understand?"

I blinked again.

Manil Datar nodded in approval. "If you are good, you will be mine, and mine only. If you are bad..." He withdrew the knife from my throat, tracing a line along my cheek with the sharp tip. "I will cut your face worse than Sanjiv's, and give you to the men to share. Do you understand?"

"Yes," I whispered, my heart thudding in my chest like a trapped thing.

His unsmiling eyes bored into mine. "You will be good?"

"Yes."

He shifted his weight off me, tugged away the sheepskin, untangled the woolen blankets, pulling me to my knees. With one hand, he opened his long coat and unlaced his thick, lined breeches. Taking my hand, he guided it to his erect phallus. With another smile that did not reach his eyes, he gestured with the dagger and uttered one of the first words he had taught me. "Mouth."

I felt sick.

The point of the dagger prodded a spot beneath my ear. "Mouth, Moirin!"

"Slow," I murmured, stroking the length of his shaft, feeling it throb in my hand. "Slow is best, yes?"

Datar's breath quickened, his lids growing heavy. "All right, yes. Slow."

Sick and horrified, I stroked him, watching his face beneath my lashes. When I cupped his heavy ballocks and began to lower my head, his eyes fluttered shut for an instant.

It was all I needed—a second without his gaze on me. Quicker than thought, faster than I'd ever done in my life, I summoned the twilight and spun it around me, taking a half-step into the spirit world.

Manil Datar uttered an involuntary cry, dropping the dagger.

Exactly what he was feeling, I couldn't say, only that it was unpleasant and unnerving. Bao had said it was like being touched by a ghost. Fury ran hot in my veins, and I tightened my grip on Datar's ballocks with grim satisfaction, feeling them shrivel and attempt to retreat into his body, his erection flagging. With my other hand, I picked up the dagger he had dropped, setting the point beneath his chin.

Datar stared frantically into the empty air before him, his eyes wide and terrified.

"You will not do this to me, Manil Datar," I said to him in a hard voice, willing him to hear. "Not tonight, not ever. Do *you* understand?"

He blinked in assent.

"Good." I shoved the knife a little. I didn't know if it would cut him while I was in the twilight and he wasn't, but whatever he felt, it made him raise his chin higher. I gave his shrinking ballocks a hard squeeze. "Never touch me again, or these..." I didn't know the word, so I squeezed them again. "No more. I make a curse. You will not be a man. Do you understand?"

His throat worked as he tried to swallow. "Yes," he said hoarsely. "Yes."

"Good." I lowered the dagger and released my death-grip on his ballocks. Manil Datar drew a ragged breath. "Now go, and do not trouble me again."

He couldn't scramble out of my tent fast enough, clutching his coat closed with one hand, holding up his unlaced breeches with the other.

Once Datar had gone, I began shaking, and couldn't stop. I clung to my grip on the twilight and wrapped my blankets around myself, wrapped my arms around my knees, and rocked.

My tent stank of his musky, cloying perfume.

I could still feel his phallus throbbing and twitching against my palm, still hear his voice saying, *Mouth, Moirin.*

Ah, gods.

Being a heroine was a very lonely affair.

In the end, I released the twilight and dozed fitfully that night, waking from time to time in a start of terror. Manil Datar did not return, but in the morning I found that the mood in the camp had changed considerably.

No one would meet my eyes.

No one brought me food to break my fast; no one saw to watering my mounts. No one aided me in striking my tent and loading my gear, all the little niceties to which I had grown accustomed, all the things that had made the caravan function with swift efficiency.

I heard one word murmured, over and over: *dakini*.

I did not need Manil Datar to translate it for me.

Witch.

Well, and so. Better that they should fear me than not. The memory of Datar's knife tracing a line along my cheek was vivid in my mind. And at least it did not seem that the caravan meant to abandon me altogether. A trader's bond was only as good as his word, and Manil Datar was not yet willing to break his.

So I dined on the *tsampa* that Nyima had packed for me, kneading roasted barley and butter together in the Tufani manner and popping balls of it into my mouth. I trudged across the meadow with the iron cooking-pot Aleksei had bought in Vralia to fill it from the waterskins the porters' yaks carried that I might water my horses, since I did not have a bucket of my own.

My saddle-horse, Lady, guzzled down a potful at one go, gazing mournfully at me with a dripping muzzle when it was empty.

Her mate Flick, my pack-horse, looked on eagerly.

I sighed. "More, eh?"

"Here," a voice said behind me. I turned to see the scarred porter, Sanjiv, a brimming leather bucket full of water in either hand. He ducked his head, embarrassed. "For your horses, Lady Dakini."

"Thank you," I said.

Sanjiv nodded without looking at me. "They should not suffer."

"No," I agreed. "They should not."

In silent accord, we watched my horses drink their fill. "Horses are good," Sanjiv offered after a time. "Yaks, too."

I nodded. "Yes."

"They like you," he said shyly.

"I like them, too." Curious, I looked at his face full on in the daylight, studying the raking scars that lacerated it, dragging his nose sideways and skewing his upper lip. Despite the disfigurement, his eyes were dark and soft, with long lashes. "Who hurt you, Sanjiv? Who did this to you?"

"No one," he said simply. "It was a snow leopard. He was hungry. I was trying to protect my yaks. It is not his fault he made me ugly."

I smiled. "I do not think you are ugly."

"No?" He met my eyes for the first time, tentative and fearful.

I shook my head. "No."

FIFTY-FIVE

Without Sanjiv's kindness, I would not have survived the journey.

For the first couple of days after Manil Datar's assault, I thought mayhap I could manage. Grueling though it was, I was accustomed to hard work and surviving on my own. Datar didn't appear inclined to deny me the share of provisions to which I was entitled; he simply ceased to ensure that any aid was given to me.

No one offered me food, but after I ran out of *tsampa*, no one attempted to stop me when I filled a plate of rice and lentils from the cooking-pot—only glanced at me sidelong and muttered under their breath. And Sanjiv took it upon himself to help care for my horses, which was a tremendous help.

And then I got sick.

I'd always been blessed with a healthy constitution, but it failed me in the mountains. I was already worn down by prolonged travel, worn down by my never-ending destiny. After Datar's assault, I had trouble sleeping, constantly waking in a start of terror. And, too, the atmosphere of suspicion and hostility in the caravan took its toll on me.

It began with a headache and a scratchiness in the back of my throat. By the second day, it hurt to swallow. My joints ached, and I suspected I was feverish.

By the third day, I was sure of it.

Manil Datar knew it, too. He came upon me struggling to hoist

Lady's saddle in place on the morning of the fourth day. Giving me a tight smile, he addressed me for the first time since he'd fled my tent. "You are sick, Moirin."

I didn't answer. My limbs felt weak, and it took all my concentration to lift the saddle.

"The caravan cannot wait," he said. "If you cannot continue, I will give back part of your money."

"No," I said shortly. If I could not continue, winter would come and I would die in the mountains. Both of us knew it.

Narrowing his eyes, Datar assessed the extent of my weakness. "Maybe I can help…for a price."

I met his gaze. I could not conceal myself in the twilight with him looking at me, but I could still call it. With an effort, I did. Seeing the air around me begin to sparkle with unexpected brightness, he paled and took a step backward. "No," I said again. "No trouble, or I make a curse."

It was a hollow threat, but Manil Datar didn't know it—and what I had done before scared him enough that he left me alone.

Even so, I was in trouble. Every little thing was a tremendous effort, even sitting upright in the saddle. My vision was blurred, and I had to struggle to focus. By the time we made camp that evening alongside a river, I felt as weak as a newborn kitten. My throat was raw and swollen, and it was excruciating to swallow. I couldn't even think about water, let alone food. I managed to get Lady unsaddled and unload Flick's packs, and then I sat helpless before the jumbled mess of my tent, unable to summon the energy to erect it.

Sanjiv came trudging over with his buckets of water. "Why do you not put up your tent, Lady Dakini?"

I closed my eyes briefly. "Tired."

He set down the buckets and squatted before me. "Tired or sick?" As gently as he tended his yaks, he touched my brow and frowned. "Sick, I think."

My pack-horse Flick wandered over to confer, thrusting his head between us. I reached up wearily to scratch the hinge of his jaw, and he snorted into my hair.

It decided the matter for Sanjiv. "I will put up your tent," he said in a firm voice. "I will take care of you, Lady Dakini. You are good to animals and they like you, so I do not think you should suffer."

I gazed at his disfigured face with profound gratitude. "Thank you, Sanjiv."

A good deal of what transpired in the days that followed is vague in my memory, a series of impressions merging into one another, all drenched in a feverish haze. Having appointed himself my guardian, Sanjiv took his role with the utmost seriousness. He struck my tent in the mornings, saddled and packed my horses, helped hoist my aching body into the saddle. In the evenings, he unsaddled and unpacked them, tended and watered them. He set up my tent and spread my blankets. All of this he managed, and his other duties, too.

He brought me food—and for a period of days when I could not bear to swallow at all, snow. I held lumps of it in my mouth, letting it melt and trickle down my throat, soothing the incessant pain.

No one spoke against his actions, not even Manil Datar. Between his skill with animals and his uncanny ability to hear an avalanche before it broke, my scarred friend Sanjiv was a lucky talisman, and the other porters regarded him with superstitious awe.

My fever waxed and waned.

On the bad days, my vision was doubled and I could barely cling to the saddle, sweating in the cold air, shivering violently as my sweat turned to ice on my skin. There were a few days when I thought I might die, and the thought didn't trouble me if it meant I could rest at last.

On the good days, when I felt more lucid and was able to string two thoughts together, I wondered if mayhap I was wrong after all, and Bao *was* suffering from a lingering illness. To be sure, mine was doggedly persistent. But when I consulted my *diadh-anam*, it was bright and unwavering within me, undeterred by my body's profound misery.

Bao's...

Bao's was unchanged, but I was growing closer to it. Closer and closer, his always calling to mine.

It kept me going, day after day.

On the cusp of this tantalizing nearness, the first deadly storm of early winter struck us. Manil Datar was minded to push on throughout the day in an effort to outpace it, but for a mercy, he listened to Sanjiv, and we broke early to make camp in a gorge where an outcropping of rock provided a natural windbreak.

The storm raged for over a full twenty-four hours, winds howling with unrelenting force, the heavens dropping an unholy amount of snow on us. I spent the time huddled in my tent, dozing fitfully. For once, I wasn't fearful of Manil Datar—even he wouldn't attempt to assault me in this tempest—but I was afraid my tent would collapse and suffocate me. And I daresay there was a good chance it would have if Sanjiv hadn't twice waded through the gathering drifts to dig me out, bringing a waterskin filled with hot, buttery tea. How and where he had managed a fire in that gale, I couldn't imagine.

The second time, even with my feverish eyes, I could see he looked weary enough to collapse himself, and he was shivering with effort and cold.

"Stay," I croaked. "Don't go back. Unless you are afraid to take sick?"

"No." Sanjiv shook his head and accepted my offer, crawling into my tent and sealing the flap behind him. "I am born here. I will not get the mountain-sickness."

I shared my blankets and my sheepskin with him. Almost instantly, he fell into a deep, exhausted sleep, his back turned to me. I curled against his back, and for the first time in more days than I could count, I slept soundly.

Somewhere in the small hours of the morning, the storm blew itself out. I awoke to stillness.

Sanjiv was asleep. I gazed at him in the faint, dull light that filtered through the tent's worn seams. Above the raking scars that disfigured his features, dragging them sideways, his long lashes broke like waves below his smooth lids, as lovely and innocent as a boy's. I wondered at a world that produced such a simple, kindhearted soul alongside a Manil Datar, a sweet boy like my Aleksei alongside a Pyotr Rostov.

And yet when Sanjiv awoke, he flinched away from me.

I smiled wryly. "It is well. Do not fear."

"Thank you, Lady Dakini!" he said breathlessly, scrambling to leave my tent and return to his duties.

Outside, the world was transformed, buried beneath a thick blanket of white snow. Overhead, the sky was a remorseless blue, and the sun shone blindingly bright on the white snow, forcing us to squint and shield our eyes.

Despite it all, I felt a little bit better. A full day's rest and a sound night's sleep had done me a world of good. Once the porters floundered through the snow, took stock of the damage, restored our camp to order, and kindled a proper cook fire, I managed to eat a full bowl of rice and lentils, managed to swallow without wincing.

Leaving the gorge was a long, hard slog. The porters and the yaks went first to break a trail, wading through chest-high snow. The rest of us followed in their wake, our mounts struggling in the churned snow.

Bao's *diadh-anam* called to mine.

Close.

So close.

Closer and closer with every step Lady took as she labored her way up the path out of the gorge, close enough that it was like a drumbeat inside me. But I had to be careful; I had to concentrate. I felt better, yes, but I was not well. If I moved my head too quickly, a wave of dizziness came over me.

I breathed the Five Styles, concentrating.

Once we passed the treeline, the path was clearer, windswept. Upward and upward we clambered, scaling the long ascent. I concentrated on Lady's bobbing head, on her pricked-forward ears. When we gained the summit on the second day after the storm, a new vista unfurled before us—and my *diadh-anam* gave a clarion call I could not ignore.

I drew rein, staring.

The Path of Heaven's Spear had led us along the shoulder of a low mountain peak. Now it would lead us downward, down a long,

long descent. In the distance, I could see forests, and more greenery beyond them, a promise of a warmer, gentler clime.

But opposite us, a higher peak towered.

To be sure, I had seen higher; snow-capped peaks wreathed in mist. But those had been the Abode of the Gods, and no one human had dared set foot there, let alone dwell there. This, this was different.

I forced my gaze to focus. Hidden in the high peaks and crags was a man-made structure, towers and crenellations challenging the sky. Humans dwelled there. The steep slope that led to the eyrie was a complex labyrinth of fissures and moraines, unnavigable to the eye at a distance, and doubtless even more confusing at close range. I remembered picking our way through the Stone Forest in Ch'in, and how we would have been hopelessly lost without the dragon's guidance. This looked much, much worse—and infinitely more dangerous.

Nonetheless, my *diadh-anam* blazed in exultation.

"Bao!" I whispered.

"So it's true," a neutral voice remarked. Manil Datar had come alongside me without my realizing it. When I reached for the twilight in unthinking panic, he raised one hand in a peaceable gesture. "Do not curse me. I mean no harm. You are god-touched. I did not know, or I would not have taken you as a passenger."

I was confused. "Why?"

He shrugged. "It is bad business when gods fight." He jerked his chin at the distant peak. "Kurugiri, eh?"

I echoed the word. "Kurugiri."

Manil Datar glanced at me sidelong. "You mean to pit your magic against hers, Lady Dakini?" He made the term a subtle insult. "Against the Spider Queen Jagrati?"

I shrugged, too. "Maybe."

His mouth hardened. "Bad luck for you. You have some tricks, yes. She has powerful magic."

"What do you know of her?" I asked him. I didn't want to be beholden to the man, but all knowledge was worth having.

Datar gestured. "She comes from the south, far south. She has stolen a great treasure there, and come to the one place where no one dares take it from her. With this treasure, she has bewitched the Falconer into marrying her even though it is forbidden, bewitched the men who serve him."

"What is this treasure?"

He lowered his voice. "It is the *kaalahiira* that Lord Shiva made from the ashes of Kamadeva."

"What is *kaalahiira* and *kamadeva*?" I knew Lord Shiva was one of the many gods of Bhodistan, but I didn't know the other words.

Manil Datar gave me a disgusted look. "You do not know the story? How can your gods send someone so ignorant?"

I touched his sleeve. "Please?"

He snorted, but he relented. "Kamadeva is the god of desire. When he disturbed Lord Shiva at his meditation, Lord Shiva burned him to ashes with his third eye. When Lord Shiva heard the grieving of Kamadeva's widow, Rati, and learned that Kamadeva was trying to awaken him to fight against a demon, he squeezed the ashes, so." He made a fist. "To make a *hiiraka*, the gem-stone that shines like ice. Only it was black because of the ashes, so it is called a *kaalahiira*."

"A diamond," I murmured to myself. "A black diamond."

"It makes desire come, very strong desire." Datar pointed toward the peak of Kurugiri. "So. The Falconer rules his nest, but the Spider Queen rules him." He shook his head. "You are beautiful, yes, but no match for the *kaalahiira* of Kamadeva."

To be sure, I didn't feel like it in my current state. "How did Jagrati steal it?"

Manil Datar turned his head and spat. "She was nobody, a no-caste nothing, a collector of night-soil. One night, she profaned the temple where the *kaalahiira* was kept and took it. I do not know how."

Shivering beneath the bright sun, I stared at the stronghold. It was a harsh place, and I couldn't imagine much grew there. "How do they live up there?"

He shrugged. "I do not know. The Falconer demands tribute for the services of his assassins." He pointed again. "You cannot see it from so far, but there is a great pot that hangs on a chain from that plateau. People who wish to hire his falcons to kill someone put messages and tributes in it. So." He gave me a mirthless smile. "Do you wish to go to Kurugiri? I will show you the way. You can send the Falconer a message or try your luck in his maze."

"No." I shivered again. If I were a great heroine from the days of yore like Phèdre nó Delaunay, that was likely exactly what I would do; but I was too scared and miserable to attempt it on my own. "I will go to Bhaktipur to ask the Rani for help."

Datar raised his brows. "In eleven years, she has not found a way to defeat the Falconer and the Spider Queen. I do not see why one sickly *dakini* will change anything."

A coughing fit took me, loose phlegm rattling in my chest. I doubled over in the saddle, swallowing hard against the pain in my throat when the fit ended. "Well," I said in a hoarse voice. "We will see."

"Why?" There was a rare note of genuine curiosity in Manil Datar's voice. "Why do you care?"

I touched my aching chest, where my *diadh-anam* called futilely to Bao's—so near, and yet so far. "Someone I love is there."

"Bad luck for him," Datar said wryly. "Or maybe not. Maybe he is happy there."

I shook my head, setting off another wave of dizziness, steadied myself against the pommel, and sneezed. "No. He's not."

Manil Datar nudged his mount, moving away from me. "Bad luck for both of you," he said over his shoulder. "Come, we are losing time."

Rounding the shoulder of the mountain, we began the long, perilous process of making our descent. By the end of the day, we were back below the treeline and the peak of Kurugiri was behind us. In our camp, I gazed at its silhouette surrounded by a nimbus of gold and crimson, the heights catching the light of the setting sun long after shadows had settled on the long, low slope we travelled.

"I will find a way, Bao," I murmured. "I promise."

FIFTY-SIX

———————

Sanjiv had called my ailment the mountain-sickness, and I'd hoped that as we left the mountains, I'd leave my sickness behind.

Not so.

It had sunk its claws too deep into me to let go that easily. Downward and downward we proceeded, travelling on a steep decline toward the valley that held the tiny kingdom of Bhaktipur. My eardrums strained and popped. Over and over, I swallowed against the pressure, even though it still hurt to swallow.

The pockets of snow dwindled.

The air grew thick and moist, and it seemed my head thickened with it. I could no longer breathe the Five Styles, forced to breathe through my mouth only.

If not for my illness and the persistent yearning of my *diadh-anam*, I would have been glad. We were venturing into inhabited territory, and after the rigors of the mountains, I was pleased to see stone houses with thatched roofs, fields of reddish soil planted with sorghum and millet, farmers working in the fields. For once in my life, I'd had a surfeit of wilderness.

As we worked our way downward, spruces and cedars gave way to more exotic flora, plants and trees I'd only seen growing in the glass pavilion in Terre d'Ange: poinsettias, oleander, towering ferns. There were forests of rhododendrons growing taller than I ever imagined they could. When they were in bloom, it must be a spectacular sight. Even on the verge of winter, the sense of lush greenery was overwhelming after the stark rigors of the mountains. There were unfamiliar gnarled trees with roots that crawled like great serpents above the ground, trees with thoughts as slow and ancient as any I'd encountered save Elua's Oak.

Birds with bright plumage flashed amid the branches, and agile little monkeys with ancient wise-man's faces chattered at us.

After so long in the heights, the kingdom of Bhaktipur seemed like a fairy-tale place, a charming city nestled in a green valley. I gazed around in wonder as we entered the narrow, bustling streets. Here and there, cows wandered untended, seemingly free to roam the city. The architecture was a mix of pagoda-style buildings familiar from Ch'in, and domes, arches, and minarets I guessed was a more traditional Bhodistani style. Folk clad in brightly colored garb made way for our caravan as we pushed through the crowded streets. We arrived at midday, and it was warm enough that I was sweltering in my thick woolen Tufani attire.

In a square, Manil Datar called a halt. "Here, our path divides, Moirin," he said, pointing south toward the far end of the valley where the mountain range rose anew. "We are continuing onward. You..." He gestured around, smiling with grim satisfaction. "You are in Bhaktipur. The debt between us is finished."

And that was that.

Sanjiv accepted my thanks with a shy smile, ducking his head and glancing at me sidelong. "Take care of your horses, Lady Dakini."

"I will," I promised.

No one else acknowledged me. Manil Datar gave the order to continue, and the caravan began filing through the city, bound for the far reaches of the Abode of the Gods.

Except for Sanjiv, I wasn't sorry to see them go; and yet once more I found myself alone and friendless in a strange place, this time with my head aching and fever addling my wits. I fingered the purse of coin that Dorje had given me, hoping it was enough to purchase lodgings as he had promised.

All I had to do was find them. Belatedly, I realized that my limited Bhodistani vocabulary did not include a word for an inn.

Dismounting, I addressed the first person to smile at me, a slender young woman carrying a live chicken under one arm. "Hello," I said politely. "Do you know where is a place and food for money?"

She nodded cheerfully and gave me directions in a dialect that differed slightly from the tongue Manil Datar had taught me. I echoed them back to her haltingly, while she nodded encouragingly.

When I had finished, she touched my face with slim fingers, her expression wondering. "You come from where?"

I pointed westward. "Far, very far. Many seas."

It seemed to impress her. For my part, I was grateful to find the folk in Bhaktipur friendly and helpful, and my first encounter a productive one. I hoped it boded well for my time here. Right now, all I wanted to do was find the inn she had described, stable my mounts, then wash weeks of travel-dirt from my skin, fall into a bed, and sleep for days.

Alas, either the young woman had misunderstood my question, or I'd misunderstood her directions. When I followed the course she had indicated along the narrow, winding streets, I found myself before a building that was unmistakably a temple of some sort—and outside the temple doors, a trio of men assaulting a young girl in rough-spun clothing.

Even as I approached, they dragged her away from the temple, thrusting her roughly against a low wall. She cried out in fear and pain, dropping a rag bundle from which a tattered bunch of dried marigolds spilled, scattering gold and saffron petals. No one else on the street did anything to intervene.

A cold anger rose in me.

I unslung my bow without thinking, nocking an arrow. The swift motion made my head swim, and when I shook it in an effort to clear it, I made it worse. "Let her go!" I called in a tight, fierce voice.

Turning, the men backed away from the girl and raised their

hands. The girl dropped to a squat, tears on her cheeks, and attempted to gather the fallen flowers.

"You do not understand," one of the men said in a sullen tone. "She tried to enter the temple."

There was a ringing in my head like the sound of bells, and I had to concentrate not to see two of him. "So?"

The man gestured aggressively toward the girl, who flinched. "She is nobody! An untouchable!"

I focused on him, training the arrow. "I do not care. Let her go!"

The sound of ringing bells grew louder. Gazing past me, the men's expressions changed. All three of them bowed their heads, pressed their palms together, and touched their fingers to their brows. The girl pressed her forehead to the ground.

"So! What is this trouble that passes here?" asked a new voice, a woman's voice, musical and lilting.

Nudging my mount with my knees, I turned slightly and beheld the Rani of Bhaktipur emerging from a palanquin. I knew at a glance it could not have been anyone else. A coterie of guards surrounded her. She was draped in an intricate garment of bright orange silk embroidered with bands of gold, vivid against her warm amber skin. There was an ornament of gold filigree twined in her black hair, a sparkling jewel hanging on her smooth forehead. Bangles jingled on her wrists, and anklets with tiny bells rang as she stepped forth onto a strip of silk cloth that two of her guards laid on the street so that her bare feet might not be sullied.

Meeting my gaze, she raised her brows in surprise, and smiled with remarkable sweetness—and I fell a little bit in love with her.

It wasn't only that she was beautiful, although she was. Though she was younger than I had expected, having been a widow for eleven years, there was a sense of profound gravity and kindness that radiated from her. She stood poised on the street, her hands clasped before her in an unfamiliar gesture, two middle fingers steepled. It was oddly calming.

"This one, highness," the man who had spoken to me pointed at the girl, squatting with her arms wrapped around her knees, head bowed over the marigolds in her lap. "This nobody sought to enter the temple."

"Is that true, little one?" the Rani asked in her musical voice. "You may speak."

The girl nodded without looking up. "My mother is very sick. I thought..."

She didn't finish the sentence. "You wanted to make an offering for her," the Rani said gently.

The girl nodded again.

I sneezed violently, barely managing to ease my drawn bowstring in time. The Rani's dark, lustrous gaze flicked back to me, another smile curving her full lips. "And what do you say, young goddess?"

"I do not know what the girl did, highness," I said honestly. "But these men were hurting her."

"So." The Rani's graceful hands shifted into a different pose, middle fingers yet steepled, index fingers and thumbs bent to form the shape of a heart. She stood in thought, and all of us waited patiently for her to speak. "You know you must not enter the temple, little one," she said at length to the girl. "Each of us must obey our own *kharma*, and it is as true for me as it is for you. But tell me, what is your mother's name?"

"Varnu," the girl whispered.

"Varnu." The Rani repeated it. "I will see that an offering is made for your mother, Varnu. Is it well?"

"Yes, great highness!" The girl looked up with a dazzling smile, then bowed her head three times, touching it to the ground. "Thank you, thank you, thank you!" Leaping to her feet, she dashed away down the street, scattering dried marigold petals in her wake.

"Highness—" one of the men began in a protesting voice.

She unclasped her hands and raised one, palm outward. It silenced him. "Do I need to remind you of honor? You have a duty to the less fortunate, and it is not to offer violence and harm, no." She shook her head. "Never."

Humbled, he looked down, as did his fellows. "Yes, highness. Please, forgive us."

"Very well." The Rani lowered her hand. "Go, and be grateful that you were prevented from doing harm."

They went, looking for all the world chastened and grateful to be spared the consequences of their own actions. I thought it was a rare gift to be able to move men's hearts with such grace and dignity.

The Rani beckoned to one of her guards and spoke to him in a low tone. I caught the word Varnu, the girl's mother's name. The man bowed and touched his steepled fingers to his brow, then hurried off to do her bidding.

"So, young goddess." She turned her attention back to me, curiosity and a spark of lively humor in her gaze, a smile hovering on her lips. "Who are you, where do you come from, and what in the world are you doing here?"

I smiled back at her. "It is a long story, highness. I am Moirin mac Fainche of the Maghuin Dhonn. And if you are the Rani of Bhaktipur, also known as the Lady of Rats, I am here looking for you."

"The Lady of Rats!" She laughed, a sound like bells chiming. "Yes, I suppose so. And you are looking for me?" Her hands shifted into a contemplative pose I'd seen in effigies of the Enlightened Ones, cupped before her, thumbs folded over one another. As her bright eyes studied me, I fought unsuccessfully to contain another sneeze, and wished that I didn't feel quite so feverish, dirty, and miserable. "Well," the Rani said in a thoughtful tone. "Then I suppose I'd better take you home with me, Moirin mac Fainche, yes?"

"Yes, please!" I agreed fervently.

FIFTY-SEVEN

Never, ever in my life had I been so glad to be ensconced in a man-made structure.

I followed the Rani's palanquin to her palace in a daze, unable to believe my good fortune. For the first time in longer than I could remember, I felt that mayhap the gods were smiling on me after all.

Behind the high walls that warded it, the palace was a charming affair built in the Bhodistani style. Dismounting from her palanquin, the Rani gave orders that my horses were to be stabled and tended, and my belongings brought to a suite of rooms. Then she reached up to touch my brow with cool fingers.

"And for you, I think, a physician." A little furrow formed between her gracefully arched brows. "Even goddesses take sick in mortal form."

I smiled. "No goddess, highness. But if it is not too much to ask, I would like a bath first."

She cocked her head, steepling her fingers in a thoughtful pose. "D'Angeline, yes?"

My eyes widened. Since leaving Vralia, I'd felt myself utterly isolated from my roots. "You know of D'Angelines?"

"Oh, yes!" The Rani laughed her chiming laugh. "Not here, no. But in Galanka, when I was a girl, yes." Her eyes sparkled, and she patted my cheek. "You will have your bath, and I will have my physician. After, you will rest. Later you will tell me your story."

I had my bath, and it was better than medicine. The Bhodistani did not believe in submerging themselves to bathe, but the Rani sent a pair of young attendants who ladled bucket after bucket of hot water over me, sluicing away weeks of accumulated dirt and dried sweat. They washed and scrubbed every inch of me with gentle thoroughness, and undertook the painstaking process of undoing the matted braids Dorje and Nyima's daughters had plaited in my locks, easing the coral and turquoise beads out of my hair, and untangling every knotted strand before combing and washing it. The steam helped clear my head, and a profound sense of lassitude suffused my aching body. I thought about Luba scouring me with lye soap and cold water, chopping off my tangled hair with her shears, and murmured a prayer of gratitude to any gods who were listening.

Afterward, they rubbed warm, scented oil into my skin and gave me clean sleeping attire to wear: a pair of loose-fitting breeches and a long tunic of sheer white linen. When they had finished with me, the Rani came with her physician. She listened gravely as he examined me and prescribed a great deal of rest, and a diet of fresh fruits and grains, yoghurt, and spoonfuls of honey.

I was almost too tired to eat anything by the time he left, my eyelids heavy and drooping. Although I was feeling better than I had at my worst, I'd pushed myself so hard for so long, my mind, body, and spirit were utterly exhausted.

And it was such a vast and unspeakable relief to be taken care of, I could have wept.

"Eat, young goddess," the Rani coaxed me. "A little honey if nothing else. Then you may sleep."

I obeyed, and found that the honey coated and soothed my sore throat. "You are very kind, highness."

She smiled in such a way that her cheeks dimpled. "I am very curious." She laid her hand on my brow. "Better, I think. Now sleep and heal, so I may hear your story."

Feeling as though I were falling down a long, dark well, I caught her hand and kissed it. "Thank you, my lady."

"D'Angeline, indeed." There was a note of amusement in her voice. She stroked my cheek. "Sleep, young one. You are safe here."

You are safe here.

The words followed me down into the darkness, followed me into my dreams, a lifeline promising me safe harbor. I dreamed the journey across the Abode of the Gods over and over again, reliving the endless trek, Manil Datar's unsmiling eyes, the feel of his phallus throbbing in my hand as the point of his dagger probed a tender spot below my ear, the enduring suspicion and hostility of the caravan. I dreamed of rockslides and avalanches, paths crumbling beneath my mount's hooves, of buffeting winds and unrelenting snowfall. Mountain peaks rising above the mist, the treacherous labyrinth that meandered down the slopes of Kurugiri.

Bao, trapped there.

The Spider Queen, Jagrati. In my dreams, she had a narrow face with elongated jaws, long, segmented limbs made of a chitinous substance, and her faceted eyes gleamed like black diamonds.

Her husband, the Falconer Tarik Khaga, watched in approval, his eyes set narrowly over a beaked nose.

I whimpered in my sleep.

You are safe here.

I saw the Rani in my dreams, placing herself between me and the Spider Queen and the Falconer, her face calm and her hands raised in a warding gesture.

I awoke, knew myself safe, and slept anew.

All in all, I slept for the better part of two days. I was sicker than I had realized, and my body needed to sweat out the last of the sickness. I was vaguely aware that the Rani's attendants cared for me solicitously, sponging my fevered skin with cool water, changing my bed-linens, and dressing me in clean clothing.

On the third day, I awoke clear-headed and ravenous. Essaying an experimental cough, I found that my lungs were clear. Swallowing, I found that it did not hurt, but only made my empty stomach grumble.

I was better.

"Ah, good!" Rousing herself from a pile of cushions, the Rani of Bhaktipur clapped her hands together with girlish pleasure, her dark eyes sleepy. "You are hungry, yes?"

"Yes," I admitted, touched by her presence. "You watched over me, highness? All this time?"

"Not *all* this time," she said. "Only some of it. I think your dreams were troubled, were they not?" She made a gesture with her hands I could not interpret. "Now you will rise and dress, and we shall have a feast, eh? And you will tell me your story, Moirin mac Fainche."

She left, and the young attendants returned to help me bathe anew and dress myself. I was glad of their assistance, for Bhodistani daytime attire was unexpectedly difficult. There was an undershirt and skirt of fine linen, and that I understood well enough, but the overgarment was an endless swathe of shimmering mustard-yellow and green silk that bewildered me. Giggling, the girls demonstrated the complicated process of wrapping, pleating, and draping the cloth, pinning it in place so that it hung gracefully.

When they were done, I felt more myself than I had since I'd left Shuntian. As a girl growing up in Alba, I'd had no use for finery, but that had changed in Terre d'Ange. I'd come to value opulence, and it was a pleasure to feel luxurious fabrics against my skin.

And, too, I was happy to see the Rani smile in appreciation when I was escorted into the dining room to join her.

"Ah, see!" she said lightly. "I have made you beautiful after the manner of my people. It suits you. I always wanted a daughter to dress."

I raised my brows at her. "I do not think you are old enough to be my mother, highness."

"No?"

I shook my head. "No."

The Rani laughed, rising to the sound of bells tinkling around her ankles. "Well, then, we shall let Ravindra decide if he wishes for a sister, for I see him beyond the door." She beckoned. "Come, my son, join us."

A slender boy some ten years of age entered the room, clad in breeches and a long tunic of maroon trimmed with blue and gold. I hadn't known there was a son, but I could see his mother's gravity in him, unleavened by her gentle mirth. He stooped and laid his hands on the tops of her bare feet in greeting, which I later learned was a sign of respect the Bhodistani showed to their elders—although sons did not always honor their mothers thusly.

When he straightened, I pressed my palms together and bowed to him. "Well met, young highness."

"Oh!" Ravindra gave me a long, startled look, then glanced at his mother. "Yes, I see."

"Not a sister then, eh?" she said to me, her eyes dancing. "Come, come, sit. We have many hours to eat and talk."

Dish after dish was brought to the table, and it was all I could do to pace myself and eat with decorum, famished as I was. There were the lentils and rice I'd eaten a great deal of in Manil Datar's caravan, only seasoned with exquisite spices and served with cooked greens and many other vegetables. There was a spicy chicken stew, rounds of flatbread, and a wide array of a condiment called *achar*, tangy pickled fruits and vegetables. In keeping with the physician's advice, there was all manner of fresh fruit—oranges and pears, mangos and bananas. After the mountains, it was an incredible bounty.

In between bites, I spun out my story.

For a mercy, I didn't have to lay out the whole complicated length of it. The traders who crossed the Abode of the Gods carrying tales of the Falconer and his Spider Queen, and the Lady of Rats, also carried tales in the opposite direction. At the first mention of Ch'in, the Rani let out a startled sound.

"Oh!" Her eyes went round, her gaze shifting from mine to the bangle on my wrist, and back. "The Emperor's jade-eyed *dakini*!"

"You heard the tale?" I asked.

"Yes." The Rani's expression turned somber, and she regarded me differently, less lightly. "I wish to hear it from you, but that, I think, will wait. What brings you here, looking for me?"

I explained about Bao's death and the Maghuin Dhonn Herself and my divided *diadh-anam*, struggling more than usual to do so in a scarce-familiar tongue. Mother and son listened attentively, hands resting on their knees, thumbs and forefingers touching in identical poses. For a boy of ten, Ravindra was uncommonly grave. I told them how I had set out after Bao and wintered among the Tatars, only to find him wed to the Great Khan's youngest daughter.

For the first time since I had mentioned Ch'in, the Rani's sparkling smile returned. "Bad boy, eh?"

"Yes," I agreed. "And yet..."

Her gaze softened. "You love him."

I nodded, and told the rest of the tale. How the Great Khan had betrayed me to the Vralians, and sent Bao on a quest in the opposite direction, one that had led him into the lair of the Falconer and the Spider Queen. How I had learned of it from the Khan's daughter, whose advice had led me here.

When I finished, mother and son exchanged a glance, both of them looking troubled.

"I wish..." Ravindra said in a plaintive tone.

"I know, little prince." The Rani tilted her head. "It is late. Go, go meet with your tutor. I will speak to Moirin, and we will speak more, later."

"Yes, Mama-ji." He went obediently.

A sense of foreboding brushed over me, light as a feather, and just as subtly barbed. I had found sanctuary in this place, but nothing else. "You cannot help, can you, highness?" I murmured.

"Amrita," she said softly. "You may call me by my name, please." There was a world of sorrow in her dark, lustrous eyes. "I am sorry, Moirin. I would like to help you very much indeed, you and your bad boy, this Bao of whom you speak. It is only..." She spread her hands, and there was nothing in the gesture but helplessness. "I do not know how. Tarik Khaga had my husband slain. Believe me, if I could have rid the world of the Falconer and his unholy bride, I would have done so by now."

It was exactly as Manil Datar had said.

I frowned, thinking. "I've seen the paths up the mountain to Kurugiri. It is a maze, yes, but there are only so many ways. Why not...?" I didn't know the word for blockade. "Put men there so no one can come or go? Would they not starve, and...?" I didn't know the word for surrender, either. "Do as you say?"

The Rani Amrita shook her head gently, the filigreed gem on her brow swaying. "You cannot see it from below, but there is a valley in Kurugiri. Not so green and good as Bhaktipur, no. It is higher, much higher. But enough grows there that they would not starve, and they raise yaks."

"So they do as they wish?" I asked, frustrated. "Take what they wish? *Who* they wish?"

"Yes," she said simply. "Here and there, the falcon takes a few lambs. Such is the cost of living. The shepherd dare not abandon his flock to the wolves in order to seek the falcon's lair; and I am the shepherd here. I am sorry, but I have no aid to give you."

"Why did he not take you?" I flushed. "Forgive me, highness. That is not a nice question. But he wanted you. I try to understand, only. He killed your husband. And you are still very beautiful. How did it go?"

Amrita was silent a moment. "There is a hidden room in the palace," she said presently. "A hidden room with a hidden passage. My lord Chakresh Sukhyhim, who was my husband, knew the risks of bringing a young bride to this place. He hid me, and hid me well, choosing to face the assassins himself. Alas, his men were unable to protect him. Afterward..." Her shoulders rose and fell. "I was widowed and with child. That is displeasing to Tarik Khaga, and he no longer wanted me."

"Oh," I said.

We gazed at one another.

"Are you really a *dakini*?" the Rani Amrita inquired.

I smiled. "Close your eyes, my lady."

She obeyed.

I looked at her because it pleased me to do so, because she was beautiful, and I liked beauty. I tried to guess her age. Twenty-seven, maybe twenty-eight. Maybe younger, even. She had wed young, I thought.

I breathed the twilight deep into my lungs, took it deep into myself. I blew it out around her, around us both, as soft as a kiss.

"Open your eyes."

"Oh!" Her eyelashes fluttered alert, her face filled with wonder. "You can do *this*?"

I nodded. "It is a gift of my people, meant for hiding. Here, no one else can see us." I sighed. "If I knew the path, I could go to Kurugiri unseen. I suppose I'll have to try," I added reluctantly. The prospect filled me with dread, but I couldn't see any other way.

The Rani frowned. "It would please me if you would stay for a time, Moirin. Many have sought the path to Kurugiri, and many have died trying. None have found it. You have been very sick; and the gods must have sent you to me for a reason. Wait, and grow stronger. Let us go to the temples and make offerings. Perhaps your purpose here will become clear." She searched my face, her dark eyes touched with silvery luster in the twilight. "Will you do this for me?"

I wanted to, oh so very much.

Bracing myself for the inevitable flare of alarm from my *diadh-anam*, I opened my mouth to refuse with regret.

My *diadh-anam* was silent.

"Yes," I said gratefully. "Yes, my lady. I will stay."

FIFTY-EIGHT

———◆———

It was the first true respite I'd known since Aleksei and I had escaped to Udinsk.

Now, as then, I knew it was only temporary. Kurugiri and its deadly maze were waiting for me; Tarik Khaga and his bedamned Spider Queen were waiting for me; to the best of my knowledge, Bao continued to languish under her spell, ensorceled by the Black Diamond of Kamadeva.

Or not; mayhap Manil Datar was right, and my stubborn peasant-boy was happy in her thrall.

I didn't believe it, but nor did I believe Bao was in imminent danger at this point. So I was more than grateful to accept this respite, and pray that the gods revealed their will.

I offered prayers of my own to the Maghuin Dhonn Herself, and to Blessed Elua and his Companions, and most especially to Naamah.

I went with the Rani Amrita to make offerings to her gods.

There were temples to Sakyamuni the Enlightened One in Bhaktipur, but like most of her folk, my lady Amrita worshipped the gods of Bhodistan, of which there were a bewildering array further complicated by the fact that many of them existed in multiple incarnations. I have to own, I never did get all of them straight in my head.

"It does not matter, Moirin," Amrita said kindly. "Only that you open your heart to them."

I tried.

We went first to the temple of the goddess Durga to whom rats were sacred. She was the patron-goddess of Amrita's husband's family, who were descended from one of her incarnations. Rats had aided the goddess in a battle against a demon that took the form of a buffalo, nipping and harrying its heels as they fought. One of Durga's later incarnations decreed that the spirits of her descendants would not go into the keeping of the god of the dead, but be housed in rats before being reborn.

It was *very* confusing.

I liked the temple, though. It made me glad to see hundreds of rats swarming over the marble floors, bright-eyed, glossy, and well fed, tame and friendly. There were tiny secret passages throughout the walls, so they darted and scurried about, emerging from unexpected nooks and crannies. The rats flocked to Amrita, scuttling around her ankles in a moving carpet of fur. When she stooped to place an offering tray of grain on the floor, a stream of rats poured over her hands as though to caress her, for which I did not blame them in the least.

"So you see, Moirin!" She smiled at me. "The Lady of Rats."

I smiled back at her. "I see."

We made an offering to the goddess herself, who was depicted as a beautiful warrior woman seated on a tiger. I thought of my warrior princess Snow Tiger, and hoped it was a good omen.

Over the course of days, we made offerings at more temples than I could remember: Brahma, Vishnu, and Shiva, who I understood formed a great triad that created the beginning, middle, and end of the world. Krishna the lover, generous Lakshmi, and fierce Kali with her out-thrust tongue and her necklace of skulls; and others I could not recall. There were gods and goddesses dancing, meditating, resting on great serpents. Hanuman, who was a monkey, which quite delighted me. Blue-skinned gods, black-skinned goddesses, many with a multitude of arms. It was all very strange, though beautiful in an unfamiliar way.

There was even one god, Ganesha, who had the head of an elephant on a man's body. When I asked Amrita why in the world it was so, she laughed and said there were different stories, and that it had never occurred to her to wonder which was true.

"Why do you think it odd?" she asked, teasing me. "You liked Hanuman. And you worship a bear!"

"Aye, but not a woman with a bear's head!" I protested.

We journeyed through the streets in Amrita's palanquin, carried by strapping fellows and surrounded by a contingent of devoted guards bearing armloads of flowers and offering goods. Everywhere we went, the folk of Bhaktipur greeted their Rani with joyful bows, and it was clear to me that she was much beloved. One thing troubled me, though.

The untouchables, the no-castes.

I came to recognize them quickly by the way they took care to avoid all contact with others, by the way they moved swiftly out of our path to ensure their shadows should not pollute the Rani's palanquin. As we made our rounds with our abundant offerings, receiving the blessing of temple priests, I found myself thinking about the no-caste girl who had wished to make an offering for her sick mother, clutching her precious armful of tattered marigolds.

On the way back to the palace, I asked Amrita why the girl wasn't allowed to enter the temple.

"Because she is unclean, her presence would profane it," she said in her lilting voice. "Only those born to the four castes are allowed to enter the temples, or to listen to the teaching of the priests and receive their blessing."

It shocked me. "Why?"

"Because that is their *kharma*, Moirin," Amrita said patiently. "All of us must obey our *kharma*. It is the way the world is ordered."

"I was not born to any caste," I observed.

"That is not true." She touched my arm. "You are descended from royalty in your own country. You and I, we are the same caste."

"Mayhap, but..." I struggled to frame my thoughts. "To deny anyone their gods is cruel."

Amrita raised her graceful brows. "Do *your* gods give themselves to everyone? Your bear-goddess and your Elua and Naamah and the others?"

I began to utter an indignant yes, but the word faltered in my mouth. I fell silent, thinking. Among the Maghuin Dhonn, not everyone who passed through the stone doorway was accepted as one of Her own children. Where did those who were rejected turn? What gods took them in, claimed them for their own? Offered them the solace of faith? I didn't know.

Blessed Elua and his Companions turned no one away, not so far as I knew. And yet...I did not recall ever hearing of anyone not of D'Angeline blood worshipping the gods of Terre d'Ange.

The bright lady stirred in my thoughts, reminding me of blessings bestowed; but when I thought on it further, I had to acknowledge that the Emperor of Ch'in's daughter and the nephew of the Patriarch of Riva met my lady Amrita's definition of caste.

It made me unsure.

"No," I said at length. "Maybe not. Yet it seems unfair, this."

"Only to us, young one." Amrita touched my arm again, stroking it gently. "The gods take a longer view, one that spans many lifetimes. The wheel of rebirth turns, and we carry our *kharma* with us, life after life. None of us can escape it. And who are you to argue against accepting your *kharma*?" She gave me a sweet, rueful smile. "It seems to me that your gods have set you a very difficult fate, and you have accepted it, no matter how unfair it is to you."

"Aye, but..."

Her dark eyes were inquiring. "Yes?"

I touched my chest. "We are different, we of the Maghuin Dhonn. She Herself, She gave us a spark to follow. A thing to guide us. Even so, we make mistakes." I shook my head, frustrated. "In Vralia, I saw. Sometimes men with a hunger for power try to shape the gods to fit their ideas. Priests, even. Maybe it happens here, too."

Amrita was quiet for a long while, the palanquin jogging beneath us. "That is a grave thought, Moirin," she said eventually.

"Aye," I agreed. "It is."

She met my gaze, fearless and steady. "I will think on it."

FIFTY-NINE

Offerings.

So many offered, so many made! I did my best to obey my lady Amrita's advice and keep my heart open, waiting for the guidance of the gods—hers or mine.

Other than the constant shadow of foreboding, it was a pleasant time. I liked visiting the temples. Although the issue of the untouchables continued to trouble me, I liked Bhaktipur and its folk.

I continued to be a little bit in love with Amrita; and I grew passing fond of her son, Ravindra, too. He was such a somber, polite young lad, more like a miniature adult than a child. At times it made me smile, but he had the keen wits to match his demeanor, and when he spoke, I took care to listen. It was understood that when Ravindra turned sixteen, his mother would relinquish the throne that had been his father's to him, and the boy took his impending duty seriously, immersing himself in his studies.

It was the custom of mother and son to converse over a game of chess after the evening meal, and it pleased them to have me join them.

It pleased me, too. The Bhodistani chess set they used was a gorgeous thing, with ornate pieces carved of ivory. I especially liked the knights, which were elephants with ruby eyes and tiny riders.

I liked to watch Amrita and Ravindra concentrate, heads bent over the black-and-white marble board. Betimes it made me think of old tales, of how Prince Imriel had disguised himself with magic and

wooed his Princess Sidonie with games of chess when she was under
Carthage's spell and did not know herself. It was a tale with a glad
ending, which made me hopeful.

Betimes it made me think of my lady Jehanne, which was poignant
and bittersweet. If she had lived, she would have been Amrita's age by
now, I thought. It grieved me to think that Jehanne's daughter would
grow up without ever knowing her enchanting, vexing mother.

"Why such a sad look tonight, Moirin?" Amrita inquired the first
time it happened, noticing my melancholy. They had finished their
game, Ravindra had departed for bed, and we were enjoying cups of
tea spiced with cardamom and sweetened with honey. "Are you worried that the gods have not spoken to you yet?"

"No." I shook my head. So long as my *diadh-anam* remained quiet
and Bao's was unchanged, I was not worried—or at least no more
than I had been. "Thinking of the past, only." I had not told her the
whole of my history. "In Terre d'Ange, I served as Queen Jehanne's
companion. When I left, she was with child."

"Ah, very good!" she exclaimed.

I smiled with sorrow. "Yes and no, my lady. I learned in Vralia that
my lady Jehanne died in childbirth. Watching you and Ravindra..."
I shrugged. "It makes me sad. Glad for you, but sad for Jehanne and
her daughter, who will never know her mother."

"Oh!" Compassion flooded her features. "I am sorry, very sorry."
Sipping her tea, Amrita studied me. "I think you loved her very much,
this queen," she said gently. "I know something of D'Angelines and
their customs, and your face is much the same as when you speak of
your young man Bao."

"Aye," I murmured. "I did."

Amrita cocked her head. "Do I remind you of her?"

It startled a soft laugh out of me. "You? No, my lady. Jehanne...
she was not always nice, not always kind." In the City of Elua, they
took wagers on how long Jehanne would go without making a cham-
bermaid cry. I couldn't even imagine the Rani uttering a cruel word,
let alone giving in to the notorious bouts of temper to which Jehanne

had been prone. "I think it may have been different after the babe was born, though," I added. "And it makes me sad that I will never see it."

"There is no secret wisdom that comes with motherhood," Amrita said ruefully. "I never felt more alone and lost than when Ravindra was born."

She had been sixteen, I knew now; they wed young in Bhodistani countries. Sixteen, a young widow, and a new mother, far from her childhood home, forced to assume rule of a tiny kingdom that lay beneath the shadow of Kurugiri.

"It must have been very, very hard," I said.

"Yes." She made an eloquent gesture. "But it was my *kharma*. Elsewhere in Bhodistan, it would have been worse. I would have been expected to follow my husband into death. However, he forbade it."

"I am very glad." I shuddered inwardly at the revelation, and inhaled the fragrant steam rising from my tea. "Did you love him?" I asked softly. "Ravindra's father?"

"My lord Chakresh?" Amrita was silent a moment. "I honored him. He was a good man, gentle and brave. A good husband, and he would have been a good father. In a way, I wish he had not been so brave, insisting on facing Khaga's assassins, for he might have lived if he had not. I miss him. But I do not think I felt what is written on your face when you speak of those you love." She gave me a faint smile. "Perhaps sometimes it is the flaws that make us fall in love, eh? Like your bad boy and your queen."

"Perhaps," I acknowledged. "Although they both had good hearts. Jehanne... I do not think being a mother was some magic that would change her. It was time, that was all. Already, before the child, she was changing, letting herself be kinder and wiser. And Bao..." I thought of the vast streak of impossible romanticism that lay beneath his seemingly careless exterior, and smiled. "Oh, he is not such a bad boy, really."

"I hope not." A troubled expression settled over her lovely face. "Moirin...I do not know what is truth and what is only a tale. But it is said that Kamadeva's diamond cannot compel false desire."

A shudder ran the length of my spine. "Are you saying Bao is a willing victim?"

Amrita tipped her head back and forth, and made an ambiguous gesture with one hand. "No. Willing, no. He crossed the Abode of the Gods in search of you, a journey as difficult as your own. Since he does not come to you, it must be that his will is not his own. But Jagrati could not bind him to her with Kamadeva's diamond if there were not a spark of true desire present."

I glanced unerringly in the direction of Kurugiri, where Bao's *diadh-anam* was a dull, guttering spark. "Is she beautiful, this Jagrati?"

"I have not seen her," Amrita admitted. "But the tales say so. Beautiful and terrible at once, like Kali dancing."

The image of the goddess Kali I had seen surfaced in my memory, her tongue thrust out in a frenzy as she danced, wearing a necklace of human skulls and a girdle of severed arms around her waist.

I shivered.

Bao had died—died, and lived. There was a shimmering darkness that hung over him that had not been there before. Mayhap such a terrible beauty spoke to him.

"Oh, Moirin!" Amrita said with dismay, reaching out to stroke my arm. "I did not mean to frighten you."

"No, I know." I raised her hand to my lips and kissed it. "Better to know, yes? There are many kinds of desire, my lady."

She shook her head at me, but she was smiling again, which pleased me. "You are a little bit of a bad girl, I think."

I smiled back at her. "I am a child of Naamah's line, and desire is my birthright. I do not need a god's ashes to make it so. I hold it sacred. It is my path. I am enough of a D'Angeline that I am not afraid to fight for love. I am not afraid to acknowledge it where I find it, including in your person, highness. And when it comes to Bao, I am not afraid to match desire for desire with the Spider Queen."

Amrita's gaze lingered on mine, caring and worried. "Is that wise, Moirin?"

I shrugged. "I don't know, my lady. I hope so. But so long as the gods remain silent, who can say?"

Ten days later, the gods broke their silence; or at least the mortal agents by which they made their will known surfaced. I found out why my *diadh-anam* had been content to allow me to linger in Bhaktipur.

The Falconer sent for me.

I would have expected high drama, a clever assassin armed to the teeth and filled with dire threats. But no, the messenger was an utterly unprepossessing fellow, not remarkable in any way in the slightest, save his utter lack of fear at being sent to deliver such a message. The assassin, I suppose, came later.

The Rani Amrita granted him an audience, sending for both her son, Ravindra, and me to attend it.

We heard him out.

"It has come to the attention of his majesty Tarik Khaga that the Rani of Bhaktipur gives shelter to a foreign *dakini* of surpassing beauty and power," the fellow droned, rocking back on his heels, his gaze raking over me with unabashed appreciation. "He demands that you send her to him immediately."

The Rani raised her brows. "Or?"

The messenger smiled, his upper lip curling to show his teeth. "I believe your highness knows the price of refusing such a request."

I glanced at Amrita, but she silenced me with a slight shake of her head. "We will take counsel, and give you our reply within a day." She raised her right hand, palm outward, and there was enough quiet strength and power in the gesture that the Falconer's messenger took an involuntary step backward. I had come to learn the meaning of some of these ritual gestures, and this one symbolized her lack of fear, and her protection of me. "Go, and return tomorrow."

The fellow pressed his palms together and bowed. "I will do so, highness." He hesitated, his gaze shifting from me to her to Ravindra. "Do not do anything foolish, highness," he murmured. "The boy has already lost his father."

"Tomorrow," the Rani repeated.

Once he had left, we met to discuss the matter. My heart was beating fast and my chest felt too tight.

Kurugiri.

It was the opportunity I had sought, and yet... I was scared. In the old tales, Phèdre nó Delaunay had entered a terrible kingdom of death and despair to rescue the missing prince, giving herself over to the kingdom's dark ruler. Now that the moment was upon me, I wasn't sure I had the same courage.

"Sit and breathe, Moirin," Amrita said gently. "Calm your thoughts." She pressed the tips of her fingers and thumbs together in a ritual gesture intended to aid in focus and concentration, and Ravindra emulated her, his young face graver than usual. "Come, let us all think."

I took the thinking-pose, too, and forced myself to cycle through the Five Styles of Breathing.

It helped settle my nerves, but it brought no insights. "I have to go with him, my lady," I said. "I cannot let Tarik Khaga send his falcons after you. I will go with him, find the path to Kurugiri, find Bao. It must be what the gods intend."

"Is that what your bear-goddess says to you?" Amrita inquired.

Frowning, I consulted my *diadh-anam*. It was flickering with eagerness, like coals blown into fresh flame, but it was not flaring with certainty. "I'm not sure."

"Then there must be another way," she said calmly. "And I would very much like to find it."

Ravindra, who was now idly pushing pieces around the chessboard, was silent.

A thought came to me, so simple and logical that I didn't know why it hadn't come to me right away. "No matter what we say, the messenger has to bring our reply back to Kurugiri, does he not? I could call the twilight and follow him."

"They know about your magic, Moirin," Ravindra said without looking up from the chessboard. "He knew you are a *dakini*. It is likely that your Bao has told them everything about you."

I winced.

"I'm sorry." He gave me an apologetic glance. "But I think we must assume this is a trap."

Amrita stroked her son's hair. "Wise boy. I think so, too. And I am not going to let you walk into it, Moirin."

"Well, I am not going to let the Falconer send assassins after you, highness!" I said in frustration. "I could not live with it."

"It is not your choice!" There was a sharp note in her musical voice I had never heard before.

I spread my hands. "Do you intend to lock me away? Unless you do, I *will* go. The gods have sent a sign. What else am I to do?"

"It is a game to them, I think," Ravindra said in a clear, precise voice, one slim finger touching the carved figure of the black king. "The Falconer and his Spider Queen. They sit atop their mountain, controlling the board with their pawns and knights. This was the opening gambit. What we must do is neither accept nor reject it, but offer a gambit of our own."

Now my *diadh-anam* flared—and I knew.

"A trade," I whispered. "Me for Bao."

Ravindra nodded in approval. "That is a very good gambit, Moirin."

"No!" Amrita shook her head. "No, I do not like it, not at all. What if Tarik Khaga accepts it?"

I swallowed. "Well, then...I go to Kurugiri and bide my time until I can escape. Sooner or later, I will find a way. After all, I am a *dakini*."

She looked unhappy. "Yes, and you are also a young woman of whom I have grown fond. You will suffer there."

"Do not worry, Mama-ji," Ravindra said in a soothing tone. "He will not accept the trade." His hovering finger moved from the black king to the black queen. "Jagrati will not let him." He picked up the piece and moved it, setting her in play. "The interesting thing will be seeing their countermove."

I eyed him. "You will make quite a ruler one day, young highness."

He smiled modestly. "Thank you."

SIXTY

The Falconer's messenger returned the following day, and the Rani Amrita delivered our reply to him.

"I can say neither yes nor no to your master," she said to him, her hands folded, middle fingers steepled. It was the ritual gesture I had seen her make the first day we met in the street outside the temple, one I now knew was meant to calm conflict. "As you noted, Moirin mac Fainche is a foreigner, and no subject of mine to compel."

The fellow opened his mouth to protest.

"However!" Amrita raised her right hand in the pose of fearlessness. "She offers a trade. There is a young Ch'in man named Bao in your master's service. He is the beloved of the *dakini* Moirin. If Tarik Khaga frees him, she will go willingly to Kurugiri." She smiled. "A touching sacrifice, do you not think?"

The messenger scowled and stared at his feet. "I do not know if that is an acceptable answer, highness."

She inclined her head. "Nonetheless, it is my reply. Go, and tell him."

He went; and we waited.

I hated waiting, the hard lesson of patience that it seemed I was fated to learn over and over.

And yet . . . I *had* learned it. And I had endured enough to be grateful that if I must be patient and wait, I was very, very fortunate to do so in this very pleasant valley kingdom, the guest of this kind and gracious ruler with her clever, thoughtful son who was wise beyond his years.

Days passed.

No one could say for a surety how long it would take. With Manil Datar's caravan, I'd made the descent from the peak opposite Kurugiri in two days; but the region was deep in winter's grip by now. Amrita assured me that the route to Kurugiri was at a low enough altitude that it would not become impassable for months on end, unlike other places in the Abode of the Gods. Still, it could be blocked for days if there were snow-storms.

And no one knew how long it took to ascend the slope itself, navigating the secret path through the torturous maze.

So we waited.

We traded tales. I told the whole long story of helping to rescue the Emperor's daughter and the dragon, and ending a civil war in Ch'in. My lady Amrita and Ravindra listened to it wide-eyed, both of them clapping excitedly at the good parts.

She told me about growing up in the coastal Bhodistani city of Galanka, where her family enjoyed great prestige. Her noble father had been the liaison to the D'Angeline embassy, which was how she had come to know my own father's folk before she was pledged in marriage to the Raja of a tiny valley kingdom far, far away to the north. Amrita was the eldest daughter in a large, sprawling family, and her voice grew wistful when she spoke of them.

"Will you ever return there, do you think?" I asked her.

"No," she said simply, her gaze settling on Ravindra. "My *kharma* is here."

I nodded, understanding.

Amrita taught me more of the *mudras*, the ritual hand gestures that focused the mind's thoughts and the body's energies, tapping into the vast harmonies of the world. It was not unlike the meditation Master Lo had taught me, and yet I could not begin to achieve Amrita's fluid grace, nor the sense of power that emanated from her slender hands when she took a pose. As clever as he was, not even young Ravindra could come close to matching his mother's grace and power.

Still, I tried.

And in turn, I taught them both the Five Styles of Breathing. It was not an unfamiliar discipline, for there were similar teachings in Bhodistan. Even so, both of them found the rhythms difficult to master.

I found myself missing Bao.

It was foolish, in a way; I missed him all the time, the yearning of my *diadh-anam* as persistent and constant as a sore tooth. But trying to teach Amrita and Ravindra reminded me of how it had all begun.

Bao and I sitting cross-legged, our knees brushing, listening to Master Lo's tutelage aboard the greatship.

We had gone from reluctant companions to comfortable ones, bonded by our long journey together and our mutual respect for Master Lo, then drifted sideways into genuine affection. I missed that familiarity and comfort. I missed his cheerful boasting. I even missed his teasing.

All of which made it that much harder when the Falconer's messenger returned to deliver Tarik Khaga's reply to our gambit.

Once again, the Rani granted him an audience with Ravindra and me in attendance, and once again, we heard him out. It was a brief reply.

"His majesty Tarik Khaga offered to release the young man Bao from his service," the fellow announced. "Bao declined his offer. He refuses to go. There will be no trade." He gave a thin smile. "His majesty's demand stands as issued."

"Very well," the Rani Amrita said in acknowledgment. "Go, and return in a day. You shall have our response."

And once again, we retired to take counsel.

Although I hadn't really expected a happier outcome, still, it was disheartening. Amrita rubbed the back of my neck, consoling me while Ravindra pored over the chessboard. "Bao's will is not his own, Moirin. You know this to be true, for he would have already found a way to you."

"I know. It's just..." I sighed. "If I could just *see* him, talk to him ... surely it would be enough to break the spell."

"That is what we will demand, then," Ravindra said calmly, moving a white pawn. "We will refute the Falconer's claim as a lie, and demand that he send Bao to Bhaktipur so Moirin may hear him refuse his freedom in his own words."

"Do you think he will agree?" I asked dubiously.

"No." Ravindra advanced a black pawn. "I think Tarik Khaga will invite you to Kurugiri to hear Bao's response in person."

"Ah!" Amrita reached down to advance a second white pawn. "And we will propose a meeting of both parties on neutral ground, eh?"

"Where both of us will seek to trick and betray the other," Ravindra agreed. "And that will be *very* interesting!"

"Perhaps, jewel of my heart, but you will not be there to see it," his mother said in a firm tone. "If it even comes to pass. You are trusting a great deal to the belief that Tarik Khaga and his queen will play this game."

"Yes, Mama-ji. I am." He steepled his fingers in the thinking-pose. "But the Falconer's men could not find *you* when they tried, thanks to the hidden room. That failure will be on his mind, and I do not think he is a man who likes to fail. And also remember, since they know of Moirin's magic, it is likely that they know she can make herself unseen, and very impossible to find and abduct on hostile ground. So I think yes, they will play the game and hope to trick us."

Amrita studied the board. "So, young chess-master! You have thought out a strategy two moves ahead of our opponent. Knowing you, I suspect there is at least one more." With one finger, she nudged a third white pawn into play, raising her brows at her son. "What is the third?"

Ravindra smiled. "An ambush. Only we must plan it now, before it is a possibility in their minds."

"My lady, my young lord..." I shook my head. The thought of either of them coming to harm made me feel ill. "This is growing too difficult and too dangerous. I cannot ask you to take such risks. Better I should go to Kurugiri."

"*No!*" mother and son said in unison, exchanging a glance.

"But—" I began.

Amrita sighed. "It is not only for you, dear one, nor for your young man. I said before that the shepherd dare not abandon his flock to hunt the falcon. But what you have given us here…" She made a gesture I didn't know. "It is a chance to lure the falcon into a trap, and I think it is a chance I cannot ignore. Perhaps this is what the gods intended in sending you here." Her face was very serious. "What does your bear-goddess say?"

My *diadh-anam* shone like a beacon, and I could not lie about it. "It seems She agrees," I murmured.

"Tarik Khaga had my father killed, Moirin," Ravindra said in a subdued tone. "And many other people, too. Will you not let us try?"

"Aye," I said reluctantly, fearful at the thought of risking them. "I will."

The following day, the Rani Amrita delivered our response to the Falconer's messenger, her demeanor calm and dignified.

"I fear the *dakini* Moirin mac Fainche does not believe your master's words," she said in a vaguely apologetic tone. "She requests that his majesty Tarik Khaga send the young man Bao to Bhaktipur that he might deliver his refusal in person. Only then will she accept this edict that there may be no trade." Amrita gave a slight, helpless shrug. "Forgive me. As I said before, the *dakini* Moirin is not mine to command."

The messenger pursed his lips and glanced at me.

Summoning my mother's best glare, I folded my arms and glowered at him under my lashes. As an added measure, I called the twilight. Although I could not vanish into it with his gaze on me, I felt it sparkle around me.

The Falconer's messenger turned pale, his throat working as he swallowed nervously. For the first time in four encounters, he was a bit afraid.

I was glad.

He bowed to Amrita, palms pressed together. "I will convey your message and return with a reply, highness."

SIXTY-ONE

———◆———

Waiting, waiting, and more waiting.

Gods, I hated it!

My lady Amrita was not idle. Guided by her preternaturally clever son's counsel, she met with the commander of the Royal Guard, which was the nearest thing to an army that Bhaktipur had. Together, they chose a spot in neutral territory suitable for an ambush, a plateau above the valley of Bhaktipur, but below the peaks of Kurugiri. It had enough open space to inspire trust, but there were copses of spruce trees that would hide a mounted battalion with a bit of creative effort.

A battalion of fifty skilled riders and archers was dispatched, hurrying to make camp and conceal it before the possibility of such an action might arise in our opponents' minds. It was important to remain three steps ahead of them.

We waited.

On the advice of the commander of her guard, we confined ourselves to the palace grounds, and Amrita and her son abandoned their sleeping-quarters to pass their nights in the hidden room her husband had commissioned before he dared to wed a beautiful, young bride.

I had to own, it was a clever design. Young Ravindra must have inherited his head for strategy from his father. The steep, narrow stair that led to the hidden room was concealed behind an elaborately embroidered wall-hanging depicting the goddess Durga on her tiger. Nothing about the architecture of the palace suggested it was there.

The room itself was small, but not unpleasant. It even had a balcony that looked out onto an interior courtyard garden with a fountain at the center, filled with growing plants, and birds and monkeys, too. Amrita invited me to join them, but I refused, feeling I'd already imposed more than enough on their lives.

I tried setting ward-stones around my room as I had learned to do travelling across the Tatar steppe, but the charm didn't work in a man-made dwelling. At least my own balcony was high and inaccessible; and clever Ravindra came up with the idea of stringing bells to the outer door of my own sleeping-chamber, so that if anyone were to succeed in forcing the lock, the clamor would awaken me before they entered, and I might summon the twilight.

In a week's time, the Falconer's messenger returned with the expected reply, delivering it with relish.

"His majesty Tarik Khaga agrees that the *dakini* Moirin is entitled to hear Bao's refusal from his own lips," he said smoothly. "His majesty invites her to accompany me to Kurugiri as his honored guest."

Clearly, the Falconer's messenger reckoned this was a counterstroke of masterful strategy on the part of the forces of Kurugiri. The Rani Amrita furrowed her brow and looked troubled, letting him believe she was at a loss for a response. "As ever, it is the *dakini* Moirin's choice," she said carefully. "Again, we will take counsel. Go, and come back tomorrow."

He bowed, and went.

There was no need to take counsel this time. Our plans were set. Amrita would have liked to use the day to make another round of temple offerings, but her commander of the guard, a handsome fellow named Hasan Dar, was adamant about not venturing beyond the palace walls.

"Tarik Khaga may tire of this game you play with him, highness," he said earnestly to her. "For all we know, he already has, and his assassins lie in wait. There are too many people in the streets, and it is too difficult to protect you. Please, take no risks. Make your offerings at the household altar. The gods will understand."

Reluctantly, Amrita agreed; and we heaped the household altar high with garlands of dried flowers, offerings of food and incense.

A day later, the Falconer's messenger returned, and Amrita delivered our final edict to him, a surprisingly stern note in her musical voice.

"Given your master's history, the *dakini* Moirin does not believe this offer is made in good faith," she said. "And I agree with her. So! We refuse."

"Then—" the messenger began.

Once again, my lady Amrita raised her right hand in the pose of fearlessness, silencing him. "I offer a compromise. I propose a meeting of both parties on neutral ground. Do you know the plateau beneath the Sleeping Calf Rock?" she inquired.

He nodded warily.

"Very good." She gave a brisk nod in reply. "Let us meet there, your master and I. The *dakini* Moirin will accompany me, and your master will bring this young man Bao. No weapons on either side. Each of us will be escorted by no more than ten unarmed guards. At a distance of five hundred paces, we will each exchange a guardsman to verify that both parties have honored these terms. Do I make myself understood?"

"Yes, highness." The messenger licked his lips. "What do you expect this meeting to accomplish?"

I answered for her. "I expect to persuade Bao to leave your master's service. If he does, I will honor my word and offer myself in his place."

His gaze slid sideways toward me. "And if you fail?"

I called the twilight, wrapping its subtle dazzle around me. "I will not fail."

The Falconer's messenger looked away.

"I am weary of this game," the Rani Amrita announced. "No more demands, no more offers. I will await your master on the plateau in one week's time. Go, and tell Tarik Khaga the Falconer that that is my final word."

"Yes, highness." He bowed to her. "I will do so."

Five days later, we set out for the plateau.

I was sick with unease. It seemed a good plan, but it was a dangerous one, too. With our hidden battalion, we would outnumber Tarik Khaga's men six to one; but the battalion would have some distance to cross once the signal was given, and Khaga's men were likely to be skilled assassins, one and all. Hasan Dar and the nine guards he had chosen to escort us were exceptional warriors, trained to fight with any weapon or none, but they were not assassins. And I had learned during my time in Bhaktipur that the Falconer was not the first to hold that dubious title, oh, no.

No, it was a hereditary mantle. For many generations, there had been a Falconer in Kurugiri, amassing years of knowledge of deadly killing arts. Until the advent of Jagrati the Spider Queen, none had killed save for hire.

This Falconer, Tarik Khaga, was different. Worse. He killed on a whim—his, or his Spider Queen's.

It was a surety that his men would have weapons hidden on them—subtle weapons, garrotes and throwing knives, mayhap poisoned darts like the one with which Black Sleeve had killed Bao.

I was afraid for myself, but the insistent blaze of my *diadh-anam* told me I had to go. More so, I was very afraid for the Rani Amrita, and I wished very, very much that she would not undertake this venture.

"I have to go, Moirin," she said calmly when I sought to dissuade her. "It is clear now that the gods sent you to me. It is my *kharma*."

"I do not see why you must risk yourself personally!" I said in frustration. "There is no sense in it."

Amrita was silent a moment. "I felt the same when my lord Chakresh insisted on facing the Falconer's assassins with his men," she said presently. "He insisted it was a matter of honor and duty. Now that the same choice is upon me, I understand." She laid a hand on my arm. "Please, do not quarrel with me, Moirin."

Reluctantly, I acceded.

It was an auspicious day when we set out, clear and bright. The Rani Amrita bade farewell to her son in private and for the first time, I saw Ravindra as a child in truth. His narrow shoulders shook as he embraced his mother and wept, his tears dampening the cloth of her sari. She held him close, kissing the top of his head.

"Be brave, jewel of my heart," she murmured. "I will draw strength from your courage."

Ravindra straightened. "I will do my best, Mama-ji."

We made our way through the streets of Bhaktipur in a splendid procession, surrounded by a hundred guards and dozens of attendants. Only ten guardsmen would accompany us to the plateau, but Hasan Dar meant to take no chances until it was necessary, especially in the crowded streets of the city.

I rode beside Amrita in her palanquin. Folks pressed as close as the guards would allow, tossing flowers and calling out blessings. Others begged the Rani not to go, echoing my sentiment. They didn't know about the ambush, of course, but they knew she meant to meet with the Falconer, and they were afraid for her.

When the outskirts of the city gave way to orchards and farmland, we abandoned the palanquin for horses and set out across the valley. Despite my pervasive fear, I was glad to be in a green, living place once more, and no longer cooped up behind the palace walls. I breathed the Breath of Trees Growing, willing my nerves to be calm.

An hour into our journey, I felt a shift occur that made me catch my breath, my *diadh-anam* flaring sharply inside me. Amrita glanced at me with concern. "What is it, Moirin?"

"Bao," I whispered. "He's moving, coming closer."

Her eyes widened. "You can tell this?"

I nodded. "Not over very vast distances, but this is near enough that I feel it. He's coming."

Amrita smiled. "Then that is very good news, is it not?"

"I don't know." Although I could sense it drawing closer, Bao's *diadh-anam* didn't quicken with eagerness like mine did. It was as sickly and guttering as it had been for all those long months since

I'd first sensed it in Vralia. I had been certain, so certain, that once we were together, no thrall could hold him. Now I wasn't so sure. "I hope so."

All throughout the day, pace by pace, I felt the distance between us lessen. I wanted to be joyful at the prospect, but I was too anxious.

By the end of the day, we had ascended into the foothills at the northern end of the valley of Bhaktipur. The warm lowland temperatures vanished quickly. Solicitous attendants brought long coats of padded, embroidered silk for Amrita and me to wear. We made camp in a meadow, where they erected tents of brightly colored silk, striped and merry. It was a festive scene, but the mood was somber. On the morrow, only twelve of us would continue—the Rani and I, and Hasan Dar and his nine handpicked guards.

Although I had no appetite, I tried to force myself to eat, reckoning I needed my strength. In contrast, Amrita ate more heartily than I'd ever seen her.

"Stop worrying, Moirin," she said, pressing a bit of flatbread with curried lamb and tangy *achar* on me. "Whatever will happen tomorrow, will happen. It does no good to worry about it."

I sighed. "I know."

"So young to be carrying the weight of the world on her shoulders!" Amrita teased me gently, coaxing a reluctant smile from me. "I think you have been doing just that for far too long, young goddess," she added in a more serious tone. "But you are not alone here. I am with you, and Hasan Dar and his men will protect your life as my own."

My throat tightened, and tears stung my eyes. "Thank you, my lady Amrita."

I was grateful, so very grateful to her; and yet I wished she were a thousand miles away, because if any harm befell this kind, beautiful, and brave Rani whom I had grown so quickly to love, I would spend the rest of my life regretting it.

I prayed it would not.

SIXTY-TWO

On the morrow, our reduced company of twelve set out for the plateau. Hasan Dar and his men left their swords behind, carrying only small knives concealed within their sashed belts. It was assumed that the Falconer's men would do the same, and worse.

I wished I had my bow, but it would have been impossible to hide.

Our path grew steeper as we climbed higher, and the air began to grow thinner. I felt dizzy at the lack, dizzy with the memory of mountain-sickness and fever, dizzy with the bright clamor of my *diadh-anam*, growing more and more insistent with each hour that passed.

Bao's name echoed in my thoughts like a drumbeat, over and over.

My aching heart felt too big for my chest, like it might burst its confines and shatter my bones.

I breathed the Breath of Earth's Pulse, grounding myself. Remembering Master Lo's teaching, I let one thought rise from another, trying not to chase them and drive myself mad with worry. I concentrated on the path, on the bobbing ears of my saddle-horse Lady, well rested and restored from her ordeal in the Abode of the Gods.

By late morning, we spotted the peak known as Sleeping Calf Rock, a jutting outcropping of stone shaped for all the world like a yak calf lying in slumber, its head stretched out and its legs folded beneath its body.

An hour later, we gained the plateau that lay beneath it. To all appearances, it was empty, an expanse of grassy meadow with a thick copse of spruce trees on the southwestern verge. I couldn't help but glance in that direction. Assuming our battalion of fifty archers was concealed within the dense copse, they were well hidden.

Gods, I hoped they were there.

Hasan Dar had a silver pipe that gave a shrill whistle on a chain around his neck. When he blew it, it would be the signal for our archers to emerge. He had argued in favor of doing so the instant the Falconer Tarik Khaga and his men were in range, ambushing them without bothering to parley with them.

The Rani Amrita had refused. "All this has come about because of Moirin and her young man," she had said firmly in her musical voice. "I fear if we do not give her the chance to save him, we defy the will of the gods."

Now, I shivered, praying that the gods did indeed intend for me to free my stubborn peasant-boy from this mess. I pushed away the memory of the boy-monk in Rasa bidding me to rescue the *tulku* Laysa. I could only bear so many burdens at once.

We took a position in the open meadow some hundred paces beyond the copse where our archers were hidden. Hasan Dar bowed to the Rani from his saddle, his palms pressed together, his eyes watchful and grave. "We are here, highness. All is in readiness. It awaits only to see if the Falconer takes our bait."

Amrita gave me an inquiring glance.

"Oh, aye," I whispered. "They are coming; or at least Bao is coming, and I doubt he is coming alone."

"How long?" she asked me.

In my mind, I measured the dwindling distance between Bao's *diadh-anam* and mine against the distance that had separated us before this journey. "Not long," I said. "Less than two hours, I think."

The sun crept across the sky; and we waited. The shadow cast by Sleeping Calf Rock shifted, obscuring the path toward the further mountains and Kurugiri.

It didn't matter.

Bao was coming. I could feel it, step by step. The nearer he got, the easier it was to gauge. My *diadh-anam* sang inside me, while his did not sing at all. Still, I felt it. When I knew he was almost upon us, I flung out my arm and pointed. "Now!"

One man on horseback rounded the curve beneath the outcropping, emerging from the shadows. He paused, surveying the plateau, then turned back and beckoned. Others followed, riding into sunlight.

Even at a distance, I spotted Bao among them. I knew him by the way he sat his mount, by the lean, tight-knit grace of his figure, by the faint shimmer of darkness that hung around him ever since his rebirth. It was stronger in the twilight, but even in daylight, I could see it. I wished I could see his face. The men spread out, forming a line, and advanced at a measured pace.

"One, two, three..." Hasan Dar squinted, counting. "Huh. Twelve, I make it. One more than allowed by our terms." He gestured to his second in command. "Pradeep, go!"

The guardsman Pradeep clapped heels to his mount, sprinting across the meadow. On the far side, the Falconer's party halted to confer. In short order, one of their men rode forward to fulfill the exchange.

It wasn't Bao. I wished it had been; I wished we could have grabbed him and fled, summoning the archers to ward our retreat. But no, it was some southern Bhodistani fellow with thick brows, a hard mouth, and a sword-belt with two empty scabbards. He scanned our company with a shrewd gaze, then gave a sharp nod, wheeled, and retreated, passing our returning guardsman Pradeep on the way.

"So?" Hasan Dar raised his brows.

"They have honored the terms, commander," Pradeep said breathlessly, leaning on his pommel. "No visible weapons. And their twelfth person...it is not an extra guard. It is Jagrati the Spider Queen herself."

A chill crawled over my skin. That had not been part of our plan;

but Pradeep was right, it was not a violation of the terms, either. It had simply not occurred to any of us that the Spider Queen would leave the safehold of Kurugiri.

Hasan Dar gave the Rani an inquiring look. She frowned, then nodded in assent. Her commander raised one arm, beckoning the Falconer's company forward.

Once again, they began to advance.

Slowly, slowly, the distance between us narrowed; and I felt my awareness narrowing, too. I tried to fight it, and couldn't. I was at the mercy of my *diadh-anam*, and nothing else in the world existed for it save its missing half. My vision dwindled to a tunnel, and at the end of the tunnel was Bao.

Closer and closer he rode, until I could make out his face. His gaze was fixed on me as surely as mine was on him...and there was nothing, nothing at all glad or joyful in it. Instead, his expression was fixed with a mix of fury and anguish, his dark eyes glittering with something that looked very much like hatred.

It struck me like a blow, hard enough that I wrenched my gaze away, breathing slowly and shivering. My vision expanded again; now it was my heart that contracted painfully, thudding in my chest.

The company reached us and drew rein a few paces away. There were ten men including Bao, each looking more deadly than the next. Mountain-folk, southern Bhodistani...others I didn't know, Akkadian, mayhap. There was even a fellow with reddish hair and grey eyes.

Tarik Khaga, the Falconer of Kurugiri, had deep-set eyes and a strong prow of a nose, black hair streaked with iron-grey. He looked to be somewhere in his fifties, a muscular fellow with the beginning of a slight paunch that didn't make him look any less dangerous.

Jagrati.

I stole a glance at the Spider Queen. Her face was gaunt and striking, dark-skinned, high cheekbones with hollows beneath them, but not so terrible a beauty as I had expected. The rest of her was draped in a black cloak fastened high around her throat.

The Rani Amrita broke the silence. "Greetings, my lord Khaga," she said, pressing her hands together, her voice clear and sincere. "I thank you for consenting to this meeting. Shall we unhorse ourselves and speak as civilized folk?"

His gaze flicked briefly to Jagrati, who gave an almost imperceptible nod. "As you wish, little Rani," he said in a dismissive tone.

Both parties dismounted. It would give our mounted archers waiting in ambush a few more seconds of time to close the distance between us; still, I felt uneasy. I kept glancing at Bao, and away from the seething hatred in his gaze. He didn't even look like himself. With the ban on weapons, his ever-present bamboo staff was missing. The unruly shock of his black hair had grown longer, caught and tamed by a clasp at the nape of his neck, and there were gold hoops in his earlobes.

"So, my lord—" the Rani began.

The Falconer cut her off with a gesture. "You shall have what you came for." He beckoned. "Bao!"

Like his master, Bao looked to Jagrati for assurance; and she nodded at him, too, her expression softening briefly. For a second, he looked grateful; and then the mask of hatred returned to his face as he moved toward me.

"Bao, please..." My voice shook as I took a step forward. My *diadh-anam* roiled and blazed in anguish.

"No!" His voice cracked like a whip. "Whoever you are, *whatever* you are, I want no part of you or whatever sick game you play! Do you understand? Go, and leave me to the service of my lord and lady Khaga!"

"Bao, it's me! Moirin!" I touched my chest, my heart aching. "How can you not know me?"

He leaned forward, nostrils flaring. I could feel the heat of his fury rolling off him, the hot-metal forge smell of his skin. His pupils were too wide, his eyes fever-bright and wild. "Because Moirin mac Fainche *died* almost a year ago!" he shouted at me, his hands clenching and unclenching. "Do you think I did not feel it? Whatever foul spirit has stolen her face, stolen the very spark of her soul, I want nothing to do with it!"

Tears blurred my eyes. "Bao, it's *me*! I wasn't killed, I was bound by magic! That's why you couldn't sense me!"

"No." Bao shook his head. "No, that is the lie the Great Khan told me, and I will not believe it twice. In Kurugiri, I learned the truth."

"No, you didn't!" I cried in frustration. "The lord and lady of Kurugiri never had anything to do with it! It was Vralian priests who took me prisoner, using Yeshuite magic! Chains, like the one the Circle of Shalomon tried to use to bind the demon-spirit they summoned, the one you and Master Lo helped me banish. Remember?"

Bao hesitated, frowning.

"The Great Khan told you a lie to send you in the opposite direction," I whispered. "But I am here now."

His *diadh-anam* flickered.

"You feel it!" I said. "You do, don't you?"

"Oh, no, no, I'm afraid that is not an acceptable outcome," another voice said—a woman's voice soft and sibilant, with a faint rasp like silk drawn over a whetstone. "This has gone on long enough, I think."

Bao glanced at Jagrati, who smiled tenderly at him.

He smiled back at her, relieved and certain once more.

And then the Spider Queen smiled at *me*, her long-fingered hands reaching up to undo the clasp of her cloak. It fell away, revealing the collar of gold filigree that adorned her long, slender throat, an immense black diamond set in the middle of it, filled with glowing hues that shifted like embers.

I was wrong.

She *was* as terrible and beautiful as Kali dancing, terrifying and compelling. She was tall, taller than me, taller than most women, with long limbs that moved with angular grace. I stood frozen as Jagrati drifted toward me, still smiling. Despite the stark beauty of her hollow-cheeked face, she had very full lips…

…and Kamadeva's diamond.

It glowed, filled with dark fire, pulsing in time with the beating of her blood. It was made from the ashes of the Bhodistani god of desire, and it called to Naamah's gift within me, setting it to rise in an endless spiral, filling my limbs with languor, sapping my will.

I opened my mouth to tell Hasan Dar to sound his whistle, to call the archers from their ambush. No words came.

Even if they had, Hasan Dar and his men were gaping, transfixed.

"So it's true." Jagrati's fingertips stroked my face, and I leaned into her touch, helpless to resist the urge. She pitched her voice low, for my ears only, fond and amused. "I thought you might respond to it. Bao has told me so very, very much about you, Moirin. I think perhaps we are not so different."

"No?" I asked mindlessly.

"No." She drew a line from my temple to the corner of my lips. "Your goddess Naamah, when she journeyed in Bhodistan, she made no distinctions when she lay down with strangers. Any caste, or nocaste. No one was untouchable to her. It was only desire that mattered. Desire that made a thing sacred. You understand this, yes? Or else you would not have let yourself love a bastard peasant-boy without so much as a family name."

I nodded. "Yes."

"Come with me, then." Jagrati's smile widened, showing perfect white teeth. "Perhaps in Kurugiri, you may convince Bao that you did not die. I did not mean to lie to him at first; it is only that I thought it must be so, that the Great Khan must have killed you. I did my best to help him through his grief, wrongly though I guessed. So, will you come?"

Unsure, I glanced sideways at the Falconer.

"Oh, do not trouble yourself with my husband." Her fingers were firm on my chin, turning me back to face her. Kamadeva's diamond and Naamah's gifts pulsed between us. "He does as I will. I am content to allow him his pleasures while I take my own with others, but he will not trouble you if I do not wish it." The Spider Queen leaned forward and kissed me, her tongue flickering against mine. "So, Moirin, will you come?"

Yes.

The word was on my lips.

"No!" Amrita's musical voice called out behind me. She tugged me away with surprising strength, wedging herself deftly between Jagrati and me, her graceful hands raised and crossed before her in an unfamiliar *mudra*. Power and conviction radiated from her small figure. "I will not allow it!"

Jagrati recoiled with a fierce expression of distaste that turned her striking face ugly. "Who will stop me, little Rani?" she asked with a sneer. "Your men?" She gestured at them, every last one transfixed by Kamadeva's diamond. "I do not think so. Your pet *dakini*?" She shook her head slowly, a sensual smile returning to her lips. "She is eager to say yes to me. It may prove quite interesting."

Desire pounded in my veins, merging confusingly with the insistent call of my *diadh-anam*. I forced myself to stare at the back of Amrita's head, clenching my teeth to keep the word "yes" from escaping.

"Nonetheless, I forbid it," Amrita said firmly. "That is a sacred object you profane, Jagrati." Her hands shifted into the soothing *mudra* that stilled conflict. "It is not too late for you to obey your *kharma*," she said in a softer tone. "Give Kamadeva's diamond to me, and I will see it restored to the temple."

The Spider Queen laughed, a sound like silk tearing; and there was dark humor in it, and hatred and loathing, too. It made my skin prickle, and the blood run cold in my veins.

"Oh, I do not think so, little Rani," she said in that low silken rasp. "I know your kind, daughter of privilege! You are so very, very concerned with the *kharma* of the less fortunate, so long as it means we will always be there to tan your leather, bury your dead, and haul away your night-soil."

"I did not choose the way the world is ordered," my lady Amrita murmured.

"No, but you are content to live in it," Jagrati observed. "You command us to carry away the shit squeezed stinking from your bowels, and then claim *we* are unclean because of it, as though it were never a part of you."

"The priests—"

"I spit on the priests!" Jagrati spat on the ground. "I spit on the gods, too! I have chosen my own destiny."

"You are only dooming yourself, Jagrati," Amrita said in a sorrowful voice.

"Ah, no." Her predatory smile returned. "I am taking quite a few others with me. Now, I shall take your oh so pretty *dakini*, and perhaps a few of your men, too. Your captain's a handsome fellow." She beckoned to Hasan Dar. "Come here."

He stepped forward obediently, the silver pipe around his neck glinting in the afternoon sunlight.

The pipe that would summon our ambush...

I couldn't move. The best I could manage was a faint, broken whisper. "The pipe! My lady Amrita...blow the pipe."

She moved without hesitation to intercept Hasan Dar, raising one hand in a gesture that halted him in his tracks. He blinked in perplexity, but he didn't protest when Amrita reached for the pipe and blew a long, shrill blast on it.

Shouts came from the copse behind us. I prayed silently that Kamadeva's diamond wasn't powerful enough to transfix fifty men charging on horseback all at once.

It seemed it wasn't, for Jagrati hissed with fury, her stark face transformed into ugliness once more.

The Falconer stirred like a man waking from a dream. "Ambush!" he shouted. "Ride!" He cast a scathing glance at Amrita as he scrambled into the saddle, jerking his mount's head around. "You will pay for this, little Rani."

She smiled grimly. "You had better ride fast, Falcon King."

"Bao!" I called his name in a choked voice. "Don't go, please!"

He looked briefly at me, and I felt his *diadh-anam* flicker again;

but then Jagrati leaned over in the saddle and spoke to him, and he turned away from me.

They fled before the onslaught of our archers, who came thundering out of hiding, sweeping across the meadow, parting to pass us by. I held my breath, fearful for Bao, unsure whether to pray for success or failure.

Beneath the shadow of Sleeping Calf Rock, at the base of the path that led higher into the mountains, two of the Falconer's men turned back, sowing confusion in the ranks of their pursuers. The air was filled with the twang of bowstrings and the hum of arrows in flight, and sparkling with the glint of throwing daggers and other hidden weapons.

Hasan Dar shook himself, dropping to one knee before the Rani and lowering his head. "My lady, forgive me," he said in a hoarse voice. "I failed you."

Amrita laid one hand on his head. "Not yet, my friend. Go after them, I beg you, and see this finished. Your men will look after me. And ʌ." She glanced at me. "Try not to kill the young man from Ch'in, please."

He nodded and sprang to his feet, striding toward his mount.

I shivered. "Thank you, my lady."

She caught my hand and squeezed it, her dark, lustrous gaze searching my face. "Are you all right, Moirin?"

"No," I said honestly. "Not even close."

SIXTY-THREE

We passed the night in the hidden encampment in the spruce copse.

I was a wreck.

It had all gone wrong, so very wrong. It had been a good plan, but it was a plan largely conceived by a ten-year-old boy who had not taken into account the possibility that Kamadeva's diamond would be set in play, rendering ten grown men and one highly susceptible daughter of Naamah's line vulnerable to desire.

Desire that would not go away.

Ah, gods! It was all entangled and complicated, my *diadh-anam* and Naamah's gifts warring against one another, my heart's yearning for Bao and the unholy wanting that Kamadeva's diamond had loosed in me doing battle. It gripped me like a fever.

Jagrati.

Her face swam before me in my dreams, gaunt, high-boned, and compelling. Although I did not trust her for an instant, some of the things she had said rang true to me. It was a cruel, unfair world that had given shape to her hatred.

Bao.

My heart ached.

I had come close, so very close, to reaching him. Now, again and again, I reached for him, reached for his *diadh-anam*, willing that faint flicker of uncertainty to kindle into a blaze, wherein he knew me once more. But although I sensed he was alive, I couldn't feel him clearly anymore. When I tried, Jagrati's face arose in my thoughts, mocking me. I would have said "yes" to her without a second thought, without a thought in my mind at all. She had taken what I believed was my strength, and turned it against me. I'd thought I could pit my *diadh-anam* and Naamah's gifts against the lure of Kamadeva's diamond and win.

I'd thought to do battle for Bao.

Instead, I was at war with myself.

"Hush, young goddess." Amrita stroked my hair, my head pillowed on her lap. "It is not your fault."

"I should have known," I murmured.

"How could you?" she asked quietly. "None of us expected it."

I sighed. "No, but at least you were not vulnerable to it. And it is probably best if you do not touch me so, my lady."

Her hands went still. "It troubles you still?"

The incessant pulse of desire beat in my veins, timed to the flickering glow trapped in Kamadeva's diamond. "Yes."

Amrita shifted gently away from me. "Very well."

In the morning, Hasan Dar and our company of archers returned, grim-faced and defeated. Once again, he knelt before the Rani and bowed his head in abject apology. "I'm sorry, highness, but I have failed you in truth. We killed several of their men, but Tarik Khaga and his cursed Queen escaped."

"Ah, no! How?" Amrita looked dismayed.

"They had weapons and armor cached along the path. One of their men held a narrow pass long enough for them to cause a rockslide above it," he said dully. "It must have been rigged to fall beforehand. We worked through the night to clear it, but by the time we succeeded, they were long gone." He glanced at me. "Your young man was with them. I do not think he was injured."

I nodded, grateful for the confirmation. I wasn't sure I could trust my desire-snarled *diadh-anam* at the moment.

"Well, then." The Rani Amrita's slender shoulders slumped. I wished I dared to comfort her, but I was barely managing to contain the maelstrom of desire raging inside me. "What do we do now?"

"We go home," Hasan Dar said in a grim voice. "And brace ourselves for assassins."

"I'm sorry," I whispered. "I'm so very sorry."

"It was not your fault." He turned his weary gaze toward me. "All of us thought the attempt worth making, and all but one of us failed in the face of Kamadeva's diamond. If her highness had not been with us, you and I would be on our way to Kurugiri, Lady Moirin." He shivered. "Willingly."

"It's a good thing I didn't let you talk me out of coming, then, isn't it?" Amrita observed with a faint spark of her usual good humor.

With an effort, I summoned a smile for her. "You were heroic, my lady. Truly."

She shook her head. "I was fortunate. Kamadeva's diamond cannot compel false desire."

It was a somber procession that made the journey back to the meadow where we had made camp the first night. We had lost five men in the effort, hewn down by the Falconer's assassins. I was afraid to ask if Bao had killed any of them, but in the end, I had to know.

"No, I don't think so," Hasan Dar said in a tired tone. "He was guarding that cursed Jagrati with some sort of fighting-staff. It must have been hidden in their caches." He rubbed at his face. "He's good, that one. I've never seen a man quick enough to bat arrows out of thin air."

"Aye, that would be Bao," I murmured.

Our somber procession met a somber welcome in the base camp, news of our failure spreading quickly. Hasan Dar posted every man he could spare around the perimeter, wary of assassins. Everyone not on guard slept fitfully that night, though perhaps none more so than I did.

The desire hadn't faded.

It didn't seem to have taken anyone else the same way, and I did not know whether it was because Jagrati had targeted me specifically, touched me and kissed me, staking a claim on me; or if it was because of Naamah's gift, sparked into unrelenting flame by the shifting fires of Kamadeva's diamond. I only knew that it racked me mercilessly, filling me with wanting, until I literally shook with it.

"Moirin..." Amrita sounded miserable. "I do not like to see you suffer. Is there nothing I can do?"

I shook my head at her, wrapping my arms around my knees. "No."

The following day, we returned to Bhaktipur. There was no tossing of flowers, no calling out of blessings. Folk in the street were silent and downcast, whispering to one another, whispering of death and cunning, skilled assassins on the way. I felt the skin between my shoulder blades grow tight and itching.

In the palace, Ravindra wept with relief to find his mother alive and well, and wept with remorse that his plan had failed us.

"Do not blame yourself, young chess-master." His mother hugged him tight. "It was a very good plan. We shall just have to continue sleeping in the hidden room for a time, you and I."

Ravindra gazed at me, eyes damp between tear-spiked lashes. "I am sorry about your Bao, Moirin."

My *diadh-anam* gave a painful flare, setting off another wave of desire, making me shudder to the bone. "So am I, young highness."

After we had bathed and eaten, and Ravindra had been sent away to sleep in the hidden room, Amrita insisted on sending for her physician to attend to me in my quarters, despite my protests that it would do no good. He felt at my brow and took my pulse, examined my tongue, and prescribed a diet of cooling foods.

"Yoghurt, cucumber, and mint," the physician said, papering over uncertainty with a decisive tone. "Yes, this will help!"

Out of courtesy, I waited until he was gone to laugh in despair. "Yoghurt?"

"Oh, Moirin!" Amrita put her arms around me, worried and concerned. "Only try it, will you not?"

I buried my face in the crook of her neck. She smelled good, like flowers and spices—not as intoxicating as my lady Jehanne, but close. I kissed her throat, opened my mouth and tasted her warm skin with my tongue.

And I hadn't the faintest idea I was doing it until I felt her stiffen in shock.

"I'm *sorry!*" I jerked away from her, hiding my face in my hands. "Amrita, I *told* you not to touch me!"

"I'm not sure I minded, actually." There was a surprisingly pragmatic note in her musical voice. "It felt rather nice. After all, the role of the sainted widow can be a lonely one." Her hands tugged at mine, lowering them. Reluctantly, I lifted my head and met her dark, lustrous gaze. A little silence came between us. "Would it help?" she asked me.

Like a shower of golden sparks, her words and their meaning fell drifting through my awareness.

"Yes," I said simply.

"Well, then." Amrita smiled at me. "You will have to show me what to do, Moirin, for I confess, I have no idea."

"Gladly," I whispered, cupping her face in my hands and kissing her. I felt her lips soften and part beneath mine.

The bright lady smiled, setting loose a flurry of doves.

"Oh!" Amrita sounded surprised. "Well, *that* is different."

I sat back on my heels. "Does it displease you?"

"No." She smiled at me beneath her lashes. "Not at all, actually. Show me more, Moirin."

I did.

Gold; she was like gold, something pure and shining in the midst of this mess. And like an alchemist's magic, her kindness transmuted the base metal of the desire that racked me into something golden and pure. I undressed her reverently until she was clad in nothing but bangles and tinkling anklets, kissing every inch of amber skin I uncovered, until she shivered and wrapped her arms around me, murmuring my name. I knew it was compassion, and not desire, that lay behind her offer, but that didn't mean I couldn't please her—and that alone would have been enough for me. But it was in Amrita's nature to be generous, and she did her best to return the gift of pleasure that I showered on her.

Bit by bit, the terrible, searing *need* drained away from me. Afterward, I couldn't find enough words to thank her.

"I am not sure it is necessary, dear one." She laughed her chiming laugh. "You have considerable skill in your art."

I smiled. "I take considerable pleasure in it."

Amrita stretched languorously. "That cursed Jagrati was right about one thing. It was certainly interesting. You are a veritable poet of desire, Moirin." She gave me a serious look. "Do you feel better now?"

"Oh, yes." I kissed the graceful curve of her bare shoulder, gleaming in the lamplight. There were still a thousand fears and worries pressing me, but in this moment, Amrita's presence held them at bay. "If there is room in the world for love, there is room for hope. Although mayhap you will have to be more fearful of Kamadeva's diamond now," I teased her.

"Do not even think it!" She tapped my lips in reproach. "I could never have done this if I did not care for you, Moirin. Never."

"I know." I caught her hand and kissed that, too. "I know the difference between kindness and genuine desire, my lady. And I am very, very grateful."

"Yes, I know," Amrita said humorously. "You do not need to demonstrate it again. I am a little worn out by your gratitude." She fell silent, thinking. Sensing her mood shift, I kept my own silence. "I think perhaps Jagrati may have said more than one true thing," she said presently. "What she said about the way the world treats those unfortunate ones born outside of a caste...they were harsh words, but they have stayed with me." She glanced at me. "I have not forgotten what you said about ambitious men attempting to shape the gods to serve their own ends. And I do not think you would disagree with what Jagrati said to me."

"No," I murmured. "I don't. But that does not give her the right to become a monster, treating the lives of others as playthings to be stolen or destroyed."

"No, but it tells us something about how the monster was made," Amrita said. "And perhaps we must take some responsibility for it." She frowned a little. "There was a *sadhu* in Galanka when I was a girl, a holy man who had renounced all things of the world, who refused to shun the untouchables. I wonder if he is still there, and if there are others like him."

"Yeshua ben Yosef went among folk you would reckon unclean and tended to them," I offered. It was one of the things Aleksei had taught me. "Lepers, beggars."

"So did your D'Angeline gods when they passed through Bhodistan. I remember my father discussing it with an ambassador, for he sent me away when he caught me listening." She sat upright and began winding her hair into a knot. "I have been thinking, trying to make sense of our failure, Moirin. Five men slain, and for nothing! I was certain that the gods sent you to me for a reason—"

"So was I, my lady," I said. "And I am so very sorry—"

"Hush." Amrita touched my lips again, gently this time. "Let me finish, young goddess. I was also certain that I *knew* the reason, that it was to rid the world of the Falconer and his Spider Queen. But perhaps I was wrong. Perhaps that was not it at all, and Jagrati's harsh words were part of the message I was meant to hear. What do you think?"

I gazed at her beautiful face, my heart feeling very full. "My lady Amrita, I cannot say. I only know for sure that if I were a Bhodistani god with a message of compassion to deliver, I could choose no one better in the world than you to hear it. However..." I glanced toward the balcony, and saw that it was fully dark outside. "There is still the matter of the Falconer's assassins, and I think it would be best if you went to the hidden room now, and we talk more in the morning."

"You will be all right?" she inquired.

I nodded. "I have Ravindra's bells to warn me, and the twilight to protect me."

"Very well, then." Amrita smiled. "I hope your sleep is peaceful."

I smiled back at her. "I daresay it will be."

For a mercy, it was. After I had helped Amrita dress and seen her safely into the custody of her guardsmen, I returned to my bed, which smelled of flowers, spices, and love-making. The bright lady was pleased, and so was I. I didn't think Amrita understood how great a gift she had given me. It wasn't just that she had quenched the fire of yearning that Kamadeva's diamond had ignited in me. I was Naamah's child, and I needed love and aye, pleasure, almost as much as food and water.

Until tonight, I hadn't known how starved I was.

Tomorrow, I thought, I would consult my *diadh-anam* and pray to every god I knew that I could figure out what to do about Bao, the bedamned Jagrati, and Kamadeva's bedamned diamond.

Tonight, I would sleep and be grateful for the profound gift I had been given.

And so I did, deep and dreamless, wrapped in the lingering grace of Naamah's approval ... until I awoke in the small hours of the night with my *diadh-anam* blazing like wildfire, and a shadowy figure in the bedchamber with me, the length of a staff strapped across its back.

I sat up and stared. *"Bao?"*

SIXTY-FOUR

"Shh!" In the space of a heartbeat, the shadowy figure crossed the room and fell upon me, pinning me to the bed and clamping one calloused hand over my mouth, setting the point of a dagger at my throat.

Bao.

It was Bao.

I stared up at him, scared and bewildered. I should have known. I should have felt him coming; but my awareness had been too entangled, first by Kamadeva's diamond, then by Amrita's loving kindness and Naamah's grace.

"I need to know!" Bao hissed at me, his eyes wild and shimmering, his expression desperate. "Who are you? What are you? Why are you here?" He prodded the hollow of my throat with the tip of his dagger. *What happened to Moirin?*"

I tried to reply, but his hand muffled my words.

Realizing it, he frowned. "Promise you won't scream?" The dagger prodded me again in warning.

I nodded.

Bao removed his hand from my mouth. "Tell me."

I took a deep breath, and then another. "Gods bedamned, Bao!" I hissed back at him. "It's *me*! And if you will not believe the proof of your eyes and the proof of my *diadh-anam* inside you, I do not know what else to say! I've spent the last year of my life following you half-way around the world, while you've been marrying Tatar princesses whose fathers betrayed us both, and falling under the spell of the bedamned Spider Queen, and do you know what? I'm very, very tired of it, you stupid, stubborn boy!"

He blinked. *"Moirin?"*

"Yes!"

Bao stood, swaying a little. "How...?"

I sat up and kindled a lamp. "I told you, it was the Vralian priests. They had chains that bound my magic. It took me a long time to escape."

His throat worked. "I thought..."

"I know," I said softly. "But it was a lie. It was always a lie. I'm here. It's me. Do you understand?"

"Uh-huh." Bao glanced around, still swaying; and I realized there was something wrong with him beyond the influence of Kamadeva's diamond. He blinked at me again. "Moirin, why does it smell of sex in here?"

And then he collapsed, sparing me the need for a reply.

Much of what passed immediately afterward is blurred in my memory. I know I went to the door of my bedchamber, rattling Ravindra's warning bells and summoning guards. The palace roused quickly, already on high alert. A pair of guards shifted Bao from the floor of my chamber into my bed.

He was weak, sweating, and racked with tremors.

Nonetheless, Hasan Dar insisted on questioning him. "Did you come as one of Tarik Khaga's assassins?" he asked in a hard voice. "Did you come to kill her highness the Rani Amrita Sukhyhim?"

"No." Bao shook his head, lolling it from side to side. "No, I said I would, but it was a lie. I do not wish your Rani or anyone else dead. I only wanted to find out about Moirin."

"How did you gain entrance to the palace and Lady Moirin's chambers?" Hasan Dar demanded.

"Vaulted the wall." Bao made a listless gesture in the direction of my balcony. "Climbed a tree in the garden, tied a rope, swung, and jumped there."

"He trained as an acrobat for many years," I murmured.

Bao nodded, closing his eyes and shuddering. It must have taken almost all of his flagging strength to accomplish the feat.

I could feel his *diadh-anam* inside him, and it was stronger and clearer than it had been, calling to mine. Whatever ailed him, it was an affliction of the body, not the spirit. I felt at his brow. Despite the sheen of sweat, his skin didn't feel fever-hot. "Are you ill?" I asked him. "Is it the mountain-sickness?"

"No." He gave another lolling shake of his head. "Opium."

"Opium causes this?" I was unsure. "Why were you smoking opium?"

Bao opened his eyes and grimaced at me. "To dull the pain of thinking you were dead, Moirin! They grow it in Kurugiri; it's everywhere. But I stopped after seeing you in the meadow, because I had to know."

"Enough!" Hasan Dar caught Bao by the front of his tunic, yanking him partially upright. "If that's what ails you, you'll live," he said grimly. "You'll want to die for a few days, but you'll live. Tell me, are there other assassins coming?" He gave Bao a shake. "Tell me everything you know!"

I winced, but I couldn't blame him. My lady Amrita's life was at stake, and mayhap Ravindra's, too. "Please, tell him anything that might help, Bao," I said. "Trust me, you definitely don't want the Rani Amrita's death on your conscience."

"What is it with you and royal ladies?" he complained, squinting at me. I had the urge to shake him myself, but Hasan Dar did it for me. "All right, all right! One moment! It is not urgent yet." Bao gestured feebly toward the north. "They will wait a few days until they're sure I failed, then they will send another. Not one you expect. Divyesh Patel is his name, and he will come by day. His weapon is poison."

Hasan Dar lowered him. "You're sure?"

Bao managed to nod. "Put a guard on your stores now. Alert your kitchen staff. Don't let them admit any strangers, don't let them serve any food or drink that hasn't been under lock and key. Sooner or later, Divyesh will approach one of them."

"Oh, I will do better than that!" Hasan Dar looked thunderous. "I will personally taste every dish that is prepared for their highnesses until this poisoner is caught."

"No, no, my friend." Amrita had entered the room unannounced, attended by several more guards. She looked ashen, but resolved. "I brought this danger on myself, and I will not allow you to risk yourself. I will taste my own dishes, and Ravindra's, too."

"Highness—" her commander protested.

She raised one hand, silencing him. Reluctantly, he acquiesced with a bow. She frowned at Bao. "It is the opium-sickness that ails him?"

"So he says," I replied.

Amrita glanced sidelong at me, raising her brows. "I take it you did not sense his presence as he approached this time."

I shook my head. "No. Kamadeva's diamond, and . . . well." I could not say aloud that the overwhelming relief of Naamah's grace had distracted me even from the approach of my own divided *diadh-anam*, but it had. "No, my lady, I did not."

Her mouth quirked. "I will send for the physician, eh? Perhaps there is something that may help your Bao through the worst of the pangs."

"That would be good," Bao said through gritted teeth, shivering violently. "Thank you, highness."

Roused from sleep, the bleary-eyed physician came to examine Bao and confirmed it was opium-sickness. "Very little will help, I fear," he said apologetically. "Give him peppermint tea to soothe his stomach when the vomiting begins. Beyond that . . ." He shrugged. "Your system must cleanse itself, young man. How long has it been since last you took opium?"

"Two days," Bao muttered. "I think."

The physician patted his shoulder helpfully. "Expect to feel like dying for a few more, then. But it will pass."

After ordering a second bed brought into my chamber, as well as clean linen and sleeping attire for Bao, who was sweating through his woolen tunic and breeches, the Rani Amrita returned to the hidden room with her escort of guards.

She took me aside, first. "I must admit, I feel a bit foolish, Moirin," she murmured. "If you had known your Bao was coming, I would not have made the offer I did, nor would you have accepted it, I think."

"Then I am glad I did not know," I said honestly.

"You do not mean that!" Amrita admonished me. I smiled at her. She tilted her head and reconsidered, flushing slightly, not entirely displeased. "Or... perhaps you do, eh?"

I touched her cheek and stroked it gently, letting my fingertips linger against her skin. "Out of the kindness of your heart, you gave me a very great gift, my lady, and Naamah's blessing is on you because of it. I hope you are not sorry for it."

She shook her head. "Not sorry, no."

I smiled again. "Well, then. Nor am I."

This time, Amrita smiled back at me, looking tired and worn and beautiful. "You are more than a little bit of a bad girl, Moirin. Go and tend to your bad boy. I think you must deserve one another."

When she had gone, I turned back to find Bao regarding me with half-lidded eyes, dark crescents glinting in the lamplight. "Ha!" he said. "I knew it."

I pointed a finger at him. "*You* do not have leave for blame, my stubborn boy. You let Jagrati make you her toy."

"You would have, too," he said. "I saw it. Only—"

"Only my lady Amrita refused to allow it." I knelt on the bed beside him, tugging at his sweat-sodden tunic. "So. If nothing else, we have established that I have far better taste in royal ladies than you do. Although I must say, your wife Erdene still loves you, and she proved helpful in the end."

"Did she?" Bao smiled faintly. "I'm glad."

"Yes." I tugged harder, to no avail. "Lift your arms, won't you? Else I'll have to summon Hasan Dar to aid me."

Bao shifted obligingly and lifted his arms, and at last I was able to ease his soaked tunic over his head, removing it.

I caught my breath.

There were new markings on his corded forearms—fresh, stark, and unfamiliar. Vivid black tattoos inked onto his skin in a complicated zig-zag pattern that forked like lightning, each turning marked with a symbol in a strange alphabet. Remembering old tales, I wondered if they were part of some charm or spell that further bound him to the Spider Queen.

I traced the pattern. "Bao? What is this?"

"What?" He glanced at his forearms. "Oh, that." He shrugged. "It is the path through the maze to Kurugiri, Moirin." He lifted his right arm a fraction. "This way is up." He let it fall, and lifted the left. "And this is down." An involuntary shudder racked him. "Do you think it will be helpful?"

I kissed him, reckoning it was best done before the vomiting began. My *diadh-anam* sang happily within me, reunited with its missing half.

"Yes," I said. "Oh, yes!"

SIXTY-FIVE

Bao was miserable for days.

He trembled and shook, racked by bone-deep pains. He tossed and turned and sweated, unable to find ease, unable to sleep. There was vomiting and worse, as though his body sought to expel every foreign substance within it along with the dregs of the opium he had smoked for months.

It was perhaps the most spectacularly unromantic lovers' reunion in the annals of history.

Still, he had done something no one else had ever done. He had walked away from the Spider Queen and Kamadeva's diamond of his own will, breaking the spell that bound him to her.

And he had brought the secret of the path to Kurugiri with him.

Hasan Dar was cautiously elated. The entire palace remained on high alert, watching for the Falconer's elusive poisoner. Guards in civilian clothes were posted over every storeroom, watched over every well, accompanied the Rani's cooks to the market. Meanwhile, the commander took counsel with the Rani and her clever son, trying to forge a plan that would take advantage of the maze's key.

Bao's presence was kept a secret that we might not alert our enemies to his betrayal. Let Tarik Khaga and Jagrati think he had failed, that he had been captured or slain, and the nature of his tattoos remained a mystery.

In between bouts of agony, Bao told Hasan Dar everything he knew about Kurugiri's vulnerabilities.

Some of the news was good. Due to the stronghold's apparent unassailability, the Falconer didn't maintain anything like an army, relying instead on his impenetrable maze and over a dozen skilled assassins.

The bad news was that the path was narrow and twisting, filled with switchbacks and blinds in which assassins could lurk alone or in pairs and defend the path against an oncoming army. Superior numbers would prevail in the end, but gaining the peak would come at a steep cost.

And the Spider Queen and Kamadeva's diamond awaited at the top, a danger not to be underestimated a second time.

Throughout his ordeal, I tended to Bao and did my best to ease his suffering. The Rani's physician was right, nothing really helped, but at least I could change his sweat-soaked linens and clothing, give him peppermint tea to drink, and see that his chamberpot was exchanged for a clean one—the cursed Jagrati's harsh words on the matter of human ordure ringing in my ears as the latter task was accomplished.

My lady Amrita was right. I did not disagree with what Jagrati had said. The stench of ordure could be washed away. It was foul deeds that made a person unclean.

Amrita visited several times a day, bringing Ravindra with her that he might witness Bao's suffering and appreciate it as a cautionary tale, lest opium tempt him one day. I was not entirely sure it worked, for despite Bao's obvious misery, Ravindra was more interested in and awed by his feat of swinging from the branch of a sprawling banyan tree in the garden to gain my balcony.

"That was a *very* long leap, Bao-ji," he said with respect.

"Heh." Bao flashed a grin at him, the first one I'd seen from him since he arrived. "I know, highness."

"Were you afraid of falling?" Ravindra inquired.

Bao scoffed. "I never fall."

Amrita shook her head in mild despair. "I fear he is not such a very good influence, your bad boy."

"No." I ruffled Bao's damp hair. "But he seldom boasts in vain."

Despite her gentle teasing, it was clear that Amrita too was kindly disposed toward Bao, solicitous of his suffering, and grateful for the warning and incredibly valuable information he brought.

Bao liked her, too. "Better be careful, Moirin," he murmured after their first visit. "Your White Queen, she will be jealous of that one."

I winced in unexpected pain.

"What?" He searched my face. "I'm sorry, was that cruel to say?"

"No." I dipped a clean cloth in a basin of cool water, wiping the sweat from his forehead. "No, you couldn't have known." The words brought a lump to my throat, but I forced them out anyway. "I learned in Vralia that Jehanne died giving birth to a daughter."

He caught his breath in a sharp hiss. "Oh, Moirin! I *am* sorry."

I nodded my thanks. "You always liked her, too, didn't you?"

"Uh-huh." Bao smiled a little. "She did whatever pleased her, and never apologized for it."

"Like Jagrati?" I asked carefully.

His face clouded. "I do not want to talk about her yet. After all, you haven't told me half of what happened to you in Vralia."

"Nor will I, until you're recovered." I wrung out the cloth. "Fair enough."

"No, not like *her*," Bao said after a time. "Your Jehanne, she was not angry at the world. There was no hatred in her, only much passion. Also, she saved you from that conceited Lord Lion Mane," he added. "And she gave much honor to Master Lo. So yes, I liked her, and I am very sorry she is gone."

I wanted to ask him more about Jagrati, but it would wait until he was ready. And I had not told him the whole truth about Vralia yet, because I was afraid it would send him into a fury that would delay his recovery. My stubborn peasant-boy and I had a great deal to talk about.

For now I was just glad to have him back.

On the fourth day after Bao's arrival, two things happened—both of them good, for once. The first was that the worst of the opium-sickness seemed to have passed, leaving Bao weary and drawn, but no longer racked with pains or afflicted by sweating, nausea, and worse.

I was grateful.

The second thing was that Hasan Dar's disguised guards had caught the poisoner Divyesh Patel.

Thanks to Bao's advice, they had been on the lookout for any strangers selling edible goods in the markets of Bhaktipur—and that was exactly what they found. One slight, nondescript, unprepossessing fellow who approached the Rani's kitchen staff with an enticing offer of fresh-caught river fish, plump and gleaming.

The Rani's staff dickered.

The slight fellow smiled when they came to accord, handing over his fish.

I daresay it took him by surprise when Hasan Dar's guards seized him, discreetly pushing up his sleeves to look for the tell-tale markings of tattoos on his forearms. By all accounts, Divyesh Patel did not fight or protest when they hustled him away. He was an assassin, not a warrior, and poison was his weapon.

My lady Amrita asked Bao to confirm his identity, and although he was a bit shaky on his feet, he did.

The little poisoner paled when he saw him in the throne room. "You!"

"Me," Bao agreed.

Divyesh Patel was indignant. "You betrayed *her*?"

"No," Bao said softly. "I traded a lie for the truth." He glanced at the Rani Amrita and her son, Ravindra. "There are two kinds of men in Kurugiri, highnesses. Those who sought to serve with their killing arts, and those caught in *her* web through no fault of their own. This one..." He gestured at the poisoner. "He is one of the former."

Amrita twined and steepled her fingers in a complex *mudra*, one that inspired trust. "Is that true?" she asked the fellow gently. "I beg of you, do not fear to answer. No one is beyond redemption."

The little poisoner coughed, bending over double and bringing his fist to his mouth. Bao swore and spun into action, his staff a blur as it swept in a horizontal arc. Something went flying and clattered on the floor. Bao's staff caught Divyesh Patel behind the knees, upending him. Before anyone else had a chance to react, he had the butt of his staff poised to crush the assassin's throat.

"What...?" Amrita was on her feet, her voice trembling slightly. "What was that?" I moved quickly to her side and she took my arm, her nails digging into my skin in an effort to maintain her composure. With her free arm, she held Ravindra close to her side.

"Poison dart, I believe," Hasan Dar said grimly, holding up the object that had gone flying, a hollow tube.

"Oh, gods!" She shivered.

"You want me to kill this one?" Bao inquired.

"No." The Rani's commander gestured to his guards to form a protective line between Amrita and the assassin. "Not until I've had a chance to question him at length."

Pinned beneath Bao's staff, Divyesh Patel flailed suddenly, his hands scrabbling at his throat. Bao swore again and gave him a sharp jab in the chest, but it was too late. The assassin hadn't been trying to escape. There was a pin-prick of blood on the side of his throat, and a tiny needle jutted from a ring on his right forefinger.

He'd taken his own life.

Whatever it was, the poison acted quickly. The fellow jerked once, then stiffened. A little froth came to his lips, and his eyes rolled back in his head.

"Is he...dead?" Ravindra whispered.

"Probably." Bao prodded the corpse with his staff, then glanced at Hasan Dar. "Better you cut his throat and make sure. He knows lots of poisons, this one. Maybe even one that makes it only *look* like he's dead." He leaned on his staff and exhaled hard, grinning wearily. "Lot of action for my first day out of bed."

Ravindra gazed at him with shining eyes. "I think you just saved my mother's life, Bao-ji!"

"I think you did," Amrita agreed. Releasing my arm, she approached

Bao and took his left hand in both of hers, pressing it warmly. "Thank you very much indeed for your swift and courageous action."

Under her lustrous regard, my incorrigible peasant-boy actually blushed. "You are welcome, highness." He shuffled his feet. "I hate poisoners. One of them killed me, you know. And...I fear you are only in danger because of Moirin and me. So I will do anything I can to protect you."

"And I am grateful for it," she said gravely, pressing his hand once more.

His blush deepened.

I raised my brows and smiled at him.

"What?" Bao scowled at me. "Don't smirk at me, Moirin. We have a lot of work to do if we're going to figure out how to save the Rani and her son."

"Yes, my hero," I said. "We do."

SIXTY-SIX

Around and around we went, trying to conceive of a plan that would get us up the path to Kurugiri without sustaining untenable losses, and deal with the problem of Kamadeva's diamond at the top.

Hasan Dar, Amrita, and Ravindra hadn't had any success, the latter chastened and made uncertain by the failure of his first plan.

Bao's knowledge was helpful, but it didn't eliminate the obstacles facing us. I listened as he discussed the treacherous path with Hasan Dar, sketching out the likeliest places for assassins to lay in waiting on a map based on his tattoos.

"The problem is that they will always have the higher ground," he said. "See, here, here, and here. We will always be coming around blind corners, where they can pick us off one by one."

I thought of an offer I had made Snow Tiger once when we faced an ambush—and a warning my mother had given me. "Unless they can't see us," I murmured.

Bao gave me a sharp look. "Your twilight."

I nodded.

"No." He shook his head. "No, Moirin. I will not risk you again."

"No, I do not like it either," Amrita said unhappily.

"What is she talking about?" Hasan Dar asked, bewildered.

It was easier to show him than explain. I had them close their eyes and summoned the twilight, wrapping it around Bao and me, then letting it fade before their open eyes. Ravindra and Hasan Dar stared in awe; the Rani Amrita, who had seen me call the twilight before, just looked worried.

"And you could kill a man thus concealed?" her commander asked. "Or Bao could?"

My mother's words echoed in my thoughts. *It is a grave gift and one never to be used lightly. Only to sustain life. Do you ever use it for sport or any idle cause, it will be stripped from you.*

Snow Tiger's, too, her voice gentle and firm as she refused my offer. *What you suggest is dishonorable.*

But when I glanced at Amrita's beautiful, worried face and her son's thin, clever one, I knew I was willing to take the risk. "I could. I cannot speak for Bao."

Bao frowned, fidgeting with the bands of steel that reinforced his bamboo fighting-staff. "I would have no trouble killing those men who serve *them* willingly," he said. "They are assassins who kill by stealth, and it is fitting that they should die thus. But I would not like to kill those who were trapped as I was."

In the end, it remained a moot point, for we could devise no plan for dealing with Kamadeva's diamond.

"I could accompany you," Amrita said quietly. "I am not affected by it, at least not with Jagrati wielding it."

"*No!*" Four voices spoke in emphatic unison.

Bao reckoned we had a few more days' grace before the Falconer and the Spider Queen decided that Divyesh Patel had failed and sent a new assassin in his place. After our initial attempts at group strategy failed, Bao suggested in private that he and I go alone. Since my *diadh-anam* had been twinned, I could hold him in the twilight as easily as myself. If I could hold it long enough, the two of us alone could approach Kurugiri without ever being seen, without alerting the Falconer's assassins.

"We could steal Kamadeva's diamond rather than take it by force," he mused, stroking my hair.

Lying in his arms, I shook my head. "I don't trust myself around it. Do *you?*"

"I don't know," Bao admitted. "Here, with you... yes. I walked away from it once. But..."

"What if Jagrati got me to betray myself utterly, Bao?" I shuddered. "What if she sent *me* against my lady Amrita and her son? *I* can summon the twilight. *I* know where the hidden room is located."

"And you are rather deadly with a bow," he added. "No, you're right. It's too dangerous." He toyed with my hair, which had grown out well below my shoulders, but was still much shorter than it had been. "Why did you cut it, Moirin?"

"It wasn't my idea."

His brows furrowed. "Whose was it?"

For the first time, I told Bao the whole of what had befallen me after the Great Khan's betrayal—the journey and the whole long, awful ordeal in Vralia, the chafing chains that bound my spirit as surely as my flesh, the Patriarch and his incessant demands that I confess the litany of my sins, Luba and her shears, cold water, and lye, the endless scrubbing of the temple floor, my knees aching, the ever-present threat of being stoned to death.

I wept.

Bao held me. "I could kill them ten times over for that!" he said fiercely, his breath warm against my temple. "Do you want me to?"

"No." I sniffled and laughed. "No, I don't ever want to go back there."

"How did you escape?"

I told him about Valentina and Aleksei, although not the part about Aleksei and Naamah's blessing.

Bao suspected it anyway, regarding me with a wry look. "I swear, Moirin, you fall in love as easily as other people fall out of a boat."

"I don't!" I protested.

"You do."

None too gently, I tugged on a hank of his longish hair. "Why did *you* let it grow? I thought it gave enemies a handhold in combat."

He didn't answer right away. I withdrew a little, propping myself on one elbow and watching his face, watching Bao decide whether or not he was ready to talk about his time in Kurugiri.

"*She* liked it that way," he said eventually.

"Jagrati?" I asked softly. Bao nodded, a muscle in his jaw twitching. "Was it terrible there?"

"No," he said after another long silence. "Or maybe it was. I don't know how to talk about it. I was in a terrible place inside myself while I was there, thinking you were dead, thinking I had only myself to blame for it." He shrugged. "It was a strange place. So much opulence, so much stolen treasure, hidden away in a stark fortress. Between *her* spell and the opium, it seems like a fever-dream now."

"How did you get there?" I wanted to keep him talking.

"There's a cauldron that hangs on a chain and a winch from a plateau above the trail," Bao said. "I heard about it during my journey there. I petitioned Tarik Khaga to take me into his service. A day later, someone came to blindfold me and lead me through the maze. I thought..." He shrugged again. "There is a kind of honor among thieves and thugs when it comes to the rules of combat. I thought perhaps there was among assassins, too. When I was granted an audience, I said I had come to claim you. I offered to fight any man among them for the right to take you away with me." He gave me a sidelong look. "Stupid plan, huh?"

"Better than none," I said. "So Jagrati ensorceled you instead?"

Bao shook his head. "Not right away, no. My story, our story... it wasn't what *she* expected. It intrigued her. *She's* the one who rules Kurugiri, you know. Not him."

"I know," I said. "I saw."

"So." He blew out his breath. "No one had ever attempted to rescue someone they had taken before. She thought it was a piece of irony that the only living soul to do so had come on a fool's errand. She wanted me to know it. She let me search to my heart's content, questioning anyone I liked. She even gave me access to the harem. And there was no trace of you anywhere. By the end of the first day,

I knew it must be true. The Great Khan had killed you, and sent me away in vain."

I stroked Bao's arm, not knowing what to say.

He glanced at the vivid zig-zag markings on his skin. "*Then* she unveiled Kamadeva's diamond. I didn't even care by that time. I was drowning in despair. Might as well drown in false desire and opium instead. And there were fights there, lots of fights. It suited my mood. I'd lost Master Lo, and then I'd lost you. The only two people I ever truly loved. I'd died a hero, and wasted the life that was given back to me on stupid choices. Running away from you, marrying Erdene. I didn't care if I got killed again."

I took a long, deep breath. "I am very, very glad that you weren't."

"Me too." Bao fell quiet once more.

I waited a while before prompting him. "So the Falconer's assassins quarrel amongst themselves?"

"Not exactly." The muscle in his jaw twitched again. "Sometimes Jagrati would choose a favorite and keep him for days on end. Other times, she liked for us to fight for the honor of her favors. To the death, if she was in a foul mood."

"Oh." I didn't know what to say about that, either.

"I don't know how long I'd been there when I felt something change," Bao mused, touching his chest. "You, your spark was back, only it was all tangled with opium dreams and the spell of that cursed diamond, and I didn't know what to believe."

I nodded. "I felt the same way the other day."

"You understand, then." He looked relieved. "Jagrati does not like to lose what is hers. I do not know if she suspected the truth, but she set out to convince me that it must be a lie of some foul magic. And... I believed it. Because I was so very sure you were dead, and it had been so very long." Bao shook his head. "When *I* died, even though it was only minutes or hours, it seemed to me that days passed in Fengdu, in the spirit world. You had been gone for months. Whatever had come back, it couldn't be Moirin. The other day in the meadow, I would gladly have killed the thing wearing your face."

I shuddered. "And I am very, very glad that you didn't."

Bao shuddered, too. "So am I. I am quite sure it would have driven me mad. But... then I began to doubt." He touched his chest again. "Your spark, I'd felt it calling to mine in the meadow. I had to know the truth. And the rest, you know." He turned to regard me, a rare vulnerability behind his eyes. "Do you hate me for it?"

"No," I murmured. "Of course not! You crossed the Abode of the Gods to find me, you dared the Falcon in his eyrie and the Spider Queen in her lair. It wasn't your fault it was all a lie. As for the rest..." I smiled ruefully. "You saw how vulnerable *I* was to Kamadeva's diamond. How can I blame *you*?"

"Well." Bao smiled a little. "Desire. It *is* a particular weakness of yours, Moirin." He laid one hand on my cheek, cupping it. "And a particular strength, too."

I leaned upward to kiss his lips in reply, softly, lightly. It felt like enough for now. Enough to feel his *diadh-anam* entwine blissfully with mine. Naamah's gift did not often counsel patience, but in these days, it did. The shadow of the Spider Queen lay between us, and there was too much yet to be done.

"So." Bao cleared his throat. "Shall we speak of *your* royal lady? I must admit, I'd rather."

"It's not what you think," I said to him.

The acerbic glint returned to his eyes, familiar and welcome. "It seems I've heard those words before. Only this time, there isn't a dragon to blame."

"No." I traced my finger down the strong column of his throat, letting my fingertip rest in the hollow, feeling the sturdy beat of his pulse. "But there is a diamond, which left me much disturbed; and my lady Amrita does not like to see anyone suffer. Out of the goodness of her heart, she has shown me many kindnesses." I kissed him again. "That was one of them."

"The Rani must care for you very much to have endured such a hardship," Bao said in a grave tone.

I thumped his chest with the heel of my hand. "You are insufferable!"

He laughed; and I could not help but be glad, dizzyingly glad, that despite everything that had happened, despite everything that had befallen us, despite the dangers and challenges we yet faced, laughter endured.

I had a feeling there would be precious little of it in the days to come.

SIXTY-SEVEN

I was right.

The next gambit from Kurugiri came sooner than expected, and it drove any thought of laughter or levity far, far from anyone's mind.

We were in another interminable counsel session in which no progress was made and everyone was miserable and frustrated. The problem of Kamadeva's diamond remained. Our young strategist Ravindra pushed chess pieces fruitlessly around the board. Hasan Dar pored over the maps he had drawn based on Bao's information—a fairly detailed map of the path and an outline of the fortress itself. Having exhausted his stores of knowledge, Bao had little left to offer. Amrita was quiet and worried, and I daresay I was much the same.

For a brief moment, it was almost a relief when one of the guardsmen interrupted the meeting.

"Hasan-ji," he said tentatively to his commander. "You said to report anything strange?"

The commander's handsome head came up. "Yes?"

"It is the night-soil collectors," the guard said in an apologetic tone. "The bucket-men. I am quite sure six came at dawn, but it seems to me only five have departed." He shrugged. "It has been some time now."

Bao tensed. "That is not good," he said quietly to Hasan Dar. "It is how Jagrati stole Kamadeva's diamond from the temple in the first place. It is a ploy any man serving *her* might use. Usually you pay no attention to those you deem beneath notice. One is now loose in the palace."

Hasan Dar swore and pounded the table with his fist, jarring Ravindra's chess pieces out of place. "In broad light of day again! Damn them. Go." He pointed at Bao. "Take the Rani and her son and your *dakini* to the hidden room." His voice turned grim. "Guard them well while we search. You seem to have a knack for it."

Bao inclined his head, no words of assent needed. We fled, Hasan Dar uttering curt orders behind us.

The concealed doorway to the hidden room was located on a landing between the first and second floors of the palace. At night, it was guarded discreetly from above and below. During the day, it was guarded not at all, the better to protect its secret. Since he had saved my lady Amrita from the poisoner, Bao had been entrusted with the secret of the hidden room. Other than Bao and me, only the guards and the Rani's most trusted attendants knew of its existence.

Even so, I felt the space between my shoulder blades itch and tingle at the thought of an assassin loose in the palace.

Bao drew back the tapestry of the goddess Durga riding a tiger, throwing open the hidden doorway. "Go quick! Hurry, hurry!"

Amrita went first, towing a stumbling Ravindra behind her. I followed them into the steep, narrow stairway. Behind me, Bao closed the door and shot the bolt, following close on my heels. I breathed a sigh of relief.

Safe, I thought.

This time I was wrong.

In the forest, in the green, wild spaces I knew so well, I might have sensed the fellow awaiting us, sensed his presence, sensed his intention. Not here, where my senses were confounded by thick marble and man-made space. Trapped in the stairwell, I couldn't even see.

All I heard was my lady Amrita's gasp as the assassin fell on her. One gasp, quickly choked.

Ahead of me, Ravindra.

Acting on panicked instinct, I drew a deep breath into my lungs, summoning the twilight with it. I blew it out, wrapping it around the boy and myself.

I don't think Ravindra even noticed. Without hesitation, the boy gave a piercing shout and flung himself against the man attempting to garrote his mother, a cord wrapped tight around her throat and throttling her. Ravindra sank his teeth into the assassin's hand, biting him hard and deep.

Bao had said it felt like being touched by a ghost. I could not imagine what it felt like to be *bitten* by one.

The assassin howled, dropping his garrote and glancing around in terror.

Scrambling out of the stairwell, I expanded my cloak of twilight and swirled it around Amrita, and the assassin released her with an involuntary hiss.

"Moirin!" Bao shouted behind me. "Get them out of the way, get them safe!"

"Come, come, come!" I whispered urgently, tugging them both to the farthest corner of the small room. Ravindra was trembling with a mix of fear and fury, and Amrita with shock, touching her abraded throat. I wrapped my arms around them both, praying I could keep them safe in the twilight, praying Bao could protect us all. In the twilight, I could actually sense the presence of Kamadeva's diamond in the distance as though it were another kind of *diadh-anam*, a god's bright spirit turned to malevolent purpose.

Bao sidled warily into the room, his staff held in a defensive pose; and that alone told me his opponent was good.

"Traitor!" The fellow spat on the ground. He had regained his composure in remarkable time. "I should have killed you in Kurugiri." His hands snatched at his belt, and in the blink of an eye, he had throwing knives fanned like playing cards in his left hand, and one poised to throw in his right. The blades twinkled like stars in the twilight. He bared his teeth in a smile. "I'll enjoy doing it now."

"You think so?" Bao feinted at him.

A flurry of glittering blades flew from the assassin's hands, one after another, quicker than the eye could follow. Bao's staff whirled, making the air whistle, and then he hurled himself sideways out of the knives' path in a horizontal spinning move that didn't seem humanly possible, landing with his battle-grin in place.

"Got more?" he asked insolently.

Unfortunately, the assassin did. He flicked a blade low, forcing Bao to parry it awkwardly, and then flicked another blade high at his unguarded face.

Amrita gave a low cry of dismay, and I tightened my arms around her and her son, fearing for all of us.

But Bao was already in motion, flinging himself backward onto the floor and rolling in a somersault. Instead of coming up into a fighting stance, he stayed in a low crouch, his staff sweeping along the floor to strike hard at the assassin's ankles while another flurry of blades flew harmlessly over his head to clatter against the wall.

The blow didn't knock the fellow off his feet, but it staggered him; and in a heartbeat, Bao was up. The fellow caught himself before Bao could strike, a lone throwing knife held up in warning.

"Heh." Bao's grin widened. "Last one, huh?"

"Maybe." The assassin's hand went to his belt again, scattering a handful of bright, sharp objects on the floor.

Bao glanced down and swore, then glanced up in time to jerk out of the way of the last blade as it flew through the air. For a moment, the men regarded each other. I didn't know what history lay between them, and I wasn't sure I wanted to. "You're done," Bao said simply, shifting his staff into an offensive pose.

Without a word, the assassin turned and dashed for the balcony.

And the purpose of the objects he'd thrown came clear as Bao went after him. They were shaped like a child's jack-toys, only larger, with long, wickedly sharp tines, forcing Bao to kick them out of the way or suffer a punctured foot. They didn't delay him long, but it was enough time for the fellow to gain the balcony and vault over it. In the garden far below, monkeys shrieked and chattered. Bao peered over the railing.

"Is it safe?" I asked him, my voice shaking a little.

"Yes." Bao sounded subdued. I released the twilight, the daylit world returning in a rush. "Best your highnesses do not look, though. It isn't pleasant."

"Is he dead?" Ravindra asked fiercely.

"Oh, yes." Bao nodded. "This time, I am very certain, young highness."

"Oh, gods!" My lady Amrita's lovely voice was hoarse from her near-garroting, and there were tears in it. "We were supposed to be safe here! How did he find this room?" Tears spilled from her eyes, streaking her face. "I cannot believe any of my people would betray us willingly!"

"Mama-ji, don't cry!" Ravindra whispered, stroking her arm.

"I don't think they did, highness." Bao's tone was as gentle as I'd ever heard it. "Not willingly, anyway."

She met his sympathetic gaze. "That's worse, isn't it?"

He nodded. "That one's name was Zoka. If he has another, I never heard it. He was a bad man, highness, one of the worst. He liked to hurt people. I am afraid he may have hurt one of yours."

"Ah, no!" The sorrow in Amrita's voice made my heart ache.

To everyone's sorrow, Bao was right.

Hasan Dar's guards found Zoka's victim in a linen storeroom in the servants' quarters. She was one of the Rani's trusted attendants, a sweet girl named Sameera who took pride in her hair-dressing skills and often sang as she worked. She couldn't have been much more than sixteen years old.

She was dead, garroted, the flesh of her slender throat swollen around the ligature mark.

And young Sameera had been tortured before she died. On her left hand, only her thumb and forefinger remained. The other three were bloody stumps with ragged bits of bone protruding from the fresh wounds. Three delicate severed fingers lay scattered on the floor of the storeroom.

Although Hasan Dar begged Amrita not to look, she insisted on it. She looked for a long, long time.

"Poor child," she murmured, stooping to touch the girl's maimed hand. "You tried to protect me, didn't you? You held out as long as you could." Raising the girl's hand to her lips, she kissed it. "Surely, you will be reborn a warrior, my little brave heart."

I wiped tears from my eyes.

Everyone was silent.

In the silence, the Rani Amrita stood. Twice in recent days, she had been frightened, badly frightened. Twice, she had nearly been killed.

Now she was angry.

I would not have thought my lovely, laughing lady Amrita could be terrible in her anger; but she was. There was a vein of dignity and quiet strength that ran deep beneath her kindness and charm, and this deed had tapped it.

"Enough!" Her voice rang, and her dark eyes flashed. "This is unacceptable. I will not remain a prisoner in my own palace, starting at shadows. I will not allow my people to be tortured and killed for their loyalty. No more fear, no more suffering. *Enough*. I do not care if we have not found the perfect plan. We are going to Kurugiri. *I* am going to Kurugiri. Once and for all, we will put an end to this!"

Ravindra swallowed hard, but he did not protest.

No one did.

I glanced at Bao, leaning on his staff. He nodded at me, promising whatever aid was required.

I glanced at Ravindra, thinking how I had flung the twilight around him.

I thought about Jagrati and Kamadeva's diamond, and how I had been able to sense them in the twilight.

I thought about how Amrita had placed herself between me and Jagrati in the meadow, her hands raised in a warding *mudra*, holding the Spider Queen herself at bay.

"My lady Amrita," I said softly. "I think I know how to take Kamadeva's diamond out of play."

Filled with fierce determination, Amrita turned her lustrous gaze on me. "Tell me."

I did.

SIXTY-EIGHT

No one loved the plan, and our young chess-master Ravindra liked it least of all.

"It's *very* dangerous, Mama-ji!" he said in an unwontedly frightened tone. "What if Moirin…" He made a helpless gesture. "Falls victim again?"

"I won't," I murmured. "Not this way."

"She won't," Amrita said with conviction. "Not with Bao-ji at her side, not with *me* there. I will not allow it."

Bao met my gaze. "If we're to survive the maze, it will require your magic after all, Moirin—even before we reach Kurugiri. There's no other way. We'll have to kill in stealth, you and I."

"I know," I said steadily. "And there is no honor in it. But I do believe that the stakes are high enough that the Maghuin Dhonn Herself will forgive me."

Ravindra's eyes narrowed. "Are you sure?"

"No, young highness," I said honestly to him. "Very little in life is certain. But I am quite sure that if we navigate the maze, I can find Jagrati and encompass her in the twilight, rendering her and Kamadeva's diamond invisible for a time."

"A time," he echoed.

"A time is long enough for us to secure the fortress," Hasan Dar said in a pragmatic voice. "That is all we need. Once it is done, there will be too many of us for her to contend with."

"Once we have gained entrance to the fortress, *she* will make her stand in a smaller place." Bao pointed at the drawing of Kurugiri's layout. "Here in the throne room is my guess. We will not be able to fit more than a score of men in there."

"How many can she control at once?" Hasan Dar inquired. "Can she force them to turn on their fellows?"

"I don't know," Bao admitted. "Only that the compulsion to do her bidding is powerful, but it can be overridden."

"How?"

"Love." Bao glanced at me, eyes crinkling in a smile of rare sweetness. "It is a force strong enough that it allowed me to walk away from her. It allowed the Rani to protect Moirin. Kamadeva's diamond commands a powerful desire, but there is no love in Jagrati, only rage and hatred. So. I suggest you meditate on those you love, commander, and advise your men to do the same, whether it be their wives and sons and daughters, mothers and fathers, priests and mentors, or their love for and loyalty to the Rani Amrita herself. Love, and love alone, is the force that will allow you to resist."

It was not a speech anyone would have expected Bao to make, me included. Hasan Dar inclined his head in surprised respect. "I will do that, Bao-ji."

"Good." Bao returned his attention to the map. "If I may make one more suggestion, I would advise dividing your men into two companies. Jagrati will have Lord Khaga and every last man standing guarding her." He tapped the map. "The harem will be unguarded."

The commander followed his thoughts. "So if everything else goes wrong, we can still rescue those poor unfortunates."

Bao nodded. "Jagrati allows Lord Khaga his harem as a sop to his pride, a place he can go to prove his manhood when she denies him to dally with his assassins. Whatever else happens, we should plan to free the harem."

"How many are there?"

"Counting the children?" Bao frowned in thought. "Twenty-five or thirty, perhaps. I do not know for sure. I was only allowed there once to search for Moirin."

"There are children in that place?" Amrita asked in horror.

"Yes, highness." Bao was silent a moment. "I do not think they were treated cruelly, at least not as children. The Falconer finds them distasteful, and avoids them. Even a woman bearing a child is repulsive to him." His mouth tightened. "I heard it said that in the harem, it was every woman's goal to conceive a son."

"Why?" I asked, perplexed.

He looked askance at me. "If a woman bears him a son, the Falconer would not return to her bed. And she would not have to worry about a daughter growing up and being forced to share his."

My stomach churned. "And you said it wasn't *terrible* there?"

"I was in a very dark place within myself, Moirin," Bao said quietly. "The hatred that Jagrati carries within her, it is like a sickness. I am still learning to live in brightness again."

"It is not your fault, Bao-ji!" Ravindra said with indignant loyalty, his narrow hands forming a *mudra* of reassurance. "The gods always test the strongest heroes, the ones they love best in the world. Surely you passed!"

Bao smiled at him with genuine affection. "You are quite the hero yourself, young highness, rushing to protect your mother as you did! It would have gone far worse for me if you hadn't."

"Truly?" Ravindra flushed with pleasure.

"Truly."

Thus for better or worse, our plan was established. It would take some days to assemble a sufficient force and arrange for supplies and other necessities, such as a battering ram that would have to be carried through the winding maze on foot.

In the meantime, we lived in fear.

Hasan Dar insisted that the Rani and her son continue to sleep in the hidden room. It made sense, for although the assassin Zoka had tortured the secret out of poor Sameera, he had taken it to his death.

Still, I could not blame either of them for being reluctant to return there.

"Would it help if Moirin and I stayed with you?" Bao offered. "I am sure it is against protocol, but..."

My lady Amrita fingered her bruised throat. "Yes," she said gratefully. "It would help very much, thank you."

I didn't think there was room in the small space for another bed. "We can put a pallet of blankets on the floor between you."

"Even better!" Ravindra clapped his hands together with glee. "Bao-ji can share my bed, and Moirin can share yours, Mama-ji. It will be as though we were a large family, like your family in Galanka, eh?" The notion delighted him. "Yes, I will pretend Bao is my older brother, and you will pretend Moirin is your little sister."

"I don't think—" I began diplomatically.

"Would that make you happy, jewel of my heart?" Amrita asked her son. He nodded. She summoned a weary smile. "Then if Moirin and Bao do not mind, we shall do so, and have a game of pretending."

Bao made a show of weighing the matter. "Do you snore, young highness?" he asked in a serious tone. "Because I cannot abide snoring. Do you steal the blankets at night? Because I do not like to be cold."

Giggling, Ravindra shook his head. "No, older brother! I promise, I do not do either thing."

Amrita touched my hand. "Do *you* mind?"

I smiled at her. "What do you think, my lady?"

She gave me a sidelong glance, a hint of her familiar, amused sparkle returning to her eyes. "I think I am very glad to see my son happy in the midst of this nightmare. I think your bad boy has a very large heart." She caught my hand and squeezed it fondly. "And I think you do not mind at all, *little sister*."

Of course I didn't.

Even so, my nerves were strung tight that evening as Bao and I ascended the narrow stairway to the hidden room to ensure it was safe, both of us wrapped in the twilight. The memory of the assassin

Zoka's attack was fresh in my mind. Bao searched every corner, peered under the beds, over the balcony, his staff at the ready. Not until he nodded at me did I kindle the lamps and release the twilight, the bright-burning wicks turning from cool silver to flickering gold.

Safe; we were safe.

This time it was true.

It was a little bit funny, a little bit awkward, and altogether sweet as we turned our backs on one another to change into sleeping attire. The beds creaked as we climbed into them, a comforting, homely sound.

I was careful not to touch my lady Amrita, not wanting to presume on her affection.

"Oh, don't be foolish, Moirin," she chided me, laying her head on my shoulder. "All of us need all the comfort we can find. I am glad you are here."

Relieved, I held her. "So am I."

Her dark eyes glimmered at me, and she put her lips close to my ear. "Listen to our boys."

Ravindra was telling Bao a tale about one of his favorite Bhodistani heroes, the great archer and warrior Arjuna, who was reluctant to do battle because of the many deaths it would cause. "But Lord Krishna convinced him it was his duty to protect his people," he said in a solemn tone. "I think that is why my mother has decided she must go to Kurugiri. Do you think you could convince her to let me come, Bao-ji? You said I was a great help today."

"So you were, little brother," Bao said soothingly. "But you have a different responsibility. You must remain here with your tutor to remind us all what we are fighting for."

Ravindra sighed. "Because I am too young?"

"You are very brave, but you are not a warrior yet." Bao tickled him. "For example, warriors do not giggle."

It was a boy's laughter, helpless and unfettered, reminding me once more to be grateful that even in the midst of fear and darkness, love and laughter could survive. Amrita smiled quietly in the dim moonlight spilling from the balcony, her thoughts echoing mine. "I think your Bao is good for my Ravindra," she murmured. "My son is such a serious boy. It is good to hear him laugh, especially during such a dreadful time."

"I think your Ravindra is good for my Bao," I said softly in reply. "He is helping him learn to live in brightness again."

Amrita shivered against me. "I pray to all the gods that we are given the chance to do so," she said in a low voice.

I thought of Sameera's severed fingers lying on the storeroom floor, of the shifting fires of Kamadeva's diamond, and Jagrati's terrible beauty; and I shivered, too. I held Amrita closer, breathing in the flowers-and-spice scent of her skin, and kissed her hair.

If I failed her in Kurugiri, I would never, ever forgive myself.

"I pray so, too, my lady," I murmured. "I pray so, too."

SIXTY-NINE

T hree days later, we departed for Kurugiri.

Although he had wept at their first parting, this time Ravindra was dry-eyed and grave, every inch the solemn young prince once more. The gravity of the situation had become all too real to him, and I think he understood that if his mother didn't return, he would be called upon to rule their people in a time of fear. He stooped to touch our feet in a gesture of respect, and embraced us all in turn.

"You will do your best to keep my mother safe, Bao-ji?" he asked.

"I will, highness." Bao pressed his palms together and bowed. "Moirin will, too," he added. "She is as skilled an archer as your Arjuna, you know."

It won the faintest of smiles from the boy. "Although I do not believe it, it is good to hear anyway."

Last of all, Ravindra embraced his mother. Amrita held him tenderly, whispering in his ear. When she turned away, there were tears in *her* eyes.

I closed mine, whispering a soft prayer to the Maghuin Dhonn Herself to grant me strength.

I would need a very great deal of it.

Once more, we set out in procession through the streets of Bhaktipur. This time the mood was altogether somber. We were riding to war, not to a parley. There was no hidden gambit to give us the upper hand. So much of our plan hinged on my ability to summon the twilight and hold it for a very long time, to use it to kill with stealth in the deadly maze, praying all the while that the Maghuin Dhonn Herself did not withdraw Her gift from me for using it thusly. If She did, I would be useless when we reached Kurugiri.

My lady Amrita had teased me once about carrying the weight of the world on my shoulders, and today it felt like it.

Folk in the street bowed as we passed, low and deep. Some went to their knees, pressing their brows to the ground. Many of them had been afraid for their much-loved Rani the first time.

This time, all of them were.

Beside me, Bao breathed the Five Styles as he rode, his expression at once fierce and calm. His *diadh-anam* burned as bright and clear as a bonfire within him, calling to mine. I took heart from it. Surely, if the Maghuin Dhonn Herself disapproved of what we meant to do, Her spark would not shine so brightly.

Although we hadn't done anything yet.

Retracing our steps, we made camp in the same meadow the first evening. I could not help but remember the last time we had been there, all of us defeated and dispirited in the wake of our failure, and me racked with unholy desire, shuddering to the marrow of my bones with it, Jagrati's predatory face swimming before my eyes.

I was afraid of her, and afraid of myself, too.

In the privacy of the tent I shared with my lady Amrita and Bao, I prayed to Naamah, begging her to have mercy on her errant daughter, begging her to let me keep her gift a blessing, and not a curse.

"I have tried to use it well, brightest of ladies," I whispered. "I know I have not always been wise or strong, but I have always tried. I am still trying. Please, help me."

In response, I had a sense of Naamah's grace enveloping me like a cloak, filled with warmth and love and desire; but there was regret in it, too. Her gift was a double-edged sword that cut both ways. Not even she could make it otherwise.

But there was another offer the bright lady Naamah could make, and I felt it, words rising through my consciousness like bubbles from the eddies of a clear-running stream, each one perfect and glistening.

One by one, the words were strung together to form a single, terrifying query, spoken as clearly to me as Naamah had ever spoken through me.

Do you wish me to take it from you?

I caught my breath, my skin prickling with awe. Tears stung my eyes; and whether they were tears of terror or relief, I couldn't have said. There was sorrow and curiosity behind the offer, but it was genuine.

Naamah could withdraw her gift from me.

My heart ached at the thought, and my *diadh-anam* flared in alarm. The Maghuin Dhonn Herself did not wish it so.

Neither did I.

I gazed at Bao, at his familiar face with its high, wide cheekbones, dark eyes glittering above them. And at my lovely lady Amrita, who gazed back at me with worried perplexity. I thought about all the people in my life I had loved and desired, from my lost Cillian slain too soon to my sweet boy Aleksei—and all that lay between them. Even the ill-advised but compelling Raphael de Mereliot with his healer's hands, and, of course, my beautiful, mercurial lady Jehanne. My valiant princess Snow Tiger, trusting me enough to reveal an unexpected playful streak that had delighted me so.

I could not betray those memories. And for whatever reason Naamah had seen fit to grant her gift to a child of the Maghuin Dhonn when she called my father to my mother, there must be some purpose in it.

"No," I murmured. "No. Please, do not take it away from me, goddess."

Naamah did not. I felt her presence fade, leaving her gift intact.

I sighed with profound relief.

"Moirin, who in the world were you talking to?" Bao inquired.

"Naamah," I said honestly. "I think...I think she offered to take her gift away from me. And I refused." I swallowed hard. "I hope that was not a very bad mistake."

Bao came over and put his strong arms around me, holding me hard. I leaned against him, feeling the steady beat of his heart, the bright flame of his *diadh-anam* entwining with mine. "Moirin without her eternal and perplexing desires would not be Moirin," he whispered against my hair. "You did the right thing."

"I think so, too," Amrita said firmly. "It is never wise to refuse a true gift of the gods. Moirin…do your gods often speak to you?"

"No." I searched for words, and found there weren't any big enough. All I could do was clear my throat. "No, my lady. Not like this."

She smiled a little. "Still, you are quite special to them, I think. I knew it the moment I saw you protecting that girl in the street. You were shaking with fever and you could barely sit up straight in the saddle, but you were not going to let those men harm her. And as sick as you were, you still looked like you'd stepped out of an ancient tale from when gods and goddesses roamed the earth."

It made me smile, too. "You are very kind, my lady."

Amrita laid one hand on Bao's shoulder and leaned in to kiss my cheek. "And you are very frightened, dear one. But you are stronger than you know. You will be strong enough to face Jagrati, I am sure of it."

I prayed she was right.

All of us slept uneasily that night, the camp on high alert, ringed about with anxious sentries. Bao positioned himself before the flap of the tent and passed the night in a restless doze. Twice, there were shouts in the night that brought him to his feet, his staff at the ready, while I reached desperately for the twilight, flinging it around myself and Amrita. But they were false alarms sounded by our uneasy guards.

There was no attack. Kurugiri, it seemed, had gone on the defensive.

The next day, we passed through the meadow where we had held our parley. As a precaution, Hasan Dar sent a company of scouts ahead to sweep through the spruce copse where our ambush had hidden, but it was empty. We filed past the Sleeping Calf Rock and began to ascend higher into the mountains, the air growing thinner and colder, pockets of snow in the windswept crags.

I breathed the Breath of Embers Glowing to warm myself, and the Breath of Earth's Pulse to center myself, letting my awareness expand as we navigated the narrow paths. I didn't sense anyone ahead of us, but I wasn't certain.

That night, we made camp on an arid plateau where the ground was so hard it took all the men's strength to pound the tent-pegs in place. Amrita was shivering in the cold, her teeth chattering. Although she didn't utter a word of complaint, she was unused to such hardship. Beneath thick woolen blankets, I did my best to warm her while Bao slept stretched before the tent-flap.

On the following day, we reached the base of Kurugiri.

The mountain seemed taller and more foreboding than I remembered, jutting into the icy blue sky. The southern face of it was sheer; indeed, only the eastern face with its complicated labyrinth was scalable. We worked our way toward it, feeling the shadow of Kurugiri looming over us. From this perspective, the fortress itself wasn't even visible, but every one of us knew it was there.

Dusk was falling by the time we passed the hanging cauldron of petition on its endless chain and reached the entrance to the maze, shadows slanting over the fissured slope. There must have been almost a dozen potential paths emerging from the maze, but Bao went unerringly toward the fifth one we encountered.

"Here." He pointed to a faint mark etched into the stone, as high as a man could reach, then pushed up his right sleeve. The same intricate symbol of curlicues and strokes was tattooed above the crook of his elbow, beginning the zig-zag path. "See?"

Hasan Dar nodded. "We'll have to camp here as best we can," he said. "Set out at dawn. You're sure it can be climbed in a day?"

Bao leaned on his staff. "I'm sure it *can* be done, yes. Whether or not *we* can do it is another matter. Depends on what we find in there."

"*I* am sure of it," Amrita said in a decisive tone, shivering. "Anything to get out of this cold!"

It made the guards smile, which I daresay was her intention; and it was the last cause anyone had to smile, for it was a truly miserable night. Due to the rocky terrain, we were unable to erect the tents and had to sleep in the open air, and it was perishing cold. But even worse was the menacing maze stretching above us, filled with possible assassins who might slip through under cover of night. Not wanting to take any chances, Hasan Dar posted sentries along every egress.

Although they were brave and loyal fellows, it was a frightening duty; and the mountain seemed like a living thing in the darkness, determined to heighten our fears. Every time a pebble shifted, someone raised an alarm. All of us slept fitfully, Bao and I with my lady Amrita between us, sharing our warmth with her, feeling horribly exposed and vulnerable all throughout the night.

Still, there was no attack.

Kurugiri was waiting.

In the dim light of predawn, I felt tired and bleary-eyed, and not at all heroic. Gazing at the deep, narrow channels etched into the mountainside, I reminded myself that I had done such a thing before in the Stone Forest.

But that had been a gentle, lovely place compared to this stark maze, and we had been able to draw our enemies away. We had had myriad paths to choose from, and a dragon to guide us.

Here, there was only one path that would not lead us astray, and we would be trapped within its confines with assassins waiting for us.

While Hasan Dar ordered his men into line, I sat cross-legged and breathed the cycle of the Five Styles. Bao sat beside me and did the same, his knee brushing against mine. I expanded my senses and drew strength from earth's pulse, from trees growing, from the memory of ocean's rolling waves, from embers glowing, and the wind's sigh.

I thought about Master Lo Feng, who had taught us both. What Master Lo had taught me had made me stronger and wiser, better able to focus the gift of the Maghuin Dhonn Herself, using it as it was meant to be used.

I felt his loss keenly, and wished he were here to counsel us, to tell me that I had done the right thing in refusing Naamah's offer.

Too soon, all was in readiness. Bao and I would take the lead, a handful of guards behind us, followed by the fellows carrying the battering ram. Hasan Dar had placed the Rani in the middle of the line lest we find ourselves ambushed from behind, and he would guard her himself, commanding from the center. Every man under his command had a copy of the map we had drawn based on Bao's tattooed arms.

"Are you ready?" Hasan Dar asked, his handsome face taut with apprehension.

Bao's gaze slid sideways toward me, his staff held loosely in his hands. "Moirin?"

I took a deep breath and stood. "Aye, I'm ready." I strode toward my mount Lady, and swung myself astride.

Bao followed suit, thrusting his bamboo staff through a thong strapped across his back. I checked my yew-wood bow and quiver, testing the draw before slinging it over my shoulder. I glanced behind us, seeing the long line of guards, the Rani Amrita looking small and cold and determined in their midst. Faint streaks of pink were emerging on the eastern horizon, making the scudding clouds blush.

I looked at Bao, my stubborn, irrepressible peasant-boy with the vast heart. "I love you, you know."

"Uh-huh." He flashed his battle-grin at me. "I love you, too, Moirin," he said, adding a familiar warning. "So try not to get yourself killed, huh?"

I smiled back at him. "You, too. Once was enough."

At my word, Hasan Dar ordered his men to avert their gazes so that I might summon the twilight to hide us from all eyes. I took another deep breath and called it, wrapping it around Bao and me.

The world turned soft and silver-dim. Behind us, there were cries of wonder at finding us vanished. In the distant heights, I felt the flicker of Kamadeva's diamond calling to me.

I ignored it, focusing on the path before us. "Let's go."

SEVENTY

The path was so narrow we were forced to ride single file, and its walls were steep and high. I'd never felt so claustrophobic in a natural place before, painfully aware of the fact that we were trapped here, that if I lost my grip on the twilight, Bao and I would be the first targets. With a hundred men behind us, there was no chance of escape.

Bao took the lead, consulting the tattoo on his right arm, matching symbols at every fork of the path.

Every path not taken made my skin tingle, for there could be assassins lurking within them, waiting to fall on our company from the side. It was unlikely, since they could do the most damage obstructing the path before us, but it was possible. And I had to keep my awareness focused on the path ahead. I couldn't afford to spread myself too thin.

According to Bao, there had been seventeen men in Jagrati's thrall, and all but two were highly trained killers.

Five had been killed during their escape from the meadow, and Bao had left. The poisoner and the fellow lurking in the Rani's hidden room were dead.

That left nine men, plus the Falconer himself. When I counted the numbers, it seemed a ridiculous few to inspire such fear... but in the maze, at the forefront of our small army, it didn't seem foolish at all.

Left, then right, then left, and left again. All the turns made me feel disoriented and dizzy. I shook my head, concentrating. The call of Kamadeva's diamond grew stronger as we climbed, the rich hues of its dark fire beckoning to Naamah's gift within me, seeking to beckon me out of the twilight.

Behind us was the clatter of hoofbeats, the jingle and creak of gear and weapons, the sounds of men breathing hard and swearing as they attempted to wrestle a battering ram through the narrow, twisting path.

I wished they would all be quiet.

We had been climbing for over an hour when I sensed the first living presence other than our own on the mountain, at a point where the path ahead of us widened around a sharp bend to the right.

"Bao, hold," I said softly, and he drew rein, waiting. Glancing behind me, I willed Hasan Dar's second in command to hear me. "Pradeep, hold and wait."

He nodded fearfully, and whether it was due to the threat of assassins, or hearing my disembodied voice, I couldn't say. But he did as we had agreed, signalling silently to the army to wait.

There was no time to hesitate. The killer ahead of us would have heard our company approaching. If Bao and I delayed, he might move to investigate. Firming my grip on the twilight, I joined Bao and we rode around the bend.

The assassin was an archer, and he had chosen his spot well. He had gone to one knee at the far end of a straight, wide stretch of path, and he had an arrow nocked and drawn. There was a tray of sand before him from which the shafts of another score of arrows bristled, points thrust into the sand, ready at hand.

Remembering how quickly the man in the Rani's chamber had thrown a flurry of knives, I shivered. I didn't doubt that this fellow was just as quick, just as deadly.

"One of the good ones or bad ones?" I asked Bao.

"Bad," he murmured. "Do you want me to take him, Moirin?"

I shook my head. "It's on me, either way." I nocked an arrow and drew, my hands shaking a little.

I had killed men twice before, but only in the heat of battle. This was murder, plain and simple. Even if the fellow would gladly have done the same to me given the opportunity, it was still murder. He had no idea I was there. His face was calm and silvery in the twilight, utterly focused. It reminded me a bit of the Tatar archer Vachir's quiet, steady confidence, which made it all the harder.

My *diadh-anam* was quiet within me, neither warning nor encouraging. The Maghuin Dhonn Herself would give me no guidance in this matter. The choice was mine to make, the risk of losing Her favor mine to take.

This, I thought, was truly an unclean deed that would leave a stain on my soul. But thinking of my lady Amrita raising poor, dead Sameera's maimed hand to her lips and kissing it, thinking of Ravindra's grave face as he bade his mother farewell, I knew it was a darkness I was willing to accept.

"Make sure it's a clean kill," Bao said quietly, reading the decision on my face. "He'll start shooting blind if you don't take him in one."

I nodded. "Get as close to the wall as you can. He's likely to loose his bowstring when he's struck."

Kneeing our mounts, we plastered ourselves as close to the walls as we could.

Breathing deeply and willing my hands to steadiness, I shot the fellow.

It was quick, so quick! There was the thrumming sound of my bowstring as I loosed it, the thump of the arrow piercing the assassin's chest indistinguishable from the second twang as his nerveless fingers loosed his own string, the hornet-buzz of an arrow speeding between Bao and me to shatter against the wall of the path.

I lost my grip on the twilight for a heartbeat. The killer's puzzled eyes met mine; then his gaze went to the feathered haft protruding from his chest. He toppled slowly sideways. And then my *diadh-anam* pulsed within me and I gasped, reclaiming the twilight.

The archer was dead.

And the Maghuin Dhonn Herself had not forsaken me. It seemed

I had guessed rightly, and the stakes were indeed high enough to call for desperate measures.

Bao dismounted and went to confirm that the killer was well and truly dead, then lugged his body as far out of the way as possible. I sat atop my mare Lady, breathing hard and shaking, fighting against a surge of nausea, feeling at once sick at heart and horribly grateful that my *diadh-anam* yet shone within me.

"It was well done, Moirin," Bao said when he returned, swinging himself back into the saddle. "A better death than that one deserved."

I swallowed. "Let's just keep going."

We alerted Pradeep and resumed our torturous climb, zigging and zagging our way up the mountain to Kurugiri. Bao consulted his tattoo and scanned the walls for symbols; behind us, Pradeep and the others consulted their maps and did the same, following our invisible progress through the endless labyrinth.

Left, right, right; left. Again and again and again.

I felt the darkness of my deed settle into me, and accepted it. I wondered if the great magician Berlik had felt the same way when he had broken his oath and slain the Cruithne princess and her unborn child to save our people.

The gods use their chosen hard.

It was true.

It was mid-day when I sensed a second living presence in the maze ahead of us, and called softly to Bao, ordering a second halt.

This time, the path was too narrow to admit us both on horseback. Bao and I dismounted, stealing around the corner together on foot. He caught his breath in a hiss at the sight of the man awaiting us.

My throat tightened. "One of the good ones?" I asked unnecessarily. This fellow was young, younger than Bao, with delicate features. His face was filled with transcendent determination, but even I could see that he held the long pike he wielded in a tentative, inexpert grip.

"Uh-huh." Bao glanced at me. "Sudhakar. I used to try to protect him."

My *diadh-anam* flickered. "We can't just kill him."

"No." He sighed. "Let him see us."

I released the twilight.

The boy yelped with alarm at the sudden sight of us, his eyes stretched wide. I nocked an arrow and trained it on him. He leveled his long pike, swinging the tip back and forth between us in an agony of indecision.

"Sudhakar, it's me," Bao said in a soothing tone, his staff tucked under one arm. "You don't want to fight, do you?"

"Our lady wills it!" His voice trembled.

"Our lady wills a great many things, none of them good," Bao said calmly. "Think, Sudhakar. She's not here now. Kamadeva's diamond is not here." He tapped his chest. "Look into your heart. You don't want to do this. Lay down your weapon and surrender, and we will take care of you, good care of you. The Rani of Bhaktipur is a good lady, a very good lady. I promise, you will be safe among us."

The boy hesitated, and I thought for a moment that Bao had reached him, but I was wrong. Jagrati and Kamadeva's diamond might not be here, but they were not far enough away, either.

"No!" young Sudhakar cried in a high-pitched voice, shaking his head frantically. "No, no, no! I am loyal to *her*!"

Pike leveled, he charged at Bao.

Despite the narrow confines, Bao spun out of his way with effortless grace, his staff lashing out to connect with the back of the boy's head as he passed. Sudhakar fell forward and measured his length on the rocky path, lying motionless.

I winced. "Dead?"

"Unconscious." Bao rolled the boy over, testing his pulse. "Broken nose, chipped front teeth. He'll live if we let him."

"Let him," I said.

Bao nodded and called for Pradeep, who procured a long length of sturdy rope from somewhere in our supply train. Together, they trussed the boy Sudhakar securely and dragged him into one of the blind alleys. Gods willing, we would retrieve him on our return journey.

"Two down," I said. "Seven to go, plus the Falconer. Do you suppose there are more in the maze ahead of us?"

"Yes," Bao said soberly. "At least one. They wouldn't have left a half-trained lad like Sudhakar as the last line of defense in here."

He was right.

For two more hours, we climbed uneventfully, the call of Kamadeva's diamond growing ever stronger. I struggled to ignore it, struggled to maintain my hold on the twilight, trying not to think about the offer Naamah had made to me, trying not to let myself get distracted by the fear that I had chosen unwisely. Nearing yet another hairpin turn, I barely sensed the presence ahead of us in time to order Pradeep to halt.

It was narrow, very narrow. Once again, Bao and I dismounted and went to investigate on foot, me with an arrow nocked.

As strained and mentally weary as I was, I couldn't make sense of the vision before me. For the space of a few seconds, I thought I was seeing one of Bhodistan's strange gods with two heads and four arms.

Then it resolved into the image of two men crowded into the narrow space together. One gestured silently to the other, who cupped his hands together. The first man put his foot in the other's cupped hands, and the other tossed him upward with a powerful heave. The fellow soared into the air, catching the ledge of the steep wall and pulling himself to his feet.

Behind us, shouts of alarm came as the assassin appeared above us; and I lost my grip on the twilight.

The fellow before us gave a hoarse cry of surprise, plucking a pair of short-handled battle-axes from his belt.

Bao shouldered past me. "The Rani, Moirin!" he shouted. "Get the other one! He's after Amrita!"

I whirled and took aim, but the fellow was already in motion, racing along the top of the deep crevasse, sure-footed and swift. He had a row of silver quoits like razor-edged bangles along one arm, plucking them free with his other hand and hurling them with deadly force as he ran. Cries of agony arose in his wake.

I shot at him and missed; and by the time I had a second arrow nocked, he was around the hairpin turn, the high walls blocking him from me. With fifty men between me and my lady Amrita, there was nothing further I could do to protect her.

Sick with fear, I turned back, only to find Bao faring poorly in his battle.

Like the archer, the axe-man had picked his spot well. The path was too narrow here for Bao to wield his long bamboo staff effectively, forcing him to parry with awkward diagonal moves, essaying cautious jabs and retreating step by step.

And step by step, the assassin advanced, the narrow space suited to his short-handled weapons, which he wielded with fearful ease, describing complex patterns in the air as they crossed and uncrossed, spun and slashed. A death's-head grin stretched his lips from his teeth, and there was a manic gleam in his eyes.

Although I had an arrow nocked, with Bao between us, I couldn't shoot the fellow, either.

"Moirin!" Bao yelled. "Call your magic!"

There was too much shouting, too much fear, too much chaos altogether. I tried and found I couldn't do it, couldn't summon the concentration.

"I *can't*!" I yelled back at him, furious and helpless. In a surge of desperate inspiration, I switched to the Shuntian scholars' tongue. "Bao, when I count to three, *duck*!"

He gave a sharp nod.

I counted. "One...two...three!"

Bao dropped like a stone into a deep crouch, ducking his head and raising his staff at a steep angle above it in a last effort to ward off the descending battle-axes. The assassin's eyes shone.

Aiming high, I loosed my bow.

The arrow caught the fellow in the throat, piercing it clean through. He staggered backward, the battle-axes falling forgotten from his hands, which rose to feel at the feathered shaft. His face softened into that bewildered look that comes when death takes a man unaware, and he sat down hard on the trail, his breath gurgling wetly in his throat.

Once again, I swallowed against a rising tide of bile.

Bao was on his feet, bending over the fellow. I looked away as he ripped the arrow free from his throat.

The sound the man made as he died was dreadful.

Bao met my gaze. "The Rani?"

I shook my head. "I don't know."

Word travelled up and down the long, twisting line of our company. One man was dead, and a half dozen more seriously injured. The Rani Amrita was alive and safe. Hasan Dar had protected her with his own body, throwing himself from the saddle. He had suffered a grievous injury in the process, one of the razor-edged quoits lodged between his ribs.

He might live—or not.

The second assassin was dead, brought down at last by our own archers. Four down altogether; five left to go, plus the Falconer.

Kurugiri was still awaiting us.

"Moirin." Bao touched my arm. "Can you continue?"

I gazed at the corpse of the axe-wielding assassin, remembering a story the trader Dorje had told me. "I think I've heard of this one, or at least one like him," I murmured. "I think he stole a Tufani yak-herder's daughter and slaughtered her family. Does that tale sound familiar to you?"

"Yes," he said quietly. "It does."

"I thought so." I remembered the weight of the prayer-urns as I turned them outside the temple of Sakyamuni in Rasa, the light touch of the boy-monk's slender fingers on my tear-stained cheeks as he sought to comfort me, the dense, fragrant scent of incense all around us. His face blurred in my memory with Ravindra's, with the boy

Dash from the caravan; his fingers blurred in memory with the image of my lady Amrita's graceful hands forming a *mudra*, with Sameera's severed fingers discarded on the storeroom floor.

Kamadeva's diamond sang to me.

I shook my head, willing it clear. I could continue because I *had* to continue.

"Moirin?" Bao nudged me.

"Aye?"

He flashed his incorrigible grin. "Marry me if we live through this?"

My heart gave an unexpected jolt, but I managed to raise my brows at him. "You already have a wife, my Tatar prince."

"Nah." Bao's grin widened. "The Great Khan dissolved our union. So?"

"Oh, fine!" I took a deep breath, drawing the twilight into my lungs, spinning it softly around us both, finding new reserves of strength. "Yes."

Bao kissed me. "Good."

SEVENTY-ONE

Hours later, we gained the summit.

There had been no further assassins awaiting us in the maze, and none awaited us atop the peak of Kurugiri. Only the fortress itself, stark, solid, and forbidding.

One by one by one, members of our company straggled out of the narrow paths—or at least most of us. One dead, another half dozen injured, Hasan Dar among them. We had been forced to leave them behind, swaddled in blankets against the cold.

I dismounted and found my lady Amrita surrounded by anxious guards, and embraced her with relief. "You're well?"

She shivered. "Well enough, young goddess. Hasan—"

"I know," I said. "I pray he survives."

Amrita laid one ice-cold hand against my cheek, shuddering uncontrollably in the thin air. "Let us make an end to this, shall we?"

I nodded. "Yes, my lady."

"Moirin has agreed to wed me if we survive," Bao informed her.

Despite everything, it made her smile, made her tired, lustrous eyes sparkle with gladness. "Well, then, we shall have to make sure of it, eh? All this effort and sacrifice must not be made in vain."

The sun was beginning to sink low in the west, streaking the horizon in tones of gold and saffron. The snow-topped mountain peaks glowed. In the valleys and deep crevasses, the shadows of night were already gathering. Taking the place of his injured commander, Pradeep rallied his troops, assigning them their duties.

The men who had worked so hard to carry the battering ram up the twisting maze gave way gratefully to a fresh crew of guards. The new men wrapped the ropes that bound it around their hands, taking firm stances. On a count of three, they surged forward, swinging the bronze-capped ram.

The sound boomed and echoed over the peaks; but the tall wooden doors held.

"Again!" Pradeep called.

Again and again, they assailed the entrance, until the doors began to bow inward, the bar that held them shut straining. At last, the bar gave way altogether with a creaking, splintery groan, and the doors crashed open. The fellows manning the battering ram backed away hastily, but no one emerged. Although the place seemed almost deserted, the flicker of lamplight within its walls told us otherwise.

Somewhere in the depths of Kurugiri, Kamadeva's diamond called to me.

Cloaked in the twilight, Bao and I made a careful survey of the entryway and found it empty. "Can you sense them?" he asked me.

I shook my head. "It doesn't work as well in man-made places. But I know where Kamadeva's diamond is." I pointed. "That way."

"The throne room," Bao said with satisfaction. "I was right."

My skin was beginning to feel warm, the call of the diamond like a caress. "Where are all the others? Surely there must be servants."

"Hiding," he said briefly. "And like as not praying we succeed."

We returned to report to Pradeep that the way was clear, and our apprehensive company filed through the doors.

The plan was to have had Hasan Dar and two dozen of his best fighters lead the attack on the Falconer and his assassins, while Pradeep led the rest in rescuing the women and children of the harem. In Hasan Dar's absence, Bao volunteered to lead the attack on the throne room, and Pradeep readily agreed to let him, not even bothering to hide his relief.

With that, our company divided.

Making our way through the empty fortress was a frightening process, all of us jumping at shadows. Even though I held myself and my lady Amrita wrapped in the twilight, I was tense and fearful. Bao was right, Kurugiri was a strange place. The architecture was plain and utilitarian, but everywhere, opulence gleamed. There were gilded braziers and lamps that burned silvery in the twilight, gorgeous woven hangings on every wall, the spoils of generations' worth of tribute—and later, outright theft.

I didn't like it, not one bit. Every wilderness-born instinct I possessed was telling me to turn and flee, that this was a bad man-made place made by bad men. And at the same time, Kamadeva's diamond was setting my blood to beating hard in my veins, setting Naamah's gift stirring in me. For once, it didn't feel like a flock of doves taking flight. Ravens, mayhap—ravens with sharp-edged wings and cruel beaks, ready to pick me apart.

"Moirin?" Amrita took my hand in concern.

It helped, and I squeezed hers in reply. "We are close, my lady. Very close."

Outside another set of tall doors, Bao gestured silently for everyone to halt. "Is she here, Moirin?" he asked in a low tone.

I stared at the doors. I could almost *see* Kamadeva's diamond through them, nestled below the hollow of Jagrati's long throat. "Yes. Oh, yes."

Bao laid one hand on the latch. "There is no lock on these doors. Are you ready?"

I shook my head, then nodded; then remembered Bao couldn't see me. Releasing Amrita's hand, I unslung my bow from my shoulder and nocked an arrow. "Are *you* ready, my lady Amrita?"

Her face was resolute. "Yes."

"We are ready," I informed Bao.

He turned the latch, shoved the door open with the butt-end of his staff, and jumped backward, cat-quick, his staff at the ready. The door swung inward silently, revealing the throne room.

And Kamadeva's diamond.

Now I *could* see it glimmering on the far side of the room; and for a moment, it and Jagrati were all I could see. The strikingly gaunt, high-boned face that had haunted my thoughts, her dark skin gleaming in the twilight. The diamond pulsing at her throat, beating in time with her blood, beating in time with my blood. Even in the twilight, the black diamond made from a god's ashes glowed with dark, shifting, blood-red fire.

I took an involuntary step forward, lowering my bow.

"No, Moirin!" Deftly, Amrita slipped past me, turning her back on the Spider Queen and raising her hands in a *mudra* to focus the will. "Be strong, dear one!"

No one could hear us in the twilight unless we willed it. I met her gaze and nodded, lifting my bow once more. "Aye, my lady."

It was strange, so very strange, stealing into the throne room, coming upon that unholy tableau unseen. They were waiting for us, they were all waiting for us, gazing fixedly at the open doorway. There was one throne and Jagrati sat in it, her long fingers curled into armrests carved in the shape of roaring tigers. Four men were arrayed before her with weapons drawn, the Falconer Tarik Khaga among them.

Two others lurked on either side of the doorway, bristling with more weapons. We were close enough that I could hear them breathing.

"Bao?" I called, willing him to hear me. "Assassins waiting to ambush you on both sides of the door."

He didn't answer.

I hoped he had heard me.

Small and fearless, my lady Amrita advanced through the twilight, past the lurking killers, all the way to the foot of the throne. I followed her.

It took every ounce of concentration I had to expand the twilight and spin it around Jagrati, but I did it.

Her head jerked up in surprise as the world dimmed around her, her face contorting with fury. "*You!* What have you done?"

Behind me, there was shouting. Later, I would learn that Bao had indeed heard my warning, had come through the doorway in a low, diving somersault that took him past the lurking killers and came up fighting, the others crowding behind him.

Now, all I knew was that the battle was engaged, Tarik Khaga and his deadly falcons rushing to join it.

I wanted to look, but I couldn't. I looked past the Spider Queen instead, keeping my arrow trained in her general direction. "No one but the Rani Amrita and I can see you, Jagrati. Give Kamadeva's diamond to her, or I will kill you."

She laughed.

A low sound, a sound at once soft and harsh. I felt it in the pit of my belly. Ravens fluttering. "No," Jagrati said fondly in her silken rasp of a voice. "No, my oh so pretty *dakini*, I do not think so." She rose from the throne, moving with that angular grace, Kamadeva's diamond glowing at her throat. "Come, put down your bow, young Moirin. Do not threaten me. It is not who you are. You were made for pleasure, not killing."

It was true; so true! With a sigh of relief, I lowered my bow.

Jagrati smiled. "Well done, child! Now release your magic."

I wanted to obey her.

"Moirin, *no*!" Amrita's voice rang out. She positioned herself deftly between us, her hands rising in a warding *mudra*. "Do not listen to her; do not look at her! Look at me, and hold fast to all you love!"

I raised my bow, blinking hard.

I held the twilight.

Jagrati hissed through her teeth, pacing with ferocious elegance. "Little Rani," she said in a guttural purr. "Do you know, you are everything I hate in this world?"

"The world has not been kind to you," my lady Amrita said steadily, her hands unwavering. "And I am sorry for it. I listened to the words you said before, and I will seek to be mindful of them in pursuit of the truth. But that does not excuse your cruelty."

"Pious mush-mouthed creature!" Jagrati reached for her, then recoiled with another hiss. "Look at you." Her voice dripped with contempt. "So brave, little daughter of the warrior caste; so proud to be doing her duty, so sanctimonious in her self-righteousness."

It made me angry.

"My lady Amrita is none of those things save brave, Jagrati," I said fiercely. "Do not project your own darkness on her."

Jagrati's glittering gaze settled on me, bringing the full force of Kamadeva's diamond to bear. My blood thundered in my ears, throbbed in my veins. I had never been afflicted with a taste for life's sharper pleasures, but that was before I had committed murder and taken darkness onto my own spirit. Now I sensed the absolution to be found in accepting punishment, in abasement and humiliation.

I was flushed and hot, aching between my thighs, beginning to shudder with the force of it. My yew-wood bow trembled in my hands. Kamadeva's diamond glowed like dark embers, like a blood-red sun setting, promising razor-edged pleasures. Jagrati's full lips curved in a smile. I wanted her to kiss me again, wanted her to touch me with those cruel, long-fingered hands, wanted her to hurt me. I wanted her to whisper foul things to me in that rasping, silken voice, compelling me to obey her, forcing me into unclean acts. Anything.

No.

No, I didn't. Because Amrita stood between us, and I would not let any harm come to my kind and lovely Rani. Because Bao fought behind me, and I could feel the force of his *diadh-anam* burning bright and clear.

I would not let Jagrati and Kamadeva's diamond turn Naamah's gift into a curse. I clung to memories of brightness, memories of love. Mayhap Bao was right, and I did fall in love as easily as other people fall out of a boat; but I loved in earnest. Well, and so? I did but obey Blessed Elua's precept, *love as thou wilt*.

Elua.

I had prayed to Naamah for aid, but the bright lady could not protect me from my own desires, even desire without love.

But mayhap Elua could.

"Blessed Elua," I whispered in D'Angeline. "In the name of everyone I have ever loved, I beg you to aid me."

Golden warmth flooded me, dispelling the darkness. The desire didn't vanish, but it grew bearable. The shudders that racked me began to lessen, and I was able to steady my hands on the bow.

Anger suffused Jagrati's face as she felt her influence waning. "What are you doing, *dakini*? What new spell do you speak?" She forced herself to calmness, coaxing again with her slithering rasp of a voice. "Come, Moirin. Do you not wish to please me? All I am asking is a small thing. Release your magic."

I shook my head. "No."

Behind me, the clashing, clamoring sounds of battle were beginning to dwindle. There were low sounds of agony, men groaning and whimpering with pain. If we had won, it would come at a price. Jagrati's gaze slid past me. I wondered what she saw.

"Bao?" I called.

"Uh-huh!" he grunted in reply, and I heard the sound of a blade clattering against his steel-wrapped bamboo staff. "Almost done, Moirin."

I kept my arrow trained on Jagrati, and although the Spider Queen of Kurugiri was as beautiful and terrible as Kali dancing, and Kamadeva's diamond shone around her throat and sang to me, there was only rage and hatred in her. I could not love her. Like my lady Amrita, I pitied her; and I saw her hate me for it.

There was a final clash behind me, then a heavy thud and two sharp thumps, followed by Bao's soft "Heh."

"It's over," I said quietly. "Give the diamond to the Rani Amrita."

Jagrati's narrow nostrils flared. "Come and take it, little Rani," she said to Amrita. "Come, unfasten it with your own hands, daughter of privilege! Or do you fear to be polluted by the touch of my skin?"

"No, Jagrati." My lady Amrita lowered her hands, her voice grave. She took a step forward. "I do not."

For the third time in two encounters, Jagrati recoiled violently from the Rani. Her hands went to the nape of her neck, working frantically at a clasp. Loosing the collar of gold filigree that held Kamadeva's black diamond, she hurled it at Amrita's feet. "Take it, then, damn you! Take it!"

Bowing her head, Amrita stooped to retrieve the necklace...

...and everything changed.

SEVENTY-TWO

The stone floor of the throne room of Kurugiri was hard beneath my knees, evoking a distant memory of scrubbing tiles in the temple of Riva.

Thinking it was odd that she seemed so tall, I gazed upward at my lady Amrita.

Upward? Yes, upward.

Taking a deep breath, I realized that I'd released the twilight and gone to my knees without thinking when Amrita picked up the necklace with Kamadeva's diamond in it. My yew-wood bow and arrow lay on the floor before me like an offering.

I was not alone.

Everyone, everyone in the throne room capable of kneeling was doing so—save for the Spider Queen Jagrati. And even as I thought it, Jagrati swayed on her feet, then crumpled helplessly to her knees, huddling there.

"Moirin?" My lady Amrita sounded forlorn and confused, the collar of gold filigree dangling from one hand, Kamadeva's diamond flickering in its setting. "What is it? What's happening, eh?"

Unable to help myself, I touched my brow to the cool flagstones. The uncertainty in her voice made my heart ache. I wanted to comfort her, to pleasure her, to assuage her every fear. For now, all I could do was reply honestly. "You hold Kamadeva's diamond and all its power, my lady."

"I do?" Amrita asked in wonder. "I do, don't I?"

My Rani was beautiful and terrible with it—but not like Kali dancing, no. Like a goddess, but a kinder, gentler one. The goddess Durga on her tiger, perhaps, her face filled with radiant light and fierce compassion.

"Yes," I whispered.

She gazed around the throne room, taking in the cost of our endeavor. The Falconer Tarik Khaga sprawled on his back, his mouth agape. Dead. He was dead; his five remaining assassins were dead. Over a dozen of her best guards were dead or dying, and it would have been worse had it not been for Bao, kneeling with his staff across his lap, gazing at her in a worshipful manner.

Amrita touched her slender fingers to her lips. "Oh, gods!"

I bent and touched my brow to the floor again. "You did what was needful, highness."

"Did I?"

I bowed low again. "Of course."

"No!" There was a fierce note in my Rani's musical voice, and her hands tugged at my shoulders. "No, no, no. Moirin, look at me. Talk to me, dear one. The gods sent you to me. Counsel me." Hope lit her eyes. "Is there some higher purpose in this? Am I meant to use Kamadeva's diamond to change the world to a kinder place?"

Fighting the urge to kneel, I sat on my heels and gazed at her.

Stone and sea! She was lovely, so lovely. Even as Kamadeva's diamond had taken all that was dark and twisted and rage-filled within Jagrati and turned it into the stuff of bitter yearning, it took all of my lady Amrita's warm, laughing, golden kindness and turned it into something far, far more powerful.

A future unspooled before my eyes…

She would be a queen such as this part of the world had never seen before: great and powerful in her compassion, terrible in her disappointment, moving men and women alike in a desire to please her, compelling love along with desire. Her influence would spread far and wide, her wisdom praised to the heavens.

But it would not last.

Ravindra's clever, narrow face swam before my eyes, the collar fixed around his throat. He would do his best to keep his mother's legacy alive; but he had been granted power, too much power.

His sons would fight and squabble. In the end, Kamadeva's diamond would bring nothing but bloodshed and war.

"No, my lady Amrita," I said with profound sorrow. "I do not believe so. It is too dangerous a tool to be wielded by mortal hands; and I do not believe you can change the world through magic. Not a change that is true, not a change that lasts."

Amrita gazed at the black diamond in her hand for a long, long time. "I believe you are right," she said at last. "It belongs in the temple from which it was taken." She glanced at me, regret in her eyes. "You are wise for one so young, Moirin. Will you take it and conceal it for now? Kamadeva's ashes should be at home with your gifts."

I swallowed. "I will try, my lady."

It was an effort to rise in her shining presence, but I made myself do it. I found a leather pouch on the belt of one of the slain assassins and untied it, dumping out a couple of unfamiliar throwing weapons. Silently, I held the open pouch out to Amrita, averting my eyes from the glorious light in her face. I heard the sound of gold filigree clinking softly, felt the pouch grow heavier, and pulled the thongs tight...

...and everything changed again.

Amrita sighed, a faint sound of loss. I braced myself for the influence of Kamadeva's diamond, wondering if *I* would become as terrible and beautiful as Naamah in all her splendor, wondering what in the world I would do if that happened; but it didn't. I felt the diamond singing softly to me, a song like a caress, but so long as I chose not to wield it, it seemed it was enough to conceal it.

I stole a glance at Amrita. She looked herself again—lovely, but ordinary and mortal. She met my eyes and gave me a rueful little smile. "I can still try to change the world, can't I, Moirin? Or at least my little corner of it?"

I smiled back at her. "Yes, my lady. You can and will."

The spell of Kamadeva's diamond broken, the reality of our situation reasserted itself. Grown men stumbled to their feet, dazed, checking themselves for injuries. Others lay moaning and bleeding on the floor.

For a mercy, Bao took charge effortlessly, ordering the living to tend to the wounded, applying compresses and tourniquets, stanching the bleeding of myriad injuries. Although he was no physician, having been Master Lo's apprentice for many years, he knew a fair bit; and I knew enough to help him.

Over a dozen dead...ah, gods!

I had seen worse, far worse, in Ch'in; but Ch'in was a vast empire, and the scale of that conflict almost unimaginable. Bhaktipur was a tiny kingdom, and the impact of the deaths that had occurred within this small throne room hit hard. I knew at least half the fallen by name, and all of them by sight.

In the midst of it all, Jagrati knelt huddled on the floor, her hands wrapped around her head, her body shivering.

We ignored her, worked around her, until there was nothing left to be done and it was impossible to ignore her any longer.

Bao nodded at her, his face tense. "What will you, highness?"

"I don't know," Amrita said uncertainly. "She is harmless now. But she has done great harm. I suppose...I suppose..." She shrugged helplessly. "We must take her with us, eh? Let the laws of justice decide her punishment."

I stooped and touched Jagrati's shoulder.

She uncoiled like a serpent, catching my hand in a hard grip and rising, her glittering gaze fixed on mine as she hauled me to my feet.

Memories, bitter memories, unfolded behind her eyes. Even without Kamadeva's diamond, Jagrati's gaunt, angular beauty was compelling. From a very early age, men had found it so, a great many men. They had used her hard, used her cruelly, taking her against the walls of alleys, over and over again, stealing away shame-faced and satisfied.

There had been no recourse, no one to protect her. Until the day she had stolen Kamadeva's diamond, she had been a helpless victim.

I caught my breath, seeing too much.

Jagrati gave me a tight smile. "You *see* things, don't you, oh so pretty *dakini*?"

"Yes."

"Untouchable." She released my hand, regarding her own, dark creases in her pale palm. "That is what they call us." Her gaze flicked toward Amrita. "That is what *you* call us."

"I am coming to believe otherwise," Amrita murmured.

"Untouchable," Jagrati repeated, a catch in her throat. She laid her palm against my cheek and I let her, my pity giving way to genuine sympathy. "And yet it never seemed to matter when no one was watching. Men were happy enough to touch me when it suited them, so long as no one saw it. It is a man's world. Men make the rules, and men decide when it is acceptable to break them. Even your precious Rani is only waiting for her son to grow old enough to take her place." She took her hand away, her expression hardening. "But I made a difference. Here, I carved out my own place. Here in Kurugiri, *I* ruled. *I* made the choices." She glanced at Bao. "Didn't I?"

He gave her an inscrutable bow, his staff tucked under one arm. "Yes, my dark lady. You most certainly did."

Another bitter smile twisted her lips. "You have an uncommon streak of willfulness. I should have cut my losses when your Moirin returned from the dead. But you...you were one of my favorites, Bao. I didn't want to lose you."

"I was not yours to keep," he said in a flat tone. "None of us were. And yet look around, my lady." He gestured. "You have lost everything."

Jagrati raised her voice to a hoarse, rasping shout. *"Do you think I don't know it?"* The words echoed off the walls, falling into a thick silence. No one answered. She glanced around the chamber, taking in the sight of the dead and wounded with no visible emotion on her face. "Is this how you mean to make the world a better place, little Rani?"

"No, Jagrati," Amrita said quietly. "This is what *you* forced me to do, you and Lord Khaga. I take responsibility for the choice, and for the deaths of my brave men. I will not take responsibility for your sins."

"So noble." Jagrati's lip curled again. "Do you know, little Rani, that the untouchables of Bhaktipur live in squalor on the outskirts of the city, tending to their dung-heaps? They are pathetically grateful to you for seeing to it that they have a well that draws clean water, since they are not allowed to use the public wells or fountains. And yet twice I had promising young lads taken to serve me, and there was no outcry, for there was nowhere for their families to turn, no one to protect them."

Amrita's brows rose. "And you are proud of this?"

She shrugged. "I treated them as human beings, not living filth. I gave them better lives than they would have had otherwise."

"You treated them as living playthings, Jagrati," Bao said. "Was it a better life for those who died fighting for the honor of sharing your bed?"

Jagrati laughed her dark tearing-silk laugh. "At least they died fighting for something they believed worth dying for, didn't they?"

"Believing a thing does not make it true." Bao shrugged. "You are not the only one in the world to have suffered, lady. The world can be cruel, even to men. I was sold into bondage when I was scarce more than a babe. I know what it is like to be used badly. I have not let it poison my heart."

She met his eyes. "But you have been fortunate in the companions life has given you, have you not?"

Bao glanced at me, and didn't answer.

"How lucky for you." Jagrati gave him her bitter smile. "The peasant-boy found a noble mentor, grew up to be a hero, and won the hand of the fair maiden." She clasped one hand over the other fist as though she meant to bow to him in the Ch'in manner. "The only luck I found, I made myself. All my old life gave me was the stink of human shit and cruelty." She looked sidelong at Amrita. "Forgive me if I am not willing to return to a world where I must grovel when you pass lest my shadow soil your pure flesh, where I can only dream of the honor of touching your perfect feet."

"Jagrati—" my lady Amrita began.

The Spider Queen's long-fingered hands tightened, driving her fist into her palm. "Good-bye."

There were jeweled rings on almost all her fingers, gleaming in the lamplight, and belatedly I remembered the poisoner and his ring with the hidden needle. But even if anyone had been minded to stop Jagrati, it was already too late. Her tall, angular body jerked and stiffened, and she fell gracelessly, a little foam rising to her lips.

The Spider Queen of Kurugiri was dead.

SEVENTY-THREE

❖

It was a long, difficult night.

There was a great deal of work to be done, little of it pleasant. But at least it began on an auspicious note as Pradeep came to report that the harem had been secured without any difficulty. The churlish messenger had been the only one to resist, and he was dead.

The Rani insisted on visiting it straightaway. It was crowded with women and children, and dozens of additional servants who had taken shelter there. None of them seemed to have been harmed in an obvious way, but they greeted us with profound gratitude, many of them weeping with joy and relief, overwhelmed at being rescued from captivity in Kurugiri.

I watched my lady Amrita go among them, talking to the women and some nine or ten children of varying ages, assuring them that they were safe and would be well cared for. It made me smile for what felt like the first time in years.

One of the women caught my eye and returned my smile. She had Tufani features, and her smile was as gentle and radiant as dawn breaking through mist. I remembered the boy-monk in Rasa giving me a message for the yak-herder's daughter.

"Are you Laysa?" I asked her.

"Yes." There was a little girl who looked to be five or six pressed against her side, and Laysa stroked her hair. "How did you know?"

"I met a young monk in Rasa, a...a *tulku*." I dredged the word from memory. "Tashi Rinpoche. He said he was one of your teachers in your last lifetime together, and that it puzzled him that he was born younger than you this time. But now it makes sense, for you have lost ten years of your life. He is waiting in Rasa to teach you again."

Her radiant smile widened. "That is very good news!" She kissed her daughter's brow. "Is it not, my little Kamala, my little lotus?" The girl nodded warily, staring at me. Her mother whispered something in her ear, making her giggle and hide her face. "She was frightened by your green eyes," Laysa said. "I told her it is because you are a magical *deva* sent to look after us. Now she is shy."

My throat tightened.

It seemed impossible that such goodness could endure and blossom in this cruel place. The world had been unkind to Laysa, mayhap not as unkind as it had been to Jagrati, but near enough. Her family had been slaughtered, and she had been forced to endure servitude in the Falconer's harem. The thought of Tarik Khaga with his hawk-nose and muscular paunch heaving and grunting atop her sickened me.

He'd gotten her with child; and she loved the child. A child she had been compelled to raise in fear that one day her daughter would be forced into an incestuous union with her own cursed father.

And still, there was joy and kindness in her smile.

"Why are you weeping, *deva*?" Laysa inquired, hugging her daughter. "Today is not a day for sorrow!"

I smiled at her through my tears. "Joy and sorrow both, I fear. Today has come at a cost. But I am honored to meet you, my lady."

"Ah." Her expression turned grave. "I am sorry for your losses. I will pray for them, and for you." She regarded me with compassion. "Your journey is a long one, I think."

"It has been," I agreed.

Laysa shook her head. "I mean the journey that yet lies ahead of you."

I sighed.

Her smile returned. "Do not fear, *deva*. You have a very great heart, and your gods love you very much."

"Moirin?" Bao appeared at my side, sliding an arm around my waist. "You have that look on your face. Who are you falling in love with now? Some new royal lady?"

"No." I leaned against him, grateful for his strength. "A yak-herder's daughter who is the reincarnation of one of the Enlightened Ones on the Path of Dharma. This is Laysa, and she says I have a long journey ahead of me yet."

"Yes," Laysa said helpfully. "A great ocean yet to cross."

Bao tightened his arm around me and kissed my temple, and I felt the flicker of his *diadh-anam* entwined with mine. "Good thing you don't have to cross it alone, huh?"

I nodded. "A very good thing."

"I remember you," Laysa said to Bao. "You came here looking for a green-eyed woman. Where did you find her after all?"

"I didn't." He smiled at her. "She found me."

That was the best part of the night. The rest of it was a nightmare of complicated logistics. We had dead and injured men within the fortress of Kurugiri, and injured men left in the winding paths of the maze where they might freeze to death. Living men who required food and rest to tend to the others. Horses left to stray outside the fortress, also requiring tending, food, and rest.

Bao shone.

He procured torches and led the expedition back into the maze to retrieve the wounded armed with blankets to serve as makeshift slings. Two of our men had not survived, but Bao's party was able to rescue four others including Hasan Dar, as well as the young lad Sudhakar, bewildered and confused at the death of Jagrati and the loss of Kamadeva's diamond's influence.

"Who is our new mistress, Bao?" Sudhakar asked uncertainly, glancing from me to Amrita. His broken nose had swollen and his eyes were beginning to blacken. "How are we meant to serve her?"

"The Rani Amrita is your new mistress," Bao said in an absent tone, examining Hasan Dar. "And you are meant to serve her by making yourself useful. Bring me all the bandages and medicines you can find. A basin of water and soap. And a sewing kit, and shears, too."

"Yes, Bao." The young man trotted away with alacrity.

When the fellow returned with the requested supplies, Bao cut Hasan's tunic away from the deadly round quoit that protruded from it. Despite his efforts to be gentle, the commander gave a stifled groan.

Amrita winced in sympathy. "Will he live?"

"I hope so, my lady." Bao pressed his ear to Hasan's back, listening. "His lungs are clear, so that is good." He met my eyes, looking worried. "I wish Master Lo were here. Or even your damned Raphael."

"Do your best, Master Lo's magpie," I murmured. "There are others waiting."

"I'll need your help to sop the blood. And maybe others to hold him still. It's going to hurt." A thought came to him. "Sudhakar!"

"Yes, Bao?"

"Fetch a pipe and a lamp. And opium, lots of opium."

"Yes, Bao!"

"He's very obedient," I observed as he trotted off again.

"He was trained to be," Bao said in a flat voice.

When Sudhakar returned a second time, Bao filled the bowl of the long, slender pipe with sticky brown poppy resin, coaxing Hasan Dar to lean on one elbow and take the mouth-piece of the pipe between his lips. He then held the oil lamp beneath the bowl until a sweet-smelling smoke arose. Hasan Dar sucked gratefully on the pipe, while Bao watched with an expression somewhere between hunger and envy.

"Don't even think about it," I warned him. "I am *not* nursing you through that twice."

"Not even a wife yet, and already you nag," he retorted, drawing a pained chuckle from Hasan.

The opium took effect quickly. Seeing the commander's limbs relax, Bao nodded in satisfaction and beckoned to Sudhakar. "Take the pipe, and see that it's given to anyone who wants it."

"Yes, Bao!"

The quoit was lodged in Hasan Dar's ribcage, closer to his back than his front, three or four inches protruding and the rest sunk deep into his flesh. After washing his hands, Bao gave it a cautious tug, wary of the razor-sharp outer edge. Hasan hissed between gritted teeth, but the thing didn't move.

"I think it struck bone," Bao muttered. He glanced around. "Are any of the household servants here?"

I shook my head. "Pradeep has them busy." He was in charge of rounding up food and bedding, not to mention a hundred horses left to stray.

"Sudhakar!" Bao called. "A change of plan. Do you know where his lordship keeps his hunting gear?" The lad came hurrying back, nodding. "Good. Fetch me a falconer's glove."

"Yes, Bao!"

"The Falconer really was a falconer?" I asked.

"Uh-huh."

"I did not know that," Amrita remarked. She looked pale and anxious. "Is there anything *I* can do to help, Bao?"

"Can you sew?" he asked.

The Rani turned even paler. "Yes, but..." Her gaze skated over the quoit sticking out of Hasan Dar's side, and her expression turned determined. "Yes, I can try."

"Sorry, my lady," Bao apologized. "I did not mean for you to sew the commander's wound." He nodded at the sewing kit, which contained curved needles and sturdy, waxed thread. "But if you could thread a needle for me, it would be a great help."

"Of course." Kneeling gracefully, Amrita bent to the task, glad to be of use, her hands calm and steady.

I rubbed Hasan Dar's back in a circular motion and breathed the Breath of Ocean's Rolling Waves, the most calming of all the Five Styles. His breathing slowed to match mine, the jutting edge of the quoit rising and falling, glinting in the lamplight.

Sudhakar returned with a falconer's glove, a thick padded affair made of tough leather. Bao donned it, flexing his fingers.

"Ready?" he asked the commander, who gave a dreamy grunt of assent. Bao took hold of the steel quoit and gave it a sharp yank.

Strong as he was, it still took three yanks to free it; and there was a sharp, cracking sound as the quoit came loose, along with a hoarse cry from Hasan Dar. The wound gaped, a white shard of bone jutting out of it, blood pulsing over the commander's skin. Bao swore, tossed the quoit aside, and stripped off the glove, plucking out the bone-shard and probing the wound for others, extracting two smaller splinters with his bare hands.

"It's clean," he said breathlessly. "My lady? Moirin?"

I blotted the wound with clean bandages, while Amrita silently handed Bao the threaded needle.

Bao sewed.

I swabbed.

When it was done, a ragged line of stitches sealed the wound shut, the flesh seeping a little. After uncorking and sniffing different unguents and ointments, Bao chose one to slather on the wound. Together, we worked to bandage it, wrapping clean cloths around Hasan Dar's torso.

"So this is what war is like," our lady Amrita said in a low tone. "It is a very terrible thing!"

"So it is, my lady." Bao swiped his forearm over his brow, which was damp with sweat, then settled onto his heels. "All right." He plunged his hands into the basin of clean water, soaping and washing them as Master Lo had taught him to do. "Sudhakar! Tell me, who is next?"

SEVENTY-FOUR

I lost count.

I do not know how many wounds I helped Bao stitch that night, how many broken bones I helped him set.

Many.

At one point, I asked him why there was no physician in the household, when surely there must have been regular injuries.

"Lord Khaga tended to them himself," he said, surprising me. "As did his father, and his grandfather before him. He took pride in his skill." Bao shrugged. "People are complicated, Moirin."

"True."

There was a rebellion on the part of the Rani's guards when Bao suggested the uninjured men should transport the bodies of the dead outdoors, where the cold would preserve them from decay.

"With all due respect, that is a pariah's work, Bao-ji," Pradeep said to him, shuddering. "Not a warrior's."

Bao narrowed his eyes at the fellow. "We are speaking of men who fought and died bravely. Those of us who survived owe them a debt of honor. Their bodies should be tended to with dignity."

"I will do it, Bao," young Sudhakar volunteered, even though he was unsteady on his feet and his nose resembled a squashed turnip. "Or at least I will try. I do not mind. I was born a no one, a no-caste."

An injured guard smoking opium from a pipe Sudhakar had prepared and handed to him coughed and lowered the pipe.

The Rani Amrita raised her hand in the *mudra* of fearlessness, stilling the room. "Bao is correct," she announced. "A debt of honor is owed to the dead, and we will see that each and every one is transported safely home and given a proper funeral—even our enemies, in the hope that they will find a greater peace in the next life. However..." She gave Bao an apologetic glance. "I fear there are predators in the mountains, are there not? Leopards and such?"

He nodded. "Yes, highness. I hadn't thought of it, but yes."

"I would not have the bodies of our dead dishonored by animals," Amrita said firmly. "So. For now, let them abide. Only know, we *will* be returning them to Bhaktipur; and it will be our honor to do so."

She lowered her hand.

In the silence that followed, the guard with the pipe let out a little sigh, returning the mouth-piece to his lips and beckoning to Sudhakar to hold the lamp for him.

I smiled at Amrita, who smiled wearily back at me. "I think that is how you change the world, my lady," I said to her. "One small step at a time."

After many long hours, at last there was nothing urgent left to be done. Everywhere, injured and uninjured men slept on the stone floors of Kurugiri, rolled in blankets. Although she could have had her choice of either Jagrati's or Tarik Khaga's chambers, the Rani chose instead to sleep in the harem. Lest he need my assistance, I stayed with Bao in the banquet hall where he had tended to the majority of the injured.

"You were very brave today, Moirin," Bao mumbled, already half-asleep, his arm around my waist and his hand resting over the hard lump of Kamadeva's diamond stashed deep within a pocket of my coat. "Facing Jagrati and that cursed thing."

"I couldn't have done it if you hadn't been there," I said. "You and Amrita."

"I know." He yawned. "But you *did* do it."

"You were beyond brave, my hero." I raised his hand to my lips and kissed his battle-scarred knuckles. "And not only for fighting boldly.

You were a healer today, Bao. Many men may owe their lives to you. Master Lo Feng would be so very, very proud of you."

A soft snore answered me. Resolving to tell him again in the morning, I fell into an exhausted sleep.

In the morning, the task before us seemed even more daunting, the scope of it revealed in the harsh light of day. There were over a score of corpses to be transported down the winding mountain path, over a score of women and children in the harem to be escorted to safety, plus dozens more servants. There were over a dozen men too badly injured to be moved yet; and one more had died in the night while we slept. There were farmers and herders in the valley nestled to the northwest of the fortress yet to be consulted. There was the question of what to do with the spoils of war, the gilded trappings and fine tapestries that adorned the fortress, the coffers of jewels found in Jagrati's chambers.

There was the question of Kurugiri itself, and who, if anyone, should lay claim to it. By right of inheritance, it should pass to the Falconer's eldest son—but none of his harem-born offspring wanted it. By right of conquest, it belonged to the Rani.

"*I* do not want it!" Amrita said, dismay in her musical voice. "It seems a cruel gift to inflict on anyone."

"So let it stand empty and crumble over time back into the mountain," Bao suggested. "Or give it to the valley-folk if they want it."

They didn't.

The Rani sent an embassy led by Pradeep to address the farmers and herders in the valley. He returned to report that the folk he had talked to were pleased to know that the Falconer and the Spider Queen were no more, but that Kurugiri had a name as a cursed place, and that they would be well content to let it stand empty and live their lives in peace without being forced to tithe the lion's share of their crops and herds to the fortress.

"They are happy to grow barley and poppies and raise yaks, highness," Pradeep said with a shrug. "I cannot blame them."

So it was decided; Kurugiri would be abandoned and left to stand empty, a stark reminder of the cruelty and self-absorption that could be bred in a place that combined deadly power and isolation.

After conferring with Hasan Dar, mercifully alive and surprisingly lucid, the Rani Amrita concluded that a swift messenger should be sent to Bhaktipur to let Ravindra know we had triumphed, requesting the aid of those guards left to ensure his safety. Meanwhile, the bulk of our guards would follow on a slower mission, escorting the Rani and members of the harem, and transporting the dead back to Bhaktipur.

Bao and I would remain to tend to the wounded, assisted by members of the household staff. We would also see that a full inventory of Kurugiri's goods was conducted. Stolen treasures that could be identified, like the fist-sized ruby called the Phoenix Stone that the Tufani trader Dorje had spoken of so long ago, would be returned in time to their rightful owners. The rest would be sold, and the proceeds divided among the victims of Kurugiri.

"I do not like leaving you in this place, Moirin," Amrita fretted. "I would prefer to know you were home safely in Bhaktipur!"

I touched her warm, smooth cheek. "I know. But the danger is over, and I will be safe with Bao, my lady. For whatever reason, the gods have seen fit to join us together. Having spent the last year of my life following him to the far ends of the earth, I'm not leaving him."

"I told you a long time ago that you would fall in love with me," Bao said with obnoxious good cheer, leaning on his staff. "Didn't I?"

I glanced sidelong at him. "Yes, O insufferable one."

He chuckled.

My lady Amrita shook her head, her lustrous eyes shining at us. "I *will* see you wed, the two of you. You most definitely deserve each other, eh?"

We gathered the dead.

It was a long, arduous process. Limbs had stiffened in the rigor of death, and it was difficult to wind linen sheets around them. Men swore, wrestling with corpses, repenting of their harsh words only when Amrita reproached them for it.

No one wanted to touch Jagrati, so Bao and I tended to her.

Even in death, she had a terrible beauty: gaunt-faced, her sunken cheeks collapsed to the bone. I wiped the dried flecks of froth from her lips, sensing Kamadeva's diamond in my pocket singing to me. Her dead skin was ashen, but it seemed to me that her spirit lingered. Hungry for vengeance against the world that had harmed her—but somewhere beneath it, I thought Jagrati hungered for acceptance, too. I remembered how she had recoiled from Amrita, and it seemed to me that it was more than the strength of the Rani's warding *mudra* at work there. It was due to a lifetime of Jagrati being taught that her touch was unclean and polluting. She'd had no problem taking her vengeance on men, no problem touching me, a foreigner and Kamadeva's victim.

It was different with the Rani Amrita. She may have been all that Jagrati had despised, but the habits of a lifetime had overridden her hatred.

I pitied the Spider Queen, mayhap more than I ought to. When Bao asked quietly if we should remove the rings and bangles that adorned her fingers and wrists, I shook my head. "Let her keep them," I said. "There's more stolen treasure than anyone needs within the walls of this bedamned place. Let her take the baubles she died wearing to the afterlife with her. Maybe it will ease her angry spirit."

Bao looked relieved. "Good."

Together, we wound Jagrati into a shroud; and both of us were relieved to have it done.

There was a blend of joy and sorrow in the procession that departed from Kurugiri when the work of gathering the dead was finished. Sorrow for the losses incurred, joy at the innocent victims liberated, the women and children of the harem who still looked happy and dazed at their good fortune. Only the *tulku* Laysa appeared serene and unsurprised, but nonetheless glad and grateful.

Amrita hugged me close in farewell, tears in her eyes. "Promise me you will be well, Moirin! I do hate leaving you here."

I returned her embrace, kissing her cheek. "It's only for a little while, my lady."

"Too long, even so." She laughed ruefully, wiping her eyes. "We must have known one another in a different life, eh? Or else how could you have become so dear to me so quickly?"

"Moirin does," Bao informed her. I gave him a sharp look, and he grinned at me. "What? You do."

"You do," Amrita agreed. "So, my bad boy Bao! You will keep her safe for all of us, eh?"

He pressed his palms together and bowed to the Rani. "I have determined it is my life's work, highness."

I rolled my eyes.

Bao snuck a glance at me, still grinning.

"He only pretends to jest," Amrita observed, her hands forming a *mudra*. "But I will hold you to your promise, Bao-ji. And I will remind you that it is Moirin who came here to rescue *you*."

He sobered. "I do not forget it, highness. I will not ever forget it."

"That is well, then." Amrita's radiant smile returned, her irrepressible laughter chiming like golden bells. "And I shall have great fun planning your wedding!"

Together, Bao and I watched the Rani Amrita and her procession depart, entering the long, winding labyrinth, men on foot and men on horseback, some riding double with women or children behind them in the saddle, some carrying terrible burdens, escorting the joyful living with care, carrying the lamented dead with dignity and honor—and the unlamented dead, too.

I sighed.

Bao kissed me, his lips lingering on mine. "The Rani was right, Moirin. I was not jesting."

"I know." I stroked the nape of his neck, feeling the strong sinew drawn tight beneath his skin. Naamah's gift stirred in me, and Kamadeva's diamond sang to it; but it was not right yet. Not here, not now. "Shall we go count some jewels?"

He nodded. "Let's."

SEVENTY-FIVE

Taking inventory of Kurugiri's treasures was a prodigious task. The coffers in Jagrati's private chambers alone revealed untold wealth.

"Stone and sea!" I plucked out an impossibly long strand of pearls the size of quail eggs, each one perfectly spherical and uniform in shape, shimmering with an iridescent pinkish hue. "How would someone even wear such a thing?"

"Looped three times around the neck, Moirin," Bao said briefly. "Sudhakar, make a note. One strand of pearls, three arm-lengths long."

"Yes, Bao!" the young man said eagerly, adding in an apologetic tone, "Only, I cannot write."

We found someone who could, since Bao could write only in Ch'in characters, and I could write only in the Western alphabet, neither of which the Bhodistani could read.

One by one, we catalogued the pieces in Jagrati's coffers.

A gold filigree hairpiece set with emeralds, another set with sapphires and seed pearls.

An ornamental dagger with three large emeralds forming the hilt, sheathed in a golden scabbard encrusted with diamonds.

Countless gold and silver bangles and anklets.

A collar wrought of rubies and diamonds crafted in the shape of glittering flowers with blood-red centers.

Rings set with every manner of gemstone.

Gaudy and elaborate brooches dripping with jewels.

On and on it went, an endless and dazzling array. We found the famous Phoenix Stone, the immense ruby for which the Maharaja of Chodur and his bride had been slain, tucked away in the corner of a coffer and forgotten.

It wasn't just jewelry, either. There were shelves of jewel-bright miniature paintings on ivory panels depicting warriors riding to battle on the backs of elephants, hunters on horseback cornering a tiger, opulent scenes of court life. There were the gilded lamps and braziers, many of the former encrusted with gems. There were decorative vessels carved from ivory and carnelian. We found an entire trunk of gilded bronze votive figures depicting the Bhodistani pantheon in intricate detail.

"Why would Jagrati want these stolen for her?" I asked in bewilderment, holding a many-armed statue of the goddess Durga. "She claimed to hate the gods."

Bao glanced at it. "I don't think this was all her doing," he said. "There was a fair bit of treasure already here. Lord Khaga let her claim what she wished, and when she tired of it, he got her more." He shrugged. "It would be like her to claim images of gods and hide them away. Having been denied access to them all her life, it would please her to deny them to others. I never knew what was in that trunk," he added. "I never saw her open it."

It reminded me in an unpleasant way that Bao must have spent a great deal of time in this bedchamber. He had been one of her favorites.

Seeing the thought on my face, he looked away. "Let's just keep going, huh?"

I nodded. "One gilded statue of Durga with..." I counted. "Eighteen arms," I said to Govind, the elderly steward who was recording the inventory for us.

After we had finished with Jagrati's hoard, there was the rest of the fortress to catalogue. Mostly its valuable furnishings consisted of furniture and wall-hangings, but there was an extensive set of gold serving-ware inlaid with precious stones that took a long time. There were still the injured men to tend to, which delayed the process, although happily, the wounded were progressing well.

Altogether, the inventory took days, and when we were done, I didn't care if I never saw another piece of jewelry or treasure again.

"No?" Bao smiled a little when I announced it. "A good thing, since I don't have any money to keep you in gold and jewels." His smile faded. "Or any money at all, really. I don't have much to offer you, Moirin."

"You have yourself, and that's enough." I hesitated, unconsciously fingering the awkward lump of Kamadeva's diamond in my pocket. "But...Bao, do you think Jagrati's shadow is always going to be between us?"

"No." He ran a hand over his hair, which he'd cropped into its former unruly shock before leaving Bhaktipur—although the gold hoops remained in his earlobes. I hadn't asked why. "No, I don't. But being here..." He shuddered. "There are too many memories. When we go, I mean to leave them behind."

"I could take them from you," I offered quietly. "If you wished it."

After only the briefest of pauses, Bao shook his head. "Good men died to remove Jagrati and Lord Khaga from this world. To rid myself of those memories would dishonor their sacrifice."

I smiled. "Funny, that's very much what Snow Tiger said when I made her the same offer."

"Her bridegroom's death?" he asked in a hushed tone. I nodded. "No, she wouldn't dishonor his memory, would she? Not our Noble Princess." Bao met my eyes. "I did not suffer anything so terrible as that here in Kurugiri. I am not proud of the things I did, or the man I was here, but since I found the strength to walk away when I needed it, on some level, I must have chosen this. So I will keep my memories, and learn to grow stronger from them. I did not murder anyone, if you are wondering," he added. "I did not become an assassin, a killer of innocents."

I had been wondering, but I didn't let him know it. "You would not have let that happen," I said firmly.

Bao's mouth quirked. "I like to think it is true. But in truth, I was never ordered to do so."

I took his hand, lacing my fingers through his. "Bao . . . there is a wellspring of relentless pride and nobility hidden in you. No matter how much you try to suppress it, it bubbles to the surface. *That* is why you did not become a killer of innocents. It is why you did your best to protect someone like poor Sudhakar; and why you walked away from your life as a prince of thugs to become Master Lo's magpie." I squeezed his hand, hard. "And it is one of the reasons I love you."

Averting his head, Bao gazed at our entwined fingers; then gave me a glinting look under his lashes. "What are the other reasons?"

"You make me laugh," I said promptly. He scoffed. "It's true! And it's worth more than you reckon. In Vralia, it helped keep me sane. I imagined you counseling me when the Patriarch was demanding my endless confession, especially when it came to you."

"What did I say?" he asked, curious.

"You said, 'Tell the stunted old pervert whatever he wants to hear, Moirin, and I will bash his head in when I have a chance.'" I smiled. "And then you grew indignant because Pyotr Rostov did not press for details about your prowess in bed."

"That does sound like me," Bao admitted.

"I know."

"What else?"

"Remember on the greatship?" I asked softly. "You said you were afraid my destiny would swallow you whole. Gods, Bao! *I'm* afraid of my own destiny. It's been a hard one thus far, and if the *tulku* is right, it's far from over. But at every crossroad, you've never hesitated. Not once."

His hand stirred in mine. "That's not true. I left you."

I shook my head. "That was a different kind of crossroad."

"Was it?"

"Yes." I freed my hand from his, laying one hand on his hard, firm chest and one on my own, feeling our shared *diadh-anam* twine and flicker. "This destiny, Master Lo laid upon us both. You had to find your own way to accept it, and I think I needed the time and distance to be certain of my own feelings, too. And ... I don't know, Bao. Mayhap the gods prompted him to do so. It has led us to bad places, dark places. Riva. Kurugiri. Even so, good things have come of it. I do believe what we have done serves the greater good."

"The no-castes," he murmured. "The untouchables."

I nodded.

Bao's eyes glittered. "We're not done here yet, are we?"

"No," I agreed. "Not yet."

Two days later, the second company of guards arrived from Bhaktipur, and we set about organizing the last exodus from the fortress. All in all, there were fourteen wounded men to transport, along with several dozen servants, and the bulk of the treasure we had inventoried, saving only for the larger pieces of furniture.

Half of the injured had recovered to the point where they could sit a horse; the other half would require litters, which the new guards had brought.

Bao's greatest concern was the cold. Hampered by the slow pace necessitated by navigating the awkward litters down the winding path without jarring the wounded, there was little chance we could manage the descent in a single day. Once night fell, we'd be trapped in the maze, the temperature plummeting. It would be a hardship for all of us, but it could take a deadly toll on the wounded men.

"Could we keep going by torchlight?" I asked.

He shook his head. "Better to rest and conserve *chi* energy. The cold will sap it and weaken them. I wish we had more blankets."

I remembered how Bao and I had slept with the Rani between us at the foot of the mountain, sharing our warmth with her. "Tell them to huddle up," I suggested. "Assign two healthy fellows to every injured man."

"Good idea." He chuckled. "It will be funny to see grown men curled up together like puppies in a litter."

"It was not funny when it was me and Amrita," I observed.

"No." Bao grinned. "That would have been quite pleasant if it were not for the freezing cold and the sentries giving false alarms all night long."

"Those are two very large 'ifs,' my magpie," I said. "But I cannot argue the point."

The following morning, we began our descent; and it was every bit as halting and torturous a process as I had imagined. Bao took the lead, with me behind him. Behind me was Hasan Dar, who insisted on riding against Bao's counsel. I could hear the breath hiss through his teeth at every jolting step as we rounded the hairpin turns.

The long train of guards, servants, litters, and pack-horses stretched behind us, abandoning the mostly empty shell of the fortress.

I would be glad to see the last of Kurugiri.

We made it a good two-thirds of the way down the mountain before the light began to fade in the sky above us and shadows settled into the deep crevasses of the maze, making it impossible to read the symbols etched on the walls.

Bao called a halt. Some of the men had laughed self-consciously when he had ordered them earlier to huddle up come nightfall, pairing two each with an injured fellow. None of them laughed now as the day's meager warmth fled.

It was an awkward business, made all the more so by the fact that our mounts were trapped in the labyrinth with us. Bao hobbled his lead mount, which was all that was needful; the path was too narrow for another horse to pass. My mare Lady gave me a mournful look, sensing no food or water in the offing.

"I'm sorry, brave heart." I stroked her muzzle. "It was too difficult to arrange in the maze. Tomorrow, I promise."

Bao squeezed past his mount to join me, and together we slipped past Lady to assist Hasan Dar, who dismounted with difficulty, his legs trembling.

"Why am I so cursed weak?" he asked in a fierce tone.

"Because you lost a great deal of blood and nearly died, commander," Bao said in a matter-of-fact tone. "And the latter is still a possibility." He spread a blanket on the stony floor of the path. "Rest, and eat if you can. Moirin and I will share our warmth with you, and hopefully the horses will not trample us in our sleep."

"They won't," I said. "Horses have more sense than that."

There were skins of water for the humans, and the roasted barley-grains mixed with yak-butter that was a staple in the mountains, reminding me of the trader Dorje and his kind wife Nyima, who had prepared a packet of the stuff for me. I rolled it into a ball, coaxing Hasan Dar to eat when he protested that he was too tired and not hungry anyway.

By the time the last traces of red had vanished from the sky, the cold intensified. Any heat lingering in the stone beneath us was gone. It was cold and hard, leaching the warmth from our flesh. Hasan Dar began to shiver violently. Bao and I pressed close against him, two blankets over us, taking turns breathing the Breath of Embers Glowing.

It was a very, very long night.

In the morning, the commander was feverish, his brow shining and damp in the cold air. "Forgive me, Bao-ji," he said. "I am not sure I have the strength to ride."

"I told you not to!" Bao scowled at him. "Now you have no choice." He cupped his hands together. "Come, I will help you into the saddle. We'll tie you in place. Moirin, there is rope in my packs."

I squeezed past Lady to retrieve it, and together Bao and I lashed Hasan Dar into his saddle.

Off we set once more, trailing guards and servants and the spoils of war, the Rani's commander lurching in the saddle behind us.

It is not a journey I would care to repeat, ever.

But we succeeded in emerging from the maze by midday, our company spreading out around the base of the mountain. Although the wounded were groaning in their litters, all had survived. Relief suffused Bao's features.

"We should keep going," I murmured to him when the last stragglers stumbled out of the maze. "We need to reach that plateau before night if we want to make a proper camp—and I think we do."

He nodded, gazing upward. "One moment."

From this vantage point, the stone fortress was hidden; but it was there. Kurugiri. The spirits of generations of rulers styling themselves the Falconer haunted it, sending assassins to do their bidding. The vengeful spirit of the Spider Queen haunted it: the dark lady Jagrati, despising the world and speaking bitter truth to it.

I watched Bao.

"Done," he said softly. "It is done. *I* am done with this place, forever."

SEVENTY-SIX

⟨✦⟩

After Kurugiri, we got Hasan Dar into a litter, where he tossed
and turned, restless with fever.

We made camp on the arid plateau, which seemed a paradise after
sleeping on the mountainside. Tents were pitched against the worst of
the cold, pegs pounded into the hard earth. Supplies were shared, our
mounts fed and watered, albeit in a miserly fashion.

Bao examined Hasan Dar's wound and found it red and inflamed,
flesh swelling around the stitches. "Stupid man," he muttered. "I *told*
you not to ride. Did you think I didn't know what I was talking
about?"

The commander's reply was incoherent.

"Listen to me!" Bao slapped his cheek lightly. "The Rani Amrita
needs you; her son, Ravindra, needs you. If they are going to change the
world, they need a strong arm beside them. So stay with us, huh?"

Hasan Dar shivered. "I will try."

"Try harder," Bao said ruthlessly.

For a mercy, Hasan was the only one of the injured to have taken
a serious turn for the worse. The others would endure.

"Pride," I murmured. "It will be his downfall if he does not survive. Take it to heart, my magpie."

Bao gave me a sidelong look. "Is that a warning, Moirin?"

"No." I shrugged, too tired to argue. "I don't know, mayhap it is. I
only know *you* would have insisted on the same in his place."

"Mayhap," Bao mused. "I will think on it."

Downward.

The air thickened and grew richer the next day, as we wound our way out of the heights, wound our way toward the meadow that lay beneath the Sleeping Calf Rock. I watched gladness settle onto the faces of the servants of Kurugiri. And two days later, as we descended into the fairy-tale valley of Bhaktipur with its warm air and lush, verdant growth, that gladness gave way to wonder.

"Is this real?" the steward Govind asked in awe.

"Oh, yes." I smiled at his expression. "And the Rani Amrita has promised that all of you will be well cared for here."

"It's been so long!" Sudhakar breathed. "I'd forgotten how lovely it was. Only I wonder..." His brows furrowed. "How shall *I* live here?"

I hadn't thought about the implications of this homecoming for him. Sudhakar was one of the no-caste lads that Jagrati had taken from the untouchable camp outside the city, the only one to have survived. Leaning over in the saddle, I laid my hand over his. "Don't worry, Sudhakar. The Rani will take care of you, too."

Sudhakar flinched away from my touch and didn't respond. In my mind, I heard the soft, tearing rasp of Jagrati's laughter. The habits of a lifetime died hard.

That and Hasan Dar's deteriorating condition were the two shadows that lay over our return to Bhaktipur. Our procession was spotted making its way along the valley, and by the time we reached the outskirts of the city, there was a royal reception awaiting us with Pradeep and a company of guards, and the Rani Amrita herself standing before her palanquin, glowing in a purple sari embroidered with gold, Ravindra resplendent beside her in a saffron tunic and loose breeches, a purple turban on his head.

Both of them were smiling so brightly, it made my heart ache.

Bao and I dismounted to approach on foot. When we were yet a few paces away, Amrita laughed and ran forward, flinging her arms around my neck and kissing me. "Oh, Moirin! I am so glad you're here. I hated leaving you in that place." She glanced around, past Bao and Ravindra exchanging bows and grinning at one another. "Is everyone here? Is everyone safe?"

"Everyone is here," I said. "But Hasan Dar is very ill, my lady."

"Ah, no!" Spotting his litter, Amrita hurried over and dropped to her knees beside it. Pradeep hurried after her with a length of silk for her to kneel on, but she ignored it, reaching into the litter to take Hasan's hand. "No, no, my friend," she chided him. "This is no good! You must get well."

His eyelids cracked open and a faint smile lifted his parched lips. "Now that you have commanded it, I'm sure I shall, highness."

Amrita rose. "Let us make haste to the palace," she said to Pradeep. "Did you tell the physician to meet us in the barracks?"

He bowed. "I did, highness."

"Good." She gave a brisk nod, then turned to address the servants of Kurugiri. "If you wish, places for all of you will be found in my household. I find we are quite shorthanded since taking in the Falconer's harem."

All save one of them looked profoundly relieved. I don't think they had let themselves believe until that moment.

Only Sudhakar was not gazing at the Rani with gratitude. He was not gazing at the Rani at all, but kneeling and touching his brow to the ground. "Highness?" he asked in a muffled voice. "You know what I am."

"Yes," Amrita said firmly. "You are the young man who assisted Bao-ji tirelessly in tending to my injured warriors. You are the young man who offered to tend to the dead with honor." Stooping, she put her hand on his shoulder and gave it a little shake. "And there is a place in my household for you, too. Perhaps you would like to be my physician's apprentice, eh?"

A great shudder racked him, and he gave a single hoarse sob. The Rani straightened. Sudhakar knelt upright, gazing at her lovely face. She smiled at him. Bowing his head once more, he reached out with trembling hands and touched her bare feet in respect and gratitude. "Thank you, highness," he whispered.

In my mind, Jagrati's dark laughter fell silent.

"Yes, yes." Amrita patted his head. "Only let us hurry, shall we? For Hasan Dar's sake."

Sudhakar leapt to his feet, his face shining. "Yes, highness!"

It wasn't really possible to hurry through the crowded, narrow streets of Bhaktipur, especially with hundreds of folk turned out to observe the royal procession and the last of the returning heroes, but we did our best. When they saw the litters and the injured men within them, the Bhaktipuri people called out blessings, laying garlands of dried flowers on them. By the time we reached the palace, Hasan Dar was half-buried beneath a carpet of blossoms.

One by one, the wounded guards were transported by their bearers into the barracks. Amrita gazed after them, worried.

"Do you think they'll be all right, Bao-ji?" Ravindra asked. "*All* of them?"

"I am worried about Hasan Dar, young highness," Bao said honestly. "But he is strong, and a fighter." He smiled at Ravindra. "And your mother has ordered him to get well. I know he wishes to obey her."

"Mama-ji said you saved many lives," Ravindra said in a respectful tone.

"I tried." Bao stretched out his hands, regarding them. "My mentor Master Lo could have done better, much better. But I did my best."

"That is all anyone can do," Ravindra said with dignity, his small face very serious beneath his purple turban. "I think you did very well indeed."

Amrita gave me a sparkling sidelong glance, and I smiled back at her, thinking that these two were truly very good for one another. "Come!" She clapped her hands together. "Let us leave the horses to the stablehands and the treasure to the porters, and get everyone inside. You must all be very tired and hungry after your journey."

To be sure, *I* was.

It was a relief, a blessed relief, to be back in this place where I had found sanctuary after a long ordeal; and with the shadow of the threat of Kurugiri's assassins lifted, it truly was a place of sanctuary once more.

I didn't know how Amrita went about settling her expanded staff within her expanded household, and I didn't care. It was enough for now to know that she did. I trusted my golden Rani to keep her word.

In the chamber I shared with Bao, I removed the pouch containing the necklace with Kamadeva's diamond from my pocket. It weighed heavy in my hand, singing softly to me. Although I'd thought myself jaded on treasure, this was no mortal gem. I had the urge to open the pouch and look at it once more, to gaze on the dark, shifting embers at the black diamond's core. In Kurugiri and on the journey, there had been no time to think about it.

Now I couldn't help but wonder how it would look around my neck, what *I* would be like wielding it.

"Tempted, Moirin?" Bao was watching me.

"No." I set the pouch down quickly on a dressing table. "Just... wondering. I can't help it."

He came over to me. "You wonder what *you* would be like?" I nodded. Bao touched my cheek with his fingertips. "You would be desirable beyond bearing," he said soberly. "You already incite powerful desire. Were you to don Kamadeva's diamond, I think no one would be able to resist you, for the diamond would reflect your own considerable passions back at them. Men would walk through fire for the chance to touch your skin—and women, too. Men would gladly fight to the death for your favor without being asked. I daresay you couldn't stop them from doing it. Is that what you want?"

"No!" I said. "Of course not." And it was true, almost entirely true; but there was a tiny piece of me that said otherwise. The vanity and pride that was wounded by the fact that I had wanted Raphael de Mereliot more than he had wanted me; by the fact that I'd failed to seduce Aleksei in Vralia; even the fact that my lady Amrita had only offered herself to me out of compassion.

But I could envision the Maghuin Dhonn Herself turning away from me in reproach, Her eyes filled with immense sorrow and regret.

I sighed. "I will ask the Rani for a coffer with a strong lock, and I will put Kamadeva's diamond in it and throw away the key. Let the priests worry about opening it when it is returned to the temple."

Bao smiled. "I think that is wise. Such powerful objects are dangerous to mere mortals, even ones with the blood of the goddess of desire running in their veins."

I put my arms around his neck. "Desirable beyond bearing, hmm?"

He nodded gravely, arms circling my waist. "Oh, yes."

I kissed him. "I would like to have a bath, and a very large meal, and then I would like to sleep in a warm bed, possibly for two days straight through. After that, I would very much like to hear more about these strong desires I incite. Does that sound reasonable to you?"

"Yes, Moirin." Bao's dark eyes glinted, and he bent his head to return my kiss. "Very, very reasonable."

His *diadh-anam* flickered against mine, gentle as a caress. Kamadeva's diamond sang in its pouch, and somewhere the bright lady smiled.

"Oh, good," I said with relief.

SEVENTY-SEVEN

As it was, it took only a single night's sleep to restore me to a semblance of normalcy; and we awoke to good news.

"Hasan Dar's fever broke in the night," the Rani Amrita informed us at the breakfast table, her face beaming. "His wound needs to drain yet, but the physician thinks he will recover fully."

"That's wonderful!" I said. "I'm so pleased to hear it, my lady."

"Yes." The light in her face faded a bit. "There have been far too many deaths already, eh?"

Bao heaped his plate with eggs cooked with vegetables and spices, warm flatbread, and savory fried lentil-cakes filled with pickled *achar*. "What of the others, highness?"

It brought back her vibrant smile. "Well, all are healing well!"

While we ate, Amrita and Ravindra told us what had transpired in our absence. It had caused a great scandal that Pradeep and the guards had transported the bodies of the fallen to the temple of funeral pyres, both their highnesses accompanying them. Although the Rani had not made a formal announcement rescinding the policy of treating no-caste persons as untouchable, the rumor was circulating, and opinion was divided.

"I have been taking counsel with priests," she said. "Some of them are quite horrified at the prospect."

"But not all of them," Ravindra added. "My tutor is of the priestly caste, and he and I have been studying the sacred Vedas." He inclined his head to me. "I think you may be right, Moirin-ji."

I bit into a sweet, fried dumpling and swallowed. "How so, highness?" I asked.

"In the oldest of the Vedas, there is no mention of no-castes," he said gravely. "Only the four castes. And in some places, one might almost infer that it is possible for someone born to one caste to rise to another through study, and worship, and clean and proper living. I would not dare to make such a claim, but my tutor thinks it is possible. So. That is why I think you may be right, and sometimes men have put words in the mouths of the gods, shaping the world to their liking."

"I have been speaking with Laysa, too," Amrita said, steepling her fingers in a *mudra* of contemplation. "She tells me that Sakyamuni the Enlightened One rejected the notion of caste when he founded the Path of Dharma." She smiled in wonderment. "Although she has no formal religious training yet in this lifetime, she has carried great wisdom with her into this incarnation. She tells me she remembers hearing the Enlightened One himself speak about this matter many lifetimes ago."

"Would you think to do the same, my lady?" I asked her. "Reject the notion of caste?"

"No." The Rani Amrita shook her head, eardrops tinkling softly. "It is the way our world is ordered, dear one, and that *is* clear in the Vedas. But I am very interested in this notion that caste is not rigid and fixed, that the challenge of one's *kharma* is not only to obey and endure one's fate, but to transcend it. And I am interested in finding ways to help people do so, especially the less fortunate ones."

"Start a school," Bao said around a mouthful of eggs. I raised my brows at him. He swallowed hastily and wiped his mouth. "Forgive me, highness. But if you wish to lift people up, the best way is to teach them. Before I met Master Lo Feng, I knew nothing but an acrobat's tricks and stick-fighting. He taught me to read and write, mathematics, enough of a physician's trade to make myself useful. He taught me the path of the Way, taught me to think and reason and meditate, to focus my mind and will. I became a different person because of what Master Lo taught me."

"Teach them," Amrita echoed.

Bao nodded. "From that one thing, ten thousand things will arise."

"I like this notion," the Rani said decisively, and Ravindra nodded in agreement. "Only...I think I shall wait until Hasan Dar is recovered to announce any sweeping changes, eh? Pradeep is a good man, but not as strong-willed and courageous."

"Do you think there will be trouble, my lady?" I asked. "That folk will protest and resist?"

"Some will," she said soberly. "It is inevitable. Both priests on high, angry at having their authority undermined, and low-caste workers, resentful at having to share their ranking with folk they despise."

"But you are minded to do this?" Bao asked softly.

"Yes." Amrita's lovely face was set and grave. "I am. The gods sent three women all bearing the same message to me. First Moirin, then Jagrati, and now the *tulku* Laysa. I cannot turn a deaf ear to them." She smiled a little. "Maybe when men fail to heed them, the gods turn at last to women, eh?"

"It took them long enough," I observed.

Amrita shook her head at me in mild reproach. "The time of gods is not like the time of mortals, dear one."

"Yes, my lady." I ate another of the sweet, fried dumplings. "So are Laysa and her daughter staying?"

"No, no. Only through the winter. When the high passes are clear, I will send them to Rasa with an escort. The others are staying," she added.

"Ah." I smiled. "So you're keeping the harem."

My lady Amrita laughed and flushed the slightest bit, narrowing her lustrous eyes at me. "I am not *keeping* the harem, Moirin. They could not return home after what they have endured, for their families would reckon them disgraced. I have offered them sanctuary here, and they have accepted it."

"Why would Mama-ji keep a harem?" Ravindra asked in bewilderment.

"Moirin was only teasing," Bao informed him.

"Oh." He continued to look puzzled.

"It is a grown-up kind of teasing, jewel of my heart," Amrita said to him. "A very D'Angeline kind of teasing."

Ravindra shrugged his narrow shoulders. "Anyway, it is very nice. It's almost as though we have the big family you always missed, isn't it, Mama-ji?" he asked. She nodded. "Would you like to come see?" he inquired. "We have opened a whole row of chambers along the lower level of the garden that have been closed for years."

"I would like that very much, young highness," I said.

After breaking our fast, we strolled in the great central courtyard garden. Although it was warm in the sunlight, there were no flowers blossoming in the winter months, but it was lush and green nonetheless, filled with towering rhododendrons that would be spectacular in bloom, and the immense banyan trees with their gnarled roots. Monkeys leapt and chattered in their branches, and birds with emerald, scarlet, and blue plumage flitted from tree to tree like living jewels.

And beneath them, children laughed and chased one another, watched by indulgent mothers. Chamber doors that had been sealed for years for lack of inhabitants opened onto patios where the women of the Falconer's harem sat and sipped tea or the spiced yoghurt drink called *lassi*, chatting with one another while keeping half an eye on the playing children.

The women greeted the Rani Amrita with glad smiles and deep bows, palms pressed together.

The young Prince Ravindra was hailed with bows and happy shouts, especially from the older boys, who quickly swarmed him and Bao, all yelling at once. It was obvious that Bao's fighting prowess had been the topic of much conversation, but only Ravindra had seen him in action.

"What's that?" Bao cupped his ear. "Surely, you don't think his highness exaggerates!" He scoffed, freeing the bamboo staff lashed across his back with a quick twist. "Stand back and watch."

Bao put on a show for them, fighting an imaginary opponent—ten imaginary opponents. He whirled like a dervish, the staff spinning in his hands until it was as blurred as a dragonfly's wings. He crouched low, his staff sweeping the grass. He leapt high, lashing out with both feet in opposite directions and his staff in a third. He hurled his body in the sideways spinning kick parallel to the ground that seemed to defy the laws of nature. Bao vaulted and somersaulted, turned hand-springs and backsprings, sending his staff soaring high into the air and catching it upon landing upright once more.

The children shrieked with delight, raising a deafening cacophony that made me smile and wince at once.

The women clapped for him.

"He's quite something, your bad boy, isn't he?" Amrita took my arm, smiling. "Moirin, would you consider staying here, you and Bao? It would please me very much if you made Bhaktipur your home."

I hesitated, not wanting to refuse outright, a part of me not wanting to refuse at all.

"Look." She squeezed my arm. "Ravindra dotes on him, eh? Your bad boy makes my serious boy smile. And you..." She searched my face, shook her head and laughed her chiming laugh. "You are a little bit of a great many things to me, young goddess, and I do not know how to name the sum of its parts. I only know that I am very, very fond of you, and I would rather not lose you."

Since Bao and I had been reunited here, I had not consulted our shared *diadh-anam*. Now I did. It whispered the same message it had at our first reunion in the Tatar encampment a year ago. And it was not urgent, but it was persistent.

West, it called to us. *Westward.*

Somewhere, oceans beckoned.

"We can't, Amrita," I whispered, tears in my eyes. "*I* can't. I wish I could, because whatever home means to me anymore, it is so very far away. If I could call any other place home, it would be this place with you and Bao and Ravindra in it. But I can't. The gods are not finished with me. And...and I miss my mother, too." I sniffled. "I hate to think of her never knowing what became of me."

"Oh, Moirin!" Amrita fussed over me, wiping my tears away with the draped hem of her sari. "Of course you do. Forgive me, I did not mean to make this harder for you."

I smiled at her through my tears. "You didn't."

"I did."

"No." I shook my head. "It was a kindness. And I am always grateful for your kindness."

"Ah." Unexpectedly, Amrita kissed my lips, sweetly and gently. "Yes, I know. I have not forgotten. Your demonstration of gratitude was very memorable. Will your gods let you stay a while, at least? Until spring comes? It will be much easier to travel then. I would be grateful for your aid in changing the world, Moirin. And I have promised to see you and your Bao wed. I would like to see it done when all the flowers are in bloom."

My *diadh-anam* did not speak against it.

"Yes," I said gratefully. "We will stay until spring."

Bao fetched up alongside us, sweat glistening on his brown skin. "I am too old for such acrobatics," he announced. "It makes my bones ache. Moirin, why are you crying?"

"Because we will have to leave this place," I said.

He frowned and glanced unerringly toward the west. "Not yet, surely?"

"No." I rubbed my face. "But it makes me sad to think on it."

"I know." Bao stroked my back. "We'll just have to make the most of our time here, all right?"

I nodded. "That we will."

SEVENTY-EIGHT

Alone in the bedchamber with Bao that night, I found myself feeling suddenly and unwontedly shy for the first time since… ever.

It had been so long since we'd been intimate, and so much had happened to us both. He had survived Kurugiri and Jagrati's favoritism. I had been the instrument of Naamah's blessing, and the near-victim of Kamadeva's diamond. As much as I wanted this, I didn't know how to be an ordinary, mortal lover anymore.

Bao sensed my uncertainty. "Do you want to wait until after we're wed?" he asked. "I can if you can. I have great strength of will, you know," he added, making me smile.

"No." I took his hand, traced the creases on his callused palm. "No, it's just…" I shrugged, lacking words. "I feel strange. Unlike myself."

"Come here." Bao tugged me close to him. I slid my arms around his waist, pressing my palms against his back, burying my face against his shoulder. He held me and breathed the Breath of Earth's Pulse, one hand sliding through my hair, lifting it and letting it fall, a motion rhythmic and soothing, as though he were petting a cat. "Do you know why I was unkind to you when we first met?"

"Because you hated Raphael de Mereliot," I said in a muffled voice. "And you didn't think I was deserving of Master Lo's attention."

He laughed deep in his chest. "True. But there was another reason.

I did not like D'Angelines very much. They think so highly of them-selves, of their beauty." His fingers slid through my hair, rising and falling. "Maybe it would have been different if I'd let myself get to know some of them. Too proud, I know."

"They probably didn't encourage it," I murmured.

"No," Bao agreed. "But I did not find them all so beautiful, either. To a Ch'in eye, it is a hard, sharp beauty, deadly as a blade. You... you were different. You looked like them and unlike them all at once, a more subtle blade, exotic to them, but a blend of the familiar and the strange to me." He lifted my face, stroked my cheekbones with his thumbs. "You wanted me to speak of desire, Moirin? You were the most desirable woman I've ever seen, and I resented you for it. Fool-ish, but true."

"Oh," I whispered.

He kissed me softly, and I felt Naamah's gift stirring at last. Doves—the wings fluttering in my belly were doves, not ravens. "If I were a poet, I would write poems of praise to your golden skin and ebony hair and green, green eyes," he said solemnly. "But I am not a poet, Moirin. Only a peasant-boy risen high above his station."

My throat tightened. "No, you are a great deal more than that, my magpie."

His mouth quirked. "Oh, aye?" he asked, mimicking my inflec-tion. "Am I?"

"Aye." I wound my arms around his neck and kissed his lips. The feeling of strangeness had fled. "You are."

Bao's eyes gleamed in the lamplight.

The bright lady smiled.

It was slow and gentle and glorious. Cupping my face, Bao kissed me until I was dizzy with pleasure, his tongue delving into my mouth, teasing my own. Our flickering *diadh-anams* entwined in a private celebration, echoing the dance of our bodies. Liquid heat uncoiled in the pit of my belly, spreading languorously to my limbs. With careful reverence, he unpinned my sari, unwinding its complicated folds, kiss-ing the skin he unveiled. The hollow of my throat, my collarbones.

Sinking to his knees before me, Bao traced patterns on my taut skin with the tip of his tongue, probing my navel and making me giggle breathlessly. He tugged down my fine linen underskirt, his deft tongue parting my nether-lips and darting between them.

"Oh!" I caught my breath, sinking my hands into his hair. My knees felt weak. "If you're going to do *that*, I cannot keep my feet."

He rose gracefully, his hands catching the hem of my cropped undershirt and easing it over my head, caressing my aching breasts in the process. "Lie down on the bed."

I did.

Bao gazed at me, hot-eyed and infinitely patient. After all, my boasting boy *did* have great strength of will. He stripped off his tunic, revealing a sculpted brown torso corded with lean muscle. He shucked his loose breeches, his tight flanks rippling, more lean muscle on his thighs and calves. Ah, gods! He had a gorgeous body, the most beautiful I'd ever seen on a man. His erect phallus was drawn as tight as a bowstring, curving toward his flat belly, the swollen head as dark and ripe as a plum.

As he slid into bed, I reached for him.

"Not yet." Bao shifted, straddling my body and pinning my arms. "I need to relearn *you*. Every part of you." He smiled down at me with rare sweetness. "It is part of learning to live in brightness, Moirin. Do you mind?"

I laughed. "Stone and sea! No!"

So many times, with so many lovers, it seemed *I* had been in charge, in control. Naamah's child, taking as much or more delight in bestowing pleasure as receiving it. It was a relief to surrender for once, to let Bao take the reins.

We kissed and kissed, until I thought I would melt. He worked his way down my body, laying a trail of kisses along my throat.

He suckled my nipples, hard. I groaned, my back arching.

He pressed kisses against the soles of my feet, the backs of my knees. He parted my thighs, kissing them. "This, here." His tongue teased the place where my thigh met my groin. His voice was thick. "I would write an ode to it."

I made a wordless sound.

His mouth moved higher, tasting me, his tongue exploring my depths and retreating to flutter against Naamah's Pearl. Pleasure broke in waves over me, my hips rising involuntarily to meet his mouth. He did not stop for a long, long time.

"Are you sufficiently reeducated?" I asked breathlessly when he finally did. "Because I feel very, very thoroughly relearned."

Bao grinned. "It's a good start, anyway." Effortlessly, he turned me in his arms, pulling me atop him. "Now I want to watch you."

Kneeling astride his waist, I leaned down to kiss him, tasting my juices on his lips, my hair falling to curtain both our faces. The tips of my nipples brushed his chest in a tantalizing manner. I bit his throat softly, sucking on the warm, smooth flesh. I kissed the hard, sleek planes of his chest, bit and sucked lightly on his small, flat nipples until he groaned, his hands clutching hard at my hips.

Only then did I sit up, rising a little on my knees and taking his phallus in my hand. It was warm and throbbing, the thin skin velvety-soft. Bao watched me, his eyes gleaming beneath heavy lids as I fitted the swollen head between my slick nether-lips. I sank down on him slowly, letting him fill me inch by delicious inch—and our shared *diadh-anams* merged in a silent starburst. I had forgotten how profoundly intense the sensation was, startling us both into a moment of stillness.

"Do you think we'll ever get used to it?" Bao whispered in awe.

I smiled. "Mayhap if we try often enough."

Slowly, the glittering intensity faded, and I began to move again, moving my hips in a small circular motion, reveling in the feeling of his shaft deep inside me, filling me, its angle changing subtly as I moved; of his strong fingers digging into my hips, encouraging me. Gasping with pleasure, I came again.

"Beautiful," Bao murmured. "So beautiful."

When I caught my breath once more, I leaned forward a bit to brace my hands on his chest and changed to a different motion, rising and sinking along the length of his phallus, creating a glorious friction that pleased us both. Finally, Bao's formidable strength of will began to crumble. With a low growl that echoed in the pit of my belly, he rolled us both over once more, his shaft still buried inside me.

He rocked between my thighs, propped on his forearms and watching my face. I closed my eyes, drinking in the sensation of being filled and emptied, rising to meet his thrusts until the waves built and built again, breaking over and over, my yielding flesh convulsing in honey-sweet spasms around his hardness, my ankles hooked around his buttocks.

It was good, so very good.

And it was good in a different way when Bao gave himself utterly over to his own desire at last, his breath coming in hard pants, his hips thrusting hard and fast, driving me to yet another climax as I felt his phallus tighten and swell within me. He gave another low growl, shuddering and coming, his chin grinding into my neck.

In the aftermath of love, his face was soft and vulnerable. I lay propped against his bare chest, stroking the unruly hair out of his dark eyes, wondering what he was thinking. "Are you happy?" I asked him.

Bao laughed. "Happy?" He trailed the fingers of one hand along the curve of my spine, making me shiver a little. "I think that is a small word for what I am feeling, Moirin. Are *you* happy?"

"Aye," I said simply. "I am."

"You should always be happy." He flattened his palm against the small of my back. "I do not tell you often enough that I love you. I am not good with pretty words and flattery. But when I hold you in my arms, I feel as though I hold everything that is good and bright in the world."

My eyes stung.

"No tears, Moirin!" Bao said in alarm. "I am not good with tears, either."

"They are happy tears," I assured him, stretching to kiss him. "I've missed you, that's all. Even though you've been right here."

He returned my kiss. "I have missed you, too."

It was enough.

Happy, sated, and languorous with pleasure in every part of my body, I drifted into sleep wrapped contentedly in Bao's arms, one leg flung over his, my head pillowed on his shoulder, breathing in the familiar hot-forge scent of his skin. My *diadh-anam* burned brightly alongside his. We were together at last, every shadow between us banished.

I slept, and dreamed.

I dreamed of Jehanne.

In my dream, she came to me clothed in the attire she had worn on the Longest Night—the costume of the Winter Queen, a collar of snow-white ermine framing her exquisite face, her silver-gilt hair piled in a high coronet. In my dream, Jehanne was alive, her blue-grey eyes sparkling at me.

"I have missed you, my beautiful girl," she said to me. "Have you missed me, too?"

I could not lie to Jehanne. "Yes. Oh, yes!"

"My sweet witchling," my dream-Jehanne said fondly, sliding one hand around the nape of my neck. "My lovely Moirin, my gorgeous savage. Preparing to wed, even!" She gazed deep into my eyes. "I do not begrudge you your pretty ruffian, my beautiful girl. Only promise me it will change nothing between us."

I paused, enveloped by her intoxicating scent. "But this is not real."

"Does it matter?" my dream-Jehanne asked, toying with the tendrils of hair at the back of my neck. "I am here with you now." Her sparkling eyes widened, searching my face. "Would you truly say no to *me*, Moirin?"

I didn't know how to answer her. A part of me knew I was dreaming, knew I was lying asleep in Bao's arms; and I did not want to betray him before I'd even wed him, even in my dreams. "Why are you haunting me, Jehanne?" I asked. "Are you angry at me for leaving you? Angry I was not there when…?" I couldn't say the words, and a part of me hoped that my dream-Jehanne would deny the entire thing, would tell me that her death was a cruel lie told me by the Patriarch to break me down and weaken me.

She didn't. Instead she pulled away from me, looking hurt. "If that is what you think, mayhap I should leave."

"No!" I couldn't bear to lose even a dream-Jehanne. I caught her hand. "No, please. Stay."

"Then you *won't* say no to me?" Jehanne asked, smiling. "I beg you, don't make me pout, Moirin! It's tiresome, and it never worked very well on you anyway."

I laughed.

Still smiling, Jehanne regarded me beneath her lashes with those star-bright eyes. My heart ached with loss and yearning, and I knew that even though none of this was real, there was no way I could ever say no to her.

"No." I touched her cheek, her skin as fine as silk. "No, Jehanne. I will not say no to you."

Her expression softened. "I only want to know you haven't forgotten me, Moirin."

I shook my head, feeling the sting of tears in my eyes once more. "Not in ten times a thousand years, my lady. I promise."

"Thank you," Jehanne whispered, and kissed me, first with infinite tenderness, and then with all the sweetness of desire, her tongue darting past my lips, the scent of night-blooming flowers and *her* all around us. Ah, gods! I had missed her so very much, and I wanted her so very badly. Sighing with pleasure, I unfastened the brooch on her ermine-collared cloak and let it fall to the ground, laying the graceful white lines of her throat and shoulders bare so I might kiss them, taste her silken skin—

And I awoke with a jolt in darkness.

My heart contracted painfully in my chest, a profound sense of loss growing so acute that an involuntary cry escaped me.

Startled out of a sound sleep, Bao scrambled wildly out of bed, reaching for his staff. "What is it?" he asked fiercely. "Moirin! What?"

An unreasoning wave of panic overcame me, words spilling out of my mouth. "Bao, I can't marry you! I can't! I'm not...I'm not a wife-type person! I love you, I do, but I can't promise to love you and you alone for the rest of my life! That's like...like asking me to love autumn, but not spring and summer! Or trees, but not flowers!"

Having determined we were in no immediate danger, Bao kindled a lamp and gazed at me with sleepy bewilderment. "Trees? Flowers? What in the world are you talking about?"

"You! Me! Us! Marriage!" I shook my head frantically. "I can't do it, Bao! I can't. I'm sorry! I may be many things, but I'm not an oath-breaker!"

He knelt on the bed and took my shoulders in his hands. "Moirin, calm down!"

"I can't!"

"You can." Bao gave me a gentle shake. "Calm down and breathe, you crazy woman, and tell me what this is about."

It helped. I forced myself to breathe slowly, my thudding heart and racing pulse easing. "I dreamed of Jehanne."

He looked confused. "Was it a bad dream?"

"No." I flushed. "Not exactly. She wanted me to promise my marriage changed nothing between us. And...I did. I promised I would never say no to her. I...um, very much began to say yes instead."

Bao's expression turned grave. "It was only a dream, Moirin. I know you loved her, and a part of your heart will always be hers. But your Jehanne is no longer with us."

"I know!" Tears spilled from my eyes, and I wiped impatiently at them. "But I wanted her—"

"Moirin," Bao interrupted me. "I am not stupid, you know. I *know* you. I do not suppose I'm wedding some dull merchant's daughter. I do not expect you to become a respectable matron. I am not asking you to swear any oath you cannot keep." He shrugged, sitting on his heels and laying his hands on his thighs. "For whatever reason, the gods have joined us together, and I cannot imagine living without you. Can you?"

"No," I murmured. "But—"

"But what?" He smiled a little. "Tomorrow, a dragon may decide to claim you as his mate. Or maybe your goddess Naamah will decide you need to seduce some spineless Yeshuite boy for his own good. I know this; and I am not afraid. It does not lessen what we are together, you and I. And since the gods have seen fit to join us, it is my thought that we should ask their blessing on our union. Is that so terrible?"

"No," I admitted.

"I will not press you if you do not wish it," Bao said. "Only know I do not expect you to be anyone but who you are."

"And that is enough?" I asked uncertainly.

He laughed. "You crossed the Abode of the Gods and rescued me from the Spider Queen, Moirin. Yes. It is more than enough."

My panic faded. "Aleksei was not spineless, you know," I said to him. "He was a gentle soul, that's all."

Bao scoffed. "Oh, please! His *mother* had to convince him to free you."

"He was very tall, with very broad shoulders," I added. "And eyes the color of rain-washed flowers the name of which I only know in Alban."

He smiled complacently at me. "Now you are only trying to make me jealous."

"It's not working very well, is it?" I observed.

"No." Bao shook his head, the gold hoops in his earlobes glinting. "Because your spineless Yeshuite boy is a thousand leagues away, and I am here. If I were going to be jealous, I would begin with our beautiful Rani, who is much closer and a much greater threat." He gave me another complacent smile. "Lucky for me, she does not share your unusual passions. Or at least not much, anyway. She *is* very fond of you."

I gazed at Bao, at his still-sleepy face, unexpectedly beautiful. At the tousled shock of his hair, his corded forearms braced against his thighs, the stark zig-zag pattern of tattoos running down them. "So you still want to wed me?"

"Yes."

I reached out and touched one of the gold hoops in his ears. "Why did you keep them? As a reminder of *her*?"

"Jagrati?" Bao stretched out his arms, regarding his tattoos. "No. I already have a reminder that cannot be removed." Reaching up, he fingered one thick hoop. "These, I couldn't figure out how to unfasten."

I laughed.

This time, it was a healing laughter; and mayhap the laughter in my dream had been, too. *Love as thou wilt,* Blessed Elua had bade his people—my father's people, and my people, too. I was a child of the Maghuin Dhonn Herself, and a daughter of Naamah, too. I had loved, and loved well.

Jehanne; always Jehanne. But so many others, too. Last and always, my great-hearted bad boy Bao, gazing at me with a quizzical look.

"Do you hate them?" he asked, touching his earlobes. "I will rip them out if you do."

I shook my head. "Let them stay. Now that I know, I do not mind."

Leaning over, Bao blew out the lamp. "Then let us sleep, Moirin, and be at peace with each other."

SEVENTY-NINE

———◆———

Once Hasan Dar was on his feet again, the Rani Amrita began to implement a plan of change.

She made a round of the temples, performing the offering rituals and prayers as we had done when I first arrived, only this time, she also announced her intention at each temple to revoke the unwritten laws regarding the untouchables within a month's time.

Although they had been forewarned, some of the priests were indeed horrified that she meant to go through with it.

"You would profane the temple with unclean persons?" one grey-bearded fellow asked in shock. "Let them lay hands on the Shiva Lingam itself?" He shuddered. "No, no, no, highness! You are a woman, and not of the priestly caste. You do not understand what you do."

"I beg to differ, brother." Ravindra's tutor, who was known as Guru-ji and whose beard was whiter than the priest's, addressed him politely. "Her highness understands it very well, and I am in agreement that it is restoring a lost tradition. I will gladly sit with you and discuss the oldest of the Vedas."

"But they are *unclean*!" the priest protested, ignoring his offer. "Highness, I beg you, do not do this thing!"

Amrita's hands were posed in a *mudra* of respect, but her face was calm and determined, and Hasan Dar and her guards stood behind her, hands on their sword-hilts. "Forgive me, Baba, but I *am* doing it."

He bowed his head in dismay. "You would seek to bend the will of the gods at the point of a sword?"

"No," the Rani said firmly. "But it is my true belief that the gods have revealed their will to me, and I will see it enforced. I will allow no bloodshed, but anyone who refuses to honor my edict will be banished."

Not all of the priests were as resistant. The Rani Amrita had done what no ruler of Bhaktipur had accomplished in generations. She had defeated the Falconer of Kurugiri; and, too, she had retrieved Kamadeva's diamond from the Spider Queen Jagrati. Clearly, the gods favored her.

So it was that some priests listened to her, listened to Guru-ji's calm arguments and heeded them, while others continued to protest.

While they were fewer in number, the monks of the Path of Dharma supported her. Word of the *tulku* Laysa's presence at the palace had emerged, and a good many followers of the Path of Dharma made pilgrimages to visit her and speak with her. Laysa welcomed them all with grave pleasure, and they carried away tales of a profound grace and wisdom undiminished by her time in Kurugiri, lending further credence to the notion that the Rani was indeed a vessel of divine will.

Among the commonfolk, the mood continued to be varied. The warrior caste stood with the Rani Amrita and her son. The merchant caste was reluctantly accepting. It was the members of the lowest caste—the servants, farmers, herders, and craftsmen—who remained bitterly resentful at the rumors of coming change.

We were returning from the temple of Hanuman, the monkey-god who delighted me so, when a scrawny boy in the street darted past the guards to hurl a rotten onion at the Rani in her palanquin, striking her in the shoulder. It gave me a brief, sick reminder of the boys in Vralia who had thrown stones at me as I was escorted in chains to Riva.

Hasan Dar roared an order, but Bao was already in motion, racing after the fleeing figure.

"Oh, Moirin!" There were unshed tears in Amrita's eyes. "None of my people has ever turned on me so!"

I patted the damp spot on her sari, wiping away bits of onion-skin. "Change comes hard, my lady," I murmured. "They are fearful of losing what humble status they possess."

"But that is not what I am doing!"

"I know." I had to own, there were times when I wondered privately if I had done the right thing in counseling our lovely Rani not to wield Kamadeva's diamond. All of this would have been so much easier with the world falling at her feet. But then I remembered the vision of bloodshed that followed, and I set aside my doubts. "You must convince them otherwise, that's all."

She nodded. "You are right, dear one."

Bao returned in short order, hauling the boy in a head-lock beneath one arm, the boy struggling ineffectually against his grip. "Here's your culprit, highness," he said in a cheerful tone. "He's a slippery one!"

"Shall I have him beaten?" Hasan Dar asked grimly.

"No." Amrita raised one hand in the *mudra* of fearlessness and stepped from the palanquin, her composure restored. "Bao-ji, let the boy go. I would speak to him."

Bao shrugged and complied.

The lad glanced around wildly, and found himself surrounded by guards. He stared defiantly at the Rani. He couldn't have been more than thirteen or fourteen years old, and there was clay in his hair and under his nails.

"What is your name, young rebel?" the Rani Amrita asked gently.

His lips thinned. "Dev."

"Dev," she echoed. "I think you must be a potter's son, eh? So tell me, young Dev, why are you so angry at me?"

He knit his dark brows in a fierce scowl. "You would make us no better than *them*!"

"How so?" Amrita inquired. "Because I mean to decree that there is no shame in attending to all aspects of life?"

The boy Dev looked away from her and spat on the ground. "I may be a potter's son, but I do not deal in *shit*."

"That is not true," Amrita said in her musical voice. "You, young rebel Dev, you and I, and bold, swift Bao-ji who captured you so handily, and my lovely *dakini* Moirin, my handsome commander Hasan Dar, my son, Ravindra, the jewel of my heart...each and every one of us are human and mortal." Her voice hardened, her words echoing Jagrati's. "Each and every one of us deals with *shit* squeezed stinking from our bowels, only we choose not to acknowledge it, even though it is part of life's great cycle."

He gaped at her, shocked by her words. Beyond the circle of guards, folk crowded close in an attempt to witness the exchange.

Amrita gestured to Hasan Dar. "Stand down, and let them hear this."

"Highness..." he protested.

She raised her hand again, and he obeyed. The guards spread out, giving the spectators an opportunity to draw closer. Unobtrusively, Bao unslung his staff and took a defensive pose at the Rani's left shoulder. I stepped out of the palanquin and stood at her other side, ready to shield her at need.

A memory teased at my thoughts, the memory of Snow Tiger attempting in vain to calm the crowd who had come to rescue her, the dragon's voice whispering in my mind. *Lend her your gift,* he had said. *Make a gateway.*

It had worked then. Without pausing to wonder, I attempted it now, calling the twilight. Instead of breathing it out, I poured it into Amrita, my fingers brushing her bare arm.

The air around her brightened visibly, drawing soft gasps from the crowd. Amrita gave me a brief, perplexed glance, and I nodded at her in silent encouragement.

The Rani took a deep breath, steepling her fingers in the soothing *mudra* that eased conflict. "Listen, then, to what I say to this potter's son, for it holds true for each and every one of you." She gazed at the boy, and he flushed beneath her shining regard. "You are not lessened by this change, young one. Is your lot in life the worse because someone else is lifted out of misery?" She shook her head. "No. The gods reward greatness of heart, not meanness of spirit. Do not seek to look at those below you and gloat. Look at those above you and aspire. I mean to build schools, good schools. If you wish to be a potter like your father, well and good. It is an honorable profession. If you wish to learn another trade, you may. You may become a merchant, or a builder of temples, or a soldier in my guard. I am placing your *kharma* in your own two hands. Is it truly a change you despise?"

Dev fell to his knees. "No."

"Good." She touched his hair. "So do not throw any more rotten onions at me, eh?"

He shook his head. "I won't."

The crowd let out a collective sigh, adoring her once more; and while their response was due in some small part to the sparkle of magic I'd lent her, mostly it was due to Amrita herself, her courage and her unfailing kindness.

The Rani Amrita smiled at the crowd. "I thank you for your patience, and for listening." Pressing her palms together, she bowed deeply to her people. "May all the gods look kindly on you."

With that, she returned to her palanquin, and I joined her, letting go my grip on the twilight. The crowds parted for us, Bao and Hasan Dar and the guards resuming their protective positions.

"That was most beautifully said, my lady," I said to her. "I do believe you swayed their hearts."

Amrita gave me a sidelong glance. "I do believe you gave me some assistance, dear one. I felt the touch of your magic."

I smiled. "Only a very little bit. A tiny push to help move change along. After all, I am not nearly as dangerous as Kamadeva's diamond."

"No?" She laughed, a merry, ringing sound that gladdened my heart, and the hearts of all who heard her. "I am not so very sure of that, Moirin," she said affectionately. "But I am grateful nonetheless."

EIGHTY

After the incident with the onion-throwing and the Rani Amrita's resounding response, the mood in Bhaktipur was calmer.

The protesting priests made one last attempt at insurrection, covertly contacting Prince Ravindra in the hopes that he would be willing to consider a coup against his mother. Clever Ravindra waited for all of those in league to show their hands before rebuffing them in a passionate public address.

"Shall I dishonor my beloved mother, who has taught me everything I know of courage, who has endured great suffering to ensure the safety of our people?" he asked in the city square, his narrow face filled with affronted dignity. "No! A thousand times, no!"

"He's quite the little speech-maker, isn't he?" Bao murmured.

Amrita smiled with rueful pride. "My young prince is quite a good many things."

I couldn't help but wonder what kind of man Ravindra would grow into; and I couldn't help but grieve at the fact that I would never know. Bao caught my eye, and I knew he was thinking the same thought. It would be very, very hard to leave this place, to leave the Rani and her son.

"Not yet," he said softly.

I shook my head. "No, not yet."

There was to be a celebration the day the proclamation was made official, a great purification ritual to symbolize the no-longer-unclean status of no-caste people. Amrita fretted over the details.

"I do not think it is wise to delay," she said. "But I wish it were spring. The river will be cold. And there will be no fresh flowers! Only dried garlands. There should be fresh flowers to mark a new beginning."

The image of a man with a seedling cupped in the palm of his hand came to me, and I drew in a sharp breath. "If my lady wishes for flowers, there shall be flowers."

Amrita raised her brows at me. "How so, dear one? Can you coax the very flowers to bloom out of season?"

I smiled. "Actually, yes."

So it was that on the day that the proclamation was issued, a month after the Rani Amrita had begun making the rounds of the temples, we traveled in procession to a fallow marigold field outside the city, escorted by the guard, trailed by half a dozen empty wagons and scores of curious Bhaktipuri folk on foot.

It was not a large field, but it was big enough that it daunted me. I had never made an attempt of such scope before, and I hoped I had not boasted out of turn. If I succeeded, there would be no doubt that the gods' blessing was on this endeavor . . . but if I failed, it would cast grave doubts on the Rani's actions.

I stood and breathed the Breath of Trees Growing, letting my awareness filter through the soil. The plants slumbered deep in the earth, not even beginning to dream of spring yet. I remembered how I had coaxed the bamboo to flower in the glass pavilion where I had first asked Master Lo to teach me.

Bao touched my arm, remembering it, too. "You can do this, Moirin."

"I hope so," I murmured.

I hitched up the folds of my sari, kneeling on the soil with bare knees. When Hasan Dar came forward to offer a square of silk, I shook my head at him. I needed to feel the earth beneath me.

"What is the *dakini* doing, highness?" someone called.

"Asking for the blessing of all the gods upon this day," Amrita replied in a firm voice. I glanced up at her. She smiled at me with perfect trust and love.

I prayed I would not fail her.

I breathed, slowly and deeply, taking the measure of the task at hand. I prayed to Anael the Good Steward, to the Maghuin Dhonn Herself, to the many Bhodistani gods, and to Sakyamuni the Enlightened One.

Lending a bit of the twilight's glamour to Amrita had been a small push. This, this would be a very large push.

In the back of my mind, I saw Jagrati's stark face, and there was a terrible, vulnerable yearning in it, a hunger that this might come to pass. If I did not fail, mayhap her angry spirit would rest.

"Please," I whispered to any gods listening, sinking my hands deep into the loose, rich earth. "Oh, please!" I took a half-step into the spirit world and held memories of languid summer sunlight in my thoughts, memories of warm, moist air, of everything good and green and fertile, breathed it all deep into my lungs.

Exhaling, I breathed summer into the soil, over the field. Over and over, I breathed summer into winter.

The earth roiled.

Plants burst forth from it with startling exuberance, unfurling ferny leaves, raising tight, hard buds toward the sky. Rows and rows of them, emerging from the soil. Somewhere, there were cries of awe and amazement. I ignored them, breathing summer, breathing the Breath of Trees Growing, willing the plants to grow, coaxing and begging them. Dark green buds opened and marigold blossoms bloomed, a riotous wave of orange, yellow, and saffron breaking across the field like a forest fire, releasing their pungent, spicy odor.

My head hung low, my hair brushing the earth. I was tired and drained, but my *diadh-anam* burned bright within me. I did not feel lessened by the effort. It was as Master Lo had taught me. When I used my gift as it was meant to be used, it would come back to me. With a weary laugh, I dragged myself upright, setting onto my heels.

Bhaktipuri folk swarmed the field, gathering blossoms. Hasan Dar and his men handed out needles and thick, waxed thread for the stringing of garlands. Men and women sang and sewed, happy to take part in a miracle.

Bao helped me to my feet and slid his arm around my waist. "Well done, Moirin."

I leaned against him, drawing strength from his presence. "Let us hope it all goes as well."

"How can it not, young goddess?" Amrita kissed my cheek. "I named you so rightly! You have made a miracle happen here."

From the miraculous field of marigolds, the Rani's procession returned to the outskirts of the city, to the slums where the untouchables dwelled. I daresay no other ruler in the history of Bhaktipur had visited the place, and I loved her all the more for doing it.

In some ways, it was not so terrible as I had expected; in others, it was worse. Young Sudhakar, who had served as the Rani's liaison to the no-caste encampment in this matter now served as our guide, as though we were visiting a foreign land. He pointed out the vast pits dug into the earth where the gathered ordure of Bhaktipur's upper castes was spread and covered with a layer of barley-straw.

"You see," he said helpfully, pointing at an older patch of ground where vines spread. "In time, it becomes fertile soil. We could not survive without it."

But ah, gods! The level of poverty was staggering. The dwellings in which they lived were crude, ramshackle affairs, in some instances nothing more than a length of ragged cloth stretched between poles. The faces that peered out at us were wary and fearful, not willing to trust to this seeming turn of fortune. A few folk had bright, hopeful eyes, but far, far more were dull and sullen with despair. All of them kept their distance, trained by a lifetime of experience not to sully folk such as us with so much as a shadow or a breath.

"People of Bhaktipur," the Rani Amrita said in a gentle tone. "The gods have seen fit to send me a message, and from this day forward, I proclaim that there shall be no more division between caste and no-caste into clean and unclean. All shall be given opportunities to rise in status through hard work and dedication. By the will of the gods, I declare the rules of untouchability are no more. All men shall be brothers, and all women sisters." She held out a garland of marigolds. "Come! I invite each and every one of you to come to the river and take part in a ritual of purification to celebrate this new beginning."

No one moved.

If I'd had the strength, I'd have lent Amrita a bit of glamour once more, but the marigold field had drained me too deeply. It would be a day or more before I was able to summon the twilight.

She stood patiently, holding out the garland, Ravindra at her side. Carts heaped with garlands waited behind them. Sudhakar shifted from foot to foot, looking earnest. The crowd that had accompanied us began to murmur, while the untouchables remained silent.

At last, beneath the shadow of a hovel consisting of a piece of rusted tin propped on a few posts, a small figure stirred, a young girl of some eleven or twelve years, turning to her mother and whispering a question. The mother nodded, and the girl stepped forth.

I recognized her. She was the girl I had seen being assaulted for attempting to enter a temple when I had first arrived in Bhaktipur.

"So, little one!" By the smile in Amrita's voice, I could tell she had recognized the child, too. "It falls to you to be bold, eh?" She beckoned. "Come, then. Be the first to accept the gods' blessing on this day."

With a tremulous smile, the girl started forward. She managed to cross half the distance between her and the Rani before falling to her knees, overwhelmed by force of habit and the enormity of the situation.

Amrita tilted her head at Sudhakar, who went to the girl's side. "Come, come, Neena!" he said cheerfully to her. "You know me, eh? There is no reason to be afraid. This is a good day, the best day." He tugged at one thin arm. "Come and be glad!"

Holding Sudhakar's hand, the girl Neena approached the Rani a second time. Her skinny legs, left bare by a garment more rags than dress, trembled like a newborn foal's. But she did it, releasing Sudhakar's hand to press her palms together and bow deeply.

"Brave girl!" the Rani Amrita congratulated her, laying the garland around her neck and kissing her cheek.

A sound like the wind sobbing through trees broke over the no-caste encampment at that kiss, that simple, sweet gesture that acknowledged the child's humanity. The girl's mother staggered out of their hovel, tears streaking her face, her arms outstretched. She fell weeping at Amrita's feet, embracing her legs.

My lady Amrita stooped and kissed her brow, then raised her up with her own hands and placed a garland around her neck. "I am glad to see you are well. Be proud of your daughter today."

One by one, others stepped forward; and then it was like a dam breaking. All at once, the untouchables of Bhaktipur surged toward the Rani and her son, mobbing them, crying out words of blessing, words of thanks, begging her to anoint them with flowers, begging her to *touch* them.

She did, each and every one of them; and there were tears in *her* eyes, too, but they were joyful ones.

When the last of seventy-odd folk had been garlanded, the Rani Amrita clapped her hands together. "To the river!"

It was a motley procession that wound its way through the city to the banks of the Bhasa River, but stone and sea! It was a joyous one. Former untouchables clad in rags and flowers walked side by side with merchants and tradefolk, escorted by members of the warrior class in all their finery.

Along the bank of the river, at the sacred bathing spot, priests were waiting with offering bowls, and the Rani's servants, many of them rescued from Kurugiri, awaited with clean, dry clothing. There were braziers smoking in the open air, and dozens of different kinds of savory foods being prepared.

I had to own, I wasn't looking forward to the ritual purification. My lady Amrita thought the gesture would be best if all took part in it, a thought with which I agreed, but the waters of the river spilled from the heights of the Abode of the Gods into this charmed valley, and I was sure they were bound to be frigid.

I was wrong.

The Bhasa River flowed slow and placid at the sacred place where broad steps went down into the water. Curling tendrils of mist rose from its gleaming waters.

Warm. The water was warm.

Amrita gave me a startled look. "More of your magic, dear one?"

I shook my head, my throat feeling tight. "No, my lady. This is truly a gift of the gods."

She smiled at me. "As are you."

We descended the steps and waded into the river, all of us. Caste and no-caste, warriors and peasants; and the water was warm, as warm as mother's milk. There was laughter and shouting and singing, and prayers intoned by priests. The soaked folds of my sari floated around me. Bao, grinning, emptied bowls of water over my head; and I did the same to him. Bedecked with garlands of flowers, everyone laughed and splashed in the warm waters of the sacred river, everyone made clean and whole by the ritual, the Rani Amrita no less than the least of her subjects.

My heart ached at the beauty of it.

And I thought of my forced, false baptism in chains in Riva, and how a portion of my life had come around full circle; how one person might truly make a difference in the world. I thought about the parallels between Aleksei and my lovely lady Amrita; and I hoped my sweet boy would prove as courageous and kind as my gentle Rani.

I hoped he would.

I thought he might.

Flowers worked their way loose from hastily strung garlands, floating down the river. We waded dripping out of the river, shivering in the cool air, glad to be met with warm blankets and clean, dry clothing.

Priests kindled the sacred fires and sang.

Everywhere, faces glowed.

Bao wrapped his arms around me, and I leaned gratefully into his embrace once more. "The world has changed a little bit today, huh?" he murmured in my ear.

I nodded. "For the better."

"I wonder what's next for us," he mused. "For there *will* be a next, Moirin."

"I know." I lifted my head to kiss him, my lips lingering on his. "But for now, can we not just be happy?"

Bao smiled at me. "For now, yes."

EIGHTY-ONE

The months that followed were a time of near-perfect happiness. A sense of benediction hovered over the valley and the celebratory mood lingered.

It was not entirely perfect; here and there, there were folk embittered by the change, folk who refused to have any dealings with the former untouchables or threatened violence against them. The Rani levied a system of steep fines against them, putting the money gathered toward the construction of a new school, and in time even the last holdouts gave way with grudging reluctance.

But for the most part, all was well. Too many people had witnessed the miracle of marigolds bursting forth from the earth and steam rising from the surface of the Bhasa River to doubt the will of the gods.

I was happy, very happy. I had the company of my lovely Rani Amrita and her clever son, who attempted in vain to teach me to play chess. I had the pleasure of spending time with the *tulku* Laysa and the other women of the harem, watching them blossom in their newfound home, watching their children run and play in the garden, free forever more from the stark tyranny of Kurugiri, watching serious Ravindra abandon his dignity to laugh and play among them.

And I had Bao.

It was a good time for us, the first time since we had been together on the greatship that there was no shadow that lay between us. No dragon's jealousy, no angry, jilted Tatar princess. No Patriarch to sully our union with his vile thoughts, no conspiracy to separate us by leagues and leagues, no hate-filled Spider Queen in her lair.

And for once, there was no destiny goading us—no princess to rescue, no assassins to thwart, no fortress to invade. Somewhere to the west, further oceans beckoned, but for now, our shared *diadh-anam* was content to let us rest.

We learned to be together as friends and lovers, learned to live with ordinary happiness as well as the divine spark that joined us.

"He is good with children, that one," my lady Amrita observed, watching Bao entertain Ravindra and the others, walking upside down on his hands and challenging them to a race. "Will you start a family after you are wed?"

"Someday, yes." I smiled wistfully. "Not for a while, I think. I fear the gods are not done with us."

She sighed. "I wish the world were not so very large! I would so like to see your children playing in this very garden."

I took her hand and squeezed it. "So would I. But our lives will always be the richer for having known you."

Having lost his absurd race and been toppled ignominiously by a horde of delighted children, Bao came over to console himself with a cool drink.

"Amrita thinks you will be a good father one day," I informed him.

Bao grinned at me. "I will be an excellent father, O queen of my heart. Our children will deserve nothing less."

I flushed at the unexpected endearment, the first Bao had ever given me. His grin softened into a lopsided smile, and we gazed foolishly at each other, still learning this business of being in love.

Amrita shook her head at us both. "I would say your wedding day cannot come too soon," she said fondly. "Except I know my D'Angeline *dakini* and my bad boy Bao have not bothered to wait for it."

"Oh, but we are looking forward to it," Bao assured her. "Very much so!"

"I am glad." She arranged her fingers in a *mudra* and took on a serious look. "There is one great favor I would ask of you, my heroes. As much as I do not like to think of your leaving, I know you must go. Will you take Kamadeva's diamond with you, and restore it to the temple from which it was taken? It is not far from your path, and there is no one else in the world I would rather trust to do it."

Bao gave me an inquiring glance, and I nodded. With the diamond locked safe in a coffer, I had not been tempted by it. "Of course." He bowed deeply to the Rani in the Ch'in manner, hand over fist. "It is the least we can do for the trouble we led to your doorstep, highness."

She smiled at him. "On the balance, you have brought far more joy than sorrow. So I will count it as a kindness, and be grateful."

One by one, the happy days fled.

A part of me wanted to cling to them, wanted the world to slow in its turning, to stay here in this charmed valley with people I had come to love, and be happy as long as I was allowed. A part of me welcomed it, yearning to return home, longing for just one glimpse of my mother's face.

I wondered what she would make of Bao.

I had a feeling they would like one another, my taciturn mother and my insolent, irrepressible magpie.

In the Rani Amrita's capable hands, the plans for our wedding proceeded apace. To be sure, it would be an untraditional affair. Family, that vast, extended web that was a cornerstone of Bhodistani society, would not come into play here. There would be no dowry, no symbolic transfer of power as I moved from my parents' household to that of my husband.

"Still!" Amrita said in a firm voice. "It will be a very, very splendid celebration, and certain things will be observed."

Certain things meant petitioning the elephant-headed god Ganesha to remove any obstacles to our union.

Certain things meant another ritual in which a priest smeared a dot of red turmeric powder on my brow and Bao's.

Certain things meant that I must sit still for hours on end while a special artist applied intricate designs of henna paste to my hands, arms, and feet, rendering me beautiful after the manner of every Bhodistani bride.

It was a good thing I had learned a great deal about patience.

I didn't mind it, though, not really. There was music and dancing, and it made me glad to hear my lady Amrita and the women of the Falconer's harem discuss men and their foibles and giggle together, finding brightness in the shadow of sorrow and suffering, weaving the strands of loss and anguish into a fabric of togetherness.

And on the eve of our wedding, certain things meant that Bao and I must spend the night apart.

"I will miss you, Moirin," he said to me. "Even for just one night."

I laid one hand on his hard chest, feeling his heart beat beneath my palm. "I will miss you, too."

Alone in the chamber we had shared, I slept…

…and dreamed of Jehanne again.

In my dream, I opened the door of the bedchamber she had had made for me, my enchanted bower, filled with growing plants. I found Jehanne naked in my bed, her pale blonde hair loose around her shoulders, her arms wrapped around her knees.

My heart pounded in my chest.

"Hello, my beautiful girl." Her eyes sparkled at me. "Won't you come and give me the kiss of greeting?"

I sat carefully on the edge of the bed. "Jehanne, you know I love you. Must you insist on tormenting me on the eve of my wedding?"

She looked away, then looked back at me with one of her unreadable expressions. "Is that what you think I'm doing?"

"I don't know." I gazed at her impossible beauty, the delicate green fern-shadows etched on her fair skin. A tickle of foreboding brushed me, as though someone had trailed a feather along my spine. "This isn't just a dream, is it?"

"I'm not meant to be here yet," Jehanne replied indirectly. "At least, I don't think so. It's hard to tell. Time moves differently on the other side, you know."

"I know," I murmured.

She nodded seriously. "You do know about such things, my lovely witch-girl. That's why I'm able to reach you. Only...if it's not time yet, I suppose you're right, and it's jealousy that draws me." She gave me a self-deprecating smile. "Are you angry?"

"No." I frowned. "But...what is this? Why? My lady, I don't even know what questions to ask."

Reaching out with one slender hand, Jehanne stroked my brow, then trailed her fingers down my cheek. "Don't scowl, Moirin," she said in a teasing tone. "You'll get wrinkles."

I pulled away from her distracting touch. "Jehanne, please! Talk to me."

She withdrew her hand, looking so disconsolate that it was all I could do not to take her in my arms and comfort her with kisses. "I can't move onward," she said. "Neither forward nor backward."

I struggled to recall what my father had told me of the D'Angeline afterlife. "You cannot pass on to the Terre d'Ange-that-lies-beyond?" I asked, and she nodded. "Nor can you be reborn in the mortal world?"

"I have to wait," she agreed.

"Oh, my lady!" I swallowed hard, feeling the sting of tears. "Why such a cruel fate?"

Her fair shoulders rose in a graceful shrug. "I don't understand it all. I only know that your business with Raphael de Mereliot is not finished. The time is coming when you will have to reckon with him, and you will need my help before the end."

A shiver ran over my skin. "Do you know how or why?"

Jehanne shook her head. "Only that it is coming. Don't cry for me, Moirin," she added, reaching out to wipe a tear from my cheek; and this time I didn't pull back from her. "Leaving was the hardest part."

"Dying?" I asked softly.

She shook her head again. "Death is not so fearful as I thought it would be. But leaving...leaving Daniel, leaving my infant daughter. Leaving a world with one such as *you* in it." She smiled at me. "Will you tell my Desirée about me when you meet her? Everyone in the

Court except her father will only tell her of the scandals and gossip I caused. You...you can tell her that her mother did a very good thing once when she rescued a beautiful young woman from her own folly."

I couldn't help my tears. "Jehanne, of course I will! You needn't ask; I would have done it anyway. I will tell her that you loved her very much, that you would have been a wonderful mother, and grown into a wise and gracious queen."

"Like your precious Rani?" Jehanne asked crossly in a mercurial mood shift that was so familiar it made me laugh through my tears.

"You *are* jealous!" I said to her.

She smiled again, taking my hand. "Yes. And a bit cheated that I didn't have the time to grow into this wise and gracious queen you dreamed I would become." Watching me beneath her lashes, she traced the intricate patterns of henna on my hand and forearm with the tip of one finger, a touch that was at once impossibly delicate and maddeningly arousing, making my skin prickle.

I took a deep breath. "Jehanne..."

Her blue-grey eyes opened wide and ingenuous. "You promised you would not say no to me. And I do not know when I will be able to reach you again, Moirin."

"Aye, and I'm getting married tomorrow!" I protested.

"Tomorrow is tomorrow." She stroked my skin with that exquisite touch. "And I am here. You used to say that to me, remember? *I am here.* It always comforted me. Will you not stay?"

I hesitated.

Jehanne's voice broke slightly, breaking my heart. "Please? It's so very lonely where I am."

And because I could no more resist her than the ocean's tides could resist the pull of the moon, I gave in to her as I had done a thousand times before; and even though it was a dream, it felt so very real, my lady Jehanne warm and alive in my arms, naked and silken, the intoxicating scent of her skin making me dizzy with longing, Jehanne winding her arms around my neck, kissing me with consummate skill and desperate ardor, whispering my name like a prayer.

I stayed; and this time the dream did not cast me out. In my dream, I fell asleep holding her.

I awoke to morning light and an empty bed, the linens rumpled.

Jehanne's scent lingered in the room.

I sighed and arose, my heart at once heavy with guilt and light with gladness, my body languid with the aftermath of pleasure.

The Rani Amrita and her attendants bustled into the chamber, laying out the bridal finery I was to wear—the crimson sari embroidered and trimmed with gold, the elaborate jewelry.

"So!" my lady Amrita said brightly to me. "The day is here at last. Are you ready to wed your bad boy, my dear one?"

With guilt, regret, and a surety of purpose, I put my dream of Jehanne aside. It was real and not-real at the same time. It was a promise of things to come; but they were things that had not happened yet.

"Yes," I said. "I am."

EIGHTY-TWO

⟨◆⟩

It was a glorious day.

The Rani's attendants helped me bathe and prepare, rubbing fragrant oils into my skin, brushing my hair until it gleamed, painting my eyelids with kohl. They helped me don the gorgeous crimson and gold sari, pinning the folds in place. Amrita insisted on adorning me with jewelry herself, sliding gold bangles onto my wrists, fastening tinkling anklets in place, pinning a gold filigree headpiece to my hair.

When she had finished, she clapped her hands together in delight. "You are the perfect bride, Moirin!"

I had a fleeting memory of my dream and smiled ruefully. "Not quite, I fear, but surely you have done your best, my lady."

She fussed with the filigree pendant hanging on my brow. "You are perfectly yourself, dear one, and that is all that matters. And you look very, very lovely."

I hugged her, holding her close. "Thank you, Amrita."

She returned my embrace, then released me. "You're very welcome. Now, do not muss your sari."

For some reason, her fussing and mothering made me laugh aloud. Amrita gave me an inquiring glance, and I shook my head, unable to explain. All I could do was gaze at her with a heart filled with a complicated mixture of affection, remembering all the many kindnesses she had shown me.

"Bad girl." She tapped my lips lovingly with one finger. "Do not look at me so. You are getting married today, remember?"

I smiled at her. "Oh, I do."

Once the preparations were finished, we adjourned to one of the palace's towers to watch the bridegroom's procession approach. The sun was high overhead, the sky was a bright, cloudless blue, and the spring air was warm and balmy.

I was getting married today.

It was an exhilarating thought—and a frightening one, too. But my heart beat surely and steadily and my *diadh-anam* called to Bao's, measuring his progress toward me. I felt him long before I saw him, resplendent in a crimson tunic and breeches, riding astride a white horse garlanded with flowers, his head held high, a crimson turban atop his unruly hair, gold hoops gleaming in his ears, his irrepressible grin in place. Hasan Dar and a handful of guards surrounded him, Sudhakar and Ravindra among them, cheering and singing love songs. The sight made my heart swell inside my chest.

My magpie, my peasant-boy, my Tatar prince.

Gods, I *did* love him very much.

How had that happened?

Bao glanced up at me as I leaned out of the turret, his grin widening, his almond-shaped eyes crinkling.

I had to tell him about Jehanne and my dream.

Later, I thought; later.

Amrita tugged at my arm. "Come, come, Moirin! You're meant to be in the garden before the bridegroom."

"Yes, my lady," I said obediently, following her.

It was spring in the charmed valley of Bhaktipur and the garden was in full bloom, filled with towering rhododendrons sporting a wealth of enormous purple blossoms, snaking lianna vines, delicate frangipani perfuming the air with fragrance, and marigolds I had coaxed to bloom early. Beneath the trees, an immense, elaborate canopy of colorful sequined fabric had been erected, sparkling in the sunlight, held up by gilded poles. There was a brazier of sacred fire, tended to by a lean priest whose kind smile belied his ascetic figure.

All the women and children of the harem were there, faces glowing on this happy day; and then the groom's party entered the garden on foot, laughing and singing, and my heart grew even fuller.

With much fanfare, Bao and I were seated opposite one another beneath the canopy, smiling at one another.

The priest beamed at all of us. "Today among friends and loved ones, in the presence of the sacred fire, upon the life-giving earth and beneath the radiant sun, we come together to seek the blessing of the gods on the marriage of Moirin and Bao," he announced.

My lady Amrita came forward and handed me a garland of flowers. Bao inclined his head, and I laid it around his neck, laughing a little as it caught and snagged on his unfamiliar turban and pulled it askew. He grinned and settled it in place. And then Ravindra, his narrow face solemn, extended a garland to Bao, who leaned forward and placed it carefully over my shoulders.

The priest intoned a sing-song series of prayers and I listened, or at least I half-listened, with my heart so very full.

If it had been a traditional Bhodistani wedding, our parents would have spoken next. I felt a pang at the absence of my beloved mother and the gracious father I had found in the City of Elua—and, too, at the absence of Bao's gentle seamstress mother and her lively daughter. I even wished the bitter non-father who had cast him out, and Tatar general who had fathered him and claimed him with pride, could be here and find gladness in this day.

But we were among loved ones; and it was enough.

"Now you shall exchange vows of devotion," the priest declared. "Moirin, it falls to you to speak first."

There were traditional words for this, too, but not vows that would make sense for such an unlikely couple as us.

I took a deep breath, gazing at Bao. "So much of what happened to thrust us together, neither of us chose. You wanted to find a way to be sure of me, my magpie? Well, today is it. We did not have to do this, you and I. You did not have to ask me to wed you, and I did not have to accept your offer." I swallowed hard, my eyes stinging. "I am here beneath this canopy, saying these words because I love you and I choose to be with you for the rest of my life. Today, I am choosing this and giving my heart to you."

Bao's dark eyes were bright with tears, and one spilled onto his cheek. I tried to remember if I'd ever seen him cry before.

I didn't think so.

The priest gestured at him. "Now you."

Bao laughed self-consciously. "Moirin." His hands clenched in his lap. "I am not good at this. Only know..." His fisted hands unknitted, lying upward and folded, and his eyes were bright, so bright, looking earnestly at me. "You have a very, very large heart. And I will do my best to take good care of it."

Shouts of laughter and approval surrounded us.

"Wait, wait!" The priest raised his hands in a good-humored protest. "We are not finished here, eh?"

So we finished.

First I cupped my hands in Bao's and the priest poured rice into our joined hands. Together we poured it into the sacred fire, a rich toasty smell arising.

Then the priest tied our wrists together with a long cord and bade us circle the brazier seven times. This we did, while he intoned a seven-fold blessing upon us, begging the gods to bless us with happiness, prosperity, and children, and a good many other things.

And then it was done.

Bao glanced sidelong at the priest. "May I kiss her now?"

The priest nodded.

Bao kissed me, smelling of sandalwood and incense, of unfamiliar oils. But beneath it, he smelled of himself, the hot-forge scent that made me feel safe and loved and protected, and I twined my arms around his neck, returning his kiss, glad he did not share the Ch'in reluctance to show affection in public.

It felt good.

It felt so very good, and right.

Our shared *diadh-anam* sang between us, and I leaned my brow against his. "Do you love me?" I asked.

He laughed. "You have to ask? Today of all days? Yes, occasionally stupid girl. I love you very much."

"Good." I smiled at him, hoping he would remember it later. "I am glad."

There was a feast that went on for many hours, servants carrying dozens of laden trays filled with spicy and savory dishes into the garden, where long tables had been erected and draped in more bright fabric. There was music and dancing, and there were games I didn't fully understand, including one in which Bao and I were made to sit back to back and answer a series of questions about each other; and yet another in which the cord that had tied us together was knotted around our wrists in a complex pattern which we had to unravel one-handed.

We did well at those.

We knew each other very well, my magpie and I. We worked well together, even at a simple task such as untying knots.

And it didn't matter that we didn't really grasp the details of the traditions, that the traditions didn't really apply to us. It didn't matter that neither of us were familiar with Bhodistani dances, gladly making fools of ourselves in the effort.

All that mattered was that we were together, and surrounded by love. Celebrating beneath the open sky, garlanded with flowers, reveling in all the joy and abundance the world had to offer.

I waited until the sun was sinking low, casting long shadows over the garden, to tell Bao about my dream—or at least the important part of it. As much as I hated to do it, I couldn't go to our bedchamber with it unspoken between us.

He listened without comment.

"Do you think it is real?" he asked gravely when I finished. "Or is it only your fear speaking to you?"

I swallowed. "I think it's real, Bao. It felt very real."

"Oh?" Bao raised his brows at me. "How real, Moirin?"

I flushed; I couldn't help it. I felt the warm blood climb into my throat and scald my cheeks, revealing my guilty secret. It wasn't always to my advantage that he knew me so well, and at such a time, Naamah's gifts felt like a curse in truth. "I'm *sorry*! But it was Jehanne," I said as though that excused me for betraying him in a dream, knowing it didn't, knowing I would do it again anyway if she came to me. "And she was lonely, so very lonely. It broke my heart! I couldn't help it. It would have broken yours, too."

He looked away from me.

I clutched his arm. "Bao? I *am* sorry. I didn't mean to do it, only..."

His shoulders shook, and I realized belatedly that he was trying not to laugh. "So!" He turned his gaze on me, his dark eyes now bright with tears of barely suppressed laughter. "Within hours of our wedding, Moirin, you are telling me that it appears I am sharing you with the ghost of the White Queen; and that together somehow you must face that idiot demon-summoning Lord Lion Mane Raphael both of you loved for no good reason. Is that right?"

I nodded, chagrined. "Aye, more or less."

Bao exhaled. "I knew I should have thumped that Raphael over the head," he remarked. "Next time, I won't hesitate."

"Have I ruined our wedding?" I asked in a miserable tone.

"No." Bao cupped my face in his hands "No," he said a second time, his breath warm on my skin. "I told you before. I love you as you are, Moirin. I would not change anything about you, even the fact that you have the will and morals of an alley-cat, because that is as your gods made you, and it is part of the reason for your very large heart." He smiled wryly. "Although I might have wished for a few days of wedded bliss before life with you got stranger."

I laughed, relieved and glad once more.

Bao kissed me—once gently, a second time with the rising heat of desire. I felt our *diadh-anam* blaze brighter than ever with the approval of the Maghuin Dhonn Herself; and then a second burst of brightness, warm and golden, a soft thunderclap all around us like a thousand doves taking flight at once, turning the blood molten in our veins and filling our mouths with a sweetness like honey.

Naamah's blessing settled over us, over the entire charmed garden and everyone in it, driving away now and forever any doubt that her gifts carried any taint of a curse. I heard soft cries of wonder as folk turned to one another and embraced spontaneously.

My magpie prince lifted his head, eyes wide with awe. "That was..."

He had removed his turban hours ago, and now I ran one hand through his thick, unruly hair, tugging his head down to kiss me again. "That," I whispered against his lips, "was Naamah's blessing. And I do believe she approves of this marriage."

Bao smiled and pulled me closer to him, one strong, lean arm snaking around my waist. "I do believe I'm ready for this party to end, Moirin."

I nodded, the golden warmth of Naamah's blessing still coursing through my veins, fanning the flames of desire. "Oh, yes!"

And so we said our thanks to our guests and our ever-gracious hostess Amrita, who regarded us with laughter in her eyes; and I couldn't help but smile fondly at her, still a little in love with her, in love with the whole world tonight. And with the heady mantle of Naamah's grace hovering over us all, it felt as though the whole love-struck, desire-smitten, intoxicated world returned the favor.

"Go, go!" Amrita said in her musical voice, making a shooing gesture at us, a rare gleam of devilry in her lustrous gaze. "I know your impatience very well, dear one."

Bao stifled a cough.

"What do you mean, Mama-ji?" Ravindra inquired in a puzzled tone.

"It is more grown-up teasing, young highness," Bao informed him. "Trust me when I tell you that you would rather not understand the jest."

"Oh." Ravindra gave him a dubious look. "All right."

Laughing, we took our leave of the party.

Our bedchamber had been filled with flowers and candles, and Bao and I made love for long hours that night, surrounded by fragrance and flickering candlelight, and it was by turns tender and sweet, and fierce and urgent, and all of it was good, so good, sanctified by Naamah's lingering blessing.

Somewhere in the small hours of the night, Bao surrendered to sleep as we lay together in a quiet moment.

I lay propped on one elbow and watched him sleep, his face as serene in repose as it never was when he was awake, as calm and beautiful as an effigy of the Enlightened One, a Dharma saint with a warrior's body.

And I thought how his journey to this moment was as long and strange as mine: a Ch'in peasant-boy sold into slavery, stubborn enough to take his destiny into his own hands no matter what the cost. A stick-fighting prince of thugs who had walked away from the entire life he'd built to become Master Lo's magpie. A leader of men, a rescuer of princesses and dragons. One called twice-born, one who had died and been restored to life.

A Tatar prince, struggling against an unwanted destiny.

Jagrati's favorite.

My husband.

Even in my thoughts, the word sounded strange to me; strange, but right. Like as not, I would be a dreadful wife. But Bao knew it and was not afraid.

For the first time in longer than I could recall, I felt the tug of destiny on my *diadh-anam*, our *diadh-anam*, grow a little more urgent, a little more insistent. Bao made a faint noise in his sleep. I glanced westward, wondering what awaited us.

Oceans; further oceans.

I wondered how many.

There was Jehanne's motherless daughter, whom I had promised to tell about her mother's courage of heart and the love and kindness and generosity she had shown to me. One day, I would tell her about the genuine fears that underlay Jehanne's foibles, and the steadily increasing joy and excitement with which she had welcomed her daughter's birth.

And there was ambitious and charismatic Raphael de Mereliot, not content with the gift of a physician's healing hands; Raphael, who had nearly been taken over entirely by the last demon he summoned.

We had saved him, Bao and I and Master Lo. We had driven away the demon Focalor, a Grand Duke of the Fallen. But I had always wondered about something I saw that day, after the demon had been forced to relinquish Raphael, after I had thrust him through the doorway and closed it. After it was all over, I thought I'd seen the briefest glimpse of Focalor's lightning flicker in Raphael's storm-grey eyes, and wondered if a trace of the demon's essence lingered in him.

If the divine spark of my *diadh-anam* could be divided, mayhap a demon's spirit could be, too.

That same feather of foreboding brushed along my spine, making me shiver.

"Moirin," Bao mumbled sleepily, half-awakened by my shudder. "Stop thinking and go to sleep. And no dreams tonight, huh?"

"It's just—"

"Sleep," he said a bit more firmly.

So I settled alongside him, my head on his shoulder, and Bao held me in his Kurugiri-marked arms, his entire body making a strong, safe haven for me, a pledge of enduring love. His breathing softened into sleep once more, a soothing and calming rhythm. Although I did not think I could sleep yet, my breathing slowed to match his as it had so many times before, and I thought that there was nowhere else I would rather be, and no one else with whom I'd rather face my everlasting destiny. Traces of Naamah's blessing lingered over us both like a promise that one day, every day would be as joyous as this one.

Somewhere, the bright lady smiled in gentle approval.

Somewhere on the far side of the stone doorway, the Maghuin Dhonn Herself paced in majesty, lifted Her mighty head, and gazed at the errant child She had loosed on the world with love and pride in Her deep, deep eyes.

A word surfaced in my thoughts. Home—the gods were calling me *home*, and I was ready to go.

Whatever came next, Bao and I would face it together.

As candles guttered low and sank into pools of wax all across the bedchamber, and I drifted down toward darkness, a sigh of happiness escaped me.

I slept, and did not dream.